The Master
of Greylands

The Master of Greylands

Mrs. Henry Wood

MINT EDITIONS

The Master of Greylands was first published in 1873.

This edition published by Mint Editions 2021.

ISBN 9781513281117 | E-ISBN 9781513286136

Published by Mint Editions®

MINT
EDITIONS
minteditionbooks.com

Publishing Director: Jennifer Newens
Design & Production: Rachel Lopez Metzger
Project Manager: Micaela Clark
Typesetting: Westchester Publishing Services

Contents

I

In the Bank Parlour

S tilborough. An old-fashioned market-town of some importance in its district, but not the chief town of the county. It was market-day: Thursday: and the streets wore an air of bustle, farmers and other country people passing and repassing from the corn-market to their respective inns, or perhaps from their visit, generally a weekly one, to the banker's.

In the heart of the town, where the street was wide and the buildings were good, stood the bank. It was nearly contiguous to the town-hall on the one hand, and to the old church of St. Mark on the other, and was opposite the new market-house, where the farmers' wives and daughters sat with their butter and poultry. For in those days—many a year ago now—people had not leaped up above their sphere; and the farmers' wives would have thought they were going to ruin outright had anybody but themselves kept market. A very large and handsome house, this bank, the residence of its owner and master, Mr. Peter Castlemaine.

No name stood higher than Mr. Peter Castlemaine's. Though of sufficiently good descent, he was, so to say, a self-made man. Beginning in a small way in early life, he had risen by degrees to what he now was—to what he had long been—the chief banker in the county. People left the county-town to bank with him; in all his undertakings he was supposed to be flourishing; in realized funds a small millionaire.

The afternoon drew to a close; the business of the day was over; the clerks were putting the last touches to their accounts previously to departing, and Mr. Peter Castlemaine sat alone in his private room. It was a spacious apartment, comfortably and even luxuriously furnished for a room devoted solely to business purposes. But the banker had never been one of those who seem to think that a hard chair and a bare chamber are necessary to the labour that brings success. The rich crimson carpet with its soft thick rug threw a warmth of colouring on the room, the fire flashed and sparkled in the grate: for the month was February and the weather yet wintry.

Before his own desk, in a massive and luxurious arm-chair, sat Mr. Peter Castlemaine. He was a tall, slender, and handsome man, fifty-one years of age this same month. His hair was dark, his eyes were brown, his good complexion was yet clear and bright. In manner he was a courteous man, but naturally a silent one; rather remarkably so; his private character and his habits were unexceptionable.

No one had ever a moment's access to this desk at which he sat: even his confidential old clerk could not remember to have been sent to it for any paper or deed that might be wanted in the public rooms. The lid of the desk drew over and closed with a spring, so that in one instant its contents could be hidden from view and made safe and fast. The long table in the middle of the room was to-day more than usually covered with papers; a small marble slab between Mr. Peter Castlemaine's left hand and the wall held sundry open ledgers piled one upon another, to which he kept referring. Column after column of figures: the very sight of them enough to give an unfinancial man the nightmare: but the banker ran his fingers up and down the rows at railroad speed, for, to him, it was mere child's-play. Seldom has there existed a clearer head for his work than that of Peter Castlemaine. But for that fact he might not have been seated where he was to-day, the greatest banker for miles round.

And yet, as he sat there, surrounded by these marks and tokens of wealth and power, his face presented a sad contrast to them and to the ease and luxury of the room. Sad, careworn, anxious, looked he; and, as he now and again paused in his work to pass his hand over his brow, a heavy sigh escaped him. The more he referred to his ledgers, and compared them with figures and papers on the desk before him, so much the more perplexed and harassed did his face become. In his eyes there was the look of a hunted animal, the look of a drowning man catching at a straw, the look that must have been in the eyes of poor Louis Dixhuit when they discovered him in his disguise and turned his horses' heads backwards. At last, throwing down his pen, he fell back in his chair, and hid his face in his hands.

"No escape," he murmured, "no escape! Unless a miracle should supervene, I am undone."

He remained in this attitude, that told so unmistakably of despair, for some minutes, revolving many things: problems working themselves in and out of his brain confusedly, as a man works in and out of a labyrinth, to which he has lost the clue. A small clock on the mantelpiece struck the hour, five, and then chimed an air once popular in France. It was a costly trifle that the banker had bought years ago. Paintings, articles of virtu, objets de luxe, had always possessed attractions for him.

The chimes aroused him. "I must talk to Hill," he muttered: "no use putting it off till another day." And he touched the spring of his small hand-bell.

In answer, the door opened, and there entered a little elderly man with snow-white hair worn long behind, and a good-looking, fair, and intellectual face, its eyes beaming with benevolence. He wore a black tail coat, according to the custom of clerks of that day, and a white cambric frilled shirt like that of his master. It was Thomas Hill; for many years Mr. Peter Castlemaine's confidential clerk and right hand.

"Come in, Hill; come in," said the banker. "Close the door—and lock it."

"The clerks are gone, sir; the last has just left," was the reply. But the old man nevertheless turned the key of the door.

Mr. Peter Castlemaine pointed to a seat close to him; and his clerk, quiet in all his movements, as in the tones of his voice, took it in silence. For a full minute they looked at each other; Thomas Hill's face reflecting the uneasiness of his master's. He was the first to speak.

"I know it, sir," he said, his manner betraying the deepest respect and sympathy. "I have seen it coming for a long while. So have you, sir. Why have you not confided in me before?"

"I could not," breathed Mr. Peter Castlemaine. "I wanted to put it from me, Hill, as a thing that could never really be. It has never come so near as it has come now, Hill; it has never been so real as at this moment of outspoken words."

"It was not my place to take the initiative, sir; but I was wishing always that you would speak to me. I could but place facts and figures before you and point to results, compare past balances with present ones, other years' speculations with last year's, and—and give you the opportunity of opening the subject with me. But you never would open it."

"I have told you why, Hill," said Peter Castlemaine. "I strove to throw the whole trouble from me. It was a weak, mistaken feeling; nine men out of every ten would have been actuated by it under similar circumstances. And yet," he continued, half in soliloquy, "I never was much like other men, and I never knew myself to be weak."

"Never weak; never weak," responded the faithful clerk, affectionately.

"I don't know, Hill; I feel so now. This has been to me long as a far-off monster, creeping onwards by degrees, advancing each day by stealthy steps more ominously near: and now it is close at hand, ready to crush me."

"I seem not to understand it," said poor Hill.

"And there are times when I cannot," returned Mr. Peter Castlemaine.

"In the old days, sir, everything you handled turned to gold. You had but to take up a speculation, and it was sure to prove a grand success. Why, sir, your name has become quite a proverb for luck. If Castlemaine the banker's name is to it, say people of any new undertaking, it must succeed. But for some time past things have changed, and instead of success, it has been failure. Sir, it is just as though your hand had lost its cunning."

"Right, Hill," sighed his master, "my hand seems to have lost its cunning. It is—I have said it over and over again to myself—just as though some curse pursued me. Ill-luck; nothing but ill-luck! If a scheme has looked fair and promising to-day, a blight has fallen on it to-morrow. And I, like a fool, as I see now, plunged into fresh ventures, hoping to redeem the last one. How few of us are there who know how to pull up in time! Were all known the public would say that the mania of gambling must have taken hold of me—"

"No, no," murmured the clerk.

"——When it was but the recklessness of a drowning man. Why, Hill—if I could get in the money at present due to me, money that I think will come in, perhaps shortly, though it is locked up now, we should weather the storm."

"I trust it will be weathered, sir, somehow. At the worst, it will not be a bad failure; there'll be twenty shillings in the pound if they will but wait. Perhaps, if you called a private meeting and pointed things out, and showed them that it is only time you want, they'd consent to let you have it. Matters would go on then, and there'd be no exposure."

"It is the want of time that will crush me," said Peter Castlemaine.

"But if they will allow you time, sir?"

"All will not," was the significant answer, and Mr. Peter Castlemaine lowered his voice as he spoke it, and looked full at his clerk. "You know those Armannon bonds?"

Whether it was the tone, the look, or the question, certain it was that in that instant an awful dread, an instinct of evil, seized upon the old man. His face turned white.

"I had to use those bonds, Hill," whispered his master. "To mortgage them, you understand. But, as I am a living man, I believed when I did it that in less than a week they would be redeemed and replaced."

"Mortgaged the Armannon bonds!" exclaimed Thomas Hill, utterly unable to take in the fact, and looking the picture of horror.

"And they are not yet redeemed."

The clerk wrung his hands. "My master! my friend and master! How could you? Surely it was done in a moment of madness!"

"Of weakness, of wickedness, if you will, Thomas, but not madness. I was as sane as I am now. You remember the large payment we had to make last August? It had to be made, you know, or things would have come to a crisis then. I used the bonds to raise the money."

"But I—I cannot comprehend," returned the clerk slowly, after casting his recollection back. "I thought you borrowed that money from Mr. Castlemaine."

"No. Mr. Castlemaine would not lend it me. I don't know whether he smelt a rat and got afraid for the rest I hold of his. What he said was, that he had not so large a sum at his disposal. Or, it may be," added the banker in a dreamy kind of tone, "that James thought I was only going into some fresh speculation, and considers I am rich enough already. How little he knows!"

"Oh, but these deeds must be redeemed!" cried the old clerk, rising from his seat in excitement. "At all sacrifice they must be got back, sir. If you have to sell up all, houses, land, and everything, they must be returned to their safe resting-place. You must not longer run this dreadful risk, sir: the fear of it would bring me down in suspense and sorrow to my grave."

"Then, what do you suppose it has been doing for me?" rejoined Mr. Peter Castlemaine. "Many a time and oft since, I have said to myself, 'Next week shall see those bonds replaced.' But the 'next week' has never come: for I have had to use all available cash to prop up the falling house and keep it from sinking. Once down, Hill, the truth about the bonds could no longer be concealed."

"You must sell all, sir."

"There's nothing left to sell, Thomas," said his master. "At least, nothing immediately available. It is time that is wanted. Given that, I could put things straight again."

A trying silence. Thomas Hill's face was full of pain and dread. "I have a little accumulated money of my own, sir: some of it I've saved, some came to me when my brother died," he said. "It is about six thousand pounds, and I have neither chick nor child. Every shilling of it shall be yours, sir, as soon as I can withdraw it from where it is invested."

His master grasped his hands. "Faithful man and friend!" he cried, the tears of emotion dimming his brown eyes. "Do you think I would accept the sacrifice and bring you to ruin as I have brought myself? Never that, Hill."

"The money shall be yours, sir," repeated the clerk firmly.

"Hush, hush!" cried Mr. Peter Castlemaine. "Though I were dying of shame and hunger, I would not take it. And, do you not see, my friend, that it would be a useless sacrifice? Six thousand pounds would be swallowed up unheeded in the vortex: it would be but as a drop of water to the heaving ocean."

It was even so. Thomas Hill saw it. They sat down together and went into the books: the banker showing him amounts and involvements that he had never suspected before. The ruin seemed to be close at hand; there seemed to be no possible way out of it. Common ruin Thomas Hill might have got over in time; but this ruin, the ruin that threatened his master, would have turned his hair white in a night had time not already turned it.

And crimes were more heavily punished in those days than they are in these.

At a quarter to six o'clock, Peter Castlemaine was in his dining-room, dressed for dinner. He often had friends to dine with him on market-days, and was expecting some that night: a small social party of half a dozen, himself included. He stood with his back to the fire, his brow smoothed, his aspect that of complete ease; he could hear his butler coming up the stairs to show in the first guest. All the dwelling-rooms were on this first floor, the ground-floor being entirely appropriated to business.

"Mr. Castlemaine."

The two brothers met in the middle of the room and shook hands. Mr. Castlemaine was the elder by two years, but he did not look so, and there was a very great likeness between them. Fine, upright, handsome men, both; with clear, fresh faces, well-cut features, and keen, flashing, dark eyes. Very pleasant men to talk to; but silent men as to their own affairs. Mr. Castlemaine had just come in from his residence, Greylands' Rest: it was in contradistinction to him that the banker was invariably called Mr. Peter Castlemaine.

"All well at home, James?"

"Quite so, thank you."

"You were not in at market, to-day."

"No: I had nothing particular to call me in. Are you expecting a large party this evening?"

"Only six of us. Here comes another."

The butler's step was again heard. But this time he came, not to announce a guest, but to bring a note, just delivered. Peter Castlemaine's hand shook slightly as he opened it. He dreaded all letters now. It proved, however, to be only an excuse from one of the expected guests: and a strange relief sat on his face as he turned to his brother.

"Lawrence can't come, James. So there'll be but five of us."

"Lawrence is not much loss," said Mr. Castlemaine, "You don't look quite yourself, Peter," he added, to his brother; something in the latter's countenance having struck his observant eye. "I think you are working too hard; have thought so for some time. Don't let the love of money take all pleasure out of life. Surely you must have made enough, and might now take some rest."

The banker laughed. "As to taking rest, that's easier recommended than done, James. I am too young to give up work yet: I should be like a fish out of water."

"Ah well—we are all, I expect, wedded to our work—whatever it may be: creatures of habit," admitted Mr. Castlemaine. "I will just go and see Mary Ursula. She in her room, I suppose. What a treasure you possess in that girl, Peter!"

"Beyond the wealth of Solomon; beyond all price," was the impulsive answer, and Peter Castlemaine's face glowed as he made it. "Yes, you will find her in her room, James."

Mr. Castlemaine went to the end of the wide and handsome passage,—its walls lined with paintings, its floor covered with a carpet, rich and soft as moss,—and knocked at a door there. A sweet voice bade him enter.

The small, choice room was brilliantly lighted with wax tapers; the fire threw a warmth on its dainty furniture. A stately lady, tall, slight, and very beautiful, who had been working at a sketch, put down her pencil, and rose. It was Miss Castlemaine, the banker's only child: as fair a picture as could be found in the world. She wore a white muslin dress, made low in the fashion of the day. On her queen-like neck was a string of pearls; bracelets of pearls clasped her pretty arms. Her face was indeed beautiful: it was like her father's face, but more delicately carved; the complexion was of a paler and fairer tint; the brown eyes, instead of flashing, as his did in his youth, had a subdued, almost a sad look in them. It was one of the sweetest faces ever seen, but altogether its pervading expression was that of sadness: an expression that in her childhood had led many an old woman to say, "She is too good to live." She had lived, however, in the best of strength and health, until now, when she was in her five-and-twentieth year. An accomplished lady, she, very much so for those days, and of great good sense; her conversational powers rare; a sound musician, and a fair linguist, fond of sketching and painting in watercolours. With it all, she was particularly gentle in manner, modest and retiring as a woman should be: there was at all times a repose upon her that seemed to exhale repose, and was most charming. Her father loved her with an ardent love; he had lost his wife, and this child was all-in-all to him. But for her sake, he might not have dreaded the coming disgrace with the intense horror he did dread it. His happiest hours were spent with her. In the twilight he would sit in the music-room, listening to her playing on the piano, or on the sweet-toned organ he had had built for her— the tones not more sweet, though, than her own voice when raised in song. Her gift of extemporising was of no mean order; and as the banker sat listening to the organ's sounds, its rise and fall, its swelling and dying away, he would forget his cares. She was engaged to William Blake-Gordon, the eldest son of Sir Richard Blake-Gordon; a poor, but very haughty baronet, unduly proud of his descent. But for the vast amount of money Miss Castlemaine was expected to inherit, Sir Richard had never condescended to give his consent to the match: but the young man loved her for her own sake. Just now Miss Castlemaine was alone: the lady, Mrs. Webb, who resided with her as chaperon and companion, having been called away by the illness of a near relative. One word as to her name—Mary Ursula. A somewhat long name to pronounce, but it was rarely shortened by her relatives. The name had been old Mrs. Castlemaine's, her grandmother's, and was revered in the Castlemaine family.

"I knew it was you, Uncle James," she said, meeting him with both hands extended. "I knew you would come in to see me."

He took her hands into one of his and touched fondly her beautiful hair, that so well set-off the small and shapely head, and kissed her tenderly. Mr. Castlemaine was fond of his niece, and very proud of her.

"Your face is cold, Uncle James."

"Fresh with the out-of-door cold, my dear. I walked in."

"All the way from Greylands!"

MRS. HENRY WOOD

He laughed at her "all the way." It was but three miles; scarcely that. "I felt inclined for the walk, Mary Ursula. The carriage will come in to take me home."

"Is Ethel well, Uncle James? And Mrs. Castlemaine?"

"Quite so, my dear. What are you doing here?"

She had sat down to the table again, and he bent his head over her to look at her drawing. There was a moment's silence.

"Why it is—it is the Friar's Keep!" exclaimed Mr. Castlemaine.

"Yes," she answered. "I sketched its outlines when at your house last summer, and I have never filled it in until now."

She sketched as she did everything else—almost perfectly. The resemblance was exact, and Mr. Castlemaine said so. "It seems to me already completed!" he observed.

"All but the shading of the sky in the back-ground."

"Why have you made those two windows darker than the rest?"

Miss Castlemaine smiled as she answered jestingly, "I thought there should be no opportunity given for the appearance of the Grey Friar in my drawing, Uncle James."

Mr. Castlemaine drew in his lips with a peculiar twist. The jest pleased him.

"Have you seen much of the Grey Sisters lately, Uncle James?"

This did not please him. And Mary Ursula, as she caught the involuntary frown that knitted his bold brow, felt vexed to have asked the question. Not for the first time, as she well recalled, had Mr. Castlemaine shown displeasure at the mention of the "Grey Sisters."

"Why do you not like them, Uncle James?"

"I cannot help thinking that Greylands might get on better if it were rid of them," was the short reply of Mr. Castlemaine. But he passed at once from the subject.

"And we are not to have this fair young lady-hostess at the dinner-table's head to-night?" he cried, in a different and a warm tone, as he gazed affectionately at his niece. "Mary Ursula, it is a sin. I wish some customs were changed! And you will be all alone!"

"'Never less alone than when alone,'" quoted Mary Ursula: "and that is true of me, uncle mine. But to-night I shall not be alone in any sense, for Agatha Mountsorrel is coming to bear me company."

"Agatha Mountsorrel! I don't care for her, Mary Ursula. She is desperately high and mighty."

"All the Mountsorrels are that—with their good descent and their wealth, I suppose they think they have cause for it—but I like her. And I fancy that is her carriage stopping now. There's six o'clock, uncle; and you will be keeping the soup waiting."

Six was striking from the room's silver-gilt timepiece. "I suppose I must go," said Mr. Castlemaine. "I'd rather stay and spend the evening with you."

"Oh, Uncle James, think of the baked meats!" she laughed. "Of the nectar-cup!"

"What are baked meats and a nectar-cup to the brightness of thine eyes, to the sweet discourse of thy lips? There's not thy peer in this world, Mary Ursula."

"Uncle, uncle, you would spoil me. Flattery is like a subtle poison, that in time destroys sound health."

"Fare you well, my dear. I will come and say goodnight to you before I leave."

As Mr. Castlemaine trod the corridor, he met Miss Mountsorrel coming up: a handsome, haughty girl in a scarlet cloak and hood. She returned his salute with a sweeping bow, and passed on her way in silence.

T tie dinner was one of those perfect little repasts that the banker was renowned for. The three other guests were Sir Richard Blake-Gordon; the Reverend John Marston, vicar of St. Mark's and also of Greylands, generally called by the public "Parson Mas'on;" and Mr. Knivett, family solicitor to the Castlemaines. The wines were excellent; the reunion was altogether sociable and pleasant; and the banker's brow gave no indication of the strife within. It's true Mr. Marston took his full share of the wine—as many a parson then appeared to think it quite religious to do—and talked rather too much accordingly. But the guests enjoyed themselves and broke up before eleven. Mr. Castlemaine, who could drink his wine with any man, but took care never to take more than he could carry as a gentleman, proceeded to his niece's room to say goodnight to her; as he had promised to do.

"I hope I have not kept you up, my dear," he began as he entered.

"Oh no, Uncle James," was Mary Ursula's answer. "I never go to bed until I have sung the evening hymn to papa."

"Where's Miss Mountsorrel?"

"The carriage came for her at ten o'clock."

"And pray where's Master William, that he has not been here this evening?"

She blushed like a summer rose. "Do you think he is here every evening, Uncle James? Mrs. Webb warned him in time that it would not be etiquette, especially while she was away. And how have you enjoyed yourself?"

"Passably. The baked meats you spoke of were tempting; the nectar good. Of which nectar, in the shape of a dinner port, the parson took slightly more than was necessary. What toast, do you suppose, he suddenly gave us?"

"How can I tell, Uncle James?" she rejoined, looking up.

"We were talking of you at the moment, and the parson rose to his legs, his glass in his hand. 'Here's to the fairest and sweetest maiden in the universe,' said he, 'and may she soon be Lady Blake-Gordon!'"

"Oh, how could he!" exclaimed Miss Castlemaine, colouring painfully in her distress. "And Sir Richard present!"

"As to Sir Richard, I thought he was going frantic. You know what he is. 'Zounds! Sir Parson,' he cried, starting up in his turn, 'do you wish me dead? Is it not enough that the young lady should first become Mistress Blake-Gordon? Am I so old and useless as to be wished out of the world for the sake of my son's aggrandisement?'—and so on. Marston pacified him at last, protesting that he had only said Mistress Blake-Gordon; or that, if he had not, he had meant to say it. And now, goodnight, my dear, for I don't care to keep my horses standing longer in the cold. When are you coming to stay at Greylands' Rest?"

"Whenever you like to invite me, Uncle James. I wish you could get papa over for a week. It would give him rest: and he has not appeared to be well of late. He seems full of care."

"Of business, my dear; not care. Though, of course, undertakings such as his must bring care with them. You propose it to him; and come with him: if he will come for anybody's asking, it is yours."

"You will give my love to Ethel; and—"

Castlemaine, stooping to kiss her, arrested the words with a whisper.

"When is it to be, Mary Ursula? When shall we be called upon to congratulate Mistress Blake-Gordon? Soon?"

"Oh uncle, I don't know." And she laughed and blushed, and felt confused at the outspoken words: but in her inmost heart was as happy as a queen.

II

The Grey Ladies

A romantic, picturesque fishing village was that of Greylands, as secluded as any English village can well be. Stilborough was an inland town; Greylands was built on the sea-coast. The London coaches, on their way from Stilborough to the great city, would traverse the nearly three miles of dreary road intervening between the town and the village, dash suddenly, as it were, upon the sea on entering the village, and then turn sharply off in its midst by the Dolphin Inn, and go on its inland road again. As to London, it was so far off, or seemed so in those quiet, non-travelling days, that the villagers would as soon have expected to undertake a journey to the moon.

The first object to be seen on drawing near to Greylands from Stilborough, was the small church; an old stone building on the left hand, with its graveyard around it. On the opposite side of the road the cliffs rose high, and the sea could not be seen for them. The Reverend John Marston held the living of Greylands in conjunction with St. Mark's at Stilborough: the two had always gone together, and the combined income was but poor. Mr. Marston was fond of fox-hunting in winter, and of good dinners at all seasons: as many other parsons were. Greylands did not get much benefit from him. He was non-resident, as the parsons there had always been, for he lived at St. Mark's. Of course, with two churches and only one parson to serve both, the services could but clash, for nobody can be doing duty in two places at once. Once a month, on the third Sunday, Mr. Marston scuffled over to Greylands to hold morning service, beginning at twelve, he having scuffled through the prayers (no sermon that day) at St. Mark's first. On the three other Sundays he held the Greylands service at three in the afternoon. So that, except for this Sunday service, held at somewhat uncertain hours—for the easy-going parson did not always keep his time, and on occasion had been known to fail altogether—Greylands was absolutely without pastoral care.

Descending onwards—an abrupt descent—past the church, the cliffs on the right soon ended abruptly; and the whole village, lying in its hollow, seemed to burst upon you all at once. It was very open, very wide just there. The beach lay flat and bare to the sea, sundry fishing-boats being high and dry there: others would be out at sea, catching fish. Huts and cottages were built on the side of the rocks; and some few on the beach. On the left stood the Dolphin Inn, looking straight across the wide road to the beach and the sea; past which inn the coach-road branched off inland again.

The village street—if it could be called a street—continued to wind on, up the village, the Dolphin Inn making a corner, as it were, between the street and the inland coach-road. Let us follow this street. It is steep and winding, and for a short distance solitary. Halfway up the ascent, on the left, and built on the sea-coast, rises the pile of old buildings called the Grey Nunnery. This pile stands back from the road across a narrow strip of waste land on which grass grows. The cliff is low there, understand, and the Grey Nunnery's built right at the edge, so that the waves dash against its lower walls at high water. The back of the building is to the road, the front to the sea. A portion of it is in ruins; but this end is quite habitable, and in it live some ladies, twelve, who are called the Grey Sisters, or sometimes the Grey Ladies, and who devote themselves to charity and to doing good. In spite of the appellation, they are of the Reformed Faith; strict, sound Protestants: a poor community as to funds, but rich in goodness. They keep a few beds for the sick among the villagers, or for accidents; and they have a day school for the village children. If they could get better children to educate, they would be glad; and some of the ladies are accomplished gentlewomen. Mr. Castlemaine, who is, so to say, head and chief of the village of Greylands, looking down on it from his mansion, Greylands' Rest, does not countenance these Sisters: he discountenances them, in fact, and has been heard to ridicule the ladies. The Master of Greylands, the title generally accorded him, is no unmeaning appellation, for in most things his will is law. Beyond the part of the building thus inhabited, there is a portion that lies in complete ruin; it was the chapel in the days of the monks, but its walls are but breast-high now; and beyond it comes another portion, still in tolerable preservation, called the Friar's Keep. The Friar's Keep was said to have gained its appellation from the fact that the confessor to the convent lived in it, together with some holy men, his brethren. A vast pile of buildings it must have been in its prime; and some of the traditions said that this Friar's Keep was in fact a monastery, divided from the nunnery by the chapel. A wild, desolate, grand place it must have been, looking down on the turbulent sea. Tales and stories were still told of those days: of the jolly monks, of the secluded nuns, some tales good, some bad—just as tales in the generations to come will be told of the present day. But, whatever scandal may have been whispered, whatever dark deeds of the dark and rude ages gone by, none could be raised of the building now. The only inhabited part of it, that occupied by the good Sisters, who were blameless and self-denying in their lives, who lived but to do good, was revered by all. That portion of it was open, and fair, and above-board; but some mysterious notions existed in regard to the other portion—the Friar's Keep. It was said to be haunted.

Now, this report, attaching to a building of any kind, would be much laughed at in these later times. For one believer in the superstition (however well it may be authenticated), ten, ay twenty, would ridicule it. The simple villagers around believed it religiously: it was said that the Castlemaines, who were educated gentlemen, and anything but simple, believed it too. The Friar's Keep was known to be entirely uninhabited, and part of it abandoned to the owls and bats. This was indisputable; nevertheless, now and again glimpses of a light would be seen within the rooms by some benighted passer-by, and people were not wanting to assert that a ghostly form, habited in a friar's light grey cowl and skirts, would appear at the casement windows, bearing a lamp. Strange noises had also been heard—or were said to have been. There was not one single inhabitant of the village, man or woman, who would have dared to cross the chapel ruins and enter the Friar's Keep alone after nightfall, had it been to save their lives. It did not lack a foundation, this superstition. Tales were whispered of a dreadful crime that had been committed by one of the monks: it transpired abroad; and, to avoid the consequences of being punished by his brethren—who of course only could punish him after public discovery, whatever they might have done without it—he had destroyed himself in a certain room, in the grey habit of his order, and was destined to "come abroad" for ever. So the story ran, and so it was credited. The good ladies at the Nunnery were grieved and vexed when allusion was made to the superstition in their presence, and would have put it down entirely if they could. They did not see anything themselves, were never disturbed by sounds: but, as the credulous villagers would remark to one another in private, the Sisters were the very last people who would be likely to see and hear. They were not near enough to the Friar's Keep for that, and the casements in the Keep could not be seen from their casements.

MRS. HENRY WOOD

The narrow common, or strip of waste land, standing between the street and the Grey Nunnery is enclosed by somewhat high palings. They run along the entire length of the building, from end to end, and have two gates of ingress. The one gate is opposite the porch door of the Grey Nunnery; the other gate leads into the chapel ruins. It should be mentioned that there was no door or communication of any kind between the Nunnery and the site of the chapel, and it did not appear that there ever had been: so that, if anyone required to pass from the Nunnery to the ruins or to the Friar's Keep, they must go round by the road and enter in at the other gate. The chapel wall, breast-high still, extended down to the palings, cutting off the Nunnery and its waste ground from the ruins.

In their secluded home lived these blameless ladies, ever searching for good to do. In a degree they served to replace the loss of a resident pastor. Many a sick and dying bed that ought to have been Mr. Marston's care, had they soothed; more than one frail infant, passing away almost as soon as it had been born, had Sister Mildred, the pious Superioress, after a few moments spent on her bended knees in silent deprecatory prayer, taken upon herself to baptize, that it might be numbered as of the Fold of Christ. They regretted that the clergyman was not more among them, but there it ended: the clergy of those days were not the active pastors of these, neither were they expected to be. The Grey Ladies paid Mr. Marston the utmost respect, and encouraged others to do so; and they were strict attendants at his irregular services on Sundays.

The origin of the sisterhood was this. Many years before, a Miss Mildred Grant, being in poor health, had gone to Greylands for change of air. As she made acquaintance with the fishermen and other poor families, she was quite struck with their benighted condition, both as to spiritual and temporal need. She resolved to do what she could to improve this; she thought it might be a solemn duty laid purposely in her path; and, she took up her abode for good at one of the cottages, and was joined by her sister, Mary Grant. In course of time other ladies, wishing to devote their lives to good works joined them; at length a regular sisterhood of twelve was formed, and they took possession of that abandoned place, the old Grey Nunnery. Six of these ladies were gentlewomen by birth and breeding; and these six had brought some portion of means with them. Six were of inferior degree. These were received without money, and in lieu thereof made themselves useful, taking it in turns to see to the housekeeping, to do the domestic work, go on errands, make and mend the clothes, and the like. All were treated alike, wearing the same dress, and taking their meals together—save the two who might be on domestic duty for the week. At first the Sisterhood had attracted much attention and caused some public talk—for such societies were then almost entirely unknown; but Greylands was a secluded place, and this soon died away. Sister Mildred remained its head, and she was getting in years now. She was a clever, practical woman, without having received much education, though a lady by birth. Latterly she had been in very ill-health; and she had always laboured under a defect, that of partial deafness. Her sister Mary had died early.

Immediately beyond the Friar's Keep the rocks rose abruptly again, and the sight of the sea was there, and for some little way onwards, inaccessible to the eye. Further on, the heights were tolerably flat, and there the preventive men were enabled to pace—which they did assiduously: for those were the days of real smuggling, when fortunes were made by it and sometimes lives marred. The coastguard had a small station just beyond the village, and the officers looked pretty sharply after the beach and the doings of the fishermen.

Just opposite the Friar's Keep, on the other side the road, was a lane, called Chapel Lane, flanking a good-sized clump of trees, almost a grove; and within these trees rose a small, low, thatched-roof building, styled the Hutt. The gentleman inhabiting this dwelling, a slight, bronzed, upright, and active man, with black eyes and black hair, was named Teague. Formerly an officer on board a man-of-war, he had saved enough for a competency through prize money and else, and had also a pension. The village called him Commodore: he would have honestly told you himself that he had no right to that exalted rank—but he did not in the least object to the appellation. He was a vast favourite with the village, from the coastguardsmen to the poor fishermen, fond of treating them in his Hutt, or of giving them a sail in his boat, or a seat in his covered spring cart—both of which articles he kept for pleasure. In habits he was somewhat peculiar; living alone without a servant of any kind, male or female, and waiting entirely on himself.

Chapel Lane—a narrow, pleasant lane, with trees meeting overhead, and wild flowers adorning its banks and hedges in summer—led into the open country, and went directly past Greylands' Rest, the residence of the Castlemaines. This lane was not the chief approach to the house;

that was by the high coach-road that branched off by the Dolphin Inn. And this brings us to speak of the Castlemaines.

Greylands' Rest, and the estate on which it stood, had been purchased and entered upon many years before by the then head and chief of the family, Anthony Castlemaine. His children grew up there. He had three sons—Basil, James, and Peter. Basil was three or four years the elder, for a little girl had died between him and James; and if he were living at the present time, he would be drawing towards sixty years of age. It was not known whether he was living or not. Anthony Castlemaine had been a harsh and hasty man; and Basil was wild and wilful. After a good deal of unpleasantness at home, and some bitter quarrelling between father and son, in which the two younger sons took part against their brother, Basil quitted his home and went abroad. He was twenty-two then, and had come into possession of a very fair sum of money, which fell to him from his late mother. The two other sons came into the same on attaining their majority. Besides this, Mr. Castlemaine handed over to Basil his portion, so that he went away rich. He went to seek his fortune and to get rid of his unnatural relatives, he informed his friends in Greylands and Stilborough, and he hoped never to come back again until Greylands' Rest was his. He never had come back all those years, something like five-and-twenty now, and they had never heard from him directly, though once or twice incidentally. The last time was about four years ago, when chance news came that he was alive and well.

James Castlemaine had remained with his father at Greylands' Rest, managing the land on the estate. Peter had taken his portion and set up as a banker at Stilborough; we have seen with what success. James married, and took his wife home to Greylands' Rest; but she died soon, leaving him a little son. Several years subsequently he married again: a widow lady; and she was the present Mrs. Castlemaine.

Old Anthony Castlemaine lived on, year after year at Greylands' Rest, wondering whether he should see his eldest son again. With all Basil's faults, he had been his father's favourite: and the old man grew to long for him. It was more than either of Basil's brothers did. Basil had had his portion from both father and mother, and so they washed their hands of him, as the two were wont to observe, and they did not want him back again. They, at least, had their wish, though Mr. Castlemaine had not. The old man lived to the age of eighty-five and then died without seeing his eldest son; without, in fact, being sure that he was still alive.

It was not so very long now since old Anthony died: they had just put off the mourning for him. James had come into Greylands' Rest on his father's death: or, at any rate, he had remained in possession; but of the real facts nothing transpired. Rumours and surmises went abroad freely: you cannot hinder people's tongues: and very frequently when nothing is known tongues flow all the faster. Some thought it was left to James In trust for Basil; but nobody knew, and the Castlemaines were close men, who never talked of their own affairs. The estate of Greylands' Rest was supposed to be worth about twelve hundred a year. It was the only portion of old Mr. Castlemaine's property that there could be any doubt or surmise about: what money he had to dispose of, he had divided during his lifetime between James and Peter; Basil having had his at starting. James Castlemaine was the only gentleman of importance living at Greylands; he was looked up to as a sort of feudal lord by its inhabitants generally, and swayed them at will.

Following the coach-road that led off by the Dolphin for about half a mile, you came to a long green avenue on the right hand, which was the chief approach to Greylands' Rest. It was an old house, built of grey stone; a straggling, in-and-out, spacious, comfortable mansion, only two stories high. Before the old-fashioned porch entrance lay a fine green lawn, with seats under its trees, and beds of flowers. Stables, barns, kitchen gardens, and more lawns and flower beds lay around. The rooms inside were many, but rather small; and most of them had to be approached by a narrow passage: as is sometimes the case in ancient houses that are substantially built. From the upper rooms at the side of the house could be seen, just opposite, the Friar's Keep, its casements and its broken upper walls; Commodore Teague's Hutt lying exactly in a line between the two buildings: and beyond all might be caught glimpses of the glorious sea.

It was a cold, bright day in February, the day following the dinner at the banker's. Mr. Castlemaine was busy in his study—a business-room, where he kept his farming accounts, and wrote his letters—which was on the upper floor of the house, looking towards the sea and the Friar's Keep, and was approached from the wide corridor by a short narrow passage having a door at either end. The inner door Mr. Castlemaine often kept locked. In a pretty room below, warm and comfortable, and called the Red Parlour from its prevailing colour, its ceiling low, its windows opening to the lawn, but closed to-day, sat the ladies of his family: Mrs. Castlemaine, her daughter Flora, and Ethel Reene.

It has been said that James Castlemaine's second wife was a widow—
she was a Mrs. Reene. Her first marriage had also been to a widower,
Mr. Reene, who had one daughter, Ethel. Mrs. Reene never took to
this stepchild; she was jealous of Mr. Reene's affection for her; and
when, on Mr. Reene's death, which occurred shortly after the marriage,
it was found that he had left considerably more money to his child
than to his new wife, Mrs. Reene's dislike was complete. A year or
two after her marriage with Mr. Castlemaine, a little girl was born to
her—Flora. On this child, her only one, she lavished all her love—but
she had none for Ethel. Mr. Castlemaine, on his part, gave the greater
portion of his affection to his son, the child of his first wife, Harry. A
very fine young man now, of some five-and-twenty years, was Harry
Castlemaine, and his father was wrapped up in him. Ethel addressed
Mr. and Mrs. Castlemaine as "papa" and "mamma," but she was in
point of fact not really related to either. She was five years old when she
came to Greylands' Rest, had grown up there as a child of the house,
and often got called, out of doors, "Miss Castlemaine."

Ethel seemed to stand alone without kith or kin, with no one
to love her; and she felt it keenly. As much as a young lady can be
put upon and snubbed in a gentleman's well-appointed family, Ethel
Reene was. Mr. Castlemaine was always kind to her, though perhaps
somewhat indifferent; Mrs. Castlemaine was unkind and tyrannical;
Flora—an indulged, selfish, ill-bred girl of twelve, forward enough in
some things for one double her age—did her best to annoy her in all
ways. And Mrs. Castlemaine permitted this: she could see no fault in
Flora, she hated Ethel. Ethel Reene was nineteen now, growing fast
into womanhood; but she was young for her years, and of a charming
simplicity—not so rare in girls then as it is now. She was good, gentle,
and beautiful; with a pale, quiet beauty that slowly takes hold of the
heart, but as surely stays there. Her large eyes, full of depth, sweetness,
and feeling, gazed out at you with almost the straightforward innocence
of a child: and no child's heart could have been more free from guile.
Her hair was dark, her pretty features were refined and delicate, her
whole appearance ladylike and most attractive.

Ethel Reene had much to put up with in her everyday life: for
Mrs. Castlemaine's conduct was trying in the extreme; Flora's worse
than trying. She seldom retaliated: having learnt how useless retaliation
from her was against them: and, besides, she loved peace. But she was
not without spirit: and only herself knew what it had cost her to learn

to keep that spirit under: sometimes when matters went too far, she would check her stepmother's angry torrent by a few firm words, and quietly leave the room to take refuge in the peace and solitude of her own chamber. Or else she would put her bonnet on and wander away to the cliffs; where, seated on the extreme edge, she would remain for hours, looking out on the sea. She had once been fond of taking her place in the chapel ruins, and sitting there, for the expanse of ocean seen from thence was most grand and beautiful; sometimes, when the water was low, so that the strip of beach beneath could be gained, she would step down the short but dangerous rock to it—which strip of beach was only accessible from the chapel ruins and at low tide. But one day Mr. Castlemaine happened to see her do this; he was very angry, and absolutely forbade her, not only to descend the rocks, but to enter, under any pretence whatsoever, the site of the chapel ruins. Ethel was not one to disobey.

But to sit on the higher rocks farther up, by the coastguard station, was not denied her; Mr. Castlemaine only enjoining her to be cautious. It had grown to be her favourite spot, and she often sat or walked there on the cliff's edge. The ever-changing water seemed to bring consolation to her spirit; it spoke to her in strange, soothing whispers; it fed the romance and the dreams that lie in a young girl's heart. When the sea was rough and the waves dashed against the cliffs, flinging up their spray mountains high, and sprinkling her face as with a mist, she would stand, lost in the grandeur and awe of the scene, her hat off and held by its ribbons, her hair floating in the wind: the sky and the waves seemed to speak to her soul of immortality; to bring nearer to her the far-off gates of heaven. And so, for want of suitable companionship, Ethel Reene shared her secrets with the sea.

The glass doors of the red parlour were closed to-day against the east wind; the lawn beyond, though bright with sunshine, lay cold under its bare and wintry trees. Mrs. Castlemaine sat by the fire working at a pair of slippers; a little woman, she, dressed in striped green silk, with light hair, and a cross look on what had once been a very pretty, though sharp-featured face. Ethel sat near the window, drawing; she wore a bright ruby winter dress of fine merino, with some white lace at its throat and sleeves; a blue ribbon, to which was suspended some small gold ornament, encircled her delicate neck; drops of gold were in her ears; and her pretty cheeks were flushed to crimson, for Mrs. Castlemaine was hot in dispute and making her feel very angry. Flora, a restless damsel, in a flounced brown frock and white pinafore, with a fair, pretty, saucy face, and her flaxen curls tied back with blue, was perched on the music-stool before Ethel's piano, striking barbarous chords with one hand and abusing Ethel alternately.

The dispute to-day was this. Miss Oldham, Flora's governess, had lately given warning precipitately, and left Greylands' Rest; tired out, as everybody but Mrs. Castlemaine knew, with her pupil's insolence. Mrs. Castlemaine had not yet found anyone willing, or whom she deemed eligible, to replace her—for it must be remembered that governesses then were somewhat rare. Weary of waiting, Mrs. Castlemaine had come to a sudden determination, and was now announcing it, that Ethel should have the honour of filling the post.

"It is of no use, mamma," said Ethel. "I could not teach; I am sure I am not fit for it. And, you know, Flora would never obey me."

"That I'd not," put in Miss Flora, wheeling herself half round on the stool. "I hate governesses; and they do me no good. I don't know half as much as I did when Miss Oldham came, twelve months ago. Do I, mamma?"

"I fear you do not, my darling," replied Mrs. Castlemaine. "Miss Oldham's system of teaching was quite a failure, and she sadly neglected her duty; but—"

"Oh, mamma," interrupted Flora, peevishly, "don't put in that horrid 'but.' I tell you I hate governesses; I'm not going to have another. Nothing but learning lessons, lessons, lessons, all day long, just as though you wanted me to be a governess!"

"If you did not learn, Flora, you would grow up a little heathen," Ethel ventured to remark. "You would not like that."

"Now don't you put in your word," retorted the girl, passionately. "It's not your place to interfere with me: is it, mamma?"

"Certainly not, my sweet child."

Miss Flora had changed her place. Quitting the music-stool for the hearthrug, she took up the poker; and now stood brandishing it around, and looking daggers at Ethel. Ethel, her sweet face still flushed, went steadily on with her drawing.

"She's as ill-natured as she can be! She'd like—mamma, she'd like— to see me toiling at geography and French grammar all night as well as all day. Nasty thing!"

"I can believe anything of Ethel that is ill-natured," equably spoke Mrs. Castlemaine, turning her slipper. "But I have made up my mind that she shall teach you, Flo, my love, under—of course, entirely under—my superintendence. Miss Oldham used to resent interference."

"I do think, mamma, you must be joking!" cried Ethel, turning her flushed face and her beautiful eyes on her stepmother.

"When do I joke?" retorted Mrs. Castlemaine. "It will save the nuisance of a governess in the house: and you shall teach Flora."

"I'll give her all the trouble I can; she's a toad," cried Miss Flora, bringing the poker within an inch of her mother's nose. "And I'll learn just what I like, and let alone what I don't like. She's not going to be set up in authority over me, as Miss Oldham was. I'll kick you if you try it, Ethel."

"Stop, stop," spoke Ethel, firmness in her tone, decision on her pretty lips. "Mamma, pray understand me; I cannot attempt to do this. My life is not very pleasant now; it would be unbearable then. You know—you see—what Flora is: how can you ask me?"

Mrs. Castlemaine half rose, in her angry spirit. It was something new for Ethel to set her mandates at defiance. Her voice turned to a scream; her small light eyes dilated.

"Do you beard me in my own house, Ethel Reene? I say that you shall do this. I am mistress here—"

Mistress she might be, but Mr. Castlemaine was master and at that moment the door opened, and he came in. Disputes were not very unusual in his home, but this seemed to be a frantic one.

"What is the meaning of this?" he inquired, halting in astonishment, and taking in the scene with his keen dark eyes. His wife unusually angry, her voice high; Ethel in tears—for they had come unbidden; Flora brandishing the poker towards Ethel, and dancing to its movements.

Mrs. Castlemaine sat down to resume her wool-work, her ruffled feathers subdued to smoothness. She never cared to give way to unseemly temper, no, nor to injustice, in the presence of her husband; for she had the grace to feel that he would be ashamed of it—ashamed for her; and that it would still further weaken the little influence she retained over him.

"Were you speaking of a governess for Flora?" he asked, advancing and taking the poker from the young lady's hand. "What has Ethel to do with that?"

"I was observing that Ethel has a vast deal of leisure time, and that she might, rather than be idle, fill it up by teaching Flora," replied

Mrs. Castlemaine, as softly as though her mouth were made of butter. "Especially as Ethel's French is so perfect. As a temporary thing, of course, if—if it did not answer."

"I do not find Ethel idle: she always seems to me to have some occupation on hand," observed Mr. Castlemaine. "As to her undertaking the teaching of Flora—would you like it, Ethel?"

"No, papa," was the brave answer, as she strove to hide her tears. "I have, I am sure, no talent for teaching; I dislike it very much: and Flora would never obey a word I said. It would make my life miserable—I was saying so when you came in."

"Then, my dear child, the task shall certainly not be put upon yon. Why need you have feared it would be? We have no more right to force Ethel to do what is distasteful to her, than we should have to force it on ourselves," he added, turning to his wife. "You must see that, Sophia."

"But—" began Mrs. Castlemaine.

"No buts, as to this," he interrupted. "You are well able to pay and keep a governess—and, as Ethel justly observes, she would not be able to do anything with Flora. Miss Oldham could not do it. My opinion is, no governess ever will do it, so long as you spoil the child."

"I don't spoil her, James."

Mr. Castlemaine lifted his dark eyebrows: the assertion was too palpably untrue to be worthy a refutation. "The better plan to adopt with Flora would be to send her to school, as Harry says—"

"That I will never do."

"Then look out for a successor to Miss Oldham. And, my strong advice to you, Sophia, is—let the governess, when she comes, hold entire control over Flora and be allowed to punish her when she deserves it. I shall not care to see her grow up the self-willed, unlovable child she seems to be now."

Mrs. Castlemaine folded up her slipper quietly and left the room; she was boiling over with rage, in spite of her apparent calmness. Flora, who stood in fear of her father, flew off to the kitchen, to demand bread and jam and worry the servants. Ethel was going on with her drawing; and Mr. Castlemaine, who had a taste for sketching himself, went and looked over her.

"Thank you, papa," she softly said, lifting to him for a moment her loving eyes. "It would have been bad both for Flora and for me."

"Of course it would," he replied: "Flora ought to have a good tight rein over her. What's this you are doing, Ethel? The Friar's Keep! Why, what a curious coincidence! Mary Ursula was filling in just the same thing last night."

"Was she, papa? It makes a nice sketch."

"You don't draw as well as Mary Ursula does, Ethel."

"I do nothing as well as she does, papa. I don't think anybody does."

"What are those figures in the foreground?"

"I meant them for two of the Grey Sisters. Their cloaks are not finished yet."

"Oh," said Mr. Castlemaine, rather shortly. "And that's a group of fishermen, I see: much the more sensible people of the two."

"What did Mary Ursula say last night, papa?"

"Say? Nothing particular. She sent her love to Ethel."

"Did she dine at table?"

"Why, of course not, child. Miss Mountsorrel spent the evening with her."

"And, papa," whispered Ethel, with a pretty little laugh and blush, "is it fixed yet?"

"Is what fixed?"

"The wedding-day."

"I don't think so—or you would have heard of it. I expect she will ask you to be her bridesmaid."

III

AT THE DOLPHIN INN

The Dolphin Inn, as already said, stood in the angle between the village street and the high road that branched off from the street to the open country. It faced the road, standing, like most of the dwellings in Greylands, somewhat back from it. A substantial, low-roofed house, painted yellow, with a flaming sign-board in front, bearing a dolphin with various hues and colours, and two low bow-windows on either side the door. Beyond lay a yard with out-houses and stables, and there was some good land behind. Along the wall, underneath the parlour windows and on either side of the entrance door, ran a bench on which wayfarers might sit; at right angles with it, near the yard, was a pump with a horse-trough beside it. Upon a pinch, the inn could supply a pair of post-horses: but they were seldom called for, as Stilborough was so near. It was the only inn of any kind at Greylands, and was frequented by the fishermen, as well as occasionally by more important guests. The landlord was John Bent. The place was his own, and had been his father's before him. He was considered to be a "warm" man; to be able to live at his ease, irrespective of custom. John Bent was independent in manner and speech, except to his wife. Mrs. Bent, a thrifty, bustling, talkative woman, had taken John's independence out of him at first setting off, so far as she was concerned; but they got on very well together. To Mr. Castlemaine especially John was given to show independence. They were civil to each other, but there was no love lost between them. Mr. Castlemaine would have liked to purchase the Dolphin and the land pertaining to it: he had made more than one strong overture to do so, which John had resisted and resented. The landlord, too, had taken up an idea that Mr. Castlemaine did not encourage the sojourn of strangers at the inn; but had done his best in a quiet way to discourage it, as was observed in regard to the Grey Ladies. Altogether John Bent did not favour the Master of Greylands.

On one of the days of this selfsame month of February, when the air was keen and frosty and the sea sparkled under the afternoon sunshine, John Bent and his wife sat in the room they mostly occupied, which was called the best kitchen. Called so in familiar parlance only, however, for it was really used as the sitting-room of the landlord and his wife, and not for cooking. The room was on the side of the house, its large, low, three-framed window and its door facing the beach. Outside this window was another of those hospitable benches, for customers to sit down on to drink their ale when it pleased them. Mrs. Bent herself liked to sit there when work was over, and criticise the doings of the village. Whatever might be the weather, this door, like the front one, stood open; and well-known guests, or neighbours stepping in for a gossip, would enter by it. But no customer attempted to call for pipe or drink in the room, unless specially permitted.

Mrs. Bent stood at the table before the window, picking shrimps for potting. She was slim and active, with dark curls on either side of her thin and comely face. Her cap had cherry-coloured ribbons in it, her favourite colour, and flying strings; her cotton gown, of a chintz pattern, was drawn through its pocket-hole, displaying a dark stuff petticoat, and neat shoes and stockings. John Bent sat at the blazing fire, as near to it as he could get his wooden chair in, reading the "Stilborough Herald."

"It's uncommon cold to-day!" he broke out presently, giving a twist to his back. "The wind comes in and cuts one like a knife. Don't you think, Dorothy, we might shut that door a bit these sharp days?"

"No, I don't," said Mrs. Bent.

"You'll get rheumatism yet before the winter's over, as sure as you're a living woman. Or I shall."

"Shall I?" retorted Mrs. Bent, in her sharply decisive tones. "Over forty years of age I am now, and I've been here nigh upon twenty, and never had a touch of it yet. I am not going to begin to shut up doors and windows, John Bent, to please you or anybody else."

Thus put down, John resigned himself to his paper again. He was a spare, middle-sized man, some few years older than his wife, with a red healthy face and scanty grey hair. Presently he laid the newspaper aside, and sat watching his wife's nimble fingers.

"Dorothy, woman, when those shrimps are done, you might send a pot of 'em over to poor Sister Mildred. She's uncommon weak, they say."

The very idea that had been running through Mrs. Bent's own mind. But she did not receive the suggestion courteously.

"Suppose you attend to your own concerns, John. If I am to supply the parish with shrimps gratis, it's about time I left off potting."

John picked up his paper again with composure: he was accustomed to all this: and just then a shadow fell across the room. A fisherman was standing at the open door with some fish for sale.

"It's you, Tim, is it?" cried Mrs. Bent, in her shrillest tones. "It's not often your lazy limbs bring me anything worth buying. What is it to-day?"

"A splendid cod, Mrs. Bent," replied the man. "Never was finer caught."

"And a fine price, I dare be bound!" returned the landlady, stepping aside to inspect the fish. "What's the price?"

Tim named it; putting on a little to allow of what he knew would ensue—the beating down. Mrs. Bent spoke loudly in her wrath.

"Now look here, Tim Gleeson!—do you think I'm made of money; or do you think I'm soft? I'll give you just half the sum. If you don't like it you may take yourself off and your fish behind you."

Mrs. Bent got the cod at her price. She had returned to her shrimps, when, after a gentle tap at the open door, there entered one of the Grey Sisters. Sister Ann—whose week it was to help in the domestic work and to go on errands—was a busy, cheerful, sensible woman, as fond of talking as Mrs. Bent herself. She was dressed entirely in grey. A grey stuff gown of a convenient length for walking, that is, just touching the ankles; a grey cloth cloak reaching down nearly as far; and a round grey straw bonnet with a white net border close to the face. When the ladies took possession of the Grey Nunnery, and constituted themselves a Sisterhood, they had assumed this attire. It was neat, suitable, and becoming; and not of a nature to attract particular attention when only one or two of them were seen abroad together. From the dress, however, had arisen the appellation applied to them—the Grey Ladies. In summer weather the stuff used was of a lighter texture. The stockings worn by Sister Ann were grey, the shoes stout, and fastened with a steel buckle. The only difference made by the superior sisters was, that the material of their gowns and cloaks was finer and softer, and their stockings were white.

"Lack-a-day! these shrimps will never get done!" cried Mrs. Bent, under her breath. "How d'ye do, Sister Ann?" she said aloud, her tones less sharp, out of respect to the Order. "You look as blue as bad news. I hope there's no fresh sickness or accident."

"It's the east wind," replied Sister Ann. "Coming round that beach corner, it does seize hold of one. I've such a pain here with it," touching her chest, "that I can hardly draw my breath."

"Cramps," said Mrs. Bent, shortly. "John," she added, turning sharply on her husband, "you'd better get Sister Ann a spoonful or two of that cordial, instead of sitting to roast your face at that fire till it's the colour of red pepper."

"Not for worlds," interposed Sister Ann, really meaning it. But John, at the hospitable suggestion, had moved away.

"I have come over to ask you if you'll be good enough to let me have a small pot of currant jelly, Mrs. Bent," continued the Grey Sister. "It is for Sister Mildred, poor thing—"

"Is she no better?" interrupted Mrs. Bent.

"Not a bit. And her lips are so parched, poor lady, and her deafness is so worrying—"

"Oh, as to her deafness, that'll never be better," cried Mrs. Bent. "It will get worse as she grows older."

"It can't be much worse than it is: it has always been bad," returned Sister Ann, who seemed slightly to resent the fact of the deafness. "We have had a good bit of sickness in the village, and our black currant jelly is all gone: not that we made much, being so poor. If you will let me buy a pot from you, Mrs. Bent, we shall be glad."

For answer, Mrs. Bent left her shrimps, unlocked a corner cupboard, and put two small pots of jelly into the Sister's hand.

"I am not sure that I can afford both to-day," said Sister Ann, dubiously. "How much are they?"

"Nothing," returned Mrs. Bent. "Not one farthing will I take from the ladies: I'm always glad to do the little I can for any of you. Give them to Sister Mildred with my respects; and say, please, that when I've done my shrimps I'll bring her over a pot of them. I was intending to do it before you came in."

The landlord returned with something in a wine-glass, and stopped the Sister's thanks by making her drink it. Putting the jelly in her basket, Sister Ann, who had no time to stay for a longer gossip that day, gratefully departed.

"It's well the Master of Greylands didn't hear you promise the shrimps and give her them two pots of jelly, wife," cried John Bent, with a queer kind of laugh. "He'd not have liked it."

"The Master of Greylands may lump it."

"It's my belief he'd like to drive the Grey Sisters away from the place, instead of having 'em helped with pots of jelly."

"What I choose to do, I do do, thank goodness, without need to ask leave of anybody," returned independent Mrs. Bent.

"I can't think what it is puts Mr. Castlemaine against 'em," debated

John Bent, thoughtfully. "Unless he fancies that if they were less busy over religion, and that, we might get the parson here more as a regular thing."

"We should be none the better for him," snapped Mrs. Bent. "For my part, I don't see much good in parsons," she candidly added. "They only get into people's way."

The silence that ensued was broken by a sound of horses in the distance, followed by the blowing of a horn. John Bent and his wife looked simultaneously at the eight-day clock, ticking in its mahogany case by the fire, and saw that it was on the stroke of four, which was the time the London coach came by. John passed through the house to the front door; his wife, after glancing at herself in the hanging glass and giving a twitch to her cap and her cherry ribbons, left her shrimps and followed him.

It was not that they expected the coach to bring visitors to them. Passengers from London and elsewhere were generally bound to Stilborough. But they as regularly went to the door to be in readiness, in case any did alight; to see it pass, and to exchange salutations with the coachman and guard.

It was an event in the Dolphin's somewhat monotonous day's existence.

"I do believe, wife, it's going to stop!" cried John.

It was doing that already. The four horses were drawing up; the guard was descending from his seat behind. He opened the door to let out a gentleman, and took a portmanteau from the boot. Before John Bent, naturally slow of movement, had well bestirred himself, the gentleman, who seemed to be remarkably quick and active, had put some money into the guard's hand and caught up his portmanteau.

"I beg your pardon, sir," said John, taking it from him. "You are welcome, sir: will you be pleased to enter?"

The stranger was on the point of stepping indoors, when he halted and looked up at the signboard—at the dolphin depicted there in all the hues of the rainbow, its tail lashing up spouts of imaginary water. Smiling to himself, almost as though the dolphin were an old acquaintance, he went in. Mrs. Bent courtesied low to him in the good old respectful fashion, and he returned it with a bow.

A fire was blazing in one of the parlours, and to this room the guest was conducted by both landlord and landlady. Taking off his upper coat, which was warmly slashed with dark Fur, they saw a slight, active man of some eight-and-twenty years, under the middle height, with a fresh, pleasant, handsome face, and bright dark eyes. Something in the face seemed to strike on a chord of the landlord's memory.

"Who the dickens is he like?" mentally questioned John. "Anyway, I like his looks."

"I can have a bedchamber, I suppose?" spoke the stranger; and they noticed that his English, though quite fluent as to words, had a foreign ring in it. "Will you show me to one?"

"At your service, sir; please step this way," said Mrs. Bent, in her most gracious tones, for she was habitually courteous to her guests, and was besides favourably impressed by this one's looks and manners. "Hot water directly, Molly," she called out in the direction of the kitchen; "and John, do you bring up the gentleman's luggage."

"I can't think who it is his face puts me in mind of," began John, when he and his wife got back to their room again, and she set on to make hasty work of the shrimps.

"Rubbish to his face," spoke Mrs. Bent. "The face is nice enough, if you mean that. It's late to get anything of a dinner up; and he has not said what he'll have, though I asked him."

"And look here, wife—that portmanteau is not an English one."

"It may be Dutch, for all it matters to us. Now John Bent, just you stir up that fire a bit, and put some coal on. I may have to bring a saucepan in here, for what I know."

"Tush!" said John, doing as he was bid, nevertheless. "A chop and a potato: that's as much as most of these chance travellers want."

"Not when they are from over the water. I don't forget the last foreign Frenchman that put up here. Fifteen dishes he wanted for his dinner, if he wanted one. And all of 'em dabs and messes."

She had gone to carry away her shrimps when the stranger came down. He walked direct into the room, and looked from the open door. The landlord stood up.

"You are Thomas Bent, I think," said the stranger, turning round.

"John Bent, sir. My father was Thomas Bent, and he has been dead many a year."

"And this is your good wife?" he added, as the landlady came bustling in. "Mistress of the inn."

"And master too," muttered John, in an undertone.

"I was about to order dinner, Mr. Bent—"

"Then you'd better order it of me, sir," put in the landlady. "His head's no better than a sieve if it has much to carry. Ask for spinach and cauliflower, and you'd get served up carrots and turnips."

"Then I cannot do better than leave my dinner to you, madam," said the young man with a pleasant laugh. "I should like some fish out of that glorious sea; and the rest I leave to you. Can I have an English plum-pudding?

"An English plum-pudding! Good gracious, sir, it could not be made and boiled!"

"That will do for to-morrow, then."

Mrs. Bent departed, calling to Molly as she went. The inn kept but two servants; Molly, and a man; the latter chiefly attending to out-of-door things: horses, pigs and such like. When further help was needed indoors, it could be had from the village.

"This must be a healthy spot," remarked the stranger, taking a chair without ceremony at John Bent's fire. "It is very open."

"Uncommon healthy, sir. A bit bleak in winter, when the wind's in the east; as it is to-day."

"Have you many good families residing about?"

"Only one, sir. The Castlemaines?"

"The Castlemaines?"

"An old family who have lived here for many a year. You'd pass their place, sir, not long before getting out here; a house of greystone on your left hand. It is called Greylands' Rest."

"I have heard of Greylands' Rest—and also of the Castlemaines. It belonged, I think, to old Anthony Castlemaine."

"It did, sir. His son has it now."

"I fancied he had more than one son."

"He had three, sir. The eldest, Mr. Basil, went abroad and never was heard of after: leastways, nothing direct from him. The second, Mr. James, has Greylands' Rest. He always lived there with his father, and he lives there still—master of all since the old gentleman died."

"How did it come to him?" asked the stranger, hastily. "By will?"

"Ah, sir, that's what no soul can tell. All sorts of surmises went about; but nobody knows how it was."

A pause. "And the third son? Where is he?"

"The third's Mr. Peter. He is a banker at Stilborough."

"Is he rich?"

John Bent laughed at the question. "Rich, sir? Him? Why, it's said he could almost buy up the world. He has one daughter; a beautiful young lady, who's going to be married to young Mr. Blake-Gordon, a son of Sir Richard. Many thought that Mr. Castlemaine—the present Master of Greylands—would have liked to get her for his own son. But—"

In burst Mrs. Bent, a big cooking apron tied on over her gown. She looked slightly surprised at seeing the stranger-seated there; but said nothing. Unlocking the corner cupboard, and throwing wide its doors, she began searching for something on the shelves.

"Here you are, Mrs. Bent! Busy as usual."

The sudden salutation came from a gentleman who had entered the house hastily. A tall, well-made, handsome, young fellow, with a ready tongue, and a frank expression in his dark brown eyes. He stood just inside the door, and did not observe the stranger.

"Is it you, Mr. Harry?" she said, glancing round.

"It's nobody else," he answered. "What an array of jam pots! Do you leave the key in the door? A few of those might be walked off and never be missed."

"I should like to see anybody attempt it," cried Mrs. Bent, wrathfully. "You are always joking, Mr. Harry."

He laughed cordially. "John," he said, turning to the landlord, "did the coach bring a parcel for me?"

"No, sir. Were you expecting one, Mr. Harry?"

Mrs. Bent turned completely round from her cupboard. "It's not a trick you are thinking to play us, is it, sir? I have not forgotten that other parcel you had left here once."

"Other parcel? Oh, that was ever so many years ago. I am expecting this from London, John, if you will take it in. It will come to-morrow, I suppose. Mrs. Bent thinks I am a boy still."

"Ah no, sir, that I don't," she said. "You've long grown beyond that, and out of my control."

"Out of everybody else's too," he laughed. "Where I used to get cuffs I now get kisses, Mrs. Bent. And I am not sure but they are the more dangerous application of the two."

"I am very sure they are," called out Mrs. Bent, as the young man went off laughing, after bowing slightly to the stranger, who was now standing up, and whose appearance bespoke him to be a gentleman.

"Who was that?" asked the stranger of John Bent.

"That was Mr. Harry Castlemaine, sir. Son of the Master of Greylands."

With one leap, the stranger was outside the door, gazing after him. But Harry Castlemaine, quick and active, was already nearly beyond view. When the stranger came back to his place again, Mrs. Bent had locked up her cupboard and was gone.

"A fine-looking young man," he remarked.

"And a good-hearted one as ever lived—though he is a bit random," said John. "I like Mr. Harry; I don't like his father."

"Why not?"

"Well, sir, I hardly know why. One is apt to take dislikes sometimes."

"You were speaking of Greylands' Rest—of the rumours that went abroad respecting it when old Mr. Castlemaine died. What were they?"

"Various rumours, sir; but all tending to one and the same point. And that was, whether Greylands' Rest had, or had not, legally come to Mr. James Castlemaine."

"Being the second son," quietly spoke the stranger. "There can be no question I should think, that the rightful heir was the eldest son, Basil."

"And it was known, too, that Basil was his father's favourite; and that the old man during his last years was always looking and longing for him to come back," spoke John Bent, warming with the subject: "and in short, sir, everybody expected it would be left to Basil. On the other hand, James was close at hand, and the old man could leave it to him if he pleased."

"One glance at the will would set all doubt at rest."

"Ay. But it was not known, sir, whether there was a will, or not."

"Not known?"

"No, sir. Some said there was a will, and that it left all to Mr. Basil; others said there was no will at all, but that old Anthony Castlemaine made Mr. James a deed of gift of Greylands' Rest. And a great many said, and still say, that old Mr. Castlemaine only handed him over the estate in trust for Mr. Basil—or for any sons Mr. Basil might leave after him."

The stranger sat in silence. On his little finger shone a magnificent diamond ring, evidently of great value; he twirled it about unconsciously.

"What is your opinion, Mr. Bent?" he suddenly asked.

"Mine, sir? Well, I can't help thinking that the whole was left to Mr. Basil, and that if he's alive the place is no more Mr. James's than it is mine. I think it particularly for two reasons: one because the old man always said it would be Basil's; and again if it was given to Mr. James, whether by will or by deed of gift, he would have taken care to show abroad the will or the deed that gave it him, and so set the rumours at rest for good. Not but what all the Castlemaines are close and haughty-natured men, never choosing to volunteer information about themselves. So that—"

"Now then, John Bent! It's about time you began to lay the cloth and see to the silver."

No need to say from whom the interruption came. Mrs. Bent, her face flushed to the colour of the cherry ribbons, whisked in and whisked out again. John followed; and set about his cloth-laying. The stranger sat where he was, in a reverie, until called to dinner.

It was a small, but most excellent repast, the wine taken with it some of the Dolphin's choice Burgundy, of which it had a little bin. John Bent waited on his guest, who dined to his complete satisfaction. He was about to leave the bottle on the table after dinner, but the guest motioned it away.

"No, no more; I do not drink after dinner. It is not our custom in France."

"Oh, very well, sir. I'll cork it up for to-morrow. I—I beg your pardon, sir," resumed the landlord, as he drew the cloth from the table, "what name shall I put down to you, sir?"

The stranger rose and stood on the hearthrug, speaking distinctly when he gave his name.

Speaking distinctly. Nevertheless John Bent seemed not to hear it, for he stared like one in a dream.

"What?" he gasped, in a startled tone of terror, as he staggered back against the sideboard; and some of the fresh colour left his face. "What name did you say, sir?"

"Anthony Castlemaine."

IV

Foreshadowings of Evil

The stone walls of Greylands' Rest lay cold and still under the pale sunshine of the February day. The air was sharp and frosty; the sun, though bright to the eye, had little warmth in it; and the same cutting east wind that John Bent had complained of to the traveller who had alighted at his house the previous afternoon, was prevailing still with an equal keenness.

Mr. Castlemaine felt it in his study, where he had been busy all the morning. He fancied he must have caught a chill, for a slight shiver suddenly stirred his tall, fine frame, and he turned to the fire and gave it a vigorous poke. The fuel was wood and coal mixed, and the blaze went roaring up the chimney. The room was not large. Standing with his back to the fire, the window was on his right hand; the door on his left; opposite to him, against the wall, stood a massive piece of mahogany furniture, called a bureau. It was a kind of closed-in desk, made somewhat in the fashion of the banker's desk at Stilborough, but larger; the inside had pigeon-holes and deep drawers, and a slab for writing on. This inside was well filled with neatly arranged bundles of papers, with account books belonging to the farm business and else, and with some few old letters: and the Master of Greylands was as cautions to keep this desk closed and locked from the possibility of the view of those about him as his brother Peter was to keep his. The Castlemaines were proud, reticent, and careful men.

For a good part of the morning Mr. Castlemaine had been busy at this desk. He had shut and locked it now, and was standing with his back to the fire, deep in thought. Two letters of the large size in vogue before envelopes were used, and sealed with the Castlemaine crest in red wax, lay on the side-table, ready to be posted. His left hand was inside his waistcoat, resting on the broad plaited shirt-frill of fine cambric; his bright dark eyes had rather a troubled look in them as they sought that old building over the fields opposite, the Friar's Keep, and the sparkling sea beyond. In reality, Mr. Castlemaine was looking neither at the Friar's Keep nor the sea, for he was deep in thought and saw nothing.

The Master of Greylands was of a superstitious nature: it may as well be stated candidly: difficult though it was to believe such of so practical a man. Not to the extent of giving credit to stories of ghosts and apparitions; the probability is, that in his heart he would have laughed at that; but he did believe in signs and warnings, in omens of ill-luck and good luck.

On this selfsame morning he had awoke with an impression of discomfort, as if some impending evil were hanging over him; he could not account for it, for there was no conducing cause; and at the time he did not connect it with any superstitions feeling or fancy, but thought he must be either out of sorts, or had had some annoyance that he did not at the moment of waking recollect; something lying latent in his mind. Three or four little hindrances, or mishaps, occurred when he was dressing. First of all, he could not find his slippers: he hunted here; he looked there; and then remembered that he had left them the previous night in his study—a most unusual thing for him to do—and he had to go and fetch them, or else dress in his stockings. Next, in putting on his shirt, he tore the buttonhole at the neck, and was obliged to change it for another. And the last thing he did was to upset all his shaving water, and had to wait while fresh was brought.

"Nothing but impediments: it seems as though I were not to get dressed to-day," muttered the Master of Greylands. "Can there be any ill-luck in store for me?"

The intelligent reader will doubtless be much surprised to hear him ask so ridiculous a question. Nevertheless, the same kind of thing—these marked hindrances—had occurred twice before in Mr. Castlemaine's life, and each time a great evil had followed in the day. Not of the present time was he thinking, now as he stood, but of one of those past days, and of what it had brought forth.

"Poor Maria!" he softly cried—alluding to his first wife, of whom he had been passionately fond. "Well, and merry, and loving in the morning; and at night stretched before me in death. It was an awful accident! and I—I have never cared quite so much for the world since. Maria was—what is it? Come in."

A knock at the door had disturbed the reflections. Mr. Castlemaine let fall his coat tails, which he had then caught up, and turned his head to it. A man servant appeared.

"Commodore Teague wants to know, sir, whether he may get those two or three barrow-loads of wood moved to the Hutt to-day. He'd like to, he says, if it's convenient."

"Yes, he can have it done. Is he here, Miles?"

"Yes, sir; he is waiting in the yard."

"I'll come and speak to him."

And the Master of Greylands, taking the two letters from the side-table, left the room to descend, shutting the door behind him.

We must turn for a few minutes to the Dolphin Inn, and to the previous evening. Nothing could well have exceeded John Bent's consternation when his guest, the unknown stranger, had revealed his name. Anthony Castlemaine! Not quite at first, but after a short interval, the landlord saw how it must be—that he was the son of the late Basil Castlemaine. And he was not the best pleased to hear it in the moment's annoyance.

"You ought to have told me, sir," he stammered in his confusion. "It was unkind to take me at a disadvantage. Here have I been using liberties with the family's name, supposing I was talking to an utter stranger!"

The frank expression of the young man's face, the pleasant look in his fine brown eyes, tended to reassure the landlord, even better than words.

"You have not said a syllable of my family that I could take exception to," he freely said. "You knew my father: will you shake hands with me, John Bent, as his son?"

"You are too good, sir; and I meant no harm by my gossip," said the landlord, meeting the offered hand. "You must be the son of Mr. Basil. It's a great many years since he went away, and I was but a youngster, but I remember him. Your face is nearly the same as his was, sir. The likeness was puzzling me beyond everything. I hope Mr. Basil is well, sir."

"No," said the young man, "he is dead. And I have come over here, as his son and heir, to claim Greylands' Rest."

It was even so. The facts were as young Anthony Castlemaine stated. And a short summary of past events must be given here.

When Basil Castlemaine went abroad so many years ago, in his hot-blooded youth, he spent some of the first years roaming about: seeing the world, he called it. Later, circumstances brought him acquainted with a young English lady, whose friends lived in France, in the province of Dauphiné: which, as the world knows, is close on the borders of Italy. They had settled near a place called Gap, and were in commerce there, owning some extensive silk-mills. Basil Castlemaine, tired probably of his wandering life, and of being a beau garçon, married this young lady, put all the money he had left (it was a very tolerably good sum) into the silk-mills, and became a partner. There he had remained. He liked the climate; he liked the French mode of life; he liked the business he had engaged in. Not once had he re-visited England. He was by nature a most obstinate man, retaining anger for ever, and he would not give token of remembrance to the father and brothers who, in his opinion, had been too glad to get rid of him. No doubt they had. But, though he did not allow them to hear of him, he heard occasionally of them. An old acquaintance of his, who was the son of one Squire Dobie, living some few miles on the other side Stilborough, wrote to him every two years, or so, and gave him news. But this correspondence (if letters written only on one side could be called such, for all Tom Dobie ever received back was a newspaper, sent in token that his letter had reached its destination) was carried on en cachette; and Tom Dobie never disclosed it to living mortal, having undertaken not to do so. Some two years before the present period, Tom Dobie had died: his letters of course ceased, and it was by the merest accident that Basil Castlemaine heard of the death of his father. He was then himself too ill to return and put in his claim to Greylands' Rest; in fact, he was near to death; but he charged his son to go to England and claim the estate as soon as he should be no more; nay, as he said, to enter into possession of it. But he made use of a peculiar warning in giving this charge to his son; and these were the words:

"Take you care what you are about, Anthony, and go to work cautiously. There may be treachery in store for you. The brothers—your uncles—who combined to drive me away from our homestead in days gone by, may combine again to keep you out of it. Take care of yourself, I say; feel your way, as it were; and beware of treachery."

Whether, as is supposed sometimes to be the case, the dying man had some prevision of the future, and saw, as by instinct, what that future would bring forth, certain it was, that he made use of this warning to young Anthony: and equally certain that the end bore out the necessity for the caution.

So here was Anthony Castlemaine: arrived in the land of his family to put in his claim to what he deemed was his lawful inheritance, Greylands' Rest, the deep black band worn for his father yet fresh upon his hat.

MRS. HENRY WOOD

Mrs. Castlemaine sat in the red parlour, reading a letter. Or, rather, re-reading it, for it was one that had arrived earlier in the morning. A lady at Stilborough had applied for the vacant place of Governess to Miss Flora Castlemaine, and had enclosed her testimonials.

"Good music, singing, drawing; no French," read Mrs. Castlemaine aloud, partly for the benefit of Miss Flora, who stood on a stool at her elbow, not at all pleased that any such application should come; for, as we have already seen, the young lady would prefer to bring herself up without the aid of any governess. "Good tempered, but an excellent disciplinarian, and very firm with her pupils—"

"I'm not going to have her, mamma," came the interruption. "Don't you think it!"

"I do not suppose you will have her, Flora. The want of French will be an insuperable objection. How tiresome it is! One seems unable to get everything. The last lady who applied was not a sufficient musician for advanced pupils, and therefore could not have undertaken Ethel's music."

"As if Ethel needed to learn music still! Why, she plays as well— as well," concluded the girl, at a loss for a simile. "Catch me learning music when I'm as old as Ethel!"

"I consider, it nonsense myself, but Ethel wishes it, and your papa so foolishly gives in to her whims in all things that of course she has to be studied in the matter as much as you. It may be months and months before we get a lady who combines all that's wanted here."

Mrs. Castlemaine spoke resentfully. What with one thing and another, she generally was in a state of resentment against Ethel.

"I hope it may be years and years!" cried Flora, leaning her arms on the table and kicking her legs about. "I hope we shall never get one at all."

"It would be easy enough to get one, but for this trouble about Ethel's music," grumbled Mrs. Castlemaine. "I have a great mind to send her to the Grey Nunnery for her lessons. Sister Charlotte, I know, is perfect on the piano; and she would be thankful for the employment."

"Papa would not let her go to the Nunnery," said the sharp girl. "He does not like the Grey Ladies."

"I suppose he'd not. I'm sure, what with this disqualification and that disqualification, a good governess is as difficult to fix upon as—— get off the table, my sweet child," hastily broke off Mrs. Castlemaine: "here's your papa."

The Master of Greylands entered the red parlour, after his short interview in the yard with Commodore Teague. Miss Flora slipped past him, and disappeared. He saw a good deal to find fault with in her rude, tomboy ways; and she avoided him when she could. Taking the paper, he stirred the fire into a blaze, just as he had, not many minutes before, stirred his own fire upstairs.

"It is a biting-cold day," he observed. "I think I must have caught a little chill, for I seem to feel cold in an unusual degree. What's that?"

Mrs. Castlemaine held the letters still in her hand; and by the expression of her countenance, bent upon the contents, he could perceive there was some annoyance.

"This governess does not do; it is as bad as the last. She lacked music; this one lacks French. Is it not provoking, James?"

Mr. Castlemaine took up the letters and read them.

"I should say she is just the sort of governess for Flora," he observed. "The testimonials are excellent."

"But her want of French! Did you not observe that?"

"I don't know that French is of so much consequence for Flora as the getting a suitable person to control her. One who will hold her under firm discipline. As it is, she is being ruined."

"French not of consequence for Flora!" repeated Mrs. Castlemaine. "What can you mean, James?"

"I said it was not of so much consequence, relatively speaking. Neither is it."

"And while Ethel's French is perfect!"

"What has that to do with it?"

"I will never submit to see Flora inferior in accomplishments to Ethel, James. French I hold especially by: I have felt the want of it myself. Better, of the two, for her to fail in music than in speaking French. If it were not for Ethel's senseless whim of continuing to take music lessons, there would be no trouble."

"Who's this, I wonder?" cried Mr. Castlemaine.

He alluded to a visitor's ring at the hall bell. Flora came dashing in.

"It's a gentleman in a fur coat," she said. "I watched him come up the avenue."

"A gentleman in a fur coat!" repeated her mother.

"Some one who has walked from Stilborough this cold day, I suppose."

Miles entered. On his small silver waiter lay a card. He presented it to his master and spoke. "The gentleman says he wishes to see you, sir. I have shown him into the drawing-room."

The Master of Greylands was gazing at the card with knitted brow and haughty lips. He did not understand the name on it.

"What farce is this?" he exclaimed, tossing the card on the table in anger. And Mrs. Castlemaine bent to read it with aroused curiosity.

"Anthony Castlemaine."

"It must be an old card of your father's, James," she remarked, "given, most likely, year's ago, to some one to send in, should he ever require to present himself here—perhaps to crave a favour."

This view, just at the moment it was spoken, seemed feasible enough to Mr. Castlemaine, and his brow lost its fierceness. Another minute, and he saw how untenable it was.

"My father never had such a card as this, Sophia. Plain 'Anthony Castlemaine,' without hold or handle. His cards had 'Mr.' before the name. And look at the strokes and flourishes—it's not like an English card. What sort of a person is it, Miles?"

"A youngish gentleman sir. He has a lot of dark fur on his coat. He asked for Mr. James Castlemaine."

"Mr. James Castlemaine!" echoed the Master of Greylands, sharply, as he stalked from the room, card in hand.

The visitor was standing before a portrait in the drawing-room contemplating it earnestly. It was that of old Anthony Castlemaine, taken when he was about fifty years of age. At the opening of the door he turned round and advanced, his hand, extended and a pleasant smile on his face.

"I have the gratification, I fancy, of seeing my Uncle James!"

Mr. Castlemaine kept his hands to himself. He looked haughtily at the intruder; he spoke frigidly.

"I have not the honour of your acquaintance, sir."

"But my card tells you who I am," rejoined the young man. "I am indeed your nephew, uncle; the son of your elder brother. He was Basil, and you are James."

"Pardon me, sir, if I tell you what I think you are. An impostor."

"Ah no, do not be afraid, uncle. I am verily your nephew, Anthony Castlemaine. I have papers and legal documents with me to prove indisputably the fact; I bring you also a letter from my father, written on his death-bed. But I should have thought you might know me by my likeness to my father; and he—I could fancy that portrait had been taken for him"—pointing to the one he had been looking at. "He always said I greatly resembled my grandfather."

There could be no dispute as to the likeness. The young man's face was the Castlemaine face exactly: the well formed, handsome features, the clear and fresh complexion, the brilliant dark eyes. All the Castlemaines had been alike, and this one was like them all; even like James, who stood there.

Taking a letter from his pocket-book, he handed it to Mr. Castlemaine. The latter broke the seal—Basil's own seal; he saw that—and began to peruse it. While he did so, he reflected a little, and made up his mind.

To acknowledge his nephew. For he had the sense to see that no other resource would be left him. He did it with a tolerably good grace, but in a reserved cold kind of manner. Folding up the letter, he asked a few questions which young Anthony freely answered, and gave a brief account of the past.

"And Basil—your father—is dead, you say! Has been dead four weeks. This letter, I see, is dated Christmas Day."

"It was on Christmas Day he wrote it, uncle. Yes, nearly four weeks have elapsed since his death: it took place on the fourteenth of January; his wife, my dear mother, had died on the same day six years before. That was curious, was it not? I had meant to come over here immediately, as he charged me to do; but there were many matters of business to be settled, and I could not get away until now."

"Have you come over for any particular purpose?" coldly asked Mr. Castlemaine.

"I have come to stay, Uncle James. To take possession of my inheritance."

"Of your inheritance?"

"The estate of Greylands' Rest."

"Greylands' Rest is not yours," said Mr. Castlemaine.

"My father informed me that it was. He brought me up to no profession: he always said that Greylands' Rest would be mine at his own death; that he should come into it himself at the death of his father, and thence it would descend to me. To make all sure, he left it to me in his will. And, as I have mentioned to you, we did not hear my grandfather was dead until close upon last Christmas. Had my father known it in the summer, he would have come over to put in his claim: he was in sufficiently good health then."

"It is a pity you should have come so far on a fruitless errand, young man. Listen. When your father, Basil, abandoned his home here in his youth, he forfeited all claim to the inheritance. He asked for his portion, and had it; he took it away with him and stayed away; stayed away for nigh upon forty years. What claim does he suppose that sort of conduct gave him on my father's affection, that he should leave to him Greylands' Rest?"

"He always said his father would leave it to no one but him: that he knew it and, was sure of it."

"What my father might have done had Basil come back during his lifetime, I cannot pretend to say: neither is it of any consequence to guess at it now. Basil did not come back, and, therefore, you cannot be surprised that he missed Greylands' Rest; that the old father left it to his second son—myself—instead of to him."

"But did he leave it to you, uncle?"

"A superfluous question, young man. I succeeded to it, and am here in possession of it."

"I am told that there are doubts upon the point abroad," returned Anthony, speaking in the same pleasant tone, but with straightforward candour.

"Doubts upon what point?" haughtily demanded Mr. Castlemaine.

"What I hear is this, Uncle James. That it is not known to the public, and never has been known, how you came into Greylands' Rest. Whether the estate was left to you by will, or handed over to you by deed of gift, or given to you in trust to hold for my father. Nobody knows, I am told, anything about it, or even whether there was or was not a will. Perhaps you will give me these particulars, uncle?"

Mr. Castlemaine's face grew dark as night. "Do you presume to doubt my word, young man? I tell you that Greylands' Rest is mine. Let it content you."

"If you will show me that Greylands' Rest is yours, Uncle James, I will never say another word upon the subject, or give you the smallest trouble. Prove this to me, and I will stay a few days in the neighbourhood, for the sake of cementing family ties—though I may never meet any of you again—and then go back to the place whence I came. But if you do not give me this proof, I must prosecute my claim, and maintain my rights."

"Rights!" scoffed Mr. Castlemaine, beginning to lose his temper. "How dare you presume to talk to me in this way? A needy adventurer—for that is what I conclude you are, left without means of your own—to come here, and—"

"I beg your pardon," interrupted the young man; "I am not needy. Though far from rich, I have a fair competency. Enough to keep me in comfort."

"It is all one to me," said Mr. Castlemaine. "You had better do as you say—go back to the place whence you came."

"If the estate be truly and lawfully yours, I should be the last to attempt to disturb you in it; I should not wish to do so. But if it be not yours, Uncle James, it must be mine; and, until I can be assured one way or the other, I shall remain here, though it be for ever."

Mr. Castlemaine drew himself up to his full height. He was perfectly calm again; perhaps somewhat vexed that he had allowed himself to betray temper; and rejoined, coolly and prudently, "I cannot pretend to control your movements; to say you shall go, or you shall come; but I tell you, frankly, that your staying will not serve you in the least. Were you to remain for ever—as you phrase it—not one tittle of proof would you get from me. Things have come to a pretty pass if I am to be bearded in my own house, and have my word doubted."

"Well, Uncle James," said the young man, still speaking pleasantly, "then nothing remains for me but to try and find out the truth for myself. I wish you had been more explicit with me, for I am sure I do not know how to set about it," he added, candidly.

A faint, proud smile curled Mr. Castlemaine's decisive lips. It seemed to say, "Do what you please; it is beneath my notice." His nephew took up his hat to depart.

"May I offer to shake hands with you, Uncle James? I hope we need not be enemies?"

A moment's hesitation, and Mr. Castlemaine shook the offered hand. It was next to impossible to resist the frank geniality; just the same frank geniality that had characterized Basil; and Mr. Castlemaine thawed a little.

"It appears to be a very strange thing that Basil should have remained stationary all those years in Franco; never once to have come home!"

"I have heard him say many a time, Uncle James, that he should never return until he returned to take possession of Greylands' Rest. And during the time of the great war travelling was dangerous and difficult."

"Neither could I have believed that he would have settled down so quietly. And to engage in commerce!"

"He grew to like the bustle of business. He had a vast capacity for business, Uncle James."

"No doubt; being a Castlemaine," was the answer, delivered with conscious superiority. "The Castlemaines lack capacity for nothing they may choose to undertake. Good-morning; and I wish you a better errand next time."

As Anthony Castlemaine, on departing, neared the gate leading to the avenue, he saw a young lady approaching it. A fisherman, to whom she was speaking, walked by her side. The latter's words, as he turned away, caught the ear of Anthony.

"You will tell the master then; please, Miss Castlemaine, and say a good word to him for me?"

"Yes, I will, Gleeson; and I am very sorry for the misfortune," the young lady answered. "Good-day."

Anthony gazed with unfeigned pleasure on the beautiful face presented to him in—as he supposed—his cousin. It was Ethel Reene. The cheeks had acquired a soft rose flush in the crisp air, the dark brown hair took a wonderfully bright tinge in the sunshine; and in the deep eyes glancing so straight and honestly through their long dark lashes into those of the stranger, there was a sweet candour that caused Anthony Castlemaine to think them the prettiest eyes he had ever seen. He advanced to her direct; said a few words indicative of his delight at meeting her; and, while Ethel was lost in astonishment, he suddenly bent his face forward, and kissed her on either cheek.

For a moment, Ethel Reene was speechless bewildered with confused indignation at the outrage; and then she burst into a flood of tears. What she said, she hardly knew; but all bespoke her shivering, sensitive sense of the insult. Anthony Castlemaine was overwhelmed. He had intended no insult, but only to give a cousinly greeting after the fashion of his adopted land; and he hastened to express his contrition.

"I beg your pardon a million times. I am so grieved to have pained or offended you. I think you cannot have understood that I am your cousin?"

"Cousin, sir," she rejoined—and Mr. Castlemaine himself could not have spoken with a more haughty contempt. "How dare you presume? I have not a cousin or a relative in the wide world."

The sweet eyes were flashing, the delicate face was flushed to crimson. It occurred to Anthony Castlemaine that he must have made some unfortunate mistake.

"I know not how to beg your pardon sufficiently," he continued. "I thought indeed you were my cousin, Miss Castlemaine."

"I am not Miss Castlemaine."

"I—pardon me!—I assuredly heard the sailor address you as Miss Castlemaine."

Ethel was beginning to recover herself. She saw that he did not look at all like a young man who would gratuitously offer any lady an insult, but like a true gentleman. Moreover there flashed upon her perception the strong likeness his face bore to the Castlemaines; and she thought that what he had done he must have done in some error.

"I am not Miss Castlemaine," she condescended to explain, her tone losing part of its anger, but not its pride. "Mr. Castlemaine's house is my home, and people often call me by the name. But—and if I were Miss Castlemaine, who are you, sir, that you should claim to be my cousin? The Castlemaines have no strange cousins."

"I am Anthony Castlemaine, young lady; son of the late Basil Castlemaine, the heir of Greylands. I come from an interview with my Uncle James; and I—I beg your pardon most heartily once more."

"Anthony Castlemaine, the son of Basil Castlemaine!" she exclaimed, nearly every emotion forgotten in astonishment; but a conviction, nevertheless, seizing upon her that it was true. "The son of the lost Basil!"

"I am, in very truth, his son," replied Anthony. "My father is dead, and I have come over to claim—and I hope, enter into—my patrimony, Greylands' Rest."

V

THE BALL

Lights gleamed from the rooms of the banker's house in Stilborough. A flood of light blazed from the hall, and was reflected on the pavement outside, and on the colours of the flowering plants just within the entrance. Mr. Peter Castlemaine and Miss Castlemaine gave a dance that night; and it was the custom to open the door early, and keep it open, for the arrival of the expected guests.

The reception-rooms were in readiness, and gay with their wax lights and flowers. They opened mostly into one another. The largest of them was appropriated to dancing. All its furniture and its carpet had been removed; benches occupied the walls under the innumerable sconces bearing lights; and the floor was chalked artistically, in a handsome pattern of flowers, after the fashion of the day.

In the small apartment that was her own sitting-room stood Mary Ursula. In her rich robes of white silk and lace, and in the jewels which had been her mother's, and which it was her father's wish she should wear on grand occasions, she looked, with her stately form and her most lovely face, of almost regal beauty. Excitement had flushed her cheeks to brightness; on her delicate and perfect features sat an animation not often seen there. Whatever evil might be overhanging the house, at least no prevision of it rested on Miss Castlemaine; and perhaps few young ladies in all the kingdom could be found who were possessed of the requisites for happiness in a degree that could vie with the banker's daughter, or who had so entire a sense of it. Beautiful, amiable, clever, rich; the darling of her father; sheltered from every care in her sumptuous home; loving and beloved by a young man worthy of her, and to whom she was soon to be united! In the days to come, Mary Ursula would look back on this time, and tell herself that the very intensity of its happiness might have warned her that it was too bright to last.

He, her lover, was by her side now. He had come early, on purpose to be for a few minutes alone with her, before the arrival of the other guests. They stood together on the hearthrug. A quiet-looking young man of middle height, with dark hair, just the shade of hers, and rather a pensive and mild cast of face: a face, however, that did not seem to proclaim much moral strength. Such was William Blake-Gordon.

They were conversing of the future; the future that to both of them looked so bright; of the home and home life that ere long would be theirs in common. Mr. Blake-Gordon had been for some little time searching for a house, and had not met with a suitable one. But he thought he had found it now.

"It seems to me to be just the thing, Mary," he was saying—for he never called her by her double name, but "Mary" simply. "Only four miles from Stilborough on the Loughton road; which will be within an easy distance of your father's home and of Sir Richard's. It was by the merest chance I heard this morning that the Wests were going; and we can secure it at once if we will, before it goes into the market."

Miss Castlemaine knew the house by sight; she had passed it many a time in her drives, and seen it nestling away amid the trees. It was called by rather a fanciful name—Raven's Priory.

"It is not to be let, you say, William; only bought."

"Only bought. There will be, I presume, no difficulty made to that by the authorities."

He spoke with a smile. She smiled too. Difficulty!—with the loads of wealth that would be theirs some time! They might well laugh at the idea.

"Only that—that it is uncertain how long we may require to live in it," she said, with a slight hesitation. "I suppose that—some time—"

"We shall have to leave it for my father's home. True. But that, I trust, may be a long while off. And then we could re-sell Raven's Priory."

"Yes, of course. It is a nice place, William?"

"Charming," he replied with enthusiasm. For, of course, all things, the proposed residence included, were to him the hue of couleur-de-rose.

"I have never been inside it," she observed.

"No. The Wests are churlish people, keeping no company. Report says that Mrs. West is a hypochondriac. They let me go in this morning, and I went over all the house. It is the nicest place, love—and not too large or too small for us; and the Wests have kept it in good condition. You will be charmed with the drawing-rooms, Mary; and the conservatory is one of the best I ever saw. They want us to take to the plants."

"Are they nice?"

"Beautiful. The Wests are moving to London, to be near good advice for her, and they do not expect to get anything of a conservatory there;

at least, that is worth the name. I wonder what your papa will think about this house, Mary? We might tell him of it now. Where is he?"

"He is out," she answered. "Just as he was going up to dress, Thomas Hill sent for him downstairs, and they went out somewhere together. Papa ran up to tell me he would be back as soon as he could, but that I must for once receive the people alone."

"I wish I might stand by your side to help receive them!" he said, impulsively. "Would any of them faint at it? Do you think Mrs. Webb would, if she were here?" he continued, with a smile. "Ah, well—a short while, my darling, and I shall have the right to stand by you."

He stole his arm round her waist, and whispered to her a repetition of those love vows that had so often before charmed her ear and thrilled her heart. Her cheek touched his shoulder; the faint perfume of her costly fan, that she swayed unconsciously as it hung from her wrist, was to him like an odour from Paradise. He recounted to her all the features he remembered of the house that neither of them doubted would be their future home; and the minutes passed, in, to both, bliss unutterable.

The crashing up of a carriage—of two carriages it seemed—warned them that this sweet pastime was at an end. Sounds of bustle in the hall succeeded to it: the servants were receiving the first guests.

"Oh, William—I forgot—I meant to tell you," she hurriedly whispered. "I had the most ugly dream last night. And you know I very rarely do dream. I have not been able to get it out of my mind all day."

"What is it, Mary?"

"I thought we were separated, you and I; separated for ever. We had quarrelled, I think; that point was not clear; but you turned off one way, and I another. It was in the gallery of this house, William, and we had been talking together. You went out at the other end, by the door near the dining-room, and I at this end; and we turned at the last and looked at one another. Oh, the look was dreadful! I shall never forget it: so full of pain and sadness! And we knew, both of us knew, that it was the last farewell look; that we should never again meet in this world."

"Oh, my love! my love!" he murmured, bending his face on hers. "And you could let it trouble you!—knowing it was but a dream! Nothing but the decree of God—death—shall ever separate us, Mary. For weal or for woe, we will go through the life here together."

He kissed away the tears that had gathered in her eyes at the remembrance; and Miss Castlemaine turned hastily into one of the larger rooms, and took up her standing there in expectation. For the feet of the gay world were already traversing the gallery.

She welcomed her guests, soon coming in thick and threefold, with the gracious manner and the calm repose of bearing that always characterised her, apologising to all for the absence of her father; telling that he had been called out unexpectedly on some matter of business, but would soon return. Amid others, came the party from Greylands' Rest, arriving rather late: Mrs. Castlemaine in black velvet, leaning on the arm of her stepson; Ethel Reene walking modestly behind, in a simple dress of white net, adorned with white ribbons. There was many a fine young man present, but never a finer or more attractive one than Harry Castlemaine; with the handsome Castlemaine features, the easy, independent bearing, and the ready tongue.

"Is it of any use to ask whether you are at liberty to honour me with your hand for the first dance, Mary Ursula?" he inquired, after leaving Mrs. Castlemaine on a sofa.

"Not the least, Harry," answered Miss Castlemaine, smiling. "I am engaged for that, and for the second as well."

"Of course. Well, it is all as it should be, I suppose. Given the presence of Mr. Blake-Gordon, and no one else has so good a right as he to open the ball with you."

"You will find a substitute for me by the asking, Harry. See all those young ladies around; not one but is glancing towards you with the hope that you may seek her."

He laughed rather consciously. He was perfectly well aware of the universal favour accorded by the ladies, young and old, to Harry Castlemaine. But this time, at any rate, he intended to disappoint them all. He turned to Miss Reene.

"Will you take compassion upon a rejected man, Ethel? Mary Ursula won't have me for the first two dances, you hear; so I appeal to you in all humility to heal the smart. Don't reject me."

"Nonsense, Harry!" was the young lady's answer. "You must not ask me for the first dance; it would be like brother and sister dancing together; all the room would resent it in you, and call it bad manners. Choose elsewhere. There's Miss Mountsorrel; she will not say you nay."

"For the dances, no but she'll not condescend to speak three words to me while they are in process," returned Mr. Harry Castlemaine. "If you do not dance them with me, Ethel, I shall sit down until the two first dances are over."

He spoke still in the same laughing, half joking manner; but, nevertheless, there was a ring of decision in the tone of the last words; and Ethel knew he meant what he said. The Castlemaines rarely broke through any decision they might announce, however lightly it was spoken; and Harry possessed somewhat of the same persistent will.

"If you make so great a point of it, I will dance with you," observed Ethel. "But I must again say that you ought to take anyone rather than me."

"I have not seen my uncle yet," remarked Miss Castlemaine to Ethel, as Harry strolled away to pay his devoirs to the room generally. "Where can he be lingering?"

"Papa is not here, Mary Ursula."

"Not here! How is that?"

"Really I don't know," replied Ethel. "When Harry came running out to get into the carriage to-night—we had been sitting in it quite five minutes waiting for him but he had been away all day, and was late in dressing—Miles shut the door. 'Don't do that,' said Harry to him, 'the master's not here.' Upon that, Mrs. Castlemaine spoke, and said papa was not coming with us."

"I suppose he will be coming in later," remarked Mary Ursula, as she moved away to meet fresh guests.

The dancing began with a country dance; or, as would have been said then, the ball opened with one. Miss Castlemaine and her lover, Mr. Blake-Gordon, took their places at its head; Harry Castlemaine and Miss Reene were next to them. For in those days, people stood much upon etiquette at these assemblies, and the young ladies of the family took precedence of all others in the opening dance.

The dance chosen was called the Triumph. Harry Castlemaine led Mary Ursula down between the line of admiring spectators; her partner, Mr. Blake-Gordon, followed, and they brought the young lady back in triumph. Such was the commencement of the figure. It was a sight to be remembered in after years; the singular good looks of at least two of the three; Harry, the sole male heir of the Castlemaines, with the tall fine form and the handsome face; and Mary Ursula, so stately and beautiful. Ethel Reene was standing alone, in her quiet loveliness, looking like a snowdrop, and waiting until her turn should come to be in like manner taken down. The faces of all sparkled with animation and happiness; the gala robes of the two young ladies added to the charm of the scene. Many recalled it later; recalled it with a pang: for, of those four, ere a year had gone by, one was not, and another's life had been blighted. No prevision, however, rested on any of them this night of what the dark future held in store; and they revelled in the moment's enjoyment, gay at heart. Heaven is too merciful to let Fate cast its ominous shade on us before the needful time.

The banker came in ere the first dance was over. Moving about from room to room among his guests, glancing with approving smile at the young dancers, seeing that the card-tables were filled, he at length reached the sofa of Mrs. Castlemaine. She happened to be alone on it just then, and he sat down beside her.

"I don't see James anywhere," he remarked. "Where is he hiding himself?"

"He has not come," replied Mrs. Castlemaine.

"No! How's that? James enjoys a ball."

"Yes, I think he does still, nearly as much as his son Harry."

"Then what has kept him away?"

"I really do not know. I had thought nearly to the last that he meant to come. When I was all but ready myself, finding James had not begun to dress, I sent Harriet to remind him of the lateness of the hour, and she brought word back that her master was not going."

"Did he say why?" asked Mr. Peter Castlemaine.

"No! I knocked at his study door afterwards and found him seated at his bureau. He seemed busy. All he said to me was, that he should remain at home; neither more nor less. You know, Peter, James rarely troubles himself to give a reason for what he does."

"Well, I am sorry. Sorry that he should miss a pleasant evening, and also because I wanted to speak to him. We may not have many more of these social meetings."

"I suppose not," said Mrs. Castlemaine, assuming that her brother-in-law alluded in an indirect way to his daughter's approaching marriage. "When once you have lost Mary Ursula, there will be nobody to hold festivities for."

"No," said the banker, absently.

"I suppose it will be very soon now."

"What will be soon?"

"The wedding. James thinks it will be after Easter."

"Oh—ay—the wedding," spoke Mr. Peter Castlemaine, with the air of a man who has just caught up some recollection that had slipped from him. "I don't know yet: we shall see: no time has been decided on."

"Close as his brother" thought Mrs. Castlemaine. "No likelihood, that he will disclose anything unless he chooses."

"Will James be coming in to Stilborough to-morrow?" asked the banker.

"I'm sure I cannot tell. He goes out and comes in, you know, without any reference to me. I should fancy he would not be coming in, unless he has anything to call him. He has not seemed well to-day; he thinks he has caught a cold."

"Ah, then I daresay that's the secret of his staying at home to-night," said Mr. Peter Castlemaine.

"Yes, it may be. I did not think of that. And he has also been very much annoyed to-day: and you know, Peter, if once James is thoroughly put out of temper, it takes some little time to put him in again."

The banker nodded assent.

"What has annoyed him?"

"A very curious thing," replied Mrs. Castlemaine: "you will hardly believe it when I tell you. Some young man—"

Breaking off suddenly, she glanced around to make sure that no one was within hearing. Then drawing nearer to the banker, went on in a lowered voice:

"Some young man presented himself this morning at Greylands' Rest, pretending to want to put in a claim to the estate."

Abstracted though the banker had been throughout the brief interview, these words aroused him to the quick. In one moment he was the calm, shrewd, attentive business man, Peter Castlemaine, his head erect, his keen eyes observant.

"I do not understand you, Mrs. Castlemaine."

"Neither do I understand," she rejoined. "James said just a word or two to me, and I gathered the rest."

"Who was the young man?"

"Flora described him as wearing a coat trimmed with fur; and Miles thought he spoke with somewhat of a foreign accent," replied Mrs. Castlemaine, deviating unconsciously from the question, as ladies sometimes do deviate.

"But don't you know who he was? Did he give no account of himself?"

"He calls himself Anthony Castlemaine."

As the name left her lips a curious kind of change, as though he were startled, passed momentarily over the banker's countenance. But he neither stirred nor spoke.

"When the card was brought in with that name upon it—James happened to be in the red parlour, talking with me about a new governess—I said it must be an old card of your father's that somebody had got hold of. But it turned out not to be that: and, indeed, it was not like the old cards. What he wants to make out is, that he is the son of Basil Castlemaine."

"Did James see him?"

"Oh dear yes, and their interview lasted more than an hour."

"And he told James he was Basil's son?—this young man."

"I think so. At any rate, the young man told Ethel he was. She happened to meet him as he was leaving the house and he introduced himself to her as Anthony Castlemaine, Basil's son, and said he had come over to claim his inheritance—Greylands' Rest."

"And where's Basil?" asked the banker, after a pause.

"Dead."

"Dead?"

"So the young man wishes to make appear. My opinion is he must be some impostor."

"An impostor no doubt," assented the banker, slowly. "At least—he may be. I only wonder that we have not, under the circumstances, had people here before, claiming to be connected with Basil."

"And I am sure the matter has annoyed James very much," pursued Mrs. Castlemaine. "He betrayed it in his manner, and was not at all like himself all the afternoon. I should make short work of it if the man came again, were I James, and threaten him with the law."

Mr. Peter Castlemaine said no more, and presently rose to join other of his guests. But as he talked to one, laughed with another, listened to a third, his head bent in attention, his eyes looking straight into their eyes, none had an idea that these signs of interest were evinced mechanically, and that his mind was far away.

He had enough perplexity and trouble of his own just then, as Heaven knew; very much indeed on this particular evening; but this other complexity, that appeared to be arising for his brother James, added to it. To Mrs. Castlemaine's scornfully expressed opinion that the man was an impostor, he had assented just in the same way that he was now talking with his guests—mechanically. For some instinct, or prevision, call it what you will, lay on the banker's heart, that the man would turn out to be no impostor, but the veritable son of the exile, Basil.

Peter Castlemaine was much attached to his brother James, and for

James's own sake he would have regretted that any annoyance or trouble should arise for him; but he had also a selfish motive for regretting it. In his dire strait as to money—for to that it had now come—he had been rapidly making up his mind that evening to appeal to James to let him have some. The appeal might not be successful under the most favourable auspices: he knew that: but with this trouble looming for the Master of Greylands, he foresaw that it must and would fail. Greylands' Rest might be James's in all legal security; but an impression had lain on the mind of Peter Castlemaine, since his father's death, that if Basil ever returned he would set up a fight for it.

Supper over—the elaborate, heavy, sit-down supper of those days—and the two dances following upon it, most of the guests departed. Mr. Blake-Gordon, seeking about for the banker to wish him goodnight, at length found him standing over the fire in the deserted card-room. Absorbed though he was in his own happiness, the young man could but notice the flood-tide of care on the banker's brow. It cleared off, as though by magic, when the banker looked up and saw him.

"Is it you, William? I thought you had left."

"I should hardly go, sir, without wishing you goodnight. What a delightful evening it has been!"

"Ay, I think you have all enjoyed yourselves."

"Oh, very, very much."

"Well, youth is the time for enjoyment," observed the banker. "We can never again find the zest in it, once youth is past."

"You look tired, sir; otherwise I—I might have ventured to trespass on you for five minutes' conversation, late though it be," pursued Mr. Blake-Gordon with some hesitation.

"Tired!—not at all. You may take five minutes; and five to that, William."

"It is about our future residence, sir. Raven's Priory is in the market: and I think—and Mary thinks—it will just suit us."

"Ay; I heard more than a week ago that the Wests were leaving."

The words took William Blake-Gordon by surprise. He looked at the banker.

"Did you, sir!—more than a week ago! And did it not strike you that it would be a very suitable place for us?"

"I cannot say that I thought much about it," was the banker's answer; and he was twirling an ornament on the mantelpiece about with his hand as he spoke: a small, costly vase of old china from Dresden.

"But don't you think it would be, sir?"

"I daresay it might be. The gardens and conservatories have been well kept up; and you and Mary Ursula have both a weakness for rare flowers."

That was perfectly true. And the "weakness" showed itself then, for the young man went off into a rapturous description of the wealth of Raven's Priory in respect of floriculture. The ten minutes slipped away to twenty; and in his own enthusiasm Mr. Blake-Gordon did not notice the absence of it in his hearer.

"But I must not keep you longer, sir," he suddenly said, as his eyes caught the hands of the clock. "Perhaps you will let me see you about it to-morrow. Or allow my father to see you—that will be better."

"Not to-morrow," said Mr. Peter Castlemaine. "I shall be particularly engaged all day. Some other time."

"Whenever you please, sir. Only—we must take care that we are not forestalled in the purchase. Much delay might—"

"We can obtain a promise of the first refusal," interrupted the banker, in a somewhat impatient tone. "That will not be difficult."

"True. Goodnight, sir. And thank you for giving us this most charming evening."

"Goodnight, William."

But Mr. Blake-Gordon had not yet said his last farewell to his betrothed wife; and lovers never think that can be spoken often enough. He found her in the music-room, seated before the organ. She was waiting for her father.

"We shall have Raven's Priory, Mary," he whispered, speaking in accordance with his thoughts, in his great hopefulness; and his voice was joyous, and his pale face had a glow on it not often seen there. "Your papa himself says how beautiful the gardens and conservatories are."

"Yes," she softly answered, "we shall be sure to have it."

"I may not stay, Mary: I only came back to tell you this. And to wish you goodnight once again."

Her hand was within his arm, and they walked together to the end of the music-room. All the lights had been put out, save two. Just within the door he halted and took his farewell. His arm was around her, his lips were upon hers.

"May all good angels guard you this happy night—my love!—my promised wife!"

MRS. HENRY WOOD

He went down the corridor swiftly; she stole her blushing face to the opening of the door, to take a last look at him. At that moment a crash, as of some frail thing broken, was heard in the card-room. Mr. Blake-Gordon turned into it Mary Ursula followed him.

The beautiful Dresden vase lay on the stone flags of the hearth, shivered into many atoms. It was one that Mary Ursula set great store by, for it had been a purchase of her mother's.

"Oh papa! How did it happen?"

"My dear, I swept it off unwittingly with my elbow: I am very sorry for it," said Mr. Peter Castlemaine.

VI

Anthony Castlemaine on his Search

The hour of dinner with all business men in Stilborough was half-past one o'clock in the day. Perhaps Mr. Peter Castlemaine was the only man who did not really dine then; but he took his luncheon; which came to the same thing. It was the recognized daily interregnum in the public doings of the town—this half hour between half-past one and two: consequently shops, banks, offices, all were virtually though not actually closed. The bank of Mr. Peter Castlemaine made no exception. On all days, except Thursday, market day, the bank was left to the care of one clerk during this half hour: the rest of the clerks and Mr. Hill would be out at their dinner. As a rule, not a single customer came in until two o'clock had struck.

It was the day after the ball. The bank had been busy all the morning, and Mr. Peter Castlemaine had been away the best part of it. He came back at half-past one, just as the clerks were filing out.

"Do you want me, sir?" asked Thomas Hill, standing back with his hat in his hand; and it was the dreadfully worn, perplexed look on his master's face that induced him to ask the question.

"Just for a few minutes," was the reply. "Come into my room."

Once there, the door was closed upon them, and they sat in grievous tribulation. There was no dinner for poor Thomas Hill that day; there was no lunch for his master: the hour's perplexities were all in all.

On the previous evening some stranger had arrived at Stilborough, had put up at the chief inn there, the Turk's Head; and then, after enquiring the private address of Mr. Peter Castlemaine's head clerk, had betaken himself to the clerk's lodgings. Thomas Hill was seated at tea when the gentleman was shown in. It proved to be a Mr. Fosbrook, from London: and the moment the clerk heard the name, Fosbrook, and realized the fact that the owner of it was in actual person before him, he turned as cold as a stone. For of all the men who could bring most danger on Mr. Peter Castlemaine, and whom the banker had most cause to dread, it was this very one, Fosbrook. That he had come down to seek explanations in person which might no longer be put off, the clerk felt sure of: and the fact of his seeking out him instead of his

MRS. HENRY WOOD

master, proved that he suspected something was more than wrong. He had had a little passing, private acquaintance with Mr. Fosbrook in the years gone by, and perhaps that induced the step.

Thomas Hill did what he could. He dared not afford explanation or information himself, for he knew not what it would be safe to say, what not. He induced Mr. Fosbrook to return to his inn, undertaking to bring his master to wait on him there. To the banker's house he would not take the stranger; for the gaiety of which it was that night the scene was not altogether a pleasant thing to show to a creditor. Leaving Mr. Fosbrook at the Turk's Head on his way, he came on to apprise Mr. Peter Castlemaine.

Mr. Peter Castlemaine went at once to the inn. He had no resource but to go: he did not dare do otherwise: and this it was that caused his absence during the arrival of the guests. The interview was not a long one; for the banker, pleading the fact of having friends at home, postponed it until the morning.

It was with this gentleman that his morning had been spent; that he had now, half-after one o'clock, just come home from. Come home with the weary look in his face, and the more than weary pain at his heart.

"And what is the result, sir?" asked Thomas Hill as they sat down together.

"The result is, that Fosbrook will wait a few days, Hill three or four, he says. Perhaps that may be made five or six: I don't know. After that— if he is not satisfied by tangible proofs that things are right and not wrong, so far as he is concerned—there will be no further waiting."

"And the storm must burst."

"The storm must burst," echoed Peter Castlemaine.

"Oh but, sir, my dear master, what can be done in those few poor days?" cried Thomas Hill, in agitation. "Nothing. You must have more time allowed you."

"I had much ado to get that much, Hill. I had to Lie for it," he added, in a low tone.

"Do you see a chance yourself, sir?"

"Only one. There is a chance; but it is a very remote one. That last venture of mine has turned up trumps: I had the news by the mail this morning: and if I can realize the funds in time, the present danger may be averted."

"And the future trouble also," spoke Thomas Hill, catching eagerly at the straw of hope. "Why, sir, that will bring you in a mine of wealth."

"Yes. The only real want now is time. Time! time! I have said it before perhaps too sanguinely; I can say it in all truth now."

"And, sir—did you not show this to be the case to Mr. Fosbrook?"

"I did. But alas, I had to deny to him my other pressing liabilities—and he questioned sharply. Nevertheless, I shall tide it over, all of it, if I can only secure the time. That account of Merrit's—we may as well go over it together now, Thomas. It will not take long."

They drew their chairs to the table side by side. A thought was running through Thomas Hill's mind, and he spoke it as he opened the ledgers.

"With this good news in store, sir, making repayment certain—for if time be given you, you will now have plenty—don't you think Mr. Castlemaine would advance you funds?"

"I don't know," said the banker. "James seems to be growing cautious. He has no notion of my real position—I shrink from telling him—and I am sure he thinks that I am quite rich enough without borrowing money from anybody for fresh speculations. And, in truth, I don't see how he can have much money at command. This new trouble, that may be looming upon him, will make him extra cautious."

"What trouble?" asked Thomas Hill.

"Some man, I hear, has made his appearance at Greylands, calling himself Anthony Castlemaine, and saying that he is a son of my brother Basil," replied the banker, confidentially.

"Never!" cried the old man. "But, sir, if he be, how should that bring trouble on Mr. Castlemaine?"

"Because the stranger says he wants to claim Greylands' Rest."

"He must be out of his mind," said Thomas Hill. "Greylands' Rest is Mr. Castlemaine's; safe enough too, I presume."

"But a man such as this may give trouble, don't you see."

"No, sir, I don't see it—with all deference to your opinion. Mr. Castlemaine has only to show him it is his, and send him to the right about—"

A knock at the room door interrupted the sentence. The clerk rose to open it, and received a card and a message, which he carried to his master. The banker looked rather startled as he read the name on it: "Anthony Castlemaine."

Somewhere about an hour before this, young Anthony Castlemaine, after a late breakfast a la fourchette, had turned out of the Dolphin Inn to walk to Stilborough. Repulsed by his Uncle James on the previous day, and not exactly seeing what his course should be, he had come to the resolution of laying his case before his other uncle, the banker. Making enquiries of John Bent as to the position of the banker's residence, he left the inn. Halting for a few seconds to gaze across beyond the beach, for he thought the sea the most beautiful object in nature and believed he should never tire of looking at it, he went on up the hill, past the church, and was fairly on his road to Stilborough. It was a lonely road enough, never a dwelling to be seen all the way, save a farm homestead or two lying away amid their buildings; but Anthony Castlemaine walked slowly, taking in all the points and features of his native land, that were so strange to his foreign eye. He stood to read the milestones; he leaned on the fences; he admired the tall fine trees, leafless though they were; he critically surveyed the two or three carts and waggons that passed. The sky was blue, the sun bright, he enjoyed the walk and did not hurry himself: but nevertheless he at length reached Stilborough, and found out the house of the banker. He rang at the private door.

The servant who opened it saw a young man dressed in a rather uncommon kind of overcoat, faced with fur. The face was that of a stranger; but the servant fancied it was a face he had seen before.

"Is my uncle Peter at home?"

"Sir!" returned the servant, staring at him. For the only nephew the banker possessed, so far as he knew, was the son of the Master of Greylands. "What name did you please to ask for, sir?"

"Mr. Peter Castlemaine. This is his residence I am told."

"Yes, sir, it is."

"Can I see him? Is he at home?"

"He is at home, in his private room, sir; I fancy he is busy. I'll ask if you can see him. What name shall I say, sir?"

"You can take my card in. And please say to your master that if he is busy, I can wait."

The man glanced at the card as he knocked at the door of the private room, and read the name: "Anthony Castlemaine."

"It must be a nephew from over the sea," he shrewdly thought: "he looks foreign. Perhaps a son of that lost Basil."

We have seen that Thomas Hill took in the card and the message to his master. He came back, saying the gentleman was to wait; Mr. Peter Castlemaine would see him in a quarter of an hour. So the servant, beguiled by the family name, thought he should do right to conduct the stranger upstairs to the presence of Miss Castlemaine, and said so, while helping him to take off his overcoat.

"Shall I say any name, sir?" asked the man, as he laid his hand on the handle of the drawing-room door.

"Mr. Anthony Castlemaine."

Mary Ursula was alone. She sat near the fire doing nothing, and very happy in her idleness, for her thoughts were buried in the pleasures of the past gay night; a smile was on her face. When the announcement was made, she rose in great surprise to confront the visitor. The servant shut the door, and Anthony came forward.

He did not commit a similar breach of good manners to the one of the previous day; the results of that had shown him that fair stranger cousins may not be indiscriminately saluted with kisses in England. He bowed, and held out his hand with a frank smile. Mary Ursula did not take it: she was utterly puzzled, and stood gazing at him. The likeness in his face to her father's family struck her forcibly. It must be premised that she did not yet know anything about Anthony, or that any such person had made his appearance in England. Anthony waited for her to speak.

"If I understood the name aright—Anthony Castlemaine—you must be, I presume, some relative of my late grandfather's, sir?" she said at length.

He introduced himself fully then; who he was, and all about it. Mary Ursula met his hand cordially. She never doubted him or his identity for a moment. She had the gift of reading countenances; and she took to the pleasant, honest face at once, so like the Castlemaines in features, but with a more open expression.

"I am sure you are my cousin," she said, in cordial welcome. "I think I should have known you for a Castlemaine had I seen your face in a crowd."

"I see, myself, how like I am to the Castlemaines, especially to my father and grandfather: though unfortunately I have not inherited their height and strength," he added, with a slight laugh. "My mother was small and slight: I take after her."

"And my poor uncle Basil is dead!"

"Alas, yes! Only a few weeks ago. These black clothes that I wear are in memorial of him."

"I never saw him," said Miss Castlemaine, gazing at the familiar—for indeed it seemed familiar—face before her, and tracing out its features. "But I have heard say my uncle Basil was just the image of his father."

"And he was," said Anthony. "When I saw the picture of my grandfather yesterday at Greylands' Rest, I thought it was my father's hanging there."

It was a long while since Miss Castlemaine had met with anyone she liked so well at a first interview as this young man; and the quarter of an hour passed quickly. At its end the servant again appeared, saying his master would see him in his private room. So he took leave of Mary Ursula, and was conducted to it.

But, as it seemed, Mr. Peter Castlemaine did not wait to receive him: for almost immediately he presented himself before his daughter.

"This person has been with you, I find, Mary Ursula! Very wrong of Stephen to have brought him up here! I wonder what possessed him to do it?"

"I am glad he did bring him, papa," was her impulsive answer. "You have no idea what a sensible, pleasant young man he is. I could almost wish he were more even than a cousin—a brother."

"Why, my dear, you must be dreaming!" cried the banker, after a pause of astonishment. "Cousin!—brother! It does not do to take strange people on trust in this way. The man may be, and I dare say is, an adventurer," he continued, testily: "no more related to the Castlemaines than I am related to the King of England."

She laughed. "You may take him upon trust, papa, without doubt or fear. He is a Castlemaine all over, save in the height. The likeness to grandpapa is wonderful; it is so even to you and to uncle James. But he says he has all needful credential proofs with him."

The banker, who was then looking from the window, stood fingering the bunch of seals that hung from his long and massive watch-chain, his habit sometimes when in deep thought. Self-interest sways us all. The young man was no doubt the individual he purported to be: but if he were going to put in a vexatious claim to Greylands' Rest, and so upset James, the banker might get no loan from him. He turned to his daughter.

"You believe, then, my dear, that he is really what he makes himself out to be—Basil's son?"

"Papa, I think there is no question of it. I feel sure there can be none. Rely upon it, the young man is not one who would lay himself out to deceive, or to countenance deception: he is evidently honest and open as the day. I scarcely ever saw so true a face."

"Well, I am very sorry," returned the banker. "It may bring a great deal of trouble upon James."

"In what way can it bring him trouble, papa?" questioned Mary Ursula, in surprise.

"This young man—as I am informed—has come over to put in a claim to Greylands' Rest."

"To Greylands' Rest!" she repeated. "But that is my uncle James's! How can anyone else claim it?"

"People may put in a claim to it; there's no law against that; as I fear this young man means to do," replied the banker, taking thought and time over his answer. "He may cost James no end of bother and expense."

"But, papa—I think indeed you must be misinformed. I feel sure this young man is not one who would attempt to claim anything that is not his own."

"But if he supposes it to be his own?"

"What, Greylands' Rest his? How can that be?"

"My dear child, as yet I know almost nothing. Nothing but a few words that Mrs. Castlemaine said to me last night."

"But why should he take up such a notion, papa?" she asked, in surprise.

"From his father, I suppose. I know Basil as much believed Greylands' Rest would descend to him as he believed In his Bible. However, I must go down and see this young man."

As soon as Peter Castlemaine entered his private room, and let his eyes rest on the face of the young man who met him so frankly, he saw the great likeness to the Castlemaines. That it was really his nephew, Basil's son, he had entertained little doubt of from the first; none, since the recent short interview with his daughter. With this conviction on his mind, it never would have occurred to him to deny or cast doubts on the young man's identity, and he accepted it at once. But though he called him "Anthony," or "Anthony Castlemaine"—and now and then by mistake "Basil"—he did not show any mark of gratification or affection, but was distant and cold; and thought it very inconvenient and ill-judged of Basil's son to be bringing trouble on James. Taking his place in his handsome chair, turned sideways to the closed desk, he faced the young man seated before him.

A few minutes were naturally spent in questions and answers, chiefly as to Basil's career abroad. Young Anthony gave every information freely—just as he had done to his uncle James on the previous day. After that, at the first pause, he passed on to the subject of the inheritance.

"Perhaps, Uncle Peter, you will not refuse to give me some information about my grandfather's estate, Greylands' Rest," he began. "My father always assured me it would be mine. He said it would come to him at his father's death, and then to me afterwards—"

"He must have spoken without justifiable warranty," interrupted the banker. "It did not necessarily lapse to Basil, or to anyone else. Your grandfather could leave it to whom he would."

"Of course: we never understood otherwise. But my father always said that it would never be left away from him."

"Then I say, that he spoke without sufficient warranty," repeated the banker. "Am I to understand that you have come over this country to put in a claim to Greylands' Rest, on this sole justification?"

"My father, on his dying bed, charged me to come and claim it, Uncle Peter. He had bequeathed it to me in his will. It was only quite at the last that he learnt his father was dead, and he made a fresh will at once, and gave me the charge to come over without delay. When I presented myself to my uncle James yesterday, he seemed much to resent the fact that I should put in any claim to the estate. He told me I had no right to do so; he said it was his."

"Well?" said the banker; for the young man had paused.

"Uncle Peter, I am not unreasonable. I come home to find my uncle James in possession of the estate, and quite ready, as I gather, to oppose my claim to it; or, I should better say, to treat me and my claim with contempt. Now I do not forget that my grandfather might have left it to uncle James; that he had the power to do so—"

"Most undoubtedly he had," again interrupted the banker. "And I can tell you that he never, to the very last, allowed anybody to interfere with his wish and will."

"Well, I say I am not unreasonable, Uncle Peter. Though I have come over to claim the estate, I should not attempt to lay claim to it in the teeth of facts. I told my uncle James so. Once let me be convinced that the estate was really and fairly bequeathed to him, and I would not, for the world, wish to disturb him in its possession. I am not a rogue."

"But he is in possession, Anthony; and it appears that you do wish to disturb him," remonstrated Mr. Peter Castlemaine.

"I beg your pardon; I think you have not quite caught my meaning. What I want is, to be assured that Greylands' Rest was left away from my father: that he was passed over for my uncle James. If uncle James came into it by will, or by legal deed, of any kind, let him just show me the deed or the will, and that will suffice."

"You doubt his word then!"

Young Anthony hesitated, before replying; and then spoke out with ingenuous candour.

"The fact is, Uncle Peter, I deem it right to assure myself by proof, of how the matter is; for my father warned me that there might be treachery—"

"Treachery!" came the quick, echoing interposition of the banker; his dark eyes flashing fire.

"My father thought it possible," quietly continued the young man; "he feared that, even though Greylands' Rest was legally mine, my claim to it might be opposed. That is one reason why I press for proof; I should press for it if there existed no other. But I find that doubts already are circulating abroad as to how Mr. James Castlemaine came into the estate, and whether it became lawfully his on my grandfather's death."

"Doubts existing abroad! Doubts where?"

"Amid the neighbours, the people of Greyland's. I have heard one and another talk of it."

"Oh, indeed!" was the cold rejoinder. "Pray where are you staying?"

"At the Dolphin Inn, Uncle Peter. When I descended at it, and saw the flaming dolphin on the signboard, splashing up the water, I could not help smiling; for my father had described it to me so accurately, that it seemed like an old acquaintance."

Mr. Peter Castlemaine made no rejoinder, and there ensued a silence. In truth, his own difficulties were so weighty that they had been pressing on his mind throughout, an undercurrent of trouble, and for the moment he was lost in them.

"Will you, Uncle Peter, give me some information of the true state of the case?" resumed the young man. "I came here purposely, intending to ask you. You see, I want to be placed at a certainty, one way or the other. I again repeat that I am not unreasonable; I only ask to be dealt with fairly and honourably. If Greylands' Rest is not mine, show me that it is not; if it is mine, I ought to have it. Perhaps you will tell me, Uncle Peter, how it was left."

The banker suddenly let drop his seals, with which he had been playing during the last appeal, and turned his full attention to the speaker, answering in a more frank tone than he had yet spoken.

"When your father, Basil, went away, he took his full portion of money with him—a third of the money we should conjointly inherit. I received my portion later; James received his. Nothing remained but Greylands' Rest and the annuity—a large one—which your grandfather enjoyed from his wife's family: which annuity had nothing to do with us, for it would go back again at his death. Greylands' Rest could be disposed of as he should please. Does it strike you as any strange thing, Anthony, that he should prefer its passing to the son who was always with him, rather than to the son who had abandoned him and his home, and whom he did not even know to be alive?"

"Uncle Peter, I have said that I see reasons why my grandfather might make his second son his heir, rather than his eldest. If he did so, I am quite ready and willing to accept the fact, but I must first of all be convinced that it is fact. It is true, is it not, that my grandfather always intended to leave the estate to his eldest son Basil?"

"That is true," assented the banker, readily. "Such no doubt was his intention at one time. But Basil crossed him, and went, besides, out of sight and out of mind, and James remained with him and was always a dutiful son. It was much more natural that he should bequeath it to James than to Basil."

"Well, will you give me the particulars of the bequest, Uncle Peter? Was the estate devised by will, or by deed of gift?"

"I decline to give you more particulars than I have already given," was the prompt reply of the banker. "The affair is not mine; it is my brother James's. You find him in secure possession of the estate; you are told that it is his; and that ought to suffice. It is a very presumptuous proceeding on the part of Basil's son, to come over in this extraordinary manner, without warning of any kind, and attempt to question the existing state of things. That is my opinion, Anthony."

"Is this your final resolve, Uncle Peter?—not to help me?"

"My final, irrevocable resolve. I have enough to do in attending to my own affairs, without interfering with my brother's!"

Anthony Castlemaine took up his hat, and put forth his hand. "I am very sorry, Uncle Peter. It might have saved so much trouble. Perhaps I shall have to go to law."

The banker shook hands with him in a sufficiently friendly spirit: but he did not ask him to remain, or to call again.

"One hint I will give you, Anthony," he said, as the young man turned to the door; and he spoke apparently upon impulse. "Were you to expend your best years and your best energies upon this search, you would be no wiser than you are now. The Castlemaines do not brook interference; neither are their affairs conducted in that loose manner that can afford a possibility of their being inquired into; and so long as Mr. Castlemaine refuses to allow you ocular proof, rely upon it you will never get to have it. The Castlemaines know how to hold their own."

"I am a Castlemaine, too, uncle, and can hold my own with the best of them. Nothing will turn me from my course in this matter, save the proofs I have asked for."

"Good-morning, Anthony."

"Good-day, Uncle Peter."

Anthony put on his coat in the hall, and went forth into the street. There he halted; looking this way and that way, as though uncertain of his route.

"A few doors on the right hand, on the other side the market-house, John Bent said," he repeated to himself. "Then I must cross the street, and so onwards."

He crossed over, went on past the market-house, and looked attentively at the doors on the other side it. On one of those doors was a brass plate: "Mr. Knivett, Attorney-at-law." Anthony Castlemaine rang the bell, asked if the lawyer was at home, and sent in one of his cards.

He was shown into a small back room. At a table strewn with papers and pens, sat an elderly man with a bald head, who was evidently regarding the card with the utmost astonishment. He turned his spectacles on Anthony.

"Do I see Mr. Knivett, the avoué?" he asked, substituting for once a French term for an English one, perhaps unconsciously.

"I am Mr. Knivett, sir, attorney-at-law."

In the frank, free way that seemed so especially to characterise him, Anthony Castlemaine put out his hand as to a friend.

"You knew my father well, sir. Will you receive his son for old memories' sake?"

"Your father?" asked Mr. Knivett, questioningly: but nevertheless meeting the hand with his own, and glancing again at the card.

"Basil Castlemaine. He who went away so long ago from Greylands' Rest."

"Bless my heart!" cried Mr. Knivett, snatching off his glasses in his surprise. "Basil Castlemaine! I never thought to hear of him again.

Why, it must be—ay—since he left, it mast be hard upon five-and-thirty years."

"About that, I suppose, sir."

"And—is he come back?"

Anthony had again to go over the old story. His father's doings abroad and his father's death, and his father's charge to him to come home and claim his paternal inheritance: he rehearsed it all. Mr. Knivett, who was very considerably past sixty, and had put his spectacles on again, never ceased gazing at the relator, as they sat nearly knee to knee. Not for a moment did any doubt occur to him that the young man was other than he represented himself to be: the face was the face of a Castlemaine, and of a truthful gentleman.

"But I have come to you, not only to show myself to a friend of my poor father's in his youth, but also as a client," proceeded Anthony, after a short while. "I have need of a lawyer's advice, sir; which I am prepared to pay for according to the charges of the English country. Will you advise me?"

"To be sure," replied Mr. Knivett. "What advice is it that you want?"

"First of all, sir—In the days when my father was at home, you were the solicitor to my grandfather, old Anthony Castlemaine. Did you continue to be so until his death?"

"I did."

"Then you can, I hope, give me some particulars that I desire to know. To whom was Greylands' Rest bequeathed—and in what manner was it devised?"

Mr. Knivett shook his head. "I cannot give you any information upon the point," he said. "I must refer you to Mr. Castlemaine."

"I have applied to Mr. Castlemaine, and to Mr. Peter Castlemaine also: neither of them will tell me anything. They met me with a point blank refusal to do so."

"Ah—I daresay. The Castlemaines never choose to be questioned."

"Why will not you afford me the information, Mr. Knivett?"

"For two reasons. Firstly, because the probability is that—pray understand me, young sir; note what I say—the probability is that I do not possess the information to give you. Secondly, if I did possess it, my relations with the family would preclude my imparting it. I am the attorney to the Castlemaines."

"Their confidential attorney?"

"Some of the business I transact for them is confidential."

"But see here, Mr. Knivett—what am I to do? I come over at the solemn command of my father, delivered to me on his death-bed, to put in my claim to the estate. I find my uncle James in possession of it. He says it is his. Well and good: I do not say it is quite unlikely to be so. But when I say to him, 'Show me the vouchers for it, the deed or the will that you hold it by,' he shuts himself metaphorically up, and says he will not show me anything—that I must be satisfied with his word. Now, is that satisfactory?"

"I daresay it does not appear so to you."

"If there was a will made, let them allow me to see the will; if it was bequeathed by a deed of gift, let me read the deed of gift. Can there be anything more fair than what I ask? If Greylands' Rest is legally my uncle James's, I should not be so foolish or so unjust as to wish to deprive him of it."

Mr. Knivett sat back in his chair, pressing the tips of his fingers together, and politely listening. But comment made he none.

"To go back home, without prosecuting my claim, is what I shall never do, unless I am convinced that I have no claim to prosecute," continued Anthony. "Well, sir, I shall want a legal gentleman to advise me how to set about the investigation of the affair; and hence I come to you."

"I have shown you why I cannot advise you," said Mr. Knivett—and his manner was ever so many shades colder than it had been at first. "I am the attorney to Mr. Castlemaine."

"You cannot help me at all, then?"

"Not at all; in this."

It sounded rather hard to the young man as he rose from his seat to depart. All he wanted was fair play, open dealing; and it seemed that he could not get it.

"My uncle Peter, with whom I have just been, said a thing that I did not like," he stayed to remark; "it rather startled me. I presume—I should think—that he is a man of strict veracity?"

"Mr. Peter Castlemaine? Undoubtedly."

"Well, sir, what he said was this. That were I to spend my best years and energies in the search after information, I should be no wiser at the end than I am now."

"That I believe to be extremely probable," cordially assented the lawyer.

"But do you see the position in which it would leave me? Years and years!—and I am not to be satisfied one way or the other?"

MRS. HENRY WOOD

The attorney froze again. "Ah, yes; true."

"Well, sir, I will say good-day to you, for it seems that I can do no good by staying, and I must not take up your time for nothing. I only wish you had been at liberty to advise me."

Mr. Knivett made some civil rejoinder about wishing that he had been. So they parted, and the young man found himself in the street again. Until now it had been one of the brightest of days; but during this short interview at the lawyer's, the weather seemed to have changed. The skies, as Anthony Castlemaine looked up, were now dull and threatening. The clouds had lowered. He buttoned his warm coat about him, and began his walk back to Greylands.

"Je crois que nous aurons de la neige," he said, in the familiar language to which he was most accustomed, "et je n'ai pas de parapluie. N'importe; je marcherai vite."

Walk fast! And to Greylands! Could poor Anthony Castlemaine have foreseen the black pall of Fate, already closing upon him like a dreadful shadow, he had turned his steps away from Greylands for ever.

VII

In the Moonlight

White clouds were passing over the face of the blue sky, casting their light and their shade on the glorious sea. Not for a minute together did the sea present the same surface; its hue, its motions, and its ripples were for ever changing. Now it would be blue and clear almost as crystal; anon, green and still; next, sparkling like diamonds under the sunlight: and each aspect seemed more beautiful than that which it had displaced.

To Anthony Castlemaine, gazing at it from his bedroom at the Dolphin Inn, no object in nature had ever seemed so beautiful. Not the vineyards of his native land; not the sunny plains of Italy; not the grand picturesque mountains of Switzerland: all these he had been accustomed to from his youth, and they were fair to look upon: but to him they were as nothing, compared with this wide, wondrous, ever-changing sea.

Some days, a very few, had elapsed since his visit to Stilborough, told of in the last chapter. Another week had come in, and this was the Tuesday in it: destined to be a most fatal day for more than one person connected with our story. The snow-storm he had anticipated, in his homeward walk that afternoon, had passed off without falling; the cold itself seemed on the next day to have taken its departure. With that variable caprice that distinguishes our insular climate, the biting frost, the keen east wind, that had almost cut people through, had given, place to the warm, cheering weather of a balmy spring.

Anthony Castlemaine had opened the casement window to admit the genial air, the fresh sea-breeze, and stood there in profound thought. On the table lay a letter he had just written. Its seal of black wax was stamped with the Castlemaine crest, and it was addressed to his native place, Gap, Dauphiné. Some shouting arose on the beach, drawing his attention. A fishing-boat was preparing to put out; one of her men had not come down, and the two others and the shrill boy were raising their voices to make tie laggard hear. He went dashing out of the Dolphin Inn, just under the view of Anthony.

Anthony Castlemaine was in perplexity. He did not see his way any clearer before him than he had seen it when he first came. That

Greylands' Rest was legally his he entertained no doubt of; but to prove it was another matter. He and Mr. Castlemaine had met one day near the Dolphin; they had talked for a few minutes, but Anthony could make out nothing. Twice since then he had presented himself at Greylands Rest, and Mr. Castlemaine had been denied to him. It was quite evident he meant to have nothing more to do with Anthony.

The waves of the sea sparkled and rippled; the sun came out from behind a fleecy cloud, and shone with renewed strength; a beautiful vessel in the distance was passing with all her sails set.

"It is very strange behaviour," mused Anthony. "If the estate belongs in truth to my uncle James, why can he not show me that it does? His not showing it almost proves of itself that it is mine. I must get to see him: I cannot stay in the dark like this."

Taking up the letter, he descended the stairs, went across to the little general shop near the beach, and dropped it into the letter-box. He was quite at home in Greylands now, had made acquaintance with its inhabitants, and was known and recognised as the grandson of old Anthony Castlemaine. In returning he met one of the Grey Sisters. Lifting his hat, he bowed to her with deep respect; for he regarded the Grey Ladies as a religious order, and in his native land these female communities are held in reverence. Little Sister Phoeby—she was very short and stout, and nearly middle-aged, and only one of the working sisters—bobbed down her grey head in return, giving him a kindly good-morrow.

"And John Bent thinks that Mr. Castlemaine derides these good ladies!" thought Anthony. "It must be fancy. John has fancies. He—Dear me! here's that charming demoiselle again!"

She was advancing swiftly, seemingly wishing to catch Sister Phoeby, her pretty figure attired becomingly in a light silk dress and short scarlet cloak with silken tassels; her strangely-beautiful eyes were cast on the sea with the same look of loving admiration that Anthony's own sometimes wore when gazing at it. He could have wished that this young lady was his sister, or really his cousin: for Anthony had not seen many faces in his life that he so believed in for truth and goodness and beauty as Ethel Reene's.

They had nearly met before she observed him. He stopped and addressed some words to her in deprecation of his former fault, keeping his hat off while he spoke. Ethel answered him frankly, and held out her hand. Since the previous encounter, she had had time to digest the offence, to understand how it had arisen and that he had not the least intention of insulting her; she had also been favourably impressed with what she had heard abroad of Anthony Castlemaine.

"Let us forget it," said Ethel, with her sweet smile. "I understand now how it happened; I know you did not intend any offence. Are you going to make a long stay at the Dolphin?"

"That must depend partly on Mr. Castlemaine," replied Anthony. "He will not give me an interview, and for myself I can scarcely see a step before my face. I must ask him once more to listen to me; I hope he will. I had some thought of going to him this afternoon."

"He is at home," said Ethel, innocently, who only very imperfectly understood the trouble looming between the young man before her and Mr. Castlemaine.

"At home now? Then I will go to him at once," said he, acting on the impulse of the moment: and he again offered his hand to Ethel. "Adieu. I hope you have quite forgiven me, Miss Castlemaine."

"I have quite forgiven you, indeed: but I am not Miss Castlemaine, you know," she said, laughing, as she let her hand rest in his. "You will know my name better soon—Ethel Reene. Good-bye."

And during her after-life Ethel was wont to look back often on this little meeting, and to feel thankful that it had taken place, and that it was a pleasant one. For she never again saw the ill-fated young man in this world.

Recrossing the road, and passing the inn corner, Anthony got into the fields on his way to Greylands' Rest. They were pleasanter than the road that sunshiny afternoon. He walked along in deep thought, deliberating on what he should say.

Ah, if he could but have seen behind him! A double shadow followed him—as the poet Hood wrote of Miss Kilmansegg going upstairs to her doom. His own natural shadow and another. Nearer and nearer it had been gradually drawing as the days went on; and now on this day it lay ready to close on him—as it would close ere the clock had told many more hours: the dark, dreadful, ominous shadow of death. Of a death done in darkness and secret.

In the last field, side by side with the avenue that led to Greylands' Rest, while Anthony was wondering whether he should be permitted to see his uncle or not, his uncle suddenly stood in front of him, coming through the little gateway that led into the field.

MRS. HENRY WOOD

The Master of Greylands, erect, well dressed, handsome, would have passed him with a slight nod, but Anthony put himself in his way.

"Uncle James, I beg your pardon; I would not wish to be rude; but will you allow me to speak a few little words to you?"

"I am in a hurry," said Mr. Castlemaine.

"Will you give me then a short interview at your house this evening? Or to-morrow morning, if that will suit you better."

"No," replied Mr. Castlemaine.

"Twice I have been to Greylands' Rest, asking to see you, Uncle James; and twice have I been denied. Though the last time I think you were at home, and that you saw me from the window."

"You cannot have anything to say to me that I wish to hear, or that would be profitable to yourself," returned the Master of Greylands "for that reason I was denied to you. Our first interview was not so satisfactory that we need wish for another."

"But it is necessary that we should converse," returned the young man. "I am waiting to have this question settled as to Greylands' Rest."

"What question?" demanded Mr. Castlemaine, with haughty indifference—just as though he had quite forgotten that anything had ever arisen in regard to it.

"Greylands' Rest is yours, Uncle James, or it is mine: I must ascertain which of us it belongs to. You decline to tell me—"

"Decline to tell you," interrupted Mr. Castlemaine. "Cannot you use your own eyes and your judgment, and see that it is mine."

"I see that you are in possession of it, Uncle James; I see no farther. You decline to show me anything of the facts: my Uncle Peter declines; Knivett, the attorney-at-law, declines."

"Have you applied to Knivett?"

"Yes, last week."

The eyes of Mr. Castlemaine flashed fire. "How dare you do such a thing, sir, as attempt to interfere in my affairs? Tamper with my man of business! By heaven, I have a great mind to give you into custody!"

"Do not let us quarrel, Uncle James; suffer me to say what little I have to say quietly. I did not go to Mr. Knivett otherwise than openly. He said he could tell me nothing; and I recognized the weight of his objection—that he is your attorney. Being so, he of course cannot act for me."

"Perhaps you tried to bribe him to act for you," scoffed Mr. Castlemaine, who was foolishly beginning to lose his temper.

"I would not do any mean or dishonourable thing, Uncle James; I am a Castlemaine, and my father's son. But what I have to say to you is this, that matters cannot rest as they are: and I wish you fully to understand what my course will be if you do not give me the satisfaction I require, as to who is the true owner of Greylands' Rest. Only show me that it is yours, and I make my bow of departure from Greylands."

"You are pretty insolent for a young man!" retorted Mr. Castlemaine, looking down on him with scorn. "Do you suppose such an application was ever made to a gentleman before? You speak of your father, my brother Basil: had some impudent stranger presented himself before him, and demanded to see title-deeds of his, what would his answer have been, think you?"

"Circumstances alter cases, Uncle James. My case is different from the imaginary one that you put. Only satisfy me that the place is yours, and I ask no more. I have a right to know so much."

"You never shall know it: for your insolence, you shall never know more than you know now. Do your best and worst."

"Then you will leave me no resource but to proceed," returned the young man, who maintained his temper and his courtesy in a notable degree. "I shall employ the best lawyer I can call to my aid, and act on his advice."

"Tush!" was the contemptuous answer. "Go and put in a claim to Parson Marston's church—to the Dolphin Inn,—to the beach itself! Claim all, and see how far a lawyer will advance you in it."

"I wish you had met me temperately, Uncle James. I only ask what's fair—to be satisfied. It is the talk of the neighbours now: they say you ought to satisfy me; they think you would do it if it were in your power."

"What?" roared Mr. Castlemaine.

Had Anthony seen the storm he was provoking, he had surely not continued. He did not wish to irritate Mr. Castlemaine: all he wanted was to show him the reasons of his proposed attempted investigation—to prove to him that he was justified in what he meant to do. The truth was, the young man, who was by nature just, honourable, and kindly, who had never in his life attempted to take a mean advantage of friend or enemy, felt half ashamed and deeply grieved to be thus thrown into adverse contact with his newly-found relatives; and he sought to show that he had justifiable excuse for it.

"It is not my fault, uncle, if the people thus give their opinion: I did not ask for it, or provoke them to it. What they say has reason in it, as it seems to me. When the popular belief prevailed that my grandfather would not leave his estate away from his eldest son, Basil, and when it was never known how he did leave it, or to whom, or anything about it, save that his second son remained in possession, why, they talked. That is what I am told. It would be a satisfaction to the public as well as to me, Uncle James, if you would suffer the truth to be known."

It was not often that the Master of Greylands allowed anger to overpower him. In his younger days he had been subject to fits of intemperate passion, but time and self-control had well-nigh stamped the failing out. Perhaps until this moment he had believed it had left him for ever. His passion rose now: his face was scarlet; his clenched hands were kept by force down to his side, lest they should deal a blow at Anthony. Them, so far, he controlled, but not his tongue: and he poured forth a torrent of abuse.

"Go back to where you came from, insolent, upstart braggart!" were the words he finished up with. "You are no true son of my brother Basil. Ill-doing though he was, he was not a fire-brand, striving to spread malignant dissension amid a peaceable community."

"Uncle James, I shall never go back until I have come to the bottom of this matter," spoke the young man, firmly: and it may be that his unruffled temper, his very calmness of bearing, only served to irritate all the more Mr. Castlemaine. "The best man of law that London will afford I shall summon to my aid: he must force you to show the title by which you hold possession of the estate; and we shall then see which has the most right to it, you or I."

The words inflamed Mr. Castlemaine almost to madness. With a fierce oath—and bad language, though common enough then, was what he was rarely, if ever, betrayed to use—he lifted his hand to strike. Anthony, startled, got away.

"What have I done to merit this treatment, Uncle James?" he remonstrated. "Is it because I am a relative? You would not, for shame, so treat a stranger."

But the Master of Greylands, flinging back a word and look of utter contempt, went striding on his way, leaving his nephew alone.

Now it happened that this contest was witnessed by the superintendent of the coastguard, Mr. Nettleby, who was walking along the path of the neighbouring field behind the far-off intervening hedge, bare at that season. He could not hear the words that passed—the whole field was between—but he saw they were angry ones, and that the Master of Greylands was in a foaming passion. Calling in at the Dolphin Inn, he related before one or two people what he had seen: and Anthony, when he returned soon after, gave the history of the interview.

"I'm sure I thought Mr. Castlemaine struck you, sir," resumed the officer.

"No, but he would have liked to strike me," said Anthony. "I stepped back from his hand. It is very foolish of him."

"I think he would like to kill Mr. Anthony, for my part, by the way he treats him," said John Bent. But the words were only spoken in the heat of partisanship, without actual meaning: just as we are all given to hasty assertions on occasion. However, they were destined to be remembered afterwards by Greylands.

Somewhat later John Bent and his guest were standing at the front door, talking together of the general perplexity of things. The sun was setting in the west in beautiful clouds of rose-colour and amber, showing the advance of evening John began to think he had better be laying the cloth for the parlour dinner, unless he wanted his wife about him. And—here she was! her cherry-coloured ribbons right over his shoulder.

At that moment, careering down the road from Greylands' Rest, came Harry Castlemaine on his spirited horse. His overcoat was rolled up and strapped on the saddle, and he looked as though mounted for a journey. On the road he was bent the Chapel Lane would have been the nearest way; but when on horseback Harry always took the front way from his house, though it might involve a round through the village.

"Going out a pleasuring, Mr. Harry?" cried the landlady, as he reined-in.

"Going out a businessing," corrected the young man, in his free and careless manner, as he nodded and smiled at Anthony—for he did not share in his father's discourteous behaviour to their new relative, though he had not yet made advances to any intimacy. "A beautiful sunset, is it not?"

"Quite very beautiful," replied Anthony.

"I am bound for Newerton, Mrs. Bent," resumed Harry. "Can I do anything for you there?"

"Nothing, thank you, sir."

"What, not even choose you some cap ribbons? Newerton ribbons, you know, take the conceit out of those at Stilborough."

"You must always have your joke, Mr. Harry! As if a fine young gentleman like you would trouble himself to choose an old woman's ribbons!"

"See if I don't bring you some! Meanwhile, John, suppose you give me a glass of ale, to speed me on my journey."

The landlord brought the ale, handing it up on a waiter; somewhat to his own discomfort, for the horse was prancing and rearing. Harry Castlemaine drank it; and with a general nod, an intimation that he should return on the morrow, and a wave of the hand to his cousin, he rode away.

Anthony went round the corner of the house to look after him. Not being anything great in horsemanship himself, he admired those who were. He admired also the tall, fine form, the handsome face, and the free, frank bearing of Harry Castlemaine; and a hope in that moment arose in his heart that they might become good friends if he remained in England. He stood and watched him up the road until its bending hid him from view. Harry's route lay past the Grey Nunnery, past the coastguard station higher up, and so onwards. Newerton was a town of some importance, at about ten miles distance.

The remaining events of the evening, so far as they concerned Anthony Castlemaine, were destined to assume importance and to be discussed for days and weeks afterwards. He took his dinner at six, John Bent waiting on him as usual; afterwards, he sat alone for an hour or two in deep thought. At least, Mrs. Bent, coming in to take away his coffee-cup, assumed him to be deep in thought as he did not speak to her, an unusual thing. He sat between the table and the fire, his elbow resting on the former and his fingers pressing his right temple. The landlady had never seen him so still, or look so solemn; there was a cloud as of some dread care upon his face—she declared so to the world afterwards. Could it have been that in those, the last few hours of his life on earth, a foreshadowing of the dreadful fate about to overtake him was presented in some vague manner to his mind? It might have been so.

About nine o'clock he suddenly asked the landlord to fetch down his inkstand and paper-case, which he had left in his bedroom; and then he wrote a letter, sealed it as he had the one in the afternoon, and put on it the same address. By-and-by, John Bent came in again to look to the fire.

"I have made up my mind to get another interview with Mr. Castlemaine before I apply for legal advice," spoke Anthony.

"Bless me!" exclaimed John Bent, for the words surprised him.

"Yes. I have been thinking it well over from beginning to end; and I see that I ought to give my uncle James one more opportunity to settle it amicably, before bringing the dispute openly before the world, and causing a scandal. He was in a passion this afternoon and perhaps did not quite understand me: when he shall have had time to reflect he may be more reasonable."

John Bent shook his head. In his own mind he did not believe that fifty fresh appeals would have any effect on Mr. Castlemaine.

"I say this to myself," went on Anthony: "Whether Greylands' Rest is his by right or not, he is in possession of it. Nobody can deny that. And I have tried to put myself in imagination in his place, and I see how cruel a blow it would seem if a stranger came to seek to deprive me of it. I might be as angry as he is."

"Then, sir, do you intend to leave him in possession of it?" returned the landlord.

"No, no; you do not comprehend. I must enforce my claim; if the estate is mine, I will never yield it—to him, or to anyone. But it may be his: and I think it is only just to offer him one more opportunity of privately satisfying me, before I take any proceedings. I shall do so. If I cannot see him to-morrow, I will write to him fully."

"The meeting might only lead to another quarrel, Mr. Anthony."

"Well—yes—I have thought of that. And I fear he would injure me if he could," added the young man, in a dreamy manner, and speaking to himself instead of to his landlord. "There: don't put more coal, please: it is too warm."

John Bent went away with his coal-scuttle. He remarked to his wife that their inmate did not seem in his usual good spirits. Mrs. Bent, trimming one of her smart caps at the round table by the fire, answered that she knew as much as that without being told; and that he (John) had better see that Molly was properly attending to the company in the public-room.

It was considerably past ten, and the company—as Mrs. Bent called them, which consisted principally of fishermen—were singing a jovial song, when Anthony Castlemaine came out of his parlour, the letter in his hand. Just as he had posted the one written in the afternoon, so he went over to the box now and posted this. After that, he took a turn up and down the beach, listening to the low murmuring of the sea, watching the moonbeams as they played on the water. It was a most beautiful night; the air still and warm, the moon rather remarkably bright. That Greylands' Rest was his own legally now, and would soon be his own practically, he entertained no doubt, and he lost himself in visions of the pleasant life he might lead there. Thus the time slipped unconsciously on, and when he got back to the Dolphin the clock had struck eleven. John Bent's company were taking their departure—for the house closed at the sober hour of eleven—John's man was shutting the shutters, and John himself stood outside his door, his hat on his head and a pipe in his mouth.

"A lovely night, sir, isn't it?" he began. "A'most like summer. I've been finishing my pipe outside on the bench here."

"Lovely indeed," replied Anthony. "I could never tire of looking at the sea yonder."

They paced about together before the bench, talking, and presently extending their stroll up the hill. Mr. Nettleby's residence, a fair-sized, pretty cottage, stood aback from the road in its garden, just opposite the Grey Nunnery; and Mr. Nettleby, smoking his pipe, was at the outer gate.

When that fatal night was gone and past, and people began to recall its events, they said how chance trifles seemed to have worked together to bring about the ill. Had Anthony Castlemaine not written that letter, the probability was that he would never have gone out at all; on returning from the post and the beach, had the landlord not been outside the inn, he would at once have entered: and finally, had the superintendent of the coastguard not been at his gate, they would not have stayed abroad.

Mr. Nettleby invited them in, hospitably offering them a pipe and glass. He had business abroad that night, and therefore had not retired to rest. They consented to enter, "just for a minute."

The minute extended itself to the best part of an hour. Once seated there by the fire, and plunged into a sea of talk, they were in no hurry to move again. Anthony Castlemaine accepted a pipe, John Bent refilled his. The former took a glass of sugar and water—at which Mr. Nettleby made a wry face; John Bent had a glass of weak Hollands, which lasted him during the visit: he was no drinker.

The conversation turned on various matters. On the claims of Anthony to Greylands' Rest, which had become quite a popular topic; on the social politics of Greylands, and on other subjects. Under a strong injunction of secrecy, Mr. Nettleby imparted certain suspicions that he was entertaining of a small hamlet called Beeton, a mile or two higher up the coast. He believed some extensive smuggling was carried on there, and he purposed paying a visit to the place that very night, to look out for anything there might be to see. Anthony inquired whether he was extensively troubled by smugglers, and the superintendent said No; very little indeed, considering that the coast lay so convenient for Holland and other suspicious countries: but he had his doubts.

They all went out together. It was twelve o'clock, or close upon it. Mr. Nettleby's road lay to the left; theirs to the right. However, they turned to accompany him a short distance, seduced to it by the beauty of the night.

"In for a penny, in for a pound," thought John Bent. "The missis can't go on more if I stay out for another hour than she'll go on now."

But they did not walk far: just to the top of the hill, and a short way beyond it. They then wished the officer goodnight, and turned back again.

The Friar's Keep looked ghastly enough in the moonlight. Anthony Castlemaine glanced up at its roof, dilapidated in places, at its dark casement windows. "Let us watch a minute," said he, jestingly, "perhaps the Grey Monk will appear."

John Bent smiled. They had passed the entrance to Chapel Lane, and were standing within the thick privet hedge and the grove of trees which overshadowed it. Not that the trees gave much shadow at that season, for their branches were bare.

"Tell me again the legend of the Grey Monk," said Anthony. "I partly forget it."

John Bent proceeded to do as he was bid, lowering his voice as befitted the time and subject. But he had scarcely begun the narrative when the sound of approaching footsteps struck on their ears, and his voice involuntarily died away into silence. At the first moment, they thought the superintendent was returning.

But no. The footsteps came from Chapel Lane. They drew more closely within the cover of the hedge, and waited. A gentleman, walking fast and firmly, emerged from the lane, crossed the road, went in at the gate of the chapel ruins, seemed to take a hasty glance out over the sea, and then passed into the Friar's Keep. Very much to the astonishment of John Bent, and somewhat to that of Anthony, they recognized Mr. Castlemaine.

"He was taking a look at the sea by moonlight," whispered Anthony. "I'll go after him. I will. And we'll have it out under the moonbeams. What's he doing now, I wonder, in that Friar's Keep?"

Before John Bent could stop him—and, as the landlord said later, an impulse prompted him to attempt it—the young man was off like a shot; entered the gate in the wake of his uncle, and disappeared amid the cloisters of the Friar's Keep.

The Master of Greylands must have emerged safely enough from those ghostly cloisters: since he was abroad and well the next day as usual: but the ill-fated Anthony Castlemaine was never again seen in this life.

VIII

Commotion at Stilborough

On that same fatal Tuesday—and fatal it might well be called, so much of evil did it bring in its train—there was commotion at Stilborough. Disagreeable rumours of some kind had got abroad, touching the solvency of the bank. Whence they arose, who had originated them, and what they precisely meant, nobody knew, nobody could tell: but they were being whispered about from one man to another, and the bank's creditors rose up in astonishment and fear.

"Is it true? It cannot be." "What is it?—what's amiss? Not possible for Peter Castlemaine to be shaky. Where did you hear it? I'd trust the bank with my life, let alone my money." "But it's said that some gigantic speculation has failed?" "Nonsense the bank would stand twenty failures: don't believe a syllable of it." "Well, rumour says the bank will stop to-morrow." "Stop to-morrow! What shall we do for our money?" "Don't know. I shall get mine out to-day."

The above sentences, and others similar to them, might be heard from different people in the streets of Stilborough. Those who were ultra-cautious went into the bank and asked for their money. At first Thomas Hill paid: he thought the demands were only in the regular course of business: but in a short while he saw what it was—that a run upon the bank was setting in; and he went into Mr. Peter Castlemaine's private room to consult his master. Fortunately the rumours had only got afloat late in the afternoon, and it was now within a few minutes of the usual time of closing. Not that, earlier or later, it could have made much difference in the calamity; but it saved some annoyance to the bank's inmates.

Had the bank been solvent, it would of course have kept its doors open, irrespective of hours and customs; being insolvent, it closed them to the minute, and the shutters too. Had Mr. Peter Castlemaine been able to meet the demands for money, he would have been in the public room with a clear face, reassuring the applicants: as it was, he bolted himself in his parlour. The clerks drew down the shutters and shut the doors against the public: two or three of the young men, who had to go out with letters or messages, got away through the private entrance. Back went Thomas Hill to his master, knocking at the door when he found it fastened.

"It is only me, sir. All's safe."

Peter Castlemaine opened it. A change, that the faithful old clerk did not like to see, was in his face. Hill's own face was scared and white enough just then, as he well knew; but it could not wear the peculiar, sickly, shrunken look he saw on his master's.

"Where are they, Thomas? Is it really a run?"

"Really and truly, sir. What an unfortunate circumstance! A few days, and you would have tided it over."

"But where are they all?"

"Outside, sir, in the street, kicking and thumping at the doors and windows; a great crowd of them by this time, and growing a bigger one every minute. We managed to get the doors shut as tie clock struck, and then put down the shutters."

Mr. Castlemaine drew his hand across his aching brow. "I think this must have been caused by Fosbrook," he remarked. "He may have let an incautious word drop."

"He'd not do it, sir."

"Not intentionally: for his own sake. I knew it boded no good when I found he meant to stay on at the Turk's Head. Alas! Alas!"

"There has not been a regular stoppage," said Thomas Hill. "And if we can manage to get assistance, and open again to-morrow morning—"

"Don't, Hill," interrupted the banker, in a tone of painful wailing. "Don't speak of hope! There's no hope left."

"But, sir, when the remittance, which we expect, comes—"

"Hush! look here."

Mr. Peter Castlemaine pushed an open letter towards his clerk. The old man's hands trembled as he held it; his face grew whiter as he mastered the contents. Hope was indeed gone. The worst had come. An embargo, or lien, had been laid in London upon the expected remittances.

"Did you get this letter this morning, sir? Why did you not tell me? It would have been better to have stopped then."

"I got it ten minutes ago, Thomas. It was sent from town by a special messenger in a post-chaise and four which, of course, the estate will be charged with. He came, by mistake, I suppose, to the private door; or perhaps he saw the crowd round the public one: and he gave the letter into my own hands, saying he would take my instructions back to town to-morrow morning, if I had any. All's over."

Too truly did Thomas Hill feel the force of the words. All was over. But for this last great misfortune, this lien upon the money that ought to have come, they might have weathered the storm. The few past days had gone on pretty quietly; and every day, passed without exposure, was so much gained. The Master of Greylands, when applied to by his brother for a loan, had listened, and placed at the bank's disposal a fairly good sum: not enough, not half enough, for what it was wanted to stop, but still a great help.

"Even now," began Thomas Hill, breaking the depressing silence, "even now, sir, if a meeting were called, and a statement of facts properly laid before the creditors, they might consent to allow time.

"Time!" echoed Mr. Peter Castlemaine. "What, with this yelling crowd clamouring at the doors!—and with Fosbrook in the place!— and with a lien on all the forthcoming remittances! And," he added, the shrunken grey look on his countenance becoming more perceptible, as his voice dropped to a whisper—"and with the discovery at hand of the use I made of the Armannon bonds! The last closing hour has come, Thomas, and nothing can save me!"

Thomas Hill took off his spectacles to wipe the mist away. The failure of the bank, and the disgrace attaching to these pecuniary misfortunes, seemed as nothing, compared with the guilty shame that must fall on his master.

"They may prosecute me criminally," breathed Mr. Peter Castlemaine, from between his dry and ashy lips.

"No, no," burst forth Thomas Hill. "They'll never do that, sir. Think how you have been respected! And besides—so far as I can understand the complication—there will be money to pay everybody."

"Every man will be paid in full to the uttermost farthing," spoke the banker emphatically. "But that's another thing. I sat up over my books nearly all last night, making my calculations, and I find that there will be funds to meet all claims. Only there's the waiting! Not any over perhaps; but there will be so much as that."

"And to think that this miserable trouble should intervene!" cried Thomas Hill, wringing his hands. "There will be my six thousand pounds to help you, sir, with the expenses, and that."

Peter Castlemaine shook his head to the last sentence, but he made no denial in words. He seemed to have neither words nor spirit left, and sat leaning his brow upon his hand. The once fine fresh colour that was natural to his cheeks had faded away, though its traces might be seen still. One might have fancied that a thin veil of grey had been flung over the healthy bloom. In all his long experience Thomas Hill had never, to his recollection, seen a man change like this.

"You look ill, sir," he said. "Let me get you something to take."

"I feel ill," was the answer. "I ought to have confronted those people just now in the other room, and should have done so, but that I felt physically incapable. While I was reading the letter brought by the London messenger, a sharp, curious pain seized me here," touching his left side. "For some minutes I could not move."

"Is the heart all right?" hesitated the clerk—as if he were afraid to breathe the question.

"I do not know. During the past twelve months, since these troubles set in, I have had a good deal of fluttering there: pain, too, at times."

"You should consult a doctor, sir. Don't, pray, delay it."

"Ay," sighed the unfortunate man. "I suppose I should. When I get a little out of this fret and turmoil—if I ever do get out of it—I'll see one. Lock the desk for me, will you, Hill? There's nothing to keep it open for: no use to pore over ledgers now."

He held out the key, sitting as he was, and Thomas Hill locked the desk and returned the key to him. Strength and health seemed suddenly to have gone out of Peter Castlemaine.

"I'll go and get you a little warm brandy and water, sir. I'm sure you ought to take it."

His master did not say Do, or Don't; and the clerk went for it. Getting it mixed by Stephen—who looked frightened out of his senses by the commotion in the street—he carried in the glass of hot liquor, and the banker sipped it. It seemed to do him a little good; he looked less entirely depressed.

"There's one thing I wanted to say, Thomas," he began. "That young man who came here last week—my brother Basil's son, you know."

"I've heard he is at Greylands, sir. Young Anthony, they say."

"Ay. Basil named him after the father. I should have done the same, had a son been born to me. He came here that day, you know, asking me to tell him the particulars of how Greylands' Rest was left; and I fear I was a little short with him. I did not wish to be, I'm sure; but this—this trouble was lying on me heavily. The young fellow spoke fairly enough; and, I daresay, I appeared cross. He wanted me to interfere between him and James; which was a thing I should not think of doing. I've thought about it since, lying awake at night; and I want you to tell Anthony for me that I meant nothing, should you ever see him."

"But surely you will be seeing him for yourself, sir!" cried the clerk, thinking this a little strange.

"I don't know that I shall. Should James show him that he has no claim, he may be going off to France again: and as to me, why, how do I know where I shall be, or how things will go with me? You'll tell him, Thomas, that Greylands' Rest, so far as I know, is legally my brother's; if I thought my father had given it to Basil, I should not deem it right in James to hold it. But it's not likely James would, were it not his."

"Did you not know, then, how the estate was left?" asked Thomas Hill, in surprise.

"No; I did not trouble myself about it," was the banker's answer: and all this while he seemed to be speaking as his faithful clerk had never before heard him speak. Instead of the shrewd, observant, intellectual man of business, whose every sense was keenly awake, he seemed weary and passive as a tired child. "I knew Greylands' Rest would not be mine; that if it was not left to Basil it would be James's. James stayed in possession of it, and I supposed it was his: I took that for granted, and did not question him. I believe surely it is his: that my father left it to him: and, Thomas, you tell the young man, this young Anthony, that such is my opinion. I don't think there can be a doubt of it. James ought to show him the vouchers for it: Basil's son has a right to so much. Only, don't say that: I do not want, I say, to interfere with James."

"It would be the easiest way of settling the matter, sir, if Mr. Castlemaine would do that."

"Of course it would. But then, you see, James never chooses to be questioned: he resents any attempt at it; always did. As a boy, I remember, nothing ever offended him like doubting his word."

At that moment there was a ring heard at the house door. The banker looked startled, and then seemed to shrink within himself.

"It is that Fosbrook!" he exclaimed. "I thought he'd be coming. I cannot see him. You go, and battle it out with him, Thomas he won't browbeat you. Go! Don't let him come in here for the world."

But it was not Mr. Fosbrook. It was only one of the clerks, returning from his errand. Thomas Hill, seeing the state of nervous depression that his master was in, proposed to proceed at once to the Turk's Head, and hold there an interview with the dreaded creditor: and the banker seized upon it eagerly.

"Do, do!" he said. "There's no one I dread as I dread him."

As the clerk went out, he saw that many angry people lingered yet around the house and doors. He went among them: he begged them to be still for that evening, to leave matters in quiet until the morning, for that Mr. Peter Castlemaine was very ill and quite unable to see anyone. The baffled creditors showered down questions on the unfortunate clerk—who certainly felt the trouble as keenly as did his master. Thomas Hill answered them to the best of his ability: and at length one by one the malcontents took their departure, leaving the street clear and the house quiet.

And no sooner was this accomplished, than the banker's handsome barouche drove to the door, containing Miss Castlemaine and her chaperone, Mrs. Webb, who had returned to her post the previous day. Opposite to them sat the young lady's lover, William Blake-Gordon. All were in the highest spirits, talking and laughing as though no such thing as care existed in the world, and utterly unconscious of the trouble that had fallen on the house and the commotion that had reigned outside it. They had, been to look over Raven's Priory, and Mary Ursula was enchanted with it.

"You will stay to dinner, William," she said, as he handed her out of the carriage. "Papa will be vexed if you do not."

He was only too ready to accept an invitation that would give him a few more hours of her sweet companionship. It was close upon the dinner-hour—six. Stephen was holding the hall-door open, with a long, grave face: they passed him, noticing nothing.

"I will not be long, William," she whispered, running up to her chamber.

A few minutes later, and she came forth again, attired for the evening. Her dress was of rich blue silk; her cheeks had more colour in them than usual, the effect of pleasurable excitement; her bright hair was disposed so as to set off the exceeding beauty of her face. Mr. Blake-Gordon stood in the gallery, looking at a new picture that some friend had recently made a present of to the banker. As she joined him, he drew her arm within his.

"It is a fine painting, Mary."

"And it is hung well for night," she observed, "for the rays of the chandelier just fall on it. By day its place is a little dark. Have you seen papa yet?"

"Not yet. There goes six o'clock."

Mrs. Webb, an elderly lady in black satin and point-lace cap, came downstairs and turned into the drawing-room. Though a very dragon of a chaperone when necessary, she knew quite well when to join the lovers, and when to leave them alone.

They began pacing the gallery, arm in arm, looking at this picture, criticising that. From paintings, their conversation turned to what just then held a deeper interest for them—the future residence they expected so soon to enter upon, Raven's Priory. This room should be the favourite morning room, and that the favourite evening room; and the beautiful conservatory should have their best care; and there should always be a blazing fire in the hall, not a cold, bare, comfortless grate, as they had seen that day; and the gravel drive should be widened, and some rocks and ferns put on the right hand in that bare space—and so the dreams went on.

The clocks went on also. Mrs. Webb, reminded probably by her appetite, looked out once or twice; the butler and Stephen, aware that the dinner was waiting, and the cook angrily demanding whether it was to be served to-day or to-morrow, passed and repassed out of the drawing-room. As to the lovers themselves, they were unconscious of clocks and reminding appetites; for love, as we all know, lives upon air. It was the custom of the house not to serve the dinner until the banker appeared in the drawing-room: on rare occasions business detained him beyond the hour.

So they paced on, those two, in their dream of happiness. And once, at the darkest end of the gallery, when there was neither step nor sound near, Mr. Blake-Gordon stole a kiss from that blushing face, so soon, as he fondly hoped, to be all his.

"My dear, is your papa out, do you know?" questioned; Mrs. Webb, appearing at the drawing-room door, as they again neared it. "It is half-past six."

"Half-past six!" repeated Mary, in surprise. "So late as that! No, I do not know whether papa is out or in. Perhaps he is busy in his parlour? There's Stephen: he may know. Stephen," she added, quitting the arm of Mr. Blake-Gordon, and advancing towards the man, "is papa below in his parlour?"

"There's no one in the parlour, ma'am, for I've been to look," was the answer. "I saw my master go up to his chamber some time ago, but I don't think he can be in it all this while."

"How long ago?"

"Just before you came home, ma'am."

"Oh, of course, your master cannot be there still," interposed Mrs. Webb, much interested in the colloquy, for she wanted her dinner frightfully. "He must have come down and gone out, Stephen."

"Very likely, ma'am."

"I am sure that Mr. Castlemaine has not come downstairs since we came in," observed Mr. Blake-Gordon. "If he had, I must have seen him. I have been here all the time."

Mary Ursula laughed. "I will tell you what it is," she said: "papa has dropped asleep on the sofa in his room. Twice lately he has done it when he has had a very tiring day." She ran lightly up the stairs as she spoke, and knocked at the chamber door. The lamp that hung in the corridor threw its light upon the oaken panels, and upon her gleaming blue dress.

"Papa!"

There was no response, and Mary gently turned the handle, intending to open the door about an inch, and call again. That her father was lying on the sofa in a sound sleep, she felt as sure of as though she had seen him. But the door would not open.

"Papa! papa!"

No: he did not awake, though she called very loudly. Hardly knowing what to do, she ran downstairs again.

"Papa must be in a very sound sleep, for I cannot make him hear, and the door is fastened inside," she said, chiefly addressing Stephen, who was nearest to her. "I daresay he has had a fatiguing day."

"Yes, ma'am, it have been fatiguing; leastways the latter part of it," replied the man, with an emphasis that they failed to catch. "Some rude people have been knocking here, and making a fine uproar."

"Rude people knocking here!" exclaimed Mrs. Webb, taking him up sharply. "What do you mean? What did they want?"

"I don't know what they wanted, ma'am: something they couldn't get, I suppose," returned the man, who had no suspicion of the real state of the case, for he believed the house to be simply a mine of wealth that could have no limit, just as children believe in the wondrous riches told of in a fairy tale. "I know I should like to have had the driving of 'em off! Master did well not to see 'em."

"But—did papa not see them?" questioned Mary Ursula, surprised into asking the question by this extraordinary story.

"No, ma'am; and that's what I fancy they made the noise over. My master was not well, either, this afternoon, for Mr. Hill came running out for hot brandy and water for him."

What more would have been said, what doubt created, was stopped by the appearance of Thomas Hill. He had just returned from his mission to the Turk's Head. Apparently it had not been a pleasant mission: for his face was pale with what looked like fear, and he, waiving ceremony, had come straight up the stairs, asking for his master.

"I must see him; I must see him instantly. I beg your pardon, dear Miss Castlemaine, but it is of the last importance."

Had Thomas Hill only waited a moment before speaking, he would have heard that the banker was fastened in his room. They told him now. He gave one scared look around while taking in the words, and then bounded to the stairs.

"Follow me," he cried, turning his livid face on the men. "We must burst open the door. I know he is ill."

Mr. Blake-Gordon, the butler and Stephen were up almost as soon as he. Mrs. Webb laid her detaining arm on the young lady.

"You must stay here, my dear: you must. They will do better without you."

"But what can it be, save sleep?" asked Mary Ursula, arresting her steps and not knowing whether there was cause for alarm or not. "When papa is very tired he sleeps heavily. On Sunday night he dropped asleep when I was at the organ, and I could not at first awaken him."

"Of course; I make no doubt he has fallen into a sound sleep; nothing else: but it will not be seemly for you to go up with them, my dear," replied Mrs. Webb, always the very essence of propriety. "Hark! the door has given way."

Sleep? Yes, at first they did think the banker was asleep. He lay on the sofa at full length, his head on the low pillow, his feet hanging down over the other end. A candle, which he must have carried up with him, stood on the drawers, and the wax candles in the dressing-glass had been previously lighted by the servants. Altogether there was a good deal of light. They looked at the banker's face by it: and saw—that the sleep was the sleep of death.

A gasping sob burst from Thomas Hill. He fell on his knees, the tears rolling down his face.

"My master! my dear master! oh, my master, my master!"

He saw what it was; perhaps felt somewhat prepared for it by the previous events of the afternoon. The others were for the moment somewhat stunned: but they did not think it could be death.

"Run for a doctor!" cried the butler to Stephen. "He's in a faint. Run for your life!"

The butler himself did not attempt to run; he was too stout. Mr. Blake-Gordon and Stephen, both slender and light of limb, sped away without their hats. The butler raised his master's head.

"Please to ring the bell, sir, for some brandy," he said to Mr. Hill. "The maids must bring up some hot flannels, too."

"Is it possible that you can be deceived?" sobbed the clerk—"that you do not see that it is death? Oh, my poor master?"

"Death! come now, don't talk in that uncomfortable way," retorted the butler; not, however, feeling very comfortable as he said it. "What should bring death to the house in this sudden way? He is warm, too. Do please ring the bell, sir."

The doctors came without delay, two of them; for Mr. Blake-Gordon brought one, and Stephen another. But nothing could be done: it was indeed death: and the medical men thought it had taken place the best part of an hour before. The great banker of Stilborough, Peter Castlemaine, had ceased to exist.

But there was one momentous, dreadful question to be solved—what had caused the death? Had it come by God's hand and will?—or had Peter Castlemaine himself wrought it? The surgeons expressed no opinion at present; they talked in an undertone, but did not let the world share their counsels. Thomas Hill overheard one word, and it nearly sent him frantic.

"How dare you say it gentlemen? Suicide! Mr. Peter Castlemaine would no more lift his hand against himself than you would lift it. I would stake all the poor bit of life I've got left—which won't be much now—that it is his heart that has killed him. This very afternoon he complained of a sharp pain there; a strange fluttering, he called it, and he looked white enough for a ghost. He told me he had felt the same pain and fluttering at times before. There cannot be a doubt, gentlemen, that it was his heart."

The doctors nodded seemingly in assent. One thing appeared to be indisputable—that if the death was natural, no other cause than the heart could be assigned for it. The face of the dead man was calm and unruffled as that of an infant. But the elder of the doctors whispered something about an "odour."

Mary Ursula came into the room when the medical men had gone. No tears were in her eyes; she was as one stunned, paralyzed: unable in her shock of bewilderment to take in the whole truth. She had deemed the room empty: but Thomas Hill turned round from the sofa at her entrance.

"He has had a good deal of trouble lately, my poor dear master, and it has been too much for him, and broken his heart," he whispered in a piteous tone, the tears running down his cheeks. "God knows I'd have saved him from it if I could, my dear young lady: I'd willingly have died for him."

"What kind of trouble has it been?" asked Mary Ursula, letting the old man take her hands, and gazing at him with a terrified and imploring countenance.

"Money trouble, money trouble," answered the clerk. "He was not used to it, and it has broken his heart. Oh, my dear, don't grieve more than you can help!—and don't think about the future, for all I have shall be yours."

"You—think—it was heart disease?" questioned Mary, in a dread, imploring whisper. "Do you really think it, Mr. Hill?"

"My dear, I am sure of it. Quite sure. And I only wonder now he did not die in my arms this afternoon in the back parlour when the pain and fluttering were upon him," added Thomas Hill, half choked with his emotion. "There was a great clamour with the creditors, and it terrified him more than I thought. The fright must have struck to his heart, and killed him."

She sighed deeply. The same appalled look of terror clung to her face: the reassurance did not seem to bring her the comfort that it ought. For Mary Castlemaine had overheard that one covert word of suspicion breathed by the medical men: and she had, and always would have, the awful doubt lying upon her heart.

It was a dreadful night for her, poor bankrupt girl—bankrupt in happiness from that hour. Mrs. Webb persuaded her to go to bed at last; and there she lay getting through the hours as the unhappy do get through them. But, miserable though it was, it would have been far more so could she have seen, as in a mirror, what had taken place that night at Greylands in the Friar's Keep—the disappearance of Anthony Castlemaine, and its cause.

IX

A Curious Story

A bright and cheery morning with a soft westerly breeze. The flowing sea sparkled in the sunlight; the little boats danced upon its waves; the birds on the land sang merry songs to one another, cheated into a belief that spring had come in.

There had been commotion in the streets of Stilborough on the previous day, and especially around the banker's door, as we have already seen; but that commotion was open and above board, as compared with the stir that was this morning agitating Greylands. For, report was running wildly about that some mysterious and unaccountable disaster had happened to Anthony Castlemaine.

Anthony Castlemaine had disappeared. There was no other word, save that, applicable to the event: he had disappeared. And as Greylands had taken a warm fancy to the young man, it rose up in great agitation. Almost with morning light the village was being searched for him and inquiry made. People turned out of their cottages, fishermen left their boats, some of the Grey Sisters even came forth from the Nunnery: all eagerly asking what and how much was true.

The originator of the rumour was John Bent. He did not seem to know a great deal more than other people; but nobody, save him, knew anything at all. The Dolphin Inn was besieged; work was at a standstill; Mrs. Bent allowed even her servant, Molly, to stand listening, with her arms akimbo, unreproved.

The story told by John Bent was a curious one. And, it should be intimated, that, but for the fears stirring within the landlord's own breast, the disappearance would not have been thought so much of at this early stage. But John Bent had caught up the fear that some fatal harm had chanced to the young man in fact, that he had been murdered! The landlord could not account for this strong impression; he acknowledged that: but it was there, and he freely spoke it out. The substance of the tale he told was as follows.

After Anthony Castlemaine had darted across the road and through the gate in the wake of his uncle the Master of Greylands, as previously related, John Bent stood still, watching for a minute or two, but could not see or hear anything of either of them. He then, finding the night air somewhat cold, stamped up and down the path, not losing sight of the opposite gate, and waiting for Anthony to come out of it. Close upon this there rang out the report of a pistol. It was accompanied, almost simultaneously, by an awful cry; the cry of a man in agony. John Bent wondered where the cry came from and what it meant, but he never thought to connect either cry or pistol with Anthony Castlemaine. The time passed: John Bent began to find this waiting wearisome; he thought what a long confab his guest was enjoying with Mr. Castlemaine, and hoped they were settling matters amicably: and he wondered somewhat at their remaining in that dark, ghostly Keep, instead of choosing the open moonlight. By-and-by a sailor staggered past—for he had been taking more grog than was good for him—towards his home in the village. He was smoking; and John Bent took his own pipe from his pocket, filled it, and lighted it by the sailor's. The pipe consoled John Bent, and the minutes passed somewhat less tediously: but when one o'clock rang out and there were no signs of the young man, he began to think it very strange. "Surely they'd not stay all this while in that haunted Friar's Keep!—and not a place to sit down on, and nothing but cold pillared cloisters to walk or stand in, and them dark!" cried John to himself—and he deliberated what he should do. The prospect of marching into the Friar's Keep in search of his guest was not altogether congenial to his taste, for John Bent did not like the chance of meeting ghosts more than Greylands did: neither did he care to proceed home himself and leave Anthony Castlemaine to follow at leisure. Another quarter of an hour elapsed; and then—finding there was no help for it and quite tired out—he put on a bold spirit, and crossed over to enter the gate. But the gate was locked.

The gate was locked. And, had John Bent seen the whole row of high, substantial palings suddenly lifted into the air, or thrown down to the earth, he would not have stood more transfixed with astonishment.

For that gate had never been known to be locked, within his remembrance. There certainly was a lock to it, but it had always lacked a key. The latch was good, and that was all the fastening used, or needed. John Bent stood with open mouth, gasping out his surprise to the air.

"What on earth does this mean?"

He shook the gate. At least, he would have shaken it, had it been less substantially firm: but it scarcely moved under his hand. And then he set on and shouted at the top of his voice, hoping his guest would hear.

MRS. HENRY WOOD

"Mr. Anthony Castlemaine! Shall you be much longer, Mr. Anthony Castlemaine?"

The light breeze took his voice over the chapel ruins and carried its echoes out to sea; but there came back no answer of any kind.

"Well, this is a rum go," cried John, looking up, and down, and round about, in his bewilderment. "Surely Mr. Anthony can't have come out and gone home!" he added, the unlikely notion flashing on him; for, when thoroughly puzzled we are all apt to catch at straws of improbability. "He couldn't have come out without my seeing him, and me never beyond view of the gate: unless it was in the minute that I was lighting my pipe by Jack Tuff's, when I had my back turned. But yet—how was it Mr. Anthony did not see me?"

Unable to solve these doubts, but still thinking that was how it must have been, the landlord went home with a rapid step. Before he gained it, he had quite made his mind up that it was so; he fully believed his guest was by this time sound asleep in his bed, and called himself a donkey for waiting out all that while. John Bent put his hand on the handle of his door to enter softly, and found it fastened. Fastened just as firmly as the gate had been.

"Where's Ned, I wonder?" he cried aloud, alluding to his man; and he knocked with his hand pretty sharply.

There was no more response to this knock than there had been to the shouts he had been lately sending forth. He knocked again and shook the door. The moonbeams still played upon the sea; a white sail or two of the night fishing boats gleamed out; he put his back against the door and gazed on the scene while he waited. No good, as he knew, to go round to the front entrance; that was sure to be closed. John knocked the third time.

The window above his head was flung open at this juncture, and Mrs. Bent's nightcapped head came out.

"Oh, it's you, is it!" she tartly cried. "I thought, for my part, you had taken up your abode in the road for the night."

"Ned's sitting up, I suppose, Dorothy. Why does he not open the door?"

"Ned will not open the door till he has my orders. There! A pretty decent thing, this is, for a respectable householder of your age to come home between one and two in the morning! If you are so fond of prancing up and down the road in the moonlight, filling a fresh pipe at every trick and turn, why don't you stay there till the house is opened to-morrow?"

"Jack Tuff must have told you that!"

"Yes, Jack Tuff did tell it me," retorted Mrs. Bent. "I stayed at the door looking for you till half after twelve. And a tidy state he was in!" added the good lady in additional wrath. "His nose touching the ground, a'most every step he took!"

"Just let me come in, Dorothy. I've not stayed out all this while for pleasure—as you may be sure."

"You've stayed for aggravation perhaps; to keep people up. Where's Mr. Anthony Castlemaine?"

"He's come home, isn't he?"

"I dare say you know very well whether he is or not!" returned Mrs. Bent from her window.

"But Dorothy, woman, it is for him I've been waiting. He went into the Friar's Keep, and he's never come out again—unless he came when I did not see him."

"The Friar's Keep!" repeated the landlady, in the most mocking tone she could use. "What excuse will you invent next?"

"It's no excuse: it's true. We saw Mr. Castlemaine go in there, and Mr. Anthony ran over and followed him, saying he'd have out the quarrel under the moonlight. And I stood cooling my heels outside, waiting for him all that while; till at last I began to think he must have come out and passed me unseen. He has come home, has he not?"

"He is not come home," said Mrs. Bent.

"Well, let the door be opened."

As the story sounded a mysterious one, and Mrs. Bent had her curiosity, and as her husband moreover was a staid man, not at all given to this kind of offence in general, she allowed him to come in, herself opening the door. He gave her a summary of the story, she wrapped in a warm shawl while she stood to listen to it and to make her comments. Anthony Castlemaine had not come home; she had seen nothing at all of him; or of anybody else, tipsy Jack Tuff excepted.

A kind of scared feeling, a presentiment of evil, crept over John Bent. For the first time, he began to wonder whether the pistol-shot he had heard had struck the young man, whether the agonised cry was his. He went into Anthony's bedroom, and saw with his own eyes that it was empty. It was not that he questioned his wife's word; but he felt confused and doubtful altogether—as though it were not possible that Anthony could be absent in this unaccountable manner.

"I must go back and look for him, Dorothy woman."

"You'll take the key with you, then," said Mrs. Bent; who, for a wonder, did not oppose the proposition: in fact, she thought it right that he should go. And back went John Bent to the Friar's Keep.

He did not at all like this solitary walking, lovely though the night was; he would rather have been asleep in bed. The Grey Nunnery lay steeped in silence and gloom; not a single light shone from any of its windows; a sure sign that just now there could be no sick inmates there. John Bent reached the gate again, and the first thing he did was to try it.

It yielded instantly. It opened at his touch. And the man stood not much less amazed than he had before been to find it fastened. At that moment the sound of approaching footsteps in the road struck on his ear; he turned swiftly, his heart beating with eager hope: for he thought they might prove to be the steps of Anthony Castlemaine.

But they were those of Mr. Nettleby. The officer was returning from his mission of night supervision, whatever it might especially be. John Bent met him, and told his tale.

"Nonsense!" cried the superintendent, after he had listened. "They would not be likely to stay in those deserted cloisters of the Friar's Keep. Are you sure it was Mr. Castlemaine you saw go in?"

"Quite sure. But I can't think what he could want there."

"You don't think you were dreaming?" asked Mr. Nettleby, who by this time evidently fancied the tale was altogether more like a dream than a reality. "I don't believe the gate has a key, or that it ever had one."

He was examining the gate as he spoke. The lock was there as usual; but of any sign that a key had been in it that night there was none. Crossing the ruins, they stood looking out over the sea; at the line of glittering moonlight, at the distant boats catching their fish. From that they went into the Friar's Keep. Its moss-eaten Gothic door lay open to the chapel ruins. Pillars of stone supported the floor—the floor which the spirit of the dead-and-gone Grey Friar was supposed to haunt. It was rather a ghostly-looking place altogether; the intersecting pillars and the arches above, and some open arches facing the sea, where a little light streamed through. They could not see the sea from this place, for the outer wall was nearly as high as they were; but not so high as the arches; and the light and the salt fresh smell of the sea came wafting in. There they stood on the stone floor of those cloisters—as people had fallen into the way of calling them—and shouted out the name of Anthony Castlemaine. Neither sight nor sound came back in answer: all was quiet and lonely as the grave; there was not the slightest sign that any one had been there.

"If they did come in here, as you say," observed Mr. Nettleby, with that same ring of disbelief in his voice, "I'll tell you what it is, Bent. They must have come out again at once, and gone home together to Greylands' Rest."

This view of the case had not presented itself to the mind of John Bent. He revolved it for an instant, and then saw that it was the most feasible solution of the problem. But he did not feel quite satisfied; for it was difficult to fancy Anthony Castlemaine would so go off without telling him. Still he accepted it; and he and the officer quitted the Keep, and turned their steps homeward. In his own mind the superintendent fully believed John Bent had been asleep and dreaming; it was so impossible to fancy any sane man promenading in the chapel ruins or the Keep at night. And the Master of Greylands, of all people!

"Did you get upon the trail of any smugglers at Beeton asked John Bent.

"No," said Mr. Nettleby, rather savagely, for he had had his night's work for nothing. "Couldn't see any traces of them. I do suspect that Beeton, though. I believe it contains a nest of the lawless wretches!"

He turned in at his own gate as he spoke. The landlord went on and was speedily at home again. Anthony Castlemaine had not come in.

Before eight o'clock in the morning, John Bent, feeling doubtful and uneasy, went up to Greylands' Rest. He noticed that all the blinds were down, and some of the shutters closed. Miles, the servant man, was outside the back-entrance door, shaking mats.

"I thought none of you could be up yet," began the landlord, "with all the blinds down! I'm sure the house looks as though somebody had died in it."

"And somebody has died, more's the pity; though not in the house," replied Miles, turning his face, full of grave concern, on the speaker. "A messenger was here soon after six this morning to fetch the master to Stilborough. Mr. Peter Castlemaine died suddenly last night."

The landlord was shocked. He could hardly believe it. "Mr. Peter Castlemaine dead!" he exclaimed. "It can't be true, Miles."

"It's too true," returned Miles.

"But he was so strong and healthy! He had not a trace of illness about him!"

"Ay. But they say it was the heart."

"Well, it's sad news any way, and I'm sorry for him," said John Bent. "Is young Mr. Castlemaine here?"

"Not just now. He'll be home some time this afternoon. He went off to Newerton yesterday on business."

"I don't mean him—Mr. Harry. I mean Mr. Anthony Castlemaine."

"What should bring that young man here?" loftily retorted Miles, who made a point of sharing in all the prejudices of his master.

John Bent told his tale. It was listened to with disbelieving and resentful ears.

"My master in at that there blessed scared place, the Friar's Keep, at twelve o'clock at night! Well, I wonder what next you'll say, Mr. Bent?"

"But I saw him go in," returned John Bent.

"It couldn't have been him. It's not likely. What should he want there? When us servants went to bed at ten, the master was in the red parlour. As to that other young man you speak of, that he has not been anigh the house I can answer for."

John Bent felt as if he were in the midst of a fog, through which no light could be seen. "You say Mr. Castlemaine is at Stilborough, Miles?"

"He went off there soon after six o'clock. And wasn't he cut up when he heard the news about his brother!" added Miles. "His lips and face had no more red in them than that"—pointing to a snowdrop under the wall. "He looked just like a man who had got a shock."

It was of no use for John Bent to linger. Anthony Castlemaine was not to be heard of at Greylands' Rest. He took his departure; and, in the absence of any other clue to follow, went making inquiries in the village. Before long, not a single inhabitant, from one end of it to the other, but had heard and was making comments on his tale.

The Dolphin Inn was a crowded place that day, and its landlord the centre of attraction. People were in and out incessantly, listening to the singular history. Numbers flocked to the Friar's Keep, and to every other spot in Greylands likely or unlikely for a man to be hidden in, dead or living; but there was no trace anywhere of the presence of Anthony Castlemaine. Setting aside the disappearance, the tale itself excited wonder; and that part of it relating to the entrance into the chapel ruins of Mr. Castlemaine, and the subsequent sound of a shot and cry, and of the locked gate, was received by some with incredulity. Opinions were hazarded that the landlord's eyes might have deceived him, his ears and his fingers played him false; that Mr. Castlemaine must have been altogether a myth; the supposed locked gate been only his awkwardness, and the shot and cry nothing but the scream of a sea bird. In this one latter point, however, John Bent's account was established by other testimony, coming, singular to say, from the Grey Ladies. It appeared that Sister Mildred was very ill that night, and two of the others sat up with her, Sisters Mona and Ann. The room of the Superioress faced the sea, and was the last room at the end next the chapel ruins. As the Sisters sat there watching in the stillness of the night, they were suddenly startled by the sound of a shot, and by a scream as from some one wounded. So, in regard to the truth of this part of John Bent's account, there could no longer be a doubt.

In the afternoon Mr. Castlemaine returned from Stilborough. The commotion Greylands was in rendered it impossible for him to remain long ignorant of what had taken place, and of the manner in which his name was mixed up with it. Being a man of quick perception, of penetrating judgment, he could not fail to see that some suspicion must attach to himself in the public mind; that the alleged story, taken in conjunction with previous facts: the pretentions of his nephew to Greylands' Rest, and their hostile meeting in the fields earlier in the day: must inevitably excite doubt and comment. Proud, haughty, and self-contained though the Master of Greylands was, this matter was of too grave a nature, and might bring too many unpleasant consequences in its train, for him to ignore it. He deemed it well to throw himself forthwith into the battle; and he went out to the Dolphin. On his way he encountered Commodore Teague. The latter had been at sea since early morning in his cutter—as he was apt to call that sailing boat of his—and had but now, on landing, had his ears assailed with the story. A few exchanged sentences between Mr. Castlemaine and the Commodore, and they parted; Mr. Castlemaine proceeding to the inn.

"What is this absurd story?" he demanded of John Bent, lifting his hat as he entered the best kitchen to the knot of people assembled there. "I cannot make head or tail of it."

For the fiftieth time at least, the landlord recounted the history. It was listened to with breathless interest, even by those who had done nothing but listen to it for many previous hours.

"And do you expect sensible people to believe this, John Bent?" were the first answering words of the Master of Greylands.

"It's true, whether they believe it or not," said John. "It was yourself, sir, was it not, that we saw pass through the gate into the chapel ruins?"

"I!" scornfully repeated Mr. Castlemaine. "What do you suppose should take me to such a place as that, at midnight? If all your points are as correct as that, Mr. Bent, your story will not hold much water."

"I said it was not likely to be Mr. Castlemaine," spoke up the superintendent of the coastguard. "I told Mr. Bent so at the time."

"I put it to you all, generally, whether it was likely," pursued Mr. Castlemaine, glancing defiantly about him.

"All I can say is this," said John Bent: "that if it was not Mr. Castlemaine, my eyes must have strangely deceived me, and young Mr. Anthony's must have deceived him. Why, the night was as light as day."

"Eyes do deceive sometimes," remarked Mr. Castlemaine. "I know that mine have on occasion deceived me at night, good though their sight is. And of all deceptive lights, the moon's light is the worst."

"Sir, if it was not you it must have been your wraith," said John Bent, evidently not inclined to give in. "You passed close by us sideways, coming out of the Chapel Lane, and crossed the road in front of us. Had you just turned your head sharp to the right, you must have seen us under the hedge."

"Was it the Grey Friar, think you?" asked Mr. Castlemaine. And John Bent did not like the bantering tone, or the suppressed laugh that went around.

"That some one crossed from the Chapel Lane may be true: for I do not see how you could purely imagine it," conceded Mr. Castlemaine, after a pause. "But it was not I. Neither can I understand nor conceive what anybody should want in the chapel ruins at that time of night. We are most of us rather given to shun the place."

"True, true," murmured the room.

"And the locked gate," proceeded Mr. Castlemaine, "how do you account for that? Where did the key come from to lock it? According to what you say, John Bent, it would appear that Mr. Anthony Castlemaine must have locked it; since you maintain that no one went in or came out subsequently to himself. If he locked it, he must have unlocked it. At least, that is the inference naturally to be drawn."

"I say that the gate never was locked," put in Superintendent Nettleby. "The latch might have caught at the minute, and caused Mr. Bent to fancy it was locked."

"You may as well tell me I don't know when a place is open and when it's shut," retorted John Bent.

"And the pistol, again!—or gun?" remonstrated Mr. Castlemaine. "It does not stand to reason that people should be firing off guns and pistols at midnight. I fancy that must be altogether a mistake—"

"The Grey Ladies can speak to that much, sir," interrupted Mrs. Bent. "As Sister Ann, here, can tell you."

Mr. Castlemaine turned on his heel and brought his eyes to bear on Sister Ann. She was sitting in the corner near the clock, her basket as usual in her hand. For she had come out to do errands, and been seduced by curiosity into the Dolphin, to take her share in the gossip.

"Yes, sir, we heard the pistol, or gun, whichever it was, and the human cry that came with it," she said to Mr. Castlemaine. "Sister Mona and I were watching in Sister Mildred's room—for the fever was very bad upon her last night, and she was restless and wandering, poor lady! It was all quite still. I was knitting and Sister Mona was reading; you might have heard a pin drop indoors or out; when there burst upon our ears a loud shot, followed by a human cry. A thrilling scream, it was, making me and sister Mona start up in terror."

"It was like a death scream," said John Bent. "And I cannot," he added, looking at Mr. Castlemaine, "get it out of my head that it was his scream—young Mr. Anthony's."

"From what direction did it come?" asked Mr. Castlemaine of the landlord.

"I can't tell, sir. I was walking about on the opposite side of the road, and at first I thought it came from seaward; but it sounded very near."

"It sounded to us as though it came from the chapel rains, or from the strip of beach below it," said Sister Aim. "We did not hear anything more."

"And I did not think at the time to connect that shot and scream with Mr. Anthony Castlemaine," pursued John Bent. "It never came anigh my mind to do it, never. It do now."

"Well, it is altogether a most extraordinary and unaccountable affair," remarked Mr. Castlemaine. "Strange to say, I was abroad last night myself and near the spot, but not as late as you describe this to have been. Between ten and eleven I went down the lane as far as the Hutt. Teague was, I had heard, purposing to go out in his boat for a few hours to-day; and I, not having been very well, lately, thought I should like to go with him, and went down to say so. I stayed and had a pipe with him, and I think it must have been half-past eleven when I left."

"And did you go straight home from the Hutt, sir?" asked John Bent, eagerly.

"I went straight home from the Hutt's door to my door," emphatically replied Mr. Castlemaine.

"And did not go anigh the other end of the lane at all?—nor the Friar's Keep?"

"Certainly not. I tell you I went straight home. I went direct from Teague's house to mine."

That Mr. Castlemaine was candid in stating this matter spontaneously, when he might have concealed it, his hearers mentally saw, and it told in his favour. But it did not lessen the perplexity, or the mist that the affair was shrouded in. He turned to depart.

"I shall at once institute a thorough search; and, if necessary, summon the law to my aid," said he. "Not that I fear any real harm has befallen my nephew Anthony; but it will be satisfactory to ascertain where he is. I fancy he must have gone off somewhere, perhaps on some sudden and uncontemplated impulse. It may be, that he is given to take these impromptu flights; as was his father before him, my brother Basil."

Mr. Castlemaine passed out as he spoke, with a bend of the head to the company. He was looking pale and ill; they could but notice it throughout the entire interview; and his face had a worn, sad cast of sorrow on it, never before seen there.

"He has brought that look back from Stilborough," remarked John Bent. "There are bad fears, it's whispered, about his brother's death: we have not got the particulars yet. But as to Mr. Anthony's having walked off in any promiscuous manner, it's the silliest thought that ever was spoken."

Commodore Teague, in his blue sailor's costume, came looming in, his hands in his pockets. He had made haste down from the Hutt (having been obliged to go there on landing, to carry his gun and sundry other articles from his boat, and to light his fires) to hear the details of the mysterious story or, as he chose to express it, the wrongs and the rights on't.

So John Bent once more recounted the particulars, assisted by the tongues of all the company—for they did not stand in awe of this listener as they did of Mr. Castlemaine. The Commodore listened with incredulity: not to say ridicule.

"Look here, John Bent, you may tell that tale to the marines. I can explain away some of it myself. Bless my heart! To think you folk should be running your head again all them marvels, when there's none to run 'em against. That gun that went off was mine," concluded the Commodore; who liked to put on a free-and-easy grammar when in familiar intercourse with Greylands, though he could be a gentleman when with such people as the Castlemaines.

"Your gun!"

"It was. And as to Mr. Castlemaine, you no more saw him go into the Friar's Keep than you saw me go. Last night, I was smoking my pipe and cleaning my gun—for I meant to shoot a few birds out at sea to-day—when who should come knocking at the Hutt door but Mr. Castlemaine. He'd been feeling out of sorts, he said, and thought a sail would do him good, and would like to go with me to-day—for it seems the whole parish had heard I was going. With all my heart, I answered; I'd be proud of his company. He sat down and took a pipe; smoking's contagious, you know: and we talked about this and that. When he left I saw him to the door, and watched him turn up the lane towards his house. It don't stand to reason he'd come down again."

"He told us all this himself, Commodore."

"Did he!—what, Mr. Castlemaine? Well, it's true. After he was gone, I got to my gun again, which I had laid aside when he entered. It struck twelve before I finished it. After that, I loaded it, took it to the door, and fired it off into the air. That was the shot you heard, landlord."

"And the cry?"

"Never was any cry to hear. 'Twas fancy. I made none, and I know I heard none."

"What time was it when your gun went off?"

"Past twelve; I don't rightly know how much. I went to bed and to sleep without looking at the clock. This morning word was brought me that Mr. Castlemaine had been fetched to Stilborough; and I took out Ben Little in the boat instead."

But this explanation did not go for so much as it might have done. The Commodore was in the habit of telling the most incredible sea yarns; and faith, in that respect, was wanting in him. Moreover, the strong impression on John Bent's mind was, that it was a pistol-shot he had heard, not a gun. Above all, there remained the one broad fact of the disappearance: Anthony Castlemaine had been alive and well and amidst them the previous night, and to-day he was not. Altogether the commotion, the dread, and the sense of some mysterious evil increased: and lying upon many a heart, more or less, was a suspicion of the part played in it by Mr. Castlemaine.

Dusk was approaching when a horseman rode past the Dolphin: Mr. Harry Castlemaine on his return from Newerton. Seeing what looked like an unusual bustle round the inn doors, he pulled up. Molly ran out.

"What's agate?" asked Mr. Harry. "You seem to have got all the world and his wife here."

"It's feared as it's murder, sir," returned simple Molly.

"Murder!"

"Well, sir, Mr. Anthony Castlemaine went into the Friar's Keep last night, and have never come out again. It's thought he was shot there. A dreadful cry was heard."

"Shot! Who shot him?"

"'Tain't known, sir. Some says it was Mr. Castlemaine that was in there along of him."

Harry Castlemaine drew up his haughty head; a dark frown knitted his brow. But that she was a woman, ignorant and stupid, and evidently unconscious of all the word's might imply, he might have struck her as she stood.

"And there's dreadful news in from Stilborough, Mr. Harry, sir," resumed the girl. "Mr. Peter Castlemaine was found dead in his chamber last night."

"What?" shouted Harry, thinking she must be playing upon him with all these horrors.

"It's true, sir. The Master of Greylands have not long got back from seeing him. He died quite sudden, poor gentleman, shut up in his room, and not a soul anigh him to watch his last breath."

It was almost too much. His uncle dead, his cousin disappeared, his father suspected he knew not yet of what. Never a more cruel moment, than that had dawned for Harry Castlemaine.

X

Just as She had Seen it in her Dream

E vils do not always come alone. It sometimes happens that before one astounding ill is barely glanced at, another has fallen. This was the case at Stilborough.

The town awoke one morning to find that the bank had stopped payment, and that the banker was dead. Never before in the memory of man had the like consternation been known. It can be better imagined than written. At once the worst was anticipated. No one had ever been so confided in as was Mr. Peter Castlemaine. His capacity for business, his honour and integrity, his immense wealth, had passed into a proverb. People not only trusted him, but forced upon him that trust. Many and many a man had placed in his hands all they possessed: the savings perhaps of half a lifetime; and now they saw themselves ruined and undone.

Never had the like excitement been known in the quiet town; never so much talking and gesticulating; metaphorically speaking, so much sighing and sobbing. And indeed it is to be doubted if this last was all metaphor. Thomas Hill had never been so sought after; so questioned and worried; so raved at and abused as now. All he could implore of them was to have a little patience until accounts could be gone into. Things might not, he represented, turn out as badly as people supposed. Nobody listened to him; and he felt that if all days were to be as this day, he should soon follow his master to the grave. Indeed, it seemed to him now, in the shock of this dreadful blow—his master's ruin and his master's untimely end—that his own existence henceforth would be little better than a death in life.

In the very midst of the commotion, there was brought to Stilborough news of that other calamity—the mysterious disappearance of young Anthony Castlemaine. He had been seen to enter the Friar's Keep the previous night, and had never come out again. The name of the Master of Greylands appeared to be mixed up in the affair; but in what manner was not yet understood. Verily misfortunes seemed to be falling heavily just now upon the Castlemaines.

This last event, however, after exciting due comment and wonder, was lost sight of in the other evil: for the first nearly concerned the interests of Stilborough, and the latter did not concern them at all. Their ruin, their ruin! That was the all-absorbing topic in the minds of the bewildered citizens.

In inquiry into the death of Peter Castlemaine ended in a decision that he had died from heart disease. This was arrived at chiefly by the testimony and the urgent representation of Thomas Hill. One of the medical men was supposed to hold a contrary opinion; and the dreadful doubt, previously spoken of, would always lie on Miss Castlemaine's mind; but the other was the accepted view. He was buried in the neighbouring churchyard, St. Mark's: Parson Marston, who had so often and so recently sat at his dinner-table, performing the service.

Gradually the first excitement diminished. Brains and tempers calmed down. For, added to that natural depression that succeeds to undue emotion, there arose a report that things would be well, after all, and everybody paid to the full.

In fact, it was so. The money that had been so long waited for— the speculation that had at last turned up trumps—was pouring in its returns. And there arose another source of means to be added to it.

One morning the great Nyndyll Mine Company, that had been looked upon as being as good as dead, took a turn for the better; received, so to say, a new lease of life. A fresh vein of surprising richness and unbounded extent, had been struck: the smallest shareholder might immediately reckon that his fortune was an accomplished fact: and those lucky enough to be largely interested might cease speculation for ever, and pass the time in building themselves castles and palaces— with more solid foundations than the air will furnish—to live in. The shares went up in the market like rockets: everyone was securing them as eagerly as we should pick up diamonds if we got the chance. In a very short time, the shares held by the house of Mr. Peter Castlemaine might have been resold for fifteen times the original amount paid for them.

"Is this true, Hill?" asked Mr. Castlemaine, who had come bounding over on horseback from Greylands' Rest at the first rumour of the news, and found the old clerk at his post as usual, before the private desk that had been his master's. "Can it be true?" repeated Mr. Castlemaine.

He was changed since his brother's death. That death, or something else, had told upon him strangely. He and Peter had been fond of each other. James had been proud of his brother's position in the country; his influence and good name. The shock had come upon him unexpectedly, as upon every one else: and, in a manner, affected him far more. Then, his interests were largely bound up with those of his brother; and though if he had lost all he had lent him he would still be a rich man, yet the thought was not to be indulged with indifference or contemplated pleasantly. But to do him justice, these considerations sank into insignificance, before the solemn fact of his brother's death, and the mystery and uncertainty enshrouding it.

"Is it true, Hill?" he reiterated before the clerk had time to speak. "Or is it all as a miserable delusion of Satan."

"It is true enough, sir," answered Thomas Hill. "The shares have gone suddenly up like nothing I ever knew. Alas, that it should be so!"

"Alas!" echoed Mr. Castlemaine. "What mean you, Hill? has trouble turned your brain?"

"I was thinking of my poor dear master," said the old man. "It was this very mine that helped to kill him. You see now, Mr. Castlemaine, how good his speculations were, how sound his judgment! Had he lived to see this turn of affairs, all would have been well."

"Too late to speak of that," said Mr. Castlemaine, with a deep sigh. "He is dead; and we must now give our attention to the living. This slice of luck will enable you to pay all demands. The shares must be realized at once.

"Enable us to pay every one, as I believe," assented Thomas Hill. "And otherwise we should not."

"What a strange chance it seems to be!" musingly observed Mr. Castlemaine. "A chance that rarely occurs in life. Well, as I say, it must be seized upon."

"And without delay, sir. The shares that have gone up so unexpectedly, may fall as suddenly. I'll write to-day." Mr. Castlemaine rose to depart. The clerk, who was settling to his papers, again looked off to ask a question.

"Have any tidings turned up, sir, of poor Mr. Anthony?"

"Not that I have heard of. Good-day, Hill."

The expected money was realized; other expected money was realized; and in an incredibly short space of time, for poor Thomas Hill worked with a will, the affairs of the bank were in a way of settlement, every creditor to be fully satisfied, and the late unfortunate banker's name to be saved. Anything that had been underhanded in his dealing, Thomas Hill and Mr. Castlemaine had contrived to keep from the public.

But one creditor, whose name did not appear on the books, and who had put in no demand to be satisfied, was passed over in silence.

Mary Ursula's fortune had been hopelessly sacrificed; and it was already known that little, if anything, would be left for her. She knew how and why her fortune had gone: Mr. Hill had explained it all to her; it had helped to save her father's honour and good name; and had it been ten times the amount, she would freely have given it for such a purpose, and been thankful that she had it to give.

Seeing what it had done, she did not as far as she herself was concerned, look upon it with one moment's regret. True she was now poor; very poor compared with the past: she would have at most but about a hundred and fifty pounds a year; but she was in too much trouble to think much of money now. One heavy weight had been lifted—the sickening dread that the creditors would lose part or all. On that one point she was now at rest. But there were other things. There was the underlying current of fear that her father had not died of heart disease; there was the mysterious perplexity attending the disappearance of her cousin Anthony; and there was her own engagement to Mr. Blake-Gordon.

Her position was now so different from what it had been when he proposed to her, and the severity, the pride, the arrogance of Sir Richard so indisputable, that she feared the worst. Moreover, she knew, from the present conduct of both father and son, that she had cause to fear it.

Twice, and twice only, had William Blake-Gordon come to her since her father's death, and he might so easily have come to her every day in her desolation! Each time he had been kind and loving as ever; not a suspicion, not a hint of separation had appeared in look or tone; but in his manner there had been something never seen before: a reticence; a keeping back, as it were, of words that ought to come out: and instinct told her that all was not as it used to be.

"How does your father take the news?—What does he say to it, and to my loss of fortune?—Is he still willing to receive me?" she had asked on each occasion; and as often he had contrived to put aside the questions without satisfactory answer.

Days went on; her position, as to lack of fortune, was known abroad; and the suspense she endured was making her ill. One morning at the breakfast table, as she finished reading some letters that had been delivered for her, Mrs. Webb, who had scanned the letters outside from the opposite side of the table, put a question that she often did put.

"Is any one of them from Mr. Blake-Gordon, my dear?"

"No," replied Mary. And no one but herself knew what it cost her to have to say it; or how trying to her was the usual silence that followed the answer.

"I will end the suspense," she said to herself, shutting herself in her own sitting-room when the meal was over. "It is Sir Richard, I know; not William: but at least they shall not find me willing to enter the family on bare sufferance. I will give them the opportunity of retiring from the engagement—if that be what they wish for."

Drawing her desk towards her, she paused with the pen in her hand, deliberating how to write. Whether in a cold formal strain, or affectionately and confidently as of yore: and she decided on the latter.

My Dearest William,

"My circumstances have so changed since the early days of our engagement, that I feel I am now, in writing to you, adopting the only course left open to me, both in fairness to you and for the sake of my own future happiness and peace of mind.

"When you proposed to me and I accepted you, I was in a very different position from that of to-day. Then I was supposed to be—nay, I supposed myself—a very rich woman. I was the daughter of a man beloved, honoured, and respected; a member of a house which, if not equal to your own in the past annals of the country, might at least mix with it on equality and hold its own amongst gentlemen. All this is now changed. My dear father is no more, my large fortune is gone, and I am left with next to nothing.

"That you have asked me to become your wife for myself alone, I feel sure of. I am certain that no thought of riches influenced you in your choice: that you would take me now as willingly as in the old days. But instinct—or presentiment tells me that others will step in to interfere between us, and to enjoin a separation. Should this be the case—should your father's consent, once given, now be withdrawn—then all must be at an end between us, and I will restore you your liberty. Without the fall approval of Sir Richard, you cannot attempt to marry me; neither should I, without it, consent to become your wife.

"If, on the other hand, that approval is still held out to us both as freely as of yore, I have only to add what you know so well—that I am yours, now as ever.

Mary Ursula Castlemaine

The letter written, she hesitated no longer about the necessity or wisdom of the step. Sealing it, she despatched it by a trusty messenger to Sir Richard's house just beyond the town.

The news of the failure of the bank and death of its master, had reached Sir Richard Blake-Gordon when he was at a dinner party. It fell upon him with startling effect. For a moment he felt half paralyzed: and then the blood once more took its free course through his veins as he remembered that his son's marriage was yet a thing of the future.

"Never," he said to himself with energy. "Never, as long as I live. I may have a battle with William; but I could always twist him round my fingers. In that respect he is his poor mother all over. No such weakness about me. Failed for millions! Good heavens, what an escape! We shall be quite justified in breaking with the daughter; and she and William have both sense enough to see it."

He was not of those who put off disagreeable things until they will be put off no longer. That very night, meeting his son when he got home, he began, after expressing regret for the banker's sudden death.

"A sad affair about the bank! Who would have expected it?"

"Who, indeed!" returned William Blake-Gordon. "Everyone thought the bank as safe as the Bank of England. Safer, if anything."

"It only shows how subject, more or less, all private concerns are to fluctuations—changes—failures—and what not," continued Sir Richard.

"Whatever this may be—failure or not—it will at least be open and straightforward," said William. "Mr. Peter Castlemaine was the soul of honour. The embarrassments must have arisen from other quarters, and Thomas Hill says the trouble and anxiety have killed him."

"Poor man! People are expecting it to be an awful failure. Not five shillings in the pound for the creditors, and all the Castlemaine family ruined. This must terminate your engagement."

The sudden mandate fell on the young man's ears with a shock. He thought at the first moment his father must be jesting.

"It must terminate my engagement?" he retorted, catching sight of the dark stern countenance. "What, give up Mary Castlemaine? Never, father! Never will I do it so long as I shall live."

"Yes, you will," said Sir Richard, quietly. "I cannot allow you to sacrifice your prospects in life."

"To give her up would be to sacrifice all the prospects I care for."

"Tush, William!"

"Think what it is you would advise, sir!" spoke the son with ill-suppressed emotion. "Putting aside my own feelings, think of the dishonour to my name! I should be shunned by all good and true men; I should shun myself. Why, I would not live through such dishonour."

Sir Richard took a pinch of snuff.

"These misfortunes only render it the more urgent for me to carry out the engagement, sir. Is it possible that you do not see it? Mary Castlemaine's happiness is, I believe, bound up in me; and mine, I freely avow it, is in hers. Surely, father, you would not part us!"

"Listen, William," spoke Sir Richard, in the calm, stern tones he could assume at will, more telling, more penetrating than the loudest passion. "Should Miss Castlemaine become portionless—as I believe it will turn out she has become—you cannot marry her. Or, if you do, it would be with my curse. I would not advise you, for your own sake, to invoke that. You can look elsewhere for a wife: there are numbers of young women as eligible as ever was Miss Castlemaine."

Long they talked together, far on into the night, the stern tones on the one hand becoming persuasive ones; the opposition sinking into silence. When they separated, Sir Richard felt that he had three parts gained his point.

"It is all right," said he mentally, as he stalked up to bed with his candle. "William was always ultra dutiful."

Sir Richard interdicted his son's visits to Miss Castlemaine; and the one or two scant calls the young man made on her, were made in disobedience. But this state of things could not last. William Blake-Gordon, with his yielding nature, had ever possessed a rather exaggerated idea of the duty a son owes his father: moreover, he knew instinctively that Mary would never consent to marry in opposition to Sir Richard, even though he brought himself to do it.

It soon became known abroad that Miss Castlemaine's fortune had certainly been sacrificed. Sir Richard was cold and distant to his son, the young man miserable.

One day the baronet returned to the charge; intending his mandate to be final. They were in the library. William's attitude was one of utter dejection as he leaned against the side of the window, looking forth on

　　　　　　　　　　　　　　　　MRS. HENRY WOOD

the spring sunshine: sunshine that brought no gladness for him. He saw too clearly what the end would be: that his own weakness, or his sense of filial duty, call it which you may, must give way before the stronger will, the commanding nature.

"Your conduct is now simply cruel to Miss Castlemaine," Sir Richard was saying. "You are keeping her all this time in suspense. Or, perhaps—worse still—allowing her to cherish the hope that her altered circumstances will not cause the engagement to terminate."

"I can't help it," replied William. "The engagement has no business to terminate. It was sacredly entered into: and, without adequate reason, it ought to be as sacredly kept."

"You are a living representation of folly," cried Sir Richard. "Adequate reason! There's reason enough for breaking off fifty engagements. Can you not see the matter in its proper light?"

"That is what I do see," replied William, sadly. "I see that the engagement ought to be maintained. For my own part, I never can go to Mary and tell her that I am to give her up."

"Coward," said Sir Richard, with a great frown. "Then I must."

"I fear you are right," returned William: "a coward I am, little better. It is a cowardly thing to break off this alliance—the world will call it by a very different name. Father," he added, appealingly, "is my happiness nothing to you? Can you sacrifice us both to your pride and vainglory."

"You will see it very differently some day," returned Sir Richard. "When you have lived in the world as long as I have, you will laugh at yourself for these ridiculously romantic ideas. Instead of marring your happiness, I am making it. Substantially, too."

"I think, sir," said Mr. Blake-Gordon, not liking the tone, "that you might leave me to be the judge of what is best for my own happiness."

"There you are mistaken, my dear William. You have but a young head on your shoulders: you see things de tort et de travers, as the French have it. The engagement with Peter Castlemaine's daughter would never have received my sanction but for her great wealth. We are poor, and it is essential that you should marry a large fortune if you marry at all. That wealth of hers has now melted, and consequently the contract is at an end. This is the common-sense view of the circumstances which the world will take. Done, it must be, William. Shall I see the young lady for you? or will you be a man and see her for yourself?"

But before Mr. Blake-Gordon had time to reply, a note was brought in. It was the one written by Miss Castlemaine; and it could not have arrived more seasonably for Sir Richard's views. The young man opened it; read it to the end: and passed it to his father in silence.

"A very sensible girl, upon my word," exclaimed Sir Richard, when he had mastered the contents by the aid of a double eye-glass. "She sees things in their right light. Castlemaine was, after all, an extremely honourable man, and put proper notions into her. This greatly facilitates matters, William. Our path is now quite smoothed out for us. I will myself write to her. You can do the same, if you are so disposed. Had this only come before, what arguments it might have saved!"

Upon which the baronet sat down, and indited the following epistle:—

My dear young Lady,

"Your note—which my son has handed to me—has given me in one sense a degree of pleasure; for I perceive in it traces of good sense and judgment, such as women do not always possess.

"You are right in supposing that under the present aspect of affairs a marriage between yourself and Mr. Blake-Gordon would be unadvisable." (She had supposed nothing of the sort, but it suited him to assume it.) "And therefore I concur with you in your opinion that the engagement should terminate.

"Deeply though I regret this personally, I have yet felt it my duty to insist upon it to my son: not only for his sake, but for your own. The very small means I am able to spare to him render it impossible for him to take a portionless wife, and I could never sanction a step that would drag him down to poverty and embarrassment. I was about to write to you, or to see you, to tell you this, for William shrank from the task, and your note has agreeably simplified what had to be done. We cordially, though reluctantly, agree to what you have had the good feeling to propose.

"At all times I shall be delighted to hear of your welfare and happiness; and, believe me, my dear Miss Castlemaine, you have not a more sincere well-wisher than your devoted friend and servant,

RICHARD BLAKE-GORDON

With much inward satisfaction the baronet folded the letter. He was wise enough not to show it to his son; who, honourable in thought and feeling as he was weak in nature, might have been prompted to tear it into shreds, and declare that come good, come ill, he would stand true to his plighted word.

"There!" said Sir Richard, with a grunt of relief, as he affixed his seal, "I have accomplished that task for you, William. As I said before, write to her yourself if you will, but be quick about it. In half an hour I shall send back my answer."

"Give me that time to myself," said William, rising to leave the room. "If I have anything to say I will write it."

At the end of the half-hour he had written the following words; and the note was despatched with his father's:—

My Darling,

I suppose we must separate; but all happiness for me is over in this world. You will, however, accord me a final interview; a moment for explanation; I cannot part without that. I will be with you this afternoon at four o'clock.

In spite of all,
I am for ever yours—and yours only,
William

Unlike his father's letter, there was no hypocrisy in this, no stupid form of words. When he wrote that all happiness for him was over, he meant it; and he wrote truly. Perhaps he deserved no less: but, if he merited blame, judgment might accord him some pity with it.

When Mary received the letters, she felt certain of their contents before a word was seen. Sir Richard would not himself have written but to break off the engagement. He had not even called upon her in all these long weary days of desolation and misery: and there could be but one motive for this unkind neglect. His note would now explain it.

But when she came to read its contents: its hollow hypocrisy, its plausible, specious argument, its profession of friendship and devotion; the pang of the death-blow gave place to the highest anger and indignation.

At that moment of bitterness the letter sounded to her desperately hollow and cruel, worse perhaps than it even was. The pain was more than her wounded spirit—so tried in the past few weeks—could bear;

and with a brief but violent storm of sobs, with which no tears came, she tore the letter in two and threw it into the fire.

"At least he might have done it differently," she said to herself in her anguish. "He might have written in a manner that would have made me feel it less."

It was one of her first lessons in the world's harshness, in the selfish nature of man. Happy for her if in her altered circumstances she had not many such to learn!

Presently, when she had grown a little calm, she opened the other note, almost wondering whether it would be a repetition of the cool falsity of Sir Richard's. Ah no, no!

"I will see him," she said, when she read the few words. "But the interview shall be brief. Of what use to prolong the agony?" So when William Blake-Gordon, true to his appointment, reached the bank at four o'clock, he was admitted.

How different an aspect the house presented from the bustle and the sociality of the days gone by! A stillness, as of a dead city, reigned. Rooms that had re-echoed with merry voices and light footsteps above, with the ring of gold and the tones of busy men below, were now silent and deserted. No change of any kind had yet been made in the household arrangements, but that was soon to come. The servants would be discharged, the costly furniture was already marked for the hammer; Mrs. Webb must leave, and—what was to be the course of Miss Castlemaine? She had not even asked herself the question, while the engagement with Mr. Blake-Gordon remained officially unbroken.

The butler opened the door to him and ushered him into the drawing-room. Mary came forward to greet him with her pale, sad face—a face that startled her lover. He clasped her to him, and she burst into sobs and tears. There are moments of anguish when pride gives way.

"Oh, my darling!" he cried, scarcely less agitated than herself, "you are feeling this cruel decision almost unto death! Why did you write that letter?—why did you not remain firm?—and thereby tacitly insist on our engagement being fulfilled?"

Never had his weakness of nature been more betrayed than then. "Why did not she insist?"—as if conscious that he was powerless to do it! She felt it keenly: she felt that in this, at least, a gulf lay between them.

"What I have done is for the best," she said, gently disengaging herself, and suppressing the signs of her emotion, as she motioned him

MRS. HENRY WOOD

to a seat. "In my altered circumstances I felt—at least I feared—that no happiness could await our marriage. Your father, in the first place, would never have given his consent."

"There are times when duty to a father should give place to duty to one's self," he returned, forgetting how singularly this argument was contradicted by his own conduct. "All my happiness in life is over."

"As you wrote to me," she said. "But by-and-by, when you shall have forgotten all this, William, and time has brought things round, you will meet with some one who will be able to make you happy: perhaps as much so as I should have done: and you will look back on these days as a dream."

"Mary!"

"And it will be better so."

"And you?" he asked, with a stifled groan of remorse.

"I?" she returned, with a smile half sad, half derisive. "I am nobody now. You have a place to fill in the world; I shall soon be heard of no more."

"But where are you going to live, Mary? You have nothing left out of the wreck."

"I have a little. Enough for my future wants. At present I shall go on a visit to Greylands' Rest. My uncle urges it, and he is the nearest representative of my father. Depend upon it, I shall meet with some occupation in life that will make me contented if not happy."

"Until you marry," he said. "Marry some man more noble than I; more worthy of you."

For a moment she looked steadily at him, and then her face flushed hot with pain. But she would not contradict it. She began to think that she had never quite understood the nature of Mr. Blake-Gordon.

"In the future, you and I will probably not meet often, William; if at all," she resumed. "But you will carry with you my best wishes, and I shall always rejoice to hear of your happiness and prosperity. The past we must, both of us, try to forget."

"I shall never forget it," was the impulsive answer.

"Do you remember my dream?" she sadly asked. "The one I told you of that ball night. How strangely it is being fulfilled! And, do you know, I think that beautiful Dresden vase, that papa broke, must have been an omen of the evil in store for the house."

He stood up now, feeling how miserable it all was, feeling his own littleness. For a short while longer they talked together: but Mary wished the interview over.

When it came to the actual parting she nearly broke down. It was very hard and bitter. Her life had not so long ago promised to be so bright! Now all was at an end. As to marriage—never for her: of that kind of happiness the future contained none. Calmness, patience in suffering, resignation, and in time even contentment, she might find in some path of duty; but beyond that, nothing.

They stood close together, her hands held in his, their hearts aching with pain and yearning, each to each, with that sad yearning that is born of utter hopelessness. A parting like this seems to be more cruel than the parting of death.

"Come what may, Mary, I shall love you, and you alone, to the end. You tell me I shall marry: it may be so; I know not: but if so, my wife, whomsoever she may be, will never have my love; never, never. We do not love twice in a lifetime. And, if those who have loved on earth are permitted to meet in Heaven, you and I, my best and dearest, shall assuredly find together in Eternity the happiness denied us here."

She was but mortal, after all; and the words sent a strange thrill of pleasure through her heart. Ah, no! he would never love another as he had loved her; she knew it: and it might be—it might be—that they should recognise each other in the bliss of a never-ending Hereafter!

And so they parted, each casting upon the other a long, last, lingering look, just as Mary had already imagined in her foreboding dream.

That evening, as Miss Castlemaine was sitting alone, musing on the past, the present, and the future, nursing her misery and her desolation, the door opened and Thomas Hill was shown in. She had seen more of him than of any one else, save Mrs. Webb, since the ruin.

"Miss Mary," said he, when they had shaken hands, "I've come to ask you whether the report can be true?"

"What report?" inquired Mary: but a suspicion of what he must mean rushed over her, ere the words had well passed her lips.

"Perhaps it is hardly a report," said the clerk, correcting himself; "for I doubt if any one else knows of it. I met Sir Richard to-day, my dear young lady," he continued, advancing and taking her hands, his tone full of indignant commiseration; "and in answer to some remark I made about your marriage, he said the marriage was not to take place; it was at an end. I did not believe him."

"It is quite true," replied Mary, with difficulty controlling her voice. "I am glad that it is at an end."

"Glad?" he repeated, looking into her face with his kindly old eyes.

"Yes. It is much better so. Sir Richard, in the altered state of my fortunes, would never think me a sufficiently good match for his son."

"But the honour, Miss Mary! Or rather the dishonour of their breaking it off! And your happiness? Is that not to be thought of?"

"All things that are wrong will right themselves," she replied with a quiet smile. "At least, Sir Richard thinks so.

"And Mr. Blake-Gordon, is he willing to submit to the separation quietly? Pardon me, Miss Mary. If your father were alive, I should know my place too well to say a word on the subject: but—but I seem to have been drawn very close to you since that time of desolation, and my heart resents all slight on you as he would have resented it. I could not rest until I knew the truth."

"Say no more about it," breathed Mary. "Let the topic be between us as one that had never had existence. It will be for my happiness."

"But can nothing be done?" persisted Thomas Hill. "Should not your uncle go and expostulate with them and expose their villainy—for I can call it by no other name?"

"Not for worlds," she said, hastily. "It is I who have broken the engagement, Mr. Hill; not they. I wrote this morning and restored Mr. Blake-Gordon his freedom: this afternoon I bade him farewell for ever. It is all over and done with: never mention it again to me."

"And you—what are your plans for the future?—And, oh, forgive me for being anxious, my dear young lady! I had you on my knee often as a little one, and in my heart you have been as dear to me and seemed to grow up as my own daughter. Where shall you live?"

"I cannot yet tell where. I am poor, you know," she added, with one of her sweet, sad smiles. "For the present I am going on a visit to my Uncle James."

"Greylands' Rest would be your most suitable home now," spoke Thomas Hill slowly and dubiously. "But—I don't know that you would like it. Mrs. Castlemaine—"

He stopped, hardly liking to say what was in his mind—that Mrs. Castlemaine was not the most desirable of women to live with. Mary understood him.

"Only on a visit," she said. "While there, I shall have leisure to think of the future. My hundred and fifty pounds a year—and that much you all say will be secured to me—"

"And the whole of what I possess, Miss Mary."

"My hundred and fifty pounds a year will seem as a sufficient income to me, once I have brought my mind down from its heights," she continued, with another faint smile, as though unmindful of the interruption. "Trust me, my dear old friend, the future shall not be as gloomy as, by the expression of your face, you seem to anticipate. I am not weak enough to throw away my life in repining, and in wishing for what Heaven sees fit to deny me."

"Heaven?" he repeated in an accent of reproof.

"Let us say circumstances, then. But in the very worst fate, it may be, that Heaven's hand may be working—overruling all for our eventual good. My future life can be a useful one; and I, if not happy, at least contented."

But that night, in the solitude of her chamber, she opened a small box, containing nothing but a few faded white rose-leaves. It was the first trembling offering William Blake-Gordon had given her, long before he dared to tell of his love. Before they were again put away out of sight, tears, bitter as any shed in her whole life, had fallen upon them.

XI

Inside the Nunnery

The time had gone on at Greylands; and its great theme of excitement, the disappearance of Anthony Castlemaine, was an event of the past. Not an iota of evidence had arisen to tell how he disappeared: but an uneasy suspicion of Mr. Castlemaine lurked in corners. John Bent had been the chief instigator in this. As truly as he believed the sun shone in the heavens, so did he believe that Anthony Castlemaine had been put out of the way by his uncle; sent out of the world, in fact, that the young man might not imperil his possession of Greylands' Rest. He did not say to the public, in so many words, Mr. Castlemaine has killed his nephew; that might not have been prudent; but the bent of his conviction could not be mistaken; and when alone with his wife he scrupled not to talk freely. All Greylands did not share in the opinion. The superstitious villagers attributed the disappearance to be due in some unconjectural manner to the dreaded spirit of the Grey Monk, haunting the Friar's Keep. The fears of the place were augmented tenfold. Not one would go at night in sight of it, save on the greatest compulsion; and Commodore Teague (a brave, fearless man, as was proved by his living so near the grim building alone) had whispered that the Grey Friar was abroad again with his lamp, for he had twice seen him glide past the casements. What with one fear and another, Greylands was not altogether in a state of calmness.

Mary Ursula had come to Greylands' Rest. The once happy home at Stilborough was given up, the furniture sold: and the affairs of the bank were virtually settled. A sufficient sum had been saved from the wreck to bring her in about a hundred and fifty pounds per annum; that income was secured to her for life and would be at her disposal at death. All claims were being paid to the uttermost shilling; liberal presents were given to the clerks and servants thrown suddenly out of employment; and not a reproach, or shadow of it, could be cast on the house of Castlemaine.

Before Mary had been a week at Greylands' Rest, she was mentally forming her plans for leaving it. Mr. Castlemaine would fain have kept her there always: he was loud and proud of her; he thought there was no other woman like her in the world. Not so Mrs. Castlemaine. She resented her husband's love and reverence for his niece; and she, little-minded, full of spite, was actually jealous of her. She had always felt a jealousy of the banker's daughter, living in her luxurious home at Stilborough, keeping the high society that Mrs. Castlemaine did not keep; she had a shrewd idea that she herself, with her little tempers, and her petty frivolities, was sometimes compared unfavourably with Mary Ursula by her husband, wife though she was; and she had far rather some disagreeable animal had taken up its abode at Greylands' Rest for good, than this grand, noble, beautiful girl. Now and again even in those first few days, she contrived to betray this feeling: and it may be that this served to hasten Mary's plans. Flora, too, was a perpetual source of annoyance to everybody but her mother; and the young lady was as rude to Miss Castlemaine as to other people.

Since her parting with Mr. Blake-Gordon, an idea had dawned upon and been growing in Mary Ursula's mind. It was, that she should join the sisterhood of the Grey Ladies. The more she dwelt upon it, the greater grew her conviction that it would be just the life now suited to her. Unlike Mr. Castlemaine, she had always held the sisters in reverence and respect. They were self-denying; they led a useful life before Heaven; they were of no account in the world: what better career could she propose, or wish, for herself, now that near and dear social ties were denied her? And she formed her resolution: though she almost dreaded to impart it to her uncle.

Mr. Castlemaine stood one morning at the window of his study, looking out on the whitened landscape, for snow covered the ground. The genial weather that came in so early had given place to winter again: not often is spring so changeable as they had it that year. The sad, worn look that might be seen lately on the Master of Greylands' face, though rarely when in company, sat on it now. He pushed his dark hair from his brow with a hasty hand, as some thought, worse than the rest, disturbed him, and a heavy groan escaped his lips. Drowning it with a cough, for at that moment somebody knocked at the study door, he held his breath but did not answer. The knock came again, and he did not know the knock: certainly it was not Miles's.

He strode to open the door with a frown. It was an understood thing in the house that this room was sacred to its master. There stood Mary, in her deep mourning.

"I have ventured to come to you here, Uncle James," she said, "as I wish to speak with you alone. Can you spare me some minutes?"

"Any number to you, Mary. And remember, my dear, that you are always welcome here."

He gave her a chair, shut down his bureau and locked it, and took a seat himself. For a moment she paused, and then began in some hesitation.

"Uncle James, I have been forming my plans."

"Plans?" he echoed.

"And I have come to tell them to you before I tell any one else."

"Well?" said Mr. Castlemaine, wondering what was coming.

"I should like—I must have some occupation in life, you know?"

"Occupation? Well?"

"And I have not been long in making up my mind what it shall be. I shall join the Sisterhood."

"Join the what?"

"The Sisters at the Grey Nunnery, uncle."

Mr. Castlemaine pushed back his chair in angry astonishment when the sense of the words fully reached him. "The Sisters at the Grey Nunnery!" he indignantly cried. "Join those Grey women who lead such an idle, gossiping, meddling life, that I have no patience when I think of them! Never shall you do that, Mary Ursula!"

"It seems to me that you have always mistaken them, uncle," she said; "have done them wrong in your heart; They are noble women, and they are leading a noble life—"

"A petty, obscure life," he interrupted.

"It is obscure; but in its usefulness and self-sacrifice it must be noble. What would Greylands be without their care?"

"A great deal better than with it."

"They help the poor, they tend the sick, they teach the young ones; they try to make the fishermen think a little of God. Who would do it if they were not here, uncle? Do you know, I have thought so much of it in the past few days that I long to join them."

"This is utter folly!" cried Mr. Castlemaine; and he had never felt so inclined to be angry with his niece. "To join this meddling Sisterhood would be to sacrifice all your future prospects in life."

"I have no prospects left to sacrifice," returned Mary. "You know that, Uncle James."

"No prospects? Nonsense! Because that dishonourable rascal, William Blake-Gordon, has chosen to forfeit his engagement, and make himself a by-word in the mouths of men, are you to renounce the world? Many a better gentleman than he, my dear, will be seeking you before a few months have gone by."

"I shall never marry," was her firm answer. "Never, never. Whether I joined the Sisters, or not; whether I retired from the world, or mixed to my dying day in all its pomps and gaieties; still I should never marry. So you see, Uncle James, I have now to make my future, and to create for myself an object in life."

"Well, we'll leave the question of marrying. Meanwhile your present home must be with me, Mary Ursula. I cannot spare you. I should like you to make up your mind to stay in it always, unless other and nearer ties shall call you forth."

"You are very kind, Uncle James; you always have been kind. But I—I must be independent," she added with a smile and a slight flush. "Forgive the seeming ingratitude, uncle dear."

"Very independent you would be, if you joined those living-by-rule women!"

"In one sense I should be thoroughly independent, uncle. My income will be most welcome to them, for they are, as you know, very poor—"

"Your income!" he interrupted, half scoffingly. "I wish—I wish, Mary—you would allow me to augment it!"

"And I shall be close to Greylands' Rest," she continued, with a slight shake of the head, for this proposal to settle money upon her had become quite a vexations question. "I shall be able to come here to see you often."

"Mary Ursula, I will hear no more of this," he cried, quite passionately. "You shall never do it with my consent."

She rose and laid her pleading hands upon his. "Uncle, pardon me, but my mind is made up. I have not decided hastily, or without due consideration. By day and by night I have dwelt upon it—I—I have prayed over it, uncle—and I plainly see it is the best thing for me. I would sooner spend my days there than anywhere, because I shall be near you."

"And I want you to be near me. But not in a nunnery."

"It is not a nunnery now you know, Uncle James, though the building happens still to bear the name. If I take up my abode there, I take no vows, remember. I do not renounce the world. Should any necessity arise—though I think it will not—for me to resume my place in society, I am at full Liberty to put off my grey gown and bonnet and do so."

"What do you think your father would have said to this, Mary Ursula?"

"Were my father alive, Uncle James, the question never could have arisen; my place would have been with him. But I think—if he could see me now under all these altered circumstances—I think he would say to me Go."

There was no turning her. James Castlemaine saw it: and when she quitted the room he felt that the step, unless some special hindrance intervened, would be carried out.

"The result of being clever enough to have opinions of one's own!" muttered Mr. Castlemaine, in reference to the, to him, most unwelcome project.

Turning to the window again, he stood there, looking out. Looking out, but seeing nothing. The Friar's Keep opposite, rising dark and grim from contrast with the intervening white landscape; the sparkling blue sea beyond, glittering in the frosty sunshine: he saw none of it. The snow must be blinding his sight, or some deep trouble his perceptive senses. Mr. Castlemaine had other motives than the world knew of for wishing to keep his niece out of the Grey Nunnery: but he did not see how it was to be done.

Mary Ursula had passed into her own chamber: the best room in the house, and luxuriously furnished. It was generally kept for distinguished guests; and Mrs. Castlemaine had thought a plainer one might have served the young lady, their relative; but, as she muttered resentfully to the empty air, if Mr. Castlemaine could load the banker's daughter with gold and precious stones, he'd go out of his way to do it.

Drawing her chair to the fire, Mary sat down and thought out her plan. And the longer she dwelt upon it, the more did she feel convinced that she was right in its adoption. A few short weeks before, and had any Nunnery and become one of the Grey Sisters, she had started back in aversion. But ideas change with circumstances. Then she had a happy home of splendour, an indulgent father, riches that seemed unbounded at command, the smiles of the gay world, and a lover to whom she was shortly to be united. Now she had none of these: all had been wrested from her at one fell swoop. To the outward world she had seemed to take her misfortunes calmly: but none knew how they had wrung her very soul. It had seemed to her that her heart was broken: it seemed to her as though some retired and quiet place to rest in were absolutely needful while she recovered, if she ever did recover, the effects of these calamities. But she did not want to sit down under her grief and nourish it: she had prayed earnestly, and did still pray, that it would please Heaven to enable her to find consolation in her future life, and that it might be one of usefulness to others, as it could not be one of happiness to herself. But a latent prevision sometimes made itself apparent, that happiness would eventually come; that in persevering in her laid-out path, she should find it.

"The sooner I enter upon it, the better," she said, rising from her chair and shaking out the crape folds of her black silk dress. "And there's nothing to wait for, now that I have broken it to my uncle."

Glancing at her own face as she passed a mirror, she halted to look at the change that trouble had made in it. Others might not notice it, but to herself it was very perceptible. The beautiful features were thinner than of yore, the cheeks bore a fainter rose-colour; her stately form had lost somewhat of its roundness. Ah, it was not her own sorrow that had mostly told upon Mary Castlemaine; it was the sudden death of her father, and the agonizing doubt attending on it.

"If I could but know that it was God's will that he should die!" she exclaimed, raising her hands in an attitude of supplication. "And there's that other dreadful trouble—that awful doubt—about poor Anthony!"

Descending the stairs, she opened the door of the red parlour, and entered on a scene of turbulence. Miss Flora was in one of her most spiteful and provoking humours. She was trying to kick Ethel, who held her at arms' length. Her pretty face was inflamed, her pretty hair hung wild—and Flora's face and hair were both as pretty as they could well be.

"Flora!" said Miss Castlemaine, advancing to the rescue. "Flora, for shame! Unless I had seen you in this passion, I had not believed it."

"I will kick her, then! It's through her I did not go with mamma in the carriage to Stilborough."

"It was mamma who would not take you," said Ethel. "She said she had some private business there, and did not want you with her."

"She would have taken me: you know she would; but for your telling her I had not done my French exercise, you ugly, spiteful thing."

"Mamma asked me whether you had done it, and I said no."

"And you ought to have said yes! You ill-natured, wicked, interfering dromedary!"

"Be still, Flora," interposed Miss Castlemaine. "Unless you are, I will call your papa. How can you so forget yourself?"

"You have no business to interfere, Mary Ursula! The house is not yours; you are only staying in it."

"True," said Miss Castlemaine, calmly. "And I shall not be very much longer in it, Flora. I am going away soon."

"I shall be glad of that," retorted the rude child; "and I am sure mamma will be. She says it is a shame that you should be let take up the best bedroom."

"Oh, Flora!" interposed Ethel.

"And she says—"

What further revelations the damsel might be contemplating, in regard to her mother, were summarily cut short. Harry Castlemaine had entered in time to hear what she was saying, and he quietly lifted her from the room. Outside, he treated her to what she dreaded, though it was not often she got it from him—a severe shaking—and she ran away howling.

"She is being ruined," said Harry. "Mrs. Castlemaine never corrects her, or allows her to be corrected. I wish my father would take it seriously in hand! She ought to be at school."

Peace restored, Mary told them what she had just been telling Mr. Castlemaine. She was about to become a Grey Sister. Harry laughed: he did not believe a syllable of it; Ethel, more clear-sighted, burst into tears.

"Don't, don't leave us!" she whispered, clinging to Mary, in her astonishment and distress. "You see what my life is here! I am without love, without sympathy. I have only my books and my music and my drawings and the sea! but for them my heart would starve. Oh, Mary; it has been so different since you came: I have had you to love."

Mary Ursula put her arm round Ethel. She herself standing in so much need of love, had felt the tender affection of this fresh young girl, already entwining itself around her heart, as the grateful tree feels the tendrils of the clinging vine.

"You will be what I shall most regret in leaving Greylands' Rest, Ethel. But, my dear, we can meet constantly. You can see me at the Nunnery when you will; and I shall come here sometimes."

"Look here, Mary Ursula," said Harry, all his lightness checked. "Sooner than you should go to that old Nunnery, I'll burn it down."

"No, you will not, Harry."

"I will. The crazy old building won't be much loss to the place, and the ruins would be picturesque."

He was so speaking only to cover his real concern. The project was no less displeasing to him than to his father.

"You do not mean this, Mary Ursula!" But the grave look of her earnest face effectually answered him.

"It is I who shall miss you," bewailed Ethel. "Oh, can nothing be done?"

"Nothing," said Mary, smiling. "Our paths, Ethel, will probably lie far apart in life. You will marry, and social ties will form about you. I—" she broke off suddenly.

"I intend to marry Ethel myself," said Harry, kicking hack a large live coal that flew far out into the hearth.

"Be quiet, Harry," said Ethel, a shade of annoyance in her tone.

"Why, you know it's true," he returned, without looking at her.

"True! When we are like brother and sister!"

Miss Castlemaine glanced from one to the other. She did not know how to take this. That Harry liked Ethel and was in the habit of paying her attention, told nothing; for he did the same by many other young ladies.

"It was only last week I asked her to fix the day," said Harry.

"And I told you to go and talk nonsense elsewhere; not to me," retorted Ethel, her tone betraying her real vexation.

"If you won't have me, Ethel, you'll drive me to desperation. I might go off and marry one of the Grey Sisters in revenge. It should be Sister Ann. She is a charming picture; one to take a young man's heart by storm."

Mary Ursula looked keenly at him. In all this there was a semblance of something not real. It struck her that he was wanting to make it appear he wished for Ethel, when in fact he did not.

"Harry," she cried, speaking upon impulse, "you have not, I hope, been falling in love with anybody undesirable?"

"But I have," said Harry, his face flushing. "Don't I tell you who it is?—Sister Ann. Mark you though, cousin mine, you shall never be allowed to make one of those Grey Sisters."

"You are very random, you know, Harry," said Miss Castlemaine, slowly. "You talk to young ladies without meaning anything—but they may not detect that. Take care you do not go too far some day, and find yourself in a mesh." Harry Castlemaine turned his bright face on his cousin. "I never talk seriously but to one person, Mary Ursula. And that's Ethel."

"Harry," cried the young girl, with flashing eyes, "you are not fair to me."

"And now, have you any commands for the Commodore?" went on Harry lightly, and taking no notice of Ethel's rebuke. "I am going to the Hutt."

They said they had none; and he left the room. Mary turned to Ethel.

"My dear—if you have no objection to confide in me—is there anything between you and Harry?"

"Nothing, Mary," was the answer, and Ethel blushed the soft blush of girlish modesty as she said it. "Last year he teased me very much, making me often angry; but latterly he has been better. The idea of my marrying him!—when we have grown up together like brother and sister! It would seem hardly proper. I like Harry very much indeed as a brother; but as to marrying him, why, I'd rather never be married at all. Here's the carriage coming back! Mamma must have forgotten something."

Mrs. Castlemaine's carriage was seen winding round the drive. They heard her get out at the door and hold a colloquy with Flora. She came to the red parlour looking angry.

"Where's Harry?" she demanded, in the sharp, unkindly tones that so often grated on the ear of those offending her, as she threw her eyes round the room.

"Harry is not here, mamma," replied Ethel.

"I understood he was here," suspiciously spoke Mrs. Castlemaine.

"He went out a minute or two ago," said Ethel. "I think he is gone to Commodore Teague's."

"He is like an eel," was the pettish rejoinder. "You never know when you have him. As to that vulgar, gossiping old Teague, that they make so much of and are always running after, I can't think what they see in him."

"Perhaps it is his gossip that they like," suggested Ethel.

"Well, I want Harry. He has been beating Flora."

"I don't think he beat her, mamma."

"Oh, you great story-teller!" exclaimed Flora, putting in her head. "He shook me till all my bones rattled."

Mrs. Castlemaine shut the door with a click. And the next that they saw, was Miss Flora dressed in her best and going off with her mamma in the carriage.

"With this injudicious treatment the child has hardly a chance to become better," murmured Mary Ursula. "Ethel, have you a mind for a walk?"

"Yes: with you."

They dressed themselves and started for the village, walking lightly over the crisp snow, under the clear blue sky. Miss Castlemaine was bound for the Grey Nunnery; Ethel protesting she would do no act or part towards helping her to enter it, went off to see some of the fishermen's wives on the cliff.

Passing through the outer gate, Mary Ursula rang at the bell, and was admitted by Sister Phoeby. A narrow passage took her into the hall. Opening from it on the left hand was a moderate-sized room, plain and comfortable. It was called the reception parlour, but was the one usually sat in by the Grey Ladies: in fact, they had no other sitting room that could be called furnished. Dinner was taken in a bare, bleak room, looking to the sea; it was used also as the schoolroom, and contained chiefly a large table and some forms. Miss Castlemaine was shown into the reception parlour. Two of the ladies were in it: Sister Margaret writing, Sister Betsey making lint.

An indication of Miss Castlemaine's wish to join the Sisters had already reached the Nunnery, and they knew not how to make enough of her. It had caused quite a commotion of delight. To number a Castlemaine amidst them, especially one so much esteemed, so high, and grand, and good as the banker's daughter, was an honour hardly to be believed in; the small fortune she would bring seemed, like riches in itself, and they coveted the companionship of the sweet and gentle lady for their own sakes. Her joining them would swell the number of the community to thirteen; but no reason existed against that.

Sister Margaret put down her pen, Sister Betsey her linen, as their visitor entered. They gave her the one arm-chair by the fire—Sister Mildred's own place—and Mary put back her crape veil as she sat down. Calm, quiet, good, looked the ladies in their simple grey gowns, their hair smoothly braided under the white cap of worked muslin; and Mary Ursula seemed to feel a foretaste of peace in the time when the like dress, the like serene life, would be hers. The Superior Sisters came flocking in on hearing she was there; all were present save sister Mildred: Margaret, Charlotte, Betsey, Grizzel, and Mona. The working Sisters were Phoeby, Ann, Rachel, Caroline, Lettice, and Ruth.

The ladies hastened to tell Miss Castlemaine of a hope, or rather project, they had been entertaining—namely, that when she joined the community, she should become its head. Sister Mildred, incapacitated by her tedious illness, had long wished to resign control; and would have done so before, but that Sister Margaret, on whom it ought to descend, declined to take it. Miss Castlemaine sat in doubt: the proposal came upon her by surprise.

"I do all the writing that has to be done, and keep the accounts; and you see that's all I'm good for," said Sister Margaret to Miss Castlemaine, in a tone of confidence. "If I were put in Sister Mildred's place, and had to order this and decide that, I should be lost. Why, if they came and asked me whether the dinner for the day should consist of fresh herrings, or pork and pease-pudding, I should never know which to say."

"Sister Mildred may regain her health," observed Miss Castlemaine.

"But she'll never regain her hearing," put in Sister Grizzel, a little quick, fresh-coloured, talkative woman. "And that tells very much against her as Superioress. In fact, her continuing as such is like a farce."

"Besides, she herself wants to give it up," said Sister Charlotte. "Oh, Miss Castlemaine, if you would but accept it in her place! You would make us happy."

Mary Ursula said she must take time for consideration. She was invited to go up to Sister Mildred, who would be sure to think it a slight if she did not. So she was conducted upstairs by the ladies, Charlotte and Mona, and found herself in a long, dark, narrow corridor, which had doors on either side—the nuns' cells of old. The Head Sister's room was at the extreme end—a neat little chamber, whose casement looked out on to the sea with a small bed in a corner. Sister Mildred was dressed and sat by the fire. She was a fair-complexioned, pleasant-looking, talkative woman, slightly deformed, and past fifty, but still very light and active. Of her own accord, she introduced the subject of resigning her post to Miss Castlemaine, and pressed her urgently to take it.

"The holding it has become a trouble to me, my dear," she said. "Instead of lying here at peace with nothing to think of—and some days I can't get up at all—I am being referred to perpetually. Sister Margaret refuses to take it; she says she's of more good for writing and account keeping. As to Sister Charlotte, she is always amid the little ones in the school; she likes teaching—and so there it is. Your taking it, my dear, would solve a difficulty; and we could hardly let one, bearing the honoured name of Castlemaine, be among us, and not be placed at our head."

"You may get better; you may regain your health," said Mary.

"And, please God, I shall," cheerfully returned Sister Mildred, when she could be made to comprehend the remark. "Mr. Parker tells me so.

But I shall be none the more competent for my post. My deafness has become so much worse since health failed that that of itself unfits me for it. The Sisters will tell you so. Why, my dear, you don't know the mistakes it leads to. I hear just the opposite of what's really said, and give orders accordingly. Sister Margaret wrote a letter and transacted some business all wrong through this, and it has caused ever so much trouble to set it to rights. It is mortifying to her and to me."

"To all of us," put in Sister Charlotte.

"Why, my dear Miss Castlemaine, just look at my facility for misapprehension! Only the other day," continued the Superioress, who dearly loved a gossip when she could get it, "Sister Ann came running up here in a flurry, her eyes sparkling, saying Parson Marston was below. 'What, below then?' I asked. 'Yes,' she said, 'below then,' and ran off again. I wondered what could have brought the parson here, for we don't see him at the Nunnery from year's end to year's end, but was grateful to him for thinking of us, and felt that I ought to get down, if possible, to receive and thank him. So I turned out of bed and scuffled into my petticoats, slipping on my best gown and a new cap, and down stairs I went. Would you believe it, my dear young lady, that it was not Parson Marston at all, but a fine sucking pig!"

Mary could not avoid a laugh.

"A beautiful sucking-pig, that lasted us two days when cooked. It came, a present, from Farmer Watson, a good, grateful man, whose little boy Sister Mona went to nurse through a fever. I had mistaken what she said, you see, and got up for nothing. But that's the way it is with me; and the sooner I am superseded by somebody who can hear, the better."

"I have said lately that you ought to change your room," cried Sister Margaret to her. "In this one you are sometimes exposed to a sharp breeze."

"Cheese?" returned the deaf lady, mistaking the word. "Bread and cheese! By all means order it into the parlour if Miss Castlemaine would like some. Dear me, I am very remiss!"

"No, no," returned Sister Margaret, laughing at the mistake, and speaking in her ear, "I only suggested it might be better for your deafness if you exchanged this room for a warmer one: one on the other side."

"Is that all! Then why did you mention cheese? No, no; I am not going to change my room. I like this one, this aspect; the sea is as good to me as a friend. And what does Miss Castlemaine say?"

Mary stood at the casement window. The grand, expansive sea lay below and around. She could see nothing else. An Indiaman was sailing majestically in the distance; on the sails of one of the fishing boats, dotting the surface nearer, some frosted snow had gathered and was sparkling in the sunshine. There she stood, reflecting.

"For the sake of constantly enjoying this scene of wondrous beauty, it would be almost worth while to come, let alone other inducements!" she exclaimed mentally in her enthusiasm. "As to acceding to their wish of taking the lead, I believe it is what I should like, what I am fitted for."

And when she quitted Sister Mildred's room she left her promise of acceptation within it.

Meanwhile an unpleasant adventure had just happened to Ethel. Her visits to the wives of the fishermen on the cliff concluded, and seeing no sign yet of Mary Ursula's leaving the Nunnery, she thought she would make a call on Mrs. Bent, and wait there: which, in truth, she was rather fond of doing. But to-day she arrived at an inopportune moment. Mr. and Mrs. Bent were enjoying a dispute.

It appeared that a letter had been delivered at the inn that morning, addressed to Anthony Castlemaine: the third letter that had come for him since his disappearance. The two first bore the postmark of Gap, this one the London postmark, and all were addressed in the same handwriting.

Mrs. Bent had urged her husband to hand over the others to the Master of Greylands: she was now urging the like as to this one. John Bent, though in most matters under his wife's finger and thumb, had wholly refused to listen to her in this: he should keep the letters in his own safe custody, he said, until the writer, or some one of Mr. Anthony's connections from over the water, appeared to claim them.

Mrs. Bent was unable to stir his decision: since the fatal night connected with the Friar's Keep, she could but notice that John had altered. He was more silent than of yore; yielded to her less, and maintained his own will better: which was, of course, not an agreeable change to Mrs. Bent.

They were in their ordinary room, facing the sea. The door stood open as usual, but a screen of two folds now intervened between the fire-place and the draught. John sat in his carved elbow-chair; Mrs. Bent stood by, folding clothes at the table; which was drawn near the fire from its place under the window.

"I tell you, then, John Bent, you might be taken up and prosecuted for it," she said, sprinkling the linen so vigorously that some splashes went on his face. "Keeping other people's letters!"

"The letters are directed here, to my house, Dorothy woman; and I shall keep them till some proper person turns up to receive them," was John's answer, delivered without irritation as he wiped his face with his pocket-handkerchief.

"The proper person is Mr. Castlemaine. Just take your elbow away: you'll be upsetting the basin. He is the young man's uncle."

"Now look here, wife. You've said that before, and once for all I tell you I'll not do it. Mr. Castlemaine is the last person in the world I'd hand the letters to. What would he do with them!—Put 'em in the fire, I dare be bound. If, as I believe; I believe it to my very heart; Mr. Castlemaine took his nephew's life that night in the Friar's Keep—"

"Hist!" said Mrs. Bent, the rosy colour on her face fading as a sound caught her ear; "hist, man!"

And, for once, more alarmed than angry, she looked behind the screen, and found herself face to face with Ethel Reene.

"Mercy be good to us!" she exclaimed, seeing by the young lady's white face that they had been overheard. And, scarcely knowing what she did, she dragged the horror-stricken girl round to the hearth, before John.

"Now you've done it!" she cried, turning upon him. "You'd better pack up and be off to jail: for if Miss Ethel tells the Master of Greylands what she has heard, he'll put you there."

"No, he won't," said John, full of contrition for the mischief he had done, but nevertheless determined not to eat his words, and believing the suspicion must have reached the young lady sooner or later.

"You cannot think this of papa!" said Ethel, sinking into a chair.

"Well, Miss Ethel, it is a great mystery, as you must know," said the landlord, who had risen. "I think the Master of Greylands could solve it if he liked."

"But—but, Mr. Bent, what you said is most dreadful!"

"I'm heartily sorry you chanced to overhear it, Miss Ethel."

"There's no cause to wink at me like that, wife. The words are said, and I cannot unsay them."

"But—do—you—believe it?" gasped Ethel.

"Yes, he does believe it," burst forth Mrs. Bent, losing sight of prudence in her anger against her husband. "If he does not get into some awful trouble one of these days through his tongue, his name's not John Bent—And there's Miss Castlemaine of Stilborough crossing over the road!"

Not less overcome by terror and dismay than Mrs. Bent had been by anger, Ethel rushed out of the house and burst into a storm of hysterical sobs. Mary Ursula, wondering much and full of concern, drew her arm within her own and went over to the little solitary bench that stood by the sea.

"Now, my dear, tell me what this means," she said, as they sat down.

But Ethel hesitated: it was not a thing to be told to Miss; Castlemaine. She stammered an incoherent word or two between her sobs, and at the best was indistinct.

"I understand, Ethel. Be calm. John Bent has been making a terrible charge against my Uncle James."

Ethel clung to her. She admitted that it was so: telling how she had unintentionally overheard the private conversation between the landlord and his wife. She said it had frightened and confused her, though she did not believe it.

"Neither do I believe it," returned Miss Castlemaine calmly. "I heard this some time ago—I mean the suspicion that is rife in Greylands— but I am sorry that you should have been startled with it. That my uncle is incapable of anything of the kind—and only to have to say as much in refutation seems a cruel insult on him—I am perfectly sure of; and I am content to wait the elucidation that no doubt time will bring."

"Bat how wicked of John Bent!" cried Ethel.

"Ethel, dear, I have gone through so much misery of late that it has subdued me, and I think I have learnt the great precept not to judge another," said Mary Ursula sadly. "I do not blame John Bent. I respect him. That a strange mystery does encompass the doings of that February night—so fatal for me as well as for poor Anthony—I cannot ignore: and I speak not now of the disappearance only. There's reason in what John Bent says—that Mr. Castlemaine is not open about it, that it might be fancied he knows more than he will say. It is so. Perhaps he will not speak because it might implicate some one—not himself, Ethel; never himself; I do not fear that."

"No, no," murmured Ethel.

"It is Mr. Castlemaine's pride, I think, that prevents his speaking. He must have heard these rumours, and naturally resents them—"

"Do you think Anthony is really dead?" interrupted Ethel.

"I have never had any hope from the first that he is not. Now and then my imagination runs away with me and suggests he may be here, he may be there, he may have done this or done that—but of real hope, that he is alive, I have none. Next to the death of my dear father, it has been the greatest weight I have had to bear. I saw him but once, Ethel, but I seemed to take to him as to a brother. I am sure he was honourable and generous, a good man and a gentleman."

"You know what they are foolish enough to say here?" breathed Ethel. "That the ghost of the Grey Friar, angry at his precincts being invaded—"

"Hush!" reproved Miss Castlemaine.

MRS. HENRY WOOD

XII

Madame Guise

It was the afternoon of this same day. The stage-coach, delayed by the snow, was very late when it was heard approaching. It's four well-fed horses drew lip at the Dolphin Lim, to set down Mr. Nettleby. The superintendent of the coastguard, who had been on some business a mile or two inland, had availed himself of the coach for returning. John Bent and his wife came running to the door. The guard, hoping, perhaps, for sixpence or a shilling gratuity, descended from his seat, and was extending a hand to help the officer down from the roof, when he found himself called to by a lady inside, who had been reconnoitring the inn, and the flaming dolphin on its signboard.

"What place is this, guard?"

"Greylands, ma'am."

"That seems a good hotel."

"It is a nice comfortable inn, ma'am."

"I will get out here. Please see to my luggage."

The guard was surprised. He thought the lady must have made a mistake.

"This is not Stilborough, ma'am. You are booked to Stilborough."

"But I will not go on to Stilborough: I will descend here instead. See my poor child"—showing the hot face of a little girl who lay half asleep upon her knee. "She has, I fear, the fever coming on, and she is so fatigued. This must be a healthy place; it has the sea, I perceive; and I think she shall rest here for a day or two before going on."

The landlord and his wife had heard this colloquy, for the lady spoke at the open window. They advanced, and the guard threw wide the door.

"Will you carry my little one?" said the lady to Mrs. Bent. "I fear she is going to be ill, and I do not care to take her on farther. Can I be accommodated with a good apartment here?"

"The best rooms we have, ma'am, are at your service; and you will find them excellent, though I say it myself," returned Mrs. Bent, receiving the child into her arms.

"Marie fatiguée," plaintively called out the little thing, who seemed about three years old. "Marie ne peut marcher."

The lady reassured her in the same language, and alighted. She was a tall, ladylike young woman of apparently some six-and-twenty years, with soft, fair hair, and a pleasing face that wore signs of care, or weariness: or perhaps both. Mrs. Bent carried the child into the parlour; John followed with a large hand-reticule made of plaited black-and-white straw, and the guard put two trunks in the passage, a large one and a small one.

"I am en voyage," said the lady, addressing Mrs. Bent—and it may be remarked that, though speaking English with fluency, and with very little foreign accent, she now and then substituted a French word, or a whole sentence as though the latter were more familiar to her in everyday life—and of which John Bent and his wife did not understand a syllable.

"But we have voyaged far, and the sea-crossing was frightfully rough, and I fear I have brought my little one on too quickly: so it may be well to halt here for a short time, and keep her quiet. I hope your hotel is not crowded with company?"

"There's nobody at all staying in it just now, ma'am," said Mrs. Bent. "We don't have many indoor visitors at the winter season."

"And this snow is not good," said the stranger; "I mean not good for voyagers. I might have put off my journey had I thought it would come. When I left my home, the warm spring sun was shining, and the trees were budding."

"We have had fine warm weather here, too," said Mrs. Bent; "it changed again a week ago to winter: not but what we had the sun out bright to-day. This dear little thing seems delicate, ma'am."

"Not generally. But she is fatigued, you see, and has a touch of fever. We must make her some tisane."

"We'll soon get her right again," said Mrs. Bent, gently; for with children, of whom she was very fond, she lost all her sharpness. "Poor little lamb! And so you've come from over the water, ma'am!—and the sea was rough!—and did this little one suffer?"

"Oh, pray do not talk of that terrible sea! I thought I must have died. To look at, nothing more beautiful; but to be on it—ah, Ciel!"

She shuddered and shrugged her shoulders with the recollection. There was something peculiarly soft and winning in the quiet tones of her voice; something attractive altogether in her features and their sad expression.

"I never was on the sea, thank goodness," said Mrs. Bent; "I have heard it's very bad. We get plenty of it as far as the looks go: and that's enough for us, ma'am. Many an invitation I've had in my life to go off sailing in people's boats—but no, not for me. One knows one's safe on land."

She had sat down, the child on her lap, and was taking off its blue woollen hood and warm woollen pelisse of fleecy grey cloth. The frock underneath was of fine black French merino. The lady wore the same kind of black dress under her cloak: it was evident that both were in mourning. Happening to look up from the semi-sleeping child, Mrs. Bent caught the traveller's eyes fixed attentively upon her, as if studying her face.

"How do you call this village, I was about to ask. Grey—"

"Greylands, ma'am. Stilborough is about three miles off. Are you going there?"

"Not to stay," said the lady, hastily. "I am come to England to see a relative, but my progress is not in any hurry. I must think first of my child: and this air seems good."

"None so good for miles and miles," returned Mrs. Bent. "A week of it will make this little lady quite another child. Pretty thing! What beautiful eyes!"

The child had woke up again in her restlessness; she was gazing up at her strange nurse with wide-open, dark brown eyes. They were not her mother's eyes, for those were blue. The hot little face was becoming paler.

"I mist make her some tisane" repeated the lady; "or show you how to make it. You have herbs, I presume. We had better get her to bed. Nothing will do her so much good as rest and sleep. Will Marie go to bed?" she said, addressing the little girl.

"Oui," replied the child, who appeared to understand English, but would not speak it. "Marie sommeil," she added in her childish patois. "Marie soif. Maman, donne Marie a boire."

"Will you take her, ma'am, for a few moments?" said Mrs. Bent, placing her in the mother's arms. "I will see after your room and make it ready."

The landlady left the parlour. The child, feverish and weary, soon began to cry. Her mother hushed her; and presently, not waiting for the reappearance of the landlady, carried her upstairs.

Which was the chamber? she wondered, on reaching the landing: but the half-open door of one, and some stir within, guided her thoughts to it, as the right. Mrs. Bent was bustling about it; and the landlord, who appeared to have been taking up the trunks, stood just inside the door. Some kind of dispute seemed to be going on, for Mrs. Bent's tones were shrill. The lady halted, not liking to intrude, and sat down on a short bench against the wall; the child, dozing again, was heavy for her.

"As if there was not another room in the house, but you must make ready this one!" John was saying in a voice of vexed remonstrance. "I told you, Dorothy, I'd never have this chamber used again until we had not space left elsewhere. What are you going to do with the things?"

"Now don't you fret yourself to fiddle-strings," retorted Mrs. Bent. "I am putting all the things into this linen-basket; his clothes and his little desk and all, even the square of scented soap he used, for he brought it with him in his portmanteau. They shall go into the small chest in our bedroom, and be locked up. And you may put a seal upon the top of it for safety."

"But I did not wish to have the things disturbed at all," urged John. "The lady might have had another room."

"The tap-room is your concern, the care of the chambers is mine, and I choose her to have this one," said independent Mrs. Bent. "As to keeping the best chamber out of use just because these things have remained in it unclaimed, is about as daft a notion as ever I heard of. If you don't take care, John, you'll go crazy over Anthony Castlemaine."

The mother outside, waiting, and hushing her child to her, had not been paying much attention: but at the last words she started, and gazed at the door. Her lips parted; her face turned white.

"Peace, wife," said the landlord. "What I say is right."

"Yes, crazy," persisted Mrs. Bent, who rarely dropped an argument of her own accord. "Look at what happened with Miss Ethel Reene to-day! I'm sure you are not in your senses on the subject, John Bent, or you'd never be so imprudent. You may believe Mr. Anthony was murdered by his uncle, but it does not do to turn yourself into a town-crier, and proclaim it."

Oh, more deadly white than before did these words turn the poor lady who was listening. Her face was as the face of one stricken with terror; her breath came in gasps; she clutched at her child, lest her trembling hands should let it fall. John Bent and his wife came forth, bearing between them the piled-up clothes-basket, a small mahogany desk on its top. She let her face drop upon her child's and kept it there, as though she too had fallen asleep.

"Dear me, there's the lady!" whispered John.

"And it's unbeknown what she has overheard," muttered Mrs. Bent. "I beg your pardon, ma'am; you'll be cold sitting there. Had you dropped asleep?"

The lady lifted her white face: fortunately the passage was in twilight: she passed a pocket-handkerchief over her brow as she spoke.

"My little child got so restless that I came up. Is the room ready?"

Letting fall her handle of the basket and leaving her husband to convey it into their chamber as he best could, Mrs. Bent took the child from the speaker's arms and preceded her into the room. A spacious, comfortable chamber, with a fine view over the sea, and a good fire burning up in the grate.

"We were as quick as we could be," said Mrs. Bent, in apology for having kept her guest waiting; "but I had to empty the chamber first of some articles that were in it. I might have given you another room at once, ma'am, for we always keep them in readiness, you see; but this is the largest and has the pleasantest look-out; and I thought if the little girl was to be ill, you'd like it best."

"Articles belonging to a former traveller?" asked the lady, who was kneeling then before her trunk to get out her child's night-things.

"Yes, ma'am. A gentleman we had here a few short weeks ago."

"And he has left?"

"Oh yes," replied Mrs. Bent, gently combing back the child's soft brown hair, before she passed the sponge of warm water over her face.

"But why did he not take his things with him?"

"Well, ma'am, he—he left unexpectedly; and so they remained here."

Now, in making this somewhat evasive answer, Mrs. Bent had no particular wish to deceive. But, what with the work she had before her, and what with the fretful child on her knee, it was not exactly the moment for entering on gossip. The disappearance of Anthony Castlemaine was too public and popular a theme in the neighbourhood for any idea of concealment to be connected with it. The lady, however, thought she meant to evade the subject, and said no more. Indeed the child claimed all their attention.

"Marie soif," said the little one, as they put her into bed. "Maman, Marie soif."

"Thirsty, always thirsty!" repeated the mother in English. "I don't much like it; it bespeaks fever."

"I'll get some milk and water," said Mrs. Bent.

"No, no, not milk," interposed the lady. "Oui, ma chérie! A spoonful or two of sugar and water while maman makes the tisane. Madame has herbs, no doubt," she added, turning to the landlady. "I could make it soon myself at this good fire if I had a little casserole: a—what you call it?—saucepan."

Mrs. Bent promised the herbs, for she had a store-room fall of different kinds, and the saucepan. A little sugared water was given to the child, who lay quiet after drinking it, and closed her eyes. Moving noiselessly about the room, the lady happened to go near the window, and her eye caught the moving sea in the distance, on which some bright light yet lingered. Opening the casement window for a moment, she put her head out, and gazed around.

"The sea is very nice to see, but I don't like to think of being on it," she said as she shut the window. "What is that great building over yonder to the left?"

"It's the Grey Nunnery, ma'am."

"The Grey Nunnery! What, have you a nunnery here in this little place? I had no idea."

"It's not a real nunnery," said Mrs. Bent, as she proceeded to explain what it was, in the intervals of folding the child's clothes, and how good the ladies were who inhabited it. "We heard a bit of news about it this afternoon," she added, her propensity for talking creeping out. "Sister Ann ran over here to borrow a baking-dish—for their own came in two in the oven with all the baked apples in it—and she said she believed Miss Castlemaine was going to join them as the Lady Superior."

"Miss—who?" cried the stranger quickly.

"Miss Castlemaine. Perhaps, ma'am, you may have heard of the Castlemaines of Greylands' Rest. It is close by."

"I do not know them," said the traveller. "Is, then, a Miss Castlemaine, of Greylands' Rest, the Lady Superior of the Nunnery?"

"Miss Castlemaine of Stilborough, ma'am. There is no Miss Castlemaine of Greylands' Rest; save a tiresome little chit of twelve. She has not joined them yet; it is only in contemplation. Sister Ann was all cock-a-hoop about it: but I told her the young lady was too beautiful to hide her head under a muslin cap in a nunnery."

"It is a grand old building," said the traveller, "and must stand out well and nobly on the edge of the cliff. And what a length! I cannot see the other end."

"The other end is nearly in ruins—part of it, at least. The chapel quite so. That lies between the Nunnery and the Friar's Keep."

"The Friar's Keep!" repeated the lady. "You have odd names here. But I like this village. It is quiet: nobody seems to pass."

"There's hardly anybody in it to pass, for that matter," cried Mrs. Bent, with disparagement. "Just the fishermen and the Grey Sisters. But here I am, talking when I ought to be doing! What would you like to have prepared for dinner, ma'am?"

"I could not eat—I feel feverish, too," was the answer given, in an accent that had a ring of piteous wail. "I will take but some tea and a tartine when I have made the tisane."

Mrs. Bent opened her eyes. "Tea and a tart, did you say, ma'am?"

"I said—I mean bread and butter," explained the stranger, translating her French word.

"And—what name—if I may ask, ma'am?" continued Mrs. Bent, as a final question.

"I am Madame Guise."

"Tea's best, after all, upon a day's travelling," were the landlady's final words as she descended the stairs. There she told her husband that the lady had rather a curious name, sounding like Madame Geese.

The small saucepan and the herbs were taken up immediately by Molly, who said she was to stay and help make the stuff, if the lady required her. The lady seemed to be glad of her help, and showed her how to pick the dried leaves from the thicker stalks.

"Do you have travellers staying here often?" asked Madame Guise, standing by Molly after she had asked her name, and doing her own portion of the work.

"A'most never in winter time," replied Molly—a round-eyed, red-cheeked, strong-looking damsel, attired in a blue linsey skirt and a cotton handkerchief crossed on her neck. "We had a gentleman for a week or two just at the turn o' January. He had this here same bedroom."

"They were his things, doubtless, that your mistress said she was removing to make space for me."

"In course they were," replied Molly. "Master said he'd not have this room used—that the coats and things should stay in it: but missis likes to take her own way. This here stalk, mum—is he too big to go in?"

"That is: we must have only the little ones. What was the gentleman's name, Mollee?"

"He was young Mr. Castlemaine: a foreign gentleman, so to say: nephew to the one at Greylands' Rest. He came over here to put in his claim to the money and lands."

"And where did he go?—where is he now?" questioned Madame Guise, with an eagerness that might have betrayed her painful interest, had the servant's suspicions been on the alert.

"It's what my master would just give his head to know," was the answer. "He went into the Friar's Keep one moon light night, and never came out on't again."

"Never came out of it again!" echoed Madame Guise "What do you mean?—How was that?"

Bit by bit Molly revealed the whole story, together with sundry items of the superstition attaching to the Friar's Keep. Very much gratified was she at the opportunity of doing it. The tale was encompassed by so many marvels, both of reality and imagination, by so much mystery, by so wide a field of wonder altogether, that others in Greylands, as well as Molly, thought it a red-letter day when they could find strange ears to impart it to.

Madame Guise sat down in a chair, her hands clasped before her, and forgetting the herbs. Molly saw how pale she looked; and felt prouder than any peacock at her own powers of narration.

"But what became of him, Mollee?" questioned the poor lady.

"Well, mum, that lies in doubt, you see. Some say he was spirited away by the Grey Monk."

Madame Guise shook her head. "That could not be," she said slowly, and somewhat in hesitation. "I don't like revenants myself—but that could not be."

"And others think," added Molly, dropping her voice, "that he was done away with by his uncle, Mr. Castlemaine. Master do, for one."

"Done away with! How?"

"Murdered," said the girl, plunging the herbs into the saucepan of water.

A shudder took Madame Guise from head to foot. Molly looked round at her: she was like one seized with ague.

"I am cold and fatigued with my long journey," she murmured, seeking to afford some plausible excuse to the round-eyed girl. "And it always startles one to hear talk of murder."

"So it do, mum," acquiesced Molly. "I dun'no which is worst to hear tell on; that or ghosts."

MRS. HENRY WOOD

"But—this Friar's Keep that you talk of, Mollee—it may be that he fell from it by accident into the sea."

"Couldn't," shortly corrected Molly. "There ain't no way to fall—no opening. They be biling up beautiful, mum."

"And—was he never—never seen again since that night?" pursued Madame Guise, casting mechanically a glance on the steaming saucepan.

"Never seen nor heard on," protested Molly emphatically. "His clothes and his portmanteau and all his other things have stayed on here; but he has never come back to claim 'em."

Madame Guise put her hands on her pallid face, as if to hide the terror there. Molly, her work done, and about to depart, was sweeping the bits of stalks and herbs from the table into her clean check apron.

"Does the voisinage know all this?" asked Madame Guise, looking up. "Is it talked of openly? May I speak of it to monsieur and madame en bas—to the host and hostess, I would say?"

"Why bless you, mum, yes! There have been nothing else talked of in the place since. Nobody hardly comes in here but what begins upon it."

Molly left with the last words. Madame Guise sat on, she knew not how long, her face buried in her hands, and the tisane was boiled too much. The little girl, soothed perhaps by the murmur of voices, had fallen fast asleep. By-and-by Mrs. Bent came up, to know when her guest would be ready for tea.

"I am ready now," was the lady's answer, after attending to the tisane. "And I wish that you and your husband, madame, would allow me to take the meal with you this one evening," added Madame Guise, with a slight shiver, as they descended the dark staircase. "I feel lonely and fatigued, and in want of companionship."

Mrs. Bent was gratified, rather than otherwise at the request. They descended; and she caused the tea-tray, already laid in their room, to be carried into the parlour. The same parlour, as the room above was the same bedroom, that had been occupied by the ill-fated Anthony Castlemaine.

"I hope you are a little less tired than you were when you arrived, madam," said John Bent, bowing, as he with deprecation took his seat at last, and stirred his tea.

"Thank you, I have been forgetting my fatigue in listening to the story of one Mr. Anthony Castlemaine's disappearance," replied Madams Guise, striving to speak with indifference. "The account is curious, and has interested me. Mollee thought you would give me the particulars."

"Oh, he'll do that, madam," put in Mrs. Bent sharply. "There's nothing he likes better than talking of that. Tell it, John."

John did as he was bid. But his account was in substance the same as Molly's. He could tell neither more nor less: some few additional small details perhaps, some trifling particulars; but of real information he could give none. The poor lady, hungering after a word of enlightenment that might tend to lessen her dread and horror, listened for it in vain.

"But what explanation can be given of it?" she urged, biting her dry lips to hide their trembling. "People cannot disappear without cause. Are you sure it was Mr. Castlemaine you saw go in at the gate, and thence into the Friar's Keep?"

"I am as sure of it, ma'am, as I am that this is a tea-cup before me. Mr. Castlemaine denies it, though."

"And you suspect—you suspect that he murdered him! That is a frightful word; I cannot bear to say it. Meurte!" she repeated in her own tongue, with a passing shiver. "Quelle chose affreuse! You suspect Mr. Castlemaine, sir, I say?"

John Bent shook his head. The encounter with Ethel had taught him caution. "I don't know, ma'am," he answered; "I can't say. That the young man was killed in some way, I have no doubt of—and I think Mr. Castlemaine must know something about it."

"Are there any places in this—what you call it?—Friar's Keep?—that he could be concealed in? Any dungeons?"

"He's not there, ma'am. The place is open enough for anybody to go in that likes. Mr. Castlemaine had a man over from Stilborough to help him search, and they went all about it together. I and Superintendent Nettleby also went over it one day, and some others with us. There wasn't a trace to be seen of young Mr. Anthony; nothing to show that he had been there."

"So it resolves itself into this much," said Madame Guise—"that you saw this Mr. Anthony Castlemaine go into the dark place, on that February night; and, so far as can be ascertained, he never came out again."

"Just that," said John Bent. "I'd give this right hand of mine"—lifting it—"to know what his fate has been. Something tells me that it will be brought to light."

Madame Guise went up to her room, and sat down there with her heavy burthen of terror and sorrow, wondering what would be the next scene in this strange mystery, and what she herself could best do towards unravelling it. Mrs. Bent, coming in by-and-by, found her weeping hysterically. Marie woke up at the moment, and they gave her some of the tisane.

"It is the reaction of the cold and long journey, ma'am," pronounced Mrs. Bent, in regard to the tears she had seen. "And perhaps the talking about this unaccountable business has startled you. You will be better after a night's rest."

"Yes, the coach was very cold. I will say goodnight to you and go to bed."

As Mrs. Bent retired, the lady sank on her knees by the side of her child, and buried her face in the white counterpane. There she prayed; prayed earnestly; for help from Above, for strength to bear.

"The good God grant that the enlightenment may be less terrible than are these my fears," she implored, with lifted hands and streaming eyes.

Back came Mrs. Bent, a wine-glass in one hand, and a hot-water bottle for the bed in the other. The glass contained some of her famous cordial—in her opinion a remedy for half the ills under the sun. Madame Guise was then quietly seated by the fire, gazing into it with a far-away look, her hands folded on her lap. She drank the glass of cordial with thanks: though it seemed of no moment what she drank or what she did not drink just then. And little Marie, her cheeks flushed, her rosy lips open sufficiently to show her pretty white teeth, had dropped off to sleep again.

XIII

A Storm of Wind

The wind was rising. Coming in gusts from across the sea, it swept round the Dolphin Inn with a force that seemed to shake the old walls and stir the windowpanes—for the corner that made the site of the inn was always an exposed one. Madame Guise, undressing slowly by the expiring fire in her chamber, shivered as she listened to it.

The wind did not howl in this fashion around her own sheltered home in the sunny Dauphine. There was no grand sea there for it to whirl and play over, and come off with a shrieking moan. Not often there did they get cold weather like this; or white snow covering the plains; or ice in the water-jugs. And never yet before in her uneventful life, had it fallen to her lot to travel all across France from South to North with a little child to take care of, and then to encounter the many hours' passage in a stifling ship on a rough and raging sea: and after a night's rest in London to come off again in the cold English stage-coach for how many miles she hew not. All this might have served to take the colour from her face and to give the shiverings to her frame—for land travelling in those days was not the easy pastime it is made now.

But there was worse behind it. Not the cold, not the want of rest, was it that was so trying to her, but the frightful whispers of a supposed tragedy that had (so to say) greeted her arrival at the Dolphin. But a few hours yet within its walls, and she had been told that him of whom she had come in secret search, her husband, had disappeared out of life.

For this poor young lady, Charlotte Guise, was in truth the wife of Anthony Castlemaine. His wife if he were still living; his widow if he were dead. That he was dead, hearing all she had heard, no doubt could exist in her mind; no hope of the contrary, not the faintest shadow of it, could enter her heart. She had come all this long journey in search of her husband, fearing some vague treachery; she had arrived to find that treachery of the deepest dye had only too probably put him out of sight for ever.

When the father, Basil Castlemaine, was on his death-bed, she had heard the charge he gave to Anthony, to come over to England and put in the claim to his right inheritance; she had heard the warning of possible treachery that had accompanied it.

Basil died. And when Anthony, in obedience to his father's last injunctions, was making ready for the journey to England, his wife recalled the warning to him. He laughed at her. He answered jokingly saying that if he never returned to Gap, she might come off to see the reason, and whether he was still in the land of the living. Ah, how many a word spoken in jest would, if we might read the future, bear a solemn meaning! That was one.

Anthony Castlemaine departed on his mission to England, leaving his wife and little child in their home at Gap. The first letter Charlotte received from her husband told her of his arrival at Greylands, and that he had put up at the Dolphin Inn. It intimated that he might not find his course a very smooth one, and that his uncle James was in possession of Greylands' Rest. Some days further on she received a second letter from him; and following closely upon it, by the next post in fact, a third. Both these letters bore the same date. The first of them stated that he was not advancing at all; that all kinds of impediments were being placed in his way by his uncles; they appeared resolved to keep him out of the estate, refusing even to show him how it was left and it ended with an expressed conviction that his Uncle James was usurping it. The last letter told her that since posting the other letter earlier in the day, he had seen his Uncle James; that the interview, which had taken place in a meadow, was an unpleasant one, his uncle even having tried to strike him that he (Anthony) really did not know what to be at, but had resolved to try for one more conference with his uncle before proceeding to take legal measures, and that he should certainly write to her again in the course of a day or two to tell her whether matters progressed or whether they did not. In this last letter there ran a vein of sadness, very perceptible to the wife. She thought her husband must have been in very bad spirits when he wrote it: and she anxiously looked for the further news promised.

It never came. No subsequent letter ever reached her. After waiting some days, she wrote to her husband at the Dolphin Inn, but she got no answer. She wrote again, and with the like result. Then, feeling strangely uneasy, not knowing how to get tidings of him, or to whom to apply, she began to think that she would have to put in practice the suggestion he had but spoken in jest, and go over to England to look after him. A short period of vacillation—for it looked like a frightfully formidable step to the untravelled young lady—and she resolved upon it. Arranging the affairs of her petit menage, as she expressed it, she started off with her child; and in due time reached London. There she stayed one night, after sending off a note to Greylands, directed to her husband at the Dolphin Inn, to tell of her intended arrival on the following day; and in the morning she took her seat in the Stilborough coach. These three letters, the two from Gap and the one from London, were those that led to the dispute between Mr. and Mrs. Bent, which Ethel Reene had disturbed. The landlord had them safely locked up in his private archives.

Forewarned, forearmed, is an old saying. Anthony Castlemaine's wife had been warned, and she strove to be armed. She would not present herself openly and in her own name at Greylands. If the Castlemaine family were dealing hardly with her husband, it would be more prudent for her to go to work warily and appear there at first as a stranger. The worst she had feared was, that Mr. James Castlemaine might be holding her husband somewhere at bay; perhaps even had put him in a prison—she did not understand the English laws—and she must seek him out and release him. So she called herself Guise as soon as she landed in England. Her name had been Guise before her marriage, and she assumed it now. Not much of an assumption: in accordance with the French customs of her native place, she retained her maiden name as an affix to her husband's, and her cards were printed Madame Castlemaine-Guise. Had her assertion of the name wanted confirmation, there it was on the small trunk; which had Guise studded on it in brass nails, for it had belonged to her father. Her intention had been to proceed to Stilborough, put up there, and come over to Greylands the following day. But when she found the coach passed through Greylands—which she had not known, and she first recognised the place by the sign of the famous dolphin, about which Anthony had written to her in his first letter—she resolved to alight there, the little girl's symptoms of feverish illness affording a pretext for it. And so, here she was, at the often-heard-of Dolphin Inn, inhabiting the very chamber that her ill-fated husband had occupied, and with the dread story she had listened to beating its terrors in her brain.

A gust of wind shook the white dimity curtain, drawn before the casement, and she turned to it with a shiver. What did this angry storm of wind mean? Why should it have arisen suddenly without apparent warning? Charlotte Guise was rather superstitious, and asked herself the question. When she got out of the coach at the inn door, the air and sea were calm. Could the angry disturbance have come to show her that the very elements were rising at the wrong dealt out to her husband? Some such an idea took hold of her.

"Every second minute I ask whether it can be true," she murmured in her native language; "or whether I have but dropped asleep in my own house, and am dreaming it all. It is not like reality. It is not like any story I ever heard before. Anthony comes over here, all those hundreds of weary miles, over that miserable sea, and finds himself amid his family; his family whom he had never seen. 'Greylands' Rest is mine, I think,' he says to them; 'will you give it to me?' And they deny that it is his. 'Then,' says he, 'what you say may be so; but you should just show me the deeds—the proofs that it is not mine.' And they decline to show them; and his uncle, James Castlemaine, at an interview in the field, seeks to strike him. Anthony comes home to the hotel here, and writes that last letter to me, and puts it in the post late at night. Then he and the landlord go walking out together in the moonlight, and by-and-by they see Mr. James Castlemaine go into a lonely place of cloisters called the Friar's Keep, and he, nay poor husband, runs in after him; and he never comes out of it again. The host, waiting for him outside, hears a shot and an awful cry, but he does not connect it with the cloisters; and so he promenades about till he's weary, thinking the uncle and nephew are talking together, and—and Anthony never at all comes out again! Yes, it is very plain: it is too plain to me: that shot took my dear husband's life. James Castlemaine, fearing he would make good his claim to the estate and turn him out of it, has murdered him."

The wind shrieked, as if it were singing a solemn requiem; the small panes of the casement seemed to crack, and the white curtain fluttered. Charlotte Guise hid her shrinking face for a moment, and then turned it on the shaking curtain, her white lips parting with some scarcely breathed words.

"If the spirits of the dead are permitted to hover in the air, as some people believe perhaps his spirit is here now, at this very window! Seeking to hold commune with mine; calling upon me to avenge him. Oh, Anthony, yes! I will never rest until I have found out the mystery of your fate. I will devote my days to doing it!"

As if to encourage the singular fancy, that the whispered story and the surroundings of the hour had called up in her over-strung nerves and brain, a gust wilder than any that had gone before swept past the house at the moment with a rushing moan. The casement shook; its fastenings seemed to strain: and the poor young lady, in some irrepressible freak of courage, born of desperation, drew aside the curtain and looked forth.

No, no; nothing was there but the wind. The white snow lay on the ground, and covered the cliff that skirted the beach on the right. The night was light, disclosing the foam of the waves as they rose and fell; clouds were sweeping madly across the face of the sky.

The little girl stirred in bed and threw out her arms. Her mother let fall the window curtain and softly approached her. The hot face wore its fever-crimson; the large brown eyes, so like her father's, opened the red lips parted with a cry.

"Maman! Marie soif; Marie veut boire."

"Oh, is she fatherless?" mentally cried the poor mother, as she took up the glass of tisane. "Oui, ma petite! ma chérie! Bois donc, Marie; bois!"

The child seized the glass with her hot and trembling little hands, and drank from it. She seemed very thirsty. Before her mother had replaced it within the fender and come back to her, her pretty face was on the pillow again, her eyes were closing.

Madame Guise—as we must continue to call her—went to bed: but not to sleep. The wind raged, the child by her side was restless, her own mind was in a chaos of horror and trouble. The words of the prophet Isaiah in Holy Writ might indeed have been applied to her: The whole head was sick and the whole heart faint.

Towards morning she dropped into a disturbed sleep, during which a dream visited her. And the dream was certainly a singular one. She thought she was alone in a strange, dark garden: gloomy trees clustered about her, ugly looking mountains rose above. She seemed to be searching for something; to be obliged to search, but she did not know for what; a great dread, or terror, lay upon her, and but for being impelled she would not have dared to put one foot before the other in the dark path. Suddenly, as she was pushing through the impeding trees, her husband stood before her. She put out her hand to greet him; but he did not respond to it, but remained where he had halted, a few paces off, gazing at her fixedly. It was not the husband who had parted from her in the sunny South; a happy man full of glad anticipations, with a bright fresh face and joyous words on his lips: but her husband with a sad, stern countenance, pale, cold, and still. Her heart seemed to sink within her, and before she could ask him what was amiss she saw

MRS. HENRY WOOD

that he was holding his waistcoat aside with his left hand, to display a shot in the region of the heart. A most dreadful sensation of terror, far more dreadful than any she could ever know in this life, seized upon her at the sight; she screamed aloud and awoke. Awoke with the drops of moisture on her face, and trembling in every limb.

Now, as will be clear to every practical mind, this dream, remarkable though it was, must have been only the result of her own imaginative thoughts, of the tale she had heard, of the fears and doubts she had been indulging before going to sleep. But she, poor distressed, lonely lady, looked upon it as a revelation. From that moment she never doubted that her husband had been shot as described; shot in the heart and killed: and that the hand that did it was Mr. Castlemaine's.

"I knew his spirit might be hovering about me," she murmured, trying to still her trembling, as she sat up in bed. "He has been permitted to appear to me to show me the truth—to enjoin on me the task of bringing the deed to light. By Heaven's help I will do it! I will never quit this spot, this Greylands, until I have accomplished it. Yes, Anthony!—can you hear me, my husband?—I vow to devote myself to the discovery; I will bring this dark wickedness into the broad glare of noonday. Country, kindred, home, friends!—I will forget them all, Anthony, in my search for you.

"Where have they hidden him?" she resumed after a little pause. "Had Mr. Castlemaine an accomplice?—or did he act alone. Oh, alone; of a certainty, alone," she continued, answering her own question. "He would not have dared it had others been present; and the landlord below says Mr. Castlemaine was by himself when he went into the cloisters. Did he fling him into the sea after he was dead?—or did he conceal him somewhere in that place—that Keep? Perhaps he buried him in it? if so, his body is lying in unconsecrated ground, and it will never rest.—Marie, then, my little one, what is it? Are you better this morning?"

The child was awaking with a moan. She had been baptised and registered in her native place as Mary Ursula. Her grandfather, Basil, never called her anything else; her father would sometimes shorten it to "Marie Ursule:" but her mother, not so well accustomed to the English tongue as they were, generally used but the one name, Marie. She looked up and put out her little hands to her mother: her eyes were heavy, her cheeks flushed and feverish.

That the child was worse than she had been the previous night, there could be little question of, and Madame Guise felt some alarm. When breakfast was over—of which meal the child refused to partake, but still complained of thirst—she inquired whether there was a doctor in the place. She asked for him as she would have asked in her own land. Is there a medecin here? and Mrs. Bent interpreted it as medicine, comprehended that medicine was requested, and rejoiced accordingly. Mrs. Bent privately put down the non-improvement to the tisane. Had a good wholesome powder been administered over night, the child, she believed, would have been all right this morning.

The doctor, Mr. Parker, came in answer to the summons: a grey-haired, pleasant-speaking man. He had formerly been in large practice at Stilborough; but after a dangerous illness which attacked him there and lasted more than a year, he took the advice of his friends and retired from the fatigues of his profession. His means were sufficient to live without it. Removing to Greylands, for change of air, and for the benefit of the salt sea-breezes, he grew to like the quietude of the place, and determined to make it his home for good. Learning that a small, pretty villa was for sale, he purchased it. It lay back from the coach road beyond the Dolphin Inn, nearly opposite the avenue that led to Greylands' Rest. The house belonged to Mr. Blackett of the Grange—the Grange being the chief residence at a small hamlet about two miles off; and Mr. Castlemaine had always intended to purchase it should it be in the market, but Mr. Blackett had hitherto refused to sell. His deciding to do so at length was quite a sudden whim; Mr. Parker heard of it, and secured the little property—which was anything but agreeable at the time to the Master of Greylands.

There Mr. Parker had since resided, and had become strong and healthy again. He had so far resumed his calling as to attend when a doctor was wanted in Greylands, for there was none nearer than Stilborough. At first Mr. Parker took to respond for humanity's sake when appealed to, and he continued it from love of his profession. Not for one visit in ten did he get paid, nor did he want to: the fishermen were poor, and he was large-hearted.

After examining the little lady traveller, he pronounced her to be suffering from a slight attack of inflammation of the chest, induced, no doubt, by the cold to which she had been exposed when travelling. Madame Guise informed him that they had journeyed from Paris (it was no untruth, for they had passed through the French capital and stayed a night in it), and the weather had become very sharp as they neared the coast—which coast it had taken them two days and a night in the diligence to reach; and the sea voyage had been fearfully hard, and had tried the little one. Yes, yes, the doctor answered, the inclement cold had attacked the little J girl, and she must stay in bed and be taken care of. Madame Guise took occasion to observe that she had been going farther on, but, on perceiving her child's symptoms of illness, had halted at this small village, called Greylands, which looked open and healthy—but the wind had got up at night. Got up very much and very suddenly, assented the doctor, got up to a gale, and it was all the better for the little one that she had not gone on. He thought he might have to put a small blister on in the afternoon, but he should see. A blister?—what was that? returned madame, not familiar with the English word. Oh, she remembered, she added a moment after—a vésicatoire.

"Yes, yes, I see it all: Heaven is helping me," mentally spoke poor Charlotte Guise, as she took up her post by Marie after the doctor's departure, and revolved matters in her mind. "This illness has been sent on purpose: a token to me that I have done right to come to Greylands, and that I am to stay in it. And by the good help of Heaven I will stay, until I shall have tracked home the fate of my husband to Mr. Castlemaine."

XIV

Plotting and Planning

The illness of little Marie Guise lasted several days. Sitting by her bed—as she did for hours together—Madame Guise had time, and to spare, to lay out her plans. That is, as far as she could lay them out. Her sole object in life now—save and except the child—was to search out the mystery of her husband's fate; her one hope to bring home the crime to Mr. Castlemaine. How to set about it she knew not. She would have to account in some plausible manner for her prolonged stay at Greylands, and to conceal her real identity. Above all, she must take care never to betray interest in the fate of Anthony Castlemaine.

To stay in Greylands, or in England at all, might be rather difficult, unless she could get some employment to eke out her means. She knew perfectly well that without her husband's signature, the cautious French bankers and men of business who held his property in their hands, would not advance much, if any, of it to her, unless proofs were forthcoming of his death. She possessed a little income of her own: it was available, and she must concert ways and means of its being transmitted to her in secret, without Greylands learning who she was, and what she was. This might be done: but the money would not be enough to support her and her child comfortably as gentlewomen.

"I think I should like to make a sojourn here in Greylands," she observed to M. Bent, cautiously opening the subject, on the first day that Marie could be pronounced convalescent, and was taken down in the parlour for a change.

"Why! should you, ma'am!" returned the landlady briskly. "Well, it's a nice place."

"I like the sea—and I should wish my little one to remain quiet now. I have suffered too much anxiety on her account to take her travelling again just yet."

"Sweet little thing!" aspirated Mrs. Bent. "Her pretty rosy colour is beginning to come back to her cheeks again. I've never seen a child with a brighter."

"It is like her—like that of some of our relatives: they have a bright colour," said Madame Guise, who only just saved herself from saying—

like her father's. "For her sake I will remain here for some two or three months. Do you think I could get an apartment?"

"An apartment!" repeated Mrs. Bent, who took the word literally, and was somewhat puzzled at it. "Did you mean one single room, ma'am."

"I mean two or three rooms—as might be enough. Or a small house—what you call a cottage."

"Oh, I see, ma'am," said the landlady. "I think you might do that. Some of the larger cottages let rooms in the summer to people coming over here from Stilborough for the sea air. And there's one pretty furnished cottage empty on the cliff."

"Would the rent of it be much?" asked Madame Guise, timorously, for a whole furnished cottage seemed a large enterprise.

"Next to nothing at this season," spoke Mrs. Bent, confidentially. "Here, John Bent—where are you?" she cried, flinging open the door. "What's the rent of that place—"

"Master's out," interrupted Molly, coming from the back kitchen to speak.

"Just like him!" retorted Mrs. Bent. "He is out when he's wanted, and at home when he's not. It's always the way with the men. Any way it's a nice little place, ma'am, and I know it would be reasonable."

The cottage she alluded to had a sitting-room, a kitchen, and two bedchambers, and was situated in the most picturesque part of all the cliff, close to the neatly kept cottage that had so long been inhabited by Miss Hallet and her very pretty niece. It was plainly furnished, and might be let at this season, including steel knives and forks, for fifteen shillings a week, Mrs. Bent thought. In summer the rent would be twenty-five: and the tenant had to find linen.

Madame Guise made a silent computation. Fifteen shillings a week! With the rent, and the cost of a servant, and housekeeping, and various little extras that are somehow never computed beforehand, but that rise up inevitably afterwards, she saw that the sum total would be more than she could command. And she hesitated to take the cottage.

Nevertheless, she went with Mrs. Bent to see it, and found it just what she would have liked. It was not quite so nice as Miss Hallet's a few yards off: but Miss Hallet took so much care that hers should be perfection.

"If I could but earn a little money!" repeated Charlotte to herself. "I wonder whether those good ladies at the Grey Nunnery could help me! I have a great mind to ask them."

After some deliberation, she went over to do so. It was a warm, pleasant day; for the capricious weather had once more changed; the snow and frost given place to soft west winds and genial sunshine—and Madame Guise was shown into the reception parlour. Sisters Margaret and Grizzel sat in it, and rose at her entrance. They had heard of this lady traveller, who had been detained on her journey by the illness of her little girl, and was staying at the Dolphin; but they had not seen her. It was with some curiosity, therefore, that the ladies gazed to see what she was like. A slender, ladylike, nice-looking, young woman, with blue eyes and fair hair, and who seemed to carry some care on her countenance.

Madame Guise introduced herself; apologising for her intrusion, and telling them at once its object. She wished to make some stay at Greylands, for she thought the pure air and sea-breezes would strengthen her child—could the ladies help her to some employment by which she might earn a trifle. She had a little income, but not quite sufficient. She could teach music and French, or do fine needlework; embroidery and the like.

The ladies answered her very kindly—they were both taken with the gentle stranger—but shook their heads to her petition: they had no help to give.

"The children we bring up here are of poor parentage and do not need accomplishments," said Sister Margaret. "If they did, we should teach them in the Nunnery: indeed we should be thankful to get pupils of a better class ourselves, for we are but poor. Sister Mona is a good French scholar; and Sister Charlotte's music is perfect. As to fine work, we do not know anyone who requires it to be done."

"Not but that we should have been glad to help you, if we could," put in Sister Grizzel, with a pleasant smile.

Madame Guise rose, stifling a sigh. She saw exactly how it was—that the Grey Nunnery was about the last place able to assist her. In leaving the parlour, she met a lady, young and stately, who was entering it; one of wondrous beauty, tall, majestic, of gracious manner and presence.

"Our Superior, Sister Mary Ursula," said Sister Grizzel.

And Madame Guise knew that it was her husband's cousin—for Miss Castlemaine had joined the Sisterhood some days past. She wore the clear muslin cap over her luxuriant hair, but not the Grey habit, for she had not put aside the mourning for her father. In the magnificent dark eyes, in the bright complexion and in the beautiful features,

Madame Guise saw the likeness to her husband and to the rest of the Castlemaines. Sister Mary Ursula bowed and said a few gracious words: Madame Guise responded with one of her elaborate French curtseys, and passed onwards through the gate.

"So that hope has failed!" she thought, as she crossed over to the inn. "I might have known it would: with so many accomplished ladies among themselves, the Sisters cannot want other people's aid."

Buried in thought, perplexed as to what her future course should be, Madame Guise did not go at once indoors, but sat down on the bench outside the house. The window of the sitting-room, occupied by John Bent and his wife, stood open—for Mrs. Bent liked plenty of fresh air—and people were talking inside. On that same bench had sat more than once her unfortunate husband, looking at the water as she was looking, at the fishermen collected on the beach, at the boats out at sea, their white sails at rest in the calm of the sunshiny day. She was mentally questioning what else she could try, now that her mission to the Grey Sisters had failed, and wondering how little she and Marie could live upon, if she got nothing to do. Gradually the talking became clearer to her ear. She heard the landlady's voice and another voice: not John Bent's, but the young, free, ready voice of a gentleman. It was in truth Harry Castlemaine's; who, passing the inn, had turned in for a gossip.

"It seems to me like a great sacrifice, Mr. Harry," were the first distinct words that fell on Madame Guise's ear. "The Grey Ladies are very good and noble; next door to angels, I'm sure, when folks are sick; but it is not the right life for Miss Castlemaine to take to."

"We told her so until we were tired of telling it," returned Harry Castlemaine. "It has cut up my father grievously. We will drop the subject, Mrs. Bent: I cannot speak of it with patience yet. How is the sick child getting on?"

"As well as can be, sir. She is just now upstairs in her midday sleep. Talking of children, though," broke off Mrs. Bent, "what is this mishap that has happened to Miss Flora? We hear she met with some accident yesterday."

"Mounted to the top of the gardener's ladder and fell off it," said Harry, with equanimity. "She is always in mischief."

"And was she hurt, sir?"

"Not much. Grazed her face in a few places and put her wrist out. She will come to greater grief unless they get somebody to take care of her. Having been so long without a governess, the young damsel is like a wild colt."

"The last time Mrs. Castlemaine passed by here on foot, Mr. Harry, she told me she had just engaged a governess. It must be a fortnight ago."

"And so she had engaged one; but the lady was taken ill and threw up the situation. Mrs. Castlemaine is hard to please in the matter of governesses. She must have perfect French and perfect music: and the two, united with other requisite qualifications, seem difficult to find. Mrs. Castlemaine was talking this morning of advertising."

"Dear me! to think that such a fine post as that should be going a begging!" cried the landlady. "A gentleman's home and a plenty of comfort in it, and—and however much pay is it a year, Mr. Harry?"

"Fifty guineas, I think," said the young man carelessly, as though fifty-guinea salaries were an every day trifle. Mrs. Bent lifted her hands and eyes.

"Fifty guineas!—and her bed and board. And only one little lady to teach; and gentlefolks to live with! My goodness! Mr. Harry, one would think half the ladies in England would jump at it."

One lady at least was ready to "jump" at it: she who sat outside, overhearing the tale. The lips of Charlotte Guise parted as she listened; her cheeks flushed red with excitement. Oh, if she herself could obtain this place!—become an inmate of the house where dwelt her husband's enemy, James Castlemaine! How seemingly clear and straightforward would be her path of discovery then, compared with what it would be in that cottage on the cliff, or with any other position she could hope to be placed in! She could daily, hourly watch Mr. Castlemaine; and it must surely be her fault if she did not track home the deed to him! As to her fitness for the post, why French was her native language, and in music she was a finished artiste: and she could certainly undertake general instruction!

While the red flush was yet on her face, the light of excitement in her eyes, Harry Castlemaine came out. Seeing her sitting there, he guessed who she was, took off his hat and politely accosted her, saying he was glad to hear the little girl was improving. Madame Guise rose. It was the first time she had spoken to him.

"I thank you, sir, for your good wishes: yes, she is getting well now. And I—I beg your pardon, sir—I think I heard you just now say to Madame Bent (the window is open) that you found it difficult to get a governess for your house."

"My people find it so. Why?—do you know of one?" he added, smiling.

"I think I do, sir."

"Mrs. Castlemaine is very difficult to please, especially as regards French," he said still smiling; "and the French of some of the ladies who have applied has turned out to be very English French, so they would not suit her. Should you chance to know of any one really eligible, madam, you would be conferring a favour in introducing the lady to the notice of Mrs. Castlemaine."

"Sir, I will think of it."

He lifted his hat again as he wished her good-day. And Madame Guise, gazing after him, thought again that Heaven was surely working for her, in thus opening a prospect of entrance to the house of Mr. Castlemaine.

XV

Getting in by Deceit

Turning out of the Dolphin Inn, by its front entrance, went Charlotte Guise, in her morning attire. It was a bright afternoon, and the fields were green again. They lay on either side her road—the inland coach road that the stage was wont to traverse. Leaving Mr. Parker's house on her left—for it was in this spot that the doctor's residence was situated—she presently came to the turning to Greylands' Rest, and passed on up the avenue. It was a wide avenue, and not far short of half a mile in length, with trees on either side; oak, elm, birch, larch, poplar, lime, and others. At its end was the gate admitting to the domain of Greylands' Rest.

The house lay still and quiet in the sunshine. Madame Guise looked at it with yearning eyes, for it was the place that had probably cost her poor husband his life. But for putting in his claim to it, he might be living yet: and whether that claim was a right or a wrong one, she hoped with her whole heart would be proved before she herself should die. Opening the gate, and passing round the fine green lawn, among the seats, the trees, the shrubs and the flower-beds, she gained the porch entrance. Miles answered her ring at the bell.

"Can I see Mrs. Castlemaine?"

"Mrs. Castlemaine is out in the carriage, ma'am. Mr. Castlemaine is at home."

Hesitating a moment, for the very name of the Master of Greylands carried to the heart of Charlotte Guise a shrinking dread, and yet fearful lest delay might cause her application to be too late, she said she would be glad to speak with Mr. Castlemaine. Miles admitted her into the hall—a good, old-fashioned room, with a wood fire blazing in it. Along a passage to the right lay the drawing-room, and into this room Miles ushered the lady.

Mrs. Castlemaine generally went out for a drive once a day. This afternoon she had taken Flora; whose face was adorned with sundry patches of sticking-plaster, the result of the fall off the ladder. In the red parlour sat Ethel Reene, painting flowers on cardboard for a hand-screen: and the Master of Greylands stood with his back to the fire, talking with her. They were speaking of Miss Castlemaine.

"Papa, I do not think we must hope it," Ethel was saying. "Rely upon it, Mary will not come out again."

Mr. Castlemaine's face darkened at the words. Though holding the same conviction himself, the step his niece had taken in entering the Nunnery was so unpalatable to him that he could not bear to hear the opinion confirmed or alluded to. He hated the Grey Sisters. He would have rid Greylands of their presence, had it been in his power.

"It is a sin, so to waste her life!" he said, his deep tones betraying his mortification. "Ethel, I think we cannot have made her happy here."

"It was nothing of that, papa. She told me she had been cherishing the idea before she came to Greylands."

"A meddling, tattling, tabby-cat set of women! Mary Ursula ought to——Well, what now, Miles?" For the man had entered the room and was waiting to speak.

"A lady has come here, sir, asking to see Mrs. Castlemaine. When I said the mistress was out, she said she would be glad to speak a few words to you. She is in the drawing-room, sir."

"What lady is it?" returned the Master of Greylands.

"Well, sir, I'm not altogether sure, but I fancy it is the one staying at the Dolphin; her with the sick child. Anyway, she's a very nice, pleasant-looking young lady, sir, whoever it is."

"I'm sure I don't know what she can want with me," remarked Mr. Castlemaine, as he walked off to the drawing-room, and laid his hand on the door. But thought is quick: and a fancy of what might have brought her here came across his mind ere he turned the handle.

She was seated near the fire in the handsome but low-ceilinged room; her face studiously turned from the one conspicuous portrait that hung opposite the chimney-glass, for its likeness to her husband had struck on her with a chill. She rose at Mr. Castlemaine's entrance and curtseyed as only a Frenchwoman can curtsey. He saw an elegant looking young woman with a pleasing countenance and somewhat shrinking manner. Mr. Castlemaine took her to be timid; probably unused to society: for in these, the opening minutes of the interview, she trembled visibly. He, of course, had heard with the rest of Greylands, of the lady traveller who had cut short her journey at the Dolphin Inn an consequence of the illness of her child, and who was supposed to be going on again as soon as she could. Mr. Castlemaine had thought no more about it than that. But the idea that crossed him now was, that this lady, having to encounter the detention at the inn, might be finding herself short of funds to pursue her journey, and had come to apply to him in the difficulty. Readily, would he have responded; for he had a generous hand, an open heart. To hear, therefore, what the real object of her visit was—that of soliciting the situation of governess, vacant in his household, surprised him not a little.

The tale she told was plausible. Mr. Castlemaine, utterly unsuspicious in regard to her, doubted nothing of its truth. The lady made a favourable impression on him, and he was very courteous to her.

She was a widow, she said: and she had come over from Paris to this country for two objects. One was to seek out a relative that she believed was somewhere in it, though she did not know for certain whether he was dead or alive; the other was to obtain employment as a governess—for she had been given to understand that good French governesses were at a premium in the English country, and her own means were but slender, not adequate to the support of herself and little girl. Journeying along by coach, she had found her child attacked with fever, which compelled her to halt at Greylands. Liking the place, perceiving that it was open and healthy, she had been thinking that she should do well to keep her child in it for a time, and therefore was hoping to make her arrangements to do so. Should she be so fortunate as to obtain the post in Mr. Castlemaine's household, the thing would be easy. Very plausibly did she tell the tale; turning, however, hot and cold alternately all the while, and detesting herself for the abhorred deceit.

"But—pardon me, madam—what, in that case, would you do with the child?" asked Mr. Castlemaine.

"I would place her at nurse with some good woman, sir. That would not be difficult. And the little thing would enjoy all the benefit of the sea-air. In my country, children are more frequently brought up at nurse than at home."

"I have heard so," observed Mr. Castlemaine. "You speak English remarkably well, madam, for a Frenchwoman. Have you been much in this country?"

"Never before, sir. My mother was English, and she always talked to me in her own tongue. I was reared in her faith—the protestant. My father was French, and a Catholic. Upon their marriage it was agreed that, of the children to be born, the boys should be brought up in his faith and the girls in hers. There came no boy, however; and only one girl—me."

All this was true. Madame Guise did not add, for it was unnecessary, that towards the close of her father's life he entered into large speculations, and became a ruined man. He and her mother were both dead now. She said just what she was obliged to say, and no more.

"And it is. I presume, to see your mother's relatives that you have come to England?" pursued Mr. Castlemaine.

"Yes, sir," she answered after a moment of hesitation; for it came indeed hard to Charlotte Guise to tell a deliberate untruth, although necessity might justify it. "My mother used to talk much of one relative that she had here—a brother. He may not be living now: I do not know."

"In what part of England did he live?"

"I think he must have been a traveller, sir, for he seemed to move about. We would hear of him, now in the south of England, now in the north, and now in the west. Mostly he seemed to be in what my mother called remote countries—Cumberland and Westmoreland."

"Cumberland and Westmoreland!" echoed Mr. Castlemaine. "Dear me! And have you no better clue to him than that?"

"No better, sir; no other. I do not, I say, know whether he is dead or alive."

"Well, it seems—pardon me—to be a somewhat wild-goose chase that you have entered on, this search for him. What is his name?"

"My mother's maiden name was Williams. He was her brother."

Mr. Castlemaine shook his head. "A not at all uncommon name," he said, "and I fear, madam, you might find some difficulty in tracing him out."

"Yes, I fear so. I find those places are very far off. At any rate, I will not think more of it for the present. My little child, I see it now, is too young to travel."

In all this account, Madame Guise had spoken the simple truth. The facts were as she stated. The only falsehood in it was, the representation that it was this relative, this never-yet-met uncle, she had come over to search out. During her long journey, through France, she had said to herself that after she had found her husband, they might perhaps go together to seek her uncle: but that was all.

"Yes, the little one is too young and delicate to travel," pursued Madame Guise, "and I dare not take her on. This illness of hers has frightened me, and I shall, if possible, remain here by the sea."

"I presume, madam—pardon me—that you were hoping to obtain help from this uncle."

"Yes," was the answer, given falteringly. "Should you admit me into your house, sir, I will do my best to help on the studies of your daughter."

"But—will you reconcile yourself to fill a situation of this kind in a stranger's house after having ruled in a home of your own?" questioned Mr. Castlemaine, considerately, as he remembered his wife's domineering and difficult temper.

"Ah, sir, the beggars, you know, must not be the choosers. I must do something to keep me, and I would like to do this."

"The salary Mrs. Castlemaine offers is fifty guineas."

"It seems a large sum to me, sir," was the truthful and candid answer. "Appointments in France, a very few excepted, are not so highly paid as in England. I should of course be permitted to go out to see my child?"

"Dear me, yes: whenever you pleased, madam. You would be quite at liberty here—be as one of ourselves entirely. Mrs. Castlemaine—but here she is; returning home."

The Master of Greylands had heard the carriage drawing up. He quitted the room, and said a few hasty words to his wife of what had occurred. Mrs. Castlemaine, much taken with the project, came in, in her black satin pelisse, coated with crape. She sat down and put a few questions as to the applicant's acquirements.

"I am a brilliant pianist, madam, as I know you sometimes phrase it in your country," said Madame Guise. "My French is of course pure; and I could teach dancing. Not drawing; I do not understand it."

"Drawing is quite a minor consideration," replied Mrs. Castlemaine. "Could you undertake the English?"

"Why not, madam? I am nearly as well read in English as in French. And I am clever at embroidery, and other kinds of fine and fancy needlework."

"Do you fully understand that you would have to undertake Miss Reene's music also? She is my stepdaughter."

"It would be a pleasure to me, madam. I am fond of music."

Mr. Castlemaine came into the room again at this juncture. "What part of France have you lived in?" he asked. "Did I understand you to say in Paris?"

Another necessary lie, or next door to one, for Charlotte Guise! Were she to say, "My native province is that of the Dauphiné, and I have lived near Gap," it might open their eyes to suspicion at once. She swallowed down a cough that rose, partly choking her.

MRS. HENRY WOOD

"Not quite in Paris, sir. A little beyond it."

"And—pardon me—could you give references?" Madame Guise looked up helplessly. The colour rose in her face; for the fear of losing the appointment became very present to her.

"I know not how. I never was a governess before; and in that respect no one could speak for me. I am of respectable family: my father was a rentier, and much considered. For myself, I am of discreet conduct and manners,—surely you cannot doubt it," she added, the tears of emotion rising to her eyes, as she looked at them.

They looked back in return: Mr. Castlemaine thinking what a nice, ladylike, earnest woman she was, one he could take on trust; Mrs. Castlemaine, entirely seduced by the prospect of the pure French for Flora, eagerly wanting to ratify the bargain. Madame Guise mistook the silence, supposing they were hesitating.

"I could have a letter written to you from Paris," she said. "I possess a friend there, who will, I am sure, satisfy you that I am of good conduct and family. Would there be more than this required?"

"Not any more, it would be quite sufficient," Mrs. Castlemaine hastened to say with emphasis. And, without waiting for the promised letter—which, as she observed could come later—she engaged the governess on the spot. Mr. Castlemaine attended Madame Guise to the door: and never a suspicion crossed him that she was—who she was. How should it? How was he likely to connect this lady-traveller— detained at the place by accident, so shy in manner, so evidently distressed for her child—with the unfortunate Anthony, lost since that fatal February night?

Madame Guise went out from the interview. In some respects it had not been satisfactory: or, rather, not in accordance with her ante-impressions. She had gone to it picturing Mr. Castlemaine as some great monster of iniquity, some crafty, cruel, sinister man, from whom the world might shrink. She found him a very good-looking, pleasing, and polished gentleman, with a high-bred air, a kind and apparently sincere manner, and with the wonderful face-resemblance to his brother Basil and to her own poor husband. How had it been possible, she asked herself, for so apparently correct a man to commit that most dreadful crime, and still be what he was? How wickedly deceitful some great criminals were!

Mrs. Bent, when consulted, made strong objection to the nursing scheme, expressing a most decided opinion against it. "Put the sweet little child to any one of those old women! Why, the next news we got would be that she had been let roll down the cliff, or had fell into the sea! I should not like to risk it for a child of mine, ma'am."

"I must do something with her," said Madame Guise, setting her lips tightly. Give up her plan, she would not; she believed Heaven itself had aided her in it; but no one knew how much it cost her to part with this great treasure, her child. From the hour of its birth, it had never been away from her. The devotion of some French women to their children seems as remarkable as is the neglect of others.

"There's one thing you might do with her, ma'am, if you chose—and a far better thing too than consigning her to any old nurse-woman."

"What is that?"

"Well, I'll take the liberty of suggesting it," cried Mrs. Bent. "Put her to the Grey Sisters."

"The Grey Sisters!" echoed Madame Guise, struck with the suggestion. "But would they take one so young, think you? A little child who can scarcely speak!"

"I think they'd take her and be glad of it. Why, ma'am, children are like playthings to them. They have the fishermen's children there by day to teach and train; and they keep 'em by night too when the little ones are sick."

No suggestion could have been more welcome to Madame Guise. The wonder was, that she had not herself thought of it: she no doubt would have done so had Marie been older. To put the matter at rest, she went over at once to the Nunnery. Sister Charlotte received her, and heard her proposal joyfully.

Admit a dear little child as boarder amongst them! Yes, that they would; and take the most loving care; and train her, they hoped, to find the road to Heaven. They would be glad to have two or three little ones of the better class, no matter what the age; the bit of money paid for them would be an assistance, for the Sisterhood was but poor. Though, indeed, now that the new Sister, Mary Ursula—Miss Castlemaine— had joined them, they were better off.

"I am so glad to hear you say she may come," said Madame Guise. "I had feared my little one was too young. She must have everything done for her, and she cannot speak plainly. English she does not speak at all, though she understands it."

"She will soon speak it with us: and we will try and make her quite happy. But I must summon our Superior," added Sister Charlotte, "for I may not take upon myself to decide this, though I know how welcome it will be."

The Superior came in, in the person of Miss Castlemaine.

Alas, no longer to be called so—but Sister Mary Ursula. She swept in, in her silk mourning dress, and with the muslin cap shading her beautiful hair, and greeted Madame Guise with all her winning and gracious manner, holding out her hand in welcome. In some turn of the face, or in some glance of the eye—it was hard to define what—so strong a likeness to the lost and ill-fated Anthony momentarily shone out from Miss Castlemaine's countenance, that poor Madame Guise felt faint. But she had to control all feeling now; she had passed into another character and left herself out of sight behind.

Seated opposite to her, giving to her her best attention, her fine head gently bent, her soft, but brilliant eyes thrown upon her, Sister Mary Ursula listened to the story Madame Guise told. She had engaged herself as governess at Greylands' Rest, and wished to be allowed to place her child with the Grey Ladies.

"Is the situation at Greylands' Rest one that you think will suit you?—do you feel that it is what you will like to undertake?" Miss Castlemaine inquired when the speaker paused: for at the first moment she had thought that it was only her opinion that was being asked.

"Yes, I do. I am very much pleased to have obtained it."

"Then I can only say that I hope you will be happy in it, and find it all you can wish. I am sure you will like my uncle. Your pupil, Miss Flora Castlemaine, is self-willed, and has been much indulged by her mother. You will be able, I trust, to bring her to better ways."

"And you will take my little girl, madam?"

"Certainly. It is very good of you to confide her to us."

"It is very good of you to agree to take her, madam. I am so glad! And how much shall I pay you for her? Say by the trimestre—the three months?"

Miss Castlemaine shook her head with a smile. "I have not been here long enough to act on my own judgment," she said: "upon all knotty points I consult Sister Mildred. We will let you know in the course of the day."

Madame Guise rose. But for the dreadful suspicion that lay upon her, the crime she was going out of her own character to track, she would have liked to throw herself into the arms of this gracious lady, and say with tears, "You are my husband's cousin. Oh, pity me, for I was

Anthony's wife!" But it might not be. She had entered on her task, and must go through with it.

And when a dainty little note in Sister Margaret's writing was brought over to the Dolphin in the evening by Sister Ann, Madame Guise found that the ladies had fixed a very small sum as payment for her child—four pounds the quarter: or, sixteen pounds the year.

"Cent francs par trimestre," commented Madame Guise in her own language. "It is quite moderate: but Marie is but a little one."

The child went over on the following day. She was entered as Mademoiselle Marie Guise. Very much astonished would those good ladies have been had they known her true name to be that of their Superior—Mary Ursula Castlemaine! There was no fear of the child betraying secrets. She was a very backward child, not only in speech; she seemed to have forgotten all about her father, and she could not have told the name of her native place, where it was, or anything about it, if questioned over so. Trouble was expected with her at the parting. Her mother was advised not to attempt to see her for some three or four days after she went over to the Nunnery: but rather to give her time to get reconciled to the change, and to this new abode.

It was cruel penance to the mother, this parting; worse than it could have been to the child. Those who understand the affection of some French mothers for their children, and who remember that the little ones never leave their side, will know what this must have been for Charlotte Guise. She saw Marie at a distance on the following day, Sunday—for it happened to be Saturday that the child went in. The little church was filled at the three o'clock afternoon service, when Parson Marston gabbled through the prayers and the sermon to the edification of his flock. Little Marie sat in the large pew with the Grey ladies, between Sister Mary Ursula in her black attire, and Sister Betsey in her grey. The latter who had a special love for children, had taken the little one under her particular charge. Marie was in black also: and a keen observer might have fancied there was some sort of likeness between her and the stately Head Sister beside her. The child looked happy and contented. To the scandal of the surrounders, no doubt far more to them than to that of the Parson himself, whose mouth widened with a laugh, she, happening to espy out her mother when they were standing up to say the belief, extended her hands, called out "Maman! maman!" and began to nod incessantly. Sister Betsey succeeded in restoring decorum.

Madame Guise sat with Mr. and Mrs. Bent, occupying the post of honour at the top of the pew. After that, she strove to hide herself from Marie. In the square, crimson-curtained pew pertaining to Greylands' Rest, the only pew in the church with any pretensions to grandeur, sat the Master of Greylands and his family: his wife with a pinched face, for she had contrived to take cold; Harry, tall as himself, free and fascinating; Flora staring about with the plaster patches on her face; and Ethel Reene, devout, modest, lovely. They were all in black: the mourning worn for Mr. Peter Castlemaine. Their servants, also in mourning, occupied a pew behind that of the Grey Ladies. It might have been noticed that Mr. Castlemaine never once turned his head towards these ladies: he had never favoured them, and the step taken by his niece in joining their society had vexed him more materially than he would have liked to say. He had his private reasons for it: he had cause to wish those ladies backs turned on Greylands; but he had no power to urge their departure openly, or to send them by force away.

Very dull was poor Charlotte Guise all that Sunday evening. She would not meet the little one on coming out of church, but mixed with the people to avoid it. Her heart yearned to give a fond word, a tender kiss; but so anxiously bent was she upon entering Greylands' Rest, that she shrank from anything that might impede it, or imperil the child's stay at the Nunnery. After taking tea in her parlour, she sat awhile in her own room above stairs indulging her sadness. It was sometimes worse than she knew how to bear. She might not give way to grief, distress, anguish in the presence of the world; that might have betrayed her to suspicion; but there were moments, when alone, that she yielded to it in all its bitterness. The fathomless sea, calm to-night, was spread out before her, grey and dull, for the rays of the setting sun had left it: did that sea cover the body of him whom she had loved more than life? To her left rose the Friar's Keep—she could almost catch a glimpse of its dark walls if she stretched her head well out at the casement; at any rate, she could see this end of the Grey Nunnery, and that was something. Did that Friar's Keep, with its dark tales, its superstitions stories—did that Keep contain the mystery? She fully believed it did. From the very first, the description of the building had seized on her mind, and left its dread there. It was there she must look for the traces of her husband's fate; perhaps even for himself. Yes, she believed that the grim walls covered him, not the heaving sea.

"Oh Anthony! my ill-fated, wronged husband!" she cried, raising her clasped hands upwards in her distress and speaking through her blinding tears, "may the good God help me to bring your fate to light!"

The shades of twilight were deepening. Fishermen, with their wives and children, were wending their way homewards after the Sunday evening's walk—the one walk taken together of the seven days. Two of the Grey Ladies came down from the cliff and went towards the Nunnery: Madame Guise, who by this time had made acquaintance with some of the inhabitants, wondered whether anybody was ill in the cottages there. A good many dwellings were scattered on this side of the cliff: some of them pretty, commodious homes, others mere huts.

Once more, as she stood there at the casement window, Charlotte Guise asked herself whether she was justified in thus entering Greylands' Rest under a false aspect—justified even by the circumstances. She had revolved the question in her mind many times during the past few days, and the answer had always been, as it was now, in the affirmative. And she was of a straightforward, honourable nature; although the reader may be disposed to judge the contrary. That Mr. Castlemaine had taken her husband's life; taken it in wilful malice and wickedness, that he might retain his usurpation of Greylands' Rest, she did not entertain a shade of doubt of: she believed, religiously believed, that the mission of tracking out this crime was laid upon her by Heaven: and she did consider herself justified in taking any steps that might forward her in it; any steps in the world, overhanded or underhanded, short of doing injury to any innocent person. Her original resolve had been, merely to stay in the village, seek out what information she could, and wait; but the opportunity having been offered her in so singularly marked a manner (as she looked upon it) of becoming an inmate of Mr. Castlemaine's home, she could not hesitate in embracing it. And yet, though she never faltered in her course, though an angel from Heaven would hardly have stopped her entrance, believing, as she did, that the entrance had been specially opened for her, every now and again qualms of conscience pricked her sharply, and she hated the whole proceeding.

"But I cannot leave Anthony alone in the unknown grave," she would piteously tell herself at these moments. "And I can see no other way to discovery; and I have no help from any one to aid me in it. If I entered upon the investigation openly, declaring who I am, that might be worse than fruitless: it would put Mr. Castlemaine on his guard; he is more clever than I, he has all power here, while I have none; and Anthony might remain where he is, unavenged, for ever. No, no, I must go on in my planned-out course."

The sea became more grey; the evening star grew bright in the sky; people had gone within their homes and the doors were shut. Madame Guise, tired with the wearily-passing hours, sick and sad at her own reflections, put on her bonnet and warm mantle to take a bit of a stroll over to the beach. Mrs. Bent happened to meet her as she gained the passage below. The landlady was looking so unusually cross that Madame Guise noticed it.

"I have been giving a word of a sort to Mr. Harry Castlemaine," she explained, as they entered her sitting-room. "You be quiet, John Bent: what I see right to do, I shall do. Mr. Harry will go too far in that quarter if he does not mind."

"Young men like to talk to pretty girls all the world over; they did in my time, I know, and they do in this," was John's peaceful answer, as he rose from his fire-side chair at his guest's entrance. "Bat I don't see, wife, that it's any good reason for your pouncing upon Mr. Harry as he was going by to his home and saying what you did."

"Prevention's better than cure," observed Mrs. Bent, in a short tone. "As to young men liking to talk to pretty girls, that's all very well when they are equals in life; but when it comes to a common sailor's daughter and a gentleman, it's a different thing."

"Jane Hallet's father was not a common sailor!"

"He was not over much above it," retorted Mrs. Bent. "Because the Grey Sisters educated her and made much of her, would you exalt her into a lady? you never had proper sense, John Bent, and never will have.

"I call Miss Hallet a lady," said John.

"You might call the moon a lantern if you chose, but you couldn't make other folks do it. As to Jane, she is too pretty to be followed by Mr. Harry Castlemaine. Why, he must have been walking with her nearly ever since tea!"

"He intends no harm, Dorothy, I'll answer for it."

"Harm comes sometimes without intention, John Bent. Mr. Harry's as thoughtless and random as a March hare. I've seen what I have seen: and Jane Hallet had better keep herself in future out of his company."

"Well, your speaking to him did no good, wife. And it was not respectful."

"Good! it's not likely it would do good with him," conceded Mrs. Bent. "He turns everything into laughter. Did you hear how he began about my Sunday cap, asking for the pattern of it, and setting Molly off in a grin! She nearly dropped the scuttle of coals she was bringing in—good evening then, ma'am, for the present, if you are going for your little stroll."

Madame Guise, leaving her host and hostess to settle their difference touching Mr. Harry Castlemaine, went over to the beach and walked about there. The shades grew deeper; the stars came out brightly: night was upon the earth when she retraced her steps. Thinking of her little one, she did not go into the inn, but walked past the Grey Nunnery: she knew she should not see the child, but it was a satisfaction only to look at the window of the room that contained her. Soon Madame Guise came to the gate of the chapel ruins; and some impulse prompted her to open it and enter. But she first of all looked cautiously around to make sure she was not being watched: once let it be known that she held any particular interest in this place, and her connection with him who had been lost within it might be suspected! When we hold a dangerous secret, the conscience is more than sensitive: and Madame Guise was no exception to the rule.

She crossed the ruins, and stood looking out on the sea, so grand from thence. It was low water; she saw the rude steps by which the little beach below might be gained, but would not have liked to venture down. The steps were hazardous for even a strong man, and perhaps were not used from one month's end to another: the slime and sea-weed made them slippery. After she had gazed her fill, she turned to the Friar's Keep, and made her way into it by the gothic door between the once firm walls.

Oh, but it was dark here! By what she could make out, when her sight got used to the gloom, she seemed to be amidst the arches of some pillared cloisters. While looking on this side and that side, striving to pierce the mysteries, taking a step this way and a step that, and trembling all the while lest she should see the revenant, said to haunt the place, a dreadful sound, like the huge fluttering of large wings, arose above in the arches. Poor Charlotte Guise, superstitious by nature and education, and but young in years yet, was seized with a perfect acme of terror; of terror too great to scream. Was it the spirit of her husband, striving to communicate with her, she wondered—and oh blame her not too greatly. She had been reared in the fear of "revenants;" she earnestly believed that the dead were sometimes permitted to revisit the earth. Silence supervened, and her terror grew somewhat less intense. "Is your grave here, Anthony?" she murmured; "are you buried in some corner of this lonesome place, away from the eye of man? Oh, hear me while I repeat my vow to search out this dreadful mystery! To the utmost of the power that circumstances and secrecy leave me, will I strive to find you, Anthony; and bring home to Mr. Castlemaine—"

A worse noise than before; an awful fluttering and flapping right above her head. She screamed out now, terrified nearly to death. The echoes repeated her scream; and the rushing wings, with another kind of scream, not half so shrill as hers, went out through the broken wall and flew across the sea. She felt just as though she were dropping into her grave. Was it the revenant of the place?—or was it the revenant of her husband?—what was it? Cowering there, her face prone against a column, Charlotte asked herself these dread questions: and never once, until her alarm was somewhat subsiding, did she think of what her reason might have shown her at first—that it was an owl. An owl, angry at its precincts being invaded: or perhaps some large sea-bird.

With her face as white as death, and her limbs shaking as though in an ague fit, she made her way to the entrance gate again; passed through it, and so got away from the Friar's Keep.

XVI

AT GREYLANDS' REST

N ow, mademoiselle, je n'eh veux pas."

"Because Ethel understands French as well as you do, that's no reason why I should. If you tell me in French what I have to do, of course I can't do it, for I don't know a word you say."

It was the first morning of the studies, Tuesday, Madame Guise having entered the previous day. She, Ethel, and Flora were seated round the table in the schoolroom, a small apartment looking to the kitchen-garden, with an old carpet on its floor, painted segged chairs, and a square piano against the wall opposite the fire. Ethel was copying music. Madame Guise was endeavouring to ascertain the advancement of Miss Flora in her studies, with a view to arranging their course in future, speaking in French, and requiring the replies to be in French. But the young lady obstinately persisted in making them in English.

"Whatever you do, Madame Guise, please speak always to Flora in French," had been Mrs. Castlemaine's first charge to the new governess. "Above all things, I wish her to be a good French scholar, and to speak it as fluently as Miss Reene does." But here, at the very outset, Miss Flora was demurring to the French, and protesting she could not understand it.

Madame Guise hesitated. She did not choose to be met by wilful disobedience; on the other hand, to issue her mandates in an unknown language would be simply waste of time. She turned her eyes questioningly on Ethel. "I am not quite sure, madame, one way or the other," said Ethel, replying in French. "Flora ought to be able to understand it; and to speak it a little too; but she has always been inattentive. Miss Oldham and the governesses who preceded her did not speak French as you do: perhaps they were not particular that Flora should speak it."

"How is it that you speak it so well?" asked Madame.

"I? Oh, I had a French nurse when I was a child, and then a French governess; and to finish my education I went to Paris for two years."

"All the three governesses I have had here did not speak French to me," interrupted Flora, resentfully. "Not one of them."

"Have you had three governesses? That is a great many, considering you are yet young," observed Madame, in English.

"They were all bad ones," said the girl.

"Or was it that you were a bad pupil You must be a better one with me."

Ethers shapely head, with its bright dark hair, was bent over her copying again: she said nothing. Madame Guise determined to speak in English to the child for at least this morning, until the studies should be put in train.

"We will begin with your English grammar"—taking up the dog-eared, untidy book. "How far have you advanced in it, Miss Flora?"

"I don't like grammar."

"How far have you advanced in it?" equably pursued Madame.

"I don't recollect."

"To begin English grammar again," spoke Madame, addressing herself, and making a note on paper with a pencil.

"I shan't begin it again."

"You will not say to me I shall or I shan't; you will do what I please," quietly corrected Madame. "This is your English History. What reign are you in?"

Miss Flora had her elbows on the table, her hands under her chin, and her pretty face pushed out defiantly opposite Madame. The patches of plaster were nearly all gone; her light curls tied back with a black ribbon, hang low behind. She wore a black frock and white pinafore.

"Which of the king's reigns are you in?" pursued Madame.

"Not in any. I know them all. Charles the Second was beheaded; and Henry the Eighth had ten wives: and Guy Faux blew up the gunpowder plot; and Elizabeth boxed people's ears."

"Oh," said Madame, "I think we shall have to begin that again. Are you good at spelling?"

"I can't spell at all. I hate it. Mamma says I need not learn to spell."

"I fancy that cannot be true. How will you write letters if you cannot spell?"

"Who wants to write letters?—I don't."

"Flora!" put in Ethel in a warning tone.

The girl turned angrily on Ethel. "Nobody asked you to speak: mind your copying."

"Mind your manners, said Ethel nodding to her.

"Not for you, or for anybody else in this room."

"It is very unpleasant to hear young ladies say these rude things," interposed Madame. "As your governess, Miss Flora, I shall not permit it."

"That's what my other governesses would say," retorted Flora. "It made no difference to me."

"If the other governesses did not do their duty by you, it is no reason why I should not do mine," said Madame. "Your papa has charged me with forming your manners; if I have trouble in doing it I am to appeal to him."

Flora was silent. The one only authority she feared, in the house or out of it, was her father's. He would not be trifled with, however her mother might be.

"I hate governesses, Madame Guise. I'd like to know what they were invented for?"

"To teach ignorant and refractory children to become good young ladies," spoke Madame, who did not seem in the least to lose her temper. Flora did not like the calmness: it augured badly for the future. It was so totally unlike her experience of former governesses. They were either driven wild, or had subsided into a state of apathy.

"I drove those other governesses away, and I'll drive you. I'll never do anything you tell me. I won't learn and I won't practise."

"The less you learn, the more persistently I will stay on to make you," said Madame, quite unruffled. "A lesson that you do not get by heart to-day, you will have to get to-morrow: the studies broken off this week, must be completed next. As to your trying to drive me away, it will be labour lost; I simply tell you I am not to be driven. If there is anything I like, and for which I think I have an especial fitness, it is the ruling of refractory children. We shall see which will be strongest, Miss Flora, you or I."

"Once, when one of my governesses wanted to make me learn, I had a fever. Mamma said it was all her fault."

"Very good," said Madame. "We will risk the fever. If you get one I will nurse you through it. I am a capital nurse."

Ethel burst out laughing. "The fever was a headache, Flora; you brought it on with crying."

"You ugly story-teller! I did have a fever. I lay in bed and had broth."

"Yes, for a day. Why, you have never had a fever in your life. Mr. Parker saw you and brought some medicine; you would not take it and got up."

"Ugh! you old tell-tale!"

"Come to my side, Miss Flora," spoke Madame. "You will stand here and read a little of French and of English that I may see how you read. And I must tell you that if we have not got through this morning what we want to get through and put the studies en train, I shall not allow you to go out this afternoon, and I shall request that you have no dinner. Instead of that, you will stay in this room with me. Mind! I never break my word."

After a few moments' delay, the young lady moved round. Probably she saw that her new mistress was not one to break her word. And, thus, a beginning made, the morning wore away rather better than its commencement had promised. Never was there a child with better abilities than Flora Castlemaine: it was only the will to use them that was lacking. She had been brought up to exercise her own will and disobey that of others. Bad training! bad training for a child.

Putting aside the difficulties attending the instruction and management of Miss Flora, Madame Guise found the residence at Greylands' Rest not at all an unpleasant one. The routine of the day was this. Breakfast—which meal was taken all together in the red parlour— at eight o'clock. Flora until dinner-time; half-past one. Ethel's music lesson of an hour, was given during the afternoon: Flora being generally out with her mamma or racing about the premises and grounds on her own account. Tea at five; one hour given to Flora afterwards, to help her to prepare her lessons or exercises for the following day: and then Madame's duties were over.

Little did Mr. Castlemaine imagine that the pleasant, though always sad young lady, who was so efficient an instructress for the young plague of the house, was his ill-fated nephew's widow. He was somewhat taken aback when he heard that Madame Guise had placed her child at the Grey Nunnery, and knitted his brow in displeasure. However, the child's being there, so long as the ladies were, could make no difference to him; it was the Sisterhood he wanted away, not the child.

Charlotte Guise never went out during the day—except on Sundays to church. Ethel would try to coax her abroad in the afternoons, but hitherto she had not succeeded. In the evening, after Flora was done with, Madame would put her bonnet on and stroll alone: sometimes to the Nunnery to see her child, whose enforced absence only made her the dearer to her mother's heart.

"Why will you not go out with me?" asked Ethel one afternoon, when she and Madame Guise rose from the piano in the red parlour—for the old square piano in the schoolroom was for the benefit of the unskilled fingers of Miss Flora only. "See how pleasant everything looks! It is quite spring weather now."

"Yes, it is spring weather, but I feel a little cold always, and I don't care to go," answered Madame Guise. "I will go when summer comes."

They sat down before the French window, Ethel opening it to the pleasant air. Madame Guise had been wishing ever since she was in the house to put a question to this fair young girl, whom she had already learned to love. But she had not yet dared to do it: conscience was always suggesting fears of her true identity being discovered: and now that she did speak it was abruptly.

"Have any tidings been heard yet of the young man said to have been lost in the Friar's Keep?"

"No, not any," replied Ethel.

"Is it true, think you, that he was killed?"

Ethel Reene flushed painfully: she could not forget what she had overheard John Bent say.

"Oh, I hope not. Of course, his disappearance is very strange; more than strange. But if—if anything did happen to him that night, it might have been by accident."

"I heard about the matter when I was at the Dolphin," observed Madame Guise, as if wishing to account for speaking of it. "It took much hold upon my interest; it seemed so strange and sad. Did you ever see that Mr. Anthony, Ethel?"

"Yes, I saw him twice. I was prejudiced against him at first, but I grew to like him. I should have liked him very much had he lived; I am sure of it: quite as a brother. Miss Castlemaine of Stilborough liked him: and I think the mystery of his loss has lain heavily upon her."

"What prejudiced you against him?" asked Charlotte.

Ethel smiled, and told the tale. She gave the history of their two meetings; gave it in detail. The tongue is ready when it has a sympathetic hearer: never a more rapt one than she who listened now.

Ethel rose as she concluded it. The disappearance was a subject she did not care to speak of, or dwell upon. Unable to believe Mr. Castlemaine otherwise than innocent, she yet saw that a prejudice had arisen against him.

"Then you will not come out with me, madame?"

"Many thanks, but no."

"What will you do with yourself all day to-morrow?" asked Ethel.

"I shall take holiday," replied Madame Guise, with a flush of colour.

For on the morrow the whole of the family were going from home, having promised to spend the day with some friends who lived near Newerton.

The flush had been caused by Charlotte Guise's self-consciousness. True, she would take holiday on the morrow from her duties; that went as a matter of course; but she was purposing to use the day, or part of it, in endeavouring to make some discovery. These twelve days had she been in the house now, and she was no farther advanced than when she entered it. She had seen Mr. Castlemaine daily; she had conversed with him, dined and taken other meals in his company; but for all the enlightenment she had obtained, or the new ideas she had gathered of the doings of that ill-fated February night, he and she might as well have been far apart as are the two poles. It was not by going on in this tame way that she could hope to obtain any clue to the past: the past to which she had made a vow to devote herself.

The morning rose brightly, and the family went off after breakfast in the carriage, Harry sitting on the box with the coachman. Madame Guise was left alone.

A feverish desire had been upon her to enter Mr. Castlemaine's room upstairs; the study where he kept the accounts pertaining to the estate, and wrote his letters. In this room he passed many hours daily, sitting in it sometimes late into the night. Charlotte Guise held an impression that if she could find tokens or records of her lost husband, it would be there. But she had never yet obtained so much as a glimpse of its interior: the room was considered sacred to Mr. Castlemaine, and the family did not approach it.

Two or three of the women servants had obtained permission to absent themselves that day to visit their friends; and the house was comparatively deserted. Madame Guise, looking forth from her chamber, found all silent and still: the upstairs work was over; the servants, those who remained at home, were shut up in the remote kitchens. Now was her time; now, if ever.

The corridor was spacious. It ran along two sides of the house, and most of the bed chambers opened from it. Mr. Castlemaine's study was the middle room in the side corridor; Madame's bedroom was nearly opposite the room; the one beyond hers being Harry Castlemaine's.

Standing outside her door, in the still silence, with a flushed face and panting breath, not liking the work she was about to do, but believing it a necessity thrown upon her, she at length softly crossed the corridor and opened the outer door leading to the study. A short, dark, narrow passage not much more than a yard in length, and there was another door. This was locked, but the key was in it; she turned the key, and entered the room. Entered it with some undefined feeling of disappointment, for it was bare and empty.

We are all apt to form ideas of places and things as yet unseen. The picture of Mr. Castlemaine's study, in the mind of Charlotte Guise, had been of a spacious apartment filled with furniture, and littered with papers. What she saw was a small square room, and no earthly thing in it, papers or else, but two tables, some chairs, and a bureau against the wall: or what would have been called in her own land a large secretaire, or office desk. She gazed around her with a blank face.

The tables and chairs were bare: no opportunity there for anything concealed. The bureau was locked. She tried it; palled it, pushed it: but the closed-down lid was firm as adamant.

"If there exists any record of him, it is in here," she said, half aloud. "I must contrive means of opening it."

She could not do that to-day. It would have to be done with a false key, she supposed; and, that, she had not in her possession. Before quitting the room, she approached the window, and looked forth cautiously. At the sea rolling in the distance; at the Friars' Keep opposite; at the fair green lands lying between that and Greylands' Rest. Charlotte Guise shuddered at a thought that crossed her.

"If he did indeed kill my poor husband and has laid him to rest in the Friars' Keep, how can he bear to be in this room, with that building in front of him to remind him of the deed?"

The day was before her: it was not yet twelve o'clock. Blankly disappointed with her failure, she put on her things to go abroad: there was nothing to stay in for. At the last moment a thought struck her that she would go to Stilborough. She wanted to make some purchases; for the wardrobe brought over from France had not been extensive, either for herself or child. Hastily attiring herself, she told Miles she should not be in to dinner, and started.

And so, just as Anthony Castlemaine had once, and but once, set off to walk to the market-town, did his poor young wife—nay, his widow—set off now. She was a good walker, and, so far, enjoyed the journey and the sweet spring day. She saw the same objects of interest (or of non-interest, as people might estimate them) that he had seen: the tall, fine trees, now budding into life: the country carts and waggons; the clumsy milestones; the two or three farm houses lying back amid their barns and orchards. Thus she reached Stilborough, and did her commissions.

It was late when she got back to Greylands; five o'clock, and she was dead tired. By the time she reached the Dolphin, she could hardly drag one foot before the other. To walk three miles on a fine day is not much; but to go about afterwards from shop to shop, and then to walk back again is something more. Mrs. Bent, standing at the inn door, saw her, brought her in, and set her down to a substantial tea-table. She told the landlady she had been to Stilborough to make purchases—which would come by the van for her on the morrow, and to be left at the Dolphin, if the Dolphin would kindly take them in.

"With pleasure," said Mrs. Bent. "Ned shall take the parcels up to Greylands' Rest."

What with the welcome rest to her tired limbs, and what with Mrs. Bent's hospitable tea and gossip, Madame Guise sat longer than she had intended. It was nearly dark when she went over to the Nunnery—for she had brought a toy and some bonbons for Marie. The Grey Sisters received her as kindly as usual; but they told her the little one did not seem very well; and Madame Guise went upstairs to look at her. Marie was in her little bed, by the side of Sister Betsey's. She seemed restless and feverish. Poor Charlotte Guise began to think that perhaps this climate did not agree with her so well as their own. Taking off her things, she sat down to stay with the child.

"Mrs. Castlemaine said it would be quite midnight before they got home, as they were to make a very long day, so I am in no hurry for an hour or two," she observed. "Miles will think I am lost; but I will tell him how it is."

"Has your little one ever had the measles?" asked Sister Mona.

"The measles?" repeated Madame Guise, puzzled for the moment. "Oh, lea rougeoles—pardon my forgetfulness—no she has not. She has never had anything."

"Then I think, but I am not sure, that she is sickening for the measles now."

"Mon Dieu!" cried the mother in consternation.

"It is nothing," said the Sister. "We have nursed dozens of children, and brought them well through it. In a week little Marie will be about again."

But Madame Guise, unused to these light ailments, and terribly anxious for her only child, whom she could but look upon, as separated from herself, in the light of a martyr, was not easily reassured. She stayed with the child as long as she dared, and begged that Mr. Parker might be sent for in the morning should Marie be no better.

It was late to go home; after eleven; but nevertheless Charlotte Guise took the lonely road past the Friars' Keep and up Chapel Lane. The way had a fascination for her. Since she had been at Greylands' Rest, in going home from the Nunnery in the evening she had always chosen it. What she expected to see or hear, that could bear upon her husband's fate, she knew not; but the vague idea ever lay upon her that she might light upon something. Could she have done it without suspicion, three parts of her time would have been spent pacing about before the chapel ruins, just as John Bent had paced the night he was waiting for his guest.

It was very lonely. All the village had long ago been in bed. The stars were bright; the night was light and clear. Looking over the chapel ruins, she could see the lights of a distant vessel out at sea. Under the hedge, in the very selfsame spot where her husband and John Bent had halted that fatal night, did she now halt, and gaze across at the Keep, Chapel Lane being close upon her left hand.

"No, they could not have been mistaken," ran her thoughts. "If Mr. Castlemaine came down the lane now and crossed over, I should know him unmistakably—and that night was lighter than this, almost like day, for the moon, they say, was never brighter. Then why, unless he were guilty, should Mr. Castlemaine deny that he was there?"

Glancing up at the windows with a shudder, almost fearing she might see the revenant of the Grey Monk pass them with his lamp, or some other revenant, Madame Guise turned up Chapel Lane. At such moments, trifles serve to unstring the nerves of a timorous woman. Sounds struck on Madame Guise's ear, and she drew back, trembling and shaking, amid the thick grove of shrubs and trees skirting one side of the lane.

"Gently, now; gently, Bess," cried a voice not far from her. "You shall go your own pace in less than five minutes, old girl. Gently now."

And to Charlotte Guise's astonishment, she saw Commodore Teague's spring-cart turn out of the dark turning that led from the Hutt, the Commodore driving. Its cover looked white in the starlight; Bess, the mare he thought so much of, had her best harness on. When nearly abreast of Madame Guise, the Commodore pulled up with an exclamation.

"The devil take it! I've forgot to lock the shed door. Stand still, old girl; stand still, Bess."

He got down and ran back. The well-trained animal stood perfectly still. In a few moments' time he was back again, had mounted, and was driving slowly away in the direction of Newerton.

"What can be taking him abroad at this night hour?" Madame said to herself in wonder.

But the encounter, though it had been a silent one, and on the man's part unsuspected, had served to restore somewhat of her courage: the proximity of a human being is so reassuring in the dark and lonely night, when superstitions fancies are running riot. And with a swift step, Charlotte Guise proceeded on her way up Chapel Lane.

XVII

OPENING THE BUREAU

G reylands' Cliff was a high cliff: and the huts of the fishermen, nestling in nooks on its side, rendered it very picturesque. Many a lover of art and nature, seeking a subject for his pencil, had sketched this cliff; some few had made it into a grand painting and sent it forth to charm the world.

The two highest cottages on it were of a superior order. Even they were not built on the top; but close under it. They stood nearly side by side; a jutting of rock stretching out between them. The walls were white: and to the side of one of these dwellings—the one nearest the sea— there was a small square piece of sunk level that served now for a little garden. Miss Hallet, to whom the cottage belonged, had caused some loads of good earth to be brought up; she planted a few flowers, a few shrubs, a few sweet herbs, and so nursed the little spot into a miniature garden. Miss Hallet herself was seated just within the open door of the dwelling, darning a rent in a pillow-case. The door opened straight upon this room; a pretty parlour, very well furnished. The kitchen was behind; and two good bedchambers and a smaller room were above. Not a large house, thinks the reader. No: but it was regarded as large by the poorer dwellers on the cliff, and Miss Hallet was looked up to by them as a lady. Having a small but sufficient income, she lived quietly and peaceably, mixing but little with other people.

Through family misfortunes she had been deprived of a home in early life, and she took a situation, half companion, half lady's-maid. The lady she served bequeathed her by will enough money to live upon. Miss Hallet had then saved money of her own; she came to Greylands, her native place, bought the cottage on the cliff, and settled herself in it. Her brother, like herself, had had to turn to and support himself. He went to sea in the merchant service, passed in time the examinations before the Board of Trade, and rose to command a vessel trading to the coast of Spain. But he never got beyond that: and one stormy night the unfortunate vessel sunk with himself and all hands. He left two orphan children, a son and daughter, not provided for; Miss Hallet adopted them, and they came home to her at Greylands. The boy, George, she sent to a good school at Stilborough; he had to walk to and fro night and morning: Jane went to the Grey Sisters. George took to the sea; in spite of all his aunt could say or do. Perhaps the liking for it was innate, and he was always about in boats and on the beach when at Greylands. He at length put himself on board Tom Dance's boat, and said he would be a fisherman, and nothing else. In vain Miss Hallet pointed out to him that he was superior to anything of the kind, and ought to look out for a higher calling in life. George would not listen. Quitting his aunt's roof—for he grew tired of the continual contentions she provoked—he went to lodge in the village, and made apparently a good living. But the treacherous sea took him, just as it had in like manner taken his father. One night during a storm, a ship was sighted in distress: Tom Dance, who was as good-hearted as he was reckless, put off in his boat with George Hallet to the rescue, and George never came back again. Handsome, light-hearted, well-mannered George Hallet was drowned. That was nearly two years ago. He was just twenty years of age; and was said to have already been given a share in Tom Dance's earnings. Tom Dance owned his own substantial boat; and his hauls of fish were good; no doubt profitable also, for he was always flush of money. His son, a silent kind of young man, was his partner now, and went out in the boat with him as George Hallet used to do. They lived in one of the cottages on the beach. Old Mrs. Dance, Tom's mother, had her dwelling in a solitary place underneath the perpendicular cliff: not on the village side of it, as the other dwellings were, but facing the sea. It was a lonely spot, inaccessible at times when the tides were high. Tom Dance, who was generous to his mother, and kept her well, would have had her quit it for a more sociably situated habitation: but the old woman was attached to her many-years homestead, and would not listen to him. When we have grown old in a home, we like it better than any other, no matter what may be its drawbacks.

Miss Hallet finished the darn, and turned the pillow-case about to look for another. She was a tall, fair, angular lady of fifty, with a cold, hard countenance; three or four prim flat curls of grey hair peeped out on her forehead from beneath her cap; tortoiseshell spectacles were stretched across her well-shaped nose. She had a fawn-coloured woollen shawl crossed about her for warmth—for, though a nice spring day, it was hardly the weather yet for one of her age to sit exposed to the open air.

"Why, this must have been cut!"

The spectacles had rested upon an almost imperceptible fray, whose edges were so keen and close as to impart a suspicion that it had never come by natural wear and tear. Miss Hallet drew in her thin lips grimly.

"And since the wash too!" she continued, when the gaze was over. "Jane must know something of this: she helped the woman to fold. Jane is frightfully heedless."

Threading a fresh needleful of the soft, fine darning cotton, she was applying herself to repair the damage, when footsteps were heard ascending the narrow zigzag path. Another minute, and Tom Dance's son loomed into view; a short, sturdy, well-meaning, but shy and silent youth of twenty.

"Father's duty, Miss Hallet, and he has sent up this fish, if you'd be pleased to accept him," said the young man, showing a good-sized fish with large scales, resting on a wicker-tray. Miss Hallet was charmed. Her hard face relaxed into as much of a smile as it could relax.

"Dear me, what a beautiful fish! How good your father is, Wally! Always thinking of somebody! Give him my best thanks back again. You have just got in, I suppose?"

"Just ten minutes ago," responded Wally. "Been out two tides."

"Well, I wonder your father does not begin to think more of his ease—and so well off as he must be! The night seems the same to him for work as the day."

"One catches the best fish under the moon," shortly remarked the young man, as he handed over the wicker-tray.

Miss Hallet took it into the house, and brought it back to him without the fish. Mr. Walter Dance caught the tray with a silent nod, and sped down the steep path at a rate, that, to unaccustomed eyes, might have seemed to put his neck in peril.

Barely had Miss Hallet taken up her sewing again, when another visitor appeared. This one's footsteps were lighter and softer than the young man's, and she was seen almost as soon as heard. A dark-haired, quick-speaking young woman in black. It was Harriet, waiting-maid to Mrs. Castlemaine.

"Is your niece at home, Miss Hallet?"

"No. She's gone to Stilborough. How are you, Harriet?"

"Oh, I'm all right, thank you. What a cliff this is to climb up!— a'most takes one's breath away. Gone to Stilborough, is she? Well, that's a bother!"

"What did you want with her?"

"Has she done any of them han'kerchers, do you know?" returned the young woman, without replying to the direct question.

"I can't say. I know she has begun them. Would you like to come in and sit down?"

"I've no time for sitting down. My missis has sent me off here on the spur of the moment: and when she sends one out on an errand for herself one had best not linger, you know. Besides, I must get back to dress my ladies."

"Oh, must you," indifferently remarked Miss Hallet; who rarely evinced curiosity as to her neighbours' doings, or encouraged gossip upon trifles.

"They are all going off to a dinner party at Stilborough; and missis took it into her head just now that she'd use one of her new fine cambric han'kerchers," continued Harriet. "So she sent me off here to get one."

"But Mrs. Castlemaine is surely not short of fine handkerchiefs!" cried Miss Hallet.

"Short of fine han'kerchers!—why, she's got a drawer fall. It was just a freak for a new thing; that's all."

"Well, I do not know whether one is done, Harriet. Jane has been working at one; she was at it last night; but I did not notice whether she finished it."

"Can't you look, please, Miss Hallet?"

Miss Hallet rose from her chair and went upstairs. She came back empty-handed.

"I don't see the handkerchiefs anywhere in Jane's room, Harriet. I daresay she has locked them up in her work-drawer: she has taken to lock up the drawer lately, I've noticed. If you could wait a few minutes she might be in: she'll not be long now."

"But I can't wait; they start off at five," was the girl's answer: "and the missis and Miss Ethel have both got to be dressed. So I'll say good afternoon, ma'am."

"Good afternoon," repeated Miss Hallet. "Should Jane return in time, if she happens to have finished one of the handkerchiefs, she shall bring it up."

The young woman turned away with a brisk step, but not at the speed Walter Dance had used. By-and-by, quite an hour later, Jane Hallet came in.

A slender, ladylike, nice-looking girl of nineteen; with a fair, soft, gentle face, mild blue eyes, hair light and bright, and almost child-like features. Jane's good looks, of which she was no doubt conscious, and Jane's propensity to dress too much were a source of continual vexation to Miss Hallet: so to say, a stumbling-block in her path. Jane wore a dark blue merino dress, a very pretty grey cloak, with a hood and tassels, and a straw bonnet trimmed with blue. Miss Hallet groaned.

"And you must walk off in all those best things to-day, Jane! Just to go to the wool shop at Stilborough! I wonder what will become of you!"

"It was so fine a day, aunt," came the cheerful, apologetic answer. "I have not hurt them.

"You've not done them good. Are any of those handkerchiefs of Mrs. Castlemaine's finished?" resumed the aunt, after a pause.

"One is."

"Then you must go up at once with it to Greylands' Rest. Don't take your cloak off—unless, indeed, you'd like to change it for your old one which would be the right thing to do," added Miss Hallet, snappishly. "And your bonnet, too!"

Jane stood still for a moment, and something like a cloud passed over her face. She did not particularly care to go to Greylands' Rest.

"I am tired with my walk, aunt."

"That can't be helped: you must take the handkerchief all the same," said Miss Hallet. And she explained the reason, and that she had promised to send one if it were done.

"You will be in time, Jane: it is hardly half-past four. The maid said the family were to start at five."

Jane went up to her chamber; a room that she took care to make look as pretty as she could. A chest of drawers stood by the bed. Taking a key from her pocket, she opened the top long drawer, the only one that was locked, and lifted out the paper of handkerchiefs. Half-a-dozen handkerchiefs of the finest and softest cambric, almost like a spider's web, that Mrs. Castlemaine had given to her to hem-stitch.

Any little job of this kind Jane Hallet was glad to undertake. The money helped to buy her clothes. Otherwise she was entirely dependent upon her aunt. The Grey Ladies had taught her all kinds of fine needlework. When she had none of that to do—and she did not have it often—she filled up her leisure time in knitting lambs' wool socks for a shop at Stilborough. There was no necessity for her to do this, and Miss Hallet did not cordially approve of it; but it gave Jane a feeling of independency.

Snatching a moment to look into the glass and put her hair in order,

Jane went down with the handkerchief, neatly folded in thin white paper. All the girls instincts were nice: she was in fact too much of a lady for her position.

"I thought you might be changing those smart things for your everyday ones," crossly spoke Miss Hallet, as Jane went through the sitting-room. "Mrs. Castlemaine wall look askance at your finery."

"There was no time for it, aunt," replied Jane, a sudden blush dyeing her face, as she hastened out.

She ran down the cliff, went past the Grey Nunnery, and so up Chapel Lane—which was the back way to Greylands' Rest, and not the front. It was not her wish or intention to see Mrs. Castlemaine, if she could avoid it; or any of the family. Presenting herself at the back door, she asked for Harriet. One of the other servants took her into a small parlour, and said she would tell the lady's maid. Five o'clock had struck before Harriet bustled in.

"The han'kercher, is it? Mrs. Castlemaine'll be glad. When she sets her mind on a thing, she do set it. Come along, Jane Hallet, she wants to see you."

No opportunity was afforded to Jane of saying no, and she followed Harriet along the passages. Mrs. Castlemaine, her rich black silk dinner dress covered by a large warm shawl, stood in the hall. Ethel Reene, in black net and white ribbons, and wearing her scarlet cloak, was also there. The carriage waited outside. Jane went forward shrinkingly, her face turning pale and red alternately.

"I just want to see it before I take it," said Mrs. Castlemaine, holding out her hand for the handkerchief. "Is it tumbled much? Oh, I see; it is very nice, quite smooth. How well you have kept it, Jane Hallet! Here, Harriet, I don't want this one now."

She tossed back an embroidered handkerchief to the maid, and swept out to the carriage. Ethel smiled at Jane, as she followed her stepmother.

"I'm sure it is very good of you, Jane, to come up with it for mamma," she said, feeling in her sensitive heart that Mrs. Castlemaine had not given one word of thanks to the girl.

Mr. Castlemaine came downstairs, an overcoat on his arm. He nodded kindly to Jane as he passed, and inquired after Miss Hallet. Miles and Harriet stood in the porch, watching the carriage away. Jane was a little behind, just within the hall.

"I thought Mr. Harry was going," observed Harriet. "What has took him not to go?"

"Don't know," said Miles. "One never can be certain of Mr. Harry—whether he goes to a place or whether he doesn't go."

"Perhaps he has walked on," remarked Harriet carelessly, as she turned round. "I say, Jane Hallet, you'll stay and take a dish o' tea, now you are here. We are just going to have it."

But Jane hastily declined. No persuasion, apparently, would induce her to accept the invitation; and she departed at once. Half an hour later Madame Guise and her pupil came home: they had been out for a long walk.

"Have they all gone?" inquired Madame of one of the housemaids.

"Oh, dear, yes, ma'am. Half an hour ago."

Now, this answer deceived Charlotte Guise. She knew the dinner engagement had been accepted by Mr. and Mrs. Castlemaine, their son, and Ethel. She had no thought or idea but what they could collectively keep it: and in saying to the servant "Have they all gone," she comprised the four, and understood that she was answered accordingly.

She and Flora took tea together. The child was growing somewhat more tractable than she used to be. Not much as yet; it was just a little shade of improvement. Flora was always better when her mamma was away; and Madame Guise had no trouble with her on this night. She even went to bed at the appointed hour, eight o'clock, without rebellion, after a regalement of what she was particularly fond of—bread and jam.

"I will take a slice of this bread and butter and jam also," remarked Madame to Miles; "and then I shall not trouble you to bring in supper for me. It will be a nice change. We like this confiture much in my country."

So Madame took her light supper that evening with Flora, and afterwards wrote a letter. At nine o'clock she rang the bell to say she was going up to her room for the night, feeling tired, and should require nothing more. Miles, who had answered the bell, saw her go up with her candle. He put out the sitting-room lights for safety, and went back to the kitchen. His master and mistress were not expected home before hall-past eleven.

In her room stood Charlotte Guise, white as a sheet. She was contemplating a deed that night, from which, in spite of what she deemed her justification for it, she shrank in horror. It was no less a step than the opening with a false key the private bureau of Mr. Castlemaine.

Some little time the best part of a fortnight, had elapsed since that walk of hers to Stilborough and Marie had had the measles—"very kindly," as Mr. Parker and the Grey Sisters expressed it—and was well again. Telling a plausible story of the loss of her keys to a Stilborough locksmith that day, Madame had obtained from him—a key that would undo, if necessary, half the locks in Mr. Castlemaine's house. No opportunity had presented itself for using it until now. Such an occasion as this, when the house was deserted by all, save the servants, might not speedily occur again.

She stood in her chamber, trembling and nervous, the light from the candle reflected on her face. The staircase clock struck the quarter past nine, and her heart beat faster as she heard it. It was the signal she had been waiting for.

For the servants would now be settled at their supper, and were not likely soon to get up from it. Nine o'clock was the nominal hour for the meal: but, as she chanced to know, they rarely sat down to it much before a quarter past. With the house free and nothing to do, they would not hurry themselves over it to-night. Half an hour—nay, an hour, she knew she might freely reckon upon while they were shut up at table in the comfortable kitchen, talking and eating.

Charlotte Guise opened the door and stood to listen. Not a sound save the ticking of the clock broke the stillness. She was quite alone. Flora was fast asleep in her room in the front corridor, next to Mrs. Castlemaine's chamber, for she had been in to see, and she had taken the precaution of turning the key on the child for safety: it would not do to be interrupted by her. Yet another minute she stood listening, candle in hand. Then, swiftly crossing the corridor, she stole into the study through the double doors. A fear had been upon her that she might find the second door a stumbling block, as Mr. Castlemaine sometimes locked it when he went abroad. It was open to-night, and she whisked through it.

The same orderly, unlittered room that she had seen before. No papers lay about, no deeds were left out that could be of use to her. Three books were stacked upon the side table; a newspaper lay on a chair; and that was positively all. The fire had long ago gone out; on the mantelpiece was a box of matches.

Putting down the candle, Charlotte Guise took out her key, and tried the bureau. It opened at once. She swung back the heavy lid and waited a moment to recover herself: her lips were white, her breath came in gasps. Oh, apart from the baseness, the dishonour of the act, which was very present to her mind, what if she were to be caught at it?

Papers were there en masse. The drawers and pigeon-holes seemed to be full of them. So far as she could judge from a short examination— and she did not dare to give a long one—these papers had reference to business transactions, to sales of goods and commercial matters— which she rather wondered at, but did not understand. But of deeds she could see none.

What did Charlotte Guise expect to find? What did she promise herself by this secret search? In truth, she could not have told. She wanted to get some record of her husband's fate, some proof that should compromise the Master of Greylands. She would also have been glad to find some will, or deed of gift, that should show to her how Greyland's Rest had been really left by old Anthony Castlemaine: whether to his son Basil or to James. If to Basil, why there would be a proof—as she, poor thing, deemed it—of the manner in which James Castlemaine had dealt with his nephew, and its urging motive.

No, there was nothing. Opening this bundle of papers, rapidly glancing into that, turning over the other, she could find absolutely nothing to help her: and in the revulsion of feeling which the disappointment caused, she said to herself how worse than foolish she had been to expect to find anything: how utterly devoid of reason she must be, to suppose Mr. Castlemaine would preserve mementos of an affair so dangerous. And where he kept his law papers, or parchments relating to his estate, she could not tell, but certainly they were not in the bureau, unless there were secret receptacles to which she knew not how to penetrate.

Not daring to stay longer, for near upon half an hour must have elapsed, she replaced the things as she had found them, so far as she could remember. All was done save one drawer; a small drawer, at the foot, next the slab. It had but a few receipted bills in it: there was one from a saddler, one from a coach maker, and such like. The drawer was very shallow; and, in closing it, the bills were forced out again. Charlotte Guise, in her trepidation and hurry, pulled the drawer forwards too forcibly, and pulled it out of its frame.

Had it chanced by accident—this little contretemps? Ah, no. When do these strange trifles pregnant with events of moment, occur by chance? At the top of the drawer, itself in the drawer, appeared a narrow, closed compartment, opening with a slide. Charlotte drew the slide back, and saw within it a folded letter and some small article wrapped in paper.

MRS. HENRY WOOD

The letter, which she opened and read, proved to be the one written by Basil Castlemaine on his death-bed—the same letter that had been brought over by young Anthony, and given to his uncle. There was nothing much to note in it—save that Basil assumed throughout it that the estate was his, and would be his son's after him. Folding it again, she opened the bit of paper: and there shone out a diamond ring that flashed in the candle's rays.

Charlotte Guise took it up and let it fall again. Let it fall in a kind of sick horror, and staggered to a chair and sat down half fainting. For it was her husband's ring.

The ring that Anthony had worn always on his left-hand little finger: the ring that he had on when he quitted Gap. It was the same ring that John Bent and his wife had often noticed and admired; the ring that was undoubtedly on his hand when he followed Mr. Castlemaine that ill-fated night into the Friar's Keep. His poor wife recognized it instantly: she knew it by its peculiar setting.

To her mind it was proof indisputable that he had indeed been put out out of the way for ever. Mr. Castlemaine must have possessed himself of the ring, unwilling that so valuable a jewel should be lost: perhaps had drawn it from Anthony's finger after death. She shuddered at the thought. But, in the midst of her distress, reason told her that this was only a negative proof, after all; not sufficient for her to act upon, to charge Mr. Castlemaine with the murder.

When somewhat recovered, she kissed the ring, and put it back into the small compartment with the letter. Pushing in the slide, she shut the drawer, and closed and locked the bureau; thus leaving all things as she had found them. Not very much result had been gained, it is true, but enough to spur her onwards on her future search. With her mind in a chaos of tumult,—with her brain in a whirl of pain,—with every vein throbbing and fevered, she left the candle on the ground where she had now lodged it, and went to the window, gasping for air.

The night was bright with stars; opposite to her, and seemingly at no distance at all, rose that dark building, the Friar's Keep. As she stood with her eyes strained upon it, though in reality not seeing it, but deep in inward thought, there suddenly shone a faint light at one of its casements. Her attention was awakened now; her heart began to throb.

The faint light grew brighter: and she distinctly saw a form in a monk's habit, the cowl drawn over his head, slowly pass the window; the light seeming to come from a lamp in his outstretched hand. All the superstitions tales she had heard of the place rushed into her mind: this must be the apparition of the Grey Friar. Charlotte Guise had an awful dread of revenants, and she turned sick and faint.

With a cry, only half suppressed, bursting from her parted lips, she caught up the candle, afraid to stay, and flew through the door into the narrow passage. The outer door was opening to her hand, when the voice of Harry Castlemaine was heard in the corridor, almost close to the door.

Ah, far more sick and faint did she turn now! Discovery seemed inevitable. Instinct led her to blow out the light and to push the door as close as she could push it. She dared not shut it: he might have heard the click of the latch. Had the others come home? Was Mr. Castlemaine ascending to his study to catch her there? Trembling, shaking, panting, the unhappy lady stood in this acme of terror, the ghost of the Friar's Keep behind her, the dread of detection before her. And the candle was making a dreadful smell!

That alone might betray her: Harry Castlemaine might push back the door to ascertain where the smell came from. Could the floor have opened and disclosed a yawning pit, the unhappy lady would thankfully have disappeared within it.

The minute seemed like an hour. Harry did not come on. He appeared to have halted close by to listen to something. Miles was speaking below.

"Thought I had gone with them to the dinner, and so put out the lights!" retorted Harry, in his, free, clear, good-natured tones. "You saw the carriage drive away, I suppose, without me. Well, light up again, and bring in some supper."

He came on now, and went into his chamber at the end of the corridor. Staying there a minute or two, as though changing his coat, he passed back, and down stairs again. Charlotte Guise, shaking, in every limb, stole out as the echo of his footsteps died away, closed the door and took refuge in her own room. There she went into hysterics: hysterics that she was totally unable to suppress, and muffled her head in a blanket to deaden the cry.

The next morning there was commotion in the house: Miss Flora Castlemaine had found herself locked in her bedroom. Given to take impromptu excursions in a morning en robe de nuit, after books, or the kitten, or into somebody's bedroom who was sure not to want her, the young lady for once found herself caged. Mrs. Castlemaine made an angry stir about it; locked doors were so dangerous in case of fire, she said. She accused the maid, Eliza, who attended on Miss Flora, and threatened her with dismissal.

"I can be upon my Bible oath that I never locked the door," cried the girl. "Why should I wish to lock it last night, more than any other night? I never touched the key. For the matter of that, I could not tell whether the key was outside or inside. You may send me away this hour, ma'am, but I am innocent, and I can't say more than that."

Poor Madame Guise, who was complaining of migrane this morning, and whose eyes were red and heavy, took the blame upon herself, to exculpate the wrongfully accused servant. In her terror of the previous night, she had totally forgotten to unlock Flora's door. She hastened now to say that she had looked in on the sleeping child when she herself went to bed: in coming out, it was possible she had turned the key. Many of the chamber doors in France shut and opened with the key only, she might have turned the key unthinkingly, meaning but to shut the door.

So the matter ended. But Charlotte Guise could not help feeling how painfully one deceit one wrong act, leads to another. And Mr. Harry, she found, had never been to the dinner at all. Some matter of business, or perhaps some whim, had led him to break his engagement, and to give due notice of it the day beforehand to the entertainers. As Miles had observed, one never could be certain of Harry Castlemaine.

XVIII

The Grey Monk

That the Grey Monk was haunting the Friar's Keep that night, and for a longer period than could be quite agreeable to any chance passer-by, appeared to be indisputable.

Some of the Grey Sisters were up that evening at the coastguard station. The wife of one of the men was very ill, her infant being only three days old: and Sister Rachel had been with her for the day. At eight o'clock Sister Rachel was relieved by Sister Mona, who would remain for the night. Sister Ann walked up from the Nunnery with Sister Mona for company, and would walk back again with Sister Rachel.

It was about half past eight that they left the station to return home, the Sisters Ann and Rachel. The night was starlight, the air somewhat frosty. Talking of the poor woman, just quitted, Sister Rachel saying the fever was getting higher, they approached the Friar's Keep. They were on the opposite side of the road, and had nearly reached Chapel Lane when something strange—some kind of glimmer or faint flash—struck on Sister Rachel's vision, and caused her to turn her eyes on the upper casements of the Keep. With a spring and a cry, she seized hold of Sister Ann and clung to her.

"Have you trod upon a stone?" asked practical Sister Ann. But the very fact of turning to her companion, who was outside, brought the windows of the Keep before her, and she saw the Grey Monk slowly gliding along, with his cowl covering his head, and his lamp in his hand. A shadowy kind of form, suggestive of terrible ideas that don't pertain to earth.

The blood of the two unfortunate Sisters seemed to turn; they nearly sank away in evaporation. They clung to each other, arm in arm, hand to hand, pushing, staggering, pressing onwards, and in a minute, as it seemed, gained the Grey Nunnery. The door was opened by Sister Caroline, and they burst into the reception parlour.

The Superior sat there, Mary Ursula; and most of the sisters with her who were not out on charitable missions. To have stopped the tongues of the two terrified grey women would have been about as feasible as to stem a rushing torrent in its overwhelming coarse. They had seen the apparition of the Grey Monk gliding past the window with their own eyes; had seen his lamp; had nearly fainted at him altogether.

"Tut, tut, tut!" reproved Sister Mildred, who was better this evening and down stairs. "I think you must have been deceived by your fears. I never saw it in my life."

But they only told their tale the more persistently, and Sister Mildred wavered. In vain Mary Ursula represented to them that there were no such things as ghosts: that people in believing in them, were misled by their fears and fancies. To this the two scared women only reiterated that they saw. They were walking quietly along, talking of the poor sick wife of the coastguardsman; nothing could have been further from their thoughts than any fears or fancies, when the figure suddenly appeared, plainly and unmistakably, before their astonished eyes.

"Sister Rachel saw it first," urged Sister Ann, anxious to defend herself against the imputation of having taken alarm unnecessarily, as though she were a foolish, timid child. "When she called out and caught hold of my arm, I thought she had trod upon a stone, or twisted her foot, or something; and, in turning to her there I saw the pale light in the window, and the figure of the Grey Monk. We stood rooted to the spot, holding on to one another, just too frightened to move, our poor eyes staring at the Keep. He glided past that window, and then past the other, his lighted lamp stretched out in his hand; just as Sister Lettice once saw him glide a year or so ago—and she knows it."

Sister Lattice, a simple woman, great in pudding-making, who had stood listening with round, frightened eyes, murmured her confirmation. One night, when she was belated, having been to a farmhouse where sickness reigned, she had seen it exactly as the two sisters were describing it now; and had come home and fainted.

"I was beginning to forget my fright," said Sister Lettice, looking pleadingly at the two Superiors. "But since the late talk there has been about that poor Mr. Anthony Castlemaine, I've not dared to go out of doors at night alone. For the ghost has been seen more frequently since he disappeared: in fact, as the ladies know, it's said by some that it is the young man's spirit that comes now, not the Grey Friar's."

"It was the Grey Friar we saw to-night, let people say what they will," rejoined Sister Ann.

The talking continued. This was a great event in the monotonous existence of the Grey ladies: and the two unfortunate Sisters were shaking still. Mary Ursula withdrew quietly from the room, and put on the grey cloak and bonnet of the order, and came down again, and let herself out at the front door.

There was something in all this gossip that disturbed and distressed Mary Ursula. Anthony's fate and the uncertainty connected with it, was more often in her mind than she would have cared to tell. Like Charlotte Guise, she—what with dwelling on it and listening to the superstitions surmises in Greylands—had grown to think that the Friar's Keep did contain some mystery not yet unsolved. As to "ghosts," Mary Castlemaine's sound good sense utterly repudiated all belief in such. What, then, she naturally asked herself, was this figure, that took the appearance of the traditional Grey Monk, and showed itself at the windows of the Keep, lamp in hand? Had it anything to do with the disappearance of Anthony?

Obeying an irresistible impulse, she was going forth to-night to look at this said apparition herself—if, indeed, it would appear again and so allow itself to be looked at. It was perhaps a foolish thing to do; but she wanted to see with her own unprejudiced eyes what and whom it was like. With her whole heart she wished the occurrences of that past February night and the mysteries of the Friar's Keep—did it in truth contain any—were thrown open to the light of day: it might tend to clear what was dark—to clear her uncle from the silent suspicions attaching to him. It was of course his place to institute this search, but he did not do it. Encasing himself in his pride, his haughty indifference, Mary supposed he was content to let the matter alone until it righted itself. But she loved her uncle and was painfully jealous for his good name.

Turning swiftly out of the gate of the Nunnery, she went up the hill, passed the Chapel Ruins, crossed the road, and stood still to gaze at the Friars' Keep. The church clock was striking nine. Taking up her position under the hedge, in almost the selfsame spot where John Bent and Anthony Castlemaine had taken theirs that unlucky night, she fixed her eyes on the windows, and waited. The old building, partly in ruins, looked grey and grim enough. Sometimes the moon lighted it up; but there was no moon to night. The stars were bright, the atmosphere was clear.

The minutes, as they went by, seemed like hours. Mary Ursula had not much more patience than other people, and it was exhausting itself rapidly. Not a shadow of a sign was there of the Grey Monk or of any other appearance. To judge by its silence and its lonely look, one might have said the Keep had not been entered since the Grey Monk was alive.

"It is hardly to be supposed it would show itself twice in one night," breathed Mary, in a spirit that was somewhat of a mocking one. But in that she was mistaken: and she went away too soon.

At the end of a quarter of an hour—which had seemed to her like two quarters—she gave it up. Crossing the road to the chapel gate, she went in, traversed the ruins to the opposite corner to the Friar's Keep, and stood looking out to sea. Mary had another vexation on her mind that night: earlier in the day a report had reached her in a letter that her recreant lover, William Blake-Gordon, was engaged again: So soon!— so soon! Whether it was true, she knew not: it could not, either way, make much difference to the pain that filled her heart: but the report wrung it cruelly. The other name, mentioned in connection with his, was Agatha Mountsorrel's; her own close friend of former days. She knew that she ought not to feel this bitter pain, this wild jealousy; that, once he was lost to her, she should have put him out of her mind for good. Ah, it is all very well for the wise to lay down laws, to say this is wrong and the other is right and you must act accordingly! human nature is but frail, and the heart must be true to itself.

Some slight movement caught her attention below. It was low water, and the strip of beach underneath was free. Mary leaned over to look. But she could not see: the shelving-out rocks hid the path as she stood. In the deep silence of the night, she thought she could distinguish whispering voices, and she waited until their owners should have passed a little farther on, where a bend inward of the rocks allowed a view to be obtained.

It brought the greatest vexation of all! A tall fine form came into sight too tall, too fine, to be any but Harry Castlemaine's. His arm was around the waist of some young girl; his head was turned to her, and they were conversing eagerly. She wore a dark cloak, its hood drawn up over her head: Mary could not see her face, for their backs were towards her, but she fancied it was Jane Hallet. They passed away under the Nunnery, as if returning to the village, and were lost to sight and hearing. Only at quite low water was that narrow strip passable.

The heaving sea stretched itself out before her eyes; the dead of the past ages were mouldering away beneath her feet; the canopy of sky, studded with stars in its vast expanse, lay above her head. But for all these signs, and the thoughts they involved, Mary Ursula Castlemaine might in that moment have lost heart and courage. The by-ways of life seemed very crooked just then; its troubles pregnant with perplexity and pain. But God was over all. The turbulent waves were held in check by His Hand; the long-ago dead had been called by Him; the sky and the stars were but emblems of His power. Yes, He was over all. From His throne in Heaven He looked down on the world; on its cares, its trials, its weaknesses, its temptations and sins; overruling all according to His will. He could set things straight; He was full of compassion, long-suffering, and mercy. The dark troubles here would be merged in a bright hereafter: in a place where there should be no cankering heart-break, where sorrow and suffering should flee away. A few more years, and—

"Dear me, ma'am! I beg your pardon."

Mary Ursula, buried in her far-off thoughts in the solitary place, was startled at the address, and turned round with a slight cry. Close at her elbow stood John Bent; a small basket in his band, covered with a white cloth.

"I'm sure I frightened you, ma'am!"

"Just for the moment you did," she said, with her sweet smile, interrupting his farther apologies. "I was standing to take a look at the sea. How grand it is from this spot!"

John Bent agreed that it was grand, and proceeded to explain his presence. His wife had dispatched him with some broth and other trifles that might be acceptable to the sick woman up at the coastguard station. In passing the chapel ruins on his way thither, he had caught sight of some one standing at the edge of the cliff, and turned in at once to see who it was.

"No wonder you did not hear me, ma'am, for I crept up on tiptoe," he acknowledged. "Since the disappearance of Mr. Anthony Castlemaine, this place is just as though it haunted me, for it is never out of my mind. To see somebody standing here in the shade of the corner wall gave me a turn. I could not imagine who it was, and meant to pounce upon 'em."

"The place lies on my mind also," said Mary Ursula. "I wish the doings of that night could be brought to light."

The landlord shook his head, she could not wish it as he wished it.

"I don't think now it ever will be," he said. "At least, I often fear it will not. There is only one person, as I believe, who could throw light upon it; and it does not seem to be his pleasure to speak."

She knew that he alluded to her uncle; and she seized on the moment for speaking a few words that she had long wished to speak to John Bent. In spite of the opinion he held, and that she knew he held, in regard to that past night, she respected the man greatly: she remembered how much her father had respected him.

"I cannot be ignorant, Mr. Bent, of the stigma you would cast on Mr. Castlemaine: the suspicion, I would rather say, lying in your mind against him. I believe that nothing can be more unjust: nothing more inconsistent with the true facts, could they be disclosed."

John Bent was silent. She stood close in the corner, within the shade cast by the slanting bit of stone wall, the blank side wall of the Grey Nunnery towering close above her. John was so near as almost to touch her. The sea was before them, a light twinkling on it here and there in the distance from some fishing vessel; the grass-grown square, once the site of the chapel, with its dottings of low crumbling walls, lay to their left, and beyond it was the Friars' Keep, its gothic door pushed to as usual. A lonely spot altogether it was to stand in, in the silence of the spring night.

"Why should you cherish this suspicion?" she asked.

John Bent tilted his hat slightly up on one side, and slowly rubbed his head. He was a very honest-minded, straightforward man; and though he might on occasion find it inexpedient to avow the truth, he yet would not, even by implication, speak an untruth; or tacitly let one be inferred.

"It is a subject, ma'am, on which my mouth ought to be closed to you."

"Not at all," she answered. "Were I Mr. Castlemaine's wife or daughter you might urge that. I am his niece, it is true; but I have now in a manner withdrawn myself from the world, and——But I will leave that argument and go to another. For my own sake, I wish you to speak openly with me. These troubles lie on my mind; sometimes I cannot sleep for thinking of them."

"I am sure I cannot sleep for them," said John.

"And I think that steps should be taken to put the doubts to flight—if we only knew what steps they could be."

John stooped to lodge the basket on the low top of the grass-grown cliff, jutting upwards before him. But he did not answer.

"Believe me when I say that no thought of reproach on you for entertaining these opinions rests on my mind," proceeded Miss Castlemaine. "I am sure that you conscientiously hold them; that you cannot divest yourself of them; and—"

"I wish I didn't," interposed John. "I only wish I had no cause to."

"There is no cause," she said in a low tone; "no true one. I am as sure of it as that I stand here. Even had it been Mr. Castlemaine whom you saw come in here that night, I feel sure his presence could have been explained away. But I think you must have been mistaken. You have no confirmation that it was he: nay, the confirmation lies rather the other way—that he was not here. Considering all this, I think you ought not to persist in your opinion, Mr. Bent; or to let the world believe you persist in it."

"As I have said before, madam, this is a matter that I don't care to talk to you upon."

"But I wish you to talk to me. I ask you to talk to me. You may see that I speak to you confidentially—do you so speak to me. There is no one else I would thus talk with about it, save you."

"Madam, it's just this—not but what I feel the honour you do me, and thank you for it; and goodness knows what honour I hold and have always held you in, Miss Castlemaine—But it's this, ma'am: your opinion lies one way and mine the other: and while I would not insist to you that Mr. Castlemaine was guilty, I yet can't let myself say he was not."

"I am as fully persuaded he was not as that those stars are above us," she said. But John made no reply.

"Mr. Anthony was made away with, madam. I—"

"No, no," she interrupted with a shiver.

"I don't accuse Mr. Castlemaine of having done it," proceeded John. "What I say, and hold to, is this, ma'am: that Mr. Castlemaine must know something of what became of him. But he does not avow it; he keeps silence: and it is that silence that strengthens the suspicions against him. I saw him come in here that night just as surely as I see you here now, Miss Castlemaine. It's true I did not see him so clearly go into the Friar's Keep; these mouldering walls, sticking up here and there a foot or two from the earth, dodge one's eyesight: still I saw the shade of him, like, go in: and in less than a minute my attention was called off Mr. Castlemaine by Mr. Anthony's own movements. I saw him go into the Keep: he made for it straight."

"But I say that the person you saw may not have been Mr. Castlemaine," she urged again, after having quietly heard him to the end.

"What other man is there in Greylands, ma'am, of the height and bearing of Mr. Castlemaine—one with the bold, free, upright walk and the gentleman's dress?" returned the landlord. "Only Mr. Harry:

and Mr. Harry is too young and slender to be mistaken for his father even in the moonlight. Mr. Harry happened to be away that night at Newerton."

"I think you are cruelly, persistently obstinate. Forgive me, Mr. Bent; I do not wish or intend to hurt your feelings," she added in a gentle, even kind tone. "It seems to me that you must have some animus against Mr. Castlemaine."

"The poor young gentleman was living under my roof, madam. I went forth with him that night, halted with him opposite this very gate, and watched him in. It has sat on my mind always since that I am in a manner accountable for him—that it lies with me to find out what became of him."

"I can understand the feeling and appreciate it," she answered quickly. "In itself it is a good and right feeling; but I think that it's very intensity tends to mislead you, and to cause this very animosity against Mr. Castlemaine. The person you saw come in here may have been a stranger: you have had no confirmation of any kind that it was Mr. Castlemaine: and the eyesight at night is so deceptive."

"Yes I have," said John, dropping his voice to a whisper, and speaking with evident reluctance. "I have had confirmation. Madam, you make me speak against my better will."

"You allude to Anthony," she rejoined somewhat impatiently. "You have said, I know, that he likewise thought it was his uncle—as indeed seems proved by the fact of his following him in. But, it may be that he was only led to think so by some exclamation of yours; that he did not see it with his own eyes. He is not here to prove it, one way or the other. In thus pressing my view of the case, I am only anxious that the fair truth should be established," she resumed after an instant's pause, as though she would explain her own persistency. "I am not wishing to mislead or bias you."

"We both saw him, ma'am, we both saw plainly that it was Mr. Castlemaine; but I did not allude to Mr. Anthony," spoke John, in the same subdued tone. "It has been confirmed by another."

"By whom?" she asked, drawing her cloak together with a sharp movement as though she were cold. "Do not hesitate; tell me all. I have said that I regard this as a confidential interview."

And perhaps John Bent, after what had passed, could find no plea of refusal. He was a very persuadable man when either his good sense or his good feeling was appealed to. As Mrs. Bent was wont to tell him, he had a soft place in his heart.

"Up to last night that ever was, ma'am, I had no idea that Mr. Castlemaine had been seen by any but us. But I find he was. I'll tell you what I've heard. You will perhaps think the evidence not worth much, Miss Castlemaine, for the man who saw him was three parts tipsy at the time: but he must have had his wits about him, for all that."

To make clear to the reader what the landlord was about to relate we must go back to the previous evening. On that evening at twilight, John Bent sauntered over to the beach, and sat down on the bench to smoke his pipe. It was a fine, still evening, favourable for the fishing-boats. While he was smoking peaceably, and gazing at the stars, beginning to show themselves in the sky, Jack Tuff, the sailor, strolled up, gave the landlord the good evening, and took his seat on the same bench. He produced his pipe, evidently wanting to smoke; but he just as evidently had no tobacco. John handed him some, and allowed him to light the pipe by his own. Talking of this and that, they somehow got upon the subject of Anthony Castlemaine's disappearance: and Mr. Tuff, perhaps out of gratitude for the good tobacco, avowed to his astonished companion that he could have confirmed his evidence, had he chosen, as to it having been Mr. Castlemaine who had crossed the road to the chapel ruins that fatal February night.

According to Mr. Jack Tuff's account, his own movements that night had been as follows. He had walked over to the little fishing hamlet, Beeton and taken a glass with a comrade there. It might have been two glasses. At any rate, it was enough to make Jack wish to pay another social visit as he went back to Greylands, instead of going straight home. In one of the three cottages situate at the back of Greylands' Rest, there lodged a sailor friend of Jack's: and accordingly Jack turned up Chapel Lane—the nearest way from where he then was—to make the call. There he stayed until late, taking other glasses, very late indeed for the quiet village; and he turned out considerably after eleven o'clock with unsteady legs. He staggered down Chapel Lane pretty safely until he neared the other end of it. When opposite the turning to the Hutt, who should emerge from that turning but some tall man. At the moment, Jack Tuff happened to be holding on with one arm to a tree trunk, to steady himself: but he made it out to be Mr. Castlemaine, and attempted to pull his old round hat off in token of respect. He did not know whether Mr. Castlemaine saw him; but fancied he did not see him. Mr. Castlemaine went up the lane towards his home, and Jack Tuff went on down it.

So far, that might be regarded as a corroboration of the Master of Greylands' statement at the time—namely, that he had left the Hutt about half-past eleven after smoking a pipe with the Commodore: and the probability seemed to be that Mr. Castlemaine had not seen Jack Tuff, or he might have called on him to confirm his testimony as to the hour.

Jack Tuff continued his progress down the small remaining portion of the lane, trying all the while to put on his hat: which he had succeeded in getting off at last. Something was undoubtedly the matter with either the head or the hat; for the hat would not go on the head, or the head into the hat. A branch of a tree, or something, caught Jack's elbow, and the hat dropped; Jack, in stooping for it, dropped also; and there he was, sitting amid the trunks of trees on the side of the lane, his back propped against one of them and his hat nowhere.

How long Jack remained there he did not pretend to say. His impression was that he fell asleep; but whether that was so, or not, Jack could not have told had he been bribed with a golden sovereign. At any rate, the next thing he heard or remembered, was, that some steps were coming down the lane. Jack looked up, and saw they were those of the Master of Greylands.

"Are you sure it was him?" interrupted John Bent, at this point of the narration, edging a little bit nearer to Jack on the bench.

"In course I'm sure," replied Jack Tuff. "The moonlight shone full upon him through the leafless branches of the trees, and I saw him plain. He didn't see me that time, for sure. I was in the dark, back amid the clump o' trees; and he went along with his head and eyes straight afore him to the end o' the lane."

"And where did he go then?"

"Don't know. He didn't come back again. Suppose he was crossing over to the Keep."

"Well, go on," said John.

There was not much more to tell. After this incident, the passing of the Master of Greylands, Mr. Tuff bethought himself that he might as well be getting homewards. To make a start, however, was not easy of accomplishment. First he had to find his hat, which took up some considerable tune: it was only when he had given it up for lost that he became conscious it was doubled up under him as he sat. Next he had to pull out his match-box and light his pipe: and that also took time. Lastly he had to get upon his legs, a work requiring skill, but accomplished by the friendly aid of the trees. Altogether from a quarter to half an hour must have been used in the process. Once fairly started and clear of the lane, he came upon Mr. Bent, pacing about opposite the ruins and waiting for Mr. Anthony Castlemaine.

"Did you hear the pistol-shot?" asked John Bent when the recital was over.

"Never heard it at all," said Jack Tuff. "I must have been feeling for my hat."

"And why did you not say at the time that you saw the Master of Greylands—and so have borne out my story?" demanded John Bent as a final question.

"I dare say!" retorted Jack Tuff: "and he laughed at for an imbecile who was drunk and saw double! Nobody'ud believe me. I'm not a going to say it now, Mr. Bent, except to you. I'm not a going to draw down Mr. Castlemaine upon me, and perhaps get put away in gaol."

And this was all John Bent got from him. That the man spoke the strict truth according to his belief—namely, that it was Mr. Castlemaine he saw both times that night—John could have staked his life upon. But that the man was equally determined not to say so much to the world, fearing the displeasure of Mr. Castlemaine: nay, that he probably would deny it in toto if the world questioned him, the landlord was equally sure of.

Miss Castlemaine heard the narrative in silence. It did not shake her belief in the innocence of her uncle; but it made it more difficult to confute John Bent, and she was now sorry to have spoken to him at all. With a deep sigh she turned to depart.

"We can only wait the elucidation that time will bring," she said to the landlord. "Rely upon it that if any ill deed was done that night, Mr. Castlemaine had no hand in it."

John Bent maintained a respectful silence. They crossed the ruins, and he held open the gate for her to pass through. Just then she remembered another topic, and spoke of it.

"What is it that appears at the casements here, in the guise of a Grey Friar? Two of the Sisters have been alarmed by it to-night."

"Something like a dozen people have been scared by it lately," said John. "As to what it is, ma'am, I don't know. Senseless idiots, to be frightened! as if a ghost could harm us! I should like to see it appear to me!"

With this answer, betraying not only his superiority to the Greylands world in general, but his inward bravery, and a mutual goodnight, they parted. John going up the hill with his basket; Miss Castlemaine turning towards the Nunnery, and pondering deeply.

Strange, perhaps, to say, considering the state Jack Tuff was avowedly in that eventful night, a conviction that his sight had not deceived him, had taken hold of her. That some mystery did attach to that night, independent of the disappearance of Anthony, she had always fancied: and this evidence only served to confirm it. Many a time the thought had arisen in her mind, but only to be driven back again, that her uncle was not as open in regard to that night's doings as he ought to be. Had it been possible that such an accusation, such a suspicion, whether openly made or only implied, had been brought against herself, she should have stood boldly forth to confront her accusers and assert her innocence, have taken Heaven to witness to it, if needs were. He had not done this; he had never spoken of it voluntarily, good or bad; in short, he shunned the subject—and it left an unsatisfactory impression. What should Mr. Castlemaine want in the chapel ruins at that midnight hour?—what could he want? But if it was he who went in why did he deny it? Put it that it was really Mr. Castlemaine, why then the inference was that he must know what became of Anthony. It seemed very strange altogether; a curious, unaccountable, mysterious affair. Mary felt it to be so. Not that she lost an iota of faith in her uncle; she seemed to trust him as she would have trusted her father; but her mind was troubled, her brain was in a chaos of confusion.

In some such confusion as she stepped bodily into a minute later. At the gate of the Nunnery she found herself in the midst of a small crowd, a small excited number of people who were running up and jostled her. Women were crying and panting, girls were pushing: a man with some object covered up in his arms, was in the midst. When the garb of Miss Castlemaine was recognized in the gloom as that of the Grey Sisters, all fell respectfully back.

"What is amiss, good people!" asked Sister Mary Ursula. And a faint moan of sympathy escaped her as she heard the answer. Polly Gleeson, one of Tim Gleeson's numerous little ones, had set her night-gown on fire and was terribly burnt. Tim was somewhere abroad, as usual: but another man had offered to bring the child to the Grey Ladies—the usual refuge for accidents and sickness.

Admitted to the Nunnery, the little sufferer was carried up to one of the small beds always kept in readiness. Sister Mildred herself, who was great in burns, came to her at once, directing two of the Sisters what was to be done. The sobbing mother, Nancy Gleeson, who was a great simpleton but had a hard life of it on the whole, asked whether she might not stay and watch by Polly for the night: but the Ladies recommended her to go home to her other children and to leave Polly to them in all confidence. Sister Mildred pronounced the burns, though bad to look at and very painful, not to be attended with danger: should the latter arise, she promised Nancy Gleeson to send for her at once. So Nancy went away pacified, the crowd attending her; and the good Ladies were left to their charge and to the night-watch it entailed.

But Sister Mary Ursula had recognized, among the women and girls pressing round the gate, the face of Jane Hallet. She recognized the dress also, as the one she had seen before that night.

Meanwhile John Bent reached the coastguard station. After chatting with the sick woman's husband, Henry Mann, who happened to be off duty and at home, John departed again with his empty basket. He chanced to be on the side opposite the Friar's Keep; for that path led direct from the preventive station—just as the two Sisters, Ann and Rachel, had taken it rather more than an hour earlier. John Bent, quite unconscious of what had happened to them, walked along leisurely, his mind full of the interview just held with Miss Castlemaine. In passing the Friar's Keep he cast his eyes up to it. Few people passed it at night without casting up their eyes—for the fascination that superstition has for most of us is irresistible. Were we told that a ghost was in the next lane, a large percentage of us would run off to see it. Even as John looked, a faint light dawned on the casement from within: and there came into view the figure, bearing its lamp. It was probably just at that selfsame moment that the eyes of Madame Guise, gazing stealthily from the window of Mr. Castlemaine's study, were regaled with the same sight. John Bent did not like it any more than madame did; any more than the Sisters did. He took to his heels, and arrived at the Dolphin in a state of cold chill indescribable.

XIX

JANE HALLET

G reylands lay, calm and monotonous, basking under the morning sun. There were no signs of any of the commotion that had stirred it the previous night: no crowding people surrounding a sad little burden; no women's cries; and John Bent's propriety had come back to him. Greylands had heard the news from one end to the other— the Grey Monk had been abroad again. It had appeared to two of the Sisters and to the landlord of the Dolphin.

The burnt child, an intelligent girl of five years old, lay in the little bed, Sister Phoebe sitting with her. The window of the room faced the road; it had upright iron bars before it: originally placed there, perhaps, to prevent the nuns putting their heads out to take a sly peep at the world. Polly Gleeson was in less pain, and lay quietly. Mr. Parker had looked in, and confirmed Sister Mildred's opinion that she would do well.

The door opened gently, and there entered Sister Mary Ursula and Miss Reene. Ethel, hearing of the accident, had come down from Greylands' Rest. Sister Phoeby rose, smiling and nodding, and they approached the bed.

"She is ever so much better," said the watching Sister. "See, she does not cry at all."

Polly was a pretty little girl. Her brown hair lay around her on the bolster; her dark eyes smiled at the ladies. The face was not touched, and nothing could be seen of the injuries as she lay: the worst of them were about the chest and shoulders. Tears stood in Ethel's eyes.

"Poor little Polly!" she said, stooping gently to kiss her. "How did it happen, little one?"

"Billy took the candle to look for a marble on the floor, and I looked too; and then there come a great light and mother screeched out."

"But were you not in bed before that time, Folly? It was past nine o'clock."

"Mother was undressing of us then: she'd been a busy washing."

"Poor little darling! Well, Polly, you will be well soon; and you must take great care of candles after this."

Polly gave as emphatic a nod as the bolster allowed her; as much as to say she would never go within wide range of a candle again. Miss Castlemaine took Sister Phoeby's place, and the latter went away.

That the child was now at ease, appeared evident; for presently her eyelids, heavy with sleep, gradually closed. She had had no sleep all night. Mary Ursula took some work from her pocket. The Sisters were making garments for this child: all she had—and a poor "all" it was—had been from the floor by the terrified mother, and caught up rolled round her to put the fire out.

"How peaceful it seems here," said Ethel in a low tone. "I think I should like to come and be a Sister with you, Mary."

Miss Castlemaine smiled one of her sad smiles. "That would never do, Ethel."

"It is so useful a life."

"You will find usefulness in another sphere. It would not be right that you should bury yourself here."

"We all told you that, Mary, you know, at Greylands' Rest. But you have done it."

"My dear, the cases are essentially different. My hopes of happiness, my prospects in the world were over: yours, Ethel, are not even yet in the bud. When some good man shall woo and win you, you will find where your proper sphere of usefulness lies."

"I don't want to be won," spoke Ethel: just as young girls are given to say. "I'm sure I would ten times be a Grey Sister than marry Harry Castlemaine."

Mary looked up with unusual quickness. The words brought to her mind one of the incidents of the past night.

"Harry does not continue to tease you, does he, Ethel?"

"Yes he does. I thought he had left it off: but this morning he brought the subject up again—and he let everybody hear him!"

"What did he say?"

"Not very much. It was when he was going out of the room after breakfast. He turned his head to me and said he hoped I should soon be ready with my answer to the question he had put to me more than once. Papa and mamma must have understood what he meant. I could have thrown the loaf after him."

"I think he must be only doing it in joke, Ethel," was the slow, thoughtful rejoinder.

"I don't know whether he is or not. Sometimes I think he is; at others

I think he is in earnest: whichever it may he, I dislike it very much. Not for the whole world would I marry Harry Castlemaine."

"Ethel, I fancy—I am not sure, but I fancy—you have no real cause to fear he will press it, or to let it trouble you. Harry is hardly staid enough yet to settle down. He does many random things."

"We have had quite a commotion at home this morning," resumed Ethel, passing to another topic. "Somebody locked Flora in her bedroom last night—when she wanted to run out this morning as usual, the door was fast. Mamma has been so angry: and when the news of Polly Gleeson's accident came up just now, she began again, saying Flora might just as well have been burnt also as not, burnt to death."

"Who locked her in?"

"I don't know—unless it was Madame Guise. Papa and mamma and I were at dinner at Stilborough—at the Barclays', Mary. Harry would not go. It was a nice party. We had singing in the evening."

"But about the door?"

"Well, Madame Guise thought she might have unintentionally done it. She said she went in last night to look at Flora. I can scarcely think she did it, for she had gone in many a time and never turned the key before. Or the keys of other doors, either."

"At least, it does not seem to have been of any consequence.

"No; only mamma made it so. I tell you every little trifle that I can, Mary," she added, laughing quietly. "Shut up here, it seems to me that you must like to hear news from the outer world."

"And so I do," was the answer. "I have not lost all interest in my fellow pilgrims, I assure you, Ethel."

"I wore my black net trimmed with white satin ribbons: you can't think how nice it looked, Mary," said Miss Ethel, some of her vanity creeping to the fore. "And a silver flower in my hair."

"I have no doubt the dress and the flower did look well, considering what a pretty girl it was adorning," was Mary's reply. And Ethel blushed slightly. She knew how nice-looking she was.

"Does Madame Guise continue to suit?"

"Oh, quite well. Mrs. Castlemaine thinks there's nobody to equal her. I like her also; but at times she puzzles me."

"How does she puzzle you?"

"Well, I can hardly explain it. She seems strange at times. But I must be going," added Ethel, rising.

"You are in a hurry, Ethel."

"I have to go up the cliff to Miss Hallet's. Jane is hem-stitching some handkerchiefs for mamma. Mamma had one of them with her last night: Mrs. Barclay saw the work, and said she would like some done for herself. So I am to tell Jane to call at Mrs. Barclay's the next time she goes to Stilborough. The work is really beautiful: it is the broad hem-stitch, you know, Mary: four or five rows of it."

A few more words spoken in the same low tone, lest the sleeping child should be disturbed, and Ethel took her departure. Opposite the beach she encountered Mrs. Bent: who was crossing back home in her cherry-ribboned cap from a purchase at Pike's tea and general shop.

"A nice day again, Miss Ethel!"

"It is a lovely day," said Ethel, stopping; for she and Mrs. Bent were great friends. "I have been in to see poor Polly Gleeson. How badly she is burnt!"

"The only wonder is that it never happened before, with that imbecile of a mother," was Mrs. Bent's tart rejoinder. "Of all incapable women, Nancy Gleeson's about the worst. Fancy her letting the children play with a candle in their night-gowns! Where could her senses have been?"

"Well, it is a sad thing for Polly. But the Sisters say she will do well. Oh, by the way, Mrs. Bent," continued Ethel, turning as she was going onward, "will you let mamma have your receipt for stewed eels again? The new cook does not do them to her mind and mamma cannot tell where the fault lies."

"It's the best receipt for eels in the three kingdoms," spoke Mrs. Bent with pride. "It was my mother's before me."

"Will you step across for it now, Miss Ethel?"

"Not now: as I come back. I am going up the cliff."

"To that Nancy Gleeson's, I suppose," cried Mrs. Bent in her free manner. "She does not deserve it. If I had twenty children about me, I'll be bound not one of 'em should ever set itself alight in my presence."

"Not there," said Ethel slightly laughing at Mrs. Bent's tartness. "I am taking a message from mamma to Jane Hallet."

"I hope it is to warn her not to make herself so free with Mr. Harry," cried Mrs. Bent, speaking on the moment's impulse. Had she taken time for thought she would not have said it.

"Warn her not to make herself so free with Mr. Harry!" repeated Ethel, somewhat haughtily. "Why, Mrs. Bent what can you mean?"

"Well, I have seen them walking together after nightfall," said Mrs. Bent, unable to eat her words.

"They may have met accidentally," returned Ethel after a pause.

"Oh, of course, they may," assented Mrs. Bent in a significant tone.

"Since when have you seen them?" pursued Ethel, feeling surprised and rather scandalized.

"Ah, well, I can't tell that. Since last autumn, though. No harm may be meant, Miss Ethel; I don't say it is; and none may come of it: but young girls in Jane Hallet's position ought to take better care of themselves than to give rise to talk."

Ethel continued her way to the cliff in some annoyance. While Mr. Harry Castlemaine made a pretence of addressing herself, it was not agreeable to hear that he was flirting with the village girls. It's true Ethel did not intend to listen to his suit: she absolutely rejected it; but that made little difference. Neither in itself was this walking with Jane Hallet the right thing. What if he made Ana fond of him? many a possibility was more unlikely than that. As to any "harm" arising, as Mrs. Bent had just phrased it, Ethel did not fear that—did not, in fact, cast a thought to it. Jane Hallet was far superior to the general run of girls at Greylands. She had been well educated by the Grey Ladies, morally and else, having gone to school to them daily for years; she was modest and reticent in manner; and Ethel would as soon believe a breath of scandal could tarnish herself as Jane. Her brother, George Hallet, who was drowned, had been made a sort of companion of by Harry Castlemaine during the last year or two of his life, as Greylands well remembered: and Ethel came to the conclusion that the intimacy Mrs. Bent talked of must be a sort of remnant of that friendship, meaning nothing: and so she dismissed it from her mind. Mrs. Bent, as Ethel knew, was rather given to find fault with her neighbours' doings.

Now it happened that as Ethel was ascending the cliff, Jane Hallet, within the pretty cottage near the top of it, was being taken to task by her aunt for the same fault that Mrs. Bent had spoken of—the staying abroad after nightfall. Miss Hallet had latterly found much occasion to speak on this score; but Jane was invariably ready with some plausible excuse; so that Miss Hallet, naturally unsuspicious, and trusting Jane as she would have trusted herself, never made much by the argument.

After taking the cambric handkerchief to Greylands' Rest the previous evening, Jane had gone home, swallowed her tea hastily, put off the best things that her aunt grumbled at her for having put on and then sat down to work. Some article was wanted in the house; and at dusk Jane ran down in her dark cloak to get it. From which expedition she did not get back until half-past nine was turned: and she seemed to have come up like one running for a wager. Miss Hallet was then ill with an attack of spasms, and Jane remained unreproved. This morning when the housework was done, and they had begun their sewing, Miss Hallet had leisure to recur to it. Jane sat by the window, busy at one of the handkerchiefs. The sun shone on her bright flaxen hair; the light print dress she wore was neat and nice—as Jane's dresses always were.

"How long does it take to get from here to Pike's shop and back again, Jane?"

"From here to Pike's shop and back again, aunt?—I could do it in a short ten minutes," said unsuspicious Jane, fancying her aunt might be wanting to send her there. "It would take you longer, of course."

"How did it happen then last night that it took you two hours and ten minutes?" demanded Miss Hallet. "You left here soon after half past seven, and you did not get back till close upon ten."

The soft colour in Jane's face grew bright on a sudden. She held her work to the window, as though some difficulty had occurred in the cambric.

"After buying the sugar, I went into the parlour to say good evening to Susan Pike, aunt. And then there came that dreadful outcry about Nancy Gleeson's poor burnt child."

The truth, but not the whole truth. Miss Jane had stayed three minutes with Susan Pike; and the commotion about the child had occurred some two hours later. The intervening time she did not allude to, or account for. Miss Hallet, never thinking to inquire minutely into time, so far accepted the explanation.

"If Nancy Gleeson's children had all been burnt, that's no reason why you should stay out all that while."

"Nearly everybody was out, aunt. It was like a fair around the Nunnery gate."

"You go off here; you go off there; pretty nigh every evening you dance out somewhere. I'm sure I never did so when I was a girl."

"When it is too dusk to see to work and too soon to light the candle, a run down the cliff does no harm," returned Jane.

"Yes, but you stay when once you are down. It comes of that propensity of yours for gossip, Jane. Once you get into the company of Susan Pike or that idle Patty Nettleby, you take as much thought of time as you might if all the clocks stopped still for you."

Jane bent to bite off a needleful of cotton—by which her flushed face was hidden.

"There you are! How often have I told you not to bite your thread! Many a set of teeth as good as yours has been ruined by it. I had the habit once; but my lady broke me of it. Use your scissors, and—Dear me! here's Miss Reene."

Ethel came in. Jane stood up to receive her and to hear her message. The girl's face was shy, and her manner was very retiring. Ethel thought of what she had just heard; certainly Jane looked pretty enough to attract Mr. Harry Castlemaine. But the blue eyes, raised to hers, were honest and good; and Ethel believed Jane was good also.

"Thank you: yes, I shall be glad to do the handkerchiefs for Mrs. Barclay," said Jane. "But I shall not be going into Stilborough for a week or so: I was there yesterday. And of course I should not begin them until I have finished Mrs. Castlemaine's."

"Very well; I suppose Mrs. Barclay is in no particular hurry," said Ethel.

"Jane might get through more work if she chose," remarked Miss Hallet. "Not that I wish her to do any: it is her own will entirely. On the other hand, I have no objection to it: and as she is fond of finer clothes than I should purchase for her, she has to get them for herself. Just before you came in, Miss Reene, I was telling her how she fritters away her time. Once dusk has set in, down she goes to her acquaintances in the village, and there she stays with one and another of them, never heeding anything else. It is a great waste of time."

Of all the hot faces, Jane's at that moment was the hottest. She was standing before Miss Reene, going on with her work as she stood. Ethel wondered why she coloured so.

"To-night she stays at Susan Pike's; to-morrow night it's at Martha Nettleby's; the next night it's at old. Mother Dance's, under the cliff!" went on Miss Hallet. "Chattering with one gossip and another, and dancing after burnt children, and what not, Jane never lacks an excuse for idling away her evenings."

"Mrs. Castlemaine said something about having her initials worked on these handkerchiefs: do you know whether she wishes it done, Miss Reene?" interposed Jane, who seemed to be flurried by the lecture. "I did not like to ask about it yesterday afternoon."

"I don't know at all," said Ethel "You had better see Mrs. Castlemaine."

"Very well, ma'am."

Ethel went down the cliff again, tripping along the zigzag path. Other paths branched off to other cottages. She took one that brought her to the door of Tim Gleeson's hut: a poor place of two rooms, with a low roof. Tim, a very idle, improvident, easy, and in general good-tempered man, sat on a stone at the door, his blue cloth legs stretched out, his rough face gloomy. "You are not in the boat to-day, Tim," remarked Ethel.

"Not to-day, Miss Castlemaine," said the man, slowly rising. "I'm a going out with the next tide. This accident have took all strength out of me! When a lot of 'em come fizzing into the Dolphin last night, a saying our Polly was afire, you might ha' knocked me down with a feather. Mrs. Bent she went on at me like anything, she did—as if it was my fault! Telling me she'd like to shut the inn doors again' me, for I went there when I ought to be elsewhere, and that I warn't good for my salt. I'd rather it had been any of 'em nor Polly: she's such a nice little thing, she is."

"Is your wife indoors?"

"No; she's off to the Nunnery. I've vowed to her that if she ever gets another end o' candle in the house, I'll make her eat it," concluded Tim, savagely.

"But she must have a candle to see with."

"I don't care: I won't have the young 'uns burnt like this. Thanks to you, miss, for turning out o' your way to think on us. The brats be a squalling indoors. I've just give 'em a licking all round."

Ethel ran on, and gained the Dolphin, entering it by the more familiar door that stood open opposite the beach. Mr. and Mrs. Bent were both in the room: he, reading his favourite weekly newspaper by the fire, the Stilborough Herald: she, sitting at the table under the window, stoning a plate of raisins. The receipt Ethel had asked for lay ready.

"You'll please tell Mrs. Castlemaine, Miss Ethel, that more or less pounded mace can be put according to taste," observed the landlady, as she handed Ethel the paper. "There's no particular quantity specified. It's strong: and a little of it goes a great way."

Ethel sat down by the table, putting a raisin into her mouth. John, who had risen to greet her, resumed his seat again. To say the truth, Miss Ethel liked running into the Dolphin: it made an agreeable interlude to the general dulness of Greylands' Rest. The screen introduced into the room during the late wintry weather, had been taken away again.

Mrs. Bent had a great mind to break it up, and burn it; but for that screen Ethel Reene would not have overheard those dangerous words. But no allusion had been made to the affair since, by any one of them: all three seemed content to ignore it.

"You must excuse my going on with my work, Miss Ethel," said Mrs. Bent. "We've got a dinner on to-night, and I had no notice of it till a few minutes ago. Some grand Inspector-General of the coastguard stations is here to-day; and he and two or three more gentlemen are going to dine here this evening. Mr. Castlemaine, I fancy, is to be one of them."

"Mr. Castlemaine is!" cried Ethel.

"Either him or Mr. Harry. I b'lieve it's him. And me with not a raisin in the house stoned for plum-pudding! I must make haste if I am to get it boiled. It's not often I'm taken unawares like this."

"If you will give me an apron to put on, I'll help you to stone them," said Ethel, taking off her black gloves.

"Now, Miss Ethel! As if I'd let you do anything of the kind! But that's just like you—always ready to do anybody a good turn."

"You give me the apron, please."

"I couldn't. If any of them from Greylands' Rest happened to look in, they'd be fit to snap at me; and at you, too, Miss Ethel. Seeing you stoning plums, indeed! There's no need, either: I am three parts through them."

Ethel began to do a few without the apron, in a desultory kind of way, and eat two or three more. John Bent came to some paragraph in the newspaper that excited his ire.

"Hear this!" he cried in anger. "Hear it, Miss Ethel! What a shame!"

"We have been given to understand that the rumour so freely circulated during this past week, of a matrimonial engagement having been made between Mr. Blake-Gordon and the heiress of Mountsorrel, has had no foundation in fact."

"The villain!" cried Mrs. Bent, momentarily forgetting her work. "He can hardly be bad enough to think of another yet."

Ethel's work was arrested too. She gazed at John Bent, a raisin in one hand, a stone in the other. That any man could be so fickle-hearted as this, she had not believed.

"I knew the tale was going about," said the landlord; "I heard it talked of in Stilborough last market day, Miss Ethel. Any way, true or untrue, they say he is a good deal over at the Mountsorrels, and—"

John Bent brought his words to a standstill; rose, and laid down his newspaper. There had entered a rather peculiar looking elderly gentleman, tall and upright yet, with a stout walking stick in his hand. He wore a long blue coat with wide skirts and brass buttons, drab breeches and top boots. His hair was long and snow white, his dark eyes were fiery.

Taking off his broad-brimmed hat with old fashioned courtesy, he looked round the room, particularly at Mrs. Bent and Ethel stoning the raisins. It is just possible he mistook the latter for a daughter of the house, dressed in her Sunday best.

"This is the Dolphin, I think!" he cried dubiously.

"At your service, sir," said John.

"Ay, I thought so. But the door seems altered. Its a good many years since I was here. Oh—ay,—I see. Front door on the other side. And you are its landlord—John Bent."

"Well, sir, I used to be."

"Just so. We shall do. I have walked over from Stilborough to see you. I want to know the truth of this dreadful report—that has but now reached my ears."

"The report, sir?" returned John—and it was perhaps natural that he should have his head filled at the moment with Mr. Blake-Gordon and the report touching him. "I believe I don't know anything about it."

"Not know anything about it! But I am told that you know all about it. Come!"

Ethel was rubbing her hands on Mrs. Bent's cloth preparatory to drawing on her gloves to depart. To help stone raisins in private at the inn was one thing; to help when visitors came in was a different thing altogether. John Bent, looked back at the stranger.

"Perhaps we are at cross-purposes, sir. If you will tell me what you mean, I may be able to answer you."

"Him that I would ask about is the son of the friend of my early days, Basil the Careless. Young Anthony Castlemaine."

The change of ideas from Mr. Blake-Gordon to the unfortunate Anthony was sudden: John Bent gave a groan, and coughed it down. The gentleman resumed, after turning to look at Ethel as she went out.

"Is it true that he, Basil Castlemaine's son, came over the seas to this place a month or two ago?—and took up his abode at this inn?—and put in a claim to his grandfather's estate, Greylands' Rest? Is that true?"

"Yes, sir."

"And where is he, this young Anthony?"

"I don't know, sir. I wish I did know."

"Is it true that he disappeared in some singular way one night—and that he has never since been seen or heard of?"

"That's true, sir—more's the pity."

The questioner took a step nearer John Bent, and dropped his voice to a low, solemn key.

"I am told that foul play has been at work."

"Foul play?" stammered John, not knowing whether this strange old man might be friend or foe—whether he might have come there to call him to account for his random words. The stranger paused to notice his changing face, and then resumed.

"That the young man has been put out of the way by his uncle—James Castlemaine."

XX

An Unwelcome Intruder

The usual dinner hour at Greylands' Rest was half past one o'clock. Mr. Castlemaine would have preferred a late dinner—but circumstances are sometimes stronger than we are. However, he never failed to put it off until evening upon the very slightest plea of excuse.

Some years before the close of old Anthony Castlemaine's life, his health failed. It was not so much a serious illness as a long and general ailing. His medical attendant insisted upon his dining early; and the dinner hour was altered from six o'clock to half past one. He recovered, and lived on: some years: but the early dinner hour was adhered to. James had never liked this early dining: and after his father's death he wished to return to the later hour. His wife, however, opposed it. She preferred the early dinner and the social supper; and she insisted upon it to Mr. Castlemaine that the interests of Ethel and Flora required that they should continue to dine early. Mr. Castlemaine said he did not see that: Ethel was old enough to dine late, and Flora might make her dinner at lunch time. Yes, poor child, and have cold meat three days out of the seven, urged Mrs. Castlemaine. The Master of Greylands yielded the point as a general rule: but on special occasion—and he made special occasions out of nothing—his edict was issued for the later dinner.

The dinner was just over to-day, and the servants had withdrawn, leaving wine and dessert on the table. Mr. Castlemaine's sitting down had been partly a matter of courtesy, though he did eat a small portion of meat: he was going to dine in the evening at the Dolphin. The early afternoon sun streamed into the dining-room: a long, comfortable room with a low ceiling, its windows on the side opposite the fire, its handsome sideboard, surmounted with plate glass, at one end; some open book-shelves, well filled with good and attractive volumes at the other. Mr. and Mrs. Castlemaine, Ethel, Flora, and Madame Guise, sat at the table. Harry Castlemaine had retired, and his chair stood vacant. As a rule, Madame Guise never sat a minute longer at any meal then she could help: as soon as she could get up without an absolute breach of good manners, she did get up. Mrs. Castlemaine called it a peculiarity. She estimated Madame Guise highly as an instructress, but she admitted to her more intimate friends that she did not understand her. To-day, as it chanced (chanced! do these things ever occur by chance?) she had stayed: and she sat in her place at Mr. Castlemaine's left hand in her perfectly-fitting black dress, with its white cuffs and collar, and her wealth of auburn hair shading her pale and quiet face. Mr. Castlemaine was in a sociable mood: latterly he had been often too silent and abstracted. His back was to the sideboard as he sat; handsome, upright, well-dressed as usual. Ethel was on his right hand, the windows behind her, Harry's empty chair between her and Mrs. Castlemaine; and Miss Flora, eating almonds and raisins as fast as she could eat them, sat on the other side of her mother with her back to the fire, and next to Madame.

Mrs. Castlemaine had introduced the subject that was very much in her thoughts just now—a visit to Paris. The Master of Greylands was purposing to make a trip thither this spring; and his wife, to her great delight, had obtained permission to accompany him. She had never been across the water in her life: the days of universal travelling had not then set in: and there were moments when she felt a jealousy of Ethel. Ethel had finished her education in the French capital; and was, so far, that much wiser than herself.

"I long to see Versailles;—and St. Cloud;—and the Palais Royal," spoke Mrs. Castlemaine in a glow of enthusiasm. "I want to walk about amid the orange-trees in pots; and in the Champs Elysées; and at Père la Chaise. And I particularly wish to see the Gobelins Tapestry, and the people working at it. You must be quite familiar with all these sights, Madame Guise."

"I have seen scarcely any of them," said Madame Guise in her gentle way. Then, perceiving the surprised look on Mrs. Castlemaine's face, she resumed hurriedly. "We did not live very near Paris, madam,—as I think I have said. And we French girls are kept so strictly:—and my mother was an invalid."

"And the bonbon shops!" pursued Mrs. Castlemaine. "I do count much on seeing the bonbon shops: they must be a sight in themselves. And the lovely bonnets!—and the jewellery! What is it that Paris has been called?—the Paradise of women?"

"May I go too?" asked Ethel with animation, these attractive allusions calling up reminiscences of her own sojourn in Paris.

"No," curtly replied Mrs. Castlemaine.

"Oh, mamma! Why, you will be glad of me to take you about and to speak French for you!"

"I shall go, mamma," quickly spoke up Flora, her mouth full of cake. "You told me I should, you know."

"We will see, my darling," said Mrs. Castlemaine, not daring to be too self-asserting just then; though her full intention was to take Flora if she could contrive it by hook or by crook. "A trip to Paris would be an excellent thing for you," she added for the benefit of Mr. Castlemaine: "it would improve your French accent and form your manners. I'll see, my dear one."

Mr. Castlemaine gave a quiet nod and smile to Ethel, as much as to say, "I will see for you." In fact he had all along meant Ethel to be of the party; though he would certainly do his best to leave Miss Flora at home.

At this moment Flora ought to be practising, instead of greedily eating of every dessert dish within her reach: but oughts did not go for much with Miss Flora Castlemaine. They might have gone for nothing but for Madame Guise. That lady, rising now from her chair, with a deprecatory bow to Mrs. Castlemaine for permission, reminded her pupil that she and the piano were both waiting her pleasure.

"I don't want to have a music lesson this afternoon; I don't want to practise," grumbled Flora.

"As you did not get your studies over this morning in sufficient time to take your lesson or to practise before dinner, you must do both now," spoke Madame in her steady way. And Mr. Castlemaine gave the young lady a nod of authority, from which she knew there might be no appeal.

"In a minute, papa. Please let me finish my orange."

She was pushing the quarters of an orange into her month with the silver fork. Just then Miles came into the room and addressed his master.

"You are wanted, sir, if you please."

"Who is it?" asked Mr. Castlemaine.

"I don't know, sir. Some oldish gentleman; a stranger. He asked—"

The man's explanation was cut short by the appearance of the visitor himself; who had followed, without permission, from the room to which he had been shown: a tall, erect, elderly man, attired in an ample blue coat and top-boots. His white hair was long, his dark eyes were keen. The latter seemed to take in the room and its inmates; his glance passing rapidly from each to each, as he stood holding his broad-brimmed hat and his stout walking-stick. Ethel knew him. instantly for the stranger who had entered the Dolphin Inn while she was helping Mrs. Bent with the raisins an hour, or so, ago: and the probability was that he recognized her, for his eyes rested on her for a few seconds.

Mr. Castlemaine had risen. He went a step or two forward as if about to speak, but seemed to be uncertain. The stranger abruptly forestalled him.

"Do you know me, James Castlemaine?"

"Why—yes—is it not Squire Dobie?" replied Mr. Castlemaine, holding out his hand.

"Just so," replied the stranger, keeping his hands down. "Perhaps you won't care to take my hand when you know that I have come here as a foe."

"As a foe?" repeated Mr. Castlemaine.

"At present. Until I get an answer to the question I have come to put. What have you done with Basil's son?"

A change passed over the face of Mr. Castlemaine: it was evident to anybody who might be looking at him; a dark look, succeeded by a flush. Squire Dobie broke the momentary silence.

"My old friend Basil's son; Basil the Careless: young Anthony Castlemaine."

The Master of Greylands was himself again. "I do not understand you," he said, with slow distinctness. "I have done nothing with the young man."

"Then rumour belies you, James Castlemaine."

"I assure you, Squire Dobie, that I know no more whither young Anthony Castlemaine went, or where he is now than you know. It has been a mystery to myself, as to every one else at Greylands."

"I got home to Dobie Hall last week," continued the stranger; "mean to stay at it, now; have only made flying visits to it since it became mine through poor Tom's death. Drove into Stilborough yesterday for the first time; put up at the Turk's Head. Landlord, old Will Heyton, waited on me himself this morning at breakfast, talking of the changes and what not, that years have brought, since I and poor Tom, and Basil the Reckless, and other rollicking blades used to torment the inn in the years gone by. We got to speak of Basil; 'twas only natural; and he told me that Basil had died abroad about last Christmas tune; and that his son, named Anthony, had come over soon after to put in his claim to his patrimony, Greylands' Rest.

He said that Anthony had suddenly disappeared one night; and was thought to have been made away with."

During this short explanation, they had not moved. The speaker stood just within the door, which Miles had closed, Mr. Castlemaine facing him a few paces distant. Madame Guise, waiting for Flora, had turned to the stranger, her face changing to the pallor of the grave. The Master of Greylands caught sight of the pallor, and it angered him: angered him that one should dare to speak of this remarkably unsatisfactory topic in the presence of the ladies of his family, startling and puzzling them. But he controlled his voice and manner to a kind of indifferent courtesy.

"If you will take a seat—and a glass of wine with me, Squire Dobie, I will give you all the information I possess on the subject of young Anthony's disappearance. It is not much; it does not really amount to anything: but such as it is, you shall hear it.—My wife, Mrs. Castlemaine. Sophia," turning to her as he made the introduction, "you had finished, I know: be so good as to leave us to ourselves."

They filed out of the room: Flora first, with Madame Guise; Ethel and her stepmother following. The latter, who knew something of the Dobie family, at least by reputation, halted to exchange a few words with the representative of it as she passed him. To judge by her manner, it seemed that she had put no offensive construction on his address to her husband: and the probability was that she did not. Mrs. Castlemaine might have been less aware than anybody of the disagreeable rumours whispered in Greylands, tacitly if not openly connecting her husband with the doings of that ill-fated night: for who would be likely to speak of them to her?

Squire Dobie, remarking that he did not like to sit with his back to the fire passed round the table and took the chair vacated by Ethel. He was the second son of the old Squire Dobie, of Dobie Hall, a fine old place and property nearly on the confines of the county. In the years gone by, as he had phrased it, he and his elder brother, Tom the heir, had been very intimate with Basil Castlemaine. Separation soon came. Basil went off on his impromptu travels abroad—from which, as the reader knows, he never returned; Tom Dobie, the heir, remained with his father at the Hall, never marrying: Alfred, this younger son, married a Yorkshire heiress, and took up his abode on her broad acres. It has been mentioned that Tom Dobie kept up a private occasional correspondence with Basil Castlemaine, and knew where he was settled, but that has nothing to do with the present moment. Some two years ago Tom died. His father, the old Squire, survived him by a year: and at his death the Hall fell to Alfred, who became Squire in his turn: he who had now intruded on Mr. Castlemaine.

"No thank you; no wine," he said, as Mr. Castlemaine was putting the decanter towards him. "I never drink between my meals; and I've ordered my dinner for six o'clock at the Turk's Head. I await your explanation, James Castlemaine. What did you do with young Anthony?"

"May I ask whether Will Heyton told you I had done anything with him?" returned Mr. Castlemaine, in as sarcastic a tone as the very extreme limit of civility allowed him to use.

"No. Will Heyton simply said the young man had disappeared; that he had been seen to enter that queer place, the Friar's Keep, at midnight, with, or closely following upon the Master of Greylands. When I inquired whether the whether the Master of Greylands was supposed to have caused him to disappear, old Will simply shrugged his shoulders, and looked more innocent than a baby. The story affected me, James Castlemaine; I went out from the breakfast-table, calling here, calling there, upon the people I had formerly known in the town. I got talking of it with them all, and heard the same tale over and over again. None accused you, mind; but I gather what their thoughts were: that you must have had a personal hand in the disappearance of Anthony; or, at least, a personal knowledge of what became of him."

Mr. Castlemaine had listened in silence; perfectly unmoved. Squire Dobie regarded him keenly with his dark and searching eyes.

"I know but little of the matter; less, apparently, than you know," he quietly said. "I am ready to tell you what that little is—but it will not help you, Squire Dobie.

"What do you mean in saying less than I know?"

"Because I never was near the Friar's Keep at all on that night. Your informants, I presume, must have been, by their assuming to know so much."

"They know nothing. It is all conjecture."

"Oh, all conjecture," returned Mr. Castlemaine, with the air of one suddenly enlightened. "And you come here and accuse me on conjecture? I ought to feel supremely indebted to you, Alfred Dobie."

"What they do say—that is not conjecture—is, that it was you who preceded Basil's son into the Keep."

"Who says it?"

"Basil's son said it, and thought it: it was only that that took him in, poor fellow. The landlord of the inn here, John Bent, saw it and says it."

"But John Bent was mistaken. And you have only his word, remember, for asserting what Basil's son saw or said."

Squire Dobie paused, looking full at his host, as if he could gather by looks whether he was deceiving him or not.

"Was it, or was it not you, who went into the Keep, James Castlemaine?"

"It was not. I have said from the first, I repeat it to you now, that I was not near the Keep that night: unless you call Teague's Hutt near it. As a matter of fact, the Hutt is near it, of course; but we estimate distances relatively—"

"I know how near it is," interrupted Squire Dobie. "I came round that way just now, up the lane; and took sounding of the places."

"Good. I went down to Teague's that night—you have no doubt heard all about the why and the wherefore. I smoked a pipe with Teague while making the arrangements to go for a sail with him on the morrow; and I came straight back again from the Hutt here, getting home at half-past eleven. I hear that Teague says he watched me up the lane: which I am sure I was not conscious of."

"You were at home here by half-past eleven?" spoke Squire Dobie.

"It had not gone the half hour."

"And did not go down the lane again?"

"Certainly not. I had nothing to go for. On the following morning, before it was light, I was roused from my bed by tidings of the death of my brother Peter, and I went off at once to Stilborough."

"Poor Peter!" exclaimed the Squire. "What a nice steady young fellow he was!—just the opposite of Basil. And what a name he afterwards made for himself!"

"When I returned to Greylands in the afternoon," quietly went on Mr. Castlemaine, "and found that Anthony was said to have disappeared unaccountably, and that my name was being bandied about in connection with it, you may imagine my astonishment."

"Yes, if you were really ignorant."

The Master of Greylands half rose from his chair, and then resumed it. His spirit, subdued hitherto, was quickening.

"Forbearance has its limits, Squire Dobie; so has courtesy. Will you inform me by what right you come into my house and persist in these most offensive and aspersive questions?"

"By the right of my former friendship for your brother Basil. I have no children of my own: never had any; and when I heard this tale, my heart warmed to poor Basil's son: I resolved to take up his cause, and try to discover what had become of him."

"Pardon me, that does not give you the right to intrude here with these outspoken suspicions."

"I think it does. The suspicions are abroad, James Castlemaine; ignore the fact to yourself as you may. Your name is cautiously used: people must be cautious, you know: not used at all perhaps in any way that could be laid hold of. One old fellow, indeed, whispered a pretty broad word; but caught it up again when half said."

"Who was he?" asked the Master of Greylands.

"I'll be shot if I tell you. John Bent? No, that it was not: John Bent seems as prudent as the rest of them. Look here, James Castlemaine: if an impression exists against you, you must not blame people, but circumstances. Look at the facts. Young Anthony comes over to claim his property which you hold, believing it to be his. You tell him it is not his, that it is yours; but you simply tell him this; you do not, in spite of his earnest request, prove it to him. There's bad blood between you: at any rate, there is on your side; and you have an open encounter in a field, where you abuse him and try to strike him. That same night he and John Bent, being abroad together, see you cross the road from this Chapel Lane, that leads direct from your house, you know, and enter the Friar's Keep; young Anthony runs over in your wake, and enters it also: and from that blessed moment he is never seen by mortal eyes again. People outside hear a shot and a scream—and that's all. Look dispassionately at the circumstances for yourself, and see if they do not afford grounds for suspicion."

"If all the facts were true—yes. The most essential link in them is without foundation—that it was I who went into the Friar's Keep. Let me put a question to you—what object can you possibly suppose I should have in quitting my house at midnight to pay a visit to that ghostly place?"

"I don't know. It puzzles everybody."

"If John Bent is really correct in his assertions, that some one did cross from the lane to the Friar's Keep, I can only assume it to have been a stranger. No inhabitant of Greylands, as I believe and now assure you Squire Dobie, would voluntarily enter that place in the middle of the night. It has an ill reputation for superstition: all kinds of ghostly fancies attach to it. I should about as soon think of quitting my house at night to pay a visit to the moon as to the Friar's Keep."

Squire Dobie sat in thought. All this was more than plausible; difficult to discredit. He began to wonder whether he had not been hard upon James Castlemaine.

"What is your opinion upon the disappearance?" he asked. "You must have formed one."

Mr. Castlemaine lifted his dark eyebrows.

"I can't form one," he said. "Sometimes I have thought Anthony must have attempted to run down the rocks by the uncertain path from the chapel ruins, and have perished in the sea; at others I think he may have left Greylands voluntarily that night, and will some day or other reappear again as unexpectedly. His father Basil was given to these impromptu flights, you know."

"But this is all supposition?"

"Undoubtedly it is. Who was it, then, they watched into the Keep, you ask?—that is the least-to-be-accounted-for statement of all. My opinion is that no one entered it; that John Bent's eyesight deceived him."

"And now one more question, James," resumed the Squire, insensibly returning to the more familiar appellation of former days: "is Greylands' Rest yours, or was it left to Basil?"

"It is mine."

"Did it come to you by will?"

For a moment Mr. Castlemaine hesitated before giving an answer. The persistent questioning annoyed him; and yet he did not know how to escape it.

"It became mine by deed of gift."

"Why did you not show the deed to Anthony?"

"I might have done so had he waited. He was too impatient. I should have done it:" and the emphasis here was marked. "To no one save yourself have I acknowledged so much, Squire Dobie. I recognize in none the right to question me."

Squire Dobie rose, taking his hat and stick from the side-table where he had laid them, and held out his hand to Mr. Castlemaine.

"If you are an innocent man, James, and I have said what cannot be justified, I heartily beg your pardon. Perhaps time will clear up the mystery. Meanwhile, if you will come over to Dobie Hall, and bring your family to stay a few days, I shall be glad to welcome you. Who was that nice-looking, delicate featured woman with the light hair?"

"With the light hair?—oh, my little daughter's governess. Madame Guise; a French lady."

"And the very pretty girl who was sitting by you?"

"Miss Reene. She is my wife's stepdaughter."

Squire Dobie took his departure, Mr. Castlemaine walking with him to the hall-door. When outside, the Squire stood for an instant as if deliberating which way to choose—the avenue, or the obscure by-way of Chapel Lane. He took the latter.

"I'll see this Commodore Teague and hear his version of it," he said to himself as he went on. "James Castlemaine speaks fairly, but doubts of him still linger on my mind: though why they should I know not."

Walking briskly up the lane, as he turned into it, came a tall, handsome young fellow, who bore a great resemblance to the Castlemaines. Squire Dobie accosted him.

"You should be James Castlemaine's son, young man."

Harry stopped.

"I am the son of the Master of Greylands."

"Ay. Can't mistake a Castlemaine. I am Squire Dobie. You've heard of the Dobies?"

"Oh dear, yes. I knew Mr. Tom Dobie and the old Squire."

"To be sure. Well, there's only me left of them. I have been to pay a visit to your father."

"I hope you found him at home, sir."

"Yes, and have been talking with him. Well you are a fine young fellow: over six feet, I suppose. I wish I had a son like you! Was that poor cousin of yours, young Anthony—who seems to have vanished more mysteriously than anybody ever vanished yet—was he a Castlemaine?"

"Not in height: he was rather short. But he had a regular Castlemaine face; as nice-looking as they say my Uncle Basil used to be."

"What has become of him?"

"I don't know. I wish I did know!" Harry added earnestly.

They parted. That this young fellow had borne no share in the business, and would be glad to find its elucidation, Squire Dobie saw. Turning down the little path, when he came to it, that led to the Hutt, he knocked at the door.

Commodore Teague was at dinner: taking it in the kitchen to save trouble. But he had the free and easy manners of a sailor, and ushered his unknown guest in without ceremony, and gave him the best seat, while the Squire introduced himself and his object in calling.

Squire Dobie?—come to know about that there business of young Mr. Castlemaine's, and how he got lost and where he went to: well, in his opinion it was all just moonshine. Yes, moonshine; and perhaps it might be also Squire Dobie's opinion that it was moonshine, if he could get to the top and bottom of it. Couldn't be a doubt that the young man had come out o' the Keep after going into it—'twarn't likely he'd stay long in that there ghostly place—and went off somewhere of his own accord. That's what he, Jack Teague, thought: though he'd not answer for it, neither, that the young fellow might not have made a false step on the slippery rock path, and gone head foremost down to Davy Jones's locker. The shot and scream? Didn't believe there ever was a scream that night; thought John Bent dreamt it; and the shot came from him, Teague; after cleaning his gun he loaded it and fired it off. The most foolish thing in it all was to suspect the Master of Greylands of marching into the Keep. As if he'd want to go there at midnight! or at any other time, for the matter of that. Mr. Castlemaine went away from his place between eleven and half-after; and he, Jack Teague, saw him go up the lane towards his house with his own eyes: 'twarn't likely he'd come down it again for the purpose of waylaying young Anthony, or what not.

Now, this was the substance of all that the anxious old friend of Basil Castlemaine could obtain from Commodore Teague. The Commodore seemed to be a rough, honest, jovial-speaking man, incapable of deceit, or of double dealing: and, indeed, as Squire Dobie asked himself, why should he be guilty of it in this matter? He went away fair puzzled, not knowing what to think; and leaving the savoury smell, proceeding from the Commodore's stew getting cold on the table. But why it should have pleased the Commodore to favour Squire Dobie with the rough and ready manners, the loose grammar, he used to the common people of Greylands, instead of being the gentleman that he could be when he chose, was best known to himself.

Crossing the road, as he emerged from the lane, the Squire entered the chapel ruins, and went to the edge of the land there. He saw the narrow, tortuous, and certainly, for those who had not a steady foot and head, dangerous path that led down to the strip of beach below: which beach was not discernible now, for it was high water. The path was rarely trodden by man: the ill reputation of the Friar's Keep kept the village away from it: and, otherwise, there was no possible inducement to tempt men down it. Neither, as some instinct taught Squire Dobie, had it been taken that night by young Anthony Castlemaine.

XXI

In the Chapel Ruins

Madam Guise sat buried in a reverie. Ethel was reading a French book aloud; Flora was practising: but Madame, supposed to be listening to both, heard neither the one nor the other.

Every minute of the hours that had passed since she saw the diamond ring of her unfortunate husband concealed in Mr. Castlemaine's bureau had been one of agony. The fright and horror she had experienced in the search was also telling upon her: her head ached, her pulses throbbed, her brain was fevered: and but for the dread of drawing attention to herself, that, in her nervousness, she feared might lead to suspicion, she would have pleaded illness and asked permission to remain that day in her chamber. No one but herself knew how she shrunk from Mr. Castlemaine: she could not be in the same room with him without feeling faint; to sit next to him at the dinner-table, to be inadvertently touched by him, was nothing less than torture. The finding of the ring was a proof to her that her husband had in truth met with the awful fate suspected; the concealment of the ring in the bureau, a sure and certain sign that Mr. Castlemaine was its author. When they were intruded upon at table by Squire Dobie with his accusing words, Charlotte Guise had been scarcely able to suppress her emotion. Mr. Castlemaine, in catching sight of the pallor of her face, had attributed it simply to the abrupt mention of the disagreeable subject: could he have suspected its true cause he had been far more put out than even by Squire Dobie's words. An idea had crossed Charlotte Guise—what if she were to declare herself to this good old gentleman, and beseech him to take up her cause.

But she did not dare. It was this she was thinking of now, when she ought to have been attending to Miss Flora's imperfect fingering. There were reasons why she might not; why, as she clearly saw, it might do her harm instead of good. With the one sole exception of the ring, there was no shadow of proof against Mr. Castlemaine: and upon the first slight breathing of hostilities, how quickly might he not do away with the ring for ever! And, once let it be declared that she was Anthony's wife, that her chief business in the house was to endeavour to track out the past, she would be expelled from it summarily and the door closed against her. How could she pursue her search then? No, she must not risk it; she must bury the ring in silence, and stay at her post.

"I should think I've practised long enough, for one afternoon, Madame!"

Flora gave a final dash at the keys as she spoke—enough to set a stoic's teeth on edge. Madame looked up languidly.

"Yes, you may shut the piano. My headache is painful and I cannot properly attend to you."

No need of further permission. Flora shut down the lid with a bang, and disappeared. Ethel closed her book.

"I beg your pardon for my thoughtlessness, Madame Guise. I ought not to have read to you: I forgot your headache. Can I get you anything for it?"

"Your reading has not hurt me at all, my dear. No, nothing: only time will cure me."

Ethel, who had moved to the window, and was standing at it suddenly burst into a laugh.

"I was thinking of that old gentleman's surprise," she said, "when he saw me here. His looks expressed it. Where do you think he had seen me to-day before, Madame Guise?"

The mention of the old gentleman—Squire Dobie—aroused Madame's interest. She lifted her languid head quickly. "I do not know."

"In Mrs. Bent's best kitchen, stoning raisins. I went into the Dolphin to get something for mamma, and began to help Mrs. Bent to do them, for she said she should be late with her pudding. Old Squire Dobie came in and saw me at them. When he found me at home here at dinner, I know he was puzzled."

"What a—strange manner he had;—what curious things he said to Mr. Castlemaine!" spoke Madame, seizing upon the opportunity.

"Yes," said Ethel, flushing scarlet. "I thought him very rude."

"He seemed to think that—that the young Mr. Anthony I have heard tell of was really killed in secret."

"You cannot help people thinking things."

"And by Mr. Castlemaine."

"It was very wrong of him; it must be very foolish. I wonder papa took it so calmly."

"You do not think it could be so then?"

"I! Is it likely, Madame Guise?"

"But suppose—my dear Miss Ethel, suppose some one were to tell you that it was so: that they had proof of it?"

"Proof of what?"

"Proof that Mr. Castlemaine did know what became of An—of the Mr. Anthony: proof that harm came to him?"

"I should laugh at them," said Ethel.

"And not believe it?"

"No, never."

Ethel left the room with the last words: perhaps to avoid the topic. Madame thought so, and sighed as she looked after her. It was only natural she thought: when we are fond of people we neither care to hear ill spoken of them, nor believe the ill; and Ethel was very fond of Mr. Castlemaine. Charlotte Guise did not wonder: but for this dreadful suspicion, she would have liked him herself. In fact she had insensibly began to like him, in spite of her prejudices, until this new and most convincing proof of his guilt was discovered in his bureau: the search for which had cost her conscience so much to set about, had taxed her fears so cruelly in the act, and was giving her so intense a torment now. "I wonder what will come of it all in the end?" she cried with a slight shiver. "Qui vivre, verra."

One of the Grey Sisters appeared at Greylands' Rest by-and-by, bringing up little Marie Guise. It was Sister Ruth. Mrs. Castlemaine had graciously invited the child to take tea with her mother. But Mrs. Castlemaine was one who rarely did a kindness without some inward motive—generally a selfish one. Marie was beginning to speak a little English now; but never willingly; never when her French could be by any possibility understood. To her mother she invariably spoke in French; and Mrs. Castlemaine had made the private discovery that, to hear the child and her mother speak together, might improve Flora's accent. So Madame Guise was quite at liberty to have Maxie up to tea as often as she liked.

"Do you remember your papa, dear?" asked Mrs. Castlemaine in English, as they sat round the tea-table; Mr. Castlemaine having gone to dine at the Dolphin.

"Sais pas, responded Marie shyly, hanging her head at the question.

"Do you like England better than France, Marie?" went on Mrs. Castlemaine.

"Sais pas," repeated the child unwillingly, as if she meant to cry.

"How is the little burnt girl? Better?"

"Sais pas, moi."

Evidently it was profitless work, the examining of Miss Marie Guise. Ethel laughed, and began talking to her in French. At best, she was but a timid little thing.

Madame Guise started at the dusk hour to take her home; proceeding to the front, open way, down the wide avenue and the high road. At the door of the Dolphin stood Mrs. Bent, a large cooking apron tied round her waist. She was wiping a cut-glass jug with a soft cloth, and apparently had stepped to the door while giving some directions to Ned, the man: who stood ready to run off somewhere without his hat.

"Mind, Ned; the very best mocha. And unless it is the best, don't bring it. I'd sooner use what I've got in the house."

Ned started off across the road in the direction of the beach: no doubt to Pike, the grocer's. Mrs. Bent was whisking in again, when she caught sight of Madame Guise and the little Marie.

"You are busy this evening," said Madame.

"We've got a dinner on," replied Mrs. Bent stooping to kiss Marie, of whom she had grown very fond during the child's sojourn and illness at the inn. "And I had no notice of it till midday—which of course makes one all the busier. I like to get things forward the day beforehand, and not leave 'em to the last minute: but if you don't know of it you can't do that."

"A dinner?—Yes, I think I heard it said at home that Mr. Castlemaine was dining at the Dolphin."

"He is here, for one. There are five of them altogether. Captain Scott—some grand man he is, they say, who goes about to look up the coastguard in places; and Superintendent Nettleby; and Mr. Blackett of the Grange. Lawyer Knivett of Stilborough makes the fifth, a friend of Captain Scott's. And I must run in, ma'am, for I'm wanted ten ways at once this evening."

Madame Guise passed on to the Nunnery, and entered it with the child. Sister Betsey shook her head, intimating that it was late for the little one to come in, considering that she had not long recovered from an illness: and she took her away at once.

This left Madame Guise alone with Miss Castlemaine. Mary Ursula sat away from the light, doing nothing: an unusual thing, for the Sisters made it a point to be always employed. The muslin cap was on her bright hair; her mourning dress, all crape, handsomer than was strictly consistent with the plain ideas of the community, fell in soft folds around her. These costly robes of Sister Mary Ursula's had been somewhat of a stumbling block in her change of existence: but, as all the Sisters said, it would be a sin against thrift to do away with them before they were worn out.

"You are thinking me very idle," she said to Madame Guise in a light tone of half apology for being caught with her hands before her. "But the truth is, I am feeling very tired this evening; unequal to work. I had a sleepless night, and got up with headache this morning."

"I too, had a sleepless night," said Madame Guise, forgetting caution in the sympathy of the moment. "Troubles were tormenting me."

"What troubles have you?" asked Mary Ursula in a kind, gentle tone. "You are satisfied with the care the Sisters give your little one?"

"Oh quite; quite. I am sure she is happy here."

"And you have told me that she and you are alone in the world."

Madame Guise untied her bonnet, and laid it on the chair beside her, before replying.

"Most of us have our troubles in one shape or another, I expect; sometimes they are of a nature that we do not care to speak of. It is that thing that the English call a skeleton in a closet. But—pardon me, Miss Castlemaine—you and I are both young to have already found the skeleton."

"True," said Mary Ursula: and for a moment she was silent from delicacy, intending to drop the subject. But her considerate goodness of heart induced her to speak at again.

"You are a lonely exile here, Madame: the land and its people are alike strange to you. If you have any source of trouble or care that it would be a comfort to you to share with another, or that I could in any way help to alleviate, impart it to me. You shall find me a true friend."

Just for one delusive instant, the impulse to take this grand and sweet and kindly lady into her confidence; to say to her I am trying to trace out my poor husband's fate; swayed Charlotte Guise. The next, she remembered that it must not be; that she was Miss Castlemaine, the niece of that great enemy.

"You are only too good and kind," she rejoined in a sad, faint tone. "I wish I could; I should ask nothing better: but there are some of our burthens we must bear alone."

"Are you quite comfortable at Greylands' Rest?" asked Mary Ursula, unable to repress the suspicion that Mrs. Castlemaine's temper or her young daughter's insolence might be rendering the governess's place a trying one.

"Yes—pretty well. That is, I should be," she hastily added, speaking on the impulse of the moment, "if I were quite sure the house was an honest one."

"The house an honest one!" echoed Mary Ursula in undisguised astonishment, a haughty flush dying her face. "What do you mean?"

"Ah, pardon me, madam!—It may be that I mistake terms—I am not English. I did not mean to say it was a thief's house."

"But what do you mean?"

Madame Guise looked full at the questioner. She spoke after a short consideration, dropping her voice to a half whisper.

"I would like to know—to feel sure—that Mr. Castlemaine did not do anything with that poor young man, his nephew."

Mary Ursula sat half confounded—the rejoinder was so very unexpected, the subject so entirely disagreeable.

"At least, Madame Guise, that cannot be any affair of yours."

"You are angry with me, madam; your words are cold, your tones resentful. The first evening that I arrived at Greylands I chanced to hear about that young man. Mollee, the servant at the inn, came up to help me make the tisane for my little child, and she talked. She told of the young man's strange disappearance, saying he was supposed to have been murdered: and that Mr. Castlemaine knew of it. Ah, it had a great effect upon me, that history; I was cold and miserable, and my little one was ill: I could not get it away from my mind."

"I think you might have done so by this time," frigidly remarked Mary Ursula.

"But it comes up now and again," she rejoined, "and that keeps alive the remembrance. Events bring it up. Only to-day, when we had not left the dinner-table, some stranger came pushing his way into the room behind Miles, asking Mr. Castlemaine what he had done with Basil's son, young Anthony. It put Mr. Castlemaine out; I saw his face change; and he sent us all from the room."

Mary Ursula forgot her coldness. It was this very subject that had deprived her past night of sleep: though she could no more confess it to Madame Guise than the latter could confess. The two were playing unconsciously at hide-and-seek with one another.

"Who was the stranger, Madame Guise?"

"Mr. Castlemaine called him Squire Dobie. They were together ever so long. Mr. Castlemaine, I say, did not like it; one might see that. Oh, when I think of what might have happened that night to the young Anthony, it makes me shudder."

"The best thing you can do is not to think of it, Madame Guise. It is nothing to you, one way or the other. And it is scarcely in good taste for you to be suspicious of Mr. Castlemaine while you are eating his bread. Rely upon it, when this matter shall have been cleared up—if it ever be cleared—Mr. Castlemaine will be found as good and honest as you are."

The bell for the Sisters' supper rang clanging out. Madame Guise put her bonnet on, and rose.

"Do forgive me," she whispered with deprecation. "I might not to have mentioned it to you; I did not wish to offend, or to hurt your feelings. But I am very lonely here; I have but my own heart to commune with."

"And thoughts are free," reflected Mary Ursula. "It was only natural that the mysterious story should lay hold of her." And in heart she excused the stranger.

"Be at ease," she said, taking Madame's hand. "Dismiss it from your mind. It is not a thing that need trouble you."

"Not trouble me!" repeated Madame Guise to herself as she went through the gate. "It is me alone that it ought to trouble, of all in the wide world."

She turned to the right, intending to go home by Chapel Lane, instead of crossing to the broad open front road; but to pass the Friar's Keep at any period of the day, and especially at night, had for Charlotte Guise an irresistible fascination. Some instinct within her, whether false or true, was always whispering that it was there she must seek for traces of her husband.

She reached the gate of the chapel ruins, hesitated, and then entered it. The same fascination that drew her to pass the Friar's Keep on her road home, caused her to enter the ruins that led to the place. A shiver, induced by nervousness, took her as she closed the gate behind her; and she did not pass into the Keep, but crossed over to the edge of the cliff. The sea and the boats on it seemed like so much company.

Not that many boats could be seen. Just two or three, fishing lower down beyond the village, rather far off, in fact; but their lights proved that they were there, and it made her feel less lonely. It was not a very light night: no moon, and the stars did not shine over brightly; but the atmosphere was clear, and the moss-covered wall of the Friar's Keep with its gothic door might be seen very distinctly.

"If I only dared go in and search about!—with a lantern or something of that!" she said to herself, glancing sideways at it. "I might come upon some token, some bit of his dress, perhaps, that had been torn away in the struggle. For a struggle there must have been. Anthony was brave, and he would not let them take his life without having a fight for it. Unless they shot him without warning!"

Burying her face in her hands, she shudderingly rehearsed over to herself what that struggle had probably been. It was foolish of her to do this, for it gave her unnecessary pain: but she had got into the habit of indulging these thoughts instead of checking them; and perhaps they came unbidden. You must not cherish your sorrow, we say to some friend who is overwhelmed with grief and despair. No, answers the poor sufferer: but how can I help it? Just so was it with Charlotte Guise. Day by day, night by night, she saw only her husband and his unhappy fate; she was as a sick person in some fever dream, whose poor brain has seized hold of one idea and rambles upon it for ever.

"There's the ring in Mr. Castlemaine's bureau!—and if I could find some other token of his person here, elucidation might come of it," she resumed, lifting her head. "A button; a glove; a torn bit of cloth?—I should know them all. It is pénible to continue to lead this false life! As I am, unknown, I can do nothing. I may not even ask John Bent to let me take just one look at his dear effects, or as much as open the lid of his small desk. While I am Madame Guise, it is no affair of mine, I should be told; I must not concern myself with it: but if I might show to the world that I am Charlotte Castlemaine, the right would be all mine. It is awkward; because I may not show it to them: and I can only search out traces in secret; that Friar's Keep may hold proofs of what his fate has been, if I could but go in and look for them."

She turned her head towards the old building, but not very courageously: at the best, it was but a ghostly-looking place at night: and then turned it back and gazed out to sea again.

"No. I should not have the bravery to go in alone; even if I could secure a lantern. There's that revenant that comes; and it might appear to me. I saw it as distinctly last night from Mr. Castlemaine's window as I ever saw anything in my life. And if I were in the place, and it appeared to me, I should die of fear.—I think I half died of fear last night when I heard the voice of Mr. Harry," she went on, after a pause:

"there was he, before me, and there was the revenant, over here, behind me; and—"

Some sound behind her at this moment nearly made Charlotte Guise start out of her skin. When buried in ghostly visions—say, for instance, in reading a frightful tale alone at night—we all know how a sudden noise will shake the nerves. The gate was opening behind Charlotte, and the fright sent her bang against the wall. There she cowered in the corner, her black clothes drawn round her, suppressing the cry that would have risen to her lips, and, praying to escape detection.

She did escape it. Thanks to the shade cast by the angle of projecting wall, and to her dark clothes, she remained unseen. It was Harry Castlemaine who had entered. He advanced to the edge of the cliff, but not near to her, and stood there for a few moments, apparently looking out to sea. Then he pushed open the gothic door, and passed into the Friar's Keep.

What was Charlotte Guise to do? Should she make a dart for the gate, to get away, running the risk of his coming out again and pouncing upon her; or should she stay where she was until he had gone again? She decided for the former, for her present situation was intolerable. After all, if he did see her, she must make the excuse that she had crossed the ruins to take a look at the beautiful sea: he could not surely suspect anything from that!

But this was not to be accomplished. She was just about to glide away from her hiding place, when the gate again opened, and some other figure, after looking cautiously about, came gliding into the ruins. A woman's light figure, enveloped in a dark cloak, its hood concealing the head and partly the face. It crossed the ruins cautiously, with a side look steadily directed to the Keep door, as if to guard against surprise, and then stood at the edge, under cover of the Keep, gazing attentively out to sea. Madame Guise was at the opposite corner close to the wall of the Nunnery, and watched all this. By the glimpse of the profile turned sideways to her, she thought it was the young girl they called Jane Hallet.

Slowly turning away from the sea, the girl was apparently about to steal back again, when she suddenly drew herself flat against the old moss-eaten wall of the Friar's Keep, and crouched down there. At the same moment, Harry Castlemaine came out of the Keep, strode with a quick step to the gate, and passed through it. The girl had evidently heard him coming out, and wished to avoid him. He crossed the road to Chapel Lane; and she, after taking another steady look across the sea, quitted the ruins also, and went scuttering down the hill in the direction of her home.

Charlotte Guise breathed again. Apart from her husband's disappearance and the tales of the revenant she so dreaded, Charlotte could not help thinking that things connected with the Friar's Keep looked romantic and mysterious. Giving ample time for Harry Castlemaine to have got half way up the lane on his road home, she entered the lane herself, after glancing up at the two windows, behind which the Grey Friar was wont to appear. All was dark and silent there to-night. She had not gone ten paces up the lane, when quick, firm footsteps were heard behind her: those of the Master of Greylands. Not caring to encounter him, still less that he should know she chose that lonely road for returning home at night, she drew aside among the trees while he passed. He turned down to the Hutt, and Madame Guise went hastening onwards.

Mr. Castlemaine was on his way homewards from the dinner at the Dolphin. When the party broke up, he had given his arm to Nettleby the superintendent; who had decidedly taken as much as he could conveniently carry. It pleased the Master of Greylands, in spite of his social superiority, to make much of the superintendent as a general rule; he was always cordial with him. Captain Scott had taken the same—for in those days hard drinking was thought less ill of than it is in these— and had fallen fast asleep in one of John Bent's good old-fashioned chairs. As Mr. Castlemaine came out of the superintendent's gate after seeing him safely indoors, he found Lawyer Knivett there.

"Why, Knivett, is it you?" he exclaimed. "I thought you and the captain were already on your road to Stilborough."

"Time enough," replied the lawyer. "Will you take a stroll on the beach? It's a nice night."

Mr. Castlemaine put his arm within the speaker's, and they crossed over in that direction. Both of them were sober as judges. It was hardly light enough to see much of the beauty of the sea; but Mr. Knivett professed to enjoy it, saying he did not get the chance of its sight or its breezes at Stilborough. In point of fact, he had something to say to the Master of Greylands, and did not care to enter upon the subject abruptly.

"Weary work, it must be, for those night fishermen!" remarked the lawyer, pointing to two or three stationary lights in the distance.

"They are used to it, Knivett."

"I suppose so. Use goes a great way in this life. By the way, Mr. Castlemaine—it has just occurred to me—I wish you'd let me give you a word of advice, and receive it in good part."

"What is it? Speak out."

"Could you not manage to show the deed of tenure by which you own Greylands' Rest?" pursued the lawyer, insensibly dropping his voice.

"I suppose I could if I chose," replied Mr. Castlemaine, after a scarcely perceptible pause.

"Then I should recommend you to do so. I have wanted to say this to you for some little time; but the truth is, I did not know how you would take it."

"Why have you wanted to say it to me?"

"Well—the fact is, people are talking. People will talk, you know—great idiots! If you could contrive to let somebody see the deed—of course you'd not seem to show it purposely—by which you hold the property, the world would be convinced that you had no cause to—to wish young Anthony out of the way, and would stop its blatant tongue. Do so, Mr. Castlemaine."

"I conclude you mean to insinuate that the world is saying I put Anthony out of the way."

"Something of that. Oh, people are foolish simpletons at the best. Of course, there's nothing in it; they are sure of that; but, don't you perceive, once let them know that young Anthony's pretensions had not a leg to stand upon, and they'd see there was no mo——in fact, they'd shut up at once," broke off the lawyer, feeling that he might be treading on dangerous ground. "If you have the deed at hand, let it be seen one of these first fine days by some worthy man whose word can be taken."

"And that would stop the tongues you say?"

"Undoubtedly it would. It would be a proof that you, at least, could have no motive for wishing Anthony elsewhere," added the lawyer more boldly.

"Then, listen to my answer, Knivett: No. I will never show it for any such purpose; never as long as I live. If the world likes to talk, let it talk."

"It does talk," urged the lawyer ruefully.

"It is quite welcome to talk, for me. I am astonished at you, Knivett; you might have known me better than to suggest such a thing. But that you were so valued by my father, and respected by me, I should have knocked you down."

The haughty spirit of the Master of Greylands had been aroused by the insinuation: he spoke coldly, proudly, and resentfully. Mr. Knivett knitted his brow: but he had partly expected this.

"The suggestion was made in friendliness," he said.

"Of course. But it was a mistake. We will forget it, Knivett."

They shook hands in silence. Mr. Knivett crossed over to the inn, where the fly waited to convey himself and Captain Scott to Stilborough; and the Master of Greylands had then commenced his walk homewards, taking the road that would lead him through Chapel Lane.

XXII

Miss Hallet in the Dust

Miss Hallet stood in the parlour of her pretty cottage on the cliff. For a wonder, she was doing nothing—being usually a most industrious body. As she stood upright in deep thought, her spare, straight, up-and-down figure motionless, her pale face still, it might be seen that some matter was troubling her mind. The matter was this: Jane (as she phrased it to herself) was getting beyond her.

A week or more had elapsed since the night Jane had made the accident to Polly Gleeson an excuse for staying out late. Children could not be burnt every night,—and yet the fault continued. Each night, since then, had she been out, and stayed later than she ought to stay: a great deal later than her aunt considered was at all proper or expedient. On the previous night, Miss Hallet had essayed to stop it. When Jane put on her cloak to take what she called her run down the cliff, Miss Hallet in her stern, quiet way, had said, "You are not going this evening, Jane." Jane's answer had been, "I must go, aunt; I have something to do"—and went.

"What's to be done if she won't mind me?" deliberated Miss Hallet. "I can't lock her up: she's too old for it. What she can possibly want, flying down the cliff night after night, passes my comprehension. As to sitting with Goody Dance or any other old fish-wife, as Jane sometimes tells me she has been doing, I don't believe a word of it. Its not in the nature of young girls to shut themselves up so much with the aged. Why, I have heard Jane call me old behind my back—and I want a good twenty or thirty years of old Dame Dance's age."

Miss Hand stopped a minute, to listen to sounds overhead. Jane was up there making the beds. She soon resumed her reflections.

"No, it's not Mother Dance, or any other old mother. It's her love of tattle and gossip. When young girls can get together, they'd talk of the moon if there was no other subject at hand—chattering geese! But that there's not a young chap in all the village that Jane would condescend to look at, I might think she had picked up a sweetheart. She holds herself too high for any of them. And quite right too: she is above them. They are but a parcel of poor fishers: and as to that young Pike, who serves in his father's shop, he has no more sense in him, and Jane knows it, than a kite's tail. No, it's not sweethearts! it's dawdling and gossip along with Susan Pike and the rest of the foolish girls. But oh, how things have changed!—to think that Jane Hallet should consort with such!"

Miss Hallet lifted her eyes to the ceiling, as though she could see through it what Jane was about. By the sound it seemed that she was sweeping the carpet.

"She is a good girl on the whole; I own that," went on Miss Hallet. "Up betimes in a morning, and keeping steady to whatever she has to do, whether it may be housework or sewing: and never gadding in the day-time. The run in the evening does her good, she says: perhaps so: but the staying late doesn't. I don't like to be harsh with her," continued Miss Hallet, after a pause. "She stands alone, save for me, now her brother's gone—and she grieves after him still. Moreover, I am not sure that Jane would stand any harsh authority, if I did put it forth. Poor George would not—though I am sure I only wanted to control him for his good: he went off and made a home for himself down in the village: and Jane has a touch of her brother's spirit. There's the difficulty."

At this moment Jane ran down the stairs with a broom and dust-pan, and went into the kitchen. Presently she came forth in her bonnet and shawl, a small basket in her hand.

"Where are you off to?" asked Miss Hallet snappishly. For if she did acknowledge to herself that Jane was a good girl, there was no necessity to let Jane know it. And Miss Hallet was one of those rigid, well-meaning people who can hardly ever speak to friend or foe without appearing cross. All for their good, of course: as this tart tone was for Jane's.

"To buy the eggs, aunt. You told me I was to go for them when I had done the rooms."

"I'll go for the eggs myself," said Miss Hallet, "I'll not be beholden to you to do my errands. Take your bonnet off and get to your work. Those handkerchiefs of Mrs. Castlemaine's don't seem to progress very quickly."

"They are all finished but one, aunt. There have been the initial letters to work—which Mrs. Castlemaine decided afterwards to have done; and the letters take time."

"Put off your things, I say."

Jane went away with her bonnet and shawl, came back, and sat down to her sewing. She did not say, Why are you so angry with me? she knew quite well why it was, and preferred to avoid unsatisfactory topics. Miss Hallet deliberately attired herself, and went out for the eggs. They kept no servant: the ordinary work of the house was light: and when rougher labour was required, washing and cleaning, a woman came in from the village to do it. The Hallets were originally of fairly good descent. Miss Hallet had been well reared, and her instincts were undoubtedly those of a gentlewoman: but when in early life she found that she would have to turn out in the world and work for her living, it was a blow that she never could get over. A feeling of blight took possession of her even now when she looked back at that time. In the course of years she retired on the money bequeathed to her, and on some savings of her own. Her brother (who had never risen higher than to be the captain of a small schooner) had then become a widower with two children. He died: and these children were left to the mercy of the world, very much as he and his sister had been left some twenty years before. Miss Hallet took to them. George was drowned: it has been already stated: Jane was with her still; and, as the reader sees, was not altogether giving satisfaction. In Miss Hallet's opinion, Jane's destiny was already fixed: she would lead a single life, and grow gradually into an old maid, as she herself had done. Miss Hallet considered it the best destiny Jane could invoke: whether it was or not, there seemed to be no help for it. Men whom she would have deemed Jane's equals, were above them in position: and she believed Jane would not look at an inferior. So Miss Hallet had continued to live on in her somewhat isolated life; civil to the people around her but associating with none; and always conscious that her fortunes and her just merits were at variance.

She attired herself in a rather handsome shawl and close straw bonnet, and went down the cliff after the required eggs. Jane sat at the open parlour window, busy over the last of Mrs. Castlemaine's handkerchiefs. She wore her neat morning print gown, with its small white collar and bow of fresh lilac ribbon, and looked cool and pretty. Miss Hallet grumbled frightfully at anything like extravagance in dress; but at the same time would have rated Jane soundly had she seen her untidy or anything but nice in any one particular. When the echo of her aunt's footsteps had fully died away, Jane laid the handkerchief on the table, and took from her pocket some other material, which she began to work at stealthily.

That's the right word for it—stealthily. For she glanced cautiously around as if the very moss on the cliff side would take note of it, and she kept her ears well on the alert, to guard against surprise. Miss Hallet had told her she did not get on very quickly with the handkerchiefs: but Miss Hallet did not know, or suspect, that when times were propitious—namely, when she herself was away from observation, or Jane safely shut up in her own room—the handkerchiefs were discarded for this other work. And yet, the work regarded casually, presented no private or ugly features. It looked like a strip of fine lawn, and was just as nice-looking and snowy as the cambric on the table.

Jane's fingers plied quickly their needle and thread. Presently she slipped a pattern of thin paper out of her pocket, unfolded it, and began to cut the lawn according to its fashion. While thus occupied, her attentive ear caught the sound of approaching footsteps: in a trice, pattern and work were in her pocket again out of sight, and she was diligently pursuing the hem-stitching of the handkerchief.

A tall, plain girl, with straggling curls of a deep red darkened the window: Miss Susan Pike, daughter of Pike, the well-to-do grocer and general dealer. Deep down in Jane Hallet's heart there had always lain an instinctive consciousness, warning her that she was superior to this girl, as well as to Matty Nettleby, of quite a different order altogether: but the young crave companionship, and will have it, suitable or unsuitable, where it is to be had. The only young lady in the place was Ethel Reene, and Jane Hallet's good sense told her that that companionship would be just as unsuitable the other way: she might as well aspire to covet an intimacy with a duchess's daughter as with Miss Reene.

"Weil, you are hard at work this morning, Jane!" was Miss Susan Pike's unceremonious and somewhat resentful salutation, as she put her hands upon the window-sill and, her head inside. For she did not at all favour work herself.

"Will you come in, Susan?" returned Jane, rising and unslipping the bolt of the door: which she had slipped after the departure of her aunt.

"Them are Mrs. Castlemaine's handkerchiefs, I suppose," observed Susan, responding to the invitation and taking a chair. "Grand fine cambric, ain't it! Well, Jane, you do hem-stitch well, I must say."

"I have to work her initials on them also," remarked Jane. "S.C."

"S.C.," repeated Miss Pike. "What do the S. stand for? What's her Chris'en name?"

"Sophia."

"Sophia!—that is a smart name. Do you work the letters in satin stitch?"

"Yes. With the dots on each side it."

"You learnt all that fine hem-stitching and braider-work at the Nunnery, Jane—and your aunt knows how to do it too, I suppose. I shouldn't have patience for it. I'd rather lade out treacle all day: and of all precious disagreeable articles our shop serves, treacle's the worst. I hate it—sticking one's hands, and messing the scales. I broke a basin yesterday morning, lading it out," continued Miss Susan: "let it slip through my fingers. Sister Phoebe came in for a pound of it, to make the ladies a pudding for dinner, she said; and I let her basin drop. Didn't mother rate me!"

"Did Sister Phoebe say how the child was getting on?—Polly Gleeson."

"Polly's three parts well, I think. Old Parker does not go across there any more. I say, Jane, I came up to ask if you'd come along with me to Stilborough this afternoon."

"I can't," said Jane. "My aunt has been very angry with me this morning. I should no more dare to ask her to let me go to Stilborough to-day than I should dare to fly."

"What has she been angry about?"

"Oh, about my not getting on with my work, and one thing or other," replied Jane carelessly. "She would not let me fetch some eggs just now; she's gone herself. And she knows that in a few days' time I shall have to go to Stilborough on my own account."

"She's a nice article for an aunt!" grumbled Miss Susan. "I've got to order in some things for the shop, and I thought it would be pleasant for us two to walk there together. You are sure you can't come Jane?"

"Quite sure. It is of no use talking of it."

"I must ask Matty Nettleby, then. But I'd rather have had you."

Miss Susan, who was somewhat younger than Jane, and wore dirty pink bonnet strings, which did not contrast well with the red curls, and a tumbled, untidy frock (but who would no doubt go off on her expedition to Stilborough finer than an African queen) fingered discontentedly, one by one, the scissors, cotton, and other articles in Jane's work-box. She was not of good temper.

"Well, it's a bother! I can't think what right aunts have to domineer over folks! And I must be off to keep shop, or I shall have mother about me. Father's got one of his liver bouts, and is lying abed till dinner-time."

"I wish you'd bring me a pound of wool from Stilborough, Susan? You know where I buy it."

"Let's have the number, then."

Jane gave her a skein of the size and colour wanted, and the money for the purchase. "I'll come down for it this evening," she said. "You'll be back then."

"All right. Good-bye, Jane."

"Good-bye," returned Jane. And as the damsel's fleet steps betook her down the cliff, Jane bolted the door again, put the cambric handkerchief aside, and took the private work out of her pocket.

Meanwhile Miss Hallet had reached the village. Not very speedily. When she went out—which was but seldom—she liked to take her leisure over it. She turned aside to Tim Gleeson's cottage, to inquire after Polly; she halted at the door of two or three more poor fishermen's huts to give the good morrow, or ask after the little ones. Miss Hallet's face was cold, her manner harsh: but she could feel for the troubles of the world, and she gave what help she could to the poor folks around her.

The old woman from whom she bought her eggs, lived in a small cottage past the Dolphin Inn. Miss Hallet got her basket filled—she and Jane often had eggs and bread and butter for dinner to save cooking—paid, and talked a bit with the woman. In returning, Mrs. Bent was at the inn door, in her chintz gown and cherry cap ribbons.

"Is it you, Miss Hallet! How are you this morning?"

"Quite well, thank you," replied Miss Hallet in her prim way.

"Been getting some eggs, I see," ran on Mrs. Bent, unceremoniously. "It's not often you come down to do your own errands. Where's Jane?"

"I left her at work," was the answer. "Jane does not get through her sewing as quickly as she might, and I have been telling her of it."

"You can't put old heads upon young shoulders," cried Mrs. Bent. "Girls like to be idle; and that's the truth. What do you suppose I caught that Molly of mine at, last night? Stuck down at the kitchen table, writing a love-letter."

Miss Hallet had her eyes bent on her eggs, as though she were counting them.

"Writing a letter, if you'll believe me! And, a fine thing of a letter it was! Smudged with ink and the writing like nothing on earth but spiders' legs in a fit. I ordered it put on the fire. She's not going to waste her time in scribbling to sweethearts while she stays with me."

"Did she rebel?" quickly asked Miss Hallet.

"Rebel! Molly! I should like to see her attempt it. She was just as sheepish as a calf at being found out, and sent the paper into the fire quicker than I could order it in."

Gossip about Mrs. Bent's Molly, or any other Molly, was never satisfactory to Miss Hallet. She broke the subject by inquiring after John Bent's health, preparatory to pursuing her way.

"Oh, he's well enough," was Mrs. Bent's answer. "It's not often men get anything the matter with them. If they were possessed of as much common sense as they are of health, I'd say it was a blessing. That weak-souled husband of mine, seeing Molly piping and sniffing last night, told me privately that he saw no harm in love-letters. He'd see no harm in a score of donkeys prancing over his young plants and other garden stuff next, leave him alone."

"I am glad Mr. Bent is well," said Miss Hallet, taking a step onwards. "Jane told me last week he was ill."

"He had a bilious attack. Jane came in the same night and saw him with his head on a cushion. By the way—look here, Miss Hallet—talking about Jane—I'd not let her be out quite so much after dark, if I were you."

No words could have been more unwelcome to Miss Hallet than these. She was a very proud woman, never brooking advice of any kind. In her heart she regarded Jane as being so infinitely superior to all Greylands, the Greylands' Rest family and the doctor's excepted, that any reproach cast on her seemed nothing less than a presumption. It might please herself to reflect upon her niece for gadding about, but it did not please her that others should.

"Young girls like their fling; I know that," went on Mrs. Bent, who never stayed her tongue for anybody. "To coop 'em up in a pen, like a parcel of old hens, doesn't do. But there's reason in all things: and it seems to me that Jane's out night after night.'

"My niece comes down the cliff for a run at dusk, when it is too dark for her to see to sew," stiffly responded Miss Hallet. "I have yet to learn, Mrs. Bent, what harm the run can do to her or to you."

"None to me, for certain; I hope none to her. I see her in Mr. Harry Castlemaine's company a little oftener than I should choose a girl of mine to be in it. I do not say it is for any harm; don't take up that notion, Miss Hallet; but Mr. Harry's not the right sort of man, being a gentleman, for Jane to make a companion of."

"And who says Jane does make him her companion?"

"I do. She is with him more than's suitable. And—look here, Miss Hallet, if I'm saying this to you, it is with a good motive and because

I have a true regard for Jane, so I hope you will take it in the friendly spirit it's meant. If they walked together by daylight, I'd not think so much of it, though in my opinion that would not be the proper thing, considering the difference between them, who he is and who she is: but it is not by daylight, it is after dark."

Miss Hallet felt a sudden chill—as though somebody were pouring cold water down her back. But she was bitterly resentful, and very hard of belief. Mrs. Bent saw the proud lines of the cold face.

"Look here, Miss Hallet. I don't say there's any harm come of it, or likely to come: if I'd thought that, I'd have told you before. Girls are more heedless than the wind, and when they are as pretty as Jane is young men like to talk to them. Mr. Harry is in and about the village at night—he often says to me how dull his own home is—and he and Jane chance to meet somewhere or other, and they talk and laugh together, roaming about while they do it. That's the worst of it, I hope: but it is not a prudent thing for Jane to do."

"Jane stays down here with her friends; she is never at a loss for companions," resentfully spoke Miss Hallet. "She sits with old Goody Dance: and she is a good deal with Miss Nettleby and with Pike's daughter; sometimes staying in one place, sometimes in another. Why, one evening last week—Thursday was it? yes, Thursday—she said she was here, helping you."

"So she was here. We had a party in the best room that night. Jane ran in; and, seeing how busy I was, she helped me to wash up the glass: she's always good-natured and ready to forward a body. She stayed here till half-past eight o'clock."

Miss Hallet's face looked doubly grim. It was nearer half-past ten than half-past eight when Miss Jane made her appearance at home—as she well remembered.

"And now don't you go blowing up Jane through what I've said," enjoined Mrs. Bent. "We were young ourselves once, and liked our liberty. She's thoughtless; that's all; if she were a few years older, she would have the sense to know that folks might get talking about her. Just give her a caution, Miss Hallet: and remind her that Mr. Harry Castlemaine is just about as far above her and us, as the moon's higher than that old weather-cock a-top of the Nunnery."

Miss Hallet went homewards with her eggs. She had perfect confidence in Jane, in her conduct and principles. Jane, as she believed, would never make a habit of walking with Mr. Harry Castlemaine, or he with her: they had both too much common sense. Unless—and a flush illumined Miss Hallet's face at the sudden thought—unless they had fallen into some foolish, fancied love affair with one another.

"Such things have happened before now, of course," reasoned Miss Hallet to herself as she began her ascent of the cliff but her tone was dubious, almost as though she would have liked to be able to tell herself that they never had happened. "But they would know better; both of them; remembering that nothing could come of it. As to the walking together—I believe that's three parts Mrs. Bent's imagination. It is not likely to be true. Good morning, Darke!"

A fisherman in a red cap, jolting down the cliff, had saluted Miss Hallet in passing. She went on with her thoughts.

"Suppose I watch Jane a bit? There's nothing I should so much hate as to speak to her upon a topic such as this, and then find I had spoken without cause. It would be derogatory to her and to me. Yes," added Miss Hallet with decision, "that will be the best plan. The next time Jane goes out at dusk, I'll follow her."

The next time happened to be that same evening. Miss Hallet gave not a word of scolding to Jane all day: and the latter kept diligently to her work at Mrs. Castlemaine's handkerchief. At dusk Jane put her warm dark cloak on, and the soft quilted bonnet.

"Where are you going to-night?" questioned Miss Hallet then, with a stress of emphasis on the to-night.

"Just down the cliff, aunt. I want to get the wool Susan Pike was to buy for me at Stilborough."

"Always an excuse for gadding out!" exclaimed Miss Hallet.

"Well, aunt, I must have the wool. I may be wanting it to-morrow."

"You'll toast me two thin bits of toast before you go," said the aunt snappishly.

Jane put off her cloak and proceeded to cut the slices of bread and toast them. But the fire was very low, and they took some considerable time to brown properly.

"Do you wish the toast buttered, aunt?"

"No. Cut it in strips. And now go and draw me my ale."

"It is early for supper, aunt."

"You do as you are bid, Jane. If I feel cold, I suppose I am at liberty to drink my ale a trifle earlier than usual, to warm me."

Jane drew the ale in a china mug that held exactly half-a-pint, and brought it in. It was Miss Hallet's evening allowance: one she never exceeded. Her supper frequently consisted of what she was about to take now: the strips of toast soaked in the ale, and eaten. It was much favoured by elderly people in those days, and was called Toast-and-ale.

Jane resumed her cloak, and was allowed to depart without farther hindrance. But during the detention, the dusk of the evening had become nearly dark. Perhaps Miss Hallet had intended this.

She ate a small portion of the toast very quickly, drank some of the ale, leaving the rest for her return, and had her own bonnet and dark shawl on in no time. Then, locking her house door for safety, she followed in the wake of Jane.

She saw Jane before she reached the foot of the cliff: for the latter's light steps had been detained by encountering Tim and Nancy Gleeson, who could not be immediately got rid of. Miss Hallet halted as a matter of precaution: it would not answer to overtake her. Jane went onwards, and darted across the road to Pike's shop. Miss Hallet stood in a shady angle underneath the cliff, and waited.

Waited for a good half hour. At the end of that time Jane came out again, a paper parcel in her hand. "The wool," thought Miss Hallet, moving her feet about, for they were getting cramped. "And now where's she going? On to the beach, I shouldn't wonder!"

Not to the beach. Jane came back by the side of the shops, the butcher's and the baker's and the little humble draper's, and turned the corner that led to the Grey Nunnery. Miss Hallet cautiously crossed the road to follow her. When Miss Hallet had her in view again, Jane had halted, and seemed to be doing something to her cloak. The aunt managed to make out that Jane was drawing its hood over her quilted bonnet, so as to shade her face. With the loose cloak hiding her figure, and the hood the best part of her face, Jane's worst enemy would not have known her speedily.

Away she sped again with a swift foot; not running, but walking lightly and quickly. The stars were very bright: night reigned. Miss Hallet, spare of form, could walk almost as quickly as Jane and she kept her in view. Onwards, past the gate of the Nunnery, went Jane to the exceeding surprise of Miss Hallet. What could her business be, in that lonely road?—a road that she herself, who had more than double the years and courage of Jane, would not have especially chosen as a promenade at night. Could Jane be going dancing up to the coastguard station, to inquire after Henry Mann's sick wife? What simpletons young girls were! They had no sense at all: and thought no more of appearances than—

A shrill noise, right over Miss Hallet's head, cut her reflections suddenly short, and sent her with a start against the Nunnery palings. It was a bird flying across, from seaward, which had chosen to make known his presence. The incident did not divert her attention from the pursuit for more than an instant: but in that instant she lost sight of Jane.

What an extraordinary thing! Where was she? How had she vanished? Miss Hallet strained her eyes as she asked the questions. When the bird suddenly diverted her attention, Jane had nearly gained the gate that led into the chapel ruins; might perhaps have been quite abreast of it. That Jane would not go in there, Miss Hallet felt quite convinced of; nobody would go in. She had not crossed the road to Chapel Lane or Miss Hallet could not have failed to see her cross it: it was equally certain that she was not anywhere in the road now.

Miss Hallet turned herself about like a bewildered woman. It was an occurrence so strangely mysterious as to savour of unreality. The highway had no trap-doors in it: Jane could not have been caught up into the air.

Miss Hallet walked slowly onwards, marvelling, and gazing about in all directions. When opposite the chapel gate, she took courage to look through the palings at that ghost-reputed place: but all there seemed lonely and silent as the grave. She raised her voice in call—just as John Bent had once raised his voice in the silent night after the ill-fated Anthony Castlemaine.

"Jane! Jane Hallet!"

"What on earth can have become of her?" debated Miss Hallet, as no response was made to the call. "She can't have gone up Chapel Lane!"

With a view to see (in spite of her conviction) whether Jane was in the lane, Miss Hallet betook herself to cross over towards it. She went slowly; glancing around and about her; and had got to the middle of the road when a faint light appeared in one of the windows of the Friar's Keep. Miss Hallet had heard that this same kind of faint light generally heralded the apparition of the Grey Monk; and she stood transfixed with horror.

Sure enough! A moment later, and the figure in his grey cowl and habit glided slowly past the window, lamp in hand. The unhappy lady gave one terror-stricken, piercing scream, and dropped down flat in the dusty highway.

XXIII

The Secret Passage

The kitchen at the Grey Nunnery was flagged with slate-coloured stone. A spacious apartment: though, it must be confessed, very barely furnished. A dresser, with its shelves, holding plates and dishes; a few pots and pans; some wooden chairs; and a large deal table in the centre of the room, were the principal features that caught the eye.

The time was evening. Three of the Sisters were ironing. Or, to be quite correct, two of them were ironing, and the other, Sister Ann, was attending to the irons at the fire, and to the horse full of fresh ironed clothes, that stood near it. The fire threw its ruddy glow around: upon the plates, of the old common willow pattern, ranged on the dresser-shelves, on the tin dish-covers, hanging against the wall, on the ironing blanket, spread on the large table. One candle only was on the board, for the Sisters were economical, and moreover possessed good eyesight; it was but a common dip in an upright iron candlestick, and required to be snuffed often. Each of the two Sisters, standing side by side, had her ironing stand on her right hand, down on which she clapped the iron continually. They wore their muslin caps, and had on ample brown-holland aprons that completely shielded their grey gowns, with over-sleeves of the same material that reached up nearly to the elbow.

The Sisters were enjoying a little friendly dispute: for such things (and sometimes not altogether friendly) will take place in the best regulated communities. Some pea-soup, that had formed a portion of the dinner that day, was not good: each of the three Sisters held her own opinion as to the cause of its defects.

"I tell you it was the fault of the peas," said Sister Caroline, who was cook that week and had made the soup. "You can't make good soup with bad peas. It's not the first time they have sent us bad peas from that place."

"There's nothing the matter with the peas," dissented fat little Sister Phoeby, who had to stand in her pattens to obtain proper command of the board whenever it was her turn to iron. "I know peas when I look at them, I hope, and I say these are good."

"Why, they would not boil at all," retorted Sister Caroline.

"That's because you did not soak them long enough."

"Soaking or not soaking does not seem to make much difference," said the aspersed Sister, shaking out a muslin kerchief violently before spreading it on the blanket. "The last time it was my week for cooking we had pea-soup twice. I soaked the peas for four-and-twenty hours; and yet the soup was grumbled at! Give me a fresh iron, please, Sister Ann."

Sister Ann, in taking one of the irons from between the bars of the grate, let it fall with a crash on the purgatory. It made a fine clatter, and both the ironers looked round. Sister Ann picked it up; rubbed it on the ironing cloth to see that it was the right heat, put it on Sister Caroline's stand, and took away the cool one.

"The fact is this," she said, putting the latter to the fire, "you can't make pea-soup, Sister Caroline. Now, it's of no use to fly out: you can't. You don't go the right way to make it. You just put on the liquor that the beef or pork has been boiled in, or from bones stewed down, as may be, and you boil the peas in that, and serve it up as pea-soup. Fine soup it is! No flavour, no goodness, no anything. The stock is good enough: we can't afford better; and nobody need have better: but if you want your pea-soup to be nice, you must stew plenty of vegetables in it—carrots especially, and the outside leaves of celery. That gives it a delicious flavour: and you need not use half the quantity of peas if you pass the pulp of the vegetables with them through the calender."

"Oh, yes!" returned Sister Caroline in a sarcastic tone. "Your pea-soup is always good: we all know that!"

"And so it is good," was easy-tempered Sister Ann's cheery answer: and she knew that she spoke the truth. "The soup I make is not a tasteless stodge that you may almost cut with the spoon, as the soup was to-day; but a delicious, palatable soup that anybody may enjoy, fit for the company-table of the Master of Greylands. Just look how your candle wants snuffing!"

Sister Caroline snuffed the candle with a fling, and put down the snuffers. She did not like to be found fault with. Sister Phoeby, who wanted a fresh iron, went clanking to the fire in her pattens, and got it for herself, leaving her own in the bars. Sister Ann was busy just then, turning the clothes on the horse.

"What I should do with that cold pea-soup is this—for I'm sure it can never be eaten as it is," suggested Sister Ann to the cook. "You've got the liquor from that boiled knuckle of ham in the larder; put it on early to-morrow with plenty of water and fresh vegetables; half an hour before dinner strain the vegetables off, and turn the pea-soup into it. It will thin it by the one half, and make it palatable."

"What's the time?" demanded Sister Caroline, making no answering comment to the advice. "Does anybody know?"

"It must have struck half-past eight."

"Was not Sister Margaret to have some arrowroot taken up?"

"Yes, I'll make it," said Sister Ann. "You two keep on, with the ironing."

Sister Margaret was temporarily indisposed; the result, Mr. Parker thought, of a chill; and was confined to her bed. Taking a small saucepan from its place, Sister Ann was reaching in the cupboard for the tin of arrowroot, when a most tremendous ringing came to the house bell. Whether it was one prolonged ring, or a succession of rings, they could not tell; but it never ceased, and it alarmed the Sisters. Cries and shrieks were also heard outside.

"It must be fire!" exclaimed the startled women.

All three rushed out of the kitchen and made for the front door, Sister Phoeby kicking off her pattens that she might ran the quicker. Old Sister Mildred, who had become so much better of late that she was about again just as the other ladies were, appeared at the door of the parlour with Sister Mary Ursula.

"Make haste, children! make haste!" she cried, as the three were fumbling at the entrance-door, and impeding one another; for "The more haste the less speed," as says the old proverb, held good here.

When it was flung open, some prostrate body in a shawl and bonnet was discovered there, uttering cries and dismal moans. The Sisters hastened to raise her, and found it was Miss Hallet. Miss Hallet covered from head to foot in dust. She staggered in, clinging to them all. Jane followed more sedately, but looking white and scared.

"Dear, dear!" exclaimed compassionating Sister Mildred, whose deafness was somewhat better with her improved health, so that she did not always need her new ear-trumpet. "Have you had an accident, Miss Hallet? Pray come into the parlour."

Seated there in Sister Mildred's own easy-chair, her shawl unfastened by sympathising hands, her bonnet removed, Miss. Hallet's gasps culminated in a fit of hysterics. Between her cries she managed to disclose the truth—the Grey Monk had appeared to her.

Some of the Sisters gave a shiver and drew closer together. The Grey Monk again!

MRS. HENRY WOOD

"But all the dust that is upon you?" asked Sister Phoeby. "Did the Grey Friar do that?"

In one sense yes, for he had caused it, was the substance of Miss Hallet's answer. The terror he gave her was so great that she had fallen flat down in the dusty road.

In half a minute after Miss Hallet's shriek and fall, as related in the last chapter, Jane had run up to her. The impression upon Miss Hallet's mind was that Jane had come up from behind her, not from before her; but Jane seemed to intimate that she had come back from Chapel Lane; and Miss Hallet's perceptions were not in a state to be trusted just then. "What brings you here, aunt?—what are you doing up here?—what's the matter?" asked Jane, essaying to raise her. "Nay," said Miss Hallet, when she could get some words out for fright, "the question is, what brings you here?" "I," said Jane; "why I was only running to the Hutt, to give Commodore Teague the muffetees I have been knitting for him," and out of Jane's pocket came the said muffetees, of a bright plum-colour, in proof of the assertion; though it might be true or it might not. "Has it gone?" faintly asked Miss Hallet. "Has what gone, aunt?" "The Grey Friar. It appeared to me at that window, and down I fell: my limbs failed me." "There—there is a faint light," said Jane, looking up for the first time. "Oh, aunt!" Jane's teeth began to chatter. Miss Hallet, in the extreme sense of terror, and not daring to get up, took a roll or two down the hill in the dust: anything to get away from that dreadful Keep. But it bumped and bruised her: she was no longer young; not to speak of the damage to her clothes, of which she was always careful. So with Jane's help she managed to get upon her feet, and reach the Nunnery somehow; where, shrieking in very nervousness, she seized upon the bell, and pulled it incessantly until admitted, as though her arm were worked by steam.

"My legs failed me," gasped Miss Hallet, explaining now to the Sisters: "I dropped like a stone in the road, and rolled there in the dust. It was an awful sight," she added, drawing unconsciously on the terrors of her imagination: "a bluish, greenish kind of light at first; and then a most dreadful, ghostly apparition with a lamp, or soft flame of some kind, in its outstretched arm. I wonder I did not die."

Sister Mildred unlocked a cupboard, and produced a bottle of cordial, a recent present from Mrs. Bent: a little of which she administered to the terrified nervous woman. Miss Hallet swallowed it in gulps. There was no end of confused chattering: a ghost is so exciting a subject to discuss, especially when it has been just seen. Sister Ann compared the present description of the Grey Friar with that which she and Sister Rachel had witnessed, not so long before, and declared the two to tally in every particular. Trembling Sister Judith added her personal testimony. Altogether there had not been so much noise and bustle within the peaceful walls of the Nunnery since that same eventful night, whose doings had been crowned by the arrival of poor little Polly Gleeson with her burns. In the midst of it an idea occurred to Sister Mildred.

"But what brought you up by the Friar's Keep at night, Miss Hallet?" she asked. "It is a lonely road: nobody takes it by choice."

Miss Hallet made no answer. She was gasping again.

"I dare say she was going to see the coastguardsman's wife, sick Emma Mann," spoke Sister Phoeby heartily. "Don't tease her." And Miss Hallet, catching at the suggestion in her extremity, gave Sister Phoeby a nod of acquiescence. It went against the grain to do so, for she was integrity itself, but she would not have these ladies know the truth for the world.

"And Jane had ran on to take the mittens to the Commodore, so that you were alone," said Sister Mildred, following out probabilities in her own mind, and nodding pleasantly to Miss Hallet. "I see. Dear me! What a dreadful thing this apparition is!—what will become of us all? I used not to believe in it much."

"Well, you see people have gone past the Keep at night lately more than they used to: I'm sure one or another seems always to be passing by it," remarked Sister Ann sensibly. "We should hear nothing about it now but for that."

When somewhat recovered, Miss Hallet asked for her bonnet and shawl: which had been taken away to be shaken and brushed. Leaving her thanks with the Sisters, she departed with Jane, and walked home in humility. Now than the actual, present fear had subsided, she felt ashamed of herself for having given way to it, and particularly for having disturbed the Nunnery in the frantic manner described. But hers had been real, genuine terror; and she could no more have helped its laying complete hold of her at the time than she could have taken wings and flown away from the spot, as an arrow flies through the air. A staid, sober-aged, well-reared woman like herself, to have made a commotion as though she had been some poor ignorant fish girl! Miss Hallet walked dumbly along, keeping her diminished head down as she toiled up the cliff.

After supper and prayers were over that night at the Nunnery, and most of the Grey Ladies had retired to their rooms—which they generally did at an early hour when there was nothing, sickness or else, to keep them up—Sisters Mildred and Mary Ursula remained alone in the parlour. That they should be conversing upon what had taken place was only natural. Mary Ursula had not, herself, the slightest faith in the supernatural adjunct of the Grey Friar; who or what it was she knew not, or why it should haunt the place and show itself as it did, lamp in hand; but she believed it would turn out to be a real presence, not a ghostly one. Sister Mildred prudently shook her head at this heterodoxy, confessing that she could not join in it; but she readily agreed that the Friar's Keep was a most mysterious place; and, in the ardour of conversation, she disclosed a secret which very much astonished Mary Ursula. There was an underground passage leading direct from the vaults of the Nunnery to the vaults of the Keep.

"I have known of it for many years," Mildred said, "and never spoken of it to any one. My Sister Mary discovered it: you have heard, I think, that she was one of us in early days: but she died young. After we took possession of this building, Mary, who was lively and active, used to go about, above ground and under it, exploring, as she called it. One day she came upon a secret door below, that disclosed a dark, narrow passage: she penetrated some distance into it, but did not cate to go on alone. At night, when the rest of the ladies had retired, she and I stayed up together—just as you and I have stayed up to-night, my dear, for it was in this very parlour—and she got me to go and explore it with her. We took a lantern to light our steps, and went. The passage was narrow, as I have said, and apparently built in a long straight line, without turnings, angles, or outlets. Not to fatigue you, I will shortly say, that after going a very long way, as it seemed to us, poor timid creatures that we were, we passed through another door, and found ourselves in a pillared place that looked not unlike cloisters, and at length made it out to be vaults under the Friar's Keep."

"What a strange thing!" exclaimed Mary Ursula, speaking into the instrument she had recently made the good Sister a present of—a small ear-trumpet, for they were talking almost in a whisper.

"Not so strange when you remember what the place was originally," dissented Sister Mildred. "Tradition says, you know, that these old religions buildings abounded in secret passages. I did not speak of the discovery, and enjoined silence on Mary; the Sisters might have been uncomfortable; and it was not a nice thing, you see, to let the public know there was a secret passage into our abode."

"Did you never enter it again?"

"Yes, once. Mary would go; and of course I could not let her go alone. It was not long before the illness came on that terminated in her death. Ah, my dear, we were young then, and such an expedition bore for us a kind of pleasurable romance."

Mary Ursula sat in thought. "It strikes me as not being a pleasant idea," she said—"the knowledge that we may be invaded at any hour by some ill-disposed or curious straggler, who chooses to frequent the Friar's Keep."

"Not a bit of it, my dear," said Sister Mildred, briskly. "Don't fear. We can go to the Keep at will, but the Keep cannot come to us. The two doors are firmly locked, and I hold the keys."

"I should like to see this passage!" exclaimed Mary Ursula. "Are you—dear Sister Mildred, do you think you are well enough to show it to me?"

"I'll make myself well enough," returned the good-natured lady: "and I think I am really so. My dear, I have always meant from, the time you joined as to tell you of this secret passage: and for two reasons. The one because the Head of our Community ought not to be in ignorance that there is such a place; the other because it was your cousin who recently has disappeared so unaccountably in the Keep—though I suppose the passage could not have had anything to do with that. But for my illness, I should have spoken before. We will go to-night, if you will."

Mary Ursula eagerly embraced the proposal on the spot. Attiring themselves in their warmest grey cloaks, the hoods well muffled about their heads, for Sister Mildred said the passage would strike cold as an ice-house, they descended to the vaults below; the elder lady carrying the keys and Mary Ursula the lighted horn lantern, which had slides to its four sides to make it lighter or darker at will.

"See, here's the door," whispered Sister Mildred, advancing to an obscure corner. "No one would ever find it; unless they had a special talent for exploring as my poor Mary had. Do you see this little nail in the wall? Well the keys were hanging up there: and it was in consequence of the keys catching her eye That Mary looked for the door."

It required the efforts of both ladies to turn the key in the rusty lock. As the small gothic door was pushed open, a rash of cold damp air blew on their faces. The passage was hardly wide enough to admit two abreast; at least without brushing against the walls on either side. The ladies held one another; Mary Ursula keeping a little in advance, her hand stretched upwards with the lantern so that its light might guide their steps.

A very long passage: no diversion in it, no turnings or angles or outlets, as Sister Mildred had described; nothing but the damp and monotonous stone walls on either hand or overhead. While Mary Ursula was wondering whether they were going on for ever, the glimmer of the lantern suddenly played on a gothic door in front, of the same size and shape as the one they had passed through.

"This is the other door, and this is the key," whispered Sister Mildred.

They put it in the lock. It turned with some difficulty and a grating sound, and the door slowly opened towards them. Another minute, and they had passed into the vaults beneath the Friar's Keep.

Very damp and cold and mouldy and unearthly. As far as Mary Ursula could judge, in the dim and confined light emitted by the small lantern, they appeared to be quite like the cloisters above: the same massive upright pillars of division forming arches against the roof, the same damp stone flooring. There was no outlet to be seen in any part; no staircase upwards or downwards. Mary Ursula carried her lantern and waved it about but could find none: none save the door they had come through.

"Is there any outlet to this place, except the passage?" she asked of Sister Mildred.

"Very, my dear; very damp indeed," was the Sister's answer. "I think we had better not stay; I am shivering with the cold air; and there's nothing, as you perceive, to see."

The ear-trumpet had been left behind, and Mary Ursula did not dare raise her voice to a loud key. She was inwardly shivering herself; not with the chilly, mildewy air, but with her own involuntary thoughts. Thoughts that she would have willingly forbidden entrance to, but could not. With these secret vaults and places under the Keep, secret because they were not generally known abroad, what facilities existed for dealing ill with Anthony Castlemaine; for putting him out of sight for ever!

"Can he be concealed here still, alive or dead?" she murmured to herself. "Surely not alive: for how—"

A sound! A sound close at hand. It was on the opposite side of the vault, and was like the striking of some metal against the wall: or it might have been the banging of a door. Instinctively Mary Ursula hid the lantern under her cloak, caught hold of Sister Mildred, and crouched down with her behind the remotest pillar. The Sister had heard nothing, of course; but she comprehended that there was some cause for alarm.

"Oh, my dear, what will become of us!" she breathed. "Whatever is it?"

Mary dared not speak. She put her hand on the Sister's lips to enjoin silence, and kept it there. Sister Mildred had gone down in a most uncomfortable position, one leg bent under her; and but for grasping the pillar for support with both hands she must have tumbled backwards. Mary Ursula, was kneeling in very close contact, which helped to prop the poor lady up behind. As to the pillar, it was nothing like wide enough to conceal them both had the place been light.

But it was pitch dark. A darkness that might almost be felt. In the midst of it; in the midst of their painful suspense, not knowing what to expect or fear, there arose a faint, distant glimmering of light over in the direction where Mary had heard the sound. A minute afterwards some indistinct, shadowy form appeared, dressed in a monk's habit and cowl. It was the apparition of the Grey Friar.

A low, unearthly moan broke from Sister Mildred. Mary Ursula, herself faint with terror, as must be confessed, but keenly alive to the necessity for their keeping still and silent, pressed the Sister's mouth more closely, and strove to reassure her by clasping her waist with the other hand. The figure, holding its lamp before it, glided swiftly across the vault amid the pillars, and vanished.

It all seemed to pass in a single moment. The unfortunate ladies— "distilled almost to jelly with the effect of fear," as Horatio says— cowered together, not knowing what was next to happen to them, or what other sight might appear. Sister Mildred went into an ague-fit.

Nothing more came; neither sight nor sound. The vaulted cloisters remained silent and inky-dark. Presently Mary Ursula ventured to show her light cautiously to guide their footsteps to the door, towards which she supported Sister Mildred: who once in the passage and the door locked behind her, gave vent to her suppressed terror in low cries and moans and groans. The light of the lantern, thrown on her face, showed it to be as damp as the wall on either side her, and ghastly white. Thus they trod the passage back to their own domains, Sister Mildred requiring substantial help.

"Take the keys," she said to Mary Ursula, when they were once more in the warm and lighted parlour, safe and sound, save for the fright. "They belong to your custody of right now; and I'm sure a saint out of heaven would never induce me to use them again. I'd rather have seen a corpse walk about in its grave-clothes."

"But, dear Sister Mildred—it was very terrifying, I admit; but it could not have been supernatural. There cannot be such things as ghosts."

"My child, we saw it," was the all-convincing answer "Perhaps if they were to get a parson into the place and let him say some prayers, the poor wandering spirit might be laid to rest."

That there was something strangely unaccountable connected with the Friar's Keep and some strange mystery attaching to it, Mary Ursula felt to her heart's core. She carried the two keys to her chamber, and locked them up in a place of safety. Her room adjoined Sister Mildred's; and she stood for some time looking out to sea before undressing. Partly to recover her equanimity; which had unquestionably been considerably shaken during the expedition; partly to indulge her thoughts and fancies, there she stood. An idea of the possibility of Anthony Castlemaine's being alive still, and kept a prisoner in some of these vaults underneath the Keep, had dawned upon her. That there were other and more secret vaults besides these cloisters they had seen, was more than probable: vaults in which men might be secretly confined for a lifetime—ay, and no doubt had been in the old days; confined until claimed by a lingering death. She did not think it likely that Anthony was there, alive: the conviction, that he was dead, had lain upon her from the first; it was upon her still: but the other idea had crept in and was making itself just sufficiently heard to render her uncomfortable.

Her chamber was rather a nice one and much larger than Sister Mildred's. Certain articles suggestive of comfort, that had belonged to her room at Stilborough, had been placed in it: a light sofa and sofa table; a pretty stand for books; a handsome reading lamp; a small cabinet with glass doors, within which were deposited some cherished ornaments and mementoes that it would have given her pain to part with; and such like. If Miss Castlemaine had renounced the world, she had not renounced some of its little vanities, its home-refinements neither did the Community she had joined require anything of the kind to be done. The window, with its most beautiful view of the sea, was kept free; curtains and draperies had been put up, no less for warmth than look: on one side it stood the cabinet, on the other the dressing-table and glass; the bed and the articles of furniture pertaining to it, drawers, washhand-stand, and such like, occupied the other end of the room. It was, in fact, a sitting-room and bedroom combined. And there, at its window, stood Mary Ursula, shivering almost as much as she had shivered in the cloisters, and full of inward discomfort.

In the course of the following morning, she was sitting with sick Sister Margaret, when word came to her that a gentleman had called. Proceeding to the reception parlour, she found the faithful old friend and clerk, Thomas Hill. He was much altered, that good old man: the unhappy death of his master and the anxiety connected with the bank affairs had told upon him perhaps also the cessation from the close routine of daily business was bearing for him its almost inevitable effect: at least, when Mary Ursula tenderly asked what it was that ailed him, he answered, Weariness, induced by having nothing to do. The tears rushed to his eyes when he inquired after her life—whether it satisfied her, whether she was not already sick to death of it, whether repentance for the step had yet set in. And Mary assured him that the contrary was the fact; that she was getting to like the seclusion better day by day.

"Can you have comforts here, my dear Miss Mary?" he inquired, not at all satisfied.

"Oh, yes, any that I please," she replied. "You should see my room above, dear old friend: it is nearly as luxurious and quite as comfortable as my chamber was at home."

"Will they let you have a fire in it, Miss Mary?"

She laughed; partly at the thought, partly to reassure him. "Of course I could if I wished for it; but the weather is coming in warm now. Sister Mildred has had a fire in her room all the winter. I am head of all, you know, and can order what I please."

"And you'll not forget, Miss Mary, that what I have is yours," he returned in a low, eager tone. "Draw upon it when you like: be sure to take care of your comforts. I should like to leave you a cheque-book: I have brought it over with its cheques signed—"

She stopped him with hasty, loving words of thanks. Assuring him that her income was enough, and more than enough, for everything she could possibly want, whether individually or for her share in the expenses of the Community. Thomas Hill, much disappointed, returned the new cheque-book to his pocket again.

"I wish to ask you one question," she resumed, after a pause, and in a tone as low as his own. "Can you tell me how the estate of Greylands' Rest was left by my grandfather?"

MRS. HENRY WOOD

"No, I cannot, Miss Mary; I have never known. Your father did not know."

"My father did not know?" she said in some surprise.

"He did not. On the very last day of his life, when he was just as ill as he could be, my dear good master, he spoke of it to me: it was while he was giving me a message to deliver to his nephew, the young man Anthony, Mr. Basil's son. He said that he had never cared to inquire the particulars, and fully believed that it became James's by legal right; he felt sure that had it been left to Basil, James would not have retained possession. Miss Mary, I say the same."

"And—what is your opinion as to what became of Anthony?" she continued after a short pause.

"I think, my dear, that young Mr. Anthony must somehow have fallen into the sea. He'd not be the first man, poor fellow, by a good many, who has met with death through taking an uncertain step in the deceptive moonlight."

Mary Ursula said no more. This was but conjecture, just as all the rest of it had been.

When the visit was over, she put on her bonnet to stroll out with him. He had walked from Stilborough, intending to dine at the Dolphin, and go back afterwards at his leisure. Mary went with him on the beach, and then parted with him at the door of the inn.

"You are sure you are tolerably happy, my dear?" he urged, as though needing to be assured of it again and again, holding both her hands in his. "Ah, my dear young lady, it is all very well for you to say you are; but I cannot get reconciled to it. I wish you could have found your happiness in a different sphere."

She knew what he meant—found it as William Blake-Gordon's wife—and something like a faintness stole over her spirit.

"Circumstances worked against it," she meekly breathed. "I am content to believe that the life I have embraced is the best for me; the one appointed by God."

How little did she think that almost close upon that minute, she should encounter him—her whilom lover! Not feeling inclined to return at once to the Nunnery, and knowing that there was yet a small space of time before dinner, she continued her way alone up the secluded road towards the church. When just abreast of the sacred edifice a lady and gentleman approached on horseback, having apparently ridden from Stilborough. She recognized them too late to turn or retreat: it was William Blake-Gordon and Miss Mountsorrel.

Miss Mountsorrel checked her horse impulsively; he could but do the same. The young lady spoke.

"Mary! is it you? How strange that we should meet you! I thought you never came beyond the convent walls."

"Did you? I go out where and when I please. Are you well, Agatha?"

"Are you well?—that is the chief question," returned Miss Mountsorrel, with a great deal of concern and sympathy in her tone. "You do not look so."

Just then Mary undoubtedly did not. Emotion had turned her as pale as death. Happening to catch sight of the countenance of Mr. Blake-Gordon, she saw that his face was, if possible, whiter than her own. A strangely yearning, imploring look went out to her from his eyes—but what it meant, she knew not.

"I shall come and see you some day, Mary, if I may," said Miss Mountsorrel.

"Certainly you may."

They prepared to ride on: Mr. Blake-Gordon's horse was restive. The young ladies wished each other good morning he bowed and lifted his hat. He had not spoken a word to her, or she to him. They had simply stood there face to face, he on horseback, she on foot, with the tale-telling emotion welling up from their hearts.

Mary opened the churchyard gate, went in, and sat down under a remote tree near the tomb of the Castlemaines, hiding her face in her hands. She felt sick and faint; and trembled as the young green leaves about her were trembling in the gentle wind. So! this was the manner of their meeting again: when he was riding by the side of another!

The noise of horses, passing by, caused her to raise her head and glance to the road again. Young Mountsorrel was riding swiftly past to catch his sister, having apparently lingered temporarily behind: and the groom clattered closely after him at a sharp trot.

MRS. HENRY WOOD

XXIV

GOING OVER IN THE TWO-HORSE VAN

August weather. For some few months had elapsed since the time of the last chapter. Stilborough lay hot and dusty under the summer sun: the pavements shone white and glistening, the roads were parched. Before the frontage of the Turk's Head on the sunny side of Cross Street, was spread a thick layer of straw to deaden the sound of horses and vehicles. A gentleman, driving into the town a few days before, was taken ill there, and lay at the hotel in a dangerous state: his doctor expressed it as "between life and death." It was Squire Dobie, of Dobie Hall.

The Turk's Head was one of those good, old-fashioned, quiet inns, not much frequented by the general public, especially by the commercial public. Its custom was chiefly confined to the county families, and to that class of people called gentlefolk. It was, therefore, very rarely in a bustle, showing but little signs of life except on Thursdays, market-day, and it would sometimes be so empty that Stilborough might well wonder how Will Heyton, its many years landlord, contrived to pay his expenses. But Will Heyton had, in point of fact, made a very nice nest-egg at it, and did not much care now whether the inn was empty or full.

In the coffee-room on this hot August morning, at a small table by the right-hand window, sat a gentleman breakfasting. A tall, slender, well-dressed young man in slight mourning, of perhaps some six-and-twenty years. He was good-looking; with a pleasing, fair, and attractive face, blue eyes, and light wavy hair that took a tinge of gold in the sunlight. This gentleman had arrived at Stilborough the previous evening by a cross-country coach, had inquired for the best hotel, and been directed to the Turk's Head. It was late for breakfast, nearly eleven o'clock: and when the gentleman—whose name was inscribed on the hotel visitors' list as Mr. George North—came down he had said something in a particularly winning way about the goodness of the bed causing him to oversleep himself. Save for him, the coffee-room was void of guests.

"Is this a large town?" he inquired of the portly head waiter, who was partly attending on him, partly rubbing up the glasses and decanters that were ranged on the mahogany stand by the wall.

"Pretty well, sir. It's next in size to the chief county town, and is quite as much frequented."

"What are the names of the places near to it?"

"We have no places of note near to us, sir: only a few small villages that count for nothing."

"Well, what are their names?"

"There's Hamley, sir; and Eastwick; and Greylands; and—"

"Are any of these places on the sea?" interrupted the stranger, as he helped himself to a mutton chop.

"Greylands is, sir. It's a poor little place in itself, nothing hardly but fishermen's huts in it; but the sea is beautiful there.—Bangalore sauce, sir?"

"Well, I don't know," said the young man, looking first at the bottle of sauce, being handed to him, and then up at the waiter, a laughing doubt in his blue eyes. "Is it good?"

"It's very good indeed, sir, as sauce; and rare too; you'd not find it in any other inn at Stilborough. Not but what some tastes prefer mutton chops plain."

"I think I do," said the stranger, declining the sauce. "Thank you; it may be better to let well alone."

His breakfast over, Mr. George North sat back in his chair, and glanced through the sunbeams at the dusty road and the white pavement. The waiter placed on the table the last number of the Stilborough Herald; and nearly at the same moment there dashed up to the inn door a phaeton and pair. The gentleman who was driving handed the reins to the groom sitting beside him, alighted, and entered the hotel.

The sun, shining right in Mr. George North's eyes, had somewhat obscured his view outwards; but as the gentleman came in and stood upright in the coffee-room, he saw a tall stately man with a remarkably handsome face. While gazing at the face, a slight emotion came suddenly into his own. "What a likeness!" he inwardly murmured. "Can it be one of them?"

"How is Squire Dobie, Hobbs?" demanded Mr. Castlemaine of the old waiter—for the new-comer was the Master of Greylands. "Any better to-day?"

"Yes, sir; the doctor thinks there's a slight improvement. He has had a fairly good night."

"That's well. Is Mr. Atherly expected in to-day, do you know?"

"No, I don't, sir. Perhaps master knows. I'll inquire."

While the waiter was gone on this errand, Mr. Castlemaine strolled to the unoccupied window, and looked out on his waiting horses. Fine animals, somewhat restive this morning, and the pride of Mr. Castlemaine's stables. He glanced at the stranger, sitting at the not yet cleared breakfast table, and was taken at once with his bright face and looks. Mr. George North was then reading the newspaper. Hobbs did not return, and Mr. Castlemaine stamped a little with one foot as though he were impatient. A sudden thought struck the young man: he rose, and held out the newspaper.

"I beg your pardon, sir; I am perhaps, keeping this from you."

"Not at all, thank you," said Mr. Castlemaine.

"I am a stranger; therefore this local news cannot interest me," persisted Mr. George North, fancying courtesy alone might have prompted the refusal. "It is of no moment whether I read the gazette or not."

"I have already seen it: I am obliged to you all the same," replied Mr. Castlemaine in his pleasantest manner, with not a shade of hauteur about it. "Are you staying here?"

"At present I am. It may be that I shall stay but for a short while. I cannot say yet. We artists travel about from village to village, from country to country, finding subjects for our pencil. I have lately been in the Channel Islands."

"Master says he is not particularly expecting Mr. Atherly to-day, sir," interposed Hobbs, returning; "but he thinks it likely he may be coming in. He'll get here about one o'clock if he does come."

The Master of Greylands nodded in reply. "I suppose, Hobbs, Squire Dobie is not allowed to see anyone?"

"Not yet, sir."

Mr. Castlemaine left the room, saluting the stranger at the breakfast table. Hobbs followed, to attend him to the door.

"What's the name of the young man in the coffee-room?" he asked, standing for a moment on the steps. "He seems to be a nice young fellow."

"North, sir. Mr. George North. He came in last night by the Swallow coach."

"He says he is an artist."

"Oh, does he, sir!" returned the waiter in an accent of mingled surprise and disappointment. "I'm sure I took him to be a gentleman."

Mr. Castlemaine smiled to himself at the words. Hobbs' ideas, he thought, were probably running on the artists who went about painting signboards.

"That accounts for his wanting to know the names of the parts about here," spoke the waiter. "He has been asking me. Them artists, sir, are rare ones for tramping about after bits of scenery."

The Master of Greylands went out to his carriage and took his seat. As he turned the horses' heads round to go back the way they came, Mr. George North, looking on from within, had for a moment the back of the phaeton pointed right towards him, with its distinguishing crest.

"The crest!" he exclaimed, under his breath. "Then it must be one of them! And I nearly knew it by the face. Shall I ask here which of them it is?—no, better not. Suppose I go out and take a look at the town?" he continued a few minutes later, waking up from a reverie.

Putting on his straw hat, which had a bit of black ribbon tied round it, and a good-sized brim, he went strolling hither and thither. It was not market day: but few people were abroad, and the streets looked almost deserted. People did not care to come abroad in the blazing sun, unless obliged. Altogether, there was not much for Mr. George North to see. Before an inn-door stood a kind of small yellow van, or omnibus—it was in fact something between the two—which was being laden to start. It made its journeys three times a week, and was called the two-horse van.

For want of something better to look at, Mr. George North stood watching the putting-to of the horses. On the sides of the van were inscribed the names of the places it called at; amidst them was Greylands. His eyes rested on the name and a sudden thought arose to him: Suppose I go over to Greylands by this yellow omnibus!

"Do you call at all these places to-day?" he asked of a man, who was evidently the driver.

"At every one of 'em, sir. And come back here through 'em again to-morrow."

"Have I time to go as far as the Turk's Head and back before you start?"

"Plenty of time, sir. We are not particular to a few minutes either way."

Mr. George North proceeded to the Turk's Head; not in the rather lazy fashion to which his movements seemed by nature inclined, but as fast as the sun allowed him. He there told the head waiter that he was going to make a little excursion into the country for the purpose of looking about him, and might not be back until evening, or even before the morrow.

"Inside or outside, sir?" questioned the driver when he got back.

"Oh, outside to-day. Can't I sit by you?"

He was welcome, the driver said, the seat not being taken; and Mr. George North mounted to the seat and put up his umbrella, which he had brought with him as a shelter against the sun. Two or three more passengers got up behind, and placed themselves amid the luggage; and there were several inside.

The two-horse van sped along very fairly; and in a short time reached the first village. After descending a hill, the glorious sea burst into view.

"What place do you call this?" asked the stranger.

"This is Greylands, sir."

"Greylands, is it? I think I'll get down here. Dear me, what a beautiful sea! How much do I pay you?"

"A shilling fare, sir. Anything you please for the driver. Thank you, sir; thank you," concluded the man pocketing the eighteen-pence given to him. "We shall stop in a minute, sir, at the Dolphin Inn."

On this hot day, which really seemed too hot for work, Mrs. Bent was stealing a few moments' idleness on the bench outside her window. John had been sitting there all the morning. The landlady was making free comments, after her wont, upon the doings, good and bad, of her neighbours; John gave an answering remark now and again, but she did not seem to wait for it.

There is not much to tell the reader of this short space of time that has elapsed without record. No very striking event had taken place in it; Greylands was much in the same condition as when we parted from it last. Poor Miss Hallet had been ill for some weeks, possibly the result of the fright, and was quite unable to look personally after the vagaries of Miss Jane: the Friar's Keep and its mysteries remained where they had been; Sister Mildred was ill again, and Mary Ursula had not plucked up courage since to penetrate anew the secret passage. Squire Dobie, red-hot at first to unravel the mystery of the disappearance of Basil's son, had finally given up the inquiry as hopeless; neither had Madame Guise advanced one jot in her discoveries touching the suspected iniquity of the Master of Greylands.

"Here comes the two-horse van," remarked Mrs. Bent.

The two-horse van drew up before the bench and close to Mr. and Mrs. Bent. Its way did not lie by that of the ordinary coach road, but straight on up the hill past the Nunnery. Whether it had parcels or passengers to descend, or whether it had not, it always halted at the Dolphin, to "give the horses a minute's breathing," as the driver said: and to give himself a minute's gossip with the landlord and landlady.

The gossip to-day lay chiefly on the score of the unusual heat, and on some refractory wheel of the van, which had persisted the previous day in dropping its spokes out. And the driver had mounted to his seat again, and the van was rattling off, before Mr. and Mrs. Bent remarked that the gentlemanly-looking man in the straw hat, who had got down, as they supposed, merely to stretch his legs, had not gone on with it.

He was standing with his back to them to look about him. At the pile of buildings rising on his left, the Grey Nunnery; at the cliff towards the right, with its nestling houses; at the dark-blue sea opposite, lying calm and lovely under its stagnant fishing boats. A long, lingering look of admiration at the latter, and he turned round to Mr. and Mrs. Bent, standing by the bench now, but not sitting, and lifted his straw bat as he addressed them.

"I beg your pardon. This seems to be a very nice place. What an expanse of sea!"

"It's a very nice place indeed—for its size, sir," said John. "And you'd not get a better sea than that anywhere."

"The place is called Greylands, I am told."

"Yes, sir: Greylands."

"I am an artist," continued the stranger in his pleasing, open manner, a manner that was quite fascinating both Mr. and Mrs. Bent. "I should fancy there must be choice bits of landscape about here well worth my taking."

"And so there is, sir. Many of 'em."

"Will you give me lodging for a few hours?—allow me to call your inn my head-quarters, while I look about for myself a little?" he continued with a most winning smile.

"And glad to receive you, sir," put in Mrs. Bent before her husband had time to reply. "Oar house is open to all, and especially to one as pleasant-speaking as you, sir."

"By the way," he said, stopping to pause when stepping before them indoors, as though he were trying to recall something—"Greylands? Greylands? Yes, that must be the name. Do you chance to know if a

French lady is living anywhere in this neighbourhood? A Madame Guise?"

"To be sure she is, sir. She is governess at Greylands Rest. Within a stone's throw—as may almost be said—of this house."

"Ah, indeed. I knew her and her husband, Monsieur Guise, in France. He was my very good friend. Dear me! how thirsty I am."

"Would you like to take anything, sir?"

"Yes, I should; but not beer, or any strong drink of that sort. Have you any lemonade?"

John Bent had; and went to fetch it. The stranger sat down near the open-window, and gazed across at the sea. Mrs. Bent was gazing at him; at his very nice-looking face, so fair and bright, and at the wavy hair, light and fine as silken threads of gold.

"Are you English, sir?" demanded free and curious Mrs. Bent.

"Why do you ask the question?" he returned with a smile, as he threw full on her the light of his laughing blue eyes.

"Well, sir—though I'm sure you are an Englishman person—and a rare good-looking one too—there's a tone in your voice that sounds foreign to me."

"I am English," he replied: "but I have lived very much abroad, in France and Italy and other countries: have roamed about from place to place. No doubt my accent has suffered. We can't be a vagabond, you see, madam, without betraying it."

Mrs. Bent shook her head at the epithet, which he spoke-with a laugh: few persons, to judge by looks, were less of a vagabond than he. John came in with the lemonade sparkling in a glass.

"Ah, that's good," said the traveller drinking it at a draught. "If your viands and wines generally are as good as that, Mr. Bent, your guests must be fortunate. I should like to call and see Madame Guise," he added rising. "I suppose I may venture to do so?"

"Why not, sir?"

"Are the people she is with dragons?" he asked, in his half laughing and wholly fascinating way. "Will they eat me up, think you? Some families do not admit visitors to their governess."

"You may call, and welcome, sir," said Mrs. Bent. "The family are of note hereabout, great gentlefolks—the Castlemaines. Madame Guise is made as comfortable there as if it were her own house and home."

"I'll venture then," said the stranger, taking his hat and umbrella. "Perhaps you will be good enough to direct the road to me."

John Bent took him out at the front door, and pointed out to him the way over the fields—which were far pleasanter and somewhat nearer than the road way: and Mr. North was soon at the gate of Greylands' Rest. Mrs. Castlemaine was seated under a shady clump of trees, doing some wool work. He raised his hat and bowed to her as he passed, but continued his way to the door. Miles opened it and asked his pleasure.

"I am told that Madame Guise lives here. May I be permitted to see her?"

"Yes, sir," replied the man, admitting him to the hall. "What name?"

"Mr. George North. I have not my cards with me."

"Mr. George North!" repeated Mrs. Castlemaine to herself, for she had been near enough to hear distinctly the conversation in the stillness of the summer's day. "What an exceedingly handsome young man! Quite a Saxon face. I wonder who he is!"

Miles conducted Mr. George North to the red parlour, where Madame Guise was sitting with Ethel. "A gentleman to see you, ma'am," was his mode of introduction: "Mr. George North."

"Mr.—who!" cried Madame, her manner hurried and startled.

"Mr. George North," repeated Miles; and ushered the gentleman in.

She turned her back upon the door, striving for courage and calmness in the one brief moment of preparation that she might dare to snatch. But that Ethel's attention was given to the stranger, she had not failed to see the agitation. Madame's pocket-handkerchief was clutched almost through in her nervous hand.

"How do you do, Madame Guise?"

She turned round then, meeting him in the middle of the room. Her face was white as death as she put out her hand to him. His own manner was unembarrassed, but his countenance at the moment looked strangely grave.

"Being in the neighbourhood I have ventured to call upon you, Madame Guise. I hope you have been well."

"Quite well, thank you," she said in a low tone, pointing to a chair, and sitting down herself. "I am so much surprised to see you."

"No doubt you are. How is the little girl?"

"She is at school with some good ladies, and she is quite happy there," replied Madame Guise, speaking rather more freely. "I thought you were in Italy, Mr. North."

"I left Italy some weeks ago. Since then I have been wandering onwards, from place to place, sketching this, sketching that, in my usual rather vagabond fashion, and have at length turned up in England."

The laughing light was coming back to his eyes again: he momentarily turned them on Ethel as he spoke. Madame Guise seemed to consider she might be under an obligation to introduce him.

"Mr. George North, my dear. Miss Ethel Reene, sir; one of my pupils."

Mr. George North rose from his chair and bowed elaborately: Ethel bowed slightly, smiled, and blushed. She was very much taken with the young man: and perhaps, if the truth were known, he was with her. Certain it was, that she was looking very pretty in her summer dress of white muslin, with the silver-grey ribbons in her hair.

"Did you come straight to England from Italy?" asked Madame Guise.

"My fashion of coming was not straight but very crooked," he answered. "I took the Channel Islands in my way."

"The Channel Islands!"

"Jersey and Guernsey and Sark. Though I am not quite sure how I got there," he added in his very charming manner, and with another glance and half smile at Ethel; who blushed again vividly as she met it, and for no earthly reason.

"But you could not fly over to them in your sleep," debated Madame Guise, taking his words literally.

"I suppose not. I was at St. Malo one day, and I presume I must have gone from thence in a boat. One of these days, when my fortune's made, I intend to take up my abode for a few months at Sark. The climate is lovely; the scenery beautiful."

"How did you know I was here?" asked Madame Guise.

"I saw—I saw Madame de Rhone in France," he replied, making a slight break, as put. "She told me you had come to England and were living with an English family at a place called Greylands," he continued. "Finding myself to-day at Greylands, I could but try to find you out."

"You are very good," murmured Madame, whose hands were again beginning to show signs of trembling.

Ethel rose to leave the room. It occurred to her that Madame might like to be alone with her friend, and she had stayed long enough for good manners. At that same moment, however, Mrs. Castlemaine came in by the open glassdoors, so Ethel's considerate thought was foiled. Mrs. Castlemaine bowed slightly as she looked at the stranger.

"Mr. North, madam; a friend of my late husband's," spoke Madame Guise, quite unable to prevent her voice from betraying agitation. "He was at Greylands to-day and has found me out."

"We are very pleased to see Mr. North," said Mrs. Castlemaine, turning to him with her most gracious tones, for the good looks and easy manners of the stranger had favourably impressed her. "Are you staying at Greylands?"

"I am travelling about, madam, from place to place, taking sketches. I have recently come from Hampshire previous to that, I was in the Channel Islands. Last night I slept at Stilborough, and came to Greylands this morning by a conveyance that I heard called the 'two-horse van' in search of objects for my pencil."

He mentioned the "two-horse van" so quaintly that Mrs. Castlemaine burst into a laugh. "I think you must have been jolted," she said, and Mr. North bowed.

"Remembering to have been told that Madame Guise, the wife of my late dear friend, Monsieur Guise was residing with a family at a place called Greylands, I made inquiries for the address at the inn here, and presumed to call."

He bowed again slightly with somewhat of deprecation to Mrs. Castlemaine as he spoke. She assured him he was quite welcome; that it was no presumption.

"Are you an artist by profession, Mr. North?—Or do you take sketches for pleasure?" she asked presently, as the conversation proceeded.

"Something of both, madam. I cannot say that I am dependent on my pencil. I once painted what my friends were pleased to call a good picture, and it was exhibited and bought—in Paris."

"A watercolour?"

"Yes, a watercolour."

"I hope you got a good price for it."

"Five thousand francs."

"How much is that in English money?" asked Mrs. Castlemaine, after an electrified pause, for at the first moment her ideas had run to five thousand pounds.

"Two hundred pounds. It was a scene taken in the Alpes-Maritimes."

"You have been much abroad, Mr. North?"

"Oh, very much. I have latterly been staying for more than a year in Italy."

"How you must have enjoyed it?"

"For the time of sojourn I did. But it will always lay on my mind in a heavy weight of repentance."

"But why?" exclaimed Mrs. Castlemaine.

"Because—" and there he made a pause. "In my unpardonable thoughtlessness, madam, I, roving about from spot to spot, omitted sometimes to give any family any address where news from them might find me."

"And you had cause to repent not doing it?"

"Bitter cause," he answered, a wrung expression resting for an instant on his face. "My father died during that time; and—there were other matters wanting me. My life, so far as that past portion of it goes, will be one of unavailing repentance."

It almost seemed—at least the fancy struck Ethel—that Mr. North gave this little bit of unusual confidence—unusual in a stranger—for the benefit of Madame Guise. Certain it was, that he looked at her two or three times as he spoke; and on her face there shone a strangely sad and regretful light.

In about half an hour he rose to depart. Mrs. Castlemaine offered luncheon, but he declined it. He had been a lazy lie-abed that morning, he said with a laughing smile, and it seemed but now almost that he had taken his breakfast at the Turk's Head. The impression he left behind him was not so much of a stranger, as of an acquaintance they had known, so pleasant and easy had been the intercourse during the interview; and an acquaintance they were sorry to part with.

Madame Guise went with him across the lawn. Mrs. Castlemaine would have gone too, but that Ethel stopped her.

"Mamma, don't," she whispered: "they may be glad to have a few moments alone. I fancy Madame Guise cannot have seen him since before her husband died: she seemed quite agitated when he came in."

"True," said Mrs. Castlemaine, for once recognising reason in words of Ethel's. "What a gentlemanly young fellow he seems—in spite of that wide straw hat."

He had put the straw hat on, and seemed to be looking at the different flower beds in his progress; Madame Guise pointing to one and another with her finger. Had Mrs. Castlemaine caught but a word of the private conversation being carried on under the semblance of admiring the flowers, she might have stolen out to listen in the gratification of her curiosity. Which would not have served her, for they spoke in French.

"How you startled me, George!" cried Madame Guise, as their heads were both bent over a rose-tree. "I thought I should have fainted. It might have made me discover all. Let us walk on!"

"Well, I suppose I ought to have written first. But I thought I should be introduced to you alone—your being here as the governess."

"How are they all at Gap?—Look at these carnations.—How is Emma? Did you get my letter through her?"

"I got it when I reached Gap. They are all well. She gave me your letter and what news she could. I cannot understand it, Charlotte. Where is Anthony?"

"Dead. Murdered. As I truly and fully believe."

Mr. North lifted his hat and passed his white handkerchief across his brow, very perplexed and stern just then.

"When can I see you alone, Charlotte?"

"This evening. As soon as dusk sets in, I will meet you in Chapel Lane:" and she directed him where to find it. "You stay at the lower end near that great building almost in ruins, the Friar's Keep, and I will come to you. Are you here at last to help me unravel the treachery, George?"

"I will try to do it."

"But why have you been so tardy?—why did you go to—what did you say—those Channel Islands?"

"I had an artist friend with me who would go over there. I did not care to show too much eagerness to come on to England—he might have suspected I had a motive. And it seems to me, Charlotte, that this investigation will be a most delicate business; one that a breath of suspicion, as to who I am, might defeat."

"And oh, why did you linger so long in Italy, George?" she asked in a low tone of painful wailing. "And to have neglected for months to let us get an address that would certainly find you! Had you been at Gap when the father died, the probability is that Anthony and you would have made the journey here in company. Surely Mr. James Castlemaine had not dared to kill him then!"

"Hush!" he answered in a voice more bitterly painful than her own. "You heard what I said just now in the salon: the regret, the self-reproach will only cease with my life. Until this evening then, Charlotte!"

"Until this evening."

"Who is that charming demoiselle?" he asked, as they shook hands in parting. "What relation is she to the house?"

"No real relation of it at all. She is Miss Reene; Mrs. Castlemaine's stepdaughter. Mrs. Castlemaine was a widow when she married into the family."

Mr. George North closed the gate behind him; took off his hat to Madame with the peculiar action of a Frenchman, and walked away.

XXV

Mr. George North

If there existed one man eminently open by nature, more truthful, devoid of guile, and less capable of deceit than his fellows, it was certainly George North. And yet he was acting a deceitful part now; inasmuch as that he had made his appearance in England and introduced himself at Greylands' Rest, under what might be called a partially false name. For the name "George North" had but been given him in baptism: the other, the chief one, was Castlemaine. He was the son of Basil Castlemaine, and the younger brother of the most unfortunate Anthony.

Four children had been born to Basil Castlemaine and his wife. They were named as follows: Anthony, Mary Ursula, George North, and Emma. The elder daughter died young: the wife died just as her other children had grown up. Anthony married Charlotte Guise; Emma married Monsieur de Rhone, a gentleman who was now the chief partner in the Silk Mills, with which Basil Castlemaine had been connected. The two young Castlemaines, Anthony and George, had both declined to engage in commerce. Their father pointed to them that a share in the Silk Mills was open to each, and no doubt a good fortune at the end of a few years' connection with the business; beyond that, he did not particularly urge the step on either of them. His sons would both inherit a modest competency under his will. Anthony would also succeed (as Basil fully believed) to his forefather's patrimony in England, Greylands' Rest, which would necessitate his residence there; and George, at the age of twenty-four, came into a fairly good fortune left to him by his uncle and godfather, Mr. North. Therefore, both of them were considered by the father to be provided for, and if they preferred to eschew commerce, they were welcome to do so. George had shown very considerable talent for drawing and painting; it had been well cultivated; and though he did not intend to make it exactly his profession, for he needed it not, he did hope to become famous as a watercolour painter. Some time after attaining the age of twenty-four, and taking possession of his bequeathed fortune, he had resolved on making a lengthened sojourn in Italy; not to stay in one part of it, but to move about as inclination dictated. And this he did.

From time to time he wrote home, saying where he then was; but rarely where he would be later, simply because he did not know himself. Two or three letters reached him in return, containing the information that all was well.

All being well seems to the young to mean always to be well; as it did to George Castlemaine: his mind was at rest, and for several months there ensued a gap of silence. It is true he wrote home; but, as to tidings from home reaching him in return, he did not afford a chance for it. He crossed to Sicily, to Corsica; he went to the Ionian Isles: it is hard to say where he did not go. When tidings from home at length reached him, he found that his family, whom he had been picturing as unchanged and happy, was totally dispersed. His father was dead. Anthony had gone over to England to see after his patrimony; and, not returning as he ought to have done, his wife and child had followed him. Emma de Rhone, who conveyed all this in writing, to her brother, confessed she did not understand what could have become of Anthony; but that she did not think he could have lost himself, though of course England was a large place, and he, being strange, might have a difficulty in making his way about it. To this portion of the letter George gave no heed; at a happier time he would have laughed at the notion of Anthony's being lost; his whole heart was absorbed in the grief for his father and in self-reproach for his own supine carelessness.

He did not hurry home: there was nothing to go for now: and it was summer weather when George once more re-entered Gap. To his intense astonishment, his concern, his perplexity, he found that Anthony really was lost: at least, that his wife seemed nimble to discover traces of him. Emma de Rhone handed him a thick letter of several sheets, which had come enclosed to her for him from Charlotte many weeks before, and had been waiting for him. When George Castlemaine broke the seal, he found it to contain a detailed account of Anthony's disappearance and the circumstances connected with it, together with her suspicions of James Castlemaine, and her residence in that gentleman's house. In short, she told him all; and she begged him to come over and see into it for himself; but to come as a stranger, en cachette, and not to declare himself to be connected with her, or as a Castlemaine. She also warned him not to tell Emma or M. de Rhone of her worst fears about Anthony, lest they should be undertaking the investigation themselves: which might ruin all hopes of discovery, for

Mr. Castlemaine was not one to be approached in that way. And the result of this was that George Castlemaine was now here as George North. He had deemed it well to obey Charlotte's behest, and come; at the same time he did not put great faith in the tale. It puzzled him extremely: and he could but recall that his brother's wife was given to be a little fanciful—romantic, in short.

Not a breath of air was stirring. The summer night seemed well-nigh as hot as the day had been. There lay a mist on the fields behind the hedge on either side Chapel Lane as Charlotte Guise hastened lightly down it. In her impatience she had come out full early to keep the appointment, and when she reached the end of the lane, George North—as for convenience' sake we must continue to call him—was but then approaching it.

"You found it readily, George?" she whispered. "Quite so. It is in a straight line from the inn."

"Are you going back to Stilborough to-night?"

"No. I shall sleep at the Dolphin, and go back to-morrow."

He offered his sister-in-law his arm. She took it; but the next moment relinquished it again. "It may be better not, George," she said. "It is not very likely that we shall meet people, but it's not impossible: and, to see me walking thus familiarly with a stranger would excite comment."

They turned to go up the hill. It was safer than Chapel Lane, as Charlotte observed; for there was no knowing but Mr. Harry Castlemaine might be going through the lane to the Commodore's, whose company both father and son seemed to favour. Mr. Castlemaine was at Stilborough: had driven over in the morning, and was no doubt staying there to dine.

"This seems to be a lonely road," remarked Mr. North, as they went on side by side.

"It is very lonely. We rarely meet any one but the preventive-men: and not often even one of them."

Almost in silence they continued their way until opposite the coastguard-station: a short line of white dwellings lying at right angles with the road on the left hand. Turning off to the right, across the waste land on the other side the road, they soon were on the edge of the cliff, with the sea lying below.

"We may walk and talk here in safety," said Charlotte. "There is never more than one man on duty: his beat is a long one, all down there"—

pointing along the line of coast in the opposite direction to that of Greylands—"and we shall see him, should he approach, long before he could reach us. Besides, they are harmless and unsuspicious, these coastguardsmen; they only look out for ships and smugglers."

"We do not get a very good view of the sea from here: that high cliff on the right is an impediment," remarked Mr. North. "What a height it is!"

"It shoots up suddenly, close on this side the Friar's Keep, and shoots down nearly as suddenly to where we are now. Ethel Reene climbs it occasionally, and sits there; but I think nobody else does."

"Not the preventive-men?"

"By day sometimes. Never by night; it would be too dangerous. Their beat commences here."

"And now, Charlotte, about this most unhappy business?" said Mr. North, as they began to pace backwards and forwards on the green brow of the coast, level there. "Where are we to look for Anthony? It cannot be that he is lost."

"But he is lost, George. He went into the Friar's Keep that unhappy night in February; and he was never seen to come out again. He never did come out again, as most people here believe; I, for one. What other word is there for it but lost?"

"It sounds like a fable," said George North. "Like a tale out of those romance books you used to read, Charlotte."

"I thought so when I came here first and heard it."

"Did that account you sent me contain all the details?"

"I think it did. One cannot give quite so elaborate a history in writing a letter as by word of mouth. Little particulars are apt to be dropped out."

"You had better go over it to me now, Charlotte: all you know from the beginning. Omit not the smallest detail."

Madame Guise obeyed at once. The opening her mouth to impart this dreadful story, dreadful and more dreadful to her day by day, was something like the relief afforded to a parched traveller in an African desert, when he comes upon the well of water he has been fainting for, and slakes his thirst. Not to one single human being had Charlotte Guise been able to pour forth by word of mouth this strange story all through these months since she heard it: the need to do it, the pain, the yearning for sympathy and counsel, had been consuming her all the while as with a fever heat.

She told the whole. The arrival of Anthony at the Dolphin Inn, and his presenting himself to his family—as heard from John Bent. The ill-reception of him by Mr. Castlemaine when he spoke of a claim to Greylands' Rest; the refusal of Mr. Castlemaine to see him subsequently, and their hostile encounter in the field; the strolling out by moonlight that same night of Anthony and the landlord; their watching (quite by chance) the entrance of Mr. Castlemaine into the Friar's Keep, and the hasty following in of Anthony, to have it out, as he impulsively said, under the moonbeams; and the total disappearance of Anthony from that hour. She told all in detail, George North listening without interruption.

"And it is supposed that the cry, following on the shot that was almost immediately heard, was my poor brother's cry?" spoke George, the first words with which he broke the silence.

"I feel sure it was his cry, George."

"And Mr. James Castlemaine denies that he was there?"

"He denies it entirely. He says he was at home at the time and in bed."

"Suppose that it was Anthony who cried; that he was killed by the shot: would it be easy to throw him into the sea out of sight?"

"Not from the Keep. They say there is no opening to the sea. Mr. Castlemaine may have dragged him across the chapel ruins and filing him from thence."

"But could he have done that without being seen? John Bent, you say, was outside the gates, waiting for Anthony."

"But John Bent was not there all the time. When he got tired of waiting he went home, thinking Anthony might have come out without his seeing him—but not in his heart believing it possible that he had. Finding Anthony had not returned to the inn, John Bent went again and searched the Keep with Mr. Nettleby, the superintendent of these coastguardsmen."

"And they did not find any trace of him?"

"Not any."

"Or of any struggle, or other ill work?"

"I believe not. Oh, it is most strange!"

"Who locked the gate—as you describe: and then opened it again?" questioned Mr. North after a moment's pause.

"Ah, I know not. Nobody can conjecture."

"Have you searched well in this Keep yourself?"

"Oh, George, I have not dared to do it! It has a revenant."

"A what!" exclaimed Mr. North.

"A revenant. I have seen it, and was nearly frightened to death."

"Charlotte!"

"I know you strong men ridicule such things," said poor Madame Guise, meekly. "Anthony would have laughed just as you do. It's true, though. The Friar's Keep is haunted by a dead monk: he appears dressed in his cowl and grey habit, the same that he used to wear in life. He passes the window sometimes with a lamp in his hand."

"Since when has this revenant taken to appear?" inquired George North, after a short period of reflection. "Since Anthony's disappearance?"

"Oh, for a long, long while before it. I believe the monk died something like two hundred years ago. Why? Were you thinking, George, that it might be the revenant of poor Anthony?"

Mr. George North drew in his disbelieving lips. At a moment like the present he would not increase her pain by showing his mockery of revenants.

"What I was thinking was this, Charlotte. Whether, if poor Anthony be really no more, his destroyers may have cause to wish the Friar's Keep to remain unexplored, lest traces of him might be found, and so have improvised a revenant, as you call it, to scare people away."

"The revenant has haunted the place for years and years, George. It has been often seen."

"Then that puts an end to my theory."

"I might have had courage to search the Keep by day for the dead, as we all believe, do not come abroad then—but that I have not dared to risk being seen there," resumed Madame Guise. "Were I to be seen going into the Friar's Keep, a place that every one shuns, it might be suspected that I had a motive, and Mr. Castlemaine would question me. Besides, my young pupil is mostly with me by day: it is only in the evening that I have unquestioned liberty."

"I wonder you reconciled yourself to go into the house as governess, Charlotte."

"For Anthony's sake," she said imploringly. "What would I not do for his sake? And then, you see, George, while Anthony does not come forward to give orders at Gap, and there is no proof that he is dead, I cannot draw money. My own income is but small."

"Why, my dear Charlotte, what are you talking of? You could have had any amount of money you pleased from me. I—"

"You forget, George: you were travelling, and could not be written to."

"Well, there was Emma," returned Mr. George, half confounded when thus confuted by his own sins.

"I did not want to give too much confidence to Emma and her husband: I have told you why. And I would have gone into Mr. Castlemaine's house, George, the opportunity offering, though I had been the richest woman in the world. But for being there, I should not have known that Mr. Castlemaine holds secret possession of Anthony's diamond ring. You remember that ring, George."

"I remember I used jokingly to say I would steal it from him—it was so beautiful. The possession of the ring is the most damaging proof of all against my Uncle James. And yet not a certain proof."

"Not a certain proof!"

"No: for it is possible that he may have picked it up in the Friar's Keep."

"Then why should he not have shown the ring? An innocent man would have done so at once, and—here comes the preventive-man," broke off Madame Guise, her quick sight detecting the officer at some distance. "Let us go down the hill again, George."

They crossed the waste land to the road, and went towards the hill. George North was lost in thought.

"There is something about it almost incomprehensible," he said aloud: "and for my own part, Charlotte, I must avow that I cannot yet believe the Uncle James to be guilty. The Castlemaines are recognised in their own land here as mirrors of honour. I have heard my father say so many a time. And this is so dreadful a crime to suspect anybody of! I think I saw the uncle to-day."

"Where?" she asked. And Mr. North explained the appearance of the gentleman that morning at the Turk's Head, whose carriage bore the Castlemaine crest. "Oh, yes, that was Mr. Castlemaine," she said, recognising him by the description.

"Well, he does not look like a man who would do a dreadful deed, Charlotte. He has a very attractive, handsome face: and I think a good face. Shall I tell you why I have more particularly faith in his innocence?—Because he is so like my father."

"And I have never doubted his guilt. You must admit, George, that appearances are strongly against him."

"Undoubtedly they are. And a sad thing it is to have to say it of one of the family. Do you see much of the younger brother—the Uncle Peter?"

"But he is dead," returned Charlotte.

"The Uncle Peter dead!"

"He died the very night that Anthony was lost: the mourning you saw Mrs. Castlemaine wearing was for him; Ethel and the little girl have gone into slighter mourning. And Madame Guise proceeded to give a brief history of Mr. Peter Castlemaine's death and the circumstances surrounding it, with the entrance of Mary Ursula to the Grey Nunnery. He listened in silence; just remarking that he had wondered in the morning which of his two uncles it was that he saw, and had felt half inclined to inquire of the waiter, but prudence kept him from it.

"This is the Friar's Keep," she said as they came to it, and her voice instinctively took a tone of awe. "Do you see those two middle windows, George? It is within them that people see the revenant of the Grey Monk."

"I wish he would show himself now!" heartily spoke George, throwing his eyes on the windows. At which wish his sister-in-law drew close enough to touch him.

"Here's the gate," she said, halting as they came to it. "Was it not a strange thing, George, that it should be locked that night!"

"If it really was locked; and is never locked at other times," replied George North, who quite seemed, what with one implied doubt and another, to be going in for some of the scepticism of his uncle, the Master of Greylands. Opening the gate, he walked in. Charlotte followed. They looked inside the Gothic door to the dark still cloisters of the Keep; they stood for some moments gazing out over the sea, so expansive to the eye from this place: but Charlotte did not care to linger there with him, lest they should be seen.

"And it was to this place of ruins Anthony came, and passed into those unearthly-looking cloisters!" he exclaimed as they were going out. "That dark, still enceinte put me in mind of nothing so much as a dead-house."

Charlotte shivered. "It is there," she said, "that we must search for traces of Anthony—"

"I suppose there is a staircase, or something of that kind, that leads to the upper rooms of the Keep?" he interrupted.

"Oh, yes: a stone staircase."

"Have you been up to the rooms?"

"I!" she exclaimed, as if he might have spared the question. "Why, it is in those upper rooms that the revenant is seen. Part of them are in ruins. Mr. Castlemaine and some men of the law he called to his aid from Stilborough went over it all after Anthony's loss, and found no traces of him. But what I think is this, George: that a search conducted by Mr. Castlemaine would not be a minute or true one: the Master of Greylands' will is law in the place: he is bowed down to like a king. How shall you manage to account plausibly for taking up your abode at Greylands, so that no suspicion may attach to you?"

"I shall be here for the purpose of sketching, you understand. An obscure travelling artist excites neither notice nor suspicion, Charlotte," he added in a half-laughing tone. "By the way—there's no danger, I hope, that the little one, Marie Greylands, will remember Uncle George?"

"Not the least; not the slightest. You left her too long ago for that. But, take you notice, George, that here she is only Marie. It would not do to let her other name, Greylands, slip out."

"I will take care," replied George North.

"I think you Will. I think you have altered, George. You are more thoughtful in mood, more sober in manner than you used to be."

"Ay," he answered. "That carelessness and its sad fruits altered me, Charlotte. It left me a lesson that will last me my lifetime."

They were opposite the entrance of the Grey Nunnery: and, in the selfsame moment, its doors opened and Ethel Reene came forth, attended by Sister Ann. The sight seemed to startle Madame Guise.

"Dear me!—but it is I who am careless to-night," she said, below her breath. "Talking with you, George, has made me forget all; even time."

In fact, Madame was to have called at the Nunnery quite an hour ago for Ethel: who had been to spend the evening there with Miss Castlemaine. Madame went forward with her apologies: saying that she had met her husband's old friend, Mr. North, and had stayed talking with him of by-gone days, forgetful of the passing moments.

"I will take charge of Miss Reene now, Sister Ann; I am so sorry you should have to put your things on," she added.

"Nay, but I am not sorry," returned Sister Ann candidly. "It is pleasant to us to get the change of a walk. Your little one has been very happy this evening, Madame Guise; playing at bo-peep and eating the grapes Miss Reene brought her."

Sister Ann retired indoors. Madame Guise and Ethel took the front way round by the Dolphin to Greylands' Rest, Mr. George North attending them. The shortest way was across the field path; though it involved a stile, Madame took it. Mr. North talked to Ethel, and made himself very agreeable—as none could do better than he: and Miss Ethel rejoiced that it was night instead of day, for she found herself blushing repeatedly at nothing, just as she had done during his visit in the morning. What could have come to her? she mentally asked; she had never been absurd before: and she felt quite angry with herself. The conversation was held in French, Madame having unconsciously resumed that language with Mr. North when they left Sister Ann.

"There are many delightful bits of scenery in this little place," said Mr. North: "I have been looking about me this afternoon. Perhaps I may bring myself and my pencils here for a short sojourn: I should much like to take some sketches."

"Yes, they are very nice views," said Ethel, blushing again. She was walking arm in arm with the governess, and Mr. North strolled along at Ethel's elbow.

"How very well you speak French!" he exclaimed. "Almost as well as we French people ourselves. There's but a slight accent."

A deeper and quite unnecessary blush at this. "But I thought you were English, monsieur."

"Well, so I am, mademoiselle. But when you come to sojourn a long while in a country, you get to identify yourself with its inhabitants,—that is to say, with their nationality."

"And you have been for a long time in France?"

"Yes."

They had come to the stile now. Mr. North got over it and assisted Madame Guise. Ethel mounted instantly, and was jumping down alone: but he turned and caught her. In the hurry she tripped, and somewhat crushed her hat against his shoulder. He made fifty thousand apologies, just as though it had been his fault; and there was much laughing. Mr. North quite forgot to release her hand until they had gone on some paces; and Ethel's blush at this was as hot as the summer's night.

At the entrance gate, where he had taken leave of Madame Guise in the morning, he took leave of them now; shaking the hand of Madame and asking whether he might be permitted to shake Ethel's, as it was the mode in England. The blushes were worst of all then: and Ethel's private conviction was that the whole world had never contained so attractive an individual as Mr. George North.

Mr. George North had all but regained the door of the Dolphin Inn, where he had dined and would lodge for the night, when a carriage and pair, with its bright lamps lighted, came spanking round the corner at a quick pace, the groom driving. George North, drawing aside as it passed him, recognized the handsome phaeton he had seen in the morning at the Turk's Head. The Master of Greylands was returning from Stilborough.

XXVI

Dining At Greylands' Rest

It was yet early morning. The sky was darkly blue, the sea indolent and calm, the air intensely hot. Mr. George North, sitting on the bench outside the Dolphin Inn, his straw hat tilted over his brows, gazed at the placid sea before him, and felt as lazy as was the atmosphere.

He had slept well, and breakfasted to his perfect content. Young, sanguine, healthy, the mystery encompassing his brother Anthony's fate had not sufficed to break his rest. The more than hinted-at doubts of Charlotte Guise—that Anthony had been vat out of the world for ever by Mr. Castlemaine—failed to find their response in George North's mind. The mere thought of it appeared to him to be absurd: the suspicion far-fetched and impossible; the implied doubt of the Master of Greylands little less than a libel on the name of Castlemaine. Men of the world are inclined to be practical in their views, rather than imaginative: and the young and hopeful look ever on the bright side of all things.

That Anthony's disappearance was most unaccountable, George North felt; his continued absence, if indeed he still lived, was more strange still. There was very much to be unravelled in connection with that past February night, and George North intended to do his best to bring its doings to light: but that his brother had been destroyed in the dreadful manner implied, he could not and would not believe. Without giving credit to anything so terrible, there existed ground enough, ay and more than enough, for distrust and uncertainty. And, just as his sister-in-law, poor bereaved Charlotte, had taken up her abode at Greylands under false colours, to devote herself to search out the mystery of that disappearance within the Friar's Keep, so did George North resolve to take up his. Nothing loth, was he, to make a sojourn there. Had Anthony presented himself before him at that moment, safe and well, George would still have felt inclined to stay; for the charms of Ethel Reene had made anything but a transient impression on him. The world was his own, too; he had no particular home in it; Greylands was as welcome to him as an abode as any other resting-place.

John Bent came forth from the open door to join his guest. Landlords and their ways in those days were different folks from what they are in these. He wore no waistcoat under his loose linen coat, and his head was bare.

"A nice stretch of water, that, sir," he said, respectfully, indicating the wide sea, shining out in the distance.

"It is indeed," replied George North. "I think the place is a nice place altogether. That sea, and the cliff, rising up there, would be worth sketching. And there must be other pretty spots also."

"True enough, sir."

"I feel inclined to bring over my pencils and take up my quarters with you for a bit, and sketch these places. What do you say to it, Mr. Bent?"

"There's nothing I could say, sir, but that it would give me and my wife pleasure if you did. We'd try and make you comfortable."

"Ay; I don't fear but you'd do that. Well, I think I shall go to Stilborough and bring back my rattletraps. I saw a charming bit of scenery yesterday when I went to call on the French lady. It is an archway covered with ivy: looking through the opening, you catch a view of a cottage with a back-ground of trees. There was a small rustic bridge also not far off, lying amid trees, and a stream of water running under it, the whole dark and sheltered. These spots would make admirable sketches."

"No doubt, sir," returned John Bent by way of answer. "But you'd have to crave the leave of the Master of Greylands before making them. And that leave might not be easy to get."

"Why not?"

"They be on his land, sir."

"What of that? Surely he would not deny it! The great Creator has not been churlish in making this world beautiful—should one man wish to keep any part of it for the enjoyment of his own sole eyesight?"

John Bent gave his head a shake. "I don't think it is that Mr. Castlemaine would do that, sir; he is not so selfish as that comes to; but he does not like to see strangers about the place. He'd keep all strange folks out of Greylands if he could: that's my belief."

"Why should he?"

"It's just his pride and his exclusive temper, sir."

"But I thought I had heard Mr. Castlemaine described as a generous man; a pleasant-tempered man," remarked Mr. North.

"Well, and so he is, sir, when he chooses to be," confessed the landlord; "I don't say to the contrary. In many things he is as easy and liberal as a man can be. But in regard to having strangers about his land, place either, he is just a despot. And I think the chances are ten ..e, sir, against your getting leave to sketch any spot of his."

"I can bat ask. If he refuses me, well and good. Of course I should not attempt to defy him—though I am by no means sure that he, or any one else, has the legal power to deny our copying nature's works, in man's possession though they may be. Never mind. Enough free objects will be left for me: such as that cliff, for example, and that glorious sea."

Mr. North rose as he spoke. At that same moment two of the Grey Ladies were crossing over from the Nunnery. Only one of them wore the dress of the community, Sister Margaret. The other was Miss Castlemaine, in her flowing mourning robes. Each of the ladies smiled kindly and gave the good-morrow to John Bent. George North lifted his straw hat with reverence, and kept it off until they should have passed.

Possibly the action, so uncharacteristic of most Englishmen, attracted particularly the attention of Mary Ursula. Bending slightly her head to acknowledge the courtesy, her eyes rested on the young man's face. Whether it was his action, whether it was anything she saw in the face that struck on her, certain it was that she half stopped to gaze upon him. She said nothing, however, but passed on.

"What a magnificent young woman!" cried Mr. North, when the ladies were out of hearing. "She is beautiful. I mean the lady in mourning: not the Sister."

"She is that, sir. It is Miss Castlemaine."

"Miss Castlemaine! Which Miss Castlemaine?"

"The late banker's daughter, sir. Niece to the Master of Greylands."

An hour later, the ladies went by again on their way homeward. John was outside his door still, but alone, with a white cap on his head. Miss Castlemaine accosted him.

"Who was that gentleman we saw here just now, Mr. Bent?"

"His name's North, madam: he is an artist."

"Thank you," said Miss Castlemaine.

"Why did you inquire?" asked Sister Margaret as they went on.

"Because something in the stranger's face seemed to be familiar to me—as though I had seen it before," replied Mary Ursula.

Meanwhile, Mr. George North, who seemed to do things rather upon impulse—or, at least, not to lose time in putting in practice any resolution he might make—had proceeded to Greylands' Rest to get the permission for sketching any particular bits of scenery he fancied, which might be owned by Mr. Castlemaine. He took the field way; the same way that he and the ladies had taken the previous night, and he was nearly at the end of his journey when he encountered Mr. Castlemaine who was coming forth from his house with Ethel Reene. Mr. North lifted his hat, and approached to accost them.

"I beg your pardon," he said to Mr. Castlemaine, bowing at the same time to Ethel, "I believe I have the honour of speaking to the Master of Greylands."

Mr. Castlemaine recognised him at once, as the young travelling artist whom he had seen the previous day at the Turk's Head; the same who had just been talked of at his breakfast-table. This Mr. George North, it turned out, was a friend of Madame Guise, or, as Madame especially put it, of her late husband's. A gentleman artist, Madame had said, for he was not dependent on his profession; he had a good patrimony, and was of good family: and Mr. Castlemaine had taken all in unsuspiciously. Apart from anything trenching on the mysteries of that certain February night and of the Friar's Keep, whatever they might be, he was the least suspicious man in the world: and it no more occurred to him to connect this young man and his appearance at Greylands with that unhappy affair, than he had connected Madame with it. Mr. Castlemaine had taken rather fancy to this young artist when at the Turk's Head: he liked the look of his bright face now, as he came up smiling: he warmed to the open, attractive manners.

George North preferred his request. He had come to Greylands the previous day in the two-horse van from Stilborough for the purpose of calling on Madame Guise; he had been struck with the pretty place and with the many charming bits of scenery it presented, fit for the pencil: some of these spots he found belonged to the Master of Greylands; would the Master of Greylands give him permission to sketch them?

And taken, it must be repeated, by the applicant's looks and words; by his winning face, his pleasing voice, his gentlemanly bearing altogether, Mr. Castlemaine gave the permission off-hand, never staying to count the cost of any after suggestions that might arise against it. Artists had come to the place before; they had stayed a week or two and departed again, leaving no traces behind: that the same would be the case with this present one, he never thought to doubt. Mr. North was somewhat different from the others, though; inasmuch as that he was known to Madame Guise (who vouched, so to say, for his being a gentleman) and also that he had gained the liking of Mr. Castlemaine.

Mr. North warmly expressed his thanks for the readily-accorded permission. Ethel had not spoken, but was blushing perpetually as she stood listening to him—and for no cause whatever, she angrily told herself. Mr. North turned to retrace his steps, and they all walked on together.

"You have been acquainted with Madame Guise and her family some time, I find," observed the Master of Greylands. "Knew them abroad."

"Oh yes. Her husband was a dear friend of mine. We were like—" Mr. North hesitated, but brought the suggestive word out, as he had led to it—"like brothers."

"Was there anything peculiar in his death?" asked Mr. Castlemaine. "Madame Guise seems to shrink so much from all mention of the subject that we can hardly help fancying there was: and it is a topic that we cannot question her upon. He died suddenly, she said one day, when some allusion was made to him, and that is all we know. Mrs. Castlemaine observed that she shivered perceptibly as she said it.

"That is what I heard—that he died suddenly," assented Mr. North. "I was roaming about Italy at the time, and did not know of it for some months afterwards. Madame Guise had left for England then. I procured her address; and, being so near, called to see her yesterday."

Mr. Castlemaine slightly nodded—as if this part scarcely needed explanation. "Then you do not know what Monsieur Guise died of, Mr. North? She has not told you?"

"No, she has not. I do not know what he died of. They were very much attached to one another, and her avoidance of the subject may be perhaps natural. He was an estimable young man, and my very good and dear friend."

Thus talking, the fields were traversed and they gained the road. Here their routes lay in opposite directions: that of the Master of Greylands and Ethel to the right, Mr. North's to the left. He was returning to the Dolphin before starting on his walk to Stilborough.

"You are staying at the inn, I presume," observed Mr. Castlemaine to him.

"Yes, I am comfortable there, and the charges are very moderate. I called for my bill this morning."

"Called for your bill! Are you going away?"

"Only to come back again this afternoon. I left my portmanteau and pencils at Stilborough."

"Well, we shall be happy to welcome you at Greylands' Rest whenever you feel inclined to call on Madame Guise," spoke Mr. Castlemaine in parting. "Will you dine with us this evening?"

"Thank you. With very much pleasure."

Mr. Castlemaine cordially shook hands, and turned away. It was rare indeed that the Master of Greylands condescended to be so free with a stranger—or, in fact, with any one. Any previous visiting-artists to the place might have looked in vain for a hand-shake. But his heart warmed to this young man; he knew not why: and there was something in Mr. North's bearing, though it was perfectly respectful to the Master of Greylands, which seemed to testify that he was, and knew himself to be, of the same social standing in society; at least, that gentleman's equal.

But that the propensity, which we all have, to take likes and dislikes seems to obey no rule or law, and is never to be accounted for, it might be noticed as a curious circumstance here. When Mr. Castlemaine first saw the unfortunate Anthony, he had taken a dislike to him. How far the avowed errand of that young man—the putting in a claim to Greylands' Rest—may have conduced to this, cannot be told: Mr. Castlemaine would have said that it had nothing to do with it; that he disliked him by instinct. Most people had seen nothing in Anthony but what was to be liked; ay, and much liked; Mr. Castlemaine was an exception. And yet, here was Anthony's brother (though Mr. Castlemaine knew it not) to whom his heart was going out as it had never yet before gone out to a stranger! Truly these instincts are more capricious than a woman's will!

George North ran into the Dolphin, caught up his umbrella to shield himself from the sun, and started on his hot walk to Stilborough. In the course of the afternoon he was back again with what he was pleased to call his rattletraps—a portmanteau and a sketching-case—having chartered a fly to Greylands. There was no two-horse van at his disposal that afternoon.

"Do you get much of this fiery weather?" he asked, throwing himself down by Mrs. Bent in her sitting-room and his hat on the table, while the landlord saw to his luggage.

"Well, we have our share of it, sir, when it's a hot summer. And this is a very hot one. Just see the sea yonder: even that looks hot."

"I shall take a dip presently and try it," returned Mr. North. "That must be the best of living at the sea-side you get glorious baths."

MRS. HENRY WOOD

"You have not told me what you'd like for dinner yet, sir," resumed Mrs. Bent, who was stripping currants into a pan, her face and the currants and the cherry cap-ribbons all one and the same colour.

"Dinner! Why, I am going to dine at Greylands' Rest. Its master asked me."

"Did he!" cried Mrs. Bent in surprise. "Well, that's a great thing for him to do. He don't favour new-comers, sir."

"He has so far favoured me. I say, Mrs. Bent," added the artist, a laughing look in his bright eyes, "what a pretty girl that is, up there!"

Mrs. Bent raised her own eyes from the stripping, and shot forth an inquiring glance. He was helping himself to the ripest bunches.

"Miss Ethel Reene! Well, so she is, sir, and as good as she is pretty. There's no love lost—as it is said—between her and her stepmother. At any rate, on Mrs. Castlemaine's part. The servants say Miss Ethel gets snubbed and put upon above a bit. She has to give way finely to the little one."

"Who is the little one?—Just look at this large bunch! Twenty on it, I know."

"You'll get a surfeit, sir, if you eat at these sharp currants like that when you are so hot.

"Not I. I never tasted any so good."

"I shall charge you for then, sir," she went on, laughing.

"All right. Charge away. I have heard my father tell a tale of going into a cherry-orchard once when he was a lad, he and three more boys. They paid sixpence each, and eat what they liked. I fancy all four had a surfeit, or something, after that."

"I dare be bound. Boys in a cherry-orchard! Do you get fine currants in France, sir?"

"We get everything that's fine there," responded Mr. North, as well as he could speak for the currants. "But what little one were you talking of, Mrs. Bent?"

"Of Miss Flora, sir: Mrs. Castlemaine's daughter. A troublesome, ill-behaved little chit, she is: always in mischief. The last time we were brewing; it's only a few days ago; my young lady was passing the door and ran in: she went rushing to the brewhouse, and fell backwards into the mash-tub. Fortunately the liquor had been drawn off; but there she was, squealing in the wet grains."

Mr. North laughed, and rose. Abandoning the currants, he put on his hat and went leisurely out to take his plunge in the sea. By-and-by, when Mrs. Bent and John were seated at tea, he came running back in a commotion, his wet towels in his hand.

"Can you tell me at what time they dine at Greylands' Rest?"

"At six o'clock, sir, when they dine late," replied John "Mostly, though, it's in the middle of the day."

"And as often five o'clock as six," put in Mrs. Bent. "The earlier Mrs. Castlemaine dines, the better she likes it. You have not half dried your hair, sir."

"I had no time for superfluous drying," he replied. "It suddenly struck me that I did not know the hour for dinner, and I came off as I could. Is that the right time?" looking at the clock. "A quarter past five?"

"Right to a minute, sir. This clock never fails."

"And you say, Mrs. Bent, that they sometimes dine at five. What will they think of me?"

He went leaping up the stairs, saying something about the thoughtless ways of wandering Arabs—by which the landlord and his wife understood him to mean artists. An incredibly short time, and he was down again, dressed, and striding off to Greylands' Rest.

The first thing Mr. North noticed, on entering the gate of the garden, was the flutter of a white dress amid a nest of trees. It was enough to assure him that the dinner had not begun. He penetrated these trees, attracted by the voices within, and found himself in sight of Ethel Reene, and the young damsel recently spoken of—Miss Flora.

The white dress he had seen was Ethel's. It was an Indian sprigged muslin, set off with black ribbons. Her rich brown hair, so bright in the flicker of sunshine, had nothing to adorn it: her delicate face wore one of its sweetest blushes as he approached. She sat in a kind of grotto formed by the trees, a book resting in her lap while she talked to Flora. That young lady, unmindful of her holiday attire—a costly and very pretty frock of grey silken gauze—for Mrs. Castlemaine had said she might dine at table—was astride on one of the branches. Ethel had in vain told her not to get up there. She jumped down at the sight of Mr. North: the frock was caught, and the result was a woful rent.

"There!" exclaimed Ethel in an undertone, for Mr. North had not quite reached them. "Your beautiful new frock! What a pity! If I were mamma I should never buy you anything but stuff and cotton."

Flora, even, looked down ruefully at the damage: the frock was new, as Ethel said, costly, and beautiful.

"Pin it up, Ethel."

"I have no pins here. Besides, pinning would not hold it. It can only be mended. You had better show it to Eliza."

The spoilt child ran past Mr. North on her way indoors. He came up to Ethel, bowed, and then held his hand out. With another bright and deeper blush she put hers into it.

"I shall get quite the English manners soon," he said, "We do not shake hands much in my country: especially with young ladies. They do not let us."

"Do you call France your country?"

"Well, I am apt to do so, having lived there so much. I have been making great haste here, Miss Reene, not knowing the hour for dinner."

"We dine at six," replied Ethel. "Mamma has but just returned from her drive, and is dressing," she added, as if in apology for being the only one to receive him. "Papa has been out all the afternoon."

"Is Madame Guise well to-day?"

"Not very. She has one of her bad headaches, I am sorry to say, and is in her room. She will be here shortly."

He sat down by Ethel, and took up the book she had been reading; a very old and attractive book indeed—the "Vicar of Wakefield."

"What an excellent story it is!" he exclaimed.

"Have you read it?" asked Ethel, rising to proceed to the house.

"Indeed I have. Twenty times, I should think. My mother had a small store of these old English works, and and my brother revelled in them."

"You have brothers and sisters?"

"Only one sister now. She is married and lives in France."

"Ah, then I can understand why you like to go thither so much," said Ethel, all unconscious that it was his native land; that he had never before been in England. "Is her husband French?"

"Yes," replied Mr. North. "Oh, what a lovely rose!" he cried, halting at a tree they were passing, perhaps to change the conversation.

It was in truth one of rare beauty: small, bright, delicate, and of exquisite fragrance. Ethel, in her impulsive good nature, in her innocent thoughtlessness, plucked it and offered it to him. As he took it from her, their eyes met: in his own shone a strangely-earnest look of gratitude for the gift, mingled with admiration. Poor Ethel became crimson at the thought of what she had done, and would have regained the flower had it been possible. She went on quickly to the glassdoors of the drawing-room; Mr. North followed, placing the rose in his buttonhole.

Madame Guise was entering the room by the inner door at the same moment. Mr. and Mrs. Castlemaine soon, appeared; lastly, Miss Flora, in her mended frock. Harry Castlemaine was not at home; some errand, either of business or pleasure, had taken him to Stilborough. Harry had been out a great deal of late: there seemed to be a restlessness upon him, and his father was beginning to notice it.

Mr. North was received (as he heard later from Madame Guise) quite en famille—which pleased him much. No alteration was made in the usual style of dinner: but the dinners at Greylands' Rest were always sufficiently good for chance company. As George North sat at table, watching the master at the head board, he could not bring himself to believe that Charlotte's suspicions were correct. Good-looking, refined, courtly, pleasing, Mr. Castlemaine appeared to be the very last man capable of committing a secret crime. Every other moment some gesture of his, or glance, or tone in the voice, put George North in mind of his father, Basil Castlemaine: and—no, he could not, he could not join in the doubts of poor Anthony's wife.

But he noticed one thing. That ever and anon Mr. Castlemaine would seem to forget where he was, forget his position as host, and fall into a fit of silent abstraction, during which, a curiously-sad expression lay on his face, and his brow was knit as with some painful care. He would rouse himself as soon as he perceived he was mentally absent, and be in an instant the grand, courtly, self-possessed Master of Greylands again. But the fits of gloom did occur, and George North observed them.

Nevertheless, he could not entertain the dread suspicions of his sister-in-law. That a vast deal of mystery attached to his brother's disappearance, and that Mr. Castlemaine was in some degree and manner connected with it, or cognizant of it, he readily saw cause, to recognize: but, of the darker accusation, he believed him to be innocent. And it went with George North very much against the grain to sit at Mr. Castlemaine's hospitable table under false colours, and not to declare the fact that he was his brother Basil's son.

Something of this he said to Madame Guise. Dinner over, the party strolled into the garden, grateful for the little breath of air it brought. Mr. North found himself momentarily alone with Madame, near the grand sweeping elm tree.

"Are you mad, George?" she hastily cried in French and in the deepest alarm, in response to the word or two he whispered. "Wish to declare yourself! not like to be here only as Mr. North! For the love of heaven, recall your senses."

"It is terrible deceit, Charlotte."

"Do you no longer care for your unfortunate brother? Have you lost all remembrance of your love for him?—of the ties of kindred?—of the time when you played together at your mother's knee! Do you think it cost me nothing to come here under a wrong name—that it costs me no self reproaches to be here under sham pretences, I who have as keen a sense of honour as you? But I do it for Anthony's sake; I bear all the feeling of disgrace for him."

"That is just it," said George, "as it seems to me. Disgrace."

"It must be borne—for my sake, and for Anthony's. Were you to say, 'I am George, Anthony's brother,' Mr. Castlemaine would take, alarm; he would turn you out of the house, and me after you: and, rely upon it, we should never, discover more of poor Anthony than we know now. It would still all be uncertain. No, mon ami, go you away from Greylands if you like, and leave me to seek on alone; but, declare yourself you must not. Anthony would rise from his grave at your unnatural conduct."

"Charlotte, you are exciting yourself for nothing," he hastily whispered, for Mrs. Castlemaine was approaching. "I did not say I was going to declare myself; I only said how unpalatable to me is the acting of this deceit. But for Anthony's sake and yours, I would not bear it for a moment; as circumstances are, I must go on with it, and be George North perhaps to the end of the chapter."

"Not to the end," she murmured, "Not to the end. Anthony's fate will be discovered before very long time has elapsed—or my prayers and tears will have found no pity in heaven."

Only at dusk did they go in to tea. Afterwards, Ethel was bade to sing some of her songs. George North—no mean musician himself, and with a soft, pleasant voice of his own—sat by the piano, listening to their melody, gazing through the twilight at her sweet face, and thinking that he had never been so nearly in an earthly paradise.

When he took his departure, they accompanied him to the gate. The stars were out, the night was clear and still, the heat yet excessive. It chanced that he and Ethel walked side by side; it chanced that he held her hand, ay, and pressed it too, longer than he had need have done when he said goodnight. That moment's parting would remain in Ethel's memory for life; the heavy perfume of the flowers lay around them, her heart and pulses were alike beating.

If she and George North had not fallen in love with one another, they were at least on the highroad towards it.

XXVII

In the Vaults

Time had again gone on. It was autumn weather. Mr. George North was making a tolerably long sojourn in the place, and seemed to be passing his days agreeably. Sketching, boating, gossiping; one would have said he had no earthly care. Perhaps he had not—save the one sweet care of making himself acceptable to Ethel Reene.

The fate of each was over and done with long ago, so far as that grand master-passion of the heart went—love. Ethel was helplessly in love with him for all time. "Ma caprice est faite," she might have said to Madame Guise in that lady's native language; and Madame would have opened her eyes to hear it. For in regard to the affection that had sprung up between those two young people, Madame was entirely in the dark. Not very observant by nature, her whole thoughts occupied with the one great trouble of her life, she remained wholly unsuspicious of what was passing in the inner life of those around her.

George North's love for Ethel made his very existence. The purest, truest affection man can feel, beat in his heart for Ethel Reene. To meet, was with both of them the one great event of the day; the hope to be looked forward to when they rose in the morning, the remembrance that glowed within their breasts at night. On the solitary cliffs up by the coastguard station: or down on the sheltered beach of the seashore, towards the Limpets; or amid the lovely scenery where he carried his pencils—in one place or another they were sure to meet. The soft wind seemed to whisper love-songs, the varying tints of the autumn foliage were as the brilliant colours of the trees on the everlasting shores, the very air was fraught with a heavenly perfume; and the world for each was as the Garden of Eden.

Mrs. Castlemaine was no more wise than Madame. She had discerned nothing. Perhaps their first intimacy grew during a few days that she was absent from home. Disappointed of the promised excursion to Paris—for Mr. Castlemaine had allowed the months to go on and on, and did not attempt to enter on it—Mrs. Castlemaine set off on a ten days' visit to some friends in the adjoining county, taking Flora with her. This was close upon the appearance of George North at Greylands.

Ethel, left at home under the chaperonage of Madame, saw a good deal of Mr. George North: and the mutual liking, already rising in either heart, perfected itself into love. Long before Mrs. Castlemaine's ten days of absence had come to an end, they were secretly conscious that they were all in all to each other.

Mrs. Castlemaine returned, and neither saw nor suspected anything. Perhaps she was not likely to suspect. People don't go about betraying the most secretive passion man can feel, or write the words, I love, in brazen letters on their foreheads. True love is essentially reticent, hiding itself away from the eye of man within the remotest folds of the shrinking heart. Neither had Mr. North breathed a word to Ethel. He was not prepared to do it. Before he could speak, he must be able to declare his own true name to her and to her step-parents, to say "I am George Castlemaine." And circumstances would not let him do that yet.

He had learned absolutely nothing in regard to his brother's fate: to unravel aught of the mystery attending it seemed to be beyond his power. He had explored, as he believed, every nook and portion of the Friar's Keep; but without success of any kind. It appeared to be a lonely, deserted, and in places a dilapidated building, affording no spots for concealment. There existed not a trace of Anthony; there was nothing to show that he had ever entered it. George North stayed on at the Dolphin, waiting patiently for the elucidation that might or might not come; listening, whenever they met, to his sister-in-law's most persistent belief that it would come: and perfectly contented so to stay on while he could see Ethel and feed his heart's love for her, though the stay had been for ever.

MIDNIGHT WAS STRIKING FROM THE old turret-clock of the Grey Nunnery. Standing at the open window of her bedchamber, was Miss Castlemaine. She had put off the mourning for her father now, and assumed the grey dress of the Sisterhood. A warm black shawl was wrapped about her shoulders, for the night air was somewhat cold, and the breeze from the sea brought a chillness with it. It was late for any of the Grey Sisters to be up; unless detained by sickness, they went to rest early: but Miss Castlemaine had come in rather late from spending the evening at Greylands' Rest, and had afterwards sat up writing a long letter. She had now been in her room some little time, and had not yet begun to undress. To use an old saying, she had no sleep in her eyes. Putting the warm shawl on, she opened the window, and stood leaning on its sill, deep in thought as she gazed out at the wide expanse of the sea. Hardly a night had passed of the past summer but she had thus stood as she was standing now. To look thus over the still sea in its calmness during this silent hour, or at its heaving waves, flashing white under the moon or starlight, and lost in thought and care, was a positive luxury to Miss Castlemaine. But these autumn nights were getting somewhat cold for it.

It was not her own proper chamber that she was in, but Sister Mildred's. Sister Mildred was away. Her health was much better; but Mr. Parker, the doctor, had said most positively that a change of a month or two was necessary to complete her cure: and Sister Mildred departed to stay with some relatives whom she had not seen for many years. She would be returning shortly now, and Mary Ursula's occupancy of her room was only temporary. The approach of cold weather had caused some necessary alterations in Mary Ursula's chamber—the old grate was being replaced by a new one, and the chimney repaired: and during its process, she occupied the chamber of Sister Mildred.

The lapse of months had not diminished the uneasiness of Mary Ursula's mind, in regard to the disappearance of her unfortunate cousin Anthony in the Friar's Keep. That Keep still wore for her an atmosphere of uncertainty and mystery. She never thought of it—and it was more often in her thoughts than she would have liked to say—but with one of those unpleasant thrills of renewed pain that arise at times with us all, when some heavy sorrow or suspense lies latent in the heart. Over and over again, since the night when Sister Mildred had discovered to her the secret passage, and she had explored with that lady its subterranean depth and length, had the wish—nay, the resolve—made itself heard within her to go again through the same passage, and look a little about the Friar's Keep. She knew not how, she knew not why, but the fear that Anthony had been treacherously dealt with grew of stronger conviction day by day. Not by Mr. Castlemaine: she could never fear that: and she resented the doubt cast upon him by the world—which he in his haughty pride would not condescend to resent—and believed that the discovery of the truth, if it could be made, would be doing her uncle the best of services. By exploring, herself, the Friar's Keep, she might be able to trace out nothing: but at least the strong desire to try lay upon her. Is it not so with all of us? In any search or complexity, do we not always mistrust others, and the capability of others, and think in our secret hearts that we could succeed where they fail? The figure Mary had seen with her own eyes, bearing its lamp, and which was religiously believed by the small community of Greylands to be the ghost of the wicked monk, long dead and gone, possessed no supernatural terrors for her. That it was some living personage, personating the dead monk for a purpose, she felt sure of; and she could not help fancying that in some unimaginable manner it must have to do with the concealment of the fate of Anthony.

Circumstances had brought all these matters more especially to her mind to-night. An old friend of hers, a Mrs. Hunter of Stilborough, had been also a visitor, though a chance one, that evening at Greylands' Rest. Mrs. Hunter was very fond of Mr. Castlemaine. She scouted the doubt thrown upon him in connection with his vanished nephew, regarding it as the height of absurdity; and to show this opinion of hers, rather liked talking of the affair. She had introduced it that evening at Greylands' Rest, asking all sorts of questions about the Keep, and about the ghost that sometimes appeared there, and about Anthony. During this conversation, Mary Ursula noticed that her uncle was remarkably silent; and once she caught a look of strangely painful uneasiness on his face. As they were walking home—for it was Mr. Castlemaine himself who had brought her back to the Grey Nunnery—she ventured to speak of it to him.

"You have never heard in any way of Anthony, I suppose, Uncle James?"

"Never," was Mr. Castlemaine's reply.

"Is it not strange that some of his friends in France do not inquire after him? He must have had friends there."

"I'm sure I don't know," was the curt answer.

"What do you think became of him, uncle?"

"My dear, the affair has altogether so annoyed me that I don't care to think. We will drop it, Mary Ursula."

Now, this was not satisfactory—and Mary felt that it was not. Of course it closed her lips upon the subject of Anthony; but she put another question not much less hazardous.

"Who is that figure that shows himself sometimes as the ghost of the Grey Monk?"

"I do not understand you."

The answer caused her to pause: the tone of it was, certainly resentful.

"He walks about with his lamp, uncle."

"Well?"

"Surely you do not believe in it—that it is really a ghost?" she exclaimed in astonishment.

"I am content not to be wiser than my neighbours," replied Mr. Castlemaine. "I suppose I have some elements of superstition within me. We are none of us responsible for our own nature, you know, Mary Ursula."

She said no more. In fact, they reached the Nunnery gate just then. Mr. Castlemaine saw her indoors, and went back again. Mary sat late, writing her letter, and then came up to her room.

She was thinking over it all now, as she stood at the window, the fresh sea air blowing upon her somewhat heated brow. There was no moon, but the night was passably light. Gentle waves stirred the surface of the water; a faint ripple might be heard from the incoming tide. It had turned some three hours since, and now covered, as Mary knew, the narrow path underneath the Nunnery, but not the strip of beach at the Friar's Keep: that beach, however, would be inaccessible for some hours, except by sea. Some night boats were out beyond Greylands, fishing as usual: she could discover their lights in the distance. Almost immediately opposite to her, and not far off, stood a two-masted vessel at anchor. She wondered why it should have stayed in that solitary spot, so close in-shore, instead of the more customary place off the beach. It may be almost said that she saw and thought these things unconsciously in her mind's preoccupation.

Nothing surprised her more—nay, half as much—as Mr. Castlemaine's implied admission of his belief in the supernatural appearance of the Grey Friar. An impression was abroad among the fishermen that the Castlemaines believed in the ghost as fully as they themselves did: but until to-night Mary had smiled at this. Look on what side she would, it seemed to be mystery upon mystery.

More food, than this subject, and quite as unpleasant, though of a different nature, had been given to Mary that night by Mrs. Hunter. One of Mary's chief friends in Stilborough had been a Mrs. Ord; she and Mary had been girls together. The husband, Colonel Ord, was in India: the young wife, who was delicate, remained at home. Sad news had now arrived from India. Colonel Ord was dead. He had died suddenly; it was supposed in consequence of excitement at the failure of an Indian Bank, in which all his property was placed. Mrs. Hunter had imparted this news at Greylands' Rest: and she had moreover whispered an announcement that had just been made public—the engagement of

William Blake-Gordon to the heiress of Mountsorrel. Little marvel that Mary's eyes had no sleep in them!

Her reflections—and they were very painful—were interrupted by some stir that appeared to be taking place on board the two-masted vessel. Suddenly, as it seemed to her, two boats shot out from it, one after the other. The men, rowing them, seemed to be steering right for this end of the Nunnery; and Mary watched with surprise. No: they were making, it was quite evident now, for the Friar's Keep higher up. Stretching out at the casement window as far as she dared stretch, Mary saw them go straight on for the little beach there; she thought she heard a bustle; she fancied she distinguished whispers. Wild ideas, devoid of reason, arose within her: in the broad matter-of-fact daylight, she might have felt ashamed of their improbability; but the imagination, when excited, soars away on curious wings. Were these boats bringing back Anthony?

The night went on. She saw other boats come: she saw boats go back; she saw them come again. Surely she was not dreaming all this! and yet it seemed an impossible pageantry. At length a powerful impulse took possession of her—she would go through the secret passage and try and solve the mystery: go then and there.

Fastening her warm black shawl more securely round her, and tying on a dark silk hood, she unlocked her drawers to get the keys of the passage, and descended softly the stairs. In descending them it had not seemed very lonely—though a sense of loneliness does strike upon one when making a solitary pilgrimage about even an inhabited house at the dead of night, when everybody else is abed and asleep. But when she came to go down the stone steps to the damp vaults below, lighted only by the solitary lantern she held, then Mary's courage deserted her. Brave and good woman though she was, she halted in a kind of terror, and asked herself whether she could go on alone. Alone she must go if she went at all: not for a great deal would she disclose the fact of this existing passage to any of the Sisters, or let them know of her errand in it. Sister Mildred was the only one who shared the secret, and Sister Mildred was not there.

Taking a few minutes to recover herself; to strive, ay, and to pray for returning courage; Mary at length went on. Arrived at the door, she unlocked it with great trouble: the lock was no less rusty than before, and now there was only one pair of hands to it; and she went swiftly along the passage in a sort of desperate perseverance. The door at the other end unlocked, but with just as much difficulty, she once more, for the second time in her life, found herself in the cloistered vaults underneath the Keep.

Pausing again to gather what bravery would come to her, her hand pressed on her beating heart, she then proceeded about the place with her lantern; throwing its light here, throwing it there. At first she could see no trace of anyone, living or dead; could hear no sound. Soon she halted abruptly; a thought had come across her, bringing a sick fear—suppose she should not be able to find her way back to the passage door, but must remain where she was until daylight? Daylight! what light of day could penetrate those unearthly vaults?—they must be always, by day and by night, as dark as the grave. As she stood undecided whether to search further or to go back at once, she became conscious of a whiff of fresh air, that brought with it a smell of the sea.

Stepping gently in its direction, she found herself at an opening. A door, it seemed: whatever it was, it was open to the strip of beach under the Friar's Keep, and to the sea beyond it. All seemed perfectly still: there was neither sight nor sound of human being; but as she stood in the stillness she caught the distant regular dip of the oars in the water, belonging no doubt to the retreating boats.

What could it mean?—what could it all be? Even this opening, in the hitherto-supposed-to-be impregnable walls—was it a new opening, or did it exist always? Mary stood wondering, listening, looking; or, rather, peering: peering into the darkness of the night, for it was not light enough to look.

These vaults, how much farther did they extend? She could not conjecture, and dared not attempt to discover, lest she lost her way back again: all the interstices of these pillared cloisters seemed one so like another that she might not risk it. Turning away from the fresh breeze and the welcome smell of the sea, she began to retrace her steps.

To retrace her steps, as she imagined, her thoughts very full. The question had been mooted, by people unacquainted with the place—were there any means by which the unfortunate Anthony Castlemaine could be effectually disposed of, if the worst had happened to him: say, any facility for throwing him into the sea? The answer had always been No, not from the Friar's Keep, for the Keep had no communication of any kind with the sea, its walls were thick and impervious. But, it seemed that there was a communication with the sea—as Mary had now just seen. Her thoughts and her breath alike came unpleasantly quick, and she groped along, and laid her disengaged hand on her bosom to still its pain.

But where was the door? Where? She thought she had been going in its direction, but she had come far enough, and to spare, and here was no sign of it. Was she indeed lost in this ghostly place? Her heart beat ten times more wildly at the thought.

She was very cautious in the use of the lantern, lest it might betray her, should anyone chance to be there: carrying it close before her, and keeping three of its sides dark. She moved it here, she moved it there: but no trace of the door did it shine upon; and in her desperation, she pushed down the three dark slides, and flung the light aloft. Nothing was to be seen but the dark stone floor of the vaults, their intersected pillars and arches above, and the openings between them. One spot, one division, was ever just like another. Lost! lost!

Her hand fell with the lantern: the drops of fear broke out on her face. At that moment a sound, as of the banging of a door, echoed among the pillars, and she hastily hid the glaring lantern under her shawl.

Other sounds came. Some door had evidently been shut, for now it was being barred and bolted. It was not very near, and Mary Ursula waited. Then, turning on the full light of her lantern again, and keeping her back to the sounds, she went swiftly, blindly about, in search of the passage door.

Ah, what a blessing! There it was, now, before her. Perhaps in all her life she had never experienced a moment of relief like that. A sound of joy faintly escaped her; an aspiration of thankfulness went up from her heart.

She had brought the keys inside with her, as a precaution, in case the door should close; they were tied together with string, and she had lodged the key belonging to this door in the lock on this side: Sister Mildred had done the same on the occasion of their first expedition. But now, as she stood there, Mary found she could not easily draw the key out: it might have got turned in the lock, and the lock was hard and unmanageable: so she had to put down the lantern, first of all closing its three sides, and take both hands to the key.

She had just got it out and pushed the door open, and was gliding softly and swiftly through, when a great bright light was thrown upon her, and a rough hand grasped her shoulder. With a cry of awful terror, Mary turned, and saw a pistol held close to her face.

"O don't!" she cried—"spare me! spare me! I am Sister Mary Ursula—I am Miss Castlemaine."

The man, who looked young, and was short and sturdy, turned in the doorway, with his dark lantern, never speaking a word. At that unlucky moment, the door swung against his elbow, and the pistol went off. Down he dropped with a hoarse scream.

Whether Mary Ursula retained her senses for the instant, she never afterwards knew. Fear, and the instinct of self-preservation, would have caused her to fly: but how could she leave the wounded man to his fate? The whole place seemed to be reeling around her; her head swam, and she stood back against the wall for support.

"Are you here alone?" she asked, bending down, when she could get her breath and some little strength into her shrinking spirit.

"I be, ma'am. The rest are all gone."

Why! surely she knew that voice! Taking her lantern, she threw its light upon his face, and recognized Walter Dance, Dance the fisherman's son: a young fellow with whom she had had a friendly chat only yesterday: and to whom she had given many a little present when he was a lad.

"Is it you, Walter!" she exclaimed, with the utmost astonishment—and to find that it was he seemed to chase away as by magic her worst fears. "What were you doing here?"

No answer—except some dismal groans.

"Are you much hurt?"

"I am just killed," he moaned. "Oh, ma'am! who is to help me?"

Who indeed! Mary Ursula had an innate dread of such calamities as this; she had a true woman's sensitive heart, shrinking terribly from the very thought of contact with these woes of life. "I do not know that I can help you, Walter," she said faintly. "Where are you hurt? Do you think you could get up?"

He began to try, and she helped him to his feet. One arm, the left, was powerless; and the young man said his left side was also. He leaned upon her, begging pardon for the liberty, and looked about him in dismay.

"Where does this here passage lead to, ma'am?"

"To the Grey Nunnery. Could you manage to walk to it?"

"I must get somewhere, lady, where I can be aided. I feel the blood a-dripping down me. If the bullet is not inside of me, it must have bedded itself in the wall."

The blood came from the arm. Beginning to feel faint again, feeling also very much as though she had been the cause of this, perhaps had cost the young man his life, Mary Ursula bound up the arm as well as she could, with her hankerchief and with his.

"Will you go on with me to the Nunnery, Walter?"

"Yes, ma'am, an' I can get there. I never knew of this here passage."

She locked the door, took the keys and the two lanterns herself, giving him the pistol, and bade Walter lean upon her. The walking seemed to hurt him very much, and he moaned frequently. In spite of his hardy fisherman's life, he was a very bad one to bear pain. When they came to the vaults of the Nunnery and, had to ascend the stairs, his face turned livid, and he clutched Miss Castlemaine tightly to save himself from falling. The pistol dropped from his hand once.

She got him into a small room off the kitchen, where accidents had been attended to before—for, indeed, the Grey Nunnery was somewhat of a hospital, and the good Sisters were its tender nurses. A wide, hard, capacious sofa was there, and down he sank upon it. Mary stayed to light a candle, and then hastened away to get help.

"You shall have a little brandy directly, Walter," she said. "I am going now to call assistance: we must get Mr. Parker here."

He only moaned in answer: the agony in his side seemed dreadful: but as Miss Castlemaine was leaving the room, he called her back again.

"Lady," he cried with feverish earnestness, and there was a wildly eager look in his eyes as they sought hers, "don't tell how it was done; don't tell where you saw me, or aught about it. I shall say my pistol went off in the chapel ruins, and that I crawled here to your door to get succour. I've got a reason for it."

"Very well: be it so," assented Miss Castlemaine, after a pause of reflection. It would be at least as inconvenient for her, were the truth confessed, as for him.

He looked frightfully pale: and, to Miss Castlemaine's horror, she saw some drops of blood dripping from his clothes, which must proceed from the wound in his side. Flying up the stairs, she entered the first chamber, where Sisters Ann and Phoeby slept; aroused them with a word or two of explanation, and was back again almost instantly with some water and the flask of brandy kept for emergencies. The Sisters were down almost as soon as she was; they were both capable women in a case such as this, almost as good themselves as a doctor. They saw to his side and bound it up, just as Mary Ursula had bound his arm. Sister Ann then ran off for Mr. Parker, and Sister Phoeby went to the kitchen to light the fire and prepare hot water, leaving Miss Castlemaine alone with the patient.

XXVIII

Out to Shoot a Night-Bird

Walter Dance's situation appeared to be critical. Miss Castlemaine (entirely unused to accidents) feared it was so, and he himself fully believed it. He thought that great common conqueror of us all, who is called the King of Terrors, was upon him, Death, and it brought to him indeed a terror belonging not to this world.

"I am dying," he moaned; "I am dying." And his frame shook as with an awful ague, and his teeth chattered, and great beads of water stood on his livid face. "Lord, pardon me! Oh, ma'am, pray for me."

The young man had been all his life so especially undemonstrative that his agitation was the more notable now from the very contrast. Mary, full of fear herself and little less agitated than he, could only strive to appear calm, as she bent over him and took his hands.

"Nay, Walter, it may not be as serious as you fear; I think it is not," she gently said. "Mr. Parker will be here presently. Don't excite yourself, my good lad; don't."

"I am dying," he reiterated; "I shall never get over this. Oh, ma'am, you ladies be like parsons for goodness: couldn't you say a prayer?"

She knelt down and put up her hands to say a few words of earnest prayer; just what she thought might best comfort him. One of his hands lay still, but he stretched the other up, suffering it to touch hers. These ladies of the Nunnery were looked upon by the fishermen as being very near to Heaven nearer (let it be said under the breath) than was Parson Marston.

"I've done a many wicked things, lady," he began when her voice ceased, apparently saying it in the light of a confession. "I've often angered father and grandmother beyond bearing: and this night work, I've never liked it. I suppose it's a wrong thing in God's sight: but father, he brought me in to't, as 'twere, and what was I to do?"

"What night work?" she asked.

But there came no answer. Mary would not repeat the question. He was lying in extreme agitation, shaking painfully. She put the brandy-and-water to his lips.

"I must tell it afore I go," he resumed, as if in response to some battle with himself. "Ma'am you'll promise me never to repeat it again?"

"I never will," she replied earnestly, remembering that death-bed confessions, made under the seal of secrecy, should, of all things, be held sacred. "If you have aught to confess, Walter, that it may comfort you to speak, tell it me with every confidence, for I promise you that it shall never pass my lips."

"It's not for my sake, you see, that it must be kept, but for their sakes: the Castlemaines."

"The what?" she cried, not catching the words.

"And for father's and the Commodore's, and all the rest of 'em. It would spoil all, you see, ma'am, for the future—and they'd never forgive me as I lay in my grave."

She wondered whether he was wandering. "I do not understand you, Walter."

"It all belongs to Mr. Castlemaine, father thinks, though the Commodore manages it, and makes believe it's his. Sometimes he comes down, the master, and sometimes Mr. Harry; but it's Teague and us that does it all."

"What is it that you are talking of?" she reiterated.

"The smuggling work," he whispered.

"The smuggling work?"

"Yes, the smuggling work. Oh, ma'am, don't ever tell of it! It would just be the ruin of father and the men, and anger Mr. Castlemaine beyond bearing."

Her thoughts ran off to Mr. Superintendent Nettleby, and to the poor fishermen, whom it was that officer's mission to suspect of possessing drams of unlawful brandy and pouches of contraband tobacco. She certainly believed the sick brain had lost its balance.

"We've run a cargo to-night," he whispered; "a good one too. The rest had cleared off, and there was only me left to lock the doors. When I see the glimmer of your light, ma'am, and somebody moving, I thought it was one of the men left behind, but when I got up and found it was a woman's garments, I feared it was a spy of the preventive officers come to betray us."

"What cargo did you run?" she inquired, putting the one question from amid her mind's general chaos.

"I fancy 'twas lace. It generally is lace, father thinks. Nothing pays like that."

Curious ideas were crowding on her, as she remembered the boats putting backwards and forwards that night from the two-masted vessel, lying at anchor. Of what strange secret was she being made cognisant? Could it be that some of the mystery attaching to the Friar's Keep was about to be thus strangely and most unexpectedly cleared to her?

"Walter, let me understand. Do you mean to say that smuggling is carried on in connection with the Friar's Keep?"

"Yes, it is. It have been for years. Once a month, or so, there's a cargo run: sometimes it's oftener. An underground passage leads from the Keep to the Hutt, and the goods are stowed away in the cellar there till the Commodore can take 'em away to the receivers in his spring cart."

"And who knows of all this?" she asked, after a pause. "I mean in Greylands."

"Only father and me," he faintly said, for he was getting exhausted. "They've not dared to trust anybody else. That's quite enough to know it—us. The sailors bring in the goods, and we wheel 'em up the passage: Teague, and me, and father. I've seen Mr. Harry put his hand to the barrow afore now. George Hallet—Jane's brother—he knew of it, and helped too. We had to be trusted with it, him and me, being on father's boat."

In the midst of her compassion and pity for this young man, a feeling of resentment at his words arose in Mary's heart. There might be truth in the tale he told in regard to the smuggling—nay, the manoeuvres of the boats that night and the unsuspected door she had seen open to the narrow beach, seemed to confirm it: but that this nefarious work was countenanced by, or even known to, the Master of Greylands, she rejected utterly. If there was, in her belief, one man more honourable than any other on the face of the earth, more proudly conscious of his own rectitude, it was her Uncle James. Pride had always been his failing. Walter Dance must be either partially wandering in mind to say it; or else must have taken up a fallacious fancy: perhaps been imposed upon by his father from some private motive. The work must be Teague's, and his only.

"Walter, you are not in a condition to be contradicted," she said gently, "but I know you are mistaken as to Mr. Castlemaine. He could not hold any cognisance of such an affair of cheating as this—or his son either."

"Why, the business is theirs, ma'am; their very own: father don't feel a doubt of it. The Commodore only manages it for 'em."

"You may have been led to suppose that: but it is not, cannot be true. My Uncle James is the soul of honour. Can you suppose it likely that a gentleman like Mr. Castlemaine would lend himself to a long continued system of fraud?"

MRS. HENRY WOOD

"I've always thought 'twas his," groaned Walter. "I've seen him there standing to look on."

"You must have been mistaken. Did you see him there to-night?"

"No, ma'am."

"Nor any other night, my poor lad, as I will venture to answer for."

"He might have been there to-night, though, without my seeing him," returned the young man, who seemed scarcely conscious of her words.

"How should you have left the vaults, but for this accident?" she asked, the question striking her.

"I had locked the door on the sea, and was going straight up the passage to the Hutt," he groaned, the pain in his side getting intolerable.

"One question, Walter, and then I will not trouble you with more," she breathed, and her voice took a trembling sound as she spoke. "Carry your thoughts back to that night, last February, when young Mr. Anthony was said to disappear within the Friar's Keep—"

"I know," he interrupted.

"Was any cargo run that night?"

"I can't tell," he answered, lifting his eyes for a moment to hers. "I was ill abed with a touch of the ague; I get it sometimes. I don't think father was abroad that night, either."

"Have you ever known, ever heard any hint, or rumour, from your father or the Commodore or the sailors who run these cargoes, that could throw light on Mr. Anthony's fate?"

"Never. Never a word."

"Who are the sailors that come?"

"Mostly foreigners. Is it very sinful?" he added in an access of agony, more bodily than mental, putting out his one hand to touch hers. "Very sinful to have helped at this, though father did lead me? Will God forgive it?"

"Oh yes, yes," she answered. "God is so merciful that He forgives every sin repented of—sins that are a vast deal blacker than this. Besides, you have not acted from your own will, it seems, but in obedience to authority."

"I think I'm dying," he murmured. "I can't bear this pain long."

She wiped the dew from his face, and again held the brandy-and-water to his lips. Walter Dance had always been in the highest degree sensitive, it may be said excruciatingly sensitive, to physical pain. Many another man, lying as he was now with these same injuries, would not have uttered a moan. Brave Tom Dance, his father, was wont to tell him that if ever he met with a sharpish hurt he'd turn out a very woman.

"If Doctor Parker would but come!" he cried restlessly. "Lady, you are sure he is sent for?"

As if to answer the doubt, the gate-bell rang out, and Mr. Parker's voice was heard, as he entered the Nunnery. Sister Ann had brought not only him, but John Bent also. Miss Castlemaine felt vexed and much surprised to see the latter: some faint idea, or hope, had been lying within her of keeping this untoward affair secret, at least for a few hours; and nobody had a longer tongue in a quiet way than the landlord of the Dolphin. She cast a look of reproach on the Sister.

"It was not my fault, madam," whispered Sister Ann, interpreting the glance. "Mr. Bent came over with us without as much as asking."

"Bless my heart, Walter Dance, here's a pretty kettle o' fish," began the surgeon, looking down on the patient. "You have shot yourself, Sister Ann says. And now, how did that come to happen?"

"Pistol went off unawares," groaned Walter. "I think I'm dying."

"Not just yet, let us hope," said the doctor cheerily, as he began to take off his coat and turn up his shirt-sleeves.

Sending Miss Castlemaine from the room, the doctor called for Sister Ann, who had helped him before in attending to accidents, and had as good a nerve as he. Mary, glad enough to be dismissed, went into the kitchen to Sister Phoeby, and there indulged in a sudden burst of tears. The events of the night had strangely unnerved her.

If Sister Ann exercised any speculation as to the cause of the displeasure visible in the Superior's face at the sight of John Bent, she set it down solely to the score of possible excitement to the patient. As she hastened to whisper, it was not her fault. Upon returning back from fetching Mr. Parker, he and she were bending their hasty steps across the road from the corner of the inn, when, to the astonishment of both, the voice of John Bent accosted them, sounding loud and clear in the silence of the night. Turning their heads, they saw the landlord standing at his open door.

"Keeping watch to see the sun rise, John?" asked the doctor jestingly.

"I am keeping watch for my lodger," replied the landlord in a grumbling tone, for he was feeling the want of his bed and, resented the being kept out of it. "Mr. North went off this afternoon to a distance with his sketch-book and things, ordering some supper to be ready at nine o'clock, as he should miss his dinner, and he has never come back again. It is to be hoped he will come; that we are not to have a second edition of the disappearance of young Anthony Castlemaine."

"Pooh!" quoth the doctor. "Mr. North has only lost his way."

"I hope it may prove so!" replied the landlord grimly: for his fears were at work, though at present they took no definite shape. "What sickness is calling you abroad at this hour, doctor?"

"Young Walter Dance has shot himself," interposed Sister Ann, who had been bursting with the strange news, and felt supremely elated at having somebody to tell it to.

"Walter Dance shot himself!" echoed the landlord, following them, upon impulse, to hear more. "How?—where? How did he do it?"

"Goodness knows!" returned Sister Ann. "He must have done it somewhere—and come to the Nunnery somehow. Sister Mary Ursula was still sitting up, we conclude—which was fortunate, as no time was lost. When we went to bed after prayers, she remained in the parlour to write letters."

In the astonishment created by the tidings, John Bent went with them to the Nunnery, leaving his own open door uncared for—but at that dead hour of the morning there was little fear of strangers finding it so. That was the explanation of his appearance. And there they were, the doctor and Sister Ann, busy with the wounded man, and John Bent satisfying his curiosity by listening to the few unconnected words of enlightenment that Walter chose to give as to the cause of the accident, and by fingering the pistol, which lay on the table.

"Will the injuries prove fatal?" asked Miss Castlemaine of the surgeon, when the latter at length came forth.

"Dear me, no!" was the reply, as he entered the parlour, at the door of which she stood. "Don't distress yourself by thinking of such a thing, my dear young lady. Blood makes a great show, you know; and no doubt the pain in the side is acute. There's no real cause for fear; not much damage, in fact: and he feels all reassured, now I have put him to rights."

"The ball was not in him?"

"Nothing of the kind. The side was torn a little and burnt, and of course was, for one who feels pain as he does, intolerably painful. When I tell you that the longest job will be the broken arm, and that it is the worse of the two, you may judge for yourself how slight it all is. Slight, of course, in comparison with what might have been, and with graver injuries."

"Did the ball go through the arm?"

"Only through the flesh. The bone no doubt snapped in falling: the arm must have got awkwardly doubled wader him somehow. We shall soon have him well again."

Mary gave vent to a little sob of thankfulness. It would have been an awful thing for her had his life been sacrificed. She felt somewhat faint herself, and sat down on the nearest chair.

"This has been too much for you," said the doctor; "you are not used to such things. And you must have been sitting up very late, my dear young lady—which is not at all right. Surely you could write your letters in the day-time!"

"I do things sometimes upon impulse; without reason," she answered with a faint smile. "Hearing sad news of an old friend of mine from Mrs. Hunter, whom I met at Greylands' Rest last evening, I sat down to write to her soon after my return."

"And spun your letter out unconsciously—it is always the case. For my part, I think there's a fascination in night work. Sit down when the house is still to pen a few minutes' letter to a friend, and ten to one but you find yourself still at it at the small hours of the morning. Well, it was lucky for young Dance that you were up. You heard him at the door at once, he says, and hastened to him."

A deep blush suffused her face. She could only tacitly uphold the deceit.

"His is rather a lame tale, though, by the way—what I can understand of it," resumed Mr. Parker. "However, it did not do to question him closely, and the lad was no doubt confused besides. We shall come to the bottom of it to-morrow."

"You are going home?" she asked.

"There's no necessity whatever for me to stay. We have made him comfortable for the rest of the night with pillows and blankets. Sister Ann means to sit up with him: not that she need do it. To-morrow we will move him to his own home."

"Will he be well enough for that?"

"Quite. He might have been carried there now had means been at hand. And do you go up to your bed at once, and get some rest," concluded the doctor, as he shook hands and took his departure.

John Bent had already gone home. To his great relief, the first object he saw was Mr. North, who arrived at the inn door, just as he himself did. The surgeon's supposition, spoken carelessly though it was proved to be correct. George North had missed his way in returning; had gone miles and miles out of the road, and then had to retrace his steps.

MRS. HENRY WOOD

"I'm dead beat," he said to the landlord, with a half laugh. "Fearfully hungry, but too tired to eat. It all comes of my not knowing the country; and there was nobody up to enquire the way of. By daylight, I should not have made so stupid a mistake."

"Well, I have been worrying myself with all sorts of fancies, Sir," said John. "It seemed just as though you had gone off for good in the wake of young Mr. Anthony Castlemaine."

"I wish to goodness I had!" was the impulsive, thoughtless rejoinder, spoken with ringing earnestness.

"Sir!"

Mr. North recollected himself, and did what he could to repair the slip.

"I should at least have had the pleasure of learning where this Mr. Anthony Castlemaine had gone—and that would have been a satisfaction to you all generally," he said carelessly.

"You are making a joke of it, sir," said the landlord, in a tone of reproach. "With some of us it is a matter all too solemn: I fear it was so with him. What will you take, sir?"

"A glass of ale—and then I will go up to bed. I am, as I say, too tired to eat. And I am very sorry indeed, Mr. Bent, to have kept you up."

"That's nothing, now you've come back in safety," was the hearty reply. "Besides, I'm not sorry it has happened so, sir, for I've had an adventure. That young Walter Dance has gone and shot himself to-night; he is lying at the Grey Nunnery, and I have but now been over there with Mr. Parker."

"Why, how did he manage to do that?" cried Mr. North, who knew young Dance very well.

"I hardly know, sir. We couldn't make top or tail of what he said: and the doctor wouldn't have him bothered. It was something about shooting a night-bird with a pistol, and he shot himself instead."

"Where?"

"In the chapel ruins."

"In the chapel ruins!" echoed Mr. North—and he had it on the tip of his tongue to say that Walter Dance would not go to the chapel ruins at night for untold gold: but the landlord went on and interrupted the words.

"He seemed to say it was the chapel ruins, sir; but we might have misunderstood him. Any way, it sounds a bit mysterious. He was in a fine tremor of pain when the doctor got in, thinking he was dying."

"Poor fellow! It was only yesterday morning I went for a sail with him. Is he seriously injured?"

"No, sir; the damages turn out to be nothing much, now they are looked into."

"I am glad of that," said Mr. North; "I like young Dance. Goodnight to you, landlord. Or, rather, good-morning," he called back, as he went up the staircase.

Miss Castlemaine also went to her bed. The first thing she did on reaching her room was to look out for the two-masted vessel. Not a trace of it remained. It must have heaved its anchor and sailed away in the silence of the night.

Mr. Parker was over betimes at the Grey Nunnery in the morning. His patient was going on quite satisfactorily.

Reassured upon the point of there being no danger, and in considerably less pain than at first, Walter Dance's spirits had gone up in a proportionate ratio. He said he felt quite well enough to be removed home—which would be done after breakfast.

"Passato il pericolo, gabbato il santo," says the Italian proverb. We have ours somewhat to the same effect, beginning "When the devil was sick"—which being well known to the reader, need not be quoted. Young Mr. Walter Dance presented an apt illustration of the same. On the previous night, when he believed himself to be dying, he was ready and eager to tell every secret pressing on his soul: this morning, finding he was going to live, his mood had changed, and he could have bitten out his unfortunate tongue for its folly.

He was well disposed, as young men go, truthful, conscientious. It would have gone against the grain with him to do an injury to any living man. He lay dwelling on the injury he might now have done, by this disclosure, to many people—and they were just those people whom, of all the world, he would most care to cherish and respect. Well, there was but one thing to do now, he thought truthful though he was by nature, he must eat his words, and so try and repair the mischief.

Mary Ursula rose rather late. Walter Dance had had his breakfast when she got down, and she was told of the doctor's good report. Much commotion had been excited in the Nunnery when the Grey Ladies heard what had happened. They had their curiosity, just as other people have theirs; and Sister Ann gave them the version of the story which she had gathered. The young man had been up at the chapel ruins to shoot a night-bird, the pistol had gone off, wounding him in the arm and side, and he came crawling on all fours to the Grey Nunnery. The superior, Sister Mary Ursula, sitting up late at her letters, heard him at the door, helped him in, and called for assistance.

Well, it was a strange affair, the ladies decided; stranger than anything that had happened at the Grey Nunnery before: but they trusted he would get over it. And did not all events happen for the best! To think that it should be just that night, of all others, that Sister Mary Ursula should have remained below!

Mary Ursula went into the sick-room, and was surprised at the improved looks of the patient. His face had lost its great anxiety and was bright again. He looked up at her gratefully, and smiled.

"They are so kind to me, lady!—and I owe it all to you."

Mary Ursula sat down by the couch. Late though it was when she went to rest, she had been unable to sleep, and had got up with one of the bad headaches to which she was occasionally subject. The strange disclosure made to her by Walter Dance, added to other matters, had troubled her brain and kept her awake. While saying to herself that so disgraceful an aspersion on the Castlemaines was worse than unjustifiable, outrageously improbable, some latent fear in her heart kept suggesting the idea—what if it should be true! With the broad light of day, she had intended to throw it quite to the winds—but she found that she could not. The anxiety was tormenting her.

"Walter," she began in a low tone, after cheerily talking a little with him about his injuries, "I want to speak to you of what you disclosed to me last night. When I got up this morning I thought in truth I had dreamt it—that it could not be true."

"Dreamt what?" he asked.

"About the smuggling," she whispered. "And about what you said, reflecting on my uncle. You are more collected this morning; tell me what is truth and what is not."

"I must have talked a deal of nonsense last night, ma'am," spoke the young man after a pause, as he turned his uneasy face to the wall—for uneasy it was growing. "I'm sure I can't remember it a bit."

She told him what he did say.

"What a fool I must have been! 'Twas the pain, lady, made me fancy it. Smugglers in the Friar's Keep! Well, that is good!"

"Do you mean to say it is not true?" she cried eagerly.

"Not a word on't, ma'am. I had a fever once, when I was a little 'un—I talked a rare lot o' nonsense then. Enough to set the place afire, grandmother said."

"And there is no smuggling carried on?—and what you said to implicate Mr. Castlemaine has no foundation save in your brain?" she reiterated, half bewildered with this new aspect.

"If I said such outrageous things, my wits must have gone clean out of me," asserted Walter. "Mr. Castlemaine would be fit to hang me, ma'am, if it came to his ears."

"But—if there is nothing of the kind carried on, what of the boats last night?" asked Mary Ursula, collecting her senses a little. "What were they doing?"

"Boats, lady!" returned Walter, showing the most supreme unconsciousness. "What boats?"

"Some boats that put off from an anchored vessel, and kept passing to and fro between it and the Keep."

"If there was boats, they must have come off for some purpose of their own," asserted the young man, looking as puzzled as you please. "And what did I do, down where you found me, you ask, ma'am? Well, I did go there to shoot a bird; that little strip o' beach is the quietest place for 'em."

Was he wandering now?—or had he been wandering then? Miss Castlemaine really could not decide the question. But for having seen and heard the boats herself, she would have believed the whole to be a disordered dream, induced by the weakness arising from loss of blood.

"But how did you get there, Walter?"

"Down that there slippery zigzag from the chapel ruins. The tide was partly up, you say, ma'am? Oh, I don't mind wet legs, I don't. The door? Well, I've always known about that there door, and I pushed it open: it don't do to talk of it, and so we don't talk of it: it mightn't be liked, you see, ma'am. 'Twas hearing a stir inside it made me go in: I said to myself, had a bird got there? and when I saw your light, ma'am, I was nigh frightened to death. As to boats—I'm sure there was none."

And that was all Mary could get from Mr. Walter Dance this morning. Press him as she might now—though she did not dare to press him too much for fear of exciting fever—she could get no other answer, no confirmatory admission of any kind. And he earnestly begged her, for the love of heaven, never to repeat a word of his "tattle" to his father, or elsewhere.

In the course of the morning, Tom Dance and two or three fishermen-friends of his came to the Grey Nunnery to convey Walter home. The rumour of what had happened had caused the greatest commotion abroad, and all the village, men and women, turned out to look for the removal. Fishermen, for that tide, abandoned their boats, women their homes and their household cares. No such excitement had arisen for Greylands since the vanishing of Anthony Castlemaine as this. The crowd attended him to Tom Dance's door with much hubbub; and after his disappearance within it, stayed to make their comments: giving praises to those good Grey Ladies who had received and succoured him.

"Now then," cried the doctor to his patient, when he had placed him comfortably in bed at his father's house and seen him take some refreshment, no one being present but themselves, "what is the true history of this matter, Walter? I did not care to question you much before."

"The true history?" faltered Walter; who was not the best hand at deception that the world could produce.

"What brought you in the chapel ruins with a loaded pistol at that untoward time of night?"

"I wanted to shoot a sea-bird: them that come abroad at night," was the uneasy answer. "A gentleman at Stilborough gave me an order for one. He's a-going to get him stuffed."

Mr. Parker looked at the speaker keenly. He detected the uneasiness at being questioned.

"And you thought that hour of the morning and that particular spot the best to shoot the bird?" he asked.

"Them birds are always hovering about the ruins there," spoke Walter, shifting his eyes in all directions. "Always a'most. One can only get at 'em at pitch dark, when things are dead still."

"I thought, too, that birds were generally shot with guns, not pistols," said the surgeon; and the young man only; groaned in answer to this: in explanation of which groan he volunteered the information that his "arm gave him a twitch."

"Where did you get the pistol?"

"Father lent it to me," said Walter, apparently in much torment, "to shoot the bird."

"And how came the pistol to go off as it did?"

"I was raising it to shoot one, a big fellow he was, and my elbow knocked again that there piece of sticking-out wall in the corner. Oh, doctor! I'm feeling rare and faint again."

Mr. Parker desisted from his investigation and went away whistling, taking in just as much as he liked of the story, and no more. There was evidently some mystery in the matter that he could not fathom.

XXIX

One More Interview

M r. and Mrs. Bent were in their sitting-room, facing the sea, as many guests around them as the room could conveniently accommodate. Much excitement prevailed: every tongue was going.

Upon the occasion of any unusual commotion at Greylands, the Dolphin, being the only inn in the place, was naturally made the centre point of the public, where expressions of marvel were freely given vent to and opinions exchanged.

Since the disappearance of Anthony Castlemaine, no event had occurred to excite the people like unto this—the shooting himself of young Walter Dance. To the primitive community this affair seemed nearly as unaccountable as that. The bare fact of the pistol's having gone off through the young man's inadvertently knocking his elbow against that bit of projecting wall, sticking itself out in the corner of the chapel ruins, was nothing extraordinary; it might have happened to anybody; but the wonder manifested lay in the attendant circumstances.

After the stir and bustle of seeing Walter Dance conveyed from the Grey Nunnery to his home had somewhat subsided, and the litter with its bearers, and the patient, and the doctor had fairly disappeared within doors, and they were barred out, the attendant spectators stayed a few minutes to digest the sight, and then moved off slowly by twos and threes to the Dolphin. The privileged among them went into Mr. and Mrs. Bent's room: the rest stayed outside. Marvel the first was, that young Dance should have gone out to shoot a bird at that uncanny hour of the morning; marvel the second was, that he should have chosen that haunted place, the chapel ruins, for nobody had evinced more fear in a silent way of the superstitions attending the Keep and the ghost that walked there than Walter Dance; marvel the third was, that he should have taken a pistol to shoot at the sea-bird, instead of a gun.

"Why couldn't he have got the bird at eight or nine o'clock at night?" debated Ben Little, quite an old oracle in the village and the father of young Ben. "That's the best hour for them sea-birds: nobody in their senses would wait till a'most the dawn."

"And look here," cried out Mrs. Bent shrilly: but she was obliged to be shrill to get a general hearing. "Why did he have a pistol with him? Tom Dance keeps a gun: he takes it out in his boat sometimes; but he keeps no pistol."

"Young Walter said in the night, to me and the doctor, that it was his father's pistol when we asked him about it," interposed John Bent.

"Rubbish!" returned the landlady. "I know better. Tom Dance never owned a pistol yet: how should he, and me not see it There's not a man in the whole place that keeps a pistol."

"Except Mr. Superintendent Nettleby," put in old Ben.

"Nobody was bringing him in," retorted the landlady, "it's his business to keep a pistol. My husband, as you all know, thought it was a pistol he heard go off the night that young Mr. Castlemaine was missed, though the Commodore stood to it that it was his gun—and, as we said then, if it was a pistol, where did the pistol come from? Pistols here, pistols there: I should like to ask what we are all coming to! We sha'n't be able to step out of our door after dark next, if pistols jump into fashion."

"At any rate, it seems it was a pistol last night, wherever he might have got it from," said Ben Little. "And downright careless it must have been of him to let it go off in the way he says it did—just for knocking his elbow again' the wall. Its to be known yet whether that there's not a lame tale; invented to excuse hisself."

Several faces were turned on old Ben Little at this. His drift was scarcely understood.

"Excuse himself from what?" demanded Mrs. Bent sharply. "Do you suppose the young fellow would shoot himself purposely, Ben Little?"

"What I think," said Ben, with calmness, "if one could come to the bottom of it, is this: that there young fellow got a fright last night—see the Grey Friar most probable; and his hand shook so that the pistol went off of itself."

This was so entirely new a view of probabilities, that the room sunk into temporary silence to revolve it. And not altogether an agreeable one. The Grey Friar did enough mischief as it was, in the matter of terrifying timid spirits: if it came to causing dreadful personal injuries with pistols and what not, Greylands was at a pretty pass!

"Now I shouldn't wonder but that was it," cried John Bent, bringing down his hand on the table emphatically. "He saw the Grey Friar, or thought he did: and it put him into more fright than mortal man could stand. You should just have seen him last night, and the terror he was in, when me and the doctor got to him—shaking the very board he lay upon."

"I'm sure he caused us fright enough," meekly interposed Sister Ann, who had been drawn into the inn (nothing loth) with the crowd. "When the Lady Superior, Sister Mary Ursula, came up to awake me and Sister Phoeby, and we saw her trembling white face, and heard that Walter Dance had taken refuge at the Nunnery, all shot about, neither of us knew how we flung our things on, to get down to him."

"Walter Dance don't like going anigh the Friar's Keep any more nor the rest of us likes it; and I can't think what should have took him there last night," spoke up young Mr. Pike from the general shop. "I was talking to him yesterday evening for a good half hour if I was talking a minute; 'twas when I was shutting up: he said nothing then about going out to shoot a bird."

"But he must have went to shoot one," insisted Ben Little. "Why say he did it if he didn't? What else took him to the ruins at all?"

A fresh comer appeared upon the scene at this juncture in the person of Mr. Harry Castlemaine. In passing the inn, he saw signs of the commotion going on, inside and outside, and turned in to see and hear. The various doubts and surmises, agitating the assembly, were poured freely into his ear.

"Oh, it's all right—that's what young Dance went up for," said he, speaking lightly. "A day or two ago I chanced to hear him say he wanted to shoot a sea-bird for stuffing."

"Well, sir that may be it; no doubt it is, else why should he say it—as I've just asked," replied Ben Little. "But what we'd like to know is—why he should ha' stayed to the little hours of morning before he went out. Why not have went just after dark?"

"He may have been busy," said Mr. Harry carelessly. "Or out in the boat."

"He wasn't out in the boat last night, sir, for I was talking to him as late as nine o'clock at our door," said young Pike. "The boat couldn't have went out after that and come back again."

"Well, I don't think it can concern us whether he went out after this bird a little later or a little earlier; or in fact that it signifies at all which it was, to the matter in question," returned the Master of Greylands' son: and it might have been noticed that his tone bore a smattering of the haughty reserve that sometimes characterised his father's. "The poor fellow has met with the accident; and that's quite enough for him without being worried with queries as to the precise half hour it happened."

"What he says is this here, Mr. Harry: that a great big sea-bird came flying off the sea, flapping its wings above the ruins; Dance cocked his pistol and raised it to take aim, when his elbow struck again' the corner wall there, and the charge went off."

"Just so, Ben; that's what Tom Dance tells me," responded Mr. Harry to old Little, for he had been the speaker. "It will be a lesson to him, I dare say, not to go out shooting birds in the dark again."

"Not to shoot 'em there, at any rate," rejoined Ben. "The conclusion we've just been and drawed is this here, Mr. Harry, sir: that the Grey Friar's shade appeared to him and set him trembling, and the dratted pistol went off of itself."

Mr. Harry's face grew long at once. "Poor fellow! it may have been so," he said: "and that alone would make his account confused. Well, my friends, the least we can do, as it seems to me, is to leave Walter Dance alone and not bother him," he continued in conclusion: and out he went as grave as a judge. Evidently the Grey Friar was not sneered at by Mr. Harry Castlemaine.

Sitting in a quiet corner of the room, obscured by the people and by the hubbub, was the Dolphin's guest, George North. Not a word, spoken, had escaped him. To every suggestive supposition, to every remark, reasonable and unreasonable, he had listened attentively. For this affair had made more impression on him than the facts might seem to warrant: and in his own mind he could not help connecting this shot and this mysterious pistol—that seemed to have come into Walter Dance's possession unaccountably—with the shot of that past February night, that had been so fatal to his brother.

Fatal, at least, in the conviction of many a one at Greylands. From John Bent to Mr. George North's sister-in-law, Charlotte Guise, and with sundry intermediate persons the impression existed and could not be shaken off. Mr. North had never given in to the belief: he had put faith in Mr. Castlemaine: he had persistently hoped that Anthony might not be dead; that he would reappear some time and clear up the mystery: but an idea had now taken sudden hold of him that this second edition of a shot, or rather the cause of it, would be found to hold some connection with the other shot: and that the two might proceed from the Grey Friar. Not the ghost of a Grey Friar, but a living and substantial one, who might wish to keep his precincts uninvaded.

We, who are in the secret of this later shot, can see how unfounded the idea was: but Mr. North was not in the secret, and it had taken (he knew not why) firm hold of him.

First of all, he had no more faith in the lame account of Mr. Walter Dance than the doctor had. It may be remembered that when the landlord was telling him of the accident the previous night, Mr. North remarked that he had been with Dance for a sail only that same morning. During this sail, which had lasted about two hours, the conversation had turned on the Friar's Keep—Mr. North frequently, in an apparently indirect manner, did turn his converse on it—and Walter Dance had expressed the most unequivocal faith in the Grey Monk that haunted it, and protested, with a shake of superstitions terror, that he would not go "anigh them parts" after dark for all the world. Therefore Mr. North did not take in the report that he had voluntarily gone to the chapel ruins to shoot a bird in the dead of the night.

The talkers around Mr. North all agreed, receiving their version of the affair from Sister Ann and John Bent, that Walter Dance's account was imperfect, confused, and not clearly to be understood; and that he was three parts beside himself with nervous fear when he gave it. All food for Mr. George North: but he listened on, saying nothing.

When Harry Castlemaine quitted the Dolphin, he turned in the direction of Stilborough; he was going to walk thither—which was nothing for his long legs. In ascending the hill past the church, which was a narrow and exceedingly lonely part of the road, the yew-trees overshadowing the gloomy churchyard on one side, the dark towering cliff on the other, he encountered Jane Hallet. She had been to Stilborough on some errand connected with her knitting-work, and was now coming back again. They met just abreast of the churchyard gate, and simultaneously stopped: as if to stop was with both of them a matter of course.

"Where have you been, Jane?" asked Mr. Harry.

"To Stilborough," she answered.

"You must have gone early."

"Yes, I went for wool"—indicating a brown-paper parcel in her hand.

"For wool!" he repeated, in a somewhat annoyed tone. "I have told you not to worry yourself with more of that needless work, Jane."

"And make my aunt more displeased than she is with me!" returned Jane sadly. "I must keep on with it as long as I can, while in her sight."

"Well, I think you must have enough to do without that," he answered, dropping the point. "How pale you are, Jane."

"I am tired. It is a long walk, there and back, without rest. I sat down on one of the shop stools while they weighed the wool, but it was not much rest."

"There again! I have told you the walk is too far. Why don't you attend to me, Jane?"

"I wish I could: but it is so difficult. You know what my aunt is."

"I am not sure, Jane, but it will be better to—to—" he stopped, seemingly intent on treading a stone into the path—"to make the change now," he went on, "and get the bother over. It must come, you know."

"Not yet; no need to do it yet," she quickly answered. "Let it be put off as long as it can be. I dread it frightfully."

"Yes, that's it: you are tormenting yourself into fiddle-strings. Don't be foolish, Jane. It is I who shall have to bear the storm, not you: and my back's broad enough, I hope."

She sighed deeply: her pale, thoughtful, pretty face cast up in sad apprehension towards the blue autumn sky. A change came over its expression: some remembrance seemed suddenly to occur to her.

"Have you heard any news about Walter Dance?" she asked with animation. "As I came down the cliff this morning, Mrs. Bent was leaving the baker's with some hot rolls in her apron, and she crossed over to tell me that Walter had shot himself accidentally at the chapel ruins in the middle of the night. Is it true?"

"Shot himself instead of a sea-bird," slightingly responded Mr. Harry.

"And in the chapel ruins?"

"I hear he says so."

"But—that is not likely to be the truth, is it?"

"How should I know, Jane?"

She lodged the paper parcel on the top of the gate, holding it with one hand, and looked wistfully across the graveyard. Harry Castlemaine whistled to a sparrow that was chirping on a branch of the nearest yew-tree.

"Was it Mr. Nettleby who did it?" she inquired, in a low, hesitating whisper.

"Mr. Nettleby!" repeated Harry Castlemaine in astonishment, breaking of his whistle to the bird. "What in the world makes you ask that Jane?"

A faint colour passed over her thin face, and she paused before answering.

"Mrs. Bent said she thought nobody in the place possessed a pistol except Superintendent Nettleby."

He looked keenly at Jane: at her evident uneasiness. She was growing pale again; paler than before; with what looked like an unnatural pallor. Mr. Harry Castlemaine's brow knitted itself into lines, with the effort to make Jane out.

"I don't like the chapel ruins: or the Friar's Keep," she went on, in the same low tone. "I wish nobody ever went near them. I wish you would not go!"

"Wish I would not go!" he exclaimed. "What do you mean, Jane?"

"It may be your turn next to be shot," she said with rising emotion, so much so that the words came out jerkily.

"I cannot tell what it is that you are driving at," he answered, regarding searchingly the evidently tired frame, the unmistakable agitation and anxiety of the thin, white face. "What have I to do with the chapel ruins? I don't go roaming about at night with a pistol to shoot sea-birds."

"If you would but make a confidante of me!" she sighed.

"What have I to confide? If you will tell me what it is, perhaps I may. I don't know."

She glanced up at him, flushing again slightly. His countenance was unembarrassed, open, and kind in its expression; but the decisive lips were set firmly. Whether he knew what she meant, or whether he did not, it was evident that he would not meet her in the slightest degree.

"Please do not be angry with me," faltered Jane.

"When am I angry with you? Simply, though, I do not understand you this morning, Jane. I think you must have tired yourself too much."

"I am tired," she replied; "and I shall be glad to get home to rest. My aunt, too, will be thinking it is time I was back."

She moved her parcel of wool off the gate, and, after another word or two, they parted: Jane going down hill, Harry Castlemaine up. Before he was quite beyond view, he stood to look back at her, and saw she had turned to look after him. A bright smile illumined his handsome face, and he waved his hand to her gaily. Few, very few, were there, so attractive as Harry Castlemaine.

Jane's lips parted with a farewell word, though he could not hear it, and her pretty dimples were all smiles as she went onwards. At the foot of the cliff she came upon little Bessy Gleeson in trouble. The child had fallen, goodness knew from what height, had cut both her knees, and was sobbing finely. Jane took the little thing up tenderly, kissed and soothed her, and then carried her up the cliff to the Gleesons' cottage. What with Bessy and what with the parcel, she could not breathe when she got there. Down she dropped on the stone by the door, her face whiter than ever.

"Where's mother?" she asked, as some of the little ones, Polly included, came running out.

But Nancy Gleeson had seen the ascent from the side window, and came forward, her hands all soap-suds. She was struck with Jane's exhausted look.

"Bessy has fallen down, Mrs. Gleeson. Her knees are bleeding."

"And how could you think of lugging her all up the cliff, Miss Jane! I declare you be as white as a sheet. A fat, heavy child like her! Fell down on your knees, have you, you tiresome little grub. There's one or another on you always a-doing of it."

"It is a warm morning, and I have been walking to and from Stilborough," remarked Jane, as she rose to go on, and not choosing to be told she looked white without accounting for it. "Wash her knees with some hot water please, Mrs. Gleeson: I dare say she is in pain, poor little thing."

"Lawk a me, Miss Jane," the woman called after her, "if you had half-a-dozen of 'em about you always you'd know better nor to take notice o' such trifles as knees." But Jane was already nearly out of hearing.

Harry was not the only one of the Castlemaine family who went that day to Stilborough. In the full brightness of the afternoon, the close carriage of the Master of Greylands, attended by its liveried servants, might have been seen bowling on its way thither, and one lady, attired in the dress of the Grey Sisters, seated inside it. A lady who was grand, and noble, and beautiful, in spite of the simple attire—Mary Ursula.

She was about to pay a visit to that friend of hers on whom misfortune had fallen—Mrs. Ord. The double calamity—loss of husband and loss of fortune—reaching Mrs. Ord by the same mail, had thrown her upon a sick-bed; and she was at all times delicate. The letter that Mary had sat up to write was despatched by a messenger early in the morning: and she had craved the loan of her uncle's close carriage to convey her on a personal visit. The close carriage: Mary shrunk (perhaps from the novelty of it) from showing herself this first time in her changed dress among her native townspeople.

The carriage left her at Mrs. Ord's house, and was directed to return for her in an hour; and Mary was shown up to the sick-chamber. It was a sad interview: this poor Mrs. Ord—whose woes, however, need not be entered upon here in detail, as she has nothing to do with the story—was but a year or two older than Mary Ursula. They had been girls together. She was very ill now: and Mary felt that at this early stage little or no consolation could be offered. She herself had had her sorrows since they last met, and it was a trying hour to both of them. Before the hour had expired, Mary took her leave and went down to the drawing-room to wait for the carriage.

She had closed the door, and was halfway across the richly-carpeted floor, before she became aware that any one was in the room. It was a gentleman—who rose from the depths of a lounging-chair at her approach. Every drop of blood in Mary's veins seemed to stand still, and then rush wildly on: her sight momentarily failed her, her senses were confused: and but that she had shut the door behind her, and come so far, she might have retreated again. For it was William Blake-Gordon.

They stood facing each other for an instant in silence, both painfully agitated. Mary's grey bonnet was in her hand; she had taken it off in the sick-chamber; he held an open letter, that he had been apparently reading to pass away the time, while the servants should carry his message to their sick mistress and bring back an answer. Mary saw the writing of the letter and recognized it for Agatha Mountsorrel's. In his confusion, as he hastily attempted to refold the letter, it escaped his hand, and fluttered to the ground. The other hand he was holding out to her.

She met it, scarcely perhaps conscious of what she did. He felt the trembling of the fingers he saw the agitation of the wan white face. Not a word did either of them speak. Mary sat down on a sofa, he took a chair near, after picking up his letter.

"What a terrible calamity this is that has fallen on Mrs. Ord!" he exclaimed, seizing upon it as something to say.

"Two calamities," answered Mary.

"Yes indeed. Her husband dead, and her fortune gone! My father sent me here to inquire personally after her; to see her if possible. He and Colonel Ord were good friends."

"I do not think she can see you. She said that I was the only one friend who would have been admitted to her."

"I did not expect she would: but Sir Richard made me come. You know his way."

Mary slightly nodded assent. She raised her hand and gently pushed from her temple the braid of her thick brown hair; as though conscious of the whiteness of her face, she would fain cover it until the colour returned. Mr. Blake-Gordon, a very bad hand at deception at all times, suffered his feelings to get the better of conventionality now, and burst forth into truth.

"Oh, Mary! how like this is to the old days! To have you by me alone!—to be sitting once more together."

"Like unto them?" she returned sadly. "No. That can never be."

"Would to heaven it could!" he aspirated.

"A strange wish, that, to hear from you now."

"And, perhaps you think, one I should not have spoken. It is always in my heart, Mary."

"Then it ought not to be."

"I see," he said. "You have been hearing tales about me."

"I have heard one tale. I presume it to be a true one. And I—I—" her lips were trembling grievously—"I wish you both happiness with all my heart."

Mr. Blake-Gordon pushed his chair back and began to pace the room restlessly. At that moment a servant came in with a message to him from her mistress. He merely nodded a reply, and the girl went away again.

"Do you know what it has all been for me, Mary?" he asked, halting before her, his brow flushed, his lips just as much agitated as hers. "Do you guess what it is? Every ray of sunshine went out of my life with you."

"At the time you—you may have thought that," she tremblingly answered. "But why recall it? The sun has surely begun to shine for you again."

"Never in this world. Never will it shine as it did then."

"Nay, but that, in the face of facts, is scarcely credible," she rejoined, striving to get up as much calmness, and to speak as quietly, as though Mr. Blake-Gordon had never been more to her than an acquaintance or friend; nerving herself to answer him now as such. "You are, I believe, about to"—a cough took her just there, and she suddenly put her hand to her throat—"marry Agatha."

"It is true. At least, partially true."

"Partially?"

"For Heaven's sake, Mary, don't speak to me in that coldly indifferent tone!" he passionately broke in. "I cannot bear it from you."

"How would you have me speak?" she asked, rapidly regaining her self-possession; and her tone was certainly kind, rather than cold, though her words were redolent of calm reasoning. "The past is past, you know, and circumstances have entirely changed. It will be better to meet them as such: to regard them as they are."

"Yes, they are changed," he answered bitterly. "You have made yourself into a lay-nun—"

"Nay, not that," she interrupted with a smile.

"A Sister of Charity, then"—pointing to her grey dress. "And I, as the world says, am to espouse Agatha Mountsorrel."

"But surely that is true."

"It is true in so far as that I have asked her to be my wife: That I should live to say that to you of another woman, Mary! She has accepted me. But, as to the marriage, I hope it will not take place yet awhile. I do not press for it."

"You shall both have my best and truest prayers for your happiness," rejoined Mary, her voice again slightly trembling. "Agatha will make you a good wife. The world calls her haughty; but she will not be haughty to her husband."

"How coolly you can contemplate it!" he cried, in reproach and pain.

Just for one single moment, in her heart's lively anguish, the temptation assailed her to tell him what it really was to her, and how deeply she loved him still. She threw it behind her, a faint smile parting her lips.

"William, you know well that what I say is all I can say. I am wedded to the life I have chosen; you will soon be wedded actually to another than me. Nothing remains for us in common: save the satisfaction of experiencing good wishes for the welfare of the other."

"It is not love, or any feeling akin to it, that has caused me to address Agatha Mountsorrel—" he was beginning; but she interrupted him with decision.

"I would rather not hear this. It is not right of you to say it."

"I will say it. Mary, be still. It is but a word or two; and I will have my way in this. It is in obedience to my father that I have addressed Miss Mountsorrel. Since the moment when you and I parted, he has never ceased to urge her upon me, to throw us together in every possible way. I resisted for a long while; but my nature is weakly yielding—as you have cause to know—and at length I was badgered into it. Forgive the word, Mary. Badgered by Sir Richard, until I went to her and said, Will you be my wife? The world had set the rumour running long before that; but the world was in haste. And now that I have told you so much, I am thankful. I meant to make the opportunity of telling you had one not offered: for the worst pain of all, to me, would be, that you should fancy I could love another. The hearing that I have engaged myself again in this indecent haste—your hearing it—is enough shame for me."

The handsome chariot of the Master of Greylands, its fine horses prancing and curvetting, passed the window and drew up at the house. Mary rose.

"I hope with all my heart that you will love her as you once loved. me," she said to him in a half whisper, as she rang the bell and caught up her bonnet. "To know that, William, will make my own life somewhat less lonely."

"Did you ever care for me?" broke from him.

"Yes. But the past is past."

He stood in silence while she tied on her grey bonnet, watching her slender fingers as they trembled with the silk strings. A servant appeared in answer to the ring. Mary was drawing on her gloves.

"The door," said Mr. Blake-Gordon.

"Good-bye," she said to him, holding out her hand.

He wrung it almost to pain. "You will allow me to see you to your carriage?"

She took the arm he held out to her and they went through the hall and down the steps together. The footman had the carriage door open, and he, her ex-lover, placed her in. Not another word was spoken. The man sprang up to his place behind, and the chariot rolled away. For a full minute after its departure, William Blake-Gordon was still standing looking after it, forgetting to put his hat on: forgetting, as it seemed, all created things.

XXX

Love's Young Dream

C ombined With Mr. Walter Dance's remorse for having betrayed to Miss Castlemaine what he did betray, in that paroxysm of fear when he thought the world was closing for him, was a wholesome dread of the consequences to himself. What his father's anger would be and what Mr. Castlemaine's punishment of him might be, when they should learn all that his foolish tongue had said, Walter did not care to contemplate. As he lay that night in the Grey Nunnery after the surgeon's visit, Sister Ann watching by his pallet, he went through nearly as much agony of fear from this source as he had just gone through from the other. While he believed his life was in peril, that that mysterious part of him, the Soul, was about to be summoned to render up its account, earth and earth's interests were as nothing: utterly lost, indeed, beside that momentous hour which he thought was at hand. But, after reassurance had set in, and the doctor had quietly convinced him there was no danger, that he would shortly be well again, then the worldly fear rose to the surface. Sister Ann assumed that his starts and turns in the bed arose from bodily pain or restlessness: in point of fact it was his mind that was tormenting him and would not let him be still.

Of course it was no fault of his that Miss Castlemaine had found him in the cloistered vaults,—or that he had found her, whichever it might be called—or that there was a door that he never knew of opening into them, or a passage between them and the Grey Nunnery, or that the pistol had gone off and shot him. For all this he could not be blamed. But what he could, and would be blamed for was, that he had committed the astounding folly of betraying the secret relating to the Friar's Keep; for it might, so to say, destroy all connected with it. Hence his resolve to undo, so far as he could, the mischief with Miss Castlemaine, by denying to her that his disclosure had reason or foundation in it: and by asserting that it must have been the effect of his disordered brain.

Believing that he had done this, when his morning interview with Sister Mary Ursula was over: believing that he had convinced her his words had been but the result of his sick fancies, he began next to ask himself why he need tell the truth at all, even to his father. The only thing to be accounted for was the shot to himself and his turning up at the Grey Nunnery: but he might just as well stand to the tale that he had told the doctor, to his father, as well as to the world: namely, that he had met with the injury in the chapel ruins, and had crawled to the Grey Nunnery for succour.

This happy thought he carried out; and Tom Dance was no wiser than other people. When once deception is entered upon, the course is comparatively easy: "ce n'est que le premier pas qui coute," say the French: and Mr. Walter Dance, truthful and honest though he loved to be, found himself quite an adept at farce-relating before the first day was over.

Not that Tom Dance, wise in his nearly fifty years, took it all in unquestioningly. There was something about the story, and about Wally's voice and face and shifting eyes when he told it, that rather puzzled him: in short, that created somewhat of a doubt: but the very impossibility (as he looked upon it) of the injuries having occurred in any other way served to dispel suspicion. The idea that there was a secret passage from the Friar's Keep to the Grey Nunnery could no more have entered into Tom Dance's imagination, than that there was a passage to the moon.

When the indoor hubbub and bustle of the removal of Walter home from the Grey Nunnery was over, and the numerous friends, admitted one at a time to see him, had gone again, and Walter had had some refreshing sleep towards sunset, then Tom Dance thought the time and opportunity had come to have a talk with him. The old grandmother, Dame Dance—who lived in her solitary abode under the cliff at some distance, and whose house at high water was not accessible except by boat—had come up to nurse and tend him, bringing her white apron and a nightcap. But Tom Dance sent his mother home again. He was a good son, and he told her that she should not have the trouble: he and Sarah could attend to Wally without further help. Sarah was his daughter, Walter's sister, and several years older than the young man. She was a cripple, poor thing, but very useful in the house; a shy, silent young woman, who could only walk with crutches; so that Greylands scarcely saw her out of doors from year's end to year's end. Now and then, on some fine Sunday she would contrive to get to church, but that was all.

Tom Dance's house was the last in the village and next the beach, its side windows facing the sea. It was twilight, but there was no candle in

Walter's room yet, and as Tom Dance sat down at the window, he saw the stars coming out over the grey waters, one by one, and heard the murmuring of the waves.

"D'ye feel that ye could peck a bit, Wally?" asked he, turning his head sideways towards the bed.

"Sarah's gone to make me some arrowroot, father."

"That's poor stuff, lad."

"It's what Dr. Parker said I was to have."

"Look here, Wally," continued Tom, after a pease, during which he had seemed to be looking out to sea again, "I can't make out what should have taken you up on to the chapel ruins. Why didn't you follow us to the Hutt?"

To account feasibly for this one particular item in the tale, was Walter's chief difficulty. He knew that: and while his father was entering upon it in the morning, had felt truly thankful that they were interrupted.

"I don't know what took me," replied Walter, with a sort of semi-wonder in his own voice, as though the fact were just as much of a puzzle to himself as it could be to his father. "I stayed behind to lock up: and the rest of you had all gone on to the Hutt ever so long: and—and so I went up and out by the chapel ruins."

"One would think you must ha' been in a dream, lad."

"It's rare and lonely up that other long passage by oneself," hazarded Walter. "You are up at the chapel ruins and out that way in no time."

"Rare and lonely!" sharply retorted the elder man, as though the words offended him. "Are you turning coward, lad?"

"Not I, father," warmly rejoined Walter, perceiving that plea would not find favour. "Any way, I don't know what it was took me to go up to the chapel ruins. I went; and that seems to be all about it."

"It was an unpardonable hazardous thing to do. Suppose you had been seen coming out o' the Keep at that time? And with a pistol!"

"I wish the pistol had been at the bottom o' the sea, I do!" groaned the invalid.

"What did you take the pistol up for?—why didn't you leave it in the usual place with the other pistols?" Walter groaned again, "I don't know."

"Tell ye what, lad: but that I know you b'ain't given to drink, I should say you'd got a drop of the crew's old Hollands into you."

"Janson did offer me some," said young Walter, from under the bedclothes.

"And you took it! Well you must ha' been a fool. Why, your grandmother 'ud be fit to—"

"I wasn't drunk: don't think that father," interrupted Walter, after a rapid mental controversy as to whether, of the two evils, it might not be better to confess to the Hollands—though, in point of fact, he had not touched a drop. "See here: it's no good talking about it, now it's done and over."

"And—if you did get out by wary of the chapel ruins, what on earth made you go letting off the pistol there?"

"Well, it was an accident, that was: I didn't go to let it off. That there wall in the corner knocked again' my elbow."

"What took you to the corner?"

"I thought I'd just give a look after the boats that were getting off," said Walter, who had spent that day as well as the night, rehearsing difficult items in his mind. "The beastly pistol went off somehow, and down I dropped."

"And of all things," continued the fisherman, "to think you should ha' knocked up the Grey Sisters! It must have been Hollands."

"I was bleeding to death, father. The Grey Nunnery is the nearest place."

"No, it's not. Nettleby's is the nearest."

"As if I should go there!" cried Walter, opening his eyes at the bare suggestion.

"And as near as any is the Hutt. That's where you ought to have come on to. Why did you not? Come!"

"I—I—never thought of the Hutt," said poor Walter, wondering when this ordeal would be over.

"You hadn't got your head upon you: that's what it was. Wally, lad, I'd a'most rather see you drownded in the sea some rough day afore my eyes, nor see you take to drink."

"'Twasn't drink, 'twas the sight of the blood," deprecatingly returned Walter. "The Grey Ladies were rare and good to me, father."

"That don't excuse your having went there. In two or three minutes more you'd have reached your home here—and we might ha' kept it all quiet. As it is, every tongue in the place is a wagging over it."

"Let 'em wag," suggested Walter. "They can't know nothing."

"How do you know what they'll find out, with their prying and their marvelling?" demanded the angry man. "Let 'em wag, indeed!"

"I could hardly get to the Nunnery," pleaded Walter. "I thought I was dying."

MRS. HENRY WOOD

"There'll be a rare fuss about it with the Castlemaines! I know that. Every knock that has come to the door this blessed day I've took to be the Master o' Greylands and shook in my shoes. A fine market you'll bring your pigs to, if you be to go on like this, a getting yourself and everybody else into trouble! George Hallet, poor fellow, would never have been such a fool."

Reproached on all sides, self-convicted of worse folly than his father had a notion of, weak in body, fainting in spirit, and at his very wits' end to ward off the home questions, Walter ended by bursting into a flood of tears. That disarmed Tom Dance; and he let the matter drop. Sarah limped in with the arrowroot, and close upon that Mr. Parker arrived.

THE BRIGHT MOON, WANTING YET some days to its full, shone down on the chapel ruins. Seated against the high, blank wall of the Grey Nunnery, his sketch-book before him, his pencil in hand, was Mr. North. He had come there to take the Friar's Keep by moonlight: at least, the side portion of it that looked that way. The chapel ruins with its broken walls made the foreground: the half-ruined Keep, with its Gothic door of entrance, the back; to the right the sketch took in a bit of the sea. No doubt it would make an attractive picture when done in watercolours, and one that must bear its own painful interest for George North.

He worked attentively and rapidly, his thoughts meanwhile as busy as his hands. The moon gave him almost as much light as he would have had by day: though it cast dark shades as well as brightness; and that would make the chief beauty of the completed painting.

Somewhere about a week had passed since the accident to Walter Dance, and the young man was three parts well again.

The occurrence had rarely been out of Mr. North's mind since. He had taken the opportunity in an easy and natural manner of calling in at Dance's to pay a visit to the invalid, to inquire after his progress and condole with him; and he that been struck during that interview with the same idea that had come to him before—namely, that the story told was not real. Putting a searching question or two, his eyes intently fixed upon the wounded man's countenance, he was surprised— or, perhaps not surprised—to see the face flush, the eyes turn away, the answering words become hesitating. Nothing, however, came of it, save this impression. Walter parried every question, telling the same tale that he had told others; but the eyes of the speaker, I say, could not look

Mr. North in the face, the ring of the voice was not true. Mr. North asked this and that; but he could not ask too pointedly or persistently, his apparent motive being concern for the accident, slightly tempered with curiosity.

"It was not the ghost of the Grey Friar that shot you, was it?" he questioned at last with a joking smile. Walter evidently took it in earnest, and shook his head gravely.

"I never saw the ghost at all, sir, that night: nor thought of it, either. I was only thinking of the bird."

"You did not get the bird, after all."

"No; he flew away when the pistol went off. It startled him, I know: you should have heard his wings a-flapping. Father says he'll shoot one the first opportunity he gets."

How much was false, and how much true, Mr. North could not discern. So far as the bird went, he was inclined to believe in it— Walter must have had some motive for going to the ruins, and, he fancied, a very strong one. It was the shot itself and the hour of its occurrence that puzzled him. But Mr. North came away from the interview no wiser than he had entered on it: except that his doubts were strengthened.

As if to give colouring to, and confirm his son's story, a day or two subsequent to the accident, Tom Dance, being in the company of some other fishermen at the time, and having his gun with him, aimed at a large grey sea-gull that came screeching over their heads, as they stood on the beach, and brought him down. The next morning, in the face and eyes of all Greylands, he went marching off with the dead bird to Stilborough, and left it with a naturalist to be stuffed: and pedestrians passing the naturalist's shop, were regaled with a sight of Le great bird exhibited there, its wings stretched out to the uttermost. But it turned out upon inquiry—far people, swayed by their curiosity, made very close inquiries, and seemed never to tire of doing it—that the bird had not been ordered by the gentleman at Stilborough, as Walter Dance was at first understood to say. Dance and his son had intended to make a present of one to him. As they would now do.

All these matters, with the various speculations they brought in their train, were swaying Mr. North's mind, as he worked on this evening by moonlight. The occurrence had certainly spurred up his intention to discover Anthony's fate, rendering him more earnest in the pursuit. It could not be said that he was not earnest in it before; but there was nothing he could lay hold of, nothing tangible. In point of fact, there was not anything now.

"Do you belong to me?" he apostrophised, casting his eyes towards the distant chimneys of Greylands' Rest, his thoughts having turned on the Master of Greylands. "Failing poor Anthony to inherit, is the property mine? I would give much to know. My Uncle James seems too honourable a man to keep what is not his own: and yet—why did he not show to Anthony the tenure by which he holds the estate?—why does he not show it now?—for he must know how people talk, and the doubts that are cast on him. I cannot tell what to think. Personally, I like him very much; and he is so like—"

A sudden shade fell on Mr. North's book, and made him look up abruptly. It was caused by a cloud passing over the face of the moon. A succession of light clouds, this cloud the vanguard of them, came sailing quickly up from beyond the sea, obscuring, until they should have dispersed, the silvery brightness of the Queen of night. Mr. North's sketch was, however, nearly done; and a few quick strokes completed it.

Putting it into his portfolio, he rose, took a look out over the sea, and passed into the Friar's Keep. Many a time, by night or by day, since his first arrival at Greylands, had he gone stealthily into that place; but never had found aught to reward him by sight or sound. Thrice he had explored it with a light: but he had seen only the monotonous space of pillared cloisters that all the world might explore at will. Silent and deserted as ever, were they now: and George North was on the point of turning out again, when the sound of light footsteps smote on his ear, and he drew back between the wall and the first pillar near the entrance.

He had left the door wide open—which was, perhaps, an incautious thing to do—and some rays of moonlight came streaming in. He was in the dark: all the darker, perhaps, the nook where he stood, from the contrast presented by these shining rays of light. George North held his breath while he looked and listened.

Darkening the shining moonlight at the entrance came a woman's figure, entering far more stealthily and softly than Mr. North had entered. She stole along amid the pillars, and then stopped suddenly, as though intent on listening. She was not quite beyond the vision of Mr. North: his eyes were accustomed to the darkness, and the rays at the open door threw a semi-light beyond: and he saw her push back her hood and bend her ear to listen. Quite two minutes passed thus they seemed like five to George North, he standing still and motionless as the grave. Then she turned, retraced her steps, and went out again. Mr. North stole to the door in her wake, and looked after her.

Yes, he thought so! It was Jane Hallet. She had gone to the edge now, and was gazing straight out to seaward, her hands raised over her eyes to steady their sight. Mr. North knew her only by the outline of her figure, for the hood of her cloak was well on; but he could not be mistaken. Being about himself of an evening, he had seen her about; had seen her more than once come to these ruins and stand as she was standing now: once only before had she entered the Keep. The precise purport of these manoeuvres he could not fathom, but felt sure that she was tracking, and yet hiding herself from, Harry Castlemaine. Another minute, and then she turned.

"Not to-night," Mr. North heard her say aloud to herself as she passed the door of the Keep. And she went through the gate and walked rapidly away towards Greylands.

Mr. North took out his watch to see the time, holding it to the moonlight. Half-past nine. Not too late, he decided, to go to Greylands' Rest and pay a short visit to Madame Guise. The family were out that evening, dining at Stilborough—which information he had picked up from Mrs. Bent: had they been at home, he would not have thought of presenting himself so late. It might be a good opportunity to get a few minutes alone with his sister-in-law, and he wanted to tell her that he had heard from Gap.

Crossing the road, he went striding quickly up the lane, and was nearly run over by Commodore Teague's spring cart, which came with a bolt unexpectedly out of the turning. The Commodore, who was driving, did not see him: he had his head bent down nearly to the off shaft, doing something to the harness. The cart clattered on its way, and Mr. North pursued his.

Turning in at the gate of Greylands' Rest, and passing round to the broad path, he heard a voice singing; a voice that he knew and loved too well. Ethel was not gone to the dinner, then! She sat alone at the piano in the red parlour, its glass doors being thrown wide open, singing a love ditty to herself in the moonlight. Mr. North, every pulse of his heart beating with its sense of bliss, drew himself up against the wall beside the window to listen.

It was a very absurdly-foolish song as to words, just as three parts of the songs mostly are; but its theme was love, and that was enough for

Ethel and for him; to both the words were no doubt nothing short of sublime. A kind of refrain followed every verse: the reader shall at least have the benefit of that.

> *"And if my love prove faithless,*
> *What will be left for me?—*
> *I'll let him think me scathless,*
> *And lay me down and dee."*

There were five or six verses in the ballad, and these lines came in after every verse. Ethel had a sweet voice and sang well. Mr. George North stood against the wall outside, his ears and his heart alike taking in the song, the words being as distinct as though they were spoken. The final refrain had two more lines added to it:

> *"But I know that he is not faithless:*
> *He'll be true to me for aye."*

Ethel left the piano with the last word and came to the window, her bright face, raised to look at the moon, glowing with a sweet, hopeful expression that seemed to tell of love.

> *"But I know that he is not faithless:*
> *He'll be true to me for aye."*

These words were repeated over to herself as she stood; not sung but spoken; repeated as though she were making the romance her own; as though the words were a fact, an assurance to herself that somebody would be true to her. George North went forward, and Ethel was startled.

"Oh, Mr. North!" she exclaimed. "How you frightened me!"

He took her hand—both hands—in his contrition, begging pardon for his thoughtlessness, and explaining that he waited there until she finished her song, not to enter and disturb it. It was one of the sweetest moments in the life of either, this unexpected meeting, all around so redolent of poetry and romance. Mr. North had to release her hands, but their pulses were thrilling with the contact.

"I thought you were gone out to dinner," he said.

"No, I was not invited. Only papa and mamma and Harry."

"Or of course I should not have attempted to intrude so late as this. I thought, believing Madame Guise alone, it would be a good opportunity to see her. I suppose she is at home."

"Oh yes; she will be glad to see you," replied Ethel, her heart beating so wildly with its love and his presence that she hardly knew what she did say. "Flora is very troublesome to-night, and Madame has had to go up to her. She will soon be back again."

Very troublesome indeed. The young lady, taking the advantage of Mr. and Mrs. Castlemaine's absence, had chosen to go into one of her wildest moods and promenade the house en robe de nuit. At this present moment she was setting Madame at defiance from various turns in the staircases, executing a kind of bo-peep dance.

George North had stepped into the room, and they were standing side by side at the open window in the moonlight, each perfectly conscious of what the companionship was to the other. He began telling her where he had been and what doing; and opened the sketch-book to show her the drawing.

"Sitting in the chapel ruins all that while alone by moonlight!" exclaimed Ethel. "It is plain you are not a native of Greylands, Mr. North. I question whether any other man in the place would do it."

"I am not a poor simple fisherman, Ethel," he laughed. He had called her "Ethel" some time now, led to it by the example of others at Greylands' Rest.

"I was not thinking altogether of the fishermen. I don't fancy even Harry Castlemaine would do it."

"No?" said Mr. North, an amused smile lingering on his

"At least, I have heard him, more than once, express a dislike of the place; that is, of going to it—had he to do such a thing—after dark. Did you see anything?"

"Only—" Mr. North suddenly arrested his words. He had been about to say, Only Jane Hallet. Various reasons prompted him to close his lips on the point to Miss Reene.

"Only shadows," he continued, amending the phrase. "The moon went under a cloud now and then. It is a most beautiful night out at sea."

Her slender fingers were trembling as she held one side of the sketch-book, he holding the other; trembling with sweet emotion. Not a word of his love had Mr. North said to her; not a word could he say to her under present circumstances; but Ethel felt that it was hers, hers for all time. Fate might part them in this life; each, it was possible, might marry apart; but he would never love another as he loved her.

"How exact it is!" she cried, looking at the page, which the bright clear moonlight fell upon. "I should know it anywhere. You have even got that one little dark stone in the middle of the wall that seems to have been put in after the other stones and is so unlike them."

"I made it darker that I may know which it is for the painting," he answered. "It will make a nice picture."

"Oh, very. When shall you paint it?"

"That I don't know. Some of these odd days."

"You are not painting at all now."

"No. I don't feel settled enough at the Dolphin for that."

A pause of silence. In changing the position of his hand, still holding the book, Mr. North somehow let it touch hers. Ethel's voice trembled slightly when next she spoke.

"Shall you be going over to France again?"

"Undoubtedly. In a letter I received this morning from some of my friends there, they inquire when it is to be. I am lingering here long, they think. It was to tell Madame Guise I had heard, for she knows them, that brought me here so late."

"You—you said one day, I remember, that you might probably settle in France," resumed Ethel, inwardly shivering as she spoke it. "Shall you do so?"

"It is quite uncertain, Ethel. If things turn out as—as they ought to turn, I should then settle in England. Probably somewhere in this neighbourhood."

Their eyes met: Ethel looking up, he down. With the yearning love, that sat in each gaze, was mingled an expression of deep sadness.

"Circumstances at present are so very doubtful," resumed Mr. North. "They may turn out well; or very ill—"

"Very ill!" involuntarily interrupted Ethel.

"Yes, they may."

The answer was given in a marked, decisive tone. For the doubt that ran through his mind—that had run through it much lately—was this: If it should indeed prove that the Master of Greylands had dealt ill with Anthony, George North could scarcely bring himself to marry one so closely connected with Greylands' Rest as Ethel.

"And—in that case?" she continued after a pause, during which he seemed to have been lost in thought.

"In that case? Oh, I should become a wandering Arab again roaming the world at large."

"And settle eventually in France?"

"Very likely—if I settled anywhere. It is all so uncertain, Ethel, that I scarcely like to glance at it. I may hold property in England some time: and that might necessitate my living on it."

"Do you mean an estate? Such as this?"

"Yes, such as this," he answered with a passing, curious smile. "Meanwhile I am so happy in the present time, in my idle life— transferring some of the beauties of your country to enrich my portfolio, with the hospitable Dolphin roof over my head, and the grand, ever-moving sea before me like a glorious panorama—that I fear I am too willing to forget the future care which may come."

Not another word did either speak: the silence, with its pleasure and its pain, was all too eloquent. The sketch-book was held between them still: and, in turning over its pages to look at former sketches, their hands could not help—or, rather, did not help—coming in contact. What bliss it was!

"Why, you are quite in the dark, my dear! Why—dear me! who is it?"

They turned at the voice—that of Madame Guise. She had just left Miss Flora.

"Not in the dark, but in the moonlight," said Mr. North, holding out his hand.

"I did not know that you were here," she answered. "It is late."

"Very late: I hope you will forgive me. But I have been here some little time. I was taking a sketch by moonlight not far off, and came on, Madame Guise, to say Bon jour, thinking you were alone."

"It is Bon soir, I think," returned Madame, with a pleasant laugh, as she rang for lights. "Will you take a chair?"

"Thank you no," he replied, putting the sketch-book into the portfolio. "I will take my departure instead, and call again to-morrow at a more seasonable hour. Goodnight to you Miss Ethel."

Ethel put her hand into his and returned the goodnight in a low tone. When he should have left, the sunshine of the evening would have left with him. Madame Guise, as she often did, stepped across the threshold to walk to the gate with him.

"Did you want anything particular with me, George?" she asked in French, waiting until they were beyond hearing—lest the walls of the house should possess ears.

"Only to tell you that I had a letter from Emma this morning. I should not have come up so late but for believing the family were all out."

"What does Emma say?"

"Not much. Emma never does, you know. She sends some kind messages to you and a kiss to Marie: and she asks how much longer I mean to linger at Greylands. That is about all."

"But does she ask nothing about Anthony?"

"She asks in a general way, whether we know more yet. Which of course we do not."

"Have you made anything out of that young Dance, George?"

"Nothing. There's nothing to be made out of him. Except that I feel convinced the tale he tells is not all true. I was in the Friar's Keep to-night—"

"And saw nothing?" she eagerly interrupted.

"And saw nothing. It was dark and silent and lonely as usual. Sometimes I ask myself what it is that I can reasonably expect to see."

"Yes, I know; you have thought that from the first," she said reproachfully. "My brain is at work always I have no rest by night or by day."

"Which is very bad for you, Charlotte: it is wearing you out. This living, restless anxiety will not bring elucidation any the surer or quicker."

"Not bring it! But it will. Will my prayers and my anguish not be heard, think you? God is good."

They parted with the last words. Charlotte Guise, leaning on the side-gate as she looked after him, raised her eyes to the blue canopy of heaven: and there and then, in her simple faith, poured forth a few words of prayer.

XXXI

CALLING IN THE BLACKSMITH

Things were swiftly coming to a crisis in Miss Hallet's house, though that lady was very far from suspecting it. Time had again gone on since the last chapter, and Walter Dance was about again.

After the evening that witnessed Miss Hallet's fright at the vision of the Grey Friar, she had been very ill. Whether it was the terror itself, or her mortification at having betrayed it, or the fall in the road that affected her, certain it was that she had a somewhat long illness, and was attended by Mr. Parker. No one could be more attentive to her than Jane was; and Miss Hallet was willing to forget that the girl had given cause for complaint. But Miss Hallet found, now that she was well, that the same cause was still in existence: at all times of unseasonably late hours Jane would be abroad. Scarcely an evening passed but Jane would make an excuse to go out; or go out without excuse if none could be framed. She had taken lately to go more to Stilborough, often without assigning any reason for it. The hour at which she would come in was uncertain; sometimes it was after ten—a very unhallowed hour in the sober estimation of her aunt. One night she had stayed out till one o'clock in the morning, sending Miss Hallet into a perfect fever of suspense and anger. She ran in, panting with the haste she had made up the cliff, and she looked worn, haggard, almost wild. Miss Hallet attacked her with some harsh words: Jane responded by a burst of tears, and declared in a tone of truth that her aunt could scarcely disbelieve, that she had only been "looking at the sea" and looking at it alone.

From that evening, Miss Hallet had taken to watch Jane as a subject of curiosity. Jane was getting nervous. More than once when Miss Hallet had gone upstairs and surprised, unintentionally, Jane in her bedroom—for that lady, since her illness, had walked about in perfectly noiseless list shoes, for comfort only, not to come upon people unawares—she had found Jane standing over a certain open drawer. Jane would shut it hastily and lock it with shaking fingers, and sometimes shake all over besides. Jane had never been nervous in her life, mentally reasoned Miss Hallet: why should she be becoming so now? Her eyes had habitually a strangely-sad look in them, something like those of a hunted hare; her face was worn and thin. The sudden appearance of anyone at the door or window would make Jane start and turn pale: she could eat nothing, and would often be so absorbed in thought as to give contrary answers. "What is the time by the clock, Jane?" her aunt might say, for instance: "No, aunt, I forgot it," might be the answer. Altogether, taking one thing with another, Miss Hallet came to the conclusion that there was some mystery about Jane, just as certain other personages of our story decided there was mystery in the Friar's Keep.

The matter troubled Miss Hallet. She knew not what to do, to whom to speak, or of whom to ask advice. Speaking to Jane herself went for nothing: for the girl invariably denied, with all the unconcern she could put on, that anything was amiss or that she was different from what she used to be. It was now that Miss Hallet felt her isolated position, and the reserve with which she had treated the village.

Her own illness had left her somewhat less strong-minded than before, or she would never have spoken of it. One day, however, when Mrs. Bent came up to pay a social visit, and Jane had gone down the cliff on some necessary errand, Miss Hallet, who had been "tried" that morning by Jane's having an hysterical fit, condescended to speak of Harry Castlemaine in connection with her niece, and to ask Mrs. Bent whether she ever saw them together now.

"Pretty nearly every other evening," was the plain and most unwelcome answer.

Miss Hallet coughed, to cover a groan of censure. "Where do they walk to?" she asked.

"Mostly under the high cliff towards the Limpets. It's lonely there at night—nobody to be met with, ever."

"Do you walk there—that you should see them?" asked keen Miss Hallet.

"To tell you the truth, I have gone there on purpose to see," was the landlady's unblushing answer. "I don't approve of it. It's very foolish of Jane."

"Foolish; yes, very: but Jane would never behave lightly!" returned Miss Hallet, a blush of resentment on her thin cheeks.

"I don't say she would: Jane ought to have better sense than that. But it is pretty nigh as bad to give rise to talk," added candid Mrs. Bent: "many a good name has been tarnished without worse cause. It's not nice news, either, to be carried up to Greylands' Rest."

"Is it carried there, Mrs. Bent?"

"Net yet, that I know of. But it will be one of these days. I should put a summary stop to it, Miss Hallet."

"Yes, yes," said the unfortunate lady, smoothing her mittened hands together nervously, as she inwardly wondered how that was to be done, with Jane in her present temper. And, perplexed with her many difficulties, she began enlarging upon Jane's new and strange moods, even mentioning the locked drawer she had surprised Jane at, and openly wondering what she kept in it.

"Love-letters," curtly observed discerning Mrs. Bent.

"Love-letters!" exclaimed Miss Hallet, who had never had a love-letter in her life, and looked upon them as no better than slow poison.

"There's not a doubt of it. His. I dare say he has got a lot of Jane's. I gave her a bit of my mind the day before yesterday, when she came to the inn to bring back the newspaper," added Mrs. Bent. "Gave it plainly, too."

"And—how did Jane receive it?"

"As meek as any lamb. 'I am not the imprudent girl you appear to think me, Mrs. Bent,' says she, with her cheeks as red as our cock's comb when he has been fighting. 'Mr. Harry Castlemaine would not like to hear you say this,' she went on. 'Mr. Harry Castlemaine might lump it,' I answered her. 'It wouldn't affect him much any way, I expect, Jane Hallet. Mr. Harry Castlemaine might set the sea afire with a trolley-load of burning tar-barrels if he so minded, and folks would just wink at him; while you would have the place about your ears if you dropped in but half a thimbleful.' Jane wished me good morning at that, and betook herself away."

Mrs. Bent's visit ended with this. Upon her departure, Miss Hallet put on her shawl and bonnet and proceeded to take her daily walk outside the door in the sun, pacing the narrow path from end to end. After Mrs. Bent's information, she could no longer doubt that Jane's changed mood must be owing to this acquaintanceship with Mr. Harry Castlemaine. A love affair, of course;—girls were so idiotic!—and Jane's trouble must arise from the knowledge that it could end in nothing. So impossible had it seemed to Miss Hallet that Jane, with her good sense, could really have anything to say, in this way, to the son of the Master of Greylands, that since the night of the expedition when she had gone after Jane to watch her, and received her fright as the result, she had suffered the idea by degrees to drop from her mind: and this revelation of Mrs. Bent's was as much a shock to her as though she had never had a former hint of it.

"Jane mast have lost her head!" soliloquised the angry lady, her face very stern. "She must know it cannot come to anything. They stand as far apart as the two poles. Our family was good in the old days; as good perhaps as that of the Castlemaines; but things altered with us. And I went out as lady's-maid, for it was that, not companion, and they know it, and I dare say put me, in their thoughts, on a level with their own servants. Mr. Castlemaine is polite when he meets me, and takes his hat off, and sometimes stays to chat for a minute: but he would no more think my niece a fit wife for his son than he would think the poorest fisherman's girl in the place fit. Jane must have lost her senses!"

Miss Hallet stopped to draw her shawl more closely round her, for the wind was brisk to-day; and then resumed her promenade and her reflections.

"Rather than the folly should continue, I would go direct to the Master of Greylands, and tell him. He would pretty soon stop it. And I will do it, if I can make no impression on Jane. I should like to know, though, before speaking to her, what footing they are upon: whether it is but a foolish fancy for each other, meaning nothing, or whether she considers it to be more serious. He cannot have been so dishonourable as to say anything about marriage! At least, I—I hope not. He might as well offer her the stars: and Jane ought to know there's as much chance of the one as the other. I wonder what is in the love-letters?"

Miss Hallet took a turn or two revolving this one point. A wish crossed her that she could read the letters. She wished it not for curiosity's sake: in truth, she would not have touched them willingly with a pair of tongs: but that their contents might guide her own conduct. If the letters really contained nothing but nonsense—boyish nonsense, Miss Hallet termed it—she might deal with the matter with Jane alone: but if Mr. Harry had been so absurd as to fill her up with notions of marriage, why then she would carry the affair up to Greylands' Rest, and leave it to be dealt with by Greylands' master.

Entering the house, she went upstairs. It was not likely that Jane had left the drawer unlocked; still it might have happened so, from inadvertence or else. But no. Miss Hallet stood in Jane's room and pulled at the drawer in question, which was the first long drawer in the chest. It resisted her efforts. Taking her own keys from her pocket, she tried every likely one, but none would fit. Nevertheless, she determined to get those letters on the first opportunity, believing it to lie in her duty. Not a shade of doubt arose in her mind, as to Mrs. Bent's clever theory: she was as sure the drawer contained Harry Castlemaine's love-letters, as though she had it open and saw them lying before her. Love-letters, and nothing else. What else, was there, that Jane should care to conceal?

"Jane's instincts are those of a lady," thought Miss Hallet, looking round the neat room approvingly at the pretty taste displayed, at the little ornamental things on the muslin-draped dressing-table. "Yes, they are. And there's her Bible and Prayer-book on their own stand; and there's—but—dear me! where on earth did these spring from?"

She had come to a glass of hot-house flowers. Not many. Half a dozen or so; but they were fresh, and of rare excellence.

"Jane must have brought them in last night. Smuggled them in, I should say, for I saw none in her hand. It is easy to know where they came from; there's only one hot-house in the whole place, and that's at Greylands' Rest."

Miss Hallet went down more vexed than she had come up. She was very precise and strait-laced: no one could deny that: but here was surely enough food to disturb her. Just after she had resumed her walk outside, her mind running upon how she could best contrive to have the drawer opened, and so get at the love-letters, Jane appeared.

Slowly and wearily was she ascending the cliff, as if she could hardly put one foot before the other. Miss Hallet could but notice it. Her face was pale; the one unoccupied arm hung down heavily, the head was bent.

"You look tired to death, Jane! What have you been doing to fatigue yourself like that?"

Jane started at the salutation, lifted her head, and saw her aunt. As if by magic, her listless manner changed, and she ran up the short bit of remaining path briskly. Her pale face had taken quite a glow of colour when she reached Miss. Hallet.

"I am not tired, aunt. I was only thinking."

"Thinking of what?" returned Miss Hallett. "You looked and walked as though you were tired: that's all I know."

"Of something Susan Pike has just told me," laughed Jane. "It might have turned out to be no laughing matter, though. Jack Tuff has taken a drop too much this morning and fallen out of a little boat he got into. Susan says he came up the beach like a drowned rat."

Jane went into the house while talking, and put down the basket she had carried. Miss Hallet followed her.

"I could only get the scrag end this morning, aunt: the best end was sold. So it must be boiled. And there's the newspaper, aunt: Mrs. Bent ran across to me with it."

"Put it on at once, then, with a sliced carrot or two," said Miss Hallet, alluding to the meat.

"And bacon," resumed Jane, "is a halfpenny a pound dearer. I think, aunt, it would be well to buy a good-sized piece of bacon at Stilborough. I am sure we give Pike a penny a pound more than we should pay there."

"Well—yes—it might be," acknowledged Miss Hallet for once: who very rarely listened to offered suggestions.

"I could bring it back this afternoon," observed Jane. "What should take you to Stilborough this afternoon, pray?"

"I want to take the socks in. And you know, aunt—I told you—that Mrs. Pugh asked me to go to tea there one day this week: I may as well stay with her to-day."

Jane had expected no end of opposition; but Miss Hallet made none. She went out to walk again without further remark, leaving Jane to the household duties. It turned out that Susan Pike was going to Stilborough, being also invited to Mrs. Pugh's. Jane mentioned it to her aunt at dinner, but Miss Hallet answered nothing.

About four o'clock, that damsel, attired in all the colours of the rainbow and as gay as a harlequin, came running up the cliff to call for Jane. Jane, dressed neatly, and looking very nice as usual, was ready for her; and they started together, Jane carrying her paper of socks and an umbrella.

"Well I never, Jane! you are not a-going to lug along that there big umbrella, are you?" cried Miss Susan, halting at the threshold, and putting up a striped parasol the size of a dinner-plate.

"I am not sure about the weather," returned Jane, looking at the sky. "I should not like to get wet. What do you think of it, aunt?"

"I think it likely to rain before you are back again: and you will either take the umbrella, Jane or you will put off that best bonnet for your old one. What is the matter with the umbrella, Susan Pike?—It will not throw discredit upon anybody."

It was, in fact, a handsome, though very large umbrella of green silk, a present to Jane from Miss Hallet. Susan shrugged her shoulders when they were out of sight; and Miss Hallet wondered for the hundredth time at Jane's making a companion of that common, illiterate girl.

She sat down to read the newspaper after they were gone, took her tea, and at dusk put on her things to go down the cliff. It was a very dull evening, dark before its time: heavy clouds of lead colour covered the sky. In a rather remote angle of the village lived the blacksmith, one Joe Brown; a small, silent, sooty kind of man in a leather apron, who might be seen at his forge from early morning to late night. He was there now, hammering at a piece of iron, as Miss Hallet entered.

"Good-evening, Brown."

Brown looked up at the address, and discerned who the speaker was by the red glare of his fire—Miss Hallet. He touched his hair in answer, and gave her back the good-evening.

She told him at once what she wanted, putting her veil aside to speak. The key of a drawer had been mislaid in her house, and she wished Brown to come and open it.

"Unlock him, or pick him, mum?" asked Brown.

"Only to unlock it."

"Won't the morrow do, mum? I be over busy to-night."

"No, to-morrow will not do," replied Miss Hallet, in one of those decisive tones that carry weight. "I want it opened to-night, and you must come at once. I shall pay you well."

So the man yielded: saying that in five minutes he would leave his forge, and be up the cliff almost as soon as she was. He kept his word: and Miss Hallet had but just got her things off when he arrived, carrying a huge bunch of keys of various sizes. It was beginning to rain. Not unfrequently was he called out on a similar errand, and would take with him either these keys, or instruments for picking a lock, as might be required.

She led the way upstairs to Jane's room, and pointed out the drawer. Brown stooped to look at the lock, holding the candle close, and at the second trial, put in a key that turned easily. He drew the drawer a little open to show that the work was done. Nothing was to be seen but a large sheet of white paper, covering the drawer half way up. The contents whatever they might be, were under it.

"Thank you," said Miss Hallet, closing the drawer again, while he took the key off the bunch at her request, to lend her until the morning. "Don't mention this little matter, Brown, will you be so good," she added, handing the man a shilling. "I do not care that my niece or the neighbours should believe me careless with my keys." And he readily promised.

The rain was now pouring down in torrents. Miss Hallet stood at the front door with the man, really sorry that he should have to go through such rain.

"It ain't nothing, mum," he said. And, taking his leather apron off to throw over his shoulders, Brown went swinging away.

As the echo of his footsteps, descending the cliff, died away on her ear, Miss Hallet slipped the bolt of the house-door, and went upstairs again. Putting the candle down on the white covering; for Miss Hallet and Jane had toilette covers in their rooms as well as their betters; she opened the drawer again. If the sheet of white paper covered only love-letters, there must be an astonishing heap of them: the colour flew into Miss Hallet's cheeks as an idea dawned upon her that there might be presents besides.

She pulled a chair forward, and drew the candle close to the edge of the drawers, preparing herself for a long sitting. Not a single letter would she leave unread: no, nor a single word in any one of them. She was safe for two good hours, for Jane was not likely to be in before nine: it might not be so soon as that, if the two girls waited at Stilborough for the storm to cease.

Setting her spectacles on her nose, Miss Hallet lifted the white paper off the contents of the drawer; and then sat gazing in surprise. There were no love-letters; no letters of any kind. The bottom of the drawer was lined with some delicate looking articles, that she took to be dolls' clothes. Pretty little cambric caps, their borders crimped with a silver knife by Jane's deft fingers; miniature frocks; small bed-gowns—and such like.

"Why, what on earth!"—began Miss Hallet, after a prolonged perplexity: and in her bewildered astonishment, she gingerly took up one of the little caps and turned it about close to her spectacles.

All in a moment, with a rush and a whirl; a rush of dread in her heart, a whirl of dreadful confusion in her brain; the truth came to the unfortunate lady. She staggered a step or two back to the waiting chair, and fell down on it, faint and sick. The appearance of the Grey Friar had brought most grievous terror to her; but it had not brought the awful dismay of this.

For the dainty wardrobe was not a doll's wardrobe but a baby's.

XXXII

MISS JANE IN TROUBLE

The Grey Ladies held fête sometimes, as well as the outside world; and it was gay this evening in the Grey Nunnery. The Sisters were en soirée: no guests, however, were present; only themselves. The occasion prompting it was the return of Sister Mildred: Sister Mildred grown young again, as she laughingly told them, so sprightly did she feel in her renewed health and strength.

She had brought some treasures back with her: contributed by the kind relatives with whom she had been staying. A basket of luscious hot-house grapes; a large, rich, home-made plum-cake; and two bottles of cowslip wine. These good things had been set out on the table of the parlour, and the whole of the Ladies sat round, listening to Sister Mildred's glowing accounts of her visit and of its pleasant doings.

"Why, my dears, they would fain have kept me till next year," she rejoined in answer to a remark: and her hearing was for the time so much improved that the small ear-trumpet, hanging by a ribbon from her waist, was scarcely ever taken up. "I had a battle, I assure you, to get away. My cousin has two charming little girls with her, her grandchildren, and the little mites hid the key of my box, so that it should not be packed; and they cried bitterly when I was ready to start."

"You will be sorry, now, that you have resigned the superiorship to me," whispered Mary Ursula, taking up the trumpet to speak. "I will give it back to you."

"Ah, my dear, no. I would not be head again for the world. I am better, as you see, thanks to our merciful Father in heaven; so much better that I can hardly believe it to be myself; but to keep well I must have no care or trouble. I shall be of less use here now than any of you."

"You will be of every use, dear Sister Mildred, if only to help me with counsel," returned Mary.

"Oh, it is pleasant to be at home again," resumed the elder lady, her face beaming from under its crisp muslin cap. "The sojourn with my relatives has been delightful; but, after all, there's no place like home. And you must give me an account, dear Sisters of all that has occurred during my absence. See to the thief in the candle!"

"There's not very-much to relate, I think," observed Sister Betsey, as she attended to the thief. "We had an adventure here, though, one night. Tom Dance's son went on to the chapel ruins to shoot a sea-bird for somebody at Stilborough, and his pistol exploded, and wounded him dreadfully. He came crawling here to be taken in."

"What do you say, dear?" asked Sister Mildred, her hand to her ear. "Tom Dance brought a sea-bird here?"

"No. His son, young Dance—"

But Sister Betsey's explanation was cut short by a loud, peremptory ring at the house-bell. Rings at that time of the evening, for it was close upon nine o'clock, generally betokened notice of illness or accident. Sister Ann hastened to the door, and the others held their breath.

"Who is ill? Is any case of calamity brought in?" quickly demanded Sister Mildred on her return.

"No ill case of any kind," replied Sister Aim, as she approached Mary Ursula. "It is a visitor for you, madam."

"For me!" exclaimed Mary, feeling surprised. "Is it my uncle—Mr. Castlemaine?"

"It is Lawyer Knivett, from Stilborough," said Sister Ann. "His business is very particular, he says."

Mary Ursula glanced around as she rose. It would scarcely be convenient for him to come in amid all the ladies; and she desired Sister Ann to take him to the dining-room. A cold, bare room it looked, its solitary candle standing at one end of the dinner-table as she entered. Mr. Knivett came forward and held out his hand.

"Will you forgive my disturbing you at this time, my dear Miss Castlemaine?" he asked. "I should have been here an hour or two ago; but first of all I waited for the violence of the storm to pass; and then, just as I was getting into my gig, a client came up from a distance, and insisted on an interview. Had I put off coming until to-morrow morning, if might have been midday before I got here."

They were sitting down as he spoke: Mary by the end of the table where the candle stood: he drew a chair so close in front of her that his knees nearly touched hers. Mary was inwardly wondering what his visit could relate to. A curious thought, bringing its latent unpleasantness, crossed her—that it might have to do with Anthony.

"My dear lady, I am the bearer of some sad news for you," he began. "People have said, you know, that a lawyer is like a magpie, a bird of ill-omen."

She caught up her breath with a sigh of pain. What was it that he had to tell her?

"It concerns your father's old friend and clerk, Thomas Hill," went on Mr. Knivett. "He was your friend too."

"Is he ill?" gasped Mary.

"He was ill, my dear Miss Castlemaine."

The stress on the one word was so peculiar that the inference seemed all too plain. Mary rose in agitation.

"Surely—surely he is not dead?"

"Sit down, my dear young lady. I know how grieved you will be; but agitation will not do any good. He died this afternoon at five o'clock."

There ensued a silence. Mary's breath was rising in gasps. "And—I—was not sent for to him," she cried, greatly agitated.

"There was no time to send," replied Mr. Knivett. "He had been ailing for several days past, but the doctor—it was Tillotson—said it was nothing; poor Hill himself thought it was not. This afternoon a change for the worse occurred, and I was sent for. There was no time for anything."

She pushed back the brown hair, braided so simply under the muslin cap. Pale memories were crowding upon her, mixing themselves up with present pain. The last time she had seen the surgeon, Tillotson, was the night when her father was found dead on his sofa, and poor Thomas Hill was mourning over him.

"Hill said more than once to me that he should not last long now his master Was gone," resumed the lawyer: "but I thought it was but an old man's talk, grieving after his many years' master and friend. He was right, however."

Regrets were stealing upon Mary. She had not, she thought, taken as much notice of this faithful old man as she ought. Why, oh, why, in that one sole visit she had made to Stilborough, to Mrs. Ord, did she not call to see him? These reproaches strike on us all when a friend passes away. The tears were trickling down her cheeks.

"And I should not have hastened over here to tell you this of itself, Miss Castlemaine; you'd have heard it soon without that; ill news travels fast. But nothing can be done without your sanction; hardly the first coffin ordered. You are left sole executor."

"I am! Executor!"

"Executrix, I should have said; but the other word comes more ready. His will does not contain ten lines, I think, for I made it; and there's not a name mentioned in it but yours. Every stick and stone is left to you; and sole, full power in all ways."

"But what shall I do, Mr. Knivett? To leave me executor!"

"My dear young lady, I knew you would be distressed at the first blush of the thing. I was surprised when he gave me the directions; but he would have it so. He had a notion, I fancy, that it might serve to take you abroad a bit out of this place: he did not like your being here."

"I know he did not. I strove to convince him I was happy when he came over here in the summer; but he could not think it."

"Just so. His money is well and safely invested, and will bring you in about three hundred and fifty pounds a year. There's some silver, too, and other knicknacks. It is all yours."

"What a good, kind, faithful man he was!" she said, her eyes streaming. "Good always, in every relation of life. He has gone to his reward."

"Ay, ay," nodded Mr. Knivett. "Hill was better than some of his neighbours, and that's a fact."

"But I can never act," she exclaimed. "I should not know what to do or how to do it."

"My dear Miss Mary, you need not trouble yourself on that score. Give me power, and I will make it all as easy for you as an old shoe. In fact, I will act instead of you. Not for gain," he added impressively: "I must do this little matter for you for friendship's sake. Nay, my dear, you must meet this as it is meant: remember my long friendship with your father."

"You are very kind," she faltered.

"Have you a pen and ink at hand?"

She brought one, and he caused her to assign to him the necessary power. Then he asked her wishes as to temporary matters and they consulted for a few minutes together: but she was glad to leave all to Mr. Knivett that she could leave.

"There has been another death at Stilborough to-day: at least, not more than a mile or two from it," observed the lawyer, as he rose to leave. "You have not heard of it, I suppose?"

He had his back to her as he spoke, having turned to take up his overcoat which lay on the children's form. Mary replied that she had not heard anything.

"Sir Richard Blake-Gordon's dead."

A great thump seemed to strike her heart. It stood still, and then went bounding on again.

"His death was very sudden," continued the lawyer, still occupied with his coat. "He fell down in a fit and never spoke again. Never recovered consciousness at all, Sir William tells me."

Mary lifted her eyes. Mr. Knivett had turned back to her then.

"Sir—William?" she stammered, feeling confused in all ways. The title was spoken too suddenly: it sounded strange to her; unnatural.

"It was he who came in and detained me: he had to see me upon an urgent matter. He is sadly cut up."

Hardly giving himself time to shake her hand, Mr. Knivett, bustled away. In passing the parlour-door, Sister Mildred was coming out of it. She and the lawyer were great friends, though they very rarely saw each other. He could not stay longer then, he said; and she and Mary went with him to the door, and walked with him across the waste ground to the gate.

The storm had entirely passed: it was the same evening, told of in the last chapter, when Miss Hallet took a trip to the blacksmith's: the sky was clear again and bright with a few stars. The storm had been one of those violent ones when the rain seems to descend in pitiless torrents. A great gutter of water was streaming along in front of the Grey Nunnery on the other side the low bank that divided the path from the road. Mr. Knivett's horse and gig waited in the road just out of the running water. The night was warm and still, balmy almost as in summer, though it was getting late in the year. Ten o'clock was striking from the Nunnery clock.

"I shall be over again in a day or two," said Mr. Knivett to the ladies, as he took a leap from the bank over the gutter, and the groom held the apron aside for him to get up.

The two ladies stood at the gate and watched him drive off. It was, indeed, a lovely night now, all around quiet and tranquil. Mary, with a sobbing sigh, said a word to Sister Mildred of the cause that had brought the lawyer over; but the good Sister heard, as the French say, à tort et à travers. Now, of all queer items of news, what should the ladies have been pouring into the ex-Superior's ear during Miss Castlemaine's absence from the parlour, but the unsatisfactory rumours just now beginning to circulate through the village to the detriment of Jane Hallet. Her mind full of this, no wonder Sister Mildred was more deaf than need have been to Mary's words.

"It is a very extraordinary thing, my dear," she responded to Mary; "and I think she must have lost her senses."

At that same moment, sounds, as of fleet footsteps, dawned on Mary's ear in the stillness of the night. A minute before, a figure might have been seen flying down the cliffs from the direction of Miss Hallet's dwelling; a panting, sobbing, crying woman: or rather, girl. She darted across the road, nobody being about, and made for the path that would take her by the Grey Nunnery. The ladies turned to her as she came into view. It looked like Jane Hallet. Jane, in her best things, too. She was weeping aloud; she seemed in desperate distress: and not until she was flying past the gate did she see the ladies standing there. Sister Mildred, her head running on what she had heard, glided out of the gateway to arrest and question her.

"Jane, what is amiss?"

Startled at the sight of the ladies, startled at their accosting her, Jane, to avoid them, made a spring off the pathway into the road. The bank was slippery with the rain, and she tried moreover to clear the running stream below it, just as Mr. Knivett had done. But her foot slipped, and she fell heavily.

Sister Mildred stooped over the bank, and held out her hand. Was Jane stunned? No: but just for the minute or two she could not stir. She put one hand to her side as Sister Mildred helped her on to the path. Of no use to try to escape now.

"Are you hurt, child?"

"I—I think I am, ma'am," panted Jane. "I fell on my side." And she burst into the sobs again.

"And now tell me what the matter is, and where you were going to."

"Anywhere," sobbed the girl. "My aunt has turned me out of doors."

"Dear me!" cried Sister Mildred. "When did she turn you out of doors?"

"Now. When I got in from Stilborough. She—she—met me with reproach and passion. Oh, she is so very violent! She frightened me. I have never seen her so before."

"But where were you running to now?" persisted Sister Mildred. "There, don't sob in that way."

"Anywhere," repeated Jane, hysterically. "I can sit under a hedge till morning, and, then go to Stilborough. I am too tired to go back to Stilborough now."

Sister Mildred, who had held her firmly by the arm all this time, considered before she spoke again. Fearing there might be too much cause to condemn the girl, she yet could not in humanity suffer her to go "anywhere." Jane was an especial favourite with all the Sisters. At least, she used to be.

"Come in, child," she said. "We will take care of you until the morning. And then—why we must see what is to be done. Your aunt, so, self-contained and calm a woman, must have had some great cause, I fear, for turning you out."

Crying, wailing, sobbing, and in a state altogether of strange agitation, Jane suffered the Sister to lead her indoors, resisting not. Mary Ursula spoke a kind word or two to encourage her. It was no time for reproach: even if the Grey Ladies had deemed it their province to administer it.

Jane was shown to a room. One or two beds were always kept made up in the Grey Nunnery. Sister Betsey, invariably cheerful and pleasant with all the world, whether they were good or bad, poor or rich, went in with Jane and stayed to help her undress, chatting while she did it. And so the evening came to an end, and the house was at length steeped in quietness.

But in the middle of the night an alarm arose. Jane Hallet was ill. Her room was next to that of Sisters Ann and Phoeby they heard her moaning, and hastened to her.

"Mercy be good to us!" exclaimed the former, startled out of all equanimity by what she saw and heard. "We must call the Lady Superior.

"No, no; not her," corrected the calmer Sister Phoeby. "It is Sister Mildred who must deal with this."

So the very unusual expedient was resorted to of disturbing the ex-Superior in her bed, who was so much older than any of them. Sister Mildred dressed herself, and proceeded to Jane's room; and then lost not a minute in despatching a summons for Mr. Parker. He came at once.

At the early dawn of morning the wail of a feeble infant was heard within the chamber. A small, sickly infant that could not possibly live. The three Sisters mentioned were alone present. None of the others had been disturbed.

"The baptismal basin," whispered the elder lady to Sister Ann. "Make haste."

A china basin of great value that had been an heirloom in the Grant family, was brought in, half-filled with water. Sister Mildred rose—she had bent for a minute or two in silent prayer—took the infant in her arms, sprinkled it with the water, and named it "Jane." Laying it down gently, those in the room knelt again. Even Mr. Parker, turning from the bed, put his one knee on a chair.

By the time the Grey Ladies generally rose, all signs and symptoms of bustle were over. Nothing remained to tell of what the night had brought forth, save the sick-bed of Jane Hallet, and a dead infant (ushered into the world all too soon), covered reverently over with a sheet in the corner.

Breakfast done with, Sister Mildred betook herself up the cliff to Miss Hallet's, her ear-trumpet hanging from her waist-band. It was a painful interview. Never had the good Sister witnessed more pitiable distress. Miss Hallet's share in the pomp and pride of life had not been much, perhaps: but such as it was, it had now passed away from her for ever.

"I had far rather have died," moaned the poor lady, in her bitter feeling, her wounded pride. "Could I have died yesterday morning before this dreadful thing was revealed, I should have been comparatively happy. Heaven hears me say it."

"It is a sad world," sighed Sister Mildred, fixing the trumpet to her ear: "and it is a dreadful thing for Jane to have been drawn into its wickedness. But we must judge her charitably, Miss Hallet; she is but young."

Miss Hallet led the Sister upstairs, undid Jane's locked drawer with the blacksmith's borrowed key, and exhibited its contents as an additional aggravation in her cup of bitterness. Sister Mildred, a lover of fine work, could not avoid expressing admiration, as she took up the things one by one.

"Why, they are beautiful!" she cried. "Look at the quality of the lace and cambric! No gentleman's child could have better things provided than these. Poor Jane! she must have known well, then, what was coming. And such sewing! She learnt that from us!"

"Never, so long as she lives, shall she darken my doors again," was the severe answer. "You must fancy what an awful shock it was to me, Sister Mildred, when I opened this drawer last evening; and what I said to Jane on her entrance, I really cannot recall. I was out of my mind. Our family has been reduced lower and lower by ill-fortune; but never yet by disgrace."

"I'm sure I can't understand it," returned the puzzled Sister. "Jane was the very last girl I could have feared for. Well, well, it cannot be mended now. We will keep her until she is about again, Miss Hallet."

"I should put her outside the Nunnery gate to-day!" came the stern reply.

"That would kill her," said Sister Mildred, shaking her head in compassion. "And the destroying of her body would not save her soul. The greater the sin, the greater, remember, was the mercy of our Lord and Master."

"She can never hold up her head in this world again. And for myself, as I say, I would far rather be dead than live."

"She won't hold it up as she has held it: it is not to be expected," assented Sister Mildred with an emphatic nod. "But—well—we must see what can be done with her when she's better. Will you come to see her, Miss Hallet?"

"I come to see her!" repeated the indignant relative, feeling the proposal as nothing less than an outrage. "I would not come to see her if she lay dying. Unless it were to reproach her with her shame."

"You are all hardness now," said indulgent Sister Mildred, "and perhaps I should be in your place: I know what a bitter blow it is. But the anguish will subside. Time heals the worst sores: and, the more we are weaned from this world, the nearer we draw to Heaven."

She dropped her trumpet, held Miss Hallet's hand in hers, and turned to depart. That ruffled lady, after escorting her to the door, turned the key and shot the bolt, as if she wanted to have no more to do with the outer world, and would fain deny it entrance.

"Oh ma'am, what a sight o' news is this!" broke forth staring Nancy Gleeson, meeting the Grey Lady face to face at a sudden turning of the cliff path, and lifting her two hands in reprobation.

It was the first instalment of the public unpleasantness: an unpleasantness that must perforce arise, and could only be met. Of no use for Sister Mildred to say "What do you mean?" or "Jane Hallet is nothing to you." The miserable news had gone flying about the village from end to end: it could neither be arrested nor the comments on it checked.

"I can't stay talking this morning, Nancy Gleeson," replied the deaf lady; who guessed, more than heard, what the theme must be. "You had better go home to your little ones; they may be setting themselves on fire again."

"'Twarn't so over long ago she was a lugging our Bessy up the path, and she looked fit to drop over it; all her breath gone, and her face the colour o' chalk," continued Nancy, disregarding the injunction. "Seemed to me, ma'am, then as if 'twas odd. Well, who'd ever ha' thought it o' Miss Jane Hallet?"

Sister Mildred was yards away, and Nancy Gleeson's words were wasted on the air. At the foot of the cliff, as she was crossing the road, Mrs. Bent saw her from the inn door, and came over with a solemn face.

"How is she doing?" asked the landlady, speaking close to Sister Mildred's ear.

"Pretty well."

"I shall never be surprised at anything after this, ma'am; never: When Molly, all agape, brought the news in this morning, I could have sent a plate at her head, for repeating what I thought was nothing but impossible scandal. Miss Hallet must be fit to hang herself."

"It is a sad, grievous thing for all parties, Mrs. Bent," spoke Sister Mildred. "Especially for Jane herself."

"One can't help pitying her, poor young thing. To have blighted her life at her age! And anything that's wanted for her while she's sick, that the Nunnery may be out of, please send over to me for. She's heartily welcome to it, Sister Mildred."

The Sister nodded her thanks, and walked on. Mr. Parker overtook her at the Nunnery door, and they went up together to the sick-room.

Jane lay, white and wan, on the pillow, Sister Mona standing by her side. She looked so still and colourless that for the moment it might have been thought she was dead. Their entrance, however, caused her eyes to open; and then a faint shade of pink tinged her face.

Mr. Parker ordered some refreshment to be administered; and Sister Mona left to get it. "See that she has it at once," he said, speaking into the trumpet. "I am in a hurry just now, and cannot stay."

"Is anyone ill?" asked Sister Mildred.

"A child up at the coastguard station is in convulsions, and they have sent for me in haste. Good-morning, madam, for the present. I'll call in on my return."

"Only one moment, doctor," cried Sister Mildred, following him out to the corridor, and speaking in a whisper. "Is Jane in danger?"

"No, I think not. She must be kept quiet."

Infinitely to the astonishment of Sister Mildred, somewhat to her scandal, Mr. Harry Castlemaine appeared on the staircase, close upon the descent of the doctor. He must have come into the Nunnery as the latter let himself out. Taking off his hat, he advanced straight to Sister

Mildred, the open door at which she was standing no doubt indicating to him the sick-room.

"By your leave, Sister Mildred," he said, with a grave and pleasant smile—and passed in.

She was too utterly astonished to stop him. But she followed him in, and laid her arresting hand on his arm.

"Mr. Harry—Harry Castlemaine, what do you mean by this? Do you think, sir, I can allow it?"

"I must speak a word or two to Jane," he whispered in her ear, catching up the trumpet of his own accord. "Dear lady, be charitable, and leave me with her just for a minute, On my honour, my stay shall not much exceed that." And, partly through his persuasive voice, and smile, and hands, for he gently forced her to the door, partly in her own anxiety to obey the doctor's injunction of keeping Jane quiet, and wholly because she felt bewildered and helpless, Sister Mildred found herself outside in the corridor again, the door shut behind her.

"My goodness!" cried the perplexed lady to herself. "It's well it's me that's here, and not the younger Sisters."

In two minutes, or little more, he came out again; his hand held forth.

"Thank you, dear Sister Mildred. I thank you from my heart."

"No, I cannot take it," she said, turning pointedly away from his proffered hand.

"Are you so offended that I should have come in!"

"Not at that: though it is wrong. You know why I cannot touch your hand in friendship, Harry Castlemaine."

He stood a moment as though about to reply; but closed his lips without making any. "God bless you, dear lady; you are all very good: I don't know what Greylands would do without you. And—please"—he added, turning back again a step or two.

"Please what?" demanded Sister Mildred.

"Do not blame her. She does not deserve it. I do."

He went softly down the stairs and let himself out. John Bent was standing at his door as Harry came in view of the Dolphin, and the young man crossed over. But, when he got up, John had disappeared indoors. There was no mistaking that the movement was intentional, or the feeling that caused the landlord to shun him. Harry Castlemaine stood still by the bench, evidently very much annoyed. Presently he began to whistle, slowly and softly, a habit of his when in deep thought, and looked up and down the road, as if uncertain which way he should take.

A knot of fishermen had gathered round the small boats on the beach, and were talking together less lazily than usual: possibly, and indeed probably, their exciting theme was the morning's news. One of them detached himself from the rest and came up towards the Dolphin, remarking that he was going to "wet his whistle." Mr. Tim Gleeson in a blue nightcap.

To judge by his flushed face and his not altogether steady gait, the whistle had been wetted already. When he saw Mr. Harry Castlemaine standing there, he came straight up to him, touching his cap. That trifling mark of respect he did observe: but when he had got a glass within him, there was no such hail-fellow-well-met in all Greylands as Tim Gleeson. He would have accosted Mr. Castlemaine himself.

"In with the tide, Gleeson?" remarked Harry—who was always pleasant with the men.

"Her's just gone out, sir," returned Gleeson, alluding to the boat. "I didn't go in her."

"Missed her, eh?" A misfortune Mr. Gleeson often met with.

"Well, I did miss of her, as might be said. I was a-talking over the news, Mr. Harry, with Tuff and one or two on 'em, and her went and put off without me."

Harry wondered he was not turned off the boat altogether. But he said nothing: he ceased to take notice of the man, and resumed his whistling. Gleeson, however, chose to enter upon the subject of the "news," and applied a hard word to Jane.

Harry's eagle glance was turned on the man like lightning. "What is that, Gleeson?" he asked, in a quiet but imperious tone.

And Mr. Tim Gleeson, owing no doubt to the wetting of the whistle, was so imprudent as to repeat it.

The next moment he seemed to have pins and needles in his eyes, and found himself flat on the ground. Struck to it by the stern hand of Mr. Harry Castlemaine.

XXXIII

A Turbulent Sea

Boisterous weather. Ethel Reene, her scarlet cloak on, and her hat tied securely over her ears, was making her way to the top of the cliff opposite the coastguard station. A somewhat adventurous expedition in such a wind; but Ethel was well used to the path. She sat down when she reached the top: dropped down, laughing heartily. For the blast seized rudely on her petticoats, and sent the silken cords and tassels of her cloak flying in the air.

A glorious sea. A sea to look at to-day: to excite awe; to impress the mind with the marvellous works of the Great Creator. "Hitherto shalt thou come, but no farther. And here shall thy proud waves be stayed."

The waves were leaping mountains high; the foam and spray dashed aloft; the sound of the roar was like prolonged thunder. Ethel sat with clasped hands and sobered face and heart, lost in contemplation of the Majesty seen and unseen. It was not the time for silent thought to-day, or for telling her secrets to the sea: wonder, praise, awe, they could alone fill the mind.

"What a grand scene!"

The words were spoken close to her ear, and she turned her head quickly, holding her hat. The fastenings of her hair had blown away, and it fell around her in a wave of curls. Mr. North was the speaker. He had made his way up the rocks to watch this wondrous sea from that elevated place, not suspecting any one was there.

"I do not think I ever saw it so rough as this," said Ethel, as he took her hand in greeting, and then sat down beside her.

"I never saw it half as rough; never: but it has not been my privilege to live near the sea," he answered. "Are you sure it is safe for you to sit here, Ethel?"

"Oh yes. I am ever so far from the edge, you see."

"I do not know," he doubtingly answered; "the blast is strong. Mr. and Mrs. Castlemaine might warn you away, did they see you here."

As if to impart weight to his words, a furious gust came sweeping along and over them. Ethel caught involuntarily to the hard ground, and bent her head down. Mr. North hastily put his arm round her for protection.

"You see, Ethel!" he spoke when the rush had subsided. "It is dangerous for you. Had I not been here, you might have been blown away."

"No, no; but—perhaps—I should not have remained after that. I do not think it was ever so fiercely rough."

As he was there, however, and holding her securely, she made no movement to go. Ah, how could she! was it not all too delicious!— bliss unutterable!—and the wind was such an excuse. In after years, whether for her they might be long or short, Ethel would never lose the remembrance of this hour. The panorama of that turbulent sea would be one of her mind's standing pictures; the clasp of his arm never cease, when recalled, to cause her heart to thrill.

They sat on, close together, speaking but a stray word now and then, for it was nearly as difficult to hear anything said as it would have been for deaf Sister Mildred. By-and-by, as if the wind wanted a temporary rest, its worst fury seemed abated.

"I wonder if I could sketch the sea?" cried Mr. North. "Perhaps I could: if you will help me to hold the book, Ethel."

He had his small sketch-book in his pocket: indeed he rarely went out without it: and he drew it forth. Ethel held the leaves down on one side the opened page, and he on the other: with his other hand he rapidly took the lines of the horizon before him, and depicted the mountainous billows of the raging sea. Just a few bold strokes—and: he left the rest to be filled in at a calmer season.

"Thank you that is enough," he said to Ethel. But it took both their efforts to close the book again securely. The wind had all but torn its pages out; a lawful prey.

"There are people existing who hate never seen the sea," remarked Ethel. "I wonder if they can form even a faint conception of the scene it presents on such a day as this?"

"Thousands and thousands have never seen it," said Mr. North. "Perhaps millions, taking the world from Pole to Pole."

Ethel laughed at a thought that came to her. "Do you know, Mr. North, there is an old woman at Stilborough who has never seen it. She has never in her life been as far as Greylands—only three miles."

"It is scarcely believable."

"No: but it is true. It is old Mrs. Fordham. Her two daughters kept a cotton and tape shop in New Street. They sell fishing-tackle, too, and writing-paper, and many other things. If you choose to go and ask Mrs. Fordham, for yourself, she would tell you she has never had the curiosity to come as far as as this to see the sea."

"But why?"

"For no reason, she says, except that she has always been a great stay-at-home. She had a good many children for one thing, and they took up all the time of her best years."

"I should like to charter a gig and bring the old lady to see it to-day," exclaimed Mr. North. "I wonder whether she would be astonished?"

"She would run away frightened," said Ethel, laughing. "Will you please to tell me what the time is?"

He took out his watch. It was past twelve o'clock; and Ethel had to go. Mr. North drew her hand within his arm, seemingly as a matter of course, remarking that he must pilot her down the cliff. Ethel's face was covered with blushes. She was too timid to withdraw her hand: but she thought what would become of her should Mr. or Mrs. Castlemaine meet them. Or even Madame! So they went on arm-in-arm.

"Should I make anything of this sketch," said Mr. North, touching his pocket that contained the book; "anything of a watercolour I mean, it shall be yours, if you accept it. A memento of this morning."

"Thank you," murmured Ethel, her lovely face all blushes again.

"You will think of me perhaps when you look at it—once in a way. I may be far away: divided from you by sea and land."

"Are you going so soon?" she stammered.

"I fear I shall have to go eventually. The—the business that is keeping me here does not advance at all; neither does it seem likely to."

"Is business keeping you here?"

"Yes."

"I had no idea of that. Of what nature?"

"It is partly connected with property."

"The property that you told me might come to you by inheritance?"

"Yes. The coming seems very far off, though; farther than ever: and I—I am doing myself no good by staying."

"No good!" exclaimed Ethel, in surprise.

"In one sense I am not: individually, I am not. For, each day that I stay will only serve to render the pain of departing more intolerable."

Their eyes met. Ethel was at no loss to understand. Whether he meant her to or not he could scarcely have decided. But for exercising some self-control, he must have spoken out plainly. And yet, to what end? This fair girl might never become more to him than she was now, and their mutual love would be flung away to die on the shoals of adverse fate; as three parts of first love is in this world.

He released her when they were on level ground, and walked side by side with her as far as Chapel Lane, Ethel's way home to-day. There they stood to shake hands.

"I wonder if we shall ever again sit together watching a sea such as this has been!" he said, retaining her hand, and gazing down at her conscious face.

"We do not get a sea like this above once or twice a year."

"No. And when you get it next, nothing may be left of me here but the memory. Good-bye, Ethel."

She made her way homewards as swiftly as the wind would allow. Mr. North, somewhat sheltered under the lee of the Grey Nunnery, once he had passed the open chapel ruins, gave his mind up to thought. The little school-children, protected by the walls of the high building, were playing on the waste ground at "You can't catch me."

His position had begun to cause him very serious reflection: in fact, to worry him. Nothing could be more uncertain than it was, nothing more unsatisfactory. Should it turn out that Mr. Castlemaine had had any hand in injuring Anthony—in killing him, in short—why, then George North must give up all hope of Ethel. Ethel was to Mr. Castlemaine as a daughter, and that would be a sufficient bar to George North's making her his wife. Long and long ago would he have declared himself to the Master of Greylands but for Charlotte Guise; he would go to him that very day, but for her, and say, "I am your nephew, sir, George Castlemaine:" and ask him candidly what he had done with Anthony. But only the bare mention of this presupposed line of conduct would upset poor Madame Guise utterly: she had implored, entreated, commanded him to be silent. He might go away from Greylands, she said, and leave all the investigation to her; she did not want him to stay; but to spoil every chance of tracing out Anthony's fate—and, as she believed, that would spoil it—was not to be heard of. This chafed Mr. North's spirit somewhat: but he felt that he could not act in defiance of his brother's widow. The morning's interview on the cliff with Ethel had not tended to lessen the uneasiness and embarrassments of his position, but rather to bring them more clearly before him.

"It would be something gained if I could only ascertain how the estate was really left," he said to himself as he glanced mechanically at the shouting children; just as so many others, including his unfortunate brother, had said before him. "If it be, de facto, my Uncle James's, why he could have had no motive for wishing Anthony out of the way: if it was left to my father, why then it was absolutely Anthony's, and the Uncle James was but a usurper. In that case—but it is very hard to think so ill of him. I wonder whether—" Mr. North made a pause to revolve the question—"whether I could get anything out of Knivett?"

Deep in, thought, the Nunnery passed, he unguardedly approached the open part by the beach. Whirr!—whew! His hat went one way, the skirts of his coat another. The latter, not being detached, had to return to their places; but the hat was nowhere.

Harry Castlemaine, chancing to pass, ran and caught it, and brought it, laughing, to Mr. North. The young men liked each other and were cordial when they met; but they had not advanced to intimacy. Each had his reasons for avoiding it: Harry Castlemaine never chose to become to friendly with any stranger sojourning at Greylands; George North, under his present pseudo aspect, rather shunned the Castlemaines.

"It is well heads are not loose, as well as hats, or they'd be gone to-day," said Harry, giving up the hat. "Where's your ribbon?"

"It had come unfastened from my buttonhole. Thank you. What a grand sea it is!"

"Wonderful. A rare sea, even for Greylands. Good-day."

Like a great many more of us, Mr. North sometimes did things upon impulse. As he crossed to the Dolphin, holding Ins hat on his head, the two-horse van came lumbering down the hill by the Nunnery on its way to Stilborough. Impulse—it certainly was not reason—induced George North to get inside and go off with it. In due course of time it conveyed him to Stilborough.

"Can you tell me where Mr. Knivett, the advocate, lives?" he asked of the driver when he was paying his fare.

"Lawyer Knivett, is it, sir, that you want? He lives close to the market-house, in the centre of the town."

"Which is my way to it?"

"Go to the end of the street, sir: take the first turning on the left, New Street, and that will bring you into the street where the marketplace is. Anybody will tell you which is Lawyer Knivett's."

Just as in the days, some months gone by, poor Anthony had been directed to the lawyer's house, and readily found it, so did the younger brother find it now. The brass-plate on the door, "Mr. Knivett, attorney-at-law," stared him in the face as he halted there. During the dinner-hour, between half-past one and two, this outer door was always shut; an intimation that clients were not wanted to call just then: at other times it was generally, though not invariably, open: impatient clients would often give it a bang behind them in escaping. Mr. North rang the bell, and was admitted to the clerk's room, where a young man, with curled black hair and a nose like a parrot's, sat behind a desk near the window, writing.

"Can I see Mr. Knivett?" asked George.

The young man stretched his neck forward to take a look at the applicant. "It's not office-hours," said he in answer, his tone superlatively distant.

"When will it be office-hours?"

"After two o'clock."

"Can I see him then—if I wait?"

"Well, yes, I suppose you can. There's a chair"—extending the feather-end of his pen to point it out: which caused the diamond ring he wore on his finger to flash in the sunlight.

"A vain young dandy," thought George, as he sat down, regarding the ring, and the curled hair, and the unexceptionable white linen. The gentleman was, in fact, a distant relative of Squire Dobie's, holding himself to be far above all the fraternity of men of the law, and deeming it an extremely hard case that his friends should have put him into it.

The silence broken only by the scratching of the pen, was interrupted by the sudden stopping before the house of a horse and gig. An active little gentleman of middle-age leaped out, came in, and opened the door of the room.

"Where's Mr. Knivett, Dobie? At his dinner?"

"Yes."

Away went the little gentleman somewhere further on in the house. Almost immediately he was back again, and Mr. Knivett with him. The latter opened the door.

"I am going out, Mr. Dobie. Don't know how long I may be detained. Old Mr. Seaton's taken ill." And, with that, he followed the little gentleman out, mounted the gig with him, and was gone.

It had all passed so quickly that George North had not space to get in a word. He supposed his chance of seeing the lawyer for that day was at an end.

Scarcely had the gig driven off, and Mr. Dobie brought back his head from gazing after it over the window blind, when there entered a gentleman in deep mourning: a good-looking man with a somewhat sad countenance. Mr. Dobie got off his stool with alacrity, and came forward.

"How are you, Sir William?"

Sir William Blake-Gordon—for it was he—returned the greeting: the two young men met occasionally in society.

"Can I see Mr. Knivett?" asked Sir William.

"No, that you can't," returned the gentleman-clerk. "Charles Seaton of the Hill has just fetched him out in a desperate hurry. Knivett, going out to the gig, put in his head to tell me old Seaton was taken ill. Wants his will altered, I suppose."

Sir William considered. "Tell Mr. Knivett, then, that I will be here at about eleven o'clock to-morrow. I wish to see him particularly."

"All right," said Mr. Dobie.

Sir William was turning away, when his eyes fell on George North, who had then risen preparatory to departure. He held out his hand cordially, and George North met it. A week or two previously, just before Sir Richard's death, it chanced that they had met at a country inn, and were detained there part of a day by a prolonged storm of rain and thunder. Each had liked the other, and quick acquaintanceship had been formed.

"Are you still at Greylands, Mr. North?"

"Yes."

"Well, do not forget that I shall be very glad to see you. Come over at any time."

"Thank you," replied George.

The new baronet went out. Mr. Dobie, witnessing all this, began to fancy that the gentleman might be somebody worth being civil to.

"I am sorry Knivett should have started off in this sudden way," he observed, his tone changed to ease, "but I suppose there was no help for it. Is there anything I can do for you?"

"No," returned George, "I fear not. I merely wanted to ask Mr. Knivett a question about a family in the neighbourhood."

"I dare say I could answer it," said Mr. Dobie. "I know all the best families as well as Knivett does, or better: been brought up among them."

"Do you know the Castlemaines?"

"Well, I ought to. My relatives, the Dobies of Dobie Hall, and the Greylands' Rest people used to be as thick as inkleweavers. Harry Castlemaine is one of my friends."

George North paused. An idea struck him that perhaps this young man might be able to give him some information: and, to tell the truth, though he had come to ask Mr. Knivett to do it, he had very little hope that the lawyer would. At least there would be no harm in his putting the question.

"I am a stranger here," he said. "Until some weeks back I never was in this part of the world or knew a soul that inhabited it. But I have become acquainted with a few people; and, amidst them, with the Castlemaines. Did you know the old grandfather, Anthony?"

"Just as well as I know my own grandfather."

"Greylands' Rest was his, I fancy?"

"Of course it was."

"To whom did he leave it?"

"Ah, that's a question," said Mr. Dobie, taking his penknife out to trim the top of one of his filbert nails. "There was a nephew made his unexpected appearance on the estate last winter—a son of the elder brother—"

"I have heard," interrupted George North: "Anthony Castlemaine."

"Just so. Well, he thought Greylands' Rest was his; wanted to put in a claim to it; but Mr. Castlemaine wouldn't allow it at any price. The claimant disappeared in some queer manner—you have no doubt heard of it—and James Castlemaine retains undisturbed possession. Which is said to be nine points of the law, you know."

"Then, you do not know how it was left? whether it is legally his?"

Mr. Dobie shook his head. "I'd not like to bet upon it, either way. If forced to do so, I'd lay it against him."

"You think it was left to Anthony Castlemaine," said George North quickly. "That is, to Anthony's father; Basil, the eldest brother."

"What I think is, that if Mr. Castlemaine could show he had any right to it, he would show it, and put an end to the bother," spoke Mr. Dobie.

"But he should be made to do this."

The clerk lifted his eyes from his nails, his eyebrows raised in surprise. "Who is to make him?"

"I'm sure I don't know. Could not the law?"

"The law must get a leg to stand upon before it can act. It has no right to interfere with Mr. Castlemaine. That young Anthony—if he's not dead—might come back and enter a process against him for restitution, and all that: in that case James Castlemaine would have to show by what tenure he holds it. But it might be an awfully long and expensive affair; and perhaps end in nothing."

"End in nothing?"

"Why, you see, if old Anthony Castlemaine simply made a present, while he was yet living, of Greylands' Rest to James, the latter would have to swear to it, and the thing would be done with. Some people think it was so. Others, and I for one, don't fancy it was his at all, but that poor young Anthony's."

"The Castlemaines have always been held to be men of honour, I believe?"

"And we should never have doubted James to be one—but for his refusal to satisfy his nephew and the public. Nothing but that raised a doubt against him. It is blowing over now."

"You do not know, then, how Greylands' Rest was left, or to whom?"

"No. I don't believe anybody does know, save Mr. Castlemaine himself. Unless it's Knivett. He may."

"But I dare say Knivett would not tell—even if he were pumped."

Mr. Dobie burst into a laugh at the idea. "Knivett tell the affairs of any of his clients!" said he. "You might as well set on and pump this high-backed chair as pump him."

The clerks, two of them, came in from dinner, and no more was said. George North walked back to Greylands, having taken nothing by his journey: just as the unfortunate Anthony had walked back to it many months before. The wind was blowing worse than ever. Several people, chiefly women, had gathered on the beach to look at the sea; but the spray and the roar nearly blinded and deafened them. Amidst others stood Mrs. Castlemaine, Ethel, and Flora: talking to them was the landlady of the Dolphin, a huge shawl tied over her head. George North approached.

"It is surely worse than it was this morning!" said George, after speaking to the ladies.

"And what'll it be when the tide is full up again!" cried Mrs. Bent, whose tongue was ever of the readiest. "Twenty years I've lived in this place, and never saw it like this. Look at that wave!—My patience!"

Almost as the words left her lips, there arose a cry of alarm. The wave, rearing itself to a towering height, came dashing in on the beach nearer than was bargained for, and engulfed Miss Flora Castlemaine.

MRS. HENRY WOOD

That young damsel, in defiance of commands, had been amusing herself by running forward to meet the waves and running back again before the water could catch her. This time she had not been quite so successful. The force of the water threw her down; and even as they looked, in the first moment of alarm, they saw her drifting rapidly out to sea with the returning tide.

Mrs. Castlemaine shrieked wildly. Nearly everybody shrieked. Some ran here, some yonder; some laid hold of one another in the nervousness induced by terror: and the child was being washed further out all the while. But the cries suddenly ceased; breaths were held in suspense: for one was going out to the rescue.

It was George North. Flinging off his coat and hat, he dashed through the waves, keeping his footing as long as he could, battling with the incoming tide. But for the boisterous state of the sea, the rescue would have been mere child's play; as it was, it cost him some work to reach and save her. He bore her back, out of the cruel water. She was quite insensible.

Ethel burst into tears. In the moment's agitation, she was not sure but she clasped his arm, wet as he was, when striving to pour forth her thanks. "Oh, how brave you are! How shall we ever repay you!"

He snatched a moment to look back into her eyes, to give her a smile that perhaps said all too much, and went on with his dripping burden. "To my house!" cried Mrs. Bent, rushing forward to lead the way. "There's a furnace of hot water there, for we've got a wash on to-day. And, Mr. North, sir, you'll just get yourself between the blankets, if you please, and I'll bring you up a dose of hot brandy-and-water."

To see them all scampering over to the Dolphin, with the picked-up coat and hat, the wind taking their petticoats behind, the two wet figures in their midst, and Mrs. Castlemaine wringing her hands in despair, was a sight for Greylands. But, at least, George North had saved the child.

The next event that happened to excite the village was the disappearance of Jane Hallet from the Nunnery. She disappeared, so to speak. In fact she ran away from it.

Something like a fortnight had elapsed since her illness, or from that to three weeks, and she was able to walk about her room and do, at her own request, some sewing for the Sisters. Mr. Harry Castlemaine had not intruded on the Nunnery again. It was getting time to think of what was to be done with her: where she was to go, how she was to live. Jane had been so meek, so humble throughout this illness, so thankful for the care and kindness shown her, and for the non-reproach, that the Grey Ladies, in spite of their inward condemnation, could not help liking her in their hearts almost as much as they had liked her before, and they felt an anxious interest in her future. Sister Mildred especially, more reflective than the others by reason of her years, often wondered what that future was to be, what it could be. Miss Hallet—shut up in her home, her cheeks pink with shame whenever she had to go abroad: which she took care should be on Sundays only; but divine service, such as it was in Greylands, she would not miss—had never been to the Nunnery to see Jane, or taken the slightest notice of her. Sister Mildred had paid another visit to the cliff, and held a second conference with Miss Hallet, but it resulted in no good for Jane.

"She has blighted her own life and embittered mine," said Miss Hallet. "Never more can I hold up my head among my neighbours. I will not willingly see her again; I hope I never shall see her."

"The worst of it is, that all this reprobation will not undo the past," returned Sister Mildred. "If it would, if it could have served to prevent it, I'd say punish Jane to the last extreme of harshness. But it won't."

"She deserves to be punished always."

"The evil has come upon her, and everybody knows it. Your receiving her again in your home will not add to it or take from it. She has nowhere else to go."

"I pray you cease, Sister Mildred," said Miss Hallet; and it was plain to be seen that she spoke with utter pain. "You cannot—pardon me—you cannot understand my feelings in this."

"What shall you do without Jane? She was very useful to you; she was a companion."

"Could I ever make a companion of her again? For the rest, I have taken a little servant—Brown the blacksmith's eldest girl—and I find her handy."

"If I could but induce you to be lenient, for Jane's sake!" urged the pleading Sister, desperately at issue between her own respect for Miss Hallet's outraged feelings and her compassion for Jane.

"I never can be," was the answer, spoken stiffly: but Miss Hallet's fingers were trembling as she smoothed back her black silk mitten. "As to receiving her under my roof again, why, if I were ever brought to do that, I should be regarded as no better than herself. I should be no better—as I look upon it. Madam, you think it right to ask me this, I know: but to entertain it is an impossibility."

Sister Mildred dropped her ear-trumpet with a click. The hardness vexed her. And yet she could but acknowledge that it was in a degree excusable. But for the difficulties lying in Jane's path, she had never urged it.

So there the matter rested. Miss Hallet had despatched her new servant to the Nunnery with a portion of Jane's wardrobe: and what on earth was to become of Jane the Sisters were unable to conjecture. They could not keep her: the Nunnery was not a reformatory, or meant to be one. Consulting together, they at last thought of a plan.

Sister Mildred went one morning into Jane's room. Jane was seated at the window in a shawl, busy at her work—some pinafores for the poor little school-children. Her face was prettier than ever and very delicate, her manner deprecating, as she rose and courtesied to the late Superior.

"How are you getting on, Jane?"

"I have nearly finished this one, madam," she answered, holding out the pinafore.

"I don't mean as to work. I mean yourself."

"Oh, I feel nearly quite well now, thank you, madam," replied Jane. "I get stronger every day."

"I was talking about you with some of the ladies last night, Jane. We wonder what you are about to do. Have you any plan, or idea of your own?"

Poor Jane's face took a shade of crimson. She did not answer.

"Not that we wish to hurry you away from us, Jane. You are welcome to stay, and we intend you to do so, for at least two weeks yet. Only it will not do to leave considerations off to the last: this is why I speak to you in time."

Sister Mildred had sat down close by Jane; by bending her ear, she could do without the trumpet. Jane's hands, slender always, and weak yet, shook as she held the pinafore.

"Have you formed any plans, Jane?"

"Oh no, ma'am."

"I thought so," returned Sister Mildred, for indeed she did not see what plans Jane, so lonely and friendless, could form. "When we cannot do what we would, we must do what we can—that used to be one of your copies in small-hand, I remember, Jane."

"Yes, ma'am."

"Well, my dear, I don't want to speak harshly, but I think you must apply it to yourself. You can no longer do what you would: you will have to do what you can. I am sorry to say that your aunt continues inexorable: she will not shelter you again."

Jane turned to the table for her handkerchief. The tears were trickling down her face.

"We—the Sisters and myself—think it will be the best for you to take an easy place as servant—"

"As servant!" echoed Jane, looking startled.

"As servant for light work in a good family far away from here. Sister Margaret thinks she can manage this—her connections are very good, you know. Of course the truth must be told to them; but you will be taken care of, and made happy—we would not else place you—and have the opportunity afforded you of redeeming the past, so far as it may be redeemed. You don't like this, I'm afraid, Jane; but what else is there that's open to you?"

Jane was sobbing bitterly. She suddenly stooped and kissed the Sister's hand; but she made no answer.

"I will talk with you again to-morrow," said Sister Mildred, rising. "Think it over, Jane—and don't sob like that, child. If you can suggest anything better, why we'll listen to it. We only want to help you, and to keep you out of harm for the future."

Jane was very sad and silent all that day. In the evening, after dark, Sister Caroline, who had been out on an errand, came in with rounded eyes, declaring she had seen Jane Hallet out of doors. The ladies reproved her. Sister Caroline often had fancies.

"If it was not Jane Hallet it was her ghost," cried Sister Caroline, lightly. "She was under the cliff by the sea. I never saw anybody so much like Jane in my life."

"Have you been down under the cliff?" questioned Sister Charlotte.

"I went there for a minute or two with poor old Dame Tuff," explained the Sister. "She was looking after Jack, who had been missing since morning: she thought he might be lying under the cliff after too much ale. While we were peering into all the holes and shady places, somebody ran by exactly like Jane."

"Ran by where?"

"Close along, between us and the sea. Towards the Limpets."

"But nobody could want anything that way. They might be drowned."

"Well, it looked like Jane."

"Hush!" said one of the graver ladies. "You know it could not be Jane Hallet. Did you find Jack Tuff?"

"No: his poor mother's gone home crying. What a trouble sons are! But—may I go and see if Jane is in her room?"

It was really very obstinate of Sister Caroline: but she was allowed to go. Down she came with a rush.

Jane was not in her room.

Several of the Sisters, excited by the news, trooped up in a body to see. Very true. The room had been made neat by Jane, but there was no trace of herself. On the table lay some lines in pencil addressed to Sister Mildred.

A few lines of grateful, heartfelt thanks for the kindness shown to her, and an imploring hope that the ladies would think of her with as little harshness as they could. But not a single word to tell of whither she had gone.

"Pray Heaven she has not done anything rash!" mentally cried Sister Mildred with pale cheeks, as she thought of the dangers of the path that led to that part of the coast called the Limpets.

XXXIV

Changed to Paradise

T he winter season was coming in, but not yet winter weather, for it was mild and balmy: more like a fine September than the close of November.

The glass doors of the red parlour at Greylands' Rest were thrown open to the garden, and to the very few autumn flowers that yet lingered around the window. Dinner was over, and the ladies were back in the parlour again. Little Marie Guise was spending the day there, and was now playing at cat's-cradle with Flora: her mother was talking with Mrs. Castlemaine. Ethel sat drawing.

"Dear me! I think this is Miss Castlemaine."

The words were Madame's, and they all looked up. Yes; advancing round from the wide garden-path in her grey dress and with her stately step, came Mary Ursula. Seeing them sitting there, and the doors open, she had turned aside on her way to the front entrance. Ethel ran out.

"How good of you, Mary! Have you come to stay the afternoon?"

"No, Ethel, dear. I want to see my uncle. Is he at home?"

"I think so. We left him at table. Come in."

Mrs. Castlemaine made much of the visitor. Disliking Mary Ursula at heart, thankful that she had joined the Grey Sisterhood for good and was out of the way of Greylands' Rest, Mrs. Castlemaine made a great show of welcome at these chance visits.

"And why can you not stay now you are here?" asked Mrs. Castlemaine, purring upon Mary as she sat down. "Do take your bonnet off."

"I would stay if I could," said Mary, "but I must be back again by four o'clock. Mr. Knivett sent me a note this morning to say he should be over at that hour with some papers that require my signature."

"Then, Mary, why did you not come some afternoon when you were not expecting Mr. Knivett?" sensibly asked Ethel.

"Because I had to come to-day, Ethel. I wish to see my uncle."

"I suppose you have been busy with your money and your executorship," spoke Mrs. Castlemaine. "You must feel quite rich."

"I do," said Mary, with earnest truth. Looking back, she had not thought herself so rich in her anticipated many, many thousands a year then, as she felt now with these two or three bequeathed hundreds of additional income. "We are rich or poor by comparison, you know," she said, smiling. "And what is Marie doing?—learning to play at cat's cradle?"

Marie snatched the thread from Flora, and ran up to her: she could speak a little English now.

"Lady play wi' Marie!

"Why, my dear little child, I think I have forgotten how to play," returned Mary. "Flora can play better than I can. Flora is none the worse for that accident, I hope?" she added to Mrs. Castlemaine. "But how serious it might have been!"

"Oh, don't, don't talk of it," cried Mrs. Castlemaine, putting her hands before her eyes to shut out the mental vision. "I shall never see a furious sea again without shuddering."

"It is beautifully calm to-day," said Mary, rising to go into the dining-room to her uncle. "Like a mill-pond."

Mr. Castlemaine was no longer in the dining-room. Miles putting the wine and dessert away, said his master had gone up to his room to write letters. So Mary went after him.

Several days had passed now since the departure of Jane Hallet from the Nunnery. And the longer the time elapsed without news of her, the greater grew the marvel of Greylands. The neighbours asked one another whether Jane had mysteriously disappeared for good, after the fashion of Anthony Castlemaine. It was rumoured that the affair altogether, connected with Jane, had much annoyed the Master of Greylands. He was supposed to have talked sharply to his son on the subject; but how Harry received it, or what he replied, was not known. Harry rather shunned home just then, and made pretext for excursions to distant places, which kept him out for a day or two at a time.

But a worse doubt than any was gaining ground: the same doubt that had crossed Sister Mildred the night of the disappearance. Had Jane committed any rash act? In short, to speak out boldly, for it is what Greylands did, people thought that Jane must have flung herself into the sea. The way to the Limpet rocks—once old Dame Dance's cottage was passed—led to nowhere but the rocks: and nobody in their senses would seek them at night if they wanted to come away alive. Clearly there was but one inference to be drawn: Jane was under the water.

Of course, it was entirely inconsistent with Greylands' neighbourly outspokenness that this dismal conviction should long be concealed from Miss Hallet. Perhaps it was considered a matter of conscience to make it known to her. Mrs. Pike at the shop was the first to run up, and undertake the communication.

Miss Hallet received it in cold silence: for all the world as if she had been a stock or a stone, as Mrs. Pike related afterwards: and for a day or two she held on in her course of high-mightiness. But it could not last. She had human feelings, as well as other people: it might have been that they were all the keener from her outward shell of impassive coldness; and they made themselves heard in spite of her injured pride. The news shocked her; the more she tried to drive it from her mind, the more persistently it came back to take up its abode there: and at length a whole flood-tide of remorse and repentance set in: for she asked herself whether she—she—had helped to drive Jane to her dreadful fate. It is one thing to browbeat our friends to within an inch of their lives: but quite another thing to shut them into their coffins.

On the second evening, when twilight was sufficiently dim to enfold her within its shade, Miss Hallet went down to seek an interview with Sister Mildred at the Nunnery; and was admitted to her. Mary Ursula Castlemaine was also in the room, writing at a table apart: but she did not interfere in any way, or take part in the conversation.

"I have come to know the truth of this," gasped Miss Hallet, whose every effort to suppress her agitation and to appear cold as usual, served to impede her breath. "At least, madam, so far as you can tell it me."

"But, my dear, good woman, I can't tell you anything," briskly returned Sister Mildred, speaking with her trumpet to her ear. "We don't know what to think ourselves. I wish we did."

They were sitting side by side on the well-worn horsehair sofa, which was drawn close to the fire. Mary was in the further corner behind them, a shade on the candle by which she wrote. Miss Hallet untied the strings of her bonnet, as if in need of air.

"Jane cannot have put an end to her life!" spoke Miss Hallet, her trembling lips betokening that she felt less assured of the fact than the words implied. "She was too religious a girl for anything so desperately wicked; too well-principled."

"That is what I tell myself ten times a day," returned Sister Mildred. "Or try to."

"Try to!" echoed Miss Hallet.

"Well, you see—you see—" Sister Mildred spoke with hesitation, between wishing to tell just the truth and dislike to say what must inflict pain—"you see, the thought that keeps intruding on me is this: having been deceived in my estimation of Jane's good principles on one point, one is obliged to feel less sure of them on another."

A groan broke from Miss Hallet; she coughed to cover it. But in another moment her misery got the better of her, and all reticence was thrown away.

"Oh, if you can help me to find her—if you can give me a hope that she is still living, do so, dear lady, for heaven's sake," she implored, placing her hands, in her irrepressible agitation, on the arm of Sister Mildred. "Let me not have her death upon my conscience!"

The good Sister took both the hands and held them in hers. "For my own sake, I would do it if I could," she gently said. "To find Jane, I would forfeit a good deal that is precious to me."

"It is killing me," said Miss Hallet. "It will kill me speedily unless this incertitude can be ended. For the past two days, I have not had one moment's peace. Night and day, night and day, the one dreadful doubt is upon me with a harrowing torment. Where is Jane?"

"We cannot think where she can be," said Sister Mildred, shaking her head. "Nobody seems to know."

A moment's silence, and then the sound of hysterics burst upon the room: cries, and sobs, and catchings of the breath. Miss Hallet had not given way like this even when her nephew died.

But, alas, they could give her no satisfaction, no comfort. Sister Mildred, shaking hands with her before departure, spoke cheerfully of hope, of "looking on the bright side of things," but it was very negative consolation.

"My dear, did you take note of what passed?" questioned Sister Mildred of Mary Ursula, when they were alone. "How distressing this is!"

Mary rose from her desk and came forward. "My heart was aching for her all the time," she said. "Miss Hallet may have acted somewhat harshly; but she has my greatest pity. I wish I could relieve her!"

"If anyone in this world knows where Jane is, it must be Mr. Harry Castlemaine," observed Sister Mildred in a cold, subdued whisper. "That is, if she be still alive. I wonder, my dear, whether we might ask him."

"Whether he would give any information, you mean," replied Mary Ursula. "He ought to; and I think he would. Though, perhaps, it might be better got at through his father."

"Through his father!" echoed Sister Mildred, quickly. "Oh, my dear, we should never dare to question the Master of Greylands."

"I would: and will," concluded Mary Ursula.

It was in pursuance of this resolve that Mary had come up this afternoon to Greylands' Rest. Harry had gone to Newerton for a day or two, this time really upon business. Mary went upstairs and knocked at her uncle's door.

The Master of Greylands was doing nothing. He had apparently been writing at his bureau, for the flap was down, one drawer stood out and some papers were lying open. He had quitted it, and sat back in a chair near the window; his eyes resting on the calm sea stretched out in the distance. Which sea, however, he never saw; his thoughts were far away.

"Nothing has gone right since that fatal night," he said to himself, his brow knitted into lines of pain. "Teague has said all the summer that suspicions are abroad—though I think he must be wrong; and now there's this miserable trouble about Harry and that girl! For myself, I seem to be treading on a volcano. The stir after Anthony is not at an end yet: I am sure of it; instinct warns me that it is not: and should a comprehensive search be instituted, who can tell where it would end, or what might come to light?"

A log of blazing wood fell on the hearth with a splutter and crash. Mr. Castlemaine looked round mechanically: but all was safe. The room was just as lonely and bare as usual: no signs of life or occupation in it, save the master himself and the papers in the open bureau.

"When men look askance at me," ran on his thoughts, "it makes my blood boil. I am living it down; I shall live it down; but I have not dared to openly resent it and that has told against me. And if the stir should arise again, and unpleasant facts come out—why then it would be all over with the good name of the Master of Greylands. The world calls me proud: and I am proud. Heaven knows, though, that I have had enough this year to take pride out of me."

A deep sigh, telling of the inward trouble, escaped him. Men whose minds are at ease cannot sigh like that.

"It has been an unlucky year for the Castlemaines: a fatal year. After a long tide of prosperity such years do come, I suppose, to a family. Peter's trouble first, and his uncertain death:—and what a near shave it was, the staving off disgrace from his name! Anthony's intrusion and the trouble he gave me, and then his death: that, unfortunately, had nothing uncertain about it. The cloud that fell upon me, and that lasts still; and now, Teague's doubts; and now again, Harry! Better for me, perhaps, to get out of it all, while the opportunity remains."

A heavy sigh broke from him, coming apparently from the very depth of his heart. He put his elbow on the arm of his chair, and leaned his brow upon his hand.

"Poor Anthony," he moaned, after a pause. "Oh, if the doings of that night could but be recalled! I would give the best years of my remaining life to undo its fatal work. Just one moment of mad, impetuous passion, and it was all over! What can his friends be about, I wonder, that they have not come to see after him? I thought he said he had a brother, at that first interview; but I have never been sure, for I was feeling resentful, half checkmated, and I would not listen to him. I am certain he said he had a sister—married, I think, to a Frenchman. They have not come; they do not write: French people don't care for their relatives, perhaps—and they must be French rather than English. If Anthony—"

A gentle knock at the door had been unheard by Mr. Castlemaine: a second knock was followed by the entrance of Mary Ursula in her Sister's dress. So entirely was Mr. Castlemaine buried in these unpleasant, far away scenes, that just for a moment he stared at the intruder, his mind completely absent. Mary could not help noticing his haggard look and the pain that sat in his eyes.

"Why, Mary Ursula, is it you?" he cried, starting up. "Come in, my dear."

With a rapid movement, as he advanced to meet her, he swept the papers back and closed the bureau. Taking her hands in his he kissed her, and put a chair for her near the fire. But Mary would not sit down. She had not time, she said: and she went and stood by the window.

It was not a pleasant matter for her to enter upon, and she spoke very slightly and briefly. Just saying that if he, her uncle, had learnt anything through his son of Jane Hallet, it would be a relief to the Grey Ladies if he would impart it, and especially to the aunt, who was in a distressing state of suspense; fears, that Jane had made away with herself, existing in Greylands.

"My dear, I know nothing whatever of her," said Mr. Castlemaine, standing at the window by the side of his niece. "The whole of the affair has been most grievous to me, most annoying—as you may well conceive. I had some words with Harry at the time; sharp ones; and it has created a sort of coolness between us. Since then, we have mutually avoided the subject."

Mary sighed. "I cannot help being sorry for Jane," she said, "whatever may be the end. She is too good to have lost herself. You do not know, Uncle James, how nice she is."

"'Sorry' is not the word for it," emphatically spoke the Master of Greylands, his stern tone meant for his absent son. "I always held the Hallets in respect."

Mary turned from the window to depart. Other things were perplexing her as well as this unfortunate business. It struck her more and more how ill her uncle looked; ill, and full of care. Lines had begun to indent themselves on his once smooth brow.

"Are you well, Uncle James?" she stayed to say.

"Why do you ask?"

"You do not look well. There is something in your face now that—that—"

"That what, child?"

"That reminds me of papa. As he looked the last month or two of his life."

"Ay. I have had some worry lately, from more sources than one. And that tries a man's looks, Mary, worse than all."

He attended her downstairs. She said farewell to the red parlour, and commenced her walk back to the Nunnery.

Somewhat later, before the dusk of the November evening came on, Madame Guise attired herself to take home Marie. The little girl was showing symptoms of a delicate chest, and the Sisters had begged her mother to let her be in betimes. To please the child they went on through the back buildings, which were at some distance from the house, that she might see the ducks, and cocks and hens.

Quitting the fold-yard to cross the meadow, which would bring them round to the avenue, they came upon Mr. North. He sat on the stump of a tree, sketching a bit of the old barn.

"Are you here, George!" spoke Madame. "What are you doing?"

He held out the sketch to show her: pulling little Marie to him at the same time, to give her a kiss.

"Why you not come to see me?" asked the child in French. For she had taken a great fancy to this pleasant gentleman, who sometimes had bonbons in his pocket for her, calling him, at the Nunnery, little incipient coquette, le joli monsieur.

"Ah, I think I must come and see Miss Marie one of these fine days. Does Marie like dolls?"

"I like four, five dolls," said Marie.

"Four, five!" laughed George. "Why it would be an army. We shall have to dismantle a shop.

"I must be going, Marie," said her mother. "And you will have to make haste with that drawing, George. You will not see very much longer."

"Oh, I shall finish it."

"Have you heard anything, George—gathered anything—that can throw light on poor Anthony?" she looked back, to ask in a whisper.

"Never a word," he answered.

"Nor I. I begin almost to despair. Au revoir."

Meanwhile, indoors, Mr. Castlemaine had gone up to his room again, and Flora in the red parlour was making herself disagreeable as usual. The young lady's insistence that Marie should stay to tea had met with no response, and she was sulky in consequence.

For some little time she relieved herself by kicking her feet about, throwing down the fire-irons, and giving shakes to the table to disturb Ethel. By-and-by, when it grew dusk, and Mrs. Castlemaine had to hold her book very close to her eyes and Ethel to put up her drawing, the young lady saw a larger field for annoyance. Advancing to the piano, she brought both her hands down on the keys with her whole might. The result was a crash that might have aroused the seven sleepers.

"How dare you, Flora?" exclaimed Ethel. "Don't you know the piano was tuned this week?"

A derisive laugh: and another crash.

"Mamma, will you speak to her?"

Crash the third. Mrs. Castlemaine, absorbed by her book of romance, took no notice whatever.

"Do you think I will have my piano served in that way and the wires broken?" cried Ethel, starting up. "What a dreadful child you are!"

A tussle—for the young lass was strong, and was leaning with her whole weight and her two arms on the keys—and then Ethel succeeded in shutting and locking it. It was Ethel's own piano: a present to her from Mr. Castlemaine, and a beautiful instrument. Mademoiselle la méchante turned to the table, took up Ethel's drawing-book and began rumpling the leaves.

"Oh, mamma, mamma, why do you not speak to her?" cried Ethel, in distress, as she tried to get possession of the book, and failed. "Mamma!"

"How tiresome you are, Ethel!" exclaimed Mrs. Castlemaine explosively: for her story was at a most interesting part, and she could not be disturbed during these last few moments of daylight. "Sit down and be quiet. The dear child would do no harm, if you only let her alone."

The dear child had retreated to the open part of the room beyond the table, and was dancing there like a little maniac, flirting over the leaves at Ethel in derision. These petty annoyances are hard to bear. Injustice is hard to bear, even where the temper is naturally as sweet as Ethel's.

"Give me that book," said Ethel, going up to Flora.

"I shan't."

"I tell you, Flora, to give it to me."

Flora was holding the book open above her head, a cover stretched in each hand, and laughing an ugly, mocking laugh. Suddenly, without warning, she dashed it full in Ethel's face: a pretty sharp blow.

Smarting, angry, Ethel seized the tiresome child by the arms. Flora shrieked, and called out in a rage that Ethel was pinching her. Very likely it might be so, for the grasp was a tight one. Flora dropped the book, and struck Ethel in the face with all the force of her wrathful hand. Her pale face tingling with the smart, agitated, indignant, but the book secured, Ethel stood before Mrs. Castlemaine.

"Am I to bear this, mamma?—and you look on and say nothing!"

"You should let her alone: it is your own fault," contemptuously retorted Mrs. Castlemaine.

Justice in that house for her!—unless Mr. Castlemaine was at hand!—Ethel had long ceased to hope for it. But the present moment was unusually bitter; it tried her terribly. She quitted the room; and, seeing the hall-door open, ran out in a storm of tears and sobs, and dashed along the path.

It was dusk but not dark; the bared trees, the wintry shrubs, the cold beds telling of the departed flowers, all spoke of loneliness. But not more lonely, they, than Ethel.

She stood when she came to the outer gate and flung her arms upon it, sobbing bitterly; gazing down the avenue, as if longing to go forth into the world for ever. Alas, there was no chance of that; she was tied to this home, so oftentimes made miserable. Had Ethel been poor she might have gone out as governess: but that plea could not be raised.

Bending her face upon her hands, which rested still upon the gate, she gave way to all the minute's gloomy anguish, weeping aloud. Not a living being was in sight or hearing; she believed herself as much alone as though it had been some unpeopled desert and could indulge her passionate grief at will.

"Oh Ethel, what is this?"

It was a soft, low, pained voice that spoke the words in her ear; a fond hand was laid upon her head; the only voice, the only hand that could have thrilled her heart.

Mr. North, passing into the avenue on his way home from sketching the piece of the old barn, his portfolio being under his arm, had come upon her thus. Opening the gate, he drew her on to the bench under the high laurel trees and sat down by her.

"Now, tell me what it is?"

Beguiled by the seduction of the moment, smarting still under the treatment she had received, contrasting his loving, gentle kindness with the cruel indifference of the only mother she had ever known, Ethel sobbed out a brief account of what had passed. His breast heaved with angry passion.

"Is it often so, Ethel?"

"Oh yes, very. It has been so for years. I have never had any one to really love me since my father died; I have never known what it is to have a securely happy home: only this one of frequent turbulence. I wish I could run away from it!"

He was no more prudent than she. He forgot wisdom, circumstances, reason: all. His breath short, his words unchosen, he poured forth the tale of his love, and asked her if she would be his wife. Ethel bent her face on his coat-sleeve, and cried silent, happy tears.

"You know, you must know, how I have loved you, Ethel. I should have spoken long ago, but that circumstances held me back. Even now I fear that I cannot speak openly to Mr. Castlemaine: it may be some little time first. But oh, my darling, you have not, you cannot have mistaken my love."

Not a word. It was early yet for confession from her. But her face was still on his arm.

"For one thing, I am not rich, Ethel. I have quite enough for comfort, but not that which would give you a home like this. And Mr. Castlemaine—"

"I would rather be in a cottage with bread, than here," she interrupted, all her candour rising to the surface.

"And Mr. Castlemaine may not choose that you shall pit this house for one less well set-up, I was about to say, my love," he went on. "What we might find sufficient competence, he might deem poverty."

"I have plenty of money of my own," said Ethel simply.

"Have you?" cried Mr. North, in a surprised and anything but a gratified tone. He had certainly never known or suspected that she had money; and he foresaw that the fact might be only an additional reason for Mr. Castlemaine's rejection of him. "It may be so much the worse for us, Ethel. I may come into money myself; quite sufficient to satisfy even Mr. Castlemaine; or I may not. It is this uncertainty that has helped to keep me silent. But come what will now, we cannot part."

No, they could never part. Heart beating against heart, knew and ratified it. He gathered her face to his, whispering his sweet love-vows as he kissed off its tears.

And, for Ethel, the lonely surroundings, the dreary paths, the bare beds, the wintry trees, seemed suddenly to have changed into the Garden of Paradise.

XXXV

The Last Cargo

At the window of her bedroom in the Grey Nunnery, steadily gazing out to sea, stood Mary Ursula Castlemaine. The night was almost as light as though the moon were shining: for a sort of light haze, partially covering the skies, seemed to illumine the earth and make things visible.

December had come in, but the weather was still balmy: people said to one another that they were going to have no winter. It had been one of those exceptional years when England seems to have borrowed some more genial climate: since the changeable spring there had been only smiles and sunshine.

As the days and weeks had gone on since that communication made to Miss Castlemaine by Walter Dance the night of his accident (to be retracted by him in the morning), the doubt in her mind and the uneasiness it caused rarely gave her rest. She had not dared to speak of it to Mr. Castlemaine: had she been perfectly sure that he was in ignorance in regard to it—in short, to speak out plainly, that he was not implicated, she would have told him all; but the uncertainty withheld her. The evidence of her own senses she could not question, therefore she did believe, that the wholesale smuggling, confessed to by young Dance in his fear of death, was an actual fact—that cargoes of lace, and what not, were periodically run. The question agitating her was—had, or had not, this treason the complicity of the Master of Greylands? If it had, she must be silent on the subject for ever; if it had not, why then she would like to communicate with himself upon it. For an idea had taken firm hold of her, arising she knew not from what instinct, that the ill-fate of Anthony—had any ill-fate in truth overtaken him—must have arisen through the doings of one of these disturbed nights when the Friar's Keep was invaded by lawless bands of sailors.

It was for this reason she could not rest; it was this never-forgotten thought that disturbed her peace by day and her sleep by night. The smuggling and the smugglers she would only have been too glad to forget; but the mysterious fate of Anthony lay on her mind like a chronic nightmare. Another thing, too, added to her disquietude. The

Grey Monk, about which nothing had been heard for some weeks past, was now, according to public rumour, appearing again.

In her heart she suspected that this Grey Monk and all the rest of the mystery had to do with the smuggling and with that only. Reason told her, or strove to tell her, that Commodore Teague was the principal in it all, the cunning man, for whom the goods were run; and she tried to put down that latent doubt of Mr. Castlemaine that would rise up unbidden. If she could but set that little doubt at rest! she was ever saying to herself. If she could but once ascertain that her uncle had nothing to do with the unlawful practices, why then she would disclose to him what she knew, and leave him to search out this clue to the disappearance of Anthony.

Many a night had she stood at her casement window as she was standing now; though not always, perhaps oftener than not. But not until to-night had she seen the same two-masted vessel—or what she took to be the same. It had certainly not been visible at sunset: but there it lay now, its masts tapering upwards, and its shape distinctly visible in the white haze, just in the same spot that it had been that other night.

Mary wrapped herself up, and put her casement window open, and sat down and watched. Watched and waited. As the clocks told midnight, some stir was discernible on board; and presently the small boats, as before, came shooting out from the ship through the water. There could be no mistake: another of those nefarious cargoes was about to be run.

With a pale face but resolute heart, Mary Ursula Castlemaine rose up. She would go forth again through the secret passage, and look on at these men. Not to denounce them; not to betray her presence or her knowledge of what they were about; but simply to endeavour to ascertain whether her uncle made one at the work.

Procuring the keys and the dark lantern, Mary started. There was some delay at setting out, in consequence of her being unable to open the first door. Try with all her force, though she would and did, she could not turn the key in the lock. And she was on the point of giving it up as hopeless, when the key yielded. At least a quarter of an hour must have been hindered over this.

It was colder by far in the passage than it had been those other nights, for the time of the year was later: cold, and damp, and wofully dreary. Mary's courage oozed out at every step. Once she paused, questioning whether she could go on with this, but she reasoned herself into it. She reached the other end, set her light on the floor, and put the key into this second door.

Meanwhile the boats had come in, been hauled up on the beach, and the goods were being landed. The men worked with a will. They wore sea-boots and waded through the water with the bales on their shoulders. Much jabbering was carried on, for some of the sailors were foreigners; but all spoke in covert tones. No one could be near enough to hear them, by land or by sea; they felt well assured of that; but it was always best to be prudent. The sailors were working as they worked on board ship, open and undisguised; Commodore Teague was undisguised; but the other three men—for there were three others—wore capes and had huge caps tied on over their ears and brows; and in the uncertain light their best friends might not have known them. Two of these, it is as well to say it, were Tom Dance and his son; the other was a tall, slender, fine-figured young man, who seemed to look on, rather than to work, and who had not the heavy sea-boots on. But there was no sign of the Master of Greylands. The bales were carried up and put down in the dry, close to the walls of the Keep. When all the goods that were to come out of the ship should be landed, then the sailors would help to carry them through the passage to the cellars of the Hutt, before finally returning on board.

"Where you lay de pistols?" asked a sailor in imperfect English, as he slung down a huge bale from his shoulder.

"Down there as usual, Jansen," replied another, pointing to some raised stone-work projecting from the walls of the Keep. "And the cutlasses too. Where should they be!"

"What do Jansen ask that for, Bill?" questioned one, of the last speaker.

"I get a bad dream last night," said Jansen, answering for himself. "I dream we all fighting, head, tail, wi' dem skulking coastguard. 'Jack,' he says to me in dream, 'where de knives, where de pistols?'—and we search about and we not find no knives, no pistols, and dey overpower us, and I call out, an' den I wake."

"I don't like them dreams," cried one of the ship's crew. "Dreams be hanged; there's nothing in 'em," struck in Tom Dance. "I dreamed one night, years ago, as my old mother was lying dead afore me: stead o' that, she told me next day she'd get married again if I didn't behave myself."

"Bear a hand here, Dance," said the Commodore.

At this moment, there was heard the sounds of a boat, clashing up through the waters.

Before the men could well look out, or discover what it meant, she was close in, and upon them. A boat that had stolen silently out from under the walls of the Grey Nunnery, where she had been lying concealed, waiting to pounce upon her prey. It was a boat belonging to the preventive service, and it contained Mr. Superintendent Nettleby and his coastguardsmen. After years of immunity the smugglers were discovered at last.

"In the King's name!" shouted the superintendent, as he sprung into the shallow water.

M. Jansen's dream had not told him true; inasmuch as the pistols and cutlasses lay ready to hand, and were at once snatched up by their owners. A desperate fight ensued; a hand-to-hand struggle: pistols were fired, oaths were hissed out, knives were put to work. But though the struggle was fierce it was very short: all the efforts of the smugglers, both sailors and landsmen, were directed to securing their own safety by escaping to the ship. And just as Mary Ursula appeared upon the scene, they succeeded in pushing the boats off, and scrambling into them.

Mary was horror-struck. She had bargained for seeing rough men running packages of goods; but she had never thought of fighting and cries and murder. Once within the vaults of the Friar's Keep the noise had guided her to the open door she had seen before, open again now; and she stood there sick and trembling.

They did not see her; she took care of that: hiding behind a pillar, her lantern darkened, she peeped out, shivering, on the scene. In the confusion she understood very little; she saw very little; though the cause of it all was plain enough to her mind—the smugglers had been surprised by the preventive men. In the preventive-service boat lay a bound and wounded sailor-prisoner, and also one of the customs' men who had been shot through the leg: not to speak of minor wounds and contusions on both sides. Of all that, however, Mary knew nothing until later. There she stood close to the scene of turmoil, hearing the harsh voices, the rough words, glancing out at the pile of goods, and at the dusky figures before her, moving about in the night. It was like a panoramic picture dimly seen.

Almost as by sleight of hand, for Mary did not see how or where they went, the men and the commotion disappeared together. The ship's boats, unfollowed, were hastening away to the ship; but what became of Mr. Nettleby and his staff? A moment ago, the small portion of the beach close before her, that was not under water, had been alive with the preventive men; Mary had recognised the superintendent's voice as he shouted out some order, and now not a soul was visible. No doubt they were exploring the inner corners of this bit of beach, never suspected of fraud, never visited by his Majesty's servants until now. She cautiously advanced a step or two and looked out. There lay, hauled up on the beach halfway, the waiting boat, which she supposed to be unoccupied: the two wounded men, one of them having fainted from loss of blood, were lying down flat in it, invisible to her.

A short while, and the officers reappeared. Mary drew back and went behind a pillar. Some of them got into the boat, and it was pushed off; three of them remained, either from want of space in the boat, or to keep guard over the goods; one of them was Mr. Nettleby.

Of what use for Mary to stay? None. She could not solve the doubt touching her uncle. Oh, that she had never come! she kept thinking to herself; that she had not had this most dreadful scene portrayed to her! Never again, she felt all too certain of it, should she attempt to enter the Keep by the subterranean passage.

Pushing up the slide of one side of the lantern to guide her steps, she was retracing her way through the vaults, when a ray of the light flashed upon a figure. A moving figure in woman's clothes, that seemed to be endeavouring to hide itself. Mary lifted her lantern, and saw the face of Jane Hallet.

Of Jane Hallet! Just for a moment or two a sickness as of some supernatural fear seized upon Miss Castlemaine. For Jane had never been heard of yet in Greylands, and very little doubt existed that she had found her bed at the bottom of the sea. The dark hood she was in the habit of wearing at night had fallen back from her face: her eyes wore a strange, terrified, appealing look in the sudden and startling light.

Recovering her better reason, Mary laid her detaining hand upon her before she could escape. Which of the two faces was the whiter, it were hard to say.

"It is you, Jane Hallet!"

"Yes, madam, it is me," gasped Jane in answer.

"Where have you been all this while, and whence do you come? And what brings you in this place now?"

The explanation was given in a few brief sentences. Jane, alarmed at the idea presented to her by the Grey Ladies of going out to service, against which step there existed private reasons, had taken straight refuge in Dame Dance's cottage under the cliff; she had been there ever since and was there still. Old Mrs. Dance was like a mother to her, she added; and had been in her entire confidence for a long while. As to what brought her in that place to-night, why—she was watching,—she told Miss Castlemaine with much emotion—watching for the dreadful evil that had to-night occurred.

"I have been dreading it always, madam," she said, her breath short in its agitation. "I knew, through my brother, of the work that was sometimes done here—though he betrayed it to me by accident, not intentionally. I have come to the chapel ruins of a night to see if there were preparations being made for running a cargo, and to look whether the vessel, whose shape I knew, was standing out at sea. One night in the autumn I saw them run the goods: I was watching all the while. It was one o'clock when I got home, and my aunt was fit to strike me: for I could not tell her why I stayed out."

"Watching for what?" imperiously spoke Miss Castlemaine.

"Oh, madam, don't you see?—for the preventive men. I was ever fearing that they would discover the work some night, and surprise it— as they have now done. I thought if I were on the watch for this (which nobody else, so far as I could guess, seemed to fear or think of) I might be in time to warn—to warn those who were doing it. But the officers were too cunning for me, too quick: as I stood just now looking over the low brink in the chapel ruins, I saw a boat shoot past from underneath the walls of the Nunnery, and I knew what it was. Before I got down here the fight had begun."

Jane had gone into a fit of trembling. Somehow Miss Castlemaine's heart was hardening to her.

"At nine o'clock this evening I thought I saw the vessel standing off in the far distance," resumed Jane: "so I came out later and watched her move up to her usual place, and have been watching since in the chapel ruins."

"May I inquire who knew of this watching of yours?" asked Mary Ursula, her tone full of resentment.

"Not any one, madam. Not any one in the world."

"Not Mr. Harry Castlemaine?"

"Oh, no. I should not dare to speak of the subject to him, unless he first spoke of it to me. I have wished he would."

"As there is nothing more that can be done here to-night, of watching or else, I think you had better return home, Jane Hallet," spoke Miss Castlemaine in the same proud, cold tone: though she inwardly wondered which way of egress Jane would take.

"I was just going," spoke the trembling girl. "There—there is not—oh! forgive me, madam!—any one lying wounded on the beach, I hope?"

"I presume not," replied Miss Castlemaine. "The superintendent and his men are there."

Jane Hallet turned meekly, and disappeared amid the pillars. Miss Castlemaine rightly conjectured that there must be some stairs leading from these lower cloisters to the cloisters above that opened on the chapel ruins. By these Jane had no doubt descended, and would now ascend. In point of fact, it was so. George Hallet had eventually made a clean breast of all the secret to Jane, including the openings and passages. But the underground passage to the Grey Nunnery neither he nor any one else had known of.

Miss Castlemaine turned to it now. She was crossing towards it, her dim lantern held aloft to steer her between the pillars, when her foot stumbled against something. Pacing slowly, she did not fall, and recovered herself at once. Bringing the light to bear, she stooped down and saw a man lying there on his back. He looked immensely tall, and wore a big cape, and had a cap muffled over his forehead and eyes, and lay still as one dead. With another faint sickness of heart, Mary pulled the cap upwards, for she thought she recognised the handsome features. Alas, yes! they were those of Harry Castlemaine: and they were set in what looked like the rigidness of death.

With a shrill cry—for her feelings got the better of her—Mary called him by name, and shook him gently. No, there was no response: he was surely dead! She tore the cape and cap off, flinging them aside; she put her hand to his heart, and could feel no pulse; she lifted one of his hands, and it fell again like a heavy weight. There could be little doubt that he must have been wounded during the fight, had run into the vaults, intending to make his escape by the chapel ruins, and had fallen down exhausted. Panting with fear and emotion, all considerations lost sight of in this one great shock, Mary went back to the beach crying for aid, and supremely astonishing Mr. Superintendent Nettleby.

Mr. Harry Castlemaine! Mr. Harry Castlemaine lying inside there as one dead! Why, how did that come about? What had brought him down there? unless, indeed, he had heard the row and the fighting? But then—how did he get down?

Mr. Nettleby spoke these problems aloud, as he proceeded by Miss Castlemaine's side to the spot, guided by her lantern, and followed by his two men. He assumed that the Grey Nunnery must have been aroused by the noise, and that the Lady Superior had come forth to see what it meant: and he politely apologised for having been the cause of disturbance to the Sisters. Mary allowed him to think this: and made no answer to his further expressed wonder of how she found her way down.

When they reached the spot where lay Harry Castlemaine, the first object the rays of the lantern flashed on was Jane Hallet. Aroused by Miss Castlemaine's cry, she had hastened back again and was now kneeling beside him, her trembling hands chafing his lifeless ones, her face a distressing picture of mute agony.

"Move away," spoke Miss Castlemaine.

Jane rose instantly, with a catching of the breath, and obeyed. Mr. Superintendent Nettleby, asking for the lantern to be held by one of his men, and to have its full light turned on, knelt down and proceeded to make what examination he could.

"I don't think he is dead, madam," he said to Mary Ursula, "but I do fear he is desperately wounded. How the dickens can it have come about?" he added, in a lower tone, meant for himself, and rising from his knees. "Could one of the fools have fired off a shot in here, and caught him as he was coming on to us? Well, we must get him up to land somehow—and my boat's gone off!"

"He had better be brought to the Grey Nunnery: it is the nearest place," spoke Mary.

"True," said the officer. "But which on earth is the way to it out of here?"

"Up these stairs. I will show you," said Jane Hallet, stepping forward again. "Please let me go on with the lantern."

She caught it up: she seemed nearly beside herself with grief and distress; and the officer and men raised Harry Castlemaine. Mary remembered the cape she had thrown aside, and could not see it, or the cap either. It was just as well, she thought, for the things had looked to her like garments worn for disguise, and they might have told tales. Even then an idea was crossing her that the worst—the complicity of the Castlemaines with the smuggling—might be kept from the world.

Yes, it was just as well: that cape and cap might have been recognised by the superintendent and his men as being the same sort that were worn by the iniquitous offenders they had surprised. No such sinners in the whole decalogue of the world's crimes, according to the estimation of Mr. Nettleby, as those who defrauded his Majesty's revenues.

"He must have come out without his hat, or else lost it," spoke the superintendent, looking down at the head he supported. "Take care, my men, that's—blood."

The stairs were soon reached: some winding steps cut in stone. Jane Hallet held the lantern to show the way; Miss Castlemaine, saying never a word of the secret passage, followed her; the men with their burden bringing up the rear. It was a difficult job to bring him up, for the staircase was very narrow. They came out by a concealed door at the end of the upper cloisters, and had to walk through them to the chapel ruins. Mr. Nettleby never supposed but that the two women, as well as Harry Castlemaine, had come down by this route.

"To think that I should never have suspected any stairs were there! or that there was another set of cloisters under these!" he exclaimed in self-humiliation, as he walked on through with the rest, avoiding the pillars. "Had I known it, and that there was a door opening to that strip of beach below, it would have been enough to tell me what might be going on. But how the deuce do they contrive to get rid of the goods after they are run?"

For Mr. Superintendent Nettleby was still ignorant of on thing— the secret passage to Commodore Teague's house. He would not be likely to discover or suspect that until the official search took place that would be made on the morrow.

Once more the Nunnery was about to be disturbed to admit a wounded man at midnight: this second man, alas! wounded unto death. Tom Dance's son had gone forth to the world again, little the worse for his wounds; for the son and heir of the Master of Greylands, earth was closing.

The clanging night-bell aroused the inmates; and Sister Rachel, who was that week portress, went down accompanied by Sister Caroline. To describe their astonishment when they saw the line of those waiting to enter, would be impossible. Harry Castlemaine, whom the motion and air had revived, borne by Mr. Nettleby and two of the coastguardsmen; the Superior, Mary Ursula; and the resuscitated Jane Hallet! Jane the erring, with the Nunnery lantern!

"Business called me abroad to-night: I did not disturb you," quietly observed Sister Mary Ursula to the round-eyed Sisters; and it was all the explanation she gave, then or later.

Harry was taken into the same room that Walter Dance had been, and laid upon the same flat, wide sofa. One of the men ran off for Mr. Parker. The other went back with the superintendent to the scene of the struggle. The captured goods, so many of them as had been landed, had to be zealously guarded: Mr. Superintendent Nettleby had never gained such a feather in his official cap as this.

Harry Castlemaine lay where he had been placed, his once fresh face bereft of its fine colour, his eyes open to the movements around.

A patient like this was altogether different from young Dance the fisherman, and the Sisters had gone to awaken and amaze the Nunnery with the news. Only Mary Ursula was with him.

"Mr. Parker will soon be here, Harry," she said gently, bending over him.

A faint smile crossed his lips. "He can do nothing for me, Mary."

"Nay, you must not think that. You feel ill, faint; I know it; but—"

Some slight stir behind her had caught Mary's senses, and caused her to turn. There was Jane Hallet, standing half in, half out at the door, a mute, deprecatory appeal for permission to enter, shining unmistakably on her sad white face.

"Back!" said Mary with calm authority, advancing to the door with her most stately step, her hand raised to repel the intruder. "I told you to go home, Jane Hallet: it is the only thing you can do. You have no right to intrude yourself into the Nunnery. Go."

And she quietly closed the door, shutting Jane out, and returned to the bedside.

Harry's hand was feebly stretched out: it fell on her arm. "Let her come in, Mary: she is my wife."

"Your wife!"

"Yes; my wife. She has been my wife all along."

"I do not understand," faltered Mary Ursula, feeling she hardly knew how.

"We were married at the beginning of last winter. Fear of my father's displeasure has prevented my declaring it."

Mary was silent. Her heart throbbed unpleasantly.

"Jane is too good a girl for aught else," he resumed, the subject seeming to impart to him some fictitious strength. "She has borne all the obloquy in patience and silence for my sake. Did you suppose, Mary, that the favourite pupil of the Grey Ladies, trained by them, could have turned out unworthily?"

"You should, at least, have confided this to Miss Hallet, Harry."

"No; to her the least of all. Miss Hallet has her pride and her notions, and would have proclaimed it in the marketplace."

"I seem not to comprehend yet," replied Mary, many remembrances crowding upon her. In point of fact, she scarcely knew whether to believe him. "Last winter—yes, and since then, Harry—you appeared to be seeking Ethel Reene for your wife."

"I once had an idea of Ethel. I knew not that the warm affection I felt for her was but that of a brother: when I fell in love with Jane I learnt the truth. My teasings of Ethel have been but jest, Mary: pursued to divert attention from my intimacy with my real love, my wife."

Mary Ursula sighed. Harry had always been random and blamable in some way or other. What a blow this would be for the Master of Greylands!

"You will let her come in, Mary! Are you doubting still?" he resumed, noting her perplexed countenance. "Why, Mary Ursula, had my relations with Jane been what the world assumed, can you imagine I should have had the hardihood to intrude my brazen face here amid the Sisters when she was taken ill? I have my share of impudence, I am told; but I have certainly not enough for that. I sought that minute's interview with Jane to bid her be firm—to bear all reproaches, spoken and unspoken, for my sake and my father's peace. The only wonder to me and to Jane also, has been that nobody ever suspected the truth."

Mary Ursula left the room. Jane was leaning against the wall outside in the semi-darkness, a picture of quiet tribulation. Too conscious of the estimation in which she was held, she did not dare assert herself. The lantern, which nobody had put out, stood on the passage slab: there was no other light. Mary drew her into the parlour—which was wholly dark, save for the reflected light that came in from the lantern. So much the better. Jealous for the honour of her family, Mary Ursula was feeling the moment bitterly, and her face would have shown that she was.

"Mr. Harry Castlemaine has been making a strange communication to me," she began. "He says he has married you."

"Oh, madam, it is true," returned Jane hysterically, the sudden revulsion of feeling at finding it was known, the relief from her miserable concealment, taking vent in a flood of tears. "We were married last November."

"By whom?"

"Parson Marston," sobbed Jane. "He married us in his church at Stilborough."

Surprise, resentment, condemnation of Parson Marston, overpowered Miss Castlemaine and kept her silent. Thinking of this inferior girl—very inferior as compared with The Castlemaines—as they had all been thinking lately, it was not in human nature that Mary should not feel it strongly. She had her share of the Castlemaine pride; though she had perhaps thought that it was laid down within her when she came out of her home at Stilborough to enter the Grey Nunnery.

"It was very strange of Mr. Marston; very wrong."

Jane's sobs did not allow her to make any rejoinder. Of course it was wrong: nobody felt more assured of that than Jane. She did not dare to tell how Harry Castlemaine's masterful will had carried all with him, including herself and the parson. Jane had perhaps been quite willing to be carried; and the parson yielded to "You must," and was besides reprehensibly indifferent. "He would only have taken the girl off to a distance and got tied up by a strange parson," was Mr. Marston's excuse later, when speaking of it. "I am not to blame; I didn't set afloat the marriage."

"How long should you have kept it secret?" asked Miss Castlemaine, looking at Jane in her distress.

"As long as my husband had wished me to keep it, madam," was the sobbing answer. "He was always hoping some occasion might arise for declaring it; but he did not like to vex Mr. Castlemaine. It was my aunt's not knowing it that grieved me most."

"I almost wonder you did not tell Sister Mildred when you were here," observed Mary, musing on the past.

"Oh if I had been able to tell her!" returned the girl, impulsively clasping her hands. "It was very hard to bear, madam, all that blame; but I tried to be patient. And many might have thought nearly as ill of me for letting one so much above me make me his wife."

"Has no one at all known it?" asked Mary.

"Only old Mrs. Dance. She has known it from the first. We used to meet at her cottage."

"Well, Jane, what is done cannot be undone. You are his wife, it seems, and have been undeserving of the reproach of light conduct passed upon you. So far I am, for your sake, glad. He has asked to see you. You can go in."

So Jane Hallet—no longer Hallet, however,—crept into the chamber, where her husband lay dying, and stood by his side, her heart breaking.

"Don't grieve, Jane, more than you can help," he said, clasping her hand. "This will answer one good end: you will be cleared."

She fell on her knees, weeping silent tears. "To save your life I would remain under the cloud for ever," she sighed. "Oh, is there no hope?—is there no hope?"

"Well, we shall see: the doctor will be here soon," said Harry evasively. "There! dry your tears, Jane; take heart, my dear."

And the doctor came without much further delay, and examined his patient, and found that a bullet had lodged itself within him.

"There must be an operation," said he, smoothing over his grave face. And he hastened to despatch a messenger on a fleet horse for Surgeon Croft, the most clever operating surgeon in Stilborough.

But Mr. Parker knew quite well that there remained no hope in this world for Harry Castlemaine.

XXXVI

Gone!

Morning dawned. The Grey Nunnery was like a fair. What with the doctors and their gigs, for two surgeons came from Stilborough, and the Sisters passing in and out on various errands, and the excited people who assembled in numbers round the gates, a stranger might have wondered at the commotion. More than once had Greylands been excited during the year now swiftly approaching its close, but never as much as now. A dreadful encounter between smugglers and the preventive men! and Harry Castlemaine shot down by one of their stray bullets! and Jane Hallet come to life again!

The Master of Greylands sat by the dying couch, giving vent now and again to his dire distress. There was no hope for his son; he knew it from the medical men: and his son had been the one only thing he had much cared for in life.

Of all the blows that had fallen on James Castlemaine, none had been like unto this. The shock alone was terrible. It reached him first through one of those Grey Sisters against whom he had been so prejudiced. Sister Ann had gone running over to knock up the Dolphin, lest cordials, or else, which the Nunnery lacked, might be required for the wounded man. After arousing John Bent and telling the news, she sped onwards under the night stars, to apprise the Master of Greylands. Greylands' Rest lay still and quiet; its doors and windows closed, the blinds drawn down. Sister Ann rang, and was immediately answered inside by the bark of a dog. "Cesar, Cesar!" she called out at the top of her voice, to assure the dog that it was a friend; and Cesar, recognising the tones, ceased his bark, which was impolitic on Sister Ann's part, for if he had kept on barking it would have aroused the inmates. Sister Ann waited and rang again; and then, terrified at the thought that the Master of Greylands might be too late to see his son, she retreated a few steps and shouted up to the windows. The Master heard it, and appeared looking out.

"Who is it?—what is it?" he asked, leaning from the window he had thrown up, and recognising with astonishment the dress of a Grey Sister.

"Oh, sir, it's bad news!" replied Sister Ann, "but I'm thankful to have awoke you. It's ill news about Mr. Harry, sir: and I've run all the way here, and am out of breath."

"What ill news about Mr. Harry?"

"He has been brought to the Nunnery wounded dreadfully. I've come up to ask you to make haste, sir, if you'd see him; for he may be bleeding to death."

"Wounded?—how?" gasped the Master, feeling as bewildered as a woman, and perhaps hard of belief.

"There has been a frightful fight to-night, they say, with smugglers, sir. Mr. Nettleby and two of the coastguardsmen brought him in. We don't know what to believe or think."

With a muttered word to the effect that he would go to the Nunnery directly, the Master of Greylands shut the window. Dressing in haste, he went forth on his errand. Of the two ways to the Nunnery, the Chapel Lane was somewhat the nearer one; and he took it. He bared his aching head to the night-air as he traversed it with fleet strides, wondering what extent of misery he might be entering upon. No very long space of time had elapsed since he sat in his room dwelling on the misfortunes and the deaths that the year had brought forth. Was there to be yet further misfortune?—another death? A death to him more cruel than any that had gone before it?

As he neared the turning to the Hutt, he dashed down the opening and tried the house-door and shouted—just as Sister Ann had tried and shouted at the door of Greylands' Rest some minutes before. The door was fast, and no response came: and the Master knocked at the little window that belonged to Teague's bedchamber. "Not back yet," he murmured to himself, after waiting barely a moment, and dashed back again and on towards the Nunnery. And there he fennel his worst fears as to Harry realised, and learnt from Mr. Parker that there was no hope of saving him.

The bleeding had been then stopped by Mr. Parker, but Harry had fainted. Before he revived and was collected enough to speak, or perhaps strong enough, the other surgeons came, and not one private word had been exchanged between father and son.

With the morning Harry was better. Better in so far as that he lay at tolerable ease and could converse at will. The surgeons had done for him what little could be done; but his life was only a question of hours. In a distress, the like of which he had never before experienced, sat the

Master of Greylands. His handsome, noble, attractive son, of whom he had been so proud, whom he had so beloved in his heart, was passing away from his sight for ever. His chair was drawn close to the couch, his hand lay on Harry's, his aching eyes rested on the pale, changed face. The whole world combined could not have wrought for him a trial such as this: his own death would have been as nothing to it: and the blow unnerved him.

They were alone together: none intruded unnecessarily on these closing hours. Harry gave briefly the history of the scene of the past night, thanking heaven aloud that his father was not present at it.

"The two first boats had not long been in, and not half their packages were landed, when another boat glided quietly up," said Harry. "I thought it was from the vessel with more goods, till I heard a shout in Nettleby's tones 'In the King's name,' and found the revenue men were leaping out of her. I ran to close the passage to Teague's, and was coming back again when I found myself struck here," touching his side. "The pain was horrible: I knew what it meant—that I was shot, and useless—and I slipped into the vaults, intending to get up to the chapel ruins, and so away. I must have fainted there, and fallen; for I remember nothing more until Nettleby and the rest were bringing me here."

"They found you lying there?"

"Not they. Mary Ursula."

"Mary Ursula!"

"It seems so. She was there with a lantern, I gather. Father, you will, doubtless, learn all the explanation you wish; I cannot give it. You know what this shot has done for me?"

The Master did not answer.

"It is my death. I forced Croft to tell me. By to-night all will be over."

Mr. Castlemaine, striving and struggling to maintain composure, broke down helplessly at the last words, and sobbed aloud with an emotion never before betrayed by him to man. The distress to Harry was all too great; he had been truly attached to his indulgent father.

"For my sake, father!—for the little time I have to stay!" he said, imploringly. And the Master smothered his grief as he best might.

With his hand held between his father's, and his sad eyes beseeching pardon for the offence which in strong life he had dreaded to tell, Harry Castlemaine made his confession: Jane Hallet was his wife. It was somewhat of a shock, no doubt, to the Master of Greylands, but it fell with comparative lightness on his ear: beside the one vast trouble close at hand, others seemed as nothing. Jane might be his son's wife; but his son would not live to own her as such to the world.

"Do you forgive me, father? That it was wrong, I am aware; but only myself know how dearly I grew to love her. The place has been heaping scorn upon her, but she bore it all for my sake, knowing she would be cleared when I could declare it to you."

"She has not deserved the scorn, then?"

"Never. I would not have sought to hurt a hair of her head. Say you forgive me, father!—the moments are passing."

"Yes, yes, I forgive you; I forgive you. Oh, my boy, I forgive all. I wish I could die instead of you."

"And—will you set her right with the world?" continued Harry, holding his father's hand against his cheek caressingly. "It is only you who can effectually do it, I think. And allow her a little income to maintain her in comfort?"

"Harry, I will do all."

"She is my wife, you see, father, and it is what should be. Your promise will ease my soul in dying. Had I lived, she would have shared my state and fortune.

"All, all; I will do all," said the Master of Greylands.

"For the past, it is not she who is to blame," continued Harry, anxious that there should be no misapprehension of Jane's conduct. "She would have held out against the marriage on account of my family, always begging of me to wait. But I would have my way. Do not visit the blame upon her, father, for she does not deserve it."

"I understand: she shall have all justice, Harry. Be at peace."

But, in spite of this one absorbing grief for his son, there was another care that kept intruding itself in no minor degree on the Master of Greylands: and that was the business connected with the smugglers. How much of that was known?—how much had good fortune been enabled to keep concealed? While the doctors were again with Harry towards midday, Mr. Castlemaine snatched a moment to go out of doors.

How strange the broad glare of day appeared to him! Coming out of the darkened room with its hushed atmosphere, its overlying sadness, into the light of the sun, high in the heavens, the hum of the crowding people, the stir of health and busy life, the Master of Greylands seemed to have passed into another world. The room he had left was as the grave, where his son would soon be; this moving scene as some passing pageantry, very redolent of mundane earth.

Which Greylands was making the most of,—the strange accident to Harry Castlemaine (every whit as strange as the self-shooting that had temporarily disabled young Dance; nay, stranger); or the astounding news touching the smugglers, or the reappearance of Jane Hallet—it was hard to say. All kinds of reports were afloat; some true, some untrue, as usual. Mr. Superintendent, Nettleby, it appeared, had for a considerable time suspected that smuggling to an extraordinary extent was carried on somewhere along this line of coast. From information supplied to him, he had little doubt that valuable goods found their contraband entrance, somewhere; within, say, the length of a dozen miles. The difficulty was—how to hit upon the spot. Surmises were chiefly directed to the little place called Beeton, a mile or two higher up. It presented unusual facilities for running contraband goods; slight incidents occurred from time to time that seemed to bear out the superintendent's suspicions of it; and his chief attention was directed to that place. It was directed to any spot rather than Greylands. Greylands, in the estimation of the revenue-men, was exempt from suspicion, or nearly exempt. Save the open beach, there was no spot at Greylands where a cargo could be run—and the superintendent took care that the beach should be protected. Not an idea existed that the little strip of beach under the old Friar's Keep could be made available for anything of the kind, or that it had a passage of communication with Commodore Teague's Hutt, or with any other place in the world. Counting on his ten fingers, Mr. Nettleby could number up fifteen months during which he had beset Beeton like a watchdog, and nothing at all had come of it. The unsuspected Greylands had been left at ease, as usual, to do what it would.

Upon Greylands the news fell like a thunderbolt. Had one of those cloud-electric missives suddenly fallen and shattered the rocks to pieces, it would not have caused more intense astonishment. The Friar's Keep been used as a place of smuggling for untold years!—and Commodore Teague was the head smuggler!—who used to stow away the goods in his big cellar till he could take them away in his spring cart! Greylands knew not how to believe this: and on the Commodore's score somewhat resented it, for he was an immense favourite. One fact seemed indisputable—the Commodore was not to be seen this morning, and his place was shut up.

The version generally believed was this. Mr. Superintendent Nettleby, observing, after dark had fallen, a suspicious-looking vessel lying nearly close in shore, and having had his attention directed to this same vessel once or twice before, had collected his men and taken up his place in the revenue-boat, under cover of the walls of the Grey Nunnery, and there waited until it was time to drop upon the smugglers: which he did, catching them in the act. Most of the men he surprised were sailors; he knew it by their attire and language; but there was at least one other man (if not two men) who was muffled up for disguise; and there was, without any disguise, working openly, Commodore Teague. The Commodore and these other men—take them at two—had escaped to the ship, and neither the superintendent nor his subordinates knew who they were. The wounded sailor-prisoner was a foreigner, who could speak but a few words of English. He gave his name as Jacob Blum, and appeared to know little about the affair, declaring solemnly that he had joined the vessel in Holland only a month before, and was not apprised that she was in the contraband trade.

But Harry Castlemaine—what caused him to be so fatally mixed up with the fight? Lacking an authorised version, the following sprung up; and, spreading from one to another, was soon accepted as truth. Mr. Harry, promenading about late in the night with his sweetheart, Jane Hallet (and sly enough she must have been, to have stayed all this while at old Goody Dance's, and never shown herself!), had his ears saluted with the noise and shots going on below. He rushed into the Keep and down the staircase to the vaults beneath (instinct having discovered the stairs to him at the right moment, as was supposed), where he was met and struck down by a stray shot, the fighters not even knowing that he was there. Jane Hallet must have followed him. Sister Mary Ursula's appearance on the scene, as mentioned by the two coastguardsmen, was accounted for in the same natural manner. She had heard the disturbance from her chamber-window—for of course the noise penetrated as far as the Grey Nunnery—and had gone forth, like a brave, good woman, to ascertain its meaning and see if succour was needed.

All these several reports—which running from one to another, grew into assured facts, as just said, in men's minds—were listened to by Mr. Castlemaine. He found that, as yet, not a shade of suspicion was directed to him or his house: he fervently hoped that it might not be. That would be one sup taken out of his cup of bitterness. Commodore Teague was regarded as the sole offender, so far as Greylands was concerned.

"To think that we should have been so deceived in any man!" exclaimed the landlord of the Dolphin, standing outside his door with his wife, and addressing Mr. Castlemaine and the crowd together. "I'd have believed anybody in the place to be a cheat, sir, rather than Teague."

"We have not had Teague's defence yet," spoke the Master of Greylands. "It is not right to entirely condemn a man unheard."

"But the coastguardsmen saw him there at work, sir," retorted ready-tongued Mrs. Bent. "Henry Mann says he was hard at it with his shirt sleeves stripped up. He'd not be helping for love: he must have had his own interest there."

The Master of Greylands was wisely silent. To defend Teague too much might have turned suspicion on himself: at least, he fancied so in his self-consciousness: and the probability was that the Commodore would never return to ascertain how he stood with Greylands.

In the course of the morning, making rather more commotion with its sail than usual, Tom Dance's fishing-boat came sailing in. Tom and his son were on board her, and a fair haul of fish. The various items of strange news were shouted out to it by half a dozen tongues as soon as it was within hailing distance. Tom gave vent to sundry surprised exclamations in return, as he found the cable and made the boat fast, and landed with a face of astonishment. The one item that seemed most to stagger him was the state of Mr. Harry Castlemaine.

"It can't be true!" he cried, standing still, while a change passed over his countenance. "Shot by smugglers!—dying! Mr. Harry Castlemaine!"

"Well, you see, Tom, it might ha' been them preventive-men,— 'twarn't obliged to ha' been they smugglers," said Jack Tuff. "Both sides was firing off, by all account, as thick as thieves. Which ever 'twas, Mr. Harry have got his death-shot. How wet your jersey is!"

Tom Dance turned in at his own door, threw off the "jersey" and other articles of his fishing toggery, flung on dry things, and went up towards the throng round the Dolphin. Mr. Castlemaine was just crossing back to the Nunnery, and looked at him, some involuntary surprise in his eyes.

"Is it you, Dance?"

"It's me, sir: just got in with the tide. I be struck stupid, pretty nigh, hearing what they've been telling me, down there," added Tom, indicating the beach.

"Ay, no doubt," said the Master of Greylands, in a subdued tone. But he walked on, saying no more.

MRS. HENRY WOOD

Tom Dance's confrères in the fishing trade had no idea but that he had sailed out in the ordinary way with the night tide. The reader knows that at midnight he was at least otherwise occupied. Tom had done a somewhat daring act. He and his son, alike uninjured in the fray, had escaped in the ship's boats; and Tom, flinging off his disguising cape and cap, his sea boots, and in fact most of his other attire, leaped into the water to swim to his fishing-boat, lying on the open beach. It was his one chance of non-discovery. He felt sure that neither he nor Walter had been recognized by Nettleby and his men; but, if they were to go off to Holland in the ship and so absent themselves from Greylands, it would at once be known that they were the two who had been seen taking part. No man in Greylands was so good a swimmer as Dance; and——he resolved to risk it. He succeeded. After somewhat of a battle, and the water was frightfully cold, he gained his boat. It had just floated with the incoming tide. By means of one of the ropes, of which there were several hanging over the side, he climbed on board, put on some of his sea-toggery that was there, and slipped the cable. The anchor was small, not at all difficult for one man to lift; but Tom Dance wanted to save both time and noise, and it was easiest to slip the cable. The moderate breeze was in his favour blowing off the land. He hoisted the staysail, and was soon nearing the ship, which was already spreading her canvas for flight. From the ship Dance took his son on board. They stayed out all night, fishing: it was necessary, to give a colouring to things and avert suspicion; and they had now, close upon midday, come in with a tolerable haul of fish. Walter had orders to stay on board, occupy himself there, and be still, while Tom landed to gather news and to see which way the wind lay.

But he had never thought to hear these sad tidings about Harry Castlemaine.

"It has a'most done me up," he said, returning on board again and speaking to his son. "He was the finest young fellow in the country, and the freest in heart and hand. And to be struck like this!"

"How much is known, father?" asked Walter, stopping in his employment of sorting the fish.

"Nothing's known that I can hear," growled Tom Dance, for he was feeling the crossness of affairs just then. "It's all laid on Teague's back—as Teague always good-naturedly said it would be, if a blow-up came."

"Can Teague ever come back, father?"

"Teague don't want to. Teague has said oftentimes that he'd as soon, or sooner, be over among the Dutch than here. He was always ready for the start, I expect. He'll be writing for us to go over and see him next summer."

"I know he liked them foreign towns: he's often been in 'em," observed Walter. "And he mist have feathered his nest pretty well."

"Yes; he won't need to look about him for his pipe and chop of a day. Our chief nest-egg is smashed though, lad. No more secret night-work for us ever again."

"Well, you must have feathered the nest too, father," returned Walter, privately glad that the said night-work was over, for he had never liked it in his heart.

"You just hold your tongue about the feathering of nests," sharply reprimanded Tom. "Once let folks fancy I've got more than fishing would bring in, and they might set on to ask where it come from. Your nest won't be feathered by me, I can tell ye, young man, unless you keep a still tongue in your head."

"There's no fear of me, father."

"And there'd better not be," concluded Tom Dance. "I'd ship ye off after Teague, short and quick, if I thought there was."

THE AFTERNOON WAS DRAWING TO its close. On the rude couch, more exhausted than he had been in the morning, getting every minute now nearer to death, lay Harry Castlemaine. His stepmother, Flora, Ethel, good old Sister Mildred, and Mary Ursula, all had taken their last farewell of him. Mrs. Bent had contrived to get in, and had taken hers with some bitter tears. Mr. Parker had just gone out again: the Sister in attendance, perceiving what was at hand, had soon followed him. The poor wife, Jane, only acknowledged to be left, had gone through her last interview with her husband and said her last adieu. Nearly paralysed with grief, suffering from undue excitement which had been repressed so long, she had relapsed into a state of alarming prostration, that seemed worse than faintness. Mr. Parker administered an opiate, and she was now lying on her old bed above, cared for by Sister Mildred. And the sole watcher by the dying bed was Mr. Castlemaine.

Oh, what sorrow was his! The only living being he had greatly cared for in the world dying before his aching eyes. It was for him he had lived, had schemed, had planned and hoped. That nefarious smuggling had been only carried on in reference to Harry's prospective wealth. But for Harry's future position, that Mr. Castlemaine had so longed to

MRS. HENRY WOOD

establish on a high footing, he had thrown it up long before. It was all over now; the secret work, the hope, and the one cherished life.

"Father, don't!" panted Harry, as Mr. Castlemaine sat catching up ever and anon his breath in sobs, though his eyes were dry. "It may be better for me to go. I used to look forward, I've often done it, to being a good son to you in your old age: but it may be best as it is."

Mr. Castlemaine could not trust himself to answer.

"And you'll forgive me for all the trouble I've cost you! As I trust God has forgiven me. I have been thinking of Him all day, father."

A terrible sob now. Mr. Castlemaine knew not how to keep down his emotion. Oh, how bitter it was to him, this closing hour, his heart aching with its pain!

"It won't be so very long, father; you'll be coming, you know: and it is a journey that we must all take. What's the matter?—it's getting dark!"

Mr. Castlemaine raised his eyes to the window. The light was certainly fading on the panes; the dusk was stealing over the winter afternoon. Harry could only speak at intervals, and the words came out with long pauses between them. Mr. Castlemaine fancied he was beginning slightly to wander: but a great many of us are apt to fancy that when watching the dying.

"And you'll take care of Jane, father? Just a little help, you know, to keep her from being thrown on the world. It's not much she'll want I don't ask it."

The damp hand, lying in Mr. Castlemaine's was, pressed almost to pain; but there was no other answer. The aching heart was well-nigh unmanned.

"And don't be angry with Marston, father: he only did what I made him do. He is a better man than we have thought him. He was very good to me when he was here to-day, and left me comfort."

Mr. Castlemaine lodged his elbow on his knee, and bent his brow upon his hand. For some time there was silence. Harry, who had none of the restlessness sometimes characteristic of the final scene, lay quite still, his eyes closed.

A very long, deep breath disturbed the silence. It startled Mr. Castlemaine. He looked up, and for a moment loosed the hand he held.

"Harry!"

Harry Castlemaine, his eyes wide open now, raised his head from the pillow. He seemed to be staring at the windowpanes with a fixed look, as though he could see the sea that lay beyond, and found something strange in it.

"Father, dear father, it is she!" he burst out in his natural tones, and with a deep, exulting joy in them. "It is my mother: I know her well. Oh, yes, mother, I am coming!"

The Master of Greylands was startled. Harry had never seen his mother to remember her; he knew her only by her picture, which hung in one of the rooms, and was a speaking likeness of her. Harry had fallen back again, and lay with a smile upon his face. One more deep respiration came slowly forth from his lips: it was the last he had to take in this world.

The bereaved father saw what it was, and all his bitter sorrow rose up within him in one long overwhelming agony. He fell upon the unconscious face lying there; his trial seeming greater than he could bear.

"Oh, Harry, my son! my son Harry! would God I could have died for thee, my son, my son!"

XXXVII

Anthony

Little explanation need be afforded in regard to the smuggling practices, so long carried on with impunity. Some ten or fifteen years before, Commodore Teague (commodore by courtesy) had taken the Hutt of old Mr. Castlemaine, on whose land it stood. Whether the Commodore had fixed on his abode there with the pre-intention to set up in the contraband trade, so much favoured then and so profitable, or whether the facilities which the situation presented for it, arising from the subterranean passage to the beach, which Teague himself discovered, and which had been unknown to the Castlemaines, first induced the thought, cannot be told. Certain it is, that Teague did organize and embark in it; and was joined in it by James Castlemaine. James Castlemaine was a young and active man then, ever about; and Teague probably thought that it would not do to run the risk of being found out by the Castlemaines. He made a merit of necessity; and by some means induced James Castlemaine to join him in the work—to be his partner in it, in fact. Half a loaf is better than no bread, runs the proverb, and the Commodore was of that opinion. His proposal was a handsome one. James Castlemaine was to take half the gross profits; he himself would take the risk, the cost, and the residue of the profits. Perhaps James Castlemaine required little urging: daring, careless, loving adventure, the prospect presented charms for him that nothing else could have brought. And the compact was made.

It was never disclosed to his father, old Anthony Castlemaine, or to Peter, the banker, or to any other of his kith and kin, his son Harry excepted. As Harry grew to manhood and settled down at Greylands' Rest, after his education was completed, the same cause that induced the Commodore to confide in James Castlemaine induced the latter to confide in his son—namely, that Harry might, one of these fine nights, be finding it out for himself. Harry delighted in it just as much as his father had, and took an active part in the fun a great deal oftener than his father did. Harry rarely allowed a cargo to be run without him; Mr. Castlemaine, especially of late years, was only occasionally present. Few men plotting against His Majesty's revenues had ever enjoyed so complete an immunity from exposure. James Castlemaine and the Commodore had, to use young Dance's expression, pretty well feathered their nests: and Tom Dance—who had been taken into confidence from the first, for the help of a strong man was needed by Teague to stow away the cargoes after they were run—had not done amiss in his small way.

It was over now. The fever and the excitement, the hidden peril and the golden harvest, all had come to an end, and Harry Castlemaine's life bad ended with them. Striding over the field path that led to Greylands' Rest, his heart softened almost like a little child's, his tears running slowly down his cheeks unchecked, went the Master of Greylands from his son's death-bed.

"Is it retribution?" he murmured, lifting his face in the gloom of the evening. "Harry's death following upon Anthony's ere the year is out!" And he struck his forehead as he walked on.

"I beg your pardon, sir, for speaking at this moment. May I say how truly I feel for you? I would not like you to think me indifferent to this great sorrow."

The speaker was George North. They had met in the most lonely part of the road, just before the turning into the avenue close to the house gates. George North did not know that the death had actually taken place; only that it was expected ere long. All his sympathies were with Mr. Castlemaine: he had been feeling truly for him and for Harry during the day; and in the impulse of the moment, meeting thus unexpectedly, he stopped to express it.

"Thank you," said Mr. Castlemaine, quite humbly, drawing his hand across his face. "Yes, it is a bitter blow. The world's sunshine has gone out for me with it."

A rapid thought came to George North. What if, in this softened mood, he were to ask for a word of Anthony? If ever the Master of Greylands could be induced to afford information of his fate, it would be now: no other moment might ever occur so favourable as this. Yes, he would; be the result what it might.

"Forgive me Mr. Castlemaine. There is a matter that I have long wished to mention to you; a question I would ask: the present, now that we are alone here, and both softened by sorrow—for believe me I do sorrow for your son more than you may suspect—seems to me to be an appropriate time. May I dare to ask it?"

"Ask anything," said the unconscious mourner.

"Can you tell me what became of young Anthony Castlemaine?"

Even in the midst of his anguish, the question gave the Master of Greylands a sharp sting. "What do you know about Anthony Castlemaine?" he rejoined.

"He was my—dear friend," spoke George in agitation. "If you would but tell me, sir, what became of him! Is he really dead?"

"Oh that he were not dead!" cried Mr. Castlemaine, unmanned by the past remembrances, the present pain. "He would have been some one to care for; I could have learnt to love him as my nephew. I have no one left now."

"You have still a nephew, sir!" returned George, deeply agitated, a sure conviction seating itself within him at the last words, that whatever might have been the adverse fate of Anthony, the sorrowing man before him had not helped to induce it. "A nephew who will ask nothing better than to serve you in all affection and duty—if you will but suffer him."

Mr. Castlemaine looked keenly at the speaker in the evening's gloaming. "Where is this nephew?" he inquired after a pause.

"I am he, sir. I am George Castlemaine."

"You?"

"Yes, Uncle James—if I may dare so to address you. I am poor Anthony's brother."

"And my brother Basil's son?"

"His younger son, Uncle James. They named me George North."

"George North Castlemaine," repeated Mr. Castlemaine, as if wishing to familiarise himself with the name. "And you have been staying here with a view of tracing out Anthony's fate?" he added, quickly arriving at the conclusion, and feeling by rapid instinct that this young man was in good truth his nephew.

"Yes, I have, sir And I had begun to despair of doing it. Is he still living?"

"No, lie is dead. He died that fatal February night that you have heard of. You have heard talk of the shot: that shot killed him."

In spite of his effort for composure, George allowed a groan to escape his lips. The Master of Greylands echoed it.

"George, my nephew, it has been an unlucky year with the Castlemaines," he said in a wailing tone. "Death has claimed three of us; two of the deaths, at least, have been violent, and all of them have been that sudden death we pray against Sunday by Sunday in the Litany. My brother Peter; my nephew Anthony; and now my son!"

The suspicion, that had been looming in George's mind since the morning, rose to the surface: a suspicion of more curious things than one.

"I think I understand it," he said; "I see it all. In some such affray with the smugglers as occurred last night, Anthony met his death. A shot killed him; as it has now killed another? A smuggler's shot?"

"A smuggler's shot—true. But there was no affray."

"Tell me all, Uncle James," said the young man, his beseeching tone amounting to pain. "Let me share all—the trouble and doings of the past. It shall be hidden in my breast for ever."

"What is it that you suspect?"

"That the smuggling trade was yours: and that the fact accounts for your having been in the Keep that night—for Harry's being there yesterday. Trust me as you have trusted your son, Uncle James: it shall be ever sacred. I will sympathise with you as he has done: am I not a Castlemaine?"

One rapid debate in his mind, and then the Master of Greylands pointed to his garden and led the way to the nearest bench there: the selfsame bench that George had sat on to whisper his love-vows to Ethel. He was about to disclose all to his new-found nephew, to whom his esteem and admiration had before been drawn as George North; whom he already liked, nay loved, by one of those subtle instincts rarely to be accounted for. Unless he made a clean breast of all things, the fate of Anthony must in some particulars still remain dark.

He first of all satisfied George upon the one point which has already been declared to the reader: they were the smugglers, the Castlemaines, in conjunction with the originator and active man, Teague: explaining to him how it was that he had been induced to join himself to the practices. And then he went on to other matters.

George Castlemaine sat by his side in the dusky night, and listened to the tale. To more than he had dared to ask, or hope for, or even to think of that eventful evening. For Mr. Castlemaine entered upon the question of the estate: speaking at first abruptly.

"Greylands' Rest is Anthony's," said he.

"Anthony's!"

"Yes. Or rather yours, now Anthony is gone; but it was his when he came over. It is necessary for me to tell you this at first: one part of the story involves another. My father knew nothing of the smuggling; never had an idea of it; and the money that I gained by it I had to invest quietly from time to time through a London agent; so that he, and others, should not know I possessed it. A few weeks before my father died, he called me to him one morning to talk about the property—"

"Did he make a will?——I beg your pardon for my interruption, Uncle James," hastily added the young man in apology for what now struck him for rudeness.

"No, he did not make a will. He never made one. Your grandfather was one of those men who shrink from making a will—there are many such in the world. It was less necessary in his case to make one than it is in some cases—at least he deemed it so. Of his available means, Basil had received his share, I had received mine, Peter had had his; all, years before. Nothing, save the estate, was left to will away. I see what you are wondering at, George—that out of twelve or thirteen hundred a year—for that is about what the estate brings in—your grandfather should have been able to live here so liberally and make the show we did: but during his lifetime he enjoyed nearly as much more from a relative of my mother's, which source of income went back at his death. Perhaps you know this. My father began that morning to talk to me— 'When do you expect Basil, James?' he asked abruptly: and the question unutterably astonished me, for we had not heard from Basil at all, and did not expect him. 'He will come,' said my father; 'he will come. Basil will know that I must be drawing near my end, and he will come over to be ready to take possession here.' 'Leave Greylands' Rest for me, father,' I burst out—for I had been hoping all along that it would be mine after him: I presume you see for why?"

But George did not see: and said so.

"On account of what went on in the Friar's Keep," explained Mr. Castlemaine. "It would not do, unless I gave up that, for me to quit this place, or for a stranger to live at it. I knew Basil of old: he would just as soon have denounced it to the world as not. And, as I was not then inclined to give up anything so profitable, I wished to have Greylands' Rest. There is no other residence within miles of the place that would have been suitable for me and my family."

"And would my grandfather not leave it to you, Uncle James?"

"He refused absolutely. He would not listen to me. Greylands' Rest must descend to Basil after him, he said, and to Basil's son—if Basil had a son—after him. I begged him to let me purchase Greylands' Rest at a fair valuation, and pay over the money to him or invest it for Basil. I said I was attached to the place, having lived in it all my life; whereas

Basil had been away from it years and years. I offered to add on to the purchase money any premium that might be named; but the old man laughed, and asked where I was to get all the money from. Of course he did not know of my private resources, and I did not dare to allude to them. I brought up Peter's name, saying he would assist me. Peter was rolling in riches then. But it was all of no use: Basil was the eldest, my father said, the rightful heir, and the estate should never pass over him for one of us. He drew up, himself, a sort of deed of gift, not a will, giving the estate to Basil then; then, during his own lifetime; and he charged me, should Basil not have appeared at the time of his demise, to remain in possession and keep it up for him. But he never charged me—mark you, George, he never charged me to seek Basil out. And, for the matter of that, we did not know where to seek him."

Mr. Castlemaine paused to take his hat off and wipe his brow. This confession must be costing him some pain. But for the greater pain at his heart, the hopeless despair that seemed to have fallen on the future, it had never been made.

"My father died. I, according to his pleasure, remained on, the Master of Greylands' Rest. People took it for granted it was left to me; I never gave a hint to the contrary, even to my brother Peter. Peter was getting into embarrassment then with his undertakings of magnitude, and came to me for money to help him. The time went on; each month as it passed and brought no sign of Basil, no tidings of him, seeming to confirm me more securely in possession of the property. My father had said to me, 'Should Basil never reappear to claim it, nor any son of Basil's, then it will be yours, James.' Before the first year came to an end, I thought it was mine; as the second year advanced, it seemed so securely my own that I never gave a thought or a fear to its being taken from me. You may judge, then, what I felt when some young fellow presented himself one day at Greylands' Rest, without warning of any kind, saying Basil was dead, that he was Basil's son, and had come to claim the property."

Again the Master of Greylands paused. But this time he remained quite still. George did not interrupt him.

"When I recall the shame connected with that period, and would fain plead an excuse for myself, I feel tempted to say that the excuse lay in the suddenness of the blow. You must not think me covetous, George Castlemaine: love of money had nothing whatever to do with the assertion to Anthony that Greylands' Rest was mine. I dreaded to

MRS. HENRY WOOD

be turned from it. I wanted, at any cost (that of honour you will say), to stay in it. At one of the interviews I had with your brother, I hinted to him that compensation might be made to him for his disappointment, even to the value of the estate, for I was rich and did not heed money. But Anthony was a true Castlemaine, I found, Basil's own son: for he at once replied that he required only justice: if the estate was his, he must have it; if not his, he did not want to be recompensed for what he had no claim to. I was angry, mortified, vexed: he kept asking me to show the Deed, or the Will, by which I held it: I could not do that, for it would have been seen at once that the property was his, not mine."

"Perhaps you have destroyed the Deed," said George.

"No, I kept it. I have it still. It was always my intention to make restitution some time, and I kept the Deed. My poor son would never have succeeded to Greylands' Rest."

"Who would then?" exclaimed George involuntarily.

"Anthony. I am speaking just now of what my thoughts and intentions were during that brief period of Anthony's sojourn at Greylands. But now listen, George. You must have heard that on the last day of your brother's life we had an encounter in yonder field."

"Oh yes, I have heard of it."

"Something indoors had put me frightfully out of temper, and I was in a haughty and angry mood. But, as Heaven is my judge, I resolved, later on in that afternoon, to make him restitution: to give up to him the estate. After leaving him, I went on; I was, I believe, in a foaming passion, and walked fast to throw it of. In passing the churchyard, I saw that some one had been flinging some dead sticks on my father's tombstone: you know it, of course: it is the large one of white marble with the iron rails round: and I went in to clear them off. How it was I know not: I suppose Heaven sends such messages to all of us: but as I stood there to read the inscription, 'Anthony Castlemaine, of Greylands' Rest,' all the folly and iniquity of my conduct rose up vividly to confront me. I saw his fine old face before me again, I seemed to hear his voice, enjoining me to hold the estate in trust for Basil, or Basil's son, and relying with the utmost implicit trust on my honour that I would do this. A revulsion of feeling came over me, my face flushed with its sense of shame. 'Father, I will obey you,' I said aloud; 'before another day shall close, Greylands' Rest shall have passed to young Anthony.' And it should so have passed. Heaven hears me say it, and knows that I would have carried it out."

"I am sure of it," said George, trustingly. It was impossible to doubt the fervent accent, the earnest tone, so replete with pain.

"I am now approaching that fatal point, the death of Anthony. When I went back home, I sat down to consider of the future. Two plans suggested themselves to me. The one was, to take Anthony into confidence as to the business transacted at the Friar's Keep; the other was to give the business up altogether, so far as I and Harry were concerned, and to make no disclosure of it to Anthony. I rather inclined to the latter course: I had realized a vast deal of money, and did not require more, and I thought it might be as well to get out of the risk while we were undiscovered. Teague, who had made money also, might give it up, or continue it on his sole score and at his own risk, as he pleased. I thought of this all the evening, and between ten and eleven o'clock, after the household had gone to bed, I went down to Teague's to speak to him about it. I had no particular motive, you understand, for going to Teague at that late hour, the morning would have been soon enough; but I had thought myself into an impatient, restless mood, and so started off upon impulse. I stayed with Teague, talking, until near half-past eleven, perhaps quite that: no decision was come to, either by me or him, as to our respective course in regard to the trade; but that made no difference to my intended communication to Anthony as to the estate; and meant to send for him to Greylands' Rest as soon as breakfast was over on the following morning. Do you believe me?"

"Fully, Uncle James. I believe every word you say."

"I am telling it before Heaven," was the solemn rejoinder. "As in the presence of my dead son."

And that was the first intimation George received that Harry was no more.

"It was, I say, about half-past eleven when I left the Hutt. In turning into Chapel Lane I saw a man standing there, holding on by one of the trees. It was Jack Tuff, one of our working fishermen. He might have noticed me, though I hoped he had not; for you will readily understand that I did not care for the village to know of any night visits I might pay Teague. Upon reaching home I went upstairs to my bureau, and sat for a few minutes, though I really can't say how many, looking over some private papers connected with the trade. Mrs. Castlemaine and the household had, I say, gone to rest. I began to feel tired; I had not been well for some days; and shut the papers up until morning. Chancing to look from the window before quitting the room, I saw a vessel at anchor, just in a line with the chapel ruins. It was a remarkably bright, moonlight night. The vessel looked like our vessel; the one engaged in the contraband trade; and I knew that if it was so, she had come over unexpectedly, without notice, to Teague. Such an occurrence was very unusual, though it had happened once or twice before. I left the house again, passed down Chapel Lane, and went straight over to the chapel ruins to take a nearer look at the vessel. Yes, I see what you are thinking of, George—your brother and John Bent did see me. Bent's assertion that they stood there and watched me across is true; though I did not see them, and had no idea anyone was there. One glance was sufficient to show me that it was in truth our vessel. I hastened through the Friar's Keep to the secret door, and ran down the staircase. The cargo was already being run: the boats were up on the beach, and the men were wading through the water with the goods. Teague was not there, nor was Dance or his son: in fact, the sailors had taken us by surprise. Without the delay of a moment, I ran up the subterranean passage to summon Teague, and met him at the other end: he had just seen the anchored vessel. Not many minutes was I away from the beach, George Castlemaine, but when I got back, the mischief had been done. Anthony was killed."

"Murdered?"

"You may call it murder, if you like. His own imprudence, poor fellow, induced it. It would appear—but we shall never know the exact truth—that he must have discovered the staircase pretty quickly, and followed me down. In my haste I had no doubt left the door open. At once he was in the midst of the scene. The boats hauled up there, the goods already landed, the sailors at their hasty work speaking together in covert whispers, must have told him what it meant. In his honest impulse, but most fatal imprudence, he dashed forward amid the sailor-smugglers. 'I have caught you, you illicit villains!' he shouted, or words to that effect. 'I see what nefarious work you are engaged in: cheating His Majesty's revenue. What, ho! coastguard!' Before the words had well left his lips, one of the men caught up a pistol, presented it at him, and shot him dead."

Mr. Castlemaine paused. His nephew, George, was silent from agitation.

"The man who shot him was the mate of the vessel, a Dutchman by birth. When Teague and I reached the beach, we saw them all standing over Anthony. He—"

"He was dead, you say?" gasped George.

"Stone dead. The bullet had gone through his heart. I cannot attempt to tell you what my sensations were; but I would freely have given all I possessed, in addition to Greylands' Rest, to recall the act. There was a short consultation as to what was to be done with him; and, during this, one of the men drew a diamond ring from poor Anthony's finger, on which the moonlight had flashed, and put it into my hand. I have it still, shut up in my bureau."

George thought of this very ring—that Charlotte Guise had discovered and told him of. She had been deeming it the one conclusive proof against Mr. Castlemaine.

"I spoke of Christian burial for Anthony: but insuperable difficulties stood in the way. It might have led to the discovery of the trade that was carried on; and Van Stan, the man who killed him, insisted on his being thrown at once into the sea."

George groaned. "Was it done?"

"It was. Van Stan, a huge, angular fellow, he was, with the strength of ten ordinary men, cleared out one of the boats. They lifted Anthony into it; he was rowed out to sea, and dropped into its midst. I can assure you, George, that for many a day I looked for the sea to cast the body ashore: but it never has cast it."

"Where is that Van Stan?"

"Van Stan has died now in his turn. Big and strong giant though he was to look at, he died in Holland not long after of nothing but a neglected cold. I ought to have told you," added Mr. Castlemaine, "that Teague went up nearly at once to lock the gate of the chapel ruins: and there he saw John Bent pacing about: which made us all the more cautious below to be as silent as might be. It was our custom to lock that gate when cargoes were being run, both to guard against surprise and against anyone coming into the ruins to look out to sea. We had three keys to the gate: Teague kept one; Harry another; Dance a third."

"I wonder you could get three keys made to it without suspicion," spoke George, amid his deeper thoughts.

"We got a fresh lock and its keys from over the water, and had it put on the gate without Greylands being the wiser. That was many a year ago."

"And—you were not present!" remarked George, his bewildered thoughts recurring to the one fatal act of the night, and speaking like a man in a dream.

"No. It was exactly as I have told you. My son was also away that night: he had gone to Newerton. Had he or I been there, I don't know that we could have hindered it: Van Stan gave no more warning of what he was about to do than does a flash of lightning. Poor Anthony's own imprudence was in fault. He no doubt supposed that he had suddenly come upon a nest of lawless wretches; and never thought to connect them in any way with the Castlemaines."

"Teague said that the shot that was heard by John Bent and others proceeded from his gun. That was not true?"

"It was not true. That he had been cleaning his gun that night, was so; for when I reached the Hutt, I found him occupied at it. It was also true that he was going out for a sail next day in his yacht—"

"And were you going with him as they said?"

"No, I was not. But if I am to tell you all, I must proceed in my own way. I went home that night, when the work was over, with Anthony's fate lying heavily upon me. After a perfectly sleepless night I was disturbed in the early morning by the news that my brother Peter was dead; and I started for Stilborough. In the afternoon, when I came back, I found Greylands in a commotion. Miles, my servant man, told me of the disappearance of Anthony, and he alluded indignantly to the rumours connecting me with it. I had to meet these rumours; prudence necessitated it; and I went to the Dolphin Inn, where the people had mostly assembled, taking the Hutt on my way. The Hutt was shut up; Teague was not in yet. On my way onwards I met him, just landed from his boat, and we stayed to exchange opinions. 'Don't let it be known that you were out at all last night, sir,' he said. 'Your man Miles sticks to it that you were not, and so must you.' I should have taken this advice but for one circumstance—in for one lie in for fifty, you know; and lies I was obliged to tell, to turn all scent from the illicit trade. I told Teague that in quitting the Hutt the previous night at half-past eleven, I had seen Tuff in the lane, and he might have recognised me. So my visit to Teague had to be acknowledged and accounted for; it was the safer plan; and in a word or two we settled what the plea should be—that I had gone down to arrange about going for a sail with him the next morning in his yacht. This I spoke of at the Dolphin; but other facts and rumours suggested against me I ignored. It was a terrible time," passionately added Mr. Castlemaine. "I never recall it without pain."

"It must have been," said George in his sympathy.

"Teague went to the Dolphin later, but I had then left the inn. He said that when he heard the people commenting on the shot, instinct prompted him to take it on himself, and he there and then avowed that the report came from his own gun. The scream he denied in toto, insisting upon it that it was all fancy. Would it had been!"

"Would it had been!" echoed George with a groan.

"It was like a fate!" burst forth the Master of Greylands, breaking the distressing pause. "Like a fate, that I should have gone into the Keep that night by way of the chapel ruins. We always avoided that way of entrance and egress, to keep observation from it. Harry, I know, had used it more than he ought: it was so much more ready a way than going into Teague's and passing through the long passage: but I was always cautioning him. The young are careless."

"The ghost of the Grey Monk?" asked George. "Who personated him? Of course I can understand that the farce was kept up to scare the world from the Friar's Keep."

"Just so. The superstition already existed in the village, and we turned it to account. I recollect when I was a boy sundry old people testified to having been at odd times scared by the apparition at the windows of the Keep when they were passing it at night. We re-organised the ghost and caused him to show himself occasionally, procuring for the purpose a monk's dress, and a lamp emitting a pale blue flame by means of spirit and salt. Teague and Harry were the actors; sometimes one, sometimes the other. It was an element of fun in my poor boy's life."

Mr. Castlemaine rose with the last words. He had need of repose.

"I will see you again in the morning, George. Come to me at what hour you please, and I will introduce you to my wife by your true name. Greylands' Rest is yours, you know, now."

"I—but I do not wish you to go out of it, Uncle James," said George in his impulse of generosity.

"I shall be only too glad to get out of it as soon as may be," was the impressive answer. "Do you think I could bear to live in it now? Would to Heaven I had gone out of it before this fatal year! George," he added, with a gasp of agitation, "as I was walking home just now I asked myself whether the finger of God had not been at work. These illicit practices of mine caused the death of Anthony; I denied that death, concealed it, have attempted to ridicule it to the world: and now my own and only son has died the same miserable death; been shot down, perhaps, by the very selfsame pistol. It is retribution, lad."

　　　　　　　　　　　　　　　　　　　　　　MRS. HENRY WOOD

"I wish I could comfort you!" whispered George.

A moment's silence and Mr. Castlemaine recovered himself; his tone changed.

"The revenues of the estate have been put by since nay father's death: left for such a moment as this: I told you I did not mean to keep possession always. They shall be paid over to you."

"They are not mine, Uncle James. Up to last February they were Anthony's."

"Anthony is dead."

"But he left a wife and child."

"A wife and child! Anthony! Was it a boy? Perhaps I have spoken too fast."

"It is a girl," said George, not deeming it well to enter on the subject of Madame Guise before the morrow. Mr. Castlemaine had been tried enough for one day.

"Oh, a girl. Then you take Greylands' Rest. At least—I suppose so," added Mr. Castlemaine doubtfully. "My brother Basil made a will?"

"Oh, yes. He made a fresh will as soon as he heard of his father's death. He bequeathed Greylands' Rest (assuming that it was then his) to Anthony and to his sons, should he have any, in succession after him: failing sons, he left it to me after Anthony."

"That is all legal then. Until to-morrow morning, George."

With a pressure of the hand, the Master of Greylands went down the path to his house, and let himself in with his latchkey. The doors were closed, the blinds were down; for tidings of Harry's death were already carried there. He went straight up to that solitary room, and shut himself in with his bitter trouble.

He was not a cruel man, or a vindictive man, or a covetous man. No, nor a false man, save in that one unhappy business relating to his nephew Anthony. All his efforts for many a year had been directed to ward off suspicion from the doings of the Friar's Keep: and when Anthony so unexpectedly appeared, his rejection of his claims had not been for the sake of retaining the revenues that were not his, but because he would not, if he could help it, quit the house. The one short sentence just spoken to George, "I have put by the revenues since my father's death," conveyed a true fact. Mr. Castlemaine did not wish for the revenues or intend to appropriate them, unless he was assured that his brother Basil and Basil's heirs had alike failed. He would have liked to send Anthony back to France, pay him what was due, and buy the estate from him. To have had the fraudulent doings discovered and brought home to him would have been to the Master of Greylands worse than death. It was to keep them secret that he discouraged the sojourn of strangers at Greylands; that he did not allow Harry to enter on an intimacy with any visitors who might be staying there: and of late he had shown an impatience, in spite of his liking for him, for the departure of the gentleman-artist, George North. His dislike of the Grey Sisters had its sole origin in this. He always dreaded that their attention might be attracted some night to the boats, putting off from the contraband vessel; and he would have shut up the Grey Nunnery had it been in his power. That Mary Ursula, with her certain income, small though it was, should have joined the Sisterhood, tried him sorely; both from this secret reason and for her own sake. Nearly as good, he thought, that she had been buried alive.

It was all over now, and the end had come. The last cargo had now been run, the lucrative trade and its dash of lawless excitement had been stopped for ever. This would not have troubled him: he was getting tired of it, he was getting afraid of it: but it had left its dreadful consequences in its train; dealt, as may be said, a final death-blow at parting. Harry Castlemaine had passed away, and with him the heart's life of the Master of Greylands.

XXXVIII

REBELLION

I t is the most ridiculously sentimental piece of business that I ever heard of in my life!" spoke Mrs. Castlemaine, in a tone between a sob and a shriek.

"Nevertheless, it is what must be," said her husband. "It is decided upon."

The morrow had come. George North—but we must put aside that name now—was at Greylands' Rest, and had held his further private conference with Mr. Castlemaine. The latter knew who Madame Guise was now, and all about it, and the motive of her residence in his house. He did not know of her having visited his bureau and seen the ring. He never would know it. Partial reticence was necessary on both sides, and each had somewhat to be ashamed of that the other did not suspect or dream of.

George Castlemaine, lying awake that night at the Dolphin Inn— his whole heart aching for his uncle, his saddest regrets, past and present, given to his brother and his cousin—had been, to use a familiar saying, turning matters about in his mind, to see what was the best that might be made of them. Greylands' Rest was his: there was no question of that; and he must and should take possession of it, and make it his abode for the future. But he hated to be the means of throwing discredit on his uncle: and this step would naturally throw on him discredit in men's minds. If Greylands' Rest was the younger brother George's now, it must have been the elder brother Anthony's before him: and all the deceit, suspected of the Master of Greylands earlier in the year, would be confirmed. Was there any way of preventing this? George thought there was. And he lay dwelling on this and other difficulties until morning, and found his way.

"The world need never know that it was Anthony's, Uncle James," he said, wringing his uncle's hand to give force to his argument. "Let it be supposed that the estate was only to lapse to him after Harry—that Harry came in first by my grandfather's will. None can dispute it. And you can make a merit, you know, of giving it up at once to me, not caring to remain here now Harry is gone."

A gleam of light, like a bit of blue sky suddenly shining out of leaden clouds, dawned on Mr. Castlemaine's face. The prospect of tacitly confessing himself a traitor before his fellow men had made a large ingredient in his cup of bitterness.

"Nothing need ever be specially proclaimed," resumed George. "Nobody in the world has a right to inquire into our affairs, to say to us, How is this? or, How is that? It can be understood that this is the case. Even to your own—your own family"—(the word on George's tongue had been "wife," but he changed it)—"you need not give other explanation. Let this be so, Uncle James. It is for the honour of the Castlemaines."

"Yes, yes; it would take a load from me—if—if it may be done," said the Master of Greylands dreamily. "I see no reason why it should not be," he added, after consideration. "It lies, George, with you. You alone know the truth."

"Then that is settled. Be assured, Uncle James, that I shall never betray it. I shall accustom myself to think that it is so; that I only came in after Harry; in time I daresay I shall quite believe it."

And so, as George said, it was a settled thing. That version of the affair went abroad, and James Castlemaine's credit was saved.

His credit had also to be saved on another score: the death of Anthony. The fact, that he was dead, could no longer be kept from the curious neighbourhood: at least, it would have been in the highest degree inexpedient not to clear it up: but the Master of Greylands' knowledge of it might still be denied and concealed. The exact truth in regard to his death, the true particulars of it, might be made known: Anthony had found his way down to the lower vaults of the Friar's Keep, that night; had pounced upon the smugglers, then running a cargo; they had shot him dead, and then flung him into the sea. The smugglers were doing their work alone that night, Commodore Teague not being with them, and they were the sole authors of the calamity. Every word of this was correct, and George would enlighten the world with this, and no more. If questions were put to him as to how he came into possession of the facts, he would avow that the smugglers had confessed it to him, now that their visits to the coast were at an end for ever. He would say that the man who shot him had taken Anthony to be a coastguardsman: and this was fact also: for Van Stan said afterwards that in the surprise and confusion he had thought this; had thought that the preventive-men were on them. The Master of Greylands would hold his own as to his ignorance and innocence: and Mr. John Bent must go on working out the puzzle, of having fancied he saw him that night, to the end.

Neither need Madame Guise be quite entirely enlightened. George, a Castlemaine himself and jealous of the family's good name, would not, even to her, throw more discredit than need be on his father's brother. He would not tell her that Mr. Castlemaine had been one with the smugglers; but he would tell her that he knew of the practices and kept silence out of regard to Commodore Teague. He would disclose to her the full details of that night, as they occurred, but not that Mr. Castlemaine had been at all upon the beach, before Anthony or after him; he would say that when Anthony's fate was disclosed to him, and the ring handed over, the most lively regret and sorrow for him took possession of his uncle, but to proclaim that he had been made cognisant of it would have done no good whatever, and ruined the Commodore. Well, so far, that was all true, and Charlotte Guise must make the best of it. Mr. Castlemaine intimated that he should settle a sum of money upon the little child, Marie; and the revenues of Greylands' Rest for the period intervening between his father's death and Anthony's death would, of course, be paid over to Charlotte. George, while this was being spoken of, privately resolved to take on himself the educational expenses of the child.

It was in Mr. Castlemaine's room that this conference with George took place. Mr. Castlemaine unlocked the bureau, produced the ring, and placed it on George's finger. George took it off.

"I think his wife should have this, Uncle James. She may like to keep it."

"Who gave it to Anthony?" asked Mr. Castlemaine.

"My mother. It had belonged to her father, and to his father before him. She gave it to Anthony before she died, telling him it was an heirloom and charging him ever to wear it in remembrance of her."

"Then I think it should now be worn by you, George; but settle it with Madame Guise as you will. Who was your mother? An Englishwoman?"

"Oh yes. Miss North. It was her brother, Mr. George North, who stood godfather to me, and who left me all his private fortune. He was in the silk mills, and died quite a young man and a bachelor."

"Ay," said Mr. Castlemaine, rather dreamily, his thoughts back with his brother Basil, "you have money, George, I know. Is it much?"

"It is altogether nearly a thousand pounds a year. Some of it came to me from my father."

"And Ethel has about seven hundred a year," remarked Mr. Castlemaine. "And there will be the revenues of Greylands' Rest: twelve hundred, or thereabouts. You will be a rich man, George, and can keep up as much state as you please here."

It will be seen by this that George Castlemaine had asked his uncle for Ethel. Mr. Castlemaine was surprised: he had not entertained the remotest suspicion of any attachment between them: but he gave a hearty consent. He had liked George; he was fond of Ethel; and the match for her was excellent.

"I would just as soon not take her away with us when we leave, except as a temporary arrangement," was his candid avowal. "Mrs. Castlemaine does not make her home too pleasant; she will be happier with you."

"Oh, I hope so!" was the hasty, fervent answer.

The conference, which had been a long one, broke up. George went away to his interview of explanation with Madame Guise, who as yet knew nothing; and the Master of Greylands summoned his wife to the room. He informed her briefly of the state of things generally: telling her who George North was, and of Anthony's death: using the version that George had suggested, and keeping himself, as to the past, on neutral ground altogether. She was not to know even as much as Madame Guise, but to understand, as the world would, that her husband only learnt the truth now. Now that poor Harry was gone, he said, George came next in the succession to Greylands' Rest, and he (Mr. Castlemaine) had resolved to give it up to him at once. Mrs. Castlemaine, who did not feel at all inclined to quit Greylands' Rest, went into a state of rebellious indignation forthwith, and retorted with the remark already given.

"Why 'must' it be?" she asked. "Where lies the obligation?"

"Nothing would induce me to remain in this house now Harry is gone," he answered. "I wish I was away from it already: the reminiscences connected with it are so painful that I can bear to stay in it for the short while that we must stay. When a blight like this falls upon a family, Sophia, it frequently brings changes in its train."

Mrs. Castlemaine, biting her lips in temper, was not ready with a rejoinder. In the face of this plea, her stepson's death, it would not be decent to say too much. Moreover, though her husband was an excellent man in regard to allowing her full sway in trifles, she knew by experience that when it came to momentous affairs, she might as well attempt to turn the sea as to interfere with his will.

"I like Greylands' Rest," she said. "I have lived in it since you brought me home. Flora was born here. It is very hard to have to hear of leaving it."

Mr. Castlemaine had his back to her, tearing up some papers that were in a drawer of his bureau. It looked exactly as though he were already making preparations for the exit.

"And I expected that this would have been my home for life," she added more angrily, his silence increasing her feelings of rebellion.

"No, you did not expect it," said he, turning round. "I heard my father inform you, the very day after you came here, that Greylands' Rest would descend to his eldest son; not to me."

"It did descend to you," was all she said.

"But it is mine no longer. Harry is gone, and I resign it to my eldest brother's only remaining son."

"It is absurd chivalry even to think of such a thing," she retorted, her lip quivering, her throat swelling. "One would fancy you had taken leave of your senses, James."

"The less said about the matter the better," he answered, turning to his papers again. "At Greylands' Rest, now my son is gone, I cannot and will not stay: and George North—George Castlemaine—comes into possession of it."

"Do you resign to him the income of the estate as well as the house?" inquired Mrs. Castlemaine, as much mockery in her tone as she dared to use.

"The arrangements I choose to make with him are my own, Sophia, and are private between himself and me. Whithersoever I may go, I shall take as good an income with me as you have enjoyed here."

"And where shall you go?"

"I think at first we will travel for a bit. You have often expressed a wish for that. Afterwards we shall see. Perhaps you would like to settle in London, and for myself I care very little where it is."

A vision of the seductions of London—its shops, its shows, its theatres, its gay life generally—rose attractively, as in a vision, before Mrs. Castlemaine. She had never been to the metropolis in her life, and quite believed its streets were paved with gold.

"One thing I am surprised at, James," she resumed quitting that bone of contention for another. "That you should give consent off hand, as you tell me you have done, to Ethel's marriage with a stranger."

"A stranger! We have seen a good deal of him in the past few months; and he is my nephew."

"But a very disreputable kind of nephew. Really I must say it! He has concealed his name from us, and has aided and abetted that governess in concealing hers! It is not reputable."

"But I have explained the cause to you. The poor woman came to the place to seek out her husband, and thought she should have a better chance of success if she dropped his name and appeared as a stranger. George came over in his turn, and at her request dropped his. Remember one thing, Sophia, the concealment has not injured us; and Madame Guise has at least been an efficient governess for Flora, and done her duty well."

"I should certainly think twice before I gave him Ethel. Such haste! I don't see" (and here a little bit of the true animus peeped out) "why Ethel should have the pleasure of staying on at Greylands' Rest for good, while I and Flora are to be forced to leave it!"

No answer.

"All the pleasant places of the dear child!—that have been hers from childhood—that she has grown up attached to! Her very swing in the garden!—the doll's house in the nursery! Everything."

"She can take her swing and her doll's house with her."

"And for that Ethel to stay, and come in for all the benefit! If she must marry George North I should at least make her wait a twelvemonth."

"They shall be married as soon as they please," said Mr. Castlemaine. "He will make her a good husband; I am sure of it: and his means are large. Her home with him will be happier than you have allowed it to be with us: I did not forget that in my decision."

The lips of Mrs. Castlemaine were being bitten to nothing. Whatever she said seemed to get twisted and turned against her. But she fully intended at some more auspicious moment, when her husband should be in a less uncompromising mood, to have another trial at retaining Greylands' Rest. If she had but known the real truth!—that it was George Castlemaine's by inheritance, and had been his since that past February night!

Meanwhile George himself was with Madame Guise, making known to her the elucidation of many things and of the manner of Anthony's death. Poor Charlotte Guise, demonstrative as are most French women sobbed and exclaimed as she listened, and found that what she had feared was indeed a certainty. It was the shot of that fatal February night that had killed her husband: the scream heard had been his death-scream. She was in truth a widow and her child fatherless.

But, when the first shock lifted itself—and it was perhaps less keenly felt in consequence of what may be called these many long months of preparation for it—her thoughts turned to Mr. Castlemaine. The certainty that he was innocent—for she implicitly believed her brother-in-law's version of the past—brought to her unspeakable relief. Prejudice apart, she had always liked Mr. Castlemaine: and she now felt ashamed for having doubted him. "If I had but taken the courage to declare myself to him at first, and what my mission was in England, I might have been spared all this dreadful suspicion and torment!" she cried, her tears dropping softly. "And it has been a torment, I assure you, George, to live in the same house with Mr. Castlemaine, believing him guilty. And oh! to think that I should have opened that bureau! Will he ever forgive me?"

"You must not tell him of that," said George gravely. "I speak in your interest alone, Charlotte. It would answer no good end to declare it; and, as it happened, no harm was done."

"No harm but to me," she moaned. "Since I saw that ring, my fears of Mr. Castlemaine and my own trouble have increased tenfold."

George held out the ring, saying that Mr. Castlemaine had just handed it to him. "He says," continued George, "that the one problem throughout it all which he could not solve, was why Anthony's friends never came over to institute a search for him, or made inquiry by letter."

"Ah, yes," said Madame Guise, "there have been problems on all sides, no doubt—and the looking back at them seems quite to bewilder me."

She had been slipping the sparkling diamond ring on and off her slender finger that wore the wedding-ring. "Take it, George," she said, giving it back to him.

"Nay, it is yours, Charlotte: not mine."

"But no," she answered in some surprise. "This is your family's ring, bequeathed to you by your mother. Anthony would have worn it always had he lived; you must wear it now. Let me put it on for you."

"It might be a consolation to you to keep it."

"I have other relics of Anthony's. There is his watch, and the chain; and there must be some little treasures in his desk. Mr. Bent will hand them over to me when he knows who I am. But as to this ring, George, I have no claim to it: nor would I keep it while you and Emma live."

"Were his watch and chain saved?" exclaimed George.

"Why yes. Did you never hear that? Mr. Bent keeps them locked up with the other things. Anthony had been writing in his parlour that night at the Dolphin, you know; it was supposed that he put off his watch to look how the time went: at any rate it was found on the table the next morning by the side of his desk."

George sighed deeply. All these trifles connected with his brother's last day on earth were so intensely painful. Never, as he fully believed, should he look at the glittering ring, now on his finger, without recalling Anthony to memory. Charlotte sat down and burst into renewed tears.

"Where is Ethel?" he asked.

"She was in the schoolroom just now, crying. Ah, George, she feels Mr. Harry's death very much: she liked him as a brother."

George proceeded to the schoolroom. As he was entering, Flora darted out, her eyes swollen, her cheeks enflamed. She, too, had loved her half-brother, for all her careless ways and his restraining hand. George would have detained her to speak a kind word, but she suddenly dipped her head and flew past, under his arm.

Ethel was not crying now. She stood by the fire, leaning her pretty head against the mantelpiece. Her back was towards the door, and she was not aware that it was George who entered.

"My darling, I fear this is a sad trial to you," he said, advancing.

His voice brought to her a start of surprise; his words caused the tears to flow again. George drew her to him, and she sobbed on his breast.

"You don't know what it is," she said quite hysterically. "I used to be at times cross and angry with him. And now I find there was no cause for it, that he was married all the while. Oh if I had but known!—he should never have heard from me an unkind word."

"Be assured of one thing, Ethel—that he appreciated your words at their proper due only, and laughed at them in his heart. He knew you loved him as a brother: and I am sure he was truly attached to you."

"Yes, I do know all that. But—I wish I had been always kind to him," she added, as she drew away and stood as before.

"I come from a long talk with Mr. Castlemaine," said George, after a minute's pause, putting his elbow on the opposite end of the mantel piece to face her while he spoke "I have been asking him for you, Ethel."

"Ye—s?" she faltered, her eyes glancing up for a moment, and then falling again. "Asking him to-day?"

"You are thinking that it is not the most appropriate day I could have chosen: and that's true. But, in one sense, I did not choose it. We had future plans of different kinds to discuss, and this one had to come in with them. I come to make a confession to you, Ethel, to crave your pardon. The name under which I have won you, George North, is not my true name. At least, not all my name. I am a Castlemaine. Mr. Castlemaine's nephew, and that poor lost Anthony's brother."

Ethel looked bewildered. "A Castlemaine!" she repeated. "How can that be?"

"My dear, it is easy to understand. Mr. Basil Castlemaine, he who settled abroad, was the eldest brother of this house, you know, years ago. Anthony was Basil's elder son, I his younger. I came over to discover what I could of Anthony's fate, and I dropped temporarily the name of Castlemaine, lest my being recognised as one of the family might impede my search. My uncle James condones it all; and I believe he thinks that I was justified. I have now resumed my name—George North Castlemaine."

Ethel drew a deep breath. She was trying to recover her astonishment.

"Would it pain you very much, Ethel, to know that you would make no change in your residence?—that you would spend your life at Greylands' Rest?"

"I—do not understand you," she faintly said, a vision of remaining under Mrs. Castlemaine's capricious control for ever, and of being separated from him, rushing over her like an ugly nightmare.

"Greylands' Rest is to be my home in future, Ethel. Mr. and Mrs. Castlemaine leave it—"

"Yours!—your own?" she interrupted in excitement. "This house! Greylands' Rest?"

"Yes; my own. It is mine now. I come in after Harry," he added very hurriedly, to cover the last sentence, which had slipped out inadvertently: "and my uncle resigns it to, me at once."

"Oh dear," said Ethel, more and more bewildered. "But it would cost so much to live here."

"Not more than I can afford to spend," he answered with a smile. "I told you, Ethel, if you remember, that I expected to come into some property, though I was not sure of it. I have come into it. What would have been poor Anthony's had he lived, is now mine."

"But—is Anthony really dead?"

"Ay. I will tell you about it later. The present question is, Ethel, whether you will share my home here at Greylands' Rest."

He spoke with a smile, crossed over, and stood before her on the shabby old hearthrug. Just one moment of maiden hesitation, of a sweet rising blush, and she bent forward to the arms that were opened to encircle her.

"One home together here," he fondly murmured, bending his face on hers. "One Heaven hereafter."

No Turning Back

Once more the whole population of Greylands turned out in commotion. A sad and silent commotion, however, this time, as befitted the cause. Voices were hushed to a low tone, faces showed sadness, the church bell was tolling. People had donned their best attire; the fishermen were in their churchgoing clothes, their boats, hauled up on the beach or lying at anchor, had rest to-day. All who could muster a scrap of mourning had put it on, though it was but an old crape hatband, or a bit of black bonnet-ribbon. Mr. Harry Castlemaine was about to be buried; and he had been a favourite with high and low.

They made their comments as they stood waiting for the funeral. The December day was raw and dull, the grey skies seeming to threaten a fall of some kind; but Mrs. Bent pronounced it not cold enough for snow. She stood at her front door, wearing a black gown, and black strings to her cap; and was condescendingly exchanging remarks with some of her inferior neighbours, and with Mrs. and Miss Pike, who had run over from the shop.

"We shall never have such a week o' surprises as this have been," pronounced Mrs. Pike, a little red-faced woman, who was this morning in what she called "the thick of a wash," and consequently had come out en déshabille, a shawl thrown over her cap, underneath which peeped out some black straggling curls. "First of all, about them smugglers and poor Mr. Harry's wound and death, and that good-hearted Commodore having to decamp himself off, through them ferreting coastguards. And now to hear that the gentleman staying here so long is one o' the Castlemaines theirselves, and heir to Greylands' Rest after Mr. Harry! It beats the news column in the Stilborough paper holla."

"'Twere a sad thing, though, about that young Mr. Anthony," exclaimed old Ben Little. "The smugglers shot him dead, ye see, and that scream Mr. Bent said he heard were his. Full o' life one moment, and shot down the next! Them wretches ought to have swung for it."

"It be a pack o' surprises, all on't, but the greatest on 'em be Jane Hallet," quoth Nancy Gleeson. "When it come out that Mr. Harry had married her, you might ha' sent me down head for'ard with a feather—

just as Mr. Harry sent down our Tim one day, when he said a word again' her."

"It was very sly of Jane," struck in Miss Susan Pike, tossing her curls. "Never saying a word to a body, and making believe as it was just talk about her and Mr. Harry, and nothing else. I'd like to know how she wheedled him over."

"It's not for you to speak against her, Susan Pike," cried Mrs. Bent in her sharpest tone. "You didn't wheedle him, and wasn't likely to. She is Mr. Harry's wife—widow, worse luck!—and by all accounts no blame's due to her. Mr. Castlemaine gives none: and we heard yesterday he was going to settle two hundred a year on her for life."

"My! won't she set up for a lady!" enviously returned Miss Pike, ignoring the reprimand.

"Don't you be jealous, and show it, Susan Pike," retorted Mrs. Bent. "Everybody liked Jane: and we are all glad—but you—that she's cleared from the scandal. I did think it odd that she should go wrong."

"Her aunt have got her home now, and have took up all her proud airs again," said Mrs. Pike, not pleased that her daughter should be put down. "That Miss Hallet have always thought none of us was good enough for her."

"Hist!" said Ben Little, in a hushed voice. "Here it comes."

On the evening of the day following the death, the remains of Harry Castlemaine, then in their first coffin, had been conveyed to his home. It was from Greylands' Rest, therefore, that the funeral procession was now advancing. The curious spectators stretched their necks aloft to watch its onward progress; but as it came near they retreated into the hedges, so to say, and compressed themselves into as small a space as possible; the men, with one accord, taking off their hats.

It was a perfectly simple funeral. The state rather loved by the Castlemaines, and hitherto maintained by the Master of Greylands, it had not pleased him to extend to the obsequies of his son. Two mutes with their batons of sable plumes were in advance; Parson Marston followed in his surplice and black hood, walking at the head of the coffin, which was covered by its pall, and carried by carriers. Close to the coffin came Mr. Castlemaine; his nephew, George, accompanying him. Squire Dobie, long recovered from his illness, and Mr. Knivett walked next; two gentlemen from Stilborough, and the doctors, Parker and Croft, brought up the rear. These comprised all the ostensible mourners: they wore crape scarfs and hat-bands that nearly swept the ground, and had white handkerchiefs in their hands; but behind them were many followers: John Bent, Superintendent Nettleby, and others, who had fallen in as the procession left the house; and Miles and the other men-servants closed it.

Whether any suspicion penetrated to Mr. Superintendent Nettleby, then or later, that it was not mere accident which had taken Harry to the secret vaults of the Keep that night, cannot be known. He never gave utterance to it, then or later.

The people came out of the hedges after it had passed, and followed it slowly to the churchyard. Mr. Marston had turned and was waiting at the gate to receive the coffin, reading his solemn words. And for once in his life Parson Marston was solemn too.

"I am the resurrection and the life, saith the Lord: he that believeth in Me, though he were dead, yet shall he live: and whosoever liveth and believeth in Me shall never die."

A sob of pain, telling what this calamity was to him, rose in the throat of the Master of Greylands. Few men could control themselves better than he: and he struggled for calmness. If he gave way at this, the commencement of the service, how should he hold out to the end? So his face took its pale impassive look again, as he followed on through the churchyard.

It was not the custom at that time for women to attend the obsequies of those in the better ranks of life. Women followed the poor, but never the rich. Neither did any, save those bidden to a funeral, attempt to enter the church as spectators: or at least, it was done but in very rare cases. The crowd who had gathered by the Dolphin Inn, to watch it pass, took up their standing in the churchyard. From time to time the voice of Mr. Marston was heard, and that of the clerk in the Amens; and soon the procession was out again.

The grave—or rather the vault—of old Anthony Castlemaine, had been opened in the churchyard, and Harry was laid there in it. His own mother was there: the coffins lay two abreast. The Master of Greylands saw his wife's as he looked in. The inscription was as plain as though she had been buried yesterday: "Maria Castlemaine. Aged twenty-six." Another sob shook his throat as Harry's was lowered on it, and for a minute or two he broke down.

It was all soon over, and they filed out of the churchyard on their way back to Greylands' Rest. Leaving the curious and sympathising crowd to watch the grave-diggers, and lament one to another that the fine, open-hearted young man had been taken away so summarily, and to elbow one another as they pushed round to see the last of his coffin, and to read its name:

"Henry Castlemaine. Aged twenty-six." So he had died at just the same age as his mother!

Miss Castlemaine sat in the parlour at the Grey Nunnery, the little Marie on her knee. Since she knew who this child was—a Mary Ursula, like herself, and a Castlemaine—a new interest had arisen for her in her heart. She was holding the little one to her, looking into her face, and tracing the resemblance to the family. A great resemblance there undoubtedly was: the features were the clearly-cut Castlemaine features, the eyes were the same dark lustrous eyes; and Mary most wondered that the resemblance had never previously struck her.

Once more Mary had put aside the simple grey dress of the Sisterhood for robes of mourning: flowing robes, they were, of silk and crape, worn for poor Harry. The cap was on her head still, shading her soft brown hair.

It was the week subsequent to the funeral. On the following day Madame Guise (as well retain the name to the last) was about to return to her own land with her child, escorted thither by George Castlemaine. It was not to be a perpetual separation, for Charlotte had faithfully promised to come over at least once in three years to stay with George and Ethel at Greylands' Rest, so as to give her child the privilege of keeping up relations with the Castlemaine family. A slab was to be placed in the church to the memory of Anthony, and that, Madame Guise said, would of itself bring her. She must afford herself the mournful satisfaction of reading it from time to time. After her departure Mary Ursula was to go to Greylands' Rest on a short farewell visit to her uncle. It would be Christmastide, and she would spend the Christmas there. Mr. and Mrs. Castlemaine were losing no time in their departure from Greylands' Rest; they would be gone, with Ethel and Flora, before the new year came in. Mr. Castlemaine would not stay in it to see the dawning of another year: the last one, he said, had been too ill-fated. George would return as soon as might be to take up his abode there—but travelling on the Continent was somewhat uncertain at that season. During the winter Mr. and Mrs. Castlemaine would remain in London; and in the spring George was to go up there for his marriage, and bring Ethel home.

"Marie must not forget her English," said Mary Ursula, pressing a kiss on the child's face.

"Marie not fordet it, lady."

"And Marie is to come sometimes and see her dear old friends here; mamma says so; and Uncle George will—"

"A gentleman to see you, madam."

Little Sister Phoeby had opened the parlour door with the announcement, and was showing the visitor in. Mary thought it must be Mr. Knivett, and wondered that she had not heard the gate-bell. The fact was, Sister Phoeby had had the front door open, to let out the school children.

It was not Mr. Knivett who entered, but a much younger man: one whom, of all the world, Mary would have least expected to see—Sir William Blake-Gordon. He came forward, holding out his hand with trepidation, his utterly colourless face betraying his inward emotion. Mary rose, putting down the child, and mechanically suffered her hand to meet his. Sister Phoeby beckoned out the little girl, and shut the door.

"Will you pardon my unauthorised intrusion?" he asked, putting his hat on the table and taking a chair near her. "I feared to write and ask permission to call, lest you should deny it to me."

"I should not have denied it—no; my friends are welcome here," replied Mary, feeling just as agitated as he, but successfully repressing its signs. "You have, no doubt, some good reason for seeking me."

She spoke with one of her sweetest smiles: the smile that she was wont to give to her best friends. How well he remembered it!

"You have heard—at least I fancy you must have heard—some news of me," resumed Sir William, speaking with considerable embarrassment and hesitation. "It has been made very public."

Mary coloured now. About a fortnight before, Mr. Knivett had told her that the projected marriage of Sir William with Miss Mountsorrel was at an end. The two lovers had quarrelled and parted. Sir William sat looking at Mary, either waiting for her answer, or because he hesitated to go on.

"I heard that something had occurred to interrupt your plans," said Mary. "It is only a temporary interruption, I trust."

"It is a lasting one," he said; "and I do not wish it to be otherwise. Oh, Mary!" he added, rising in agitation, "you know, you must know, how hateful it was to me! I entered into it to please my father; I never had an iota of love for her. Love! the very word is desecrated in connection with what I felt for Miss Mountsorrel. I really and truly had not even friendship for her; I could not feel it. When we parted, I felt like a man who has been relieved from some heavy weight of dull despair; it was as though I had shaken off a felon's chains."

"What caused it?" questioned Mary, feeling that she must say something.

"Coolness caused it. For the very life of me I was unable to behave to her as I ought—as I suppose she had a right to expect me to behave. Since my father's death I had been more distant than ever, for I could not help remembering the fact that, had I held out against his will until then, I should have been free: and I resented it bitterly in my heart. Resented it on her, I fear. She reproached me with my coolness one day—some two or three weeks ago, it is. One word led to another; we had a quarrel and she threw me up."

"I am sorry to hear it," said Mary.

"Can you say that from your heart?"

He put the subdued question so pointedly, and there was so wistful an expression of reproach in his face that she felt confused. Sir William came up close, and took her hands.

"You know what I have come for," he cried, his voice hoarse with agitation. "I should have come a week ago but that it was the period of your deep mourning. Oh, Mary! let it be with us as it used to be! There can be no happiness for me in this world apart from you. Since the day of my father's death I have never ceased to—to—I had almost said to curse the separation that he forced upon us; or, rather to curse my weakness in yielding to it. Oh, my darling, forgive me!—my early and only love, forgive me I Come to me Mary, and be my dear wife!"

The tears were running down her face. Utterly unnerved, feeling how entirely the old love was holding sway in her heart, she let her hands lie in his.

"I am not rich, as you know, Mary; but we shall have enough for comfort. Your position at least, as Lady Blake Gordon, will be assured, and neither of us cares for riches. Our tastes are alike simple. Do you remember how we both used to laugh at undue parade and show?"

"Hush, William! Don't tempt me."

"Not tempt you! My dear one, you must be mine. It was a sin to separate us: it would be a worse sin to prolong the separation now that impediments are removed."

"I cannot turn back," she said. "I have cast my lot in here, and must abide by it. I—I—seem to see—to see more surely and clearly day by day as the days go on"—she could scarcely speak for agitation—"that

God Himself has led me to this life; that He is showing me hour by hour how to be more useful in it. I may not quit it now."

"Do you recall the fact, Mary, that your father gave you to me? It was his will that we should be man and wife. You cannot refuse to hear my prayer."

None knew, or ever would know, what that moment was to Mary Ursula: how strong was the temptation that assailed her; how cruelly painful to resist it. But, while seductive love showed her the future, as his wife, in glowing colours, reason forbade her yielding to it. Argument after argument against it crowded into her mind. She had cast in her lot with these good ladies; she had made the poor patient community, struggling before with need and privation, happy with her means. How could she withdraw those means from them? She had, in her own heart, and doing it secretly as to Christ, taken up her cross and her work in this life that she had entered upon. When she embraced it, she embraced it for ever: to turn away from it now would be like a mockery of Heaven. Involuntarily there arose in her mind a warning verse of Holy Writ, strangely applicable. She thought it might almost have been written for her; and a breathed word of silent prayer went up from her heart that she might be helped and strengthened.

"You know, Mary, that Mr. Peter Castlemaine—"

"Just a moment, William," she interrupted, lifting her hand pleadingly. "Let me think it out."

There were worldly reasons also why she should not yield, she went on to think: ay, and perhaps social ones. What would the public say if, during this temporary estrangement from Agatha Mountsorrel, this trumpery quarrel, she were to seize upon him again with indecent haste, and make him her own? What would her own sense of right say to it?—her maidenly propriety?—her untarnished spirit of honour? No, it could not be: the world might cry shame on her, and she should cry it on herself. Sir William Blake-Gordon interrupted her with his impassioned words. This moment, as it should be decided, seemed to be to him as one of life or death.

"William, hush!" she said, gazing at him through her blinding tears, and clasping his hands, in which hers still rested, almost to pain in her mind's anguish. "It may not be."

"Sit you down, my love, and be calm. I am sure you are hardly conscious of what you say. Oh, Mary, reflect! It is our whole life's happiness that is at stake: yours and mine."

They sat down side by side; and when her emotion had subsided she told him why it might not, giving all the reasons for her decision, and speaking quietly and firmly. He pleaded as though he were pleading for life itself, as well as its happiness: but he pleaded in vain. All the while she was repeating to herself that verse of warning, as if she dreaded letting it go from her for a moment.

"We will be as dear brother and sister, William, esteeming each other unto our lives' end, and meeting occasionally. You will still marry Agatha—"

"Mary!"

"Yes, I think it will be so; and I hope and trust you will be happy together. I am sure you will be."

"Our time together is short enough to-day, Mary. Do not waste it in these idle words. If you knew how they grate on me!"

"Well, I will leave that. But you must not waste your life in impossible thoughts of me and of what might have been. It would render impracticable our intercourse as friends. Thank you for what you have come this day to say: it will make my heart happier when its tumult and agitation shall be over."

Once more, by every argument in his power to call up, by the deep love and despair at his heart, he renewed his pleading. But it did not answer. The interview was prolonged to quite an unusual period, and was painful on both sides, but it terminated at length; and when William Blake-Gordon left her presence he left it as her lover for ever.

MRS. HENRY WOOD

Conclusion

Winter had passed: summer had come round again. Greylands basked in the light and heat of the June sun; the sea lay sleeping under the fishing boats.

There's not much to tell. Greylands' Rest had its new inmates: George Castlemaine and his wife. Ethel told her secrets to her husband now instead of to the sea: but they both were fond of sitting on the high cliffs together and watching its waves. Mr. and Mrs. Castlemaine were somewhere abroad, intending to stay there until autumn: and Miss Flora was where poor Harry always said she ought to be—at a good school. Mr. Castlemaine had carried his point, in spite of the opposition of his wife. It must be one of two things, he said: either that Mrs. Castlemaine stayed in England herself, or else that she disposed in some way of Flora; for Flora he was fully determined not to have abroad with him. So, being bent upon the foreign travel, Mrs. Castlemaine had to yield.

Jane Hallet—old names stand by us—had taken up her abode again with her aunt, in the pretty home on the cliff. It would probably be her dwelling-place for life. Unless, indeed, she carried out the project she had been heard once to mention—that, whenever her aunt should be called away, she hoped to join the community of the Grey Sisters. Very sad and gentle and subdued did Jane look in her widow's cap. There was a little stone now in the churchyard to the memory of "Jane, infant child of Harry Castlemaine:" it had been placed there, unasked, by the Master of Greylands; and just as Jane used to steal down the cliff in the dusk of evening to meet her husband, so did she now often steal down at the same silent hour to weep over the graves of her child and its father, lying side by side. Not yet did Greylands, as a rule, give her her true name: old names, it has been just observed, stand by us: and Hallet, as applied to Jane, was more familiar to the tongue than Castlemaine. The income settled on Jane was ample for every comfort: she and her aunt now lived as quiet gentle-people, keeping a good servant. Jane had dropped her intimacy with Miss Susan Pike, though she would stay and speak cordially to her when by chance they met. Which implied distance, or reserve, or whatever it might be, was not at all agreeable to that damsel, and she consoled herself by telling Greylands that Jane was "stuck-up." Little cared poor Jane. Her young life had always been a sad one: and now, before she was twenty years of age, its happiness had been blighted out of it. George Castlemaine and his wife, at Greylands' Rest, were becoming fond of Jane: Ethel had always liked her. Jane visited them now sometimes; and Greylands was shown that they respected and regarded her.

"It is as it should be: Jane's manners and ways were always too high for her pocket—as are Miss Hallet's, too, for that matter," remarked Mrs. Bent to her husband, one day that they sat sunning themselves on the bench outside the inn, and saw Jane pass with Ethel. John only nodded in reply. With the elucidation of the fate of Anthony Castlemaine, and the delivering over of his effects to his widow, Charlotte Guise, John's mind was at rest, and he had returned to his old easy apathy. By dint of much battling with strong impressions, John had come to the conclusion that the tall man he saw cross from the Chapel Lane to the ruins, that February night, might have been one of the smugglers on his way from the Hutt, who bore an extraordinary resemblance to the Master of Greylands. Jack Tuff held out still that it was he; but Jack Tuff was told his eyesight that night could not be trusted.

News came from Commodore Teague pretty often. He appeared to be flourishing in his new abode over the water, and had set up a pleasure-boat on the Scheldt. He sent pressing messages for Greylands to visit him and Tom Dance and his son intended to avail themselves of the invitation. The Commodore inquired after old friends, even to the ghost of the Grey Monk, whether it "walked" as much as it used to walk, or whether it didn't. The Hutt remained without a tenant. Not a soul would take it. Events had severely shaken the bravery of Greylands; the ghost had shown itself much in the last year, and the Hutt was too near its haunting place, the Friar's Keep, to render it a comfortable residence. So it remained untenanted, and was likely to remain so. Greylands would almost as soon have parted with its faith in the Bible as in the Grey Monk.

And the participation of the Master of Greylands in those illicit practices was not disclosed or suspected, and the name and reputation of the Castlemaines had never a tarnish on it. It was believed that he had behaved in a remarkably handsome and liberal manner to his nephew George, in giving up to him Greylands' Rest during his own lifetime: George himself spoke feelingly of it: and what with that, and what with the sympathy felt for the loss of his son, and what with regret for the suspicions cast on him in regard to Anthony, Mr. Castlemaine stood higher in men's estimation than ever he had stood originally. And that was saying a great deal.

And she—Mary Ursula! Some further good fortune had come to her in the shape of money. A heavy debt due to her father since long years, which had been looked upon as a total loss, was suddenly repaid. It amounted, with the interest, to many thousands of pounds. As Mr. Peter Castlemaine had himself not a creditor in the world, all his obligations having been paid in full, it lapsed of course to his daughter. So, even on the score of fortune, she might not have been so unequal a match for Sir William Blake-Gordon. Sir William, knowing how utterly at an end was all hope of Mary, had, after some tardy delay, renewed his engagement with Miss Mountsorrel: and this month, June, they had been married. Mary sent them a loving letter of good wishes, and a costly present: and she told them that she and they should always be the best of friends.

She was too rich now, she was wont to say, laughingly, to the Sisters: and she introduced some changes for comfort into the Nunnery. One of the rooms hitherto shut up, a spacious apartment with the lovely sea view, she had caused to be renovated and furnished for the Ladies, leaving the parlour still as the reception-room. A smaller apartment with the same sea aspect was fitted up for herself, and her own fine piano placed in it: the Superior's private sitting-room. Sister Mildred had neither the means nor had she been educated with the tastes of Mary Ursula. The door leading from the Nunnery into the secret passage was bricked-up for ever.

A grand, stately Superior-mistress made Miss Castlemaine; and the Grey Ladies, under her wise and gracious sway, enlarged their sphere of benevolence. Using her means, they sought out their fellow-pilgrims, entangled amid the thorns of this world, and helped them on the road to a better. For herself, though anxiously fulfilling all the social obligations of her sphere here, she kept her feet and her heart set ever towards the eternal shore. And if—for she was but human—a regret came over her for the position she had persisted in resigning, or a vision rose of the earthly bliss that would have been hers as William Blake-Gordon's wife, that one verse of the loving MASTER's, delivered to His people during His sojourn on earth, was sure to suggest itself for her consolation. As it had come into her mind, uncalled for and unbidden, during that hour of her temptation, so would it return to cheer and comfort her now.

"No man, having put his hand to the plough, and looking back, is fit to enter the kingdom of God."

THE END

A Note About the Author

Ellen Price (1814–1887) was an English novelist and translator, better known by her penname, Mrs. Henry Wood. Wood lived with her husband, Henry Wood, and four children in Southern France for twenty years, until moving back to England when Henry's business failed. In England, Wood supported her family with her writing, becoming an international bestseller. Wood was praised for her masterful storytelling of middle-class lives, and often advocated for faith and strong morals in her work. Wood's most celebrated work was *East Lynne*, a sensation novel popular for its elaborate plot. In 1867, Wood became the owner and editor of Argosy Magazine, which she continued to publish until her death in 1887. By the end of her career, Wood published over thirty novels, many of which were immensely popular in England, the United States, and in Australia.

A Note from the Publisher

Spanning many genres, from non-fiction essays to literature classics to children's books and lyric poetry, Mint Edition books showcase the master works of our time in a modern new package. The text is freshly typeset, is clean and easy to read, and features a new note about the author in each volume. Many books also include exclusive new introductory material. Every book boasts a striking new cover, which makes it as appropriate for collecting as it is for gift giving. Mint Edition books are only printed when a reader orders them, so natural resources are not wasted. We're proud that our books are never manufactured in excess and exist only in the exact quantity they need to be read and enjoyed.

Discover more of your favorite classics with Bookfinity™.

- Track your reading with custom book lists.
- Get great book recommendations for your personalized Reader Type.
- Add reviews for your favorite books.
- AND MUCH MORE!

Visit **bookfinity.com** and take the fun Reader Type quiz to get started.

Enjoy our classic and modern companion pairings!

Printed in the USA
CPSIA information can be obtained
at www.ICGtesting.com
JSHW022202140824
68134JS00018B/820

9 781513 281117